Nathaniel Hawthorne

SELECTED TALES AND SKETCHES

Third Edition
WITH INTRODUCTIONS
BY HYATT H. WAGGONER

HOLT, RINEHART AND WINSTON

NEW YORK · CHICAGO · SAN FRANCISCO · ATLANTA
DALLAS · MONTREAL · TORONTO · LONDON · SYDNEY

The text of this edition is that of the still standard Riverside Edition of 1883, with certain obvious misprints silently corrected.

Introductions and Notes
Copyright 1950, © 1964, 1970 by Hyatt H. Waggoner
All rights reserved
Library of Congress Catalog Card Number: 74-94894
ISBN 0-03-079790-X
Printed in the United States of America

567 073 2019181716

Introduction to Third Edition

In the more than a century since Hawthorne's death his work has continued to be widely read and greatly respected by readers whose opinions are recorded. Of course his reputation has fluctuated somewhat from generation to generation, but one of the signs of his greatness is that each new generation of readers has been able to find in his work something to admire, if not what their fathers admired, something that answered a new need and satisfied different expectations.

During the twenty-year period between the writing of the Introduction to the original 1950 edition of this collection and the present much has happened in Hawthorne criticism and scholarship and, as a direct consequence, to our understanding and appreciation of Hawthorne's writing. In the middle years of the fifties, the critical studies of R. H. Fogle, the present writer, and others laid the groundwork for the great outpouring of "New Critical" analyses of Hawthorne's work that have largely dominated Hawthorne study for the past dozen years. Studies by Roy Male and Harry Levin assimilated the new critical probings and enlarged the perspective in which Hawthorne should be understood. Randall Stewart, the most prominent Hawthorne scholar of his generation, calling attention to what he called the "renaissance" of Hawthorne studies in the middle fifties, described the period as "The Golden Age of Hawthorne Criticism." The work of such critics as Daniel Hoffman, R. P. Adams, R. W. B.

Lewis, Marius Bewley, Seymour Gross, A. N. Kaul, and others in the years following Stewart's article has fully justified the encomium.

But history, including literary history, seems to move at an ever-increasing tempo. Beginning with the deaths of the great modernist writers—Eliot, Hemingway, Faulkner, Cummings, and others—in the sixties, the "New Criticism" which had arisen in part as a response to the challenge offered by their "difficult" writing and which had proved equally serviceable when applied to Hawthorne's work, began to fall into disfavor. A new historicism and a new Freudianism turned away from symbolic and mythic analyses of the stories to attempts to place Hawthorne in literary and cultural history or else to elicit his "latent" meanings, the meanings that emerge when his tales are read as dreams.

Whatever the ultimate outcome of the present revisionist stirrings in Hawthorne study may be, it at least seems clear that the increased interest in relating the man Hawthorne to the work he produced, to his age, and to the processes and conditions of artistic creation anywhere at any time will continue for some time. The best of Hawthorne's tales, including some that were first made widely known by the original edition of this collection, no longer seem in need of any defense of their literary merit. That Hawthorne's tales, as the original Introduction to this book put it, "represent a literary achievement of the first order" is now commonly assumed. What an apparently increasing number of readers would like to read now, along with the greatest of the tales and sketches, is some of the lesser pieces including the more revealing failures, the false starts, the obsessive repetitions, that they may better understand Hawthorne's career as a whole and its relation to the careers of other writers of his time and ours, Melville and Faulkner for example, who often worked with similar materials and developed similar themes.

This new edition, therefore, has been revised by enlargement, not by subtraction or replacement. A dozen tales and sketches and a lengthy segment of "Chiefly About War Matters," the last piece of writing Hawthorne completed, have been added to the original twenty-five tales and sketches, with the selections from the Prefaces left unchanged. The result is a collection much more representative of the whole range of Hawthorne's achievement and more suggestive of the Hawthorne his own age knew and valued.

Some, but by no means all, of the additions would probably still be excluded by a rigid application of an "only the best" criterion. "Sunday at Home," for instance, has been included chiefly for the way it reveals Hawthorne working in the tradition of the "personal essay" and for the light it throws on his religious ideas and feelings, showing a side of him closer to the attitudes of such contemporaries as Emerson and Thoreau than one would guess from reading only his "darker"—and generally greater—works. "A Virtuoso's Collection," for another example, might hold little interest for a reader who had read nothing else by Hawthorne, but to a student of Hawthorne it is enjoyable not only for its judgments of some of Hawthorne's contemporaries like Jones Very but for what it reveals of Hawthorne's miscellaneous reading, his chief literary sources, and his thematic preoccupations. Granted only an initial interest in Hawthorne's work, one need not be a collector of versions of the legend of the Wandering Jew to find this light sketch continuously interesting.

Similarly, "The Hall of Fantasy," though it lacks something of the controlled development and power of such sketches as "Earth's Holocaust" or "The Celestial Railroad," is likely to strike a reader already acquainted with Hawthorne's major works as a helpful aid toward gaining an understanding and just evaluation of them. In it Hawthorne defines the area in which his imagination moves most freely, the "region which lies above, below, or beyond the actual" and which may be entered by the imagination, in fortunate moments, or by "the universal passport of a dream." Once again, as in "A Virtuoso's Collection," we find interesting comments on Hawthorne's reading and some of the best evidence to be found anywhere in the works that Hawthorne, at least at this period in his life, understood and could distance his obsessive concerns and so could use them creatively instead of being victimized by them as he was in his last years.

I have written elsewhere at some length on the importance of that overlooked sketch "The Old Apple Dealer" as a revelation both of Hawthorne's ideas about the art and the limits of fiction as he wished to practice it, and of his moral and religious ideas, so I shall add here only this: that the sketch now strikes me as an impressive literary *tour de force* in its own right, so that even a collection aimed at presenting "only the best" of Hawthorne, as the original edition of this book aimed at doing, ought to have included it. The fact that the sketch very probably inspired Melville to write "Bartleby the Scrivener" gives us another reason for being interested in it today.

"Night Sketches," too, it now seems to me, ought to have been included originally. Its beautifully controlled expression of Hawthorne's ever-present concern with the relations between the Ideal and the Real, or dream and actuality, its revelation of that "dark" side of Hawthorne that Melville responded to, its gentle humor and self-directed irony, its memorable symbolization of the sort of darkness into which Hawthorne, unlike Melville, chose not to wander—all these and other features of this revealing sketch ought to give it a place in any collection of Hawthorne's shorter works.

Of the remaining additions to this collection, three—"Fire Worship," "Sights from a Steeple," and "Feathertop"—now seem to me to have more merit in their own right than they once did, and five others seemed to demand inclusion because of the insights into Hawthorne and his career they provide. "An Old Woman's Tale" complements "The Hollow of the Three Hills" both in being one of the earliest of the surviving tales and in revealing how quickly after he began to write Hawthorne found the subjects and themes that were to remain his hallmark throughout his career. "The Gentle Boy" was Hawthorne's best-known and best-liked tale during his lifetime. Rewarding for its recreation of the Puritan scene, it also reminds us that the temptation to think of Hawthorne as totally alienated from his own time ought to be avoided.

"Main Street" is important for what it reveals about Hawthorne's acute sense of history, his strong feeling for *place,* and his attitudes toward his ancestors. Indeed, for an understanding of the springs of the power of Hawthorne's fiction considered as historical romance, it is essential. A somewhat similar claim to importance might be made for "Chiefly About War Matters," though it reveals aspects of Hawthorne's personality not likely to appeal strongly to most younger readers today. Here we meet the Hawthorne who was a Democrat in politics but could not shake off the feeling of being a sort of disinherited aristocrat, and a rather fastidious one at that, remarking on President Lincoln's carpet slippers and apparently uncombed hair and amused by his rustic manners and general lack of reserve. Here we catch a glimpse of the handsome youth continuously gazing at himself in the mirror, the young Narcissus of "Monsieur du Miroir" that Malcolm Cowley called to our attention years ago in "Hawthorne in the Looking-Glass."

But "Alice Doane's Appeal" is the prime example of the way this revised edition has been expanded to include pieces of writing that are more important as documents than as finished works of art. The story as we have it is incoherent on the literal or manifest level; there are gaps, inconsistencies, unexplained shifts of scene and bits of action. Hawthorne was trying, apparently, by adding a frame to an earlier unframed tale, to salvage for publication a dream fantasy that in many remarkable ways foreshadows the breakdown in control so evident in the late romances he could never finish. Significantly, he never reprinted the tale after its magazine publication, whether because he recognized its literary weaknesses or because he found its revelations of the preoccupations of his fantasy life embarrassing, we do not know. We may guess that he felt dissatisfied with the tale on both counts.

Yet nothing else Hawthorne ever chose to publish is more

interesting and useful to the modern student of Hawthorne
who wants to try to understand the shape and significance of
his whole career, its failures and limitations as well as its
great achievements, its early triumphs and its late collapse.
The incest motif, though of course a common enough theme
in the Romantic movement, here seems to be more personal
and compulsive than a literary borrowing. The picture of the
dead enemy-father is unlike anything in our literature at the
time. It moves Hawthorne closer to Poe than we have realized
and at the same time closer to the practice of some of our
contemporary antirealists. The world of "Alice Doane's Appeal" is not only—as in some sense much of Hawthorne's
most impressive work is—a world of dream, it is a world of
nightmare from which the awakening is compulsive because
the dream-fantasy has become at once too transparent and too
close to the forbidden. As the original Introduction to this
collection put it, "The story almost certainly means more to
the modern reader than Hawthorne consciously intended it
should." Today the "almost certainly" seems unnecessary.

To say so much about the relatively unsuccessful pieces
Hawthorne left us, the false starts and abortive experiments,
or the simply dull things that can be used as "documents"
helpful toward an understanding of the greater works, and to
pass over Hawthorne's artistic triumphs in silence would
seem a strange tactic indeed were it not that, at this juncture
in time, two conditions having to do with literary and cultural
history seem to unite to suggest the appropriateness of such
a procedure in an Introduction designed for college students
beginning a study of Hawthorne's work.

The first condition was glanced at in the opening paragraphs of this Introduction. What it amounts to is the existence of a very large and still growing body of "close readings," *explications de texte,* of most of the major Hawthorne
tales and sketches and many of the admittedly minor ones
too. The original Introduction's call for a—then nonexistent

—"close reading" of Hawthorne's tales has been answered many times over—too many, it sometimes begins to seem—until there is some danger that the student may so exhaust his energy wading through the piled-up bulk of multiple interpretations that he has little energy left to give to the tale itself in the form of his own personal response—if he ever actually gets to the tale. At the very least, he may find a tale too much interpreted before he has experienced it lacking in freshness. After all, he already knows, he thinks, what it "means."

The remarkable accumulation of Hawthorne criticism during the past fifteen years or so will stand as one of the lasting achievements of the New Critical period in literary study. Hawthorne's work has engaged many of the best critical minds of the period with the result that the critical work that has been done on him is vastly more impressive, more likely to continue to seem useful to future readers than, for example, what has been done on Emerson's poetry and prose or on Whitman's poetry. It is an encumbrance only insofar as a student may be tempted to take the shortcut to "inside" knowledge and "authoritative" opinion offered by the accumulated criticism listed and described in convenient form by Buford Jones in *A Checklist of Hawthorne Criticism: 1951–1966*. In the bibliographical note at the end of this Introduction, suggestions are made for critical reading on some of the greatest of the tales. Coming to them *after* reading the tale, the student may be sent back to it to find what he missed or to check on why he disagrees with the critics. Such is the proper use of criticism.

The second condition that contributed something to the shaping of this new Introduction, also glanced at earlier, is at once less apparent and less important though it seems worthy of some comment. It consists of the apparently growing tendency among young critics and readers to be attracted to psychological modes of criticism rather than to philosophical, theological, or moral ones. Among its most extreme practitioners, this fashion produces criticism that professedly "explains" the genesis of a literary work by reducing its meaning to the author's psychic mechanisms and compulsive preoccupations. Thus we are told by one of the new psychological critics that Hawthorne's "Egotism, or The Bosom Serpent" is "about" masturbation!

This is critical reductionism with a vengeance! Even if it could be proved to be true that Hawthorne's guilty feelings about masturbation had something to do with the shaping of this tale—and it can't, though the speculation has always seemed to this writer to be a likely one—it would still be a grossly naive critical fallacy to equate the origin and the finished product. Works of art, like other products of man's creative efforts, have all sorts of "origins," most of which we cannot know with any precision. A work of fiction grows from and reflects both the writer's conscious waking experience of the inner and outer worlds including, often most importantly, his reading and the experience he has repressed, of which he may be partially, dimly conscious or wholly unconscious at the time of writing. Psychological readings that isolate the supposed unconscious elements that went into the creation of a work of literary art and deny either the existence or the relevance both of other "shaping" aspects of the writer's experience and of the resultant work's *manifest* as opposed to *latent* meanings and values insult our critical intelligence and impoverish the stories they pretend to "explain."

To say so much is not to deny the uses of psychological insights. When a story falls into certain types of incoherence, or when the work of a whole career exhibits repeated failure to be able to deal successfully with certain subjects or situations, "Freudian" analysis may offer the only available explanation. (The classic example of this kind of highly valuable literary exploration is Henry Murray's Introduction to the Hendricks House edition of Melville's *Pierre*.) The ambivalent way Hawthorne so often treats the father figures in his stories— both in his successes and in his failures—is a case in point. Noting it may help us to understand better the nature of Hawthorne's breakdown in his final years and thus throw some light on the indecision and incoherence that are the most striking features of all but one fragment of the late unfinished romances. Nevertheless, it still seems truer to say that there is *both* a "logic of compulsion" in "Roger Malvin's Burial" *and* the religious and moral meanings Hawthorne must have thought he had succeeded in embodying in the tale than that there is *only* one or the other type of meaning. Types of meaning in art coexist as frames of reference and systems of discourse do in our everyday lives.

The speculative, mythic, and moral meanings that may be found in Hawthorne's successful tales and sketches have been treated fully and repeatedly not only by the present writer in the original Introduction to this book, in *Hawthorne, A Critical Study* (1955; revised edition, 1963), in the Minnesota Pamphlet *Nathaniel Hawthorne* (1962), and in "Art and Belief" in the *Hawthorne Centenary Essays,* but by a host of other critics, most notably perhaps by Randall Stewart, R. H. Fogle, Roy Male, Austin Warren, Marius Bewley, R. W. B. Lewis, Seymour Gross, and David Levin. Since the body of critical interpretation produced by these and other writers is readily available, and since the present writer has, at the moment, no new interpretations to offer or changes of mind to record, it has seemed appropriate to offer comments only on the new additions to this collection, and particularly on those that, like "Alice Doane's Appeal," throw a special kind of light on the unique qualities of the Hawthorne corpus and on the problems that arise when we contemplate the shape of the career.

For a generation or more now, most readers have been more strongly attracted to the expressions of the tragic vision found in the work of Hawthorne, Melville, the late James, Eliot, Faulkner, and R. P. Warren, among others, with its insistence on irony, complexity, and the ambiguity of experience, than to the Adamic or prelapsarian hopefulness of the tradition first brought to full expression by Emerson, continued without diminishment by Whitman, and kept alive in the recent past by such poets as Williams and Cummings. To adopt for a moment the classifications codified by R. W. B. Lewis in *The American Adam,* modern experience has been such as to predispose most of us to finding tragic and ironic writings "relevant," and transcendental or other forms of hopefulness "irrelevant." The "party of irony" has been "in" for a long time, the "party of hope" "out."

There have been many signs recently that this situation is changing rapidly. Emerson is being studied afresh and found to have something to say that is relevant to our condition. It no longer seems necessary to think of him as naive merely because he hoped to find a way of transcending the shifting illusions and ambiguous contraries of experience. Extreme spokesmen for the new sensibility go so far as to suggest that Hawthorne's special appeal to the modern reader has been no more than a by-product of our ignorance of, or our inability to read, Emerson. However exaggerated and simplistic such a view may be, it would seem to contain a certain kind of limited truth. At any rate it seems clear that at present Emerson is on the way to becoming the "in" writer that Hawthorne has been for so long.

The "tides of taste" move with a pendulumlike regularity that those who prize private judgment and the right to differ are likely to find repugnant. There is, it would seem, no really good reason why we should feel obliged to belittle Hawthorne merely because we are discovering the values Emerson holds for us. If our experience is wide enough and our minds and hearts open enough, we shall be able to see that the visions of both men were valid responses to a reality whose limits can be drawn by no set of clearly articulated doctrines, whether they be those of Emerson's metaphysic of Absolute Idealism, of Hawthorne's unchurched but privately cherished version of Unitarian Christianity, or of the naturalistic "humanists" who thrive today.

It was Whitman, following Emerson's lead, who said that arguments fail to convince when they contradict immediate, uninterpreted experience. Reading through the selections in this volume will, hopefully, do more than any argument could to persuade us that to be unable to respond gratefully to the full range of values present in Hawthorne's work would be evidence that we are cut off not only from our national past but also from much of the meaning potentially present for us in our own experience.

A Biographical Note

Born in 1804 in Salem, Massachusetts, Hawthorne came of the oldest New England stock. One of his ancestors was a judge in the witchcraft trials in Salem in 1692–1693. (For Hawthorne's feeling on this matter, see his introduction to *The Scarlet Letter;* for his judgment of the Puritans, see "Main Street" and "The Gentle Boy.") For several generations his paternal ancestors followed the sea, while the family declined in wealth and social importance; his father, Captain Nathaniel Hathorne,[1] died at Surinam, Dutch Guiana, when his son was four years old. He was brought up in the households of his mother's family in Salem and the back country of Maine and sent to Bowdoin College by his uncles. He graduated in 1825, determined to become a writer of fiction. For more than a decade he devoted himself to learning his craft, living at the family home, reading much, writing much, destroying some of his productions, sending stories to the magazines and "annuals" or Christmas gift books of the time, where they were published anonymously. After some ventures in editing and literary hackwork undertaken in an effect to support himself—for the many stories he published in these years brought him little income—and after a brief period of employment in the Boston Custom House and another period as a member of the experimental Socialist community at Brook Farm, he married, at the age

[1] Hawthorne added the *w* to the spelling of the family name after he graduated from college.

of thirty-eight, Miss Sophia Peabody. Thereafter, anticipating the later American pattern, he was never to know a home which he could think of as permanent. Several happy years in the Old Manse in Concord brought him into close contact with Emerson and Thoreau. Later, back in Salem again, he was employed as Surveyor in the Salem Custom House until, losing his job for political reasons, he tried the experiment of devoting himself wholly to literature and wrote *The Scarlet Letter* very quickly, following it soon after with *The House of the Seven Gables, The Blithedale Romance,* and other works. In Lenox in the Berkshires he formed what is for us his most significant literary friendship when he became a neighbor of Herman Melville, then at work on *Moby Dick* which Melville dedicated to Hawthorne. For seven years he was abroad, in England, where he tried to solve the financial problem by serving as United States Consul in Liverpool, and in Italy, adding steadily to his notebooks but unable to do any creative work until, at the end of his stay, he wrote *The Marble Faun*. Returning to Concord in 1860, he died after four unhappy years during which, working against failing health and flagging creative energies which were probably attributable to a breakdown of his psychic health, he tried to bring to satisfactory conclusion several late romances which he left unfinished at his death.

Selected Bibliography

1. HAWTHORNE'S LIFE AND WORK

Arvin, Newton, *Hawthorne*. Boston: Little, Brown, 1929.

Bridge, Horatio, *Personal Recollections of Nathaniel Hawthorne.* New York: Harper and Brothers, 1893.

Conway, Moncure D., *Life of Nathaniel Hawthorne.* London: Walter Scott, Ltd., 1895.

Cady, Edwin H., "The Wizard Hand: Hawthorne, 1864–1900," in Pearce (ed.), *Hawthorne Centenary Essays.* Columbus, Ohio: State University Press, 1964.

Cowley, Malcolm, "Hawthorne in the Looking Glass," *Sewanee Review,* 56 (October, 1948), 545–63.

Hawthorne, Julian, *Hawthorne and His Wife.* Boston: Ticknor, 1888.

Hoeltje, Hubert H., *Inward Sky: The Mind and Heart of Nathaniel Hawthorne.* Durham: Duke University Press, 1962.

James, Henry, *Hawthorne.* London: Macmillan, 1879. Many reprints available, e.g., Ithaca, N.Y.: Cornell University Press, "Great Seal Books" ed., 1963.

Lathrop, George Parsons, *A Study of Hawthorne.* Boston: James R. Osgood, 1876.

Lathrop, Rose Hawthorne. *Memories of Hawthorne.* Boston: Houghton Mifflin, 1897.

Levin, Harry, *The Power of Blackness.* New York: Alfred A. Knopf, 1958; Vintage Book, 1960.

Loggins, Vernon, *The Hawthornes: The Story of Seven Generations of an American Family.* New York: Columbia University Press, 1951.

Lowell, Robert, "Hawthorne," in Pearce (ed.), *Hawthorne Centenary Essays*. (A poem interpreting Hawthorne's personality.) Also published in Lowell's *For the Union Dead,* New York: Farrar, Straus & Giroux, 1964, pp. 38–39.

Stewart, Randall, *Nathaniel Hawthorne: A Biography*. New Haven: Yale University Press, 1948.

Van Doren, Mark, *Nathaniel Hawthorne*. New York: William Sloane Associates, 1949.

Wagenknecht, Edward, *Nathaniel Hawthorne: Man and Writer*. New York: Oxford University Press, 1961.

Waggoner, Hyatt H., *Nathaniel Hawthorne*. Minneapolis: The University of Minnesota Pamphlets on American Writers, 1962.

II. CRITICAL STUDIES

GENERAL

Crews, Frederick C., *The Sons of the Fathers: Hawthorne's Psychological Themes*. New York, Oxford University Press; 1966.

Fogle, Richard Harter, *Hawthorne's Fiction: The Light and the Dark*. Norman, University of Oklahoma Press, 1952, paperback ed., revised, 1964.

Male, Roy R., *Hawthorne's Tragic Vision*. Austin, University of Texas Press, 1957. Paperback ed. published by Norton.

Pearce, Roy Harvey (ed.), *Hawthorne Centenary Essays:* Columbus, Ohio State University Press, 1964.

Waggoner, Hyatt H., *Hawthorne: A Critical Study*. Cambridge, Harvard University Press, 1955; revised ed., 1963.

In addition, the following books contain valuable discussions of Hawthorne's work:

Bewley, Marius, *The Complex Fate*. London: Chatto and Windus, 1952. Reprinted in New York, Gordian Press ed., 1967.

———, *The Eccentric Design: Form in the Classic American Novel.* New York: Columbia University Press, 1959. Available also in a Columbia University Press paperback ed.

Feidelson, Jr., Charles. *Symbolism and American Literature*. Chicago: University of Chicago Press, 1953. Also available in a paperback ed.

Fiedler, Leslie A., *Love and Death in the American Novel*. Revised edition, New York, Dell, 1966.

Hoffman, Daniel G., *Form and Fable in American Fiction*. New York: Oxford University Press, 1961. Also available in an Oxford University Press "Galaxy Book" paperback, 1965.

Kaul, A. N., *The American Vision: Actual and Ideal Society in Nineteenth Century Fiction*. New Haven, Yale University Press 1963.

Lewis, R. W. B., *The American Adam: Innocence, Tragedy, and Tradition in the Nineteenth Century*. Chicago: University of Chicago Press, 1955. Also available in a University of Chicago Press "Phoenix Books" paperback ed., 1964.

Marx, Leo, *The Machine in the Garden: Technology and the Pastoral Ideal in America*. New York, Oxford University Press, 1964; Galaxy (paperback) ed., 1967.

Matthiessen, F. O., *American Renaissance*. New York: Oxford University Press, 1941. Also available in an Oxford University Press paperback ed., 1968.

Poirier, Richard, *A World Elsewhere: The Place of Style in American Literature*. New York, Oxford University Press, 1966. Also available in a paperback ed.

SPECIFIC WORKS

RECOMMENDED INTERPRETATIONS OF SOME MAJOR TALES

"My Kinsman, Major Molineux"

Gross, Seymour L., "Hawthorne's 'My Kinsman, Major Molineux' as Moral Adventure," *Nineteenth Century Fiction,* 12 (September, 1957), pp. 97–109.

Daniel G. Hoffman, "Yankee Bumpkin and Scapegoat King," *The Sewanee Review,* 69 (January–March 1961), p. 48, Reprinted in *Form and Fable in American Fiction.*

Pearce, Roy Harvey, "Hawthorne and the Sense of the Past, or, The Immortality of Major Molineux," *English Literary History,* 21 (December 1954), pp. 327–340.

Trilling, Lionel, *The Experience of Literature*. New York, Holt, Rinehart and Winston, 1967, pp. 438–440.

Waggoner, Hyatt H., *Hawthorne, A Critical Study;* and "Art and Belief," in *Hawthorne Centenary Essays.*

"Roger Malvin's Burial"

Crews, Frederick C., "The Logic of Compulsion," in *The Sins of the Fathers*. Published as "The Logic of Compulsion in

'Roger Malvin's Burial' " in *Publication of Modern Language Association,* 79 (1964), pp. 457–465.

Stock, Ely, "History and the Bible in Hawthorne's 'Roger Malvin's Burial.' " *Essex Institute Historical Collections,* 100 (October 1964), 279–296.

Thompson, W. R., "The Biblical Sources of Hawthorne's 'Roger Malvin's Burial,' " *PMLA,* 77 (March 1962), pp. 92–96.

Waggoner, Hyatt H., *Hawthorne, a Critical Study.*

"Young Goodman Brown"

Adams, Richard P., "Hawthorne's 'Provincial Tales,' " *New England Quarterly,* 30 (March 1957), pp. 39–57.

Fogle, Richard Harter, *Hawthorne's Fiction: The Light and the Dark.* Norman, University of Oklahoma Press, 1952, paperback edition, revised, 1964.

Levin, David, "Shadows of Doubt: Specter Evidence in Hawthorne's 'Young Goodman Brown,' " *American Literature,* 34 (November 1962), pp. 344–352.

Roy R. Male, *Hawthorne's Tragic Vision.* Austin, University of Texas Press, 1957. Paperback edition published by Norton.

"The Maypole of Merrymount"

Fogle, Richard Harter, *Hawthorne's Fiction: The Light and the Dark.* Norman, University of Oklahoma Press, 1952, paperback edition, revised, 1964.

Hoffman, Daniel, *Form and Fable in American Fiction.* New York, Oxford University Press, 1961.

Leavis, Q. D., "Hawthorne As Poet," Part I, *Sewanee Review,* 59 (Spring 1951), 179–205; reprinted in A. N. Kaul, ed., *Hawthorne, Twentieth Century Views.* Englewood Cliffs, Prentice-Hall, 1966.

Vickery, John B., "The Golden Bough at Merry Mount," *Nineteenth Century Fiction,* 12 (December 1957), pp. 203–214.

"The Birthmark"

Fogle, Richard Harter, *Hawthorne's Fiction: The Light and Dark,* 1964 ed. Norman: University of Oklahoma Press.

Heilman, Robert B. "Science as Religion," *The South Atlantic Quarterly,* Vol. 48, No. 4 (October 1949).

Lesser, Simon O., "The Attitude of Fiction," *Modern Fiction Studies,* 2 (May 1956), pp. 52–55.

Reid, Alfred S., "Hawthorne's Humanism: 'The Birthmark' and Sir Kenelm Digby," *American Literature,* 38 (November 1966), pp. 337–351.

"Rappaccini's Daughter"

Michael J. Colacurcio, "A Better Mode of Evidence: The Transcendental Problem of Faith and Spirit," *Emerson Society Quarterly,* No. 54, 1969, pp. 12–22.

Crews, Frederick C., *The Sins of the Fathers.* New York: Oxford University Press, 1961.

Oliver Evans, "Allegory and Incest in 'Rappaccini's Daughter,'" *Nineteenth Century Fiction,* XIX (September 1964), 185–195; and "The Cavern and the Fountain: Paradox and Double Paradox in 'Rappaccini's Daughter,'" *College English,* 24 (March 1963), 461–463.

Male, Roy R., *Hawthorne's Tragic Vision.* Austin: University of Oklahoma Press. Paperback ed., published by Norton.

Waggoner, Hyatt H., *Hawthorne, A Critical Study.* Cambridge: Harvard University Press, 1955; revised ed., 1963.

"Ethan Brand"

Fogle, Richard Harter, *Hawthorne's Fiction: The Light and the Dark.* Norman: University of Oklahoma Press, 1952; paperback ed., revised, 1964.

Kaul, A. N., *The American Vision: Actual and Ideal Society in Nineteenth Century Fiction.* New Haven: Yale University Press, 1963.

Stock, Ely, "The Biblical Context of 'Ethan Brand,'" *American Literature,* 37 (May 1965), 115–134.

Additional critical studies of individual tales and sketches are most easily found in the following bibliographical aids:

Jones, Buford, (ed.), *A Checklist of Hawthorne Criticism, 1951–1966.* Hartford, Transcendental Books, 1957. (The listings contain brief descriptive and summary comments.)

Woodress, James, (ed.), *American Literary Scholarship.* Durham, Duke University Press, annually since 1963. (The chapter devoted to Hawthorne surveys, summarizes, and evaluates the year's scholarly and critical writing on Hawthorne.)

Contents

TALES

SKETCHES

PREFACES

JOURNALISM

The dates in parentheses following titles are those of first publication.

Tales

THE HOLLOW OF THE
THREE HILLS

In those strange old times, when fantastic dreams and madmen's reveries were realized among the actual circumstances of life, two persons met together at an appointed hour and place. One was a lady, graceful in form and fair of feature, though pale and troubled, and smitten with an untimely blight in what should have been the fullest bloom of her years; the other was an ancient and meanly-dressed woman, of ill-favored aspects, and so withered, shrunken, and decrepit, that even the space since she began to decay must have exceeded the ordinary term of human existence. In the spot where they encountered, no mortal could observe them. Three little hills stood near each other, and down in the midst of them sunk a hollow basin, almost mathematically circular, two or three hundred feet in breadth, and of such depth that a stately cedar might but just be visible above the sides. Dwarf pines were numerous upon the hills, and partly fringed the outer verge of the intermediate hollow, within which there was nothing but the brown grass of October, and here and there a tree trunk that had fallen long ago, and lay mouldering with no green successor from its roots. One of these masses of decaying wood, formerly a majestic oak, rested close beside a pool of green and sluggish water at the bottom of the basin. Such scenes as this (so gray tradition tells) were once the resort of the Power of Evil and his plighted subjects;

First published in *The Salem Gazette*, November 12, 1830.

and here, at midnight or on the dim verge of evening, they were said to stand round the mantling pool, disturbing its putrid waters in the performance of an impious baptismal rite. The chill beauty of an autumnal sunset was now gilding the three hill-tops, whence a paler tint stole down their sides into the hollow.

"Here is our pleasant meeting come to pass," said the aged crone, "according as thou hast desired. Say quickly what thou wouldst have of me, for there is but a short hour that we may tarry here."

As the old withered woman spoke, a smile glimmered on her countenance, like lamplight on the wall of a sepulchre. The lady trembled, and cast her eyes upward to the verge of the basin, as if meditating to return with her purpose unaccomplished. But it was not so ordained.

"I am a stranger in this land, as you know," said she at length. "Whence I come it matters not; but I have left those behind me with whom my fate was intimately bound, and from whom I am cut off forever. There is a weight in my bosom that I cannot away with, and I have come hither to inquire of their welfare."

"And who is there by this green pool that can bring thee news from the ends of the earth?" cried the old woman, peering into the lady's face. "Not from my lips mayst thou hear these tidings; yet, be thou bold, and the daylight shall not pass away from yonder hill-top before thy wish be granted."

"I will do your bidding though I die," replied the lady desperately.

The old woman seated herself on the trunk of the fallen tree, threw aside the hood that shrouded her gray locks, and beckoned her companion to draw near.

"Kneel down," she said, "and lay your forehead on my knees."

She hesitated a moment, but the anxiety that had long been kindling burned fiercely up within her. As she knelt down, the border of her garment was dipped into the pool; she laid her forehead on the old woman's knees, and the latter drew a cloak about the lady's face, so that she was in darkness. Then she heard the muttered words of prayer, in the midst of which she started, and would have arisen.

"Let me flee,—let me flee and hide myself, that they may not look upon me!" she cried. But, with returning recollection, she hushed herself, and was still as death.

For it seemed as if other voices—familiar in infancy, and unforgotten through many wanderings, and in all the vicissitudes of her heart and fortune—were mingling with the accents of the prayer. At first the words were faint and indistinct, not rendered so by distance, but rather resembling the dim pages of a book which we strive to read by an imperfect and gradually brightening light. In such a manner, as the prayer proceeded, did those voices strengthen upon the ear; till at length the petition ended, and the conversation of an aged man, and of a woman broken and decayed like himself, became distinctly audible to the lady as she knelt. But those strangers appeared not to stand in the hollow depth between the three hills. Their voices were encompassed and reëchoed by the walls of a chamber, the windows of which were rattling in the breeze; the regular vibration of a clock, the crackling of a fire, and the tinkling of the embers as they fell among the ashes, rendered the scene almost as vivid as if painted to the eye. By a melancholy hearth sat these two old people, the man calmly despondent, the woman querulous and tearful, and their words were all of sorrow. They spoke of a daughter, a wanderer they knew not where, bearing dishonor along with her, and leaving shame and affliction to bring their gray heads to the grave. They alluded also to other and more recent woe, but in the midst of their talk their voices seemed to melt into the sound of the wind sweeping mournfully among the autumn leaves; and when the lady lifted her eyes, there was she kneeling in the hollow between three hills.

"A weary and lonesome time yonder old couple have of it," remarked the old woman, smiling in the lady's face.

"And did you also hear them?" exclaimed she, a sense of

intolerable humiliation triumphing over her agony and fear.

"Yea; and we have yet more to hear," replied the old woman. "Wherefore, cover thy face quickly."

Again the withered hag poured forth the monotonous words of a prayer that was not meant to be acceptable in heaven; and soon, in the pauses of her breath, strange murmurings began to thicken, gradually increasing so as to drown and overpower the charm by which they grew. Shrieks pierced through the obscurity of sound, and were succeeded by the singing of sweet female voices, which, in their turn, gave way to a wild roar of laughter, broken suddenly by groanings and sobs, forming altogether a ghastly confusion of terror and mourning and mirth. Chains were rattling, fierce and stern voices uttered threats, and the scourge resounded at their command. All these noises deepened and became substantial to the listener's ear, till she could distinguish every soft and dreamy accent of the love songs that died causelessly into funeral hymns. She shuddered at the unprovoked wrath which blazed up like the spontaneous kindling of flame, and she grew faint at the fearful merriment raging miserably around her. In the midst of this wild scene, where unbound passions jostled each other in a drunken career, there was one solemn voice of a man, and a manly and melodious voice it might once have been. He went to and fro continually, and his feet sounded upon the floor. In each member of that frenzied company, whose own burning thoughts had become their exclusive world, he sought an auditor for the story of his individual wrong, and interpreted their laughter and tears as his reward of scorn or pity. He spoke of woman's perfidy, of a wife who had broken her holiest vows, of a home and heart made desolate. Even as he went on, the shout, the laugh, the shriek, the sob, rose up in unison, till they changed into the hollow, fitful, and uneven sound of the wind, as it fought among the pine-trees on those three lonely hills. The lady looked up, and there was the withered woman smiling in her face.

"Couldst thou have thought there were such merry times in a madhouse?" inquired the latter.

"True, true," said the lady to herself; "there is mirth within its walls, but misery, misery without."

"Wouldst thou hear more?" demanded the old woman.

"There is one other voice I would fain listen to again," replied the lady, faintly.

"Then, lay down thy head speedily upon my knees, that thou mayst get thee hence before the hour be past."

The golden skirts of day were yet lingering upon the hills, but deep shades obscured the hollow and the pool, as if sombre night were rising thence to overspread the world. Again that evil woman began to weave her spell. Long did it proceed unanswered, till the knolling of a bell stole in among the intervals of her words, like a clang that had travelled far over valley and rising ground, and was just ready to die in the air. The lady shook upon her companion's knees as she heard that boding sound. Stronger it grew and sadder, and deepened into the tone of a death bell, knolling dolefully from some ivy-mantled tower, and bearing tidings of mortality and woe to the cottage, to the hall, and to the solitary wayfarer, that all might weep for the doom appointed in turn to them. Then came a measured tread, passing slowly, slowly on, as of mourners with a coffin, their garments trailing on the ground, so that the ear could measure the length of their melancholy array. Before them went the priest, reading the burial service, while the leaves of his book were rustling in the breeze. And though no voice but his was heard to speak aloud, still there were revilings and anathemas, whispered but distinct, from women and from men, breathed against the daughter who had wrung the aged hearts of her parents,—the wife who had betrayed the trusting fondness of her husband,—the mother who had sinned against natural affection, and left her child to die. The sweeping sound of the funeral train faded away like a thin vapor, and the wind, that just before had seemed to shake the coffin pall, moaned sadly round the verge of the Hollow between three Hills. But when the old woman stirred the kneeling lady, she lifted not her head.

"Here has been a sweet hour's sport!" said the withered crone, chuckling to herself.

AN OLD
WOMAN'S TALE

In the house where I was born, there used to be an old woman crouching all day long over the kitchen fire, with her elbows on her knees and her feet in the ashes. Once in a while she took a turn at the spit, and she never lacked a coarse gray stocking in her lap, the foot about half finished; it tapered away with her own waning life, and she knit the toe-stitch on the day of her death. She made it her serious business and sole amusement to tell me stories at any time from morning till night, in a mumbling, toothless voice, as I sat on a log of wood, grasping her check-apron in both my hands. Her personal memory included the better part of a hundred years, and she had strangely jumbled her own experience and observation with those of many old people who died in her young days; so that she might have been taken for a contemporary of Queen Elizabeth, or of John Rogers in the Primer. There are a thousand of her traditions lurking in the corners and by-places of my mind, some more marvellous than what is to follow, some less so, and a few not marvellous in the least, all of which I should like to repeat, if I were as happy as she in having a listener. But I am humble enough to own, that I do not deserve a listener half so well as that old tooth-less woman, whose narratives possessed an excellence attributable neither to herself, nor to any single individual. Her ground-plots, seldom within the widest scope of probability,

First published in *The Salem Gazette*, December 21, 1830.

8

were filled up with homely and natural incidents, the gradual accretions of a long course of years, and fiction hid its grotesque extravagance in this garb of truth, like the Devil (an appropriate simile, for the old woman supplies it) disguising himself, cloven-foot and all, in mortal attire. These tales generally referred to her birthplace, a village in the valley of the Connecticut, the aspect of which she impressed with great vividness on my fancy. The houses in that tract of country, long a wild and dangerous frontier, were rendered defensible by a strength of architecture that has preserved many of them till our own times, and I cannot describe the sort of pleasure with which, two summers since, I rode through the little town in question, while one object after another rose familiarly to my eye, like successive portions of a dream becoming realized. Among other things equally probable, she was wont to assert that all the inhabitants of this village (at certain intervals, but whether of twenty-five or fifty years, or a whole century, remained a disputable point) were subject to a simultaneous slumber, continuing one hour's space. When that mysterious time arrived, the parson snored over his half-written sermon, though it were Saturday night and no provision made for the morrow,—the mother's eyelids closed as she bent over her infant, and no childish cry awakened,— the watcher at the bed of mortal sickness slumbered upon the death-pillow,—and the dying man anticipated his sleep of ages by one as deep and dreamless. To speak emphatically, there was a soporific influence throughout the village, stronger than if every mother's son and daughter were reading a dull story; notwithstanding which the old woman professed to hold the substance of the ensuing account from one of those principally concerned in it.

One moonlight summer evening, a young man and a girl sat down together in the open air. They were distant relatives, sprung from a stock once wealthy, but of late years so poverty-stricken, that David had not a penny to pay the marriage fee, if Esther should consent to wed. The seat they had chosen was in an open grove of elm and walnut-trees, at a right angle of the road; a spring of diamond water just bubbled into the moonlight beside them, and then whimpered away through the bushes and long grass, in search of a neighboring mill-stream. The nearest house (situated within twenty yards of them, and the residence of their great-grandfather in his life-time) was a venerable old edifice, crowned with many high and narrow peaks, all overrun by innumerable creeping plants, which hung curling about the roof like a nice young wig on an elderly gentleman's head. Opposite to this estab-lishment was a tavern, with a well and horse-trough before it, and a low green bank running along the left side of the door. Thence, the road went onward, curving scarce percepti-bly, through the village, divided in the midst by a narrow lane of verdure, and bounded on each side by a grassy strip of twice its own breadth. The houses had generally an odd look. Here, the moonlight tried to get a glimpse of one, a rough old heap of ponderous timber, which, ashamed of its dilapidated aspect, was hiding behind a great thick tree; the lower story of the next had sunk almost under ground, as if the poor little house were a-weary of the world, and retiring into the seclusion of its own cellar; farther on stood one of the few recent structures, thrusting its painted face conspicuously into the street, with an evident idea that it was the fairest thing there. About midway in the village was a grist-mill, partly concealed by the descent of the ground towards the stream which turned its wheel. At the southern extremity, just so far distant that the window-panes dazzled into each other, rose the meeting-house, a dingy old barnlike building, with an enormously disproportioned steeple sticking up straight into heaven, as high as the Tower of Babel, and the cause of nearly as much confusion in its day. This steeple, it must be understood, was an afterthought, and its addition to the main edifice, when the latter had already begun to decay, had excited a vehement quarrel, and almost a schism in the church, some fifty years before. Here the road wound down a hill, and was seen no more, the remotest object in view being the graveyard gate, beyond the meeting-house.

The youthful pair sat hand in hand beneath the trees, and for several moments they had not spoken, because the breeze was hushed, the brook scarce tinkled, the leaves had ceased their rustling, and everything lay motionless and silent as if Nature were composing herself to slumber.

"What a beautiful night it is, Esther!" remarked David, somewhat drowsily.

"Very beautiful," answered the girl, in the same tone.

"But how still!" continued David.

"Ah, too still!" said Esther, with a faint shudder, like a modest leaf when the wind kisses it.

Perhaps they fell asleep together, and, united as their spirits were by close and tender sympathies, the same strange dream might have wrapped them in its shadowy arms. But they conceived, at the time, that they still remained wakeful by the spring of bubbling water, looking down through the village, and all along the moon-lighted road, and at the queer old houses, and at the trees, which thrust their great twisted branches almost into the windows. There was only a sort of mistiness over their minds like the smoky air of an early autumn night. At length, without any vivid astonishment, they became conscious that a great many people were either entering the village or already in the street, but whether they came from the meeting-house, or from a little beyond it, or where the devil they came from, was more than could be determined. Certainly a crowd of people seemed to be there, men, women, and children, all of whom were yawning and rubbing their eyes, stretching their limbs, and staggering from side to side of the road, as if but partially awakened from a sound slumber. Sometimes they stood stock-still, with their hands over their brows to shade their sight from the moonbeams. As they drew near, most of their countenances appeared familiar to Esther and David, possessing the peculiar features of families in the village, and that general air and aspect by which a person would recognize his own townsmen in the remotest ends of the earth. But though the whole multitude might have been taken, in the mass, for neighbors and acquaintances, there was not a single individual whose exact likeness they had ever before seen. It was a noticeable circumstance, also, that the newest fashioned garment on the backs of these people might have been worn by the great-grandparents of the existing generation. There was one figure behind all the rest, and not yet near enough to be perfectly distinguished.

"Where on earth, David, do all these odd people come from?" said Esther, with a lazy inclination to laugh.

"Nowhere on earth, Esther," replied David, unknowing why he said so.

As they spoke, the strangers showed some symptoms of dis-quietude, and looked towards the fountain for an instant, but immediately appeared to assume their own trains of thought and previous purposes. They now separated to different parts of the village, with a readiness that implied intimate local knowledge, and it may be worthy of remark, that, though they were evidently loquacious among themselves, neither their footsteps nor their voices reached the ears of the beholders. Wherever there was a venerable old house, of fifty years' standing and upwards, surrounded by its elm or walnut-trees, with its dark and weather-beaten barn, its well, its orchard and stone-walls, all ancient and all in good repair around it, there a little group of these people assembled. Such parties were mostly composed of an aged man and woman, with the younger members of a family; their faces were full of joy, so deep that it assumed the shade of melancholy; they pointed to each other the minutest objects about the homesteads, things in their hearts, and were now comparing them with the originals. But where hollow places by the wayside, grass-grown, and uneven, with unsightly chimneys rising ruinous in the midst, gave indications of a fallen dwelling and of hearths long cold, there did a few of the strangers sit them down on the mouldering beams, and on the yellow moss that had overspread the door-stone. The men folded their arms, sad and speechless; the women wrung their hands with a more vivid expression of grief; and the little children tottered to their knees, shrinking away from the open grave of domestic love. And wherever a recent edifice reared its white and flashy front on the foundation of an old one, there a gray-haired man might be seen to shake his staff in anger at it, while his aged dame and their offspring appeared to join in their maledictions, forming a fearful picture in the ghostly moonlight. While these scenes were passing, the one figure in the rear of all the rest was descending the hollow towards the mill, and the eyes of David and Esther were drawn thence to a pair with whom they could fully sympathize. It was a youth in a sailor's dress and a pale slender maiden, who met each other with a sweet embrace in the middle of the street.

"How long it must be since they parted," observed David.

"Fifty years at least," said Esther.

They continued to gaze with wondering calmness and quiet interest, as the dream (if such it were) unrolled its quaint and motley semblance before them, and their notice was now attracted by several little knots of people apparently engaged in conversation. Of these one of the earliest collected and most characteristic was near the tavern, the persons who composed it being seated on the low green bank along the left side of the door. A conspicuous figure here was a fine corpulent old fellow in his shirt-sleeves and flame-colored breeches, and with a stained white apron over his paunch, beneath which he held his hands, and wherewith at times he wiped his ruddy face. The stately decrepitude of one of his companions, the scar of an Indian tomahawk on his crown, and especially his worn buff-coat, were appropriate marks of a veteran belonging to an old Provincial garrison, now deaf to the roll-call. Another showed his rough face under a tarry hat and wore a pair of wide trousers, like an ancient mariner who had tossed away his youth upon the sea, and was returned, hoary and weather-beaten, to his inland home. There was also a thin young man, carelessly dressed, who ever and anon cast a sad look towards the pale maiden above mentioned. With these there sat a hunter, and one or two others, and they were soon joined by a miller, who came upward from the dusty mill, his coat as white as if besprinkled with powdered starlight. All these (by the aid of jests, which might indeed be old, but had not been recently repeated) waxed very merry, and it was rather strange, that just as their sides shook with the heartiest laughter, they appeared greatly like a group of shadows flickering in the moonshine. Four personages, very different from these, stood in front of the large house with its periwig of creeping plants. One was a little elderly figure, distinguished by the gold on his three-cornered hat and sky-blue coat, and by the seal of arms annexed to his great gold watch-chain; his air and aspect befitted a Justice of Peace and County Major, and all earth's pride and pomposity were squeezed into this small gentleman of five feet high. The next in importance was a grave person of sixty or seventy years, whose black suit and band sufficiently indicated his character, and the polished baldness of whose head was worthy of a famous preacher in the village, half a century before, who had made wigs a subject of pulpit denunciation. The two other figures, both clad in dark gray, showed the sobriety of Deacons; one was ridiculously tall and thin, like a man of ordinary bulk infinitely produced, as the mathematicians say; while the brevity and thickness of his colleague seemed a compression of the same man. These four talked with great earnestness, and their gestures intimated that they had revived the ancient dispute about the meeting-house steeple. The grave person in black spoke with composed solemnity, as if he were addressing a Synod; the short deacon grunted out occasional sentences, as brief as himself; his tall brother drew the long thread of his argument through the whole discussion, and (reasoning from analogy) his voice must indubitably have been small and squeaking. But the little old man in gold-lace was evidently scorched by his own red-hot eloquence; he bounced from one to another, shook his cane at the steeple, at the two deacons, and almost in the parson's face, stamping with his foot fiercely enough to break a hole through the very earth; though, indeed, it could not exactly be said that the green grass bent beneath him. The figure, noticed as coming behind all the rest, had now surmounted the ascent from the mill, and proved to be an elderly lady with something in her hand.

"Why does she walk so slow?" asked David.

"Don't you see she is lame?" said Esther.

This gentlewoman, whose infirmity had kept her so far in the rear of the crowd, now came hobbling on, glided unobserved by the polemic group, and paused on the left brink of the fountain, within a few feet of the two spectators. She was a magnificent old dame, as ever mortal eye beheld. Her spangled shoes and gold-clocked stockings shone gloriously within the spacious circle of a red hoop-petticoat, which swelled to the very point of explosion, and was bedecked all over with embroidery a little tarnished. Above the petticoat, and parting in front so as to display it to the best advantage, was a figured blue damask gown. A wide and stiff ruff encircled her neck, a cap of the finest muslin, though rather dingy, covered her head, and her nose was bestridden by a pair of gold-bowed spectacles with enormous glasses. But the old lady's face was pinched, sharp, and sallow, wearing a niggardly and avaricious expression, and forming an odd contrast to the splendor of her attire, as did likewise the implement which she held in her hand. It was a sort of iron shovel (by housewives termed a "slice"), such as is used in clearing the oven, and with this, selecting a spot between a walnut-tree and the fountain, the good dame made an earnest attempt to dig. The tender sods, however, possessed a strange impenetrability. They resisted her efforts like a quarry of living granite, and, losing her breath, she cast down the shovel and seemed to bemoan herself most piteously, gnashing her teeth (what few she had) and wringing her thin yellow hands. Then, apparently with new hope, she resumed her toil, which still had the same result,—a circumstance the less surprising to David and Esther, because at times they would catch the moonlight shining through the old woman, and dancing in the fountain beyond. The little man in gold-lace now happened to see her, and made his approach on tiptoe.

"How hard this elderly lady works!" remarked David.

"Go and help her, David," said Esther, compassionately.

As their drowsy voices spoke, both the old woman and the pompous little figure behind her lifted their eyes, and for a moment they regarded the youth and damsel with something like kindness and affection; which, however, were dim and uncertain, and passed away almost immediately. The old woman again betook herself to the shovel, but was startled by a hand suddenly laid upon her shoulder; she turned round in great trepidation, and beheld the dignitary in the blue coat; then followed an embrace of such closeness as would indicate no remoter connection than matrimony between these two decorous persons. The gentleman next pointed to the shovel, appearing to inquire the purpose of his lady's occupation; while she as evidently parried his interrogatories, maintaining a demure and sanctified visage as every good woman ought, in similar cases. Howbeit, she could not forbear looking askew, behind her spectacles, towards the spot of stubborn turf. All the while, their figures had a strangeness in them, and it seemed as if some cunning jeweller had made their golden ornaments of the yellowest of the setting sunbeams, and that the blue of their garments was brought from the dark sky near the moon, and that the gentleman's silk waistcoat was the bright side of a fiery cloud, and the lady's scarlet petticoat a remnant of the blush of morning,—and that they both were two unrealities of colored air. But now there was a sudden movement throughout the multitude. The Squire drew forth a watch as large as the dial on the famous steeple, looked at the warning hands and got him gone, nor could his lady tarry; the party at the tavern door took to their heels, headed by the fat man in the flaming breeches; the tall deacon stalked away immediately, and the short deacon waddled after, making four steps to the yard; the mothers called their children about them and set forth, with a gentle and sad glance behind. Like cloudy fantasies that hurry by a viewless impulse from the sky, they all were fled, and the wind rose up and followed them with a strange moaning down the

lonely street. Now whither these people went is more than
may be told; only David and Esther seemed to see the shadowy
splendor of the ancient dame, as she lingered in the moonshine at the graveyard gate, gazing backward to the fountain.

"O Esther! I have had such a dream!" cried David, starting
up, and rubbing his eyes.

"And I such another!" answered Esther, gaping till her
pretty red lips formed a circle.

"About an old woman with gold-bowed spectacles," continued David.

"And a scarlet hoop-petticoat," added Esther. They now
stared in each other's eyes, with great astonishment and some
little fear. After a thoughtful moment or two, David drew
a long breath and stood upright.

"If I live till to-morrow morning," said he, "I'll see what
may be buried between that tree and the spring of water."

"And why not to-night, David?" asked Esther; for she was
a sensible little girl, and bethought herself that the matter
might as well be done in secrecy.

David felt the propriety of the remark, and looked round
for the means of following her advice. The moon shone
brightly on something that rested against the side of the old
house, and, on a nearer view, it proved to be an iron shovel,
bearing a singular resemblance to that which they had seen
in their dreams. He used it with better success than the old
woman, the soil giving way so freely to his efforts, that he had
soon scooped a hole as large as the basin of the spring. Suddenly, he poked his head down to the very bottom of this
cavity. "Oho!—what have we here?" cried David.

THE WIVES
OF THE DEAD

Τhe following story, the simple and domestic incidents of which may be deemed scarcely worth relating, after such a lapse of time, awakened some degree of interest, a hundred years ago, in a principal seaport of the Bay Province. The rainy twilight of an autumn day,—a parlor on the second floor of a small house, plainly furnished, as beseemed the middling circumstances of its inhabitants, yet decorated with little curiosities from beyond the sea, and a few delicate specimens of Indian manufacture,—these are the only particulars to be premised in regard to scene and season. Two young and comely women sat together by the fireside, nursing their mutual and peculiar sorrows. They were the recent brides of two brothers, a sailor and a landsman, and two successive days had brought tidings of the death of each, by the chances of Canadian warfare and the tempestuous Atlantic. The universal sympathy excited by this bereavement drew numerous condoling guests to the habitation of the widowed sisters. Several, among whom was the minister, had remained till the verge of evening, when, one by one, whispering many comfortable passages of Scripture that were answered by more abundant tears, they took their leave, and departed to their own happier homes. The mourners, though not insensible to the kindness of their friends, had yearned to be left alone. United, as they had been, by the relationship of the living,

First published in *The Token,* 1832.

and now more closely so by that of the dead, each felt as if whatever consolation her grief admitted were to be found in the bosom of the other. They joined their hearts, and wept together silently. But after an hour of such indulgence, one of the sisters, all of whose emotions were influenced by her mild, quiet, yet not feeble character, began to recollect the precepts of resignation and endurance which piety had taught her, when she did not think to need them. Her misfortune, besides, as earliest known, should earliest cease to interfere with her regular course of duties; accordingly, having placed the table before the fire, and arranged a frugal meal, she took the hand of her companion.

"Come, dearest sister; you have eaten not a morsel to-day," she said. "Arise, I pray you, and let us ask a blessing on that which is provided for us."

Her sister-in-law was of a lively and irritable temperament, and the first pangs of her sorrow had been expressed by shrieks and passionate lamentation. She now shrunk from Mary's words, like a wounded sufferer from a hand that revives the throb.

"There is no blessing left for me, neither will I ask it!" cried Margaret, with a fresh burst of tears. "Would it were His will that I might never taste food more!"

Yet she trembled at these rebellious expressions, almost as soon as they were uttered, and, by degrees, Mary succeeded in bringing her sister's mind nearer to the situation of her own. Time went on, and their usual hour of repose arrived. The brothers and their brides, entering the married state with no more than the slender means which then sanctioned such a step, had confederated themselves in one household, with equal rights to the parlor, and claiming exclusive privileges in two sleeping-rooms contiguous to it. Thither the widowed ones retired, after heaping ashes upon the dying embers of their fire, and placing a lighted lamp upon the hearth. The doors of both chambers were left open, so that a part of the interior of each, and the beds, with their unclosed curtains, were reciprocally visible. Sleep did not steal upon the sisters at one and the same time. Mary experienced the effect often consequent upon grief quietly borne, and soon sunk into temporary forgetfulness; while Margaret became more disturbed and feverish, in proportion as the night advanced with its deepest and stillest hours. She lay listening to the drops of rain that came down in monotonous succession, unswayed by a breath of wind; and a nervous impulse continually caused her to lift her head from the pillow, and gaze into Mary's chamber and the intermediate apartment. The cold light of the lamp threw the shadows of the furniture up against the wall, stamping them immovably there, except when they were shaken by a sudden flicker of the flame. Two vacant arm-chairs were in their old positions on opposite sides of the hearth, where the brothers had been wont to sit in young and laughing dignity, as heads of families; two humbler seats were near them, the true thrones of that little empire, where Mary and herself had exercised in love a power that love had won. The cheerful radiance of the fire had shone upon the happy circle, and the dead glimmer of the lamp might have befitted their reunion now. While Margaret groaned in bitterness, she heard a knock at the street-door.

"How would my heart have leapt at that sound but yesterday!" thought she, remembering the anxiety with which she had long awaited tidings from her husband. "I care not for it now; let them begone, for I will not arise."

But even while a sort of childish fretfulness made her thus resolve, she was breathing hurriedly, and straining her ears to catch a repetition of the summons. It is difficult to be convinced of the death of one whom we have deemed another self. The knocking was now renewed in slow and regular strokes, apparently given with the soft end of a doubled fist, and was accompanied by words, faintly heard through several thicknesses of wall. Margaret looked to her sister's chamber, and beheld her still lying in the depths of sleep. She arose, placed her foot upon the floor, and slightly arrayed herself, trembling between fear and eagerness as she did so.

"Heaven help me!" sighed she. "I have nothing left to fear,

and methinks I am ten times more a coward than ever."

Seizing the lamp from the hearth, she hastened to the window that overlooked the street-door. It was a lattice, turning upon hinges; and having thrown it back, she stretched her head a little way into the moist atmosphere. A lantern was reddening the front of the house, and melting its light in the neighboring puddles, while a deluge of darkness overwhelmed every other object. As the window grated on its hinges, a man in a broadbrimmed hat and blanket-coat stepped from under the shelter of the projecting story, and looked upward to discover whom his application had aroused. Margaret knew him as a friendly innkeeper of the town.

"What would you have, Goodman Parker?" cried the widow.

"Lackaday, is it you, Mistress Margaret?" replied the innkeeper. "I was afraid it might be your sister Mary; for I hate to see a young woman in trouble, when I haven't a word of comfort to whisper her."

"For Heaven's sake, what news do you bring?" screamed Margaret.

"Why, there has been an express through the town within this half-hour," said Goodman Parker, "travelling from the eastern jurisdiction with letters from the governor and council. He tarried at my house to refresh himself with a drop and a morsel, and I asked him what tidings on the frontiers. He tells me we had the better in the skirmish you wot of, and that thirteen men reported slain are well and sound, and your husband among them. Besides, he is appointed of the escort to bring the captivated Frenchers and Indians home to the province jail. I judged you wouldn't mind being broke of your rest, and so I stepped over to tell you. Good night."

So saying, the honest man departed; and his lantern gleamed along the streets, bringing to view indistinct shapes of things, and the fragments of a world, like order glimmering through chaos, or memory roaming over the past. But Margaret stayed not to watch these picturesque effects. Joy flashed into her heart, and lighted it up at once; and breathless, and with winged steps, she flew to the bedside of her sister. She paused, however, at the door of the chamber, while a thought of pain broke in upon her.

"Poor Mary!" said she to herself. "Shall I waken her, to feel her sorrow sharpened by my happiness? No; I will keep it within my own bosom till the morrow."

She approached the bed, to discover if Mary's sleep were peaceful. Her face was turned partly inward to the pillow, and had been hidden there to weep; but a look of motionless contentment was now visible upon it, as if her heart, like a deep lake, had grown calm because its dead had sunk down so far within. Happy is it, and strange, that the lighter sorrows are those from which dreams are chiefly fabricated. Margaret shrunk from disturbing her sister-in-law, and felt as if her own better fortune had rendered her involuntarily unfaithful, and as if altered and diminished affection must be the consequence of the disclosure she had to make. With a sudden step she turned away. But joy could not long be repressed, even by circumstances that would have excited heavy grief at another moment. Her mind was thronged with delightful thoughts, till sleep stole on, and transformed them to visions, more delightful and more wild, like the breath of winter (but what a cold comparison!) working fantastic tracery upon a window.

When the night was far advanced, Mary awoke with a sudden start. A vivid dream had latterly involved her in its unreal life, of which, however, she could only remember that it had been broken in upon at the most interesting point. For a little time, slumber hung about her like a morning mist, hindering her from perceiving the distinct outline of her situation. She listened with imperfect consciousness to two or three volleys of a rapid and eager knocking; and first she deemed the noise a matter of course, like the breath she drew; next, it appeared a thing in which she had no concern; and lastly, she became aware that it was a summons necessary to be obeyed. At the same moment, the pang of recollection darted into her mind; the pall of sleep was thrown back from the face of grief; the dim light of the chamber, and the objects therein revealed, had retained all her suspended ideas, and restored them as soon as she unclosed her eyes. Again there was a quick peal upon the street-door. Fearing that her sister would also be disturbed, Mary wrapped herself in a cloak and hood, took the lamp from the hearth, and hastened to the window. By some accident, it had been left unhasped, and yielded easily to her hand.

"Who's there?" asked Mary, trembling as she looked forth.

The storm was over, and the moon was up; it shone upon broken clouds above, and below upon houses black with moisture, and upon little lakes of the fallen rain, curling into silver beneath the quick enchantment of a breeze. A young man in a sailor's dress, wet as if he had come out of the depths of the sea, stood alone under the window. Mary recognized him as one whose livelihood was gained by short voyages along the coast; nor did she forget that, previous to her marriage, he had been an unsuccessful wooer of her own.

"What do you seek here, Stephen?" said she.

"Cheer up, Mary, for I seek to comfort you," answered the rejected lover. "You must know I got home not ten minutes ago, and the first thing my good mother told me was the news about your husband. So, without saying a word to the old woman, I clapped on my hat, and ran out of the house. I couldn't have slept a wink before speaking to you, Mary, for the sake of old times."

"Stephen, I thought better of you!" exclaimed the widow, with gushing tears and preparing to close the lattice; for she was no whit inclined to imitate the first wife of Zadig.

"But stop, and hear my story out," cried the young sailor. "I tell you we spoke a brig yesterday afternoon, bound in from old England. And whom do you think I saw standing on deck, well and hearty, only a bit thinner than he was five months ago?"

Mary leaned from the window, but could not speak.

"Why, it was your husband himself," continued the generous seaman. "He and three others saved themselves on a spar, when the Blessing turned bottom upwards. The brig will beat into the bay by daylight, with this wind, and you'll see him here tomorrow. There's the comfort I bring you, Mary, and so good night."

He hurried away, while Mary watched him with a doubt of waking reality, that seemed stronger or weaker as he alternately entered the shade of the houses, or emerged into the broad streaks of moonlight. Gradually, however, a blessed flood of conviction swelled into her heart, in strength enough to overwhelm her, had its increase been more abrupt. Her first impulse was to rouse her sister-in-law, and communicate the new-born-gladness. She opened the chamber-door, which had been closed in the course of the night, though not latched, advanced to the bedside, and was about to lay her hand upon the slumberer's shoulder. But then she remembered that Margaret would awake to thoughts of death and woe, rendered not the less bitter by their contrast with her own felicity. She suffered the rays of the lamp to fall upon the unconscious form of the bereaved one. Margaret lay in unquiet sleep, and the drapery was displaced around her; her young cheek was rosy-tinted, and her lips half opened in a vivid smile; an expression of joy, debarred its passage by her sealed eyelids, struggled forth like incense from the whole countenance.

"My poor sister! you will waken too soon from that happy dream," thought Mary.

Before retiring, she set down the lamp, and endeavored to arrange the bedclothes so that the chill air might not do harm to the feverish slumberer. But her hand trembled against Margaret's neck, a tear also fell upon her cheek, and she suddenly awoke.

MY KINSMAN,
MAJOR MOLINEUX

After the kings of Great Britain had assumed the right of appointing the colonial governors, the measures of the latter seldom met with the ready and generous approbation which had been paid to those of their predecessors, under the original charters. The people looked with most jealous scrutiny to the exercise of power which did not emanate from themselves, and they usually rewarded their rulers with slender gratitude for the compliances by which, in softening their instructions from beyond the sea, they had incurred the reprehension of those who gave them. The annals of Massachusetts Bay will inform us, that of six governors in the space of about forty years from the surrender of the old charter, under James II., two imprisoned by a popular insurrection; a third, as Hutchinson inclines to believe, was driven from the province by the whizzing of a musket-ball; a fourth, in the opinion of the same historian, was hastened to his grave by continual bickerings with the House of Representatives; and the remaining two, as well as their successors, till the Revolution, were favored with few and brief intervals of peaceful sway. The inferior members of the court party, in times of high political excitement, led scarcely a more desirable life. These remarks may serve as a preface to the following adventures, which chanced upon a summer night, not

First published in *The Token*, 1832.

far from a hundred years ago. The reader, in order to avoid a long and dry detail of colonial affairs, is requested to dispense with an account of the train of circumstances that had caused much temporary inflammation of the popular mind.

It was near nine o'clock of a moonlight evening, when a boat crossed the ferry with a single passenger, who had obtained his conveyance at that unusual hour by the promise of an extra fare. While he stood on the landing-place, searching in either pocket for the means of fulfilling his agreement, the ferryman lifted a lantern, by the aid of which, and the newly risen moon, he took a very accurate survey of the stranger's figure. He was a youth of barely eighteen years, evidently country-bred, and now, as it should seem, upon his first visit to town. He was clad in a coarse gray coat, well worn, but in excellent repair; his under garments were durably constructed of leather, and fitted tight to a pair of serviceable and well-shaped limbs; his stockings of blue yarn were the incontrovertible work of a mother or a sister; and on his head was a three-cornered hat, which in its better days had perhaps sheltered the graver brow of the lad's father. Under his left arm was a heavy cudgel formed of an oak sapling, and retaining a part of the hardened root; and his equipment was completed by a wallet, not so abundantly stocked as to incommode the vigorous shoulders on which it hung. Brown, curly hair, well-shaped features, and bright, cheerful eyes were nature's gifts, and worth all that art could have done for his adornment.

The youth, one of whose names was Robin, finally drew from his pocket the half of a little province bill of five shillings, which, in the depreciation in that sort of currency, did but satisfy the ferryman's demand, with the surplus of a sexangular piece of parchment, valued at three pence. He then walked forward into the town, with as light a step as if his day's journey had not already exceeded thirty miles, and with as eager an eye as if he were entering London city, instead of the little metropolis of a New England colony. Before Robin had proceeded far, however, it occurred to him that he knew not whither to direct his steps; so he paused, and looked up and down the narrow street, scrutinizing the small and mean wooden buildings that were scattered on either side.

"This low hovel cannot be my kinsman's dwelling," thought he, "nor yonder old house, where the moonlight enters at the broken casement; and truly I see none hereabouts that might be worthy of him. It would have been wise to inquire my way of the ferryman, and doubtless he would have gone with me, and earned a shilling from the Major for his pains. But the next man I meet will do as well."

He resumed his walk, and was glad to perceive that the street now became wider, and the houses more respectable in their appearance. He soon discerned a figure moving on moderately in advance, and hastened his steps to overtake it. As Robin drew nigh, he saw that the passenger was a man in years, with a full periwig of gray hair, a wide-skirted coat of dark cloth, and silk stockings rolled above his knees. He carried a long and polished cane, which he struck down perpendicularly before him at every step; and at regular intervals he uttered two successive hems, of a peculiarly solemn and sepulchral intonation. Having made these observations, Robin laid hold of the skirt of the old man's coat, just when the light from the open door and windows of a barber's shop fell upon both their figures.

"Good evening to you, honored sir," said he, making a low bow, and still retaining his hold of the skirt. "I pray you tell me whereabouts is the dwelling of my kinsman, Major Molineux."

The youth's question was uttered very loudly; and one of the barbers, whose razor was descending on a well-soaped chin, and another who was dressing a Ramillies wig, left their occupations, and came to the door. The citizen, in the mean time, turned a long-favored countenance upon Robin, and answered him in a tone of excessive anger and annoyance. His two sepulchral hems, however, broke into the very centre of his rebuke, with most singular effect, like a thought of the cold grave obtruding among wrathful passions.

"Let go my garment, fellow! I tell you, I know not the

man you speak of. What! I have authority, I have—hem, hem —authority; and if this be the respect you show for your betters, your feet shall be brought acquainted with the stocks by daylight, tomorrow morning!"

Robin released the old man's skirt, and hastened away, pursued by an ill-mannered roar of laughter from the barber's shop. He was at first considerably surprised by the result of his question, but, being a shrewd youth, soon thought himself able to account for the mystery.

"This is some country representative," was his conclusion, "who has never seen the inside of my kinsman's door, and lacks the breeding to answer a stranger civilly. The man is old, or verily—I might be tempted to turn back and smite him on the nose. Ah, Robin, Robin! even the barber's boys laugh at you for choosing such a guide! You will be wiser in time, friend Robin."

He now became entangled in a succession of crooked and narrow streets, which crossed each other, and meandered at no great distance from the water-side. The smell of tar was obvious to his nostrils, the masts of vessels pierced the moonlight above the tops of the buildings, and the numerous signs, which Robin paused to read, informed him that he was near the centre of business. But the streets were empty, the shops were closed, and lights were visible only in the second stories of a few dwelling-houses. At length, on the corner of a narrow lane, through which he was passing, he beheld the broad countenance of a British hero swinging before the door of an inn, whence proceeded the voices of many guests. The casement of one of the lower windows was thrown back, and a very thin curtain permitted Robin to distinguish a party at supper, round a well-furnished table. The fragrance of the good cheer steamed forth into the outer air, and the youth could not fail to recollect that the last remnant of his travelling stock of provision had yielded to his morning appetite, and that noon had found and left him dinnerless.

"Oh, that a parchment three-penny might give me a right to sit down at yonder table!" said Robin, with a sigh. "But the Major will make me welcome to the best of his victuals;

so I will even step boldly in, and inquire my way to his dwelling."

He entered the tavern, and was guided by the murmur of voices and the fumes of tobacco to the public-room. It was a long and low apartment, with oaken walls, grown dark in the continual smoke, and a floor which was thickly sanded, but of no immaculate purity. A number of persons—the larger part of whom appeared to be mariners, or in some way connected with the sea—occupied the wooden benches, or leather-bottomed chairs, conversing on various matters, and occasionally lending their attention to some topic of general interest. Three or four little groups were draining as many bowls of punch, which the West India trade had long since made a familiar drink in the colony. Others, who had the appearance of men who lived by regular and laborious handicraft, preferred the insulated bliss of an unshared potation, and became more taciturn under its influence. Nearly all, in short, evinced a predilection for the Good Creature in some of its various shapes, for this is a vice to which, as Fast Day sermons of a hundred years ago will testify, we have a long hereditary claim. The only guests to whom Robin's sympathies inclined him were two or three sheepish countrymen, who were using the inn somewhat after the fashion of a Turkish caravansary; they had gotten themselves into the darkest corner of the room, and heedless of the Nicotian atmosphere, were supping on the bread of their own ovens, and the bacon cured in their own chimney-smoke. But though Robin felt a sort of brotherhood with these strangers, his eyes were attracted from them to a person who stood near the door, holding whispered conversation with a group of ill-dressed associates. His features were separately striking almost to grotesqueness, and the whole face left a deep impression on the memory. The forehead bulged out into a double prominence, with a vale between; the nose came boldly forth in an irregular curve, and its bridge was of more than a finger's breadth; the eyebrows were deep and shaggy, and the eyes glowed beneath them like fire in a cave.

While Robin deliberated of whom to inquire respecting his

kinsman's dwelling, he was accosted by the innkeeper, a little man in a stained white apron, who had come to pay his professional welcome to the stranger. Being in the second generation from a French Protestant, he seemed to have inherited the courtesy of his parent nation; but no variety of circumstances was ever known to change his voice from the one shrill note in which he now addressed Robin.

"From the country, I presume, sir?" said he, with a profound bow. "Beg leave to congratulate you on your arrival, and trust you intend a long stay with us. Fine town here, sir, beautiful buildings, and much that may interest a stranger. May I hope for the honor of your commands in respect to supper?"

"The man sees a family likeness! the rogue has guessed that I am related to the Major!" thought Robin, who had hitherto experienced little superfluous civility.

All eyes were now turned on the country lad, standing at the door, in his worn three-cornered hat, gray coat, leather breeches, and blue yarn stockings, leaning on an oaken cudgel, and bearing a wallet on his back.

Robin replied to the courteous innkeeper, with such an assumption of confidence as befitted the Major's relative. "My honest friend," he said, "I shall make it a point to patronize your house on some occasion, when"—here he could not help lowering his voice—"when I may have more than a parchment three-pence in my pocket. My present business," continued he, speaking with lofty confidence, "is merely to inquire my way to the dwelling of my kinsman, Major Molineux."

There was a sudden and general movement in the room, which Robin interpreted as expressing the eagerness of each individual to become his guide. But the innkeeper turned his eyes to a written paper on the wall, which he read, or seemed to read, with occasional recurrences to the young man's figure.

"What have we here?" said he, breaking his speech into little dry fragments. "'Left the house of the subscriber, bounden servant, Hezekiah Mudge,—had on, when he went away, gray coat, leather breeches, master's third-best hat. One pound currency reward to whosoever shall lodge him in any jail of the province.' Better trudge, boy; better trudge!''

Robin had begun to draw his hand towards the lighter end of the oak cudgel, but a strange hostility in every countenance induced him to relinquish his purpose of breaking the courteous innkeeper's head. As he turned to leave the room, he encountered a sneering glance from the bold-featured personage whom he had before noticed; and no sooner was he beyond the door, than he heard a general laugh, in which the innkeeper's voice might be distinguished, like the dropping of small stones into a kettle.

"Now, is it not strange," thought Robin, with his usual shrewdness,—"is it not strange that the confession of an empty pocket should outweigh the name of my kinsman, Major Molineux? Oh, if I had one of those grinning rascals in the woods, where I and my oak sapling grew up together, I would teach him that my arm is heavy though my purse be light!''

On turning the corner of the narrow lane, Robin found himself in a spacious street, with an unbroken line of lofty houses in each side, and a steepled building at the upper end, whence the ringing of a bell announced the hour of nine. The light of the moon, and the lamps from the numerous shop-windows, discovered people promenading on the pavement, and amongst them Robin had hoped to recognize his hitherto inscrutable relative. The result of his former inquiries made him unwilling to hazard another, in a scene of such publicity, and he determined to walk slowly and silently up the street, thrusting his face close to that of every elderly gentleman, in search of the Major's lineaments. In his progress, Robin encountered many gay and gallant figures. Embroidered garments of showy colors, enormous periwigs, gold-laced hats, and silver-hilted swords glided past him and dazzled his optics. Travelled youths, imitators of the European fine gentlemen of the period, trod jauntily along, half dancing to the fashionable tunes which they hummed, and making poor Robin ashamed of his quiet and natural gait. At length, after many pauses to examine the gorgeous display of goods in the shop-windows, and after suffering some rebukes for the impertinence of his scrutiny into people's faces, the Major's kinsman found himself near the steepled building, still unsuccessful in his search. As yet, however, he had seen only one side of the thronged street; so Robin crossed, and continued the same sort of inquisition down the opposite pavement, with stronger hopes than the philosopher seeking an honest man, but with no better fortune. He had arrived about midway towards the lower end, from which his course began, when he overheard the approach of some one who struck down a cane on the flag-stones at every step, uttering at regular intervals, two sepulchral hems.

"Mercy on us!" quoth Robin, recognizing the sound.

Turning a corner, which chanced to be close at his right hand, he hastened to pursue his researches in some other part of the town. His patience now was wearing low, and he seemed to feel more fatigue from his rambles since he crossed the ferry, than from his journey of several days on the other side. Hunger also pleaded loudly within him, and Robin began to balance the propriety of demanding, violently, and with lifted cudgel, the necessary guidance from the first solitary passenger whom he should meet. While a resolution to this effect was gaining strength, he entered a street of mean appearance, on either side of which a row of ill-built houses was straggling towards the harbor. The moonlight fell upon no passenger along the whole extent, but in the third domicile which Robin passed there was a half-opened door, and his keen glance detected a woman's garment within.

"My luck may be better here," said he to himself.

Accordingly, he approached the door, and beheld it shut closer as he did so; yet an open space remained, sufficing for the fair occupant to observe the stranger, without a corresponding display on her part. All that Robin could discern was a strip of scarlet petticoat, and the occasional sparkle of an eye, as if the moonbeams were trembling on some bright thing.

"Pretty mistress," for I may call her so with a good conscience, thought the shrewd youth, since I know nothing to the contrary,—"my sweet pretty mistress, will you be kind enough to tell me whereabouts I must seek the dwelling of my kinsman, Major Molineux?"

Robin's voice was plaintive and winning, and the female, seeing nothing to be shunned in the handsome country youth, thrust open the door, and came forth into the moonlight. She was a dainty little figure, with a white neck, round arms, and a slender waist, at the extremity of which her scarlet petticoat jutted out over a hoop, as if she were standing in a balloon. Moreover, her face was oval and pretty, her hair dark beneath the little cap, and her bright eyes possessed a sly freedom, which triumphed over those of Robin.

"Major Molineux dwells here," said this fair woman.

Now, her voice was the sweetest Robin had heard that night, yet he could not help doubting whether that sweet voice spoke Gospel truth. He looked up and down the mean street, and then surveyed the house before which they stood. It was a small, dark edifice of two stories, the second of which projected over the lower floor, and the front apartment had the aspect of a shop for petty commodities.

"Now, truly, I am in luck," replied Robin, cunningly, "and so indeed is my kinsman, the Major, in having so pretty a housekeeper. But I prithee trouble him to step to the door; I will deliver him a message from his friends in the country, and then go back to my lodgings at the inn."

"Nay, the Major has been abed this hour or more," said the lady of the scarlet petticoat; "and it would be to little purpose to disturb him to-night, seeing his evening draught was of the strongest. But he is a kind-hearted man, and it would be as much as my life's worth to let a kinsman of his turn away from the door. You are the good old gentleman's very picture, and I could swear that was his rainy-weather hat. Also he has garments very much resembling those leather small-clothes. But come in, I pray, for I bid you hearty welcome in his name."

So saying, the fair and hospitable dame took our hero by the hand; and the touch was light, and the force was gentleness, and though Robin read in her eyes what he did not hear in her words, yet the slender-waisted woman in the scarlet petticoat proved stronger than the athletic country youth. She had drawn his half-willing footsteps nearly to the threshold, when the opening of a door in the neighborhood startled the Major's housekeeper, and, leaving the Major's kinsman, she vanished speedily into her own domicile. A heavy yawn preceded the appearance of a man, who, like the Moonshine of Pyramus and Thisbe, carried a lantern, needlessly aiding his sister luminary in the heavens. As he walked sleepily up the street, he turned his broad, dull face on Robin, and displayed a long staff, spiked at the end.

"Home, vagabond, home!" said the watchman, in accents that seemed to fall asleep as soon as they were uttered. "Home, or we'll set you in the stocks by peep of day!"

"This is the second hint of the kind," thought Robin. "I wish they would end my difficulties, by setting me there to-night."

Nevertheless, the youth felt an instinctive antipathy towards the guardian of midnight order, which at first prevented him from asking his usual question. But just when the man was about to vanish behind the corner, Robin resolved not to lose the opportunity, and shouted lustily after him,—

"I say, friend! will you guide me to the house of my kinsman, Major Molineux?"

The watchman made no reply, but turned the corner and was gone; yet Robin seemed to hear the sound of drowsy laughter stealing along the solitary street. At that moment, also, a pleasant titter saluted him from the open window above his head; he looked up, and caught the sparkle of a saucy eye; a round arm beckoned to him, and next he heard light footsteps descending the staircase within. But Robin, being of the household of a New England clergyman, was a good youth, as well as a shrewd one; so he resisted temptation, and fled away.

He now roamed desperately, and at random, through the town, almost ready to believe that a spell was on him, like that by which a wizard of his country had once kept three pursuers wandering, a whole winter night, within twenty paces of the cottage which they sought. The streets lay before him, strange and desolate, and the lights were extinguished in almost every house. Twice, however, little parties of men, among whom Robin distinguished individuals in outlandish attire, came hurrying along; but, though on both occasions, they paused to address him, such intercourse did not at all enlighten his perplexity. They did but utter a few words in some language of which Robin knew nothing, and perceiving his inability to answer, bestowed a curse upon him in plain English and hastened away. Finally, the lad determined to knock at the door of every mansion that might appear worthy to be occupied by his kinsman, trusting that perseverance would overcome the fatality that had hitherto thwarted him. Firm in this resolve, he was passing beneath the walls of a church, which formed the corner of two streets, when, as he turned into the shade of its steeple, he encountered a bulky stranger, muffled in a cloak. The man was proceeding with the speed of earnest business, but Robin planted himself full before him, holding the oak cudgel with both hands across his body as a bar to further passage.

"Halt, honest man, and answer me a question," said he, very resolutely. "Tell me, this instant, whereabouts is the dwelling of my kinsman, Major Molineux!"

"Keep your tongue between your teeth, fool, and let me pass!" said a deep, gruff voice, which Robin partly remembered. "Let me pass, or I'll strike you to the earth!"

"No, no, neighbor!" cried Robin, flourishing his cudgel, and then thrusting its larger end close to the man's muffled face. "No, no, I'm not the fool you take me for, nor do you pass till I have an answer to my question. Whereabouts is the dwelling of my kinsman, Major Molineux?"

The stranger, instead of attempting to force his passage, stepped back into the moonlight, unmuffled his face, and stared full into that of Robin.

"Watch here an hour, and Major Molineux will pass by," said he.

Robin gazed with dismay and astonishment on the unprecedented physiognomy of the speaker. The forehead with its double prominence, the broad hooked nose, the shaggy eyebrows, and fiery eyes were those which he had noticed at the inn, but the man's complexion had undergone a singular, or, more properly, a twofold change. One side of the face blazed an intense red, while the other was black as midnight, the division line being in the broad bridge of the nose; and a mouth which seemed to extend from ear to ear was black or red, in contrast to the color of the cheek. The effect was as if two individual devils, a fiend of fire and a fiend of darkness, had united themselves to form this infernal visage. The stranger grinned in Robin's face, muffled his party-colored features, and was out of sight in a moment.

"Strange things we travellers see!" ejaculated Robin.

He seated himself, however, upon the steps of the church-door, resolving to wait the appointed time for his kinsman. A few moments were consumed in philosophical speculations upon the species of man who had just left him; but having settled this point shrewdly, rationally, and satisfactorily, he was compelled to look elsewhere for his amusement. And first he threw his eyes along the street. It was of more respectable appearance than most of those into which he had wandered; and the moon, creating, like the imaginative power, a beautiful strangeness in familiar objects, gave something of romance to a scene that might not have possessed it in the light of day. The irregular and often quaint architecture of the houses, some of whose roofs were broken into numerous little peaks, while others ascended, steep and narrow, into a single point, and others again were square; the pure snow-white of some of their complexions, the aged darkness of others, and the thousand sparklings, reflected from bright substances in the walls of many; these matters engaged Robin's attention for a while, and then began to grow wearisome. Next he endeavored to define the forms of distant objects, starting away, with almost ghostly indistinctness, just as his eye appeared to grasp them; and finally he took a minute survey of an edifice which stood on the opposite side of the street, directly in front of the church-door, where he was stationed. It was a large, square mansion, distinguished from its neighbors by a balcony, which rested on tall pillars, and by an elaborate Gothic window, communicating therewith.

"Perhaps this is the very house I have been seeking," thought Robin.

Then he strove to speed away the time, by listening to a murmur which swept continually along the street, yet was scarcely audible, except to an unaccustomed ear like his; it was a low, dull, dreamy sound, compounded of many noises, each of which was at too great a distance to be separately heard. Robin marvelled at this snore of a sleeping town, and marvelled more whenever its continuity was broken by now and then a distant shout, apparently loud where it originated. But altogether it was a sleep-inspiring sound, and, to shake off its drowsy influence, Robin arose, and climbed a window-frame, that he might view the interior of the church. There the moonbeams came trembling in, and fell down upon the deserted pews, and extended along the quiet aisles. A fainter yet more awful radiance was hovering around the pulpit, and one solitary ray had dared to rest upon the open page of the great Bible. Had nature, in that deep hour, become a worshipper in the house which man had builded? Or was that heavenly light the visible sanctity of the place,—visible because no earthly and impure feet were within the walls? The scene made Robin's heart shiver with a sensation of loneliness stronger than he had ever felt in the remotest depths of his native woods; so he turned away and sat down again before the door. There were graves around the church, and now an uneasy thought obtruded into Robin's breast. What if the object of his search, which had been so often and so strangely thwarted, were all the time mouldering in his shroud? What if his kinsman should glide through yonder gate, and nod and smile to him in dimly passing by?

"Oh that any breathing thing were here with me!" said Robin.

Recalling his thoughts from this uncomfortable track, he

sent them over forest, hill, and stream, and attempted to imagine how that evening of ambiguity and weariness had been spent by his father's household. He pictured them assembled at the door, beneath the tree, the great old tree, which had been spared for its huge twisted trunk and venerable shade, when a thousand leafy brethren fell. There, at the going down of the summer sun, it was his father's custom to perform domestic worship, that the neighbors might come and join with him like brothers of the family, and that the wayfaring man might pause to drink at that fountain, and keep his heart pure by freshening the memory of home. Robin distinguished the seat of every individual of the little audience; he saw the good man in the midst, holding the Scriptures in the golden light that fell from the western clouds; he beheld him close the book and all rise up to pray. He heard the old thanksgivings for daily mercies, the old supplications for their continuance, to which he had so often listened in weariness, but which were now among his dear remembrances. He perceived the slight inequality of his father's voice when he came to speak of the absent one; he noted how his mother turned her face to the broad and knotted trunk; how his elder brother scorned, because the beard was rough upon his upper lip, to permit his features to be moved; how the younger sister drew down a low hanging branch before her eyes; and how the littlest one of all, whose sports had hitherto broken the decorum of the scene, understood the prayer for her playmate, and burst into clamorous grief. Then he saw them go in at the door; and when Robin would have entered also, the latch tinkled into its place, and he was excluded from his home.

"Am I here, or there?" cried Robin, starting; for all at once, when his thoughts had become visible and audible in a dream, the long, wide, solitary street shone out before him.

He aroused himself, and endeavored to fix his attention steadily upon the large edifice which he had surveyed before. But still his mind kept vibrating between fancy and reality; by turns, the pillars of the balcony lengthened into the tall, bare stems of pines, dwindled down to human figures, settled

Robin can't see clearly

again into their true shape and size, and then commenced a new succession of changes. For a single moment, when he deemed himself awake, he could have sworn that a visage— one which he seemed to remember, yet could not absolutely name as his kinsman's—was looking towards him from the Gothic window. A deeper sleep wrestled with and nearly overcame him, but fled at the sound of footsteps along the opposite pavement. Robin rubbed his eyes, discerned a man passing at the foot of the balcony, and addressed him in a loud, peevish, and lamentable cry.

"Hallo, friend! must I wait here all night for my kinsman, Major Molineux?"

The sleeping echoes awoke, and answered the voice; and the passenger, barely able to discern a figure sitting in the oblique shade of the steeple, traversed the street to obtain a nearer view. He was himself a gentleman in his prime, of open, intelligent, cheerful, and altogether prepossessing countenance. Perceiving a country youth, apparently homeless and without friends, he accosted him in a tone of real kindness, which had become strange to Robin's ears.

"Well, my good lad, why are you sitting here?" inquired he. "Can I be of service to you in any way?"

"I am afraid not, sir," replied Robin, despondingly; "yet I shall take it kindly, if you'll answer me a single question. I've been searching, half the night, for one Major Molineux; now, sir, is there really such a person in these parts, or am I dreaming?"

"Major Molineux! The name is not altogether strange to me," said the gentleman, smiling. "Have you any objection to telling me the nature of your business with him?"

Then Robin briefly related that his father was a clergyman, settled on a small salary, at a long distance back in the country, and that he and Major Molineux were brothers' children. The Major, having inherited riches, and acquired civil and military rank, had visited his cousin, in great pomp, a year or two before; had manifested much interest in Robin and an elder brother, and, being childless himself, had thrown out hints respecting the future establishment of one of them in life. The elder brother was destined to succeed to the farm which his father cultivated in the interval of sacred duties; it was therefore determined that Robin should profit by his kinsman's generous intentions, especially as he seemed to be rather the favorite, and was thought to possess other necessary endowments.

"For I have the name of being a shrewd youth," observed Robin, in this part of his story.

"I doubt not you deserve it," replied his new friend, good-naturedly; "but pray proceed."

"Well, sir, being nearly eighteen years old, and well grown, as you see," continued Robin, drawing himself up to his full height, "I thought it high time to begin in the world. So my mother and sister put me in handsome trim, and my father gave me half the remnant of his last year's salary, and five days ago I started for this place, to pay the Major a visit. But, would you believe it, sir! I crossed the ferry a little after dark, and have yet found nobody that would show me the way to his dwelling; only, an hour or two since, I was told to wait here, and Major Molineux would pass by."

"Can you describe the man who told you this?" inquired the gentleman.

"Oh, he was a very ill-favored fellow, sir," replied Robin, "with two great bumps on his forehead, a hook nose, fiery eyes; and, what struck me as the strangest, his face was of two different colors. Do you happen to know such a man, sir?"

"Not intimately," answered the stranger, "but I chanced to meet him a little time previous to your stopping me. I believe you may trust his word, and that the Major will very shortly pass through this street. In the mean time, as I have a singular curiosity to witness your meeting, I will sit down here upon the steps and bear you company."

He seated himself accordingly, and soon engaged his companion in animated discourse. It was but of brief continuance, however, for a noise of shouting, which had long been remotely audible, drew so much nearer that Robin inquired its cause.

"What may be the meaning of this uproar?" asked he. "Truly, if your town be always as noisy, I shall find little sleep while I am an inhabitant."

"Why, indeed, friend Robin, there do appear to be three or four riotous fellows abroad to-night," replied the gentleman. "You must not expect all the stillness of your native woods here in our streets. But the watch will shortly be at the heels of these lads and"—

"Ay, and set them in the stocks by peep of day," interrupted Robin, recollecting his own encounter with the drowsy lantern-bearer. "But, dear sir, if I may trust my ears, an army of watchmen would never make head against such a multitude of rioters. There were at least a thousand voices went up to make that one shout."

"May not a man have several voices, Robin, as well as two complexions?" said his friend.

"Perhaps a man may; but Heaven forbid that a woman should!" responded the shrewd youth, thinking of the seductive tones of the Major's housekeeper.

The sounds of a trumpet in some neighboring street now became so evident and continual, that Robin's curiosity was strongly excited. In addition to the shouts, he heard frequent bursts from many instruments of discord, and a wild and confused laughter filled up the intervals. Robin rose from the steps, and looked wistfully towards a point whither people seemed to be hastening.

"Surely some prodigious merry-making is going on," exclaimed he. "I have laughed very little since I left home, sir, and should be sorry to lose an opportunity. Shall we step round the corner by that darkish house, and take our share of the fun?"

"Sit down again, sit down, good Robin," replied the gentleman, laying his hand on the skirt of the gray coat. "You forget that we must wait here for your kinsman; and there is reason to believe that he will pass by, in the course of a very few moments."

The near approach of the uproar had now disturbed the

neighborhood; windows flew open on all sides; and many heads, in the attire of the pillow, and confused by sleep suddenly broken, were protruded to the gaze of whoever had leisure to observe them. Eager voices hailed each other from house to house, all demanding the explanation, which not a soul could give. Half-dressed men hurried towards the unknown commotion, stumbling as they went over the stone steps that thrust themselves into the narrow footwalk. The shouts, the laughter, and the tuneless bray, the antipodes of music, came onwards with increasing din, till scattered individuals, and then denser bodies, began to appear round a corner at the distance of a hundred yards.

"Will you recognize your kinsman, if he passes in this crowd?" inquired the gentleman.

"Indeed, I can't warrant it, sir; but I'll take my stand here, and keep a bright lookout," answered Robin, descending to the outer edge of the pavement.   *overwhelming*

A mighty stream of people now emptied into the street, and came rolling slowly towards the church. A single horseman wheeled the corner in the midst of them, and close behind him came a band of fearful wind-instruments, sending forth a fresher discord now that no intervening buildings kept it from the ear. Then a redder light disturbed the moonbeams, and a dense multitude of torches shone along the street, concealing, by their glare, whatever object they illuminated. The single horseman, clad in a military dress, and bearing a drawn sword, rode onward as the leader, and, by his fierce and variegated countenance, appeared like war personified; the red of one cheek was an emblem of fire and sword; the blackness of the other betokened the mourning that attends them. In his train were wild figures in the Indian dress, and many fantastic shapes without a model, giving the whole march a visionary air, as if a dream had broken forth from some feverish brain, and were sweeping visibly through the midnight streets. A mass of people, inactive, except as applauding spectators, hemmed the procession in; and several women ran along the sidewalk, piercing the confusion of heavier sounds with their shrill voices of mirth or terror.

"The double-faced fellow has his eye upon me," muttered Robin, with an indefinite but an uncomfortable idea that he was himself to bear a part in the pageantry.

The leader turned himself in the saddle, and fixed his glance full upon the country youth, as the steed went slowly by. When Robin had freed his eyes from those fiery ones, the musicians were passing before him, and the torches were close at hand; but the unsteady brightness of the latter formed a veil which he could not penetrate. The rattling of wheels over the stones sometimes found its way to his ear, and confused traces of a human form appeared at intervals, and then melted into the vivid light. A moment more, and the leader thundered a command to halt: the trumpets vomited a horrid breath, and then held their peace; the shouts and laughter of the people died away, and there remained only a universal hum, allied to silence. Right before Robin's eyes was an uncovered cart. There the torches blazed the brightest, there the moon shone out like day, and there, in tar-and-feathery dignity, sat his kinsman, Major Molineux!

He was an elderly man, of large and majestic person, and strong, square features, betokening a steady soul; but steady as it was, his enemies had found means to shake it. His face was pale as death, and far more ghastly; the broad forehead was contracted in his agony, so that his eyebrows formed one grizzled line; his eyes were red and wild, and the foam hung white upon his quivering lip. His whole frame was agitated by a quick and continual tremor, which his pride strove to quell, even in those circumstances of overwhelming humiliation. But perhaps the bitterest pang of all was when his eyes met those of Robin; for he evidently knew him on the instant, as the youth stood witnessing the foul disgrace of a head grown gray in honor. They stared at each other in silence, and Robin's knees shook, and his hair bristled, with a mixture of pity and terror. Soon, however, a bewildering excitement began to seize upon his mind; the preceding adventures of the night, the unexpected appearance of the crowd, the torches, the confused din and the hush that followed, the spectre of his kinsman reviled by that great multitude,—all this, and, more than all, a perception of tremendous ridicule in the whole scene, affected him with a sort of mental inebriety. At that moment a voice of sluggish merriment saluted Robin's ears; he turned instinctively, and just behind the corner of the church stood the lantern-bearer, rubbing his eyes, and drowsily enjoying the lad's amazement. Then he heard a peal of laughter like the ringing of silvery bells; a woman twitched his arm, a saucy eye met his, and he saw the lady of the scarlet petticoat. A sharp, dry cachinnation appealed to his memory, and standing on tiptoe in the crowd, with his white apron over his head, he beheld the courteous little innkeeper. And lastly, there sailed over the heads of the multitude a great, broad laugh, broken in the midst by two sepulchral hems; thus, "Haw, haw, haw,—hem, hem,—haw, haw, haw, haw!"

The sound proceeded from the balcony of the opposite edifice, and thither Robin turned his eyes. In front of the Gothic window stood the old citizen, wrapped in a wide gown, his gray periwig exchanged for a nightcap, which was thrust back from his forehead, and his silk stockings hanging about his legs. He supported himself on his polished cane in a fit of convulsive merriment, which manifested itself on his solemn old features like a funny inscription on a tombstone. Then Robin seemed to hear the voices of the barbers, of the guests of the inn, and of all who had made sport of him that night. The contagion was spreading among the multitude, when all at once, it seized upon Robin, and he sent forth a shout of laughter that echoed through the street,—every man shook his sides, every man emptied his lungs, but Robin's shout was the loudest there. The cloud-spirits peeped from their silvery islands, as the congregated mirth went roaring up the sky! The Man in the Moon heard the far bellow. "Oho," quoth he, "the old earth is frolicsome to-night!"

When there was a momentary calm in that tempestuous sea of sound, the leader gave the sign, the procession resumed its march. On they went, like fiends that throng in mockery around some dead potentate, mighty no more, but majestic still in his agony. On they went, in counterfeited pomp, in senseless uproar, in frenzied merriment, trampling all on an old man's heart. On swept the tumult, and left a silent street behind.

———————

"Well, Robin, are you dreaming?" inquired the gentleman, laying his hand on the youth's shoulder.

Robin started, and withdrew his arm from the stone post to which he had instinctively clung, as the living stream rolled by him. His cheek was somewhat pale, and his eye not quite as lively as in the earlier part of the evening.

"Will you be kind enough to show me the way to the ferry?" said he, after a moment's pause.

"You have, then, adopted a new subject of inquiry?" observed his companion, with a smile.

"Why, yes, sir," replied Robin, rather dryly. "Thanks to you, and to my other friends, I have at last met my kinsman, and he will scarce desire to see my face again. I begin to grow weary of a town life, sir. Will you show me the way to the ferry?"

"No, my good friend Robin,—not to-night, at least," said the gentleman. "Some few days hence, if you wish it, I will speed you on your journey. Or, if you prefer to remain with us, perhaps, as you are a shrewd youth, you may rise in the world without the help of your kinsman, Major Molineux."

Things aren't what they seem he has to make his own way. Suggest human condition. He sees what the human condition.

ROGER MALVIN'S BURIAL

Oﾠne of the few incidents of Indian warfare naturally susceptible of the moonlight of romance was that exhibition undertaken for the defence of the frontiers in the year 1725, which resulted in the well-remembered "Lovell's Fight." Imagination, by casting certain circumstances judicially into the shade, may see much to admire in the heroism of a little band who gave battle to twice their number in the heart of the enemy's country. The open bravery displayed by both parties was in accordance with civilized ideas of valor; and chivalry itself might not blush to record the deeds of one or two individuals. The battle, though so fatal to those who fought, was not unfortunate in its consequences to the country; for it broke the strength of a tribe and conduced to the peace which subsisted during several ensuing years. History and tradition are unusually minute in their memorials of their affair; and the captain of a scouting party of frontier men has acquired as actual a military renown as many a victorious leader of thousands. Some of the incidents contained in the following pages will be recognized, notwithstanding the substitution of fictitious names, by such as have heard, from old men's lips, the fate of the few combatants who were in a condition to retreat after "Lovell's Fight."

First published in *The Token*, 1832.

The early sunbeams hovered cheerfully upon the tree-tops, beneath which two weary and wounded men had stretched their limbs the night before. Their bed of withered oak leaves was strewn upon the small level space, at the foot of a rock, situated near the summit of one of the gentle swells by which the face of the country is there diversified. The mass of granite, rearing its smooth, flat surface fifteen or twenty feet above their heads, was not unlike a gigantic gravestone, upon which the veins seemed to form an inscription in forgotten characters. On a tract of several acres around this rock, oaks and other hard-wood trees had supplied the place of the pines, which were the usual growth of the land; and a young and vigorous sapling stood close beside the travellers.

The severe wound of the elder man had probably deprived him of sleep; for, so soon as the first ray of sunshine rested on the top of the highest tree, he reared himself painfully from his recumbent posture and sat erect. The deep lines of his countenance and the scattered gray of his hair marked him as past the middle age; but his muscular frame would, but for the effect of his wound, have been as capable of sustaining fatigue as in the early vigor of life. Languor and exhaustion now sat upon his haggard features; and the despairing glance which he sent forward through the depths of the forest proved his own conviction that his pilgrimage was at an end. He next turned his eyes to the companion who reclined by his side. The youth—for he had scarcely attained the years of manhood—lay, with his head upon his arm, in the embrace of an unquiet sleep, which a thrill of pain from his wounds seemed each moment on the point of breaking. His right hand grasped a musket; and, to judge from the violent action of his features, his slumbers were bringing back a vision of the conflict of which he was one of the few survivors. A shout—deep and loud in his dreaming fancy—found its way in an imperfect murmur to his lips; and, starting even at the slight sound of his own voice, he suddenly awoke. The first act of reviving recollection was to make anxious inquiries respecting the condition of his wounded fellow-traveller. The latter shook his head.

"Reuben, my boy," said he, "this rock beneath which we sit will serve for an old hunter's gravestone. There is many and many a long mile of howling wilderness before us yet; nor would it avail me anything if the smoke of my own chimney were but on the other side of that swell of land. The Indian bullet was deadlier than I thought."

"You are weary with our three days' travel," replied the youth, "and a little longer rest will recruit you. Sit you here while I search the woods for the herbs and roots that must be our sustenance; and, having eaten, you shall lean on me, and we will turn our faces homeward. I doubt not that, with my help, you can attain to some one of the frontier garrisons."

"There is not two days' life in me, Reuben," said the other, calmly, "and I will no longer burden you with my useless body, when you can scarcely support your own. Your wounds are deep and your strength is failing fast; yet, if you hasten onward alone, you may be preserved. For me there is no hope, and I will await death here."

"If it must be so, I will remain and watch by you," said Reuben, resolutely.

"No, my son, no," rejoined his companion. "Let the wish of a dying man have weight with you; give me one grasp of your hand and get you hence. Think you that my last moments will be eased by the thought that I leave you to die a more lingering death? I have loved you like a father, Reuben; and at a time like this I should have something of a father's authority. I charge you to be gone that I may die in peace."

"And because you have been a father to me, should I therefore leave you to perish and to lie unburied in the wilderness?" exclaimed the youth. "No; if your end be in truth approaching, I will watch by you and receive your parting words. I will dig a grave here by the rock, in which, if my weakness overcome me, we will rest together; or, if Heaven gives me strength, I will seek my way home."

"In the cities and wherever men dwell," replied the other, "they bury their dead in the earth; they hide them from the sight of the living; but here, where no step may pass perhaps for a hundred years, wherefore should I not rest beneath the open sky, covered only by the oak leaves when the autumn winds shall strew them? And for a monument, here is this gray rock, on which my dying hand shall carve the name of Roger Malvin; and the traveller in days to come will know that here sleeps a hunter and a warrior. Tarry not, then, for a folly like this, but hasten away, if not for your own sake, for hers who will else be desolate."

Malvin spoke the last few words in a faltering voice, and their effect upon his companion was strongly visible. They reminded him that there were other and less questionable duties than that of sharing the fate of a man whom his death could not benefit. Nor can it be affirmed that no selfish feeling strove to enter Reuben's heart, though the consciousness made him more earnestly resist his companion's entreaties.

"How terrible to wait the slow approach of death in this solitude!" exclaimed he. "A brave man does not shrink in the battle; and, when friends stand round the bed, even women may die composedly; but here"—

"I shall not shrink even here, Reuben Bourne," interrupted Malvin. "I am a man of no weak heart, and, if I were, there is a surer support than that of earthly friends. You are young, and life is dear to you. Your last moments will need comfort far more than mine; and when you have laid me in the earth, and are alone, and night is settling on the forest, you will feel all the bitterness of the death that may now be escaped. But I will urge no selfish motive to your generous nature. Leave me for my sake, that, having said a prayer for your safety, I may have space to settle my account undisturbed by worldly sorrows."

"And your daughter,—how shall I dare to meet her eye?" exclaimed Reuben. "She will ask the fate of her father, whose life I vowed to defend with my own. Must I tell her that he travelled three days' march with me from the field of battle and that then I left him to perish in the wilderness? Were it not better to lie down and die by your side than to return safe and say this to Dorcas?"

"Tell my daughter," said Roger Malvin, "that, though yourself sore wounded, and weak, and weary, you led my tottering footsteps many a mile, and left me only at my earnest entreaty, because I would not have your blood upon my soul. Tell her that through pain and danger you were faithful, and that, if your lifeblood could have saved me, it would have flowed to its last drop; and tell her that you will be something dearer than a father, and that my blessing is with you both, and that my dying eyes can see a long and pleasant path in which you will journey together."

As Malvin spoke he almost raised himself from the ground, and the energy of his concluding words seemed to fill the wild and lonely forest with a vision of happiness; but, when he sank exhausted upon his bed of oak leaves, the light which had kindled in Reuben's eye was quenched. He felt as if it were both sin and folly to think of happiness at such a moment. His companion watched his changing countenance, and sought with generous art to wile him to his own good.

"Perhaps I deceive myself in regard to the time I have to live," he resumed. "It may be that, with speedy assistance, I might recover of my wound. The foremost fugitives must, ere this, have carried tidings of our fatal battle to the frontiers, and parties will be out to succor those in like condition with ourselves. Should you meet one of these and guide them hither, who can tell but that I may sit by my own fireside again?"

A mournful smile strayed across the features of the dying man as he insinuated that unfounded hope,—which, however, was not without its effect on Reuben. No merely selfish motive, nor even the desolate condition of Dorcas, could have induced him to desert his companion at such a moment—but his wishes seized on the thought that Malvin's life might be preserved, and his sanguine nature heightened almost to certainty the remote possibility of procuring human aid.

"Surely there is reason, weighty reason, to hope that friends are not far distant," he said, half aloud. "There fled one coward, unwounded, in the beginning of the fight, and most probably he made good speed. Every true man on the frontier would shoulder his musket at the news; and, though no party may range so far into the woods as this, I shall perhaps encounter them in one day's march. Counsel me faithfully," he added, turning to Malvin, in distrust of his own motives. "Were your situation mine, would you desert me while life remained?"

"It is now twenty years," replied Roger Malvin,—sighing, however, as he secretly acknowledged the wide dissimilarity between the two cases,—"it is now twenty years since I escaped with one dear friend from Indian captivity near Montreal. We journeyed many days through the woods, till at length overcome with hunger and weariness, my friend lay down and besought me to leave him; for he knew that, if I remained, we both must perish; and, with but little hope of obtaining succor, I heaped a pillow of dry leaves beneath his head and hastened on."

"And did you return in time to save him?" asked Reuben, hanging on Malvin's words as if they were to be prophetic of his own success.

"I did," answered the other. "I came upon the camp of a hunting party before sunset of the same day. I guided them to the spot where my comrade was expecting death; and he is now a hale and hearty man upon his own farm, far within the frontiers, while I lie wounded here in the depths of the wilderness."

This example, powerful in affecting Reuben's decision, was aided, unconsciously to himself, by the hidden strength of many another motive. Roger Malvin perceived that the victory was nearly won.

"Now, go, my son, and Heaven prosper you!" he said. "Turn not back with your friends when you meet them, lest your wounds and weariness overcome you; but send hitherward two or three, that may be spared, to search for me; and believe me, Reuben, my heart will be lighter with every step you take towards home." Yet there was, perhaps, a change both in his countenance and voice as he spoke thus; for, after all, it was a ghastly fate to be left expiring in the wilderness.

Reuben Bourne, but half convinced that he was acting rightly, at length raised himself from the ground and prepared himself for his departure. And first, though contrary to Malvin's wishes, he collected a stock of roots and herbs, which had been their only food during the last two days. This useless supply he placed within reach of the dying man, for whom, also, he swept together a bed of dry oak leaves. Then climbing to the summit of the rock, which on one side was rough and broken, he bent the oak sapling downward, and bound his handkerchief to the topmost branch. This precaution was not unnecessary to direct any who might come in search of Malvin; for every part of the rock, except its broad, smooth front, was concealed at a little distance by the dense undergrowth of the forest. The handkerchief had been the bandage of a wound upon Reuben's arm; and, as he bound it to the tree, he vowed by the blood that stained it that he would return, either to save his companion's life or to lay his body in the grave. He then descended, and stood, with downcast eyes, to receive Roger Malvin's parting words.

The experience of the latter suggested much and minute advice respecting the youth's journey through the trackless forest. Upon this subject he spoke with calm earnestness, as if he were sending Reuben to the battle or the chase while he himself remained secure at home, and not as if the human countenance that was about to leave him were the last he would ever behold. But his firmness was shaken before he concluded.

"Carry my blessing to Dorcas, and say that my last prayer shall be for her and you. Bid her to have no hard thoughts because you left me here,"—Reuben's heart smote him,—"for that your life would not have weighed with you if its sacrifice could have done me good. She will marry you after she has mourned a little while for her father; and Heaven grant you long and happy days, and may your children's children stand round your death bed! And, Reuben," added he, as the weakness of mortality made its way at last, "return, when your wounds are healed and your weariness refreshed,—return to this wild rock, and lay my bones in the grave, and say a prayer over them."

An almost superstitious regard, arising perhaps from the customs of the Indians, whose war was with the dead as well as the living, was paid by the frontier inhabitants to the rites of sepulture; and there are many instances of the sacrifice of life in the attempt to bury those who had fallen by the "sword of the wilderness." Reuben, therefore, felt the full importance of the promise which he most solemnly made to return and perform Roger Malvin's obsequies. It was remarkable that the latter, speaking his whole heart in his parting words, no longer endeavored to persuade the youth that even the speediest succor might avail to the preservation of his life. Reuben was internally convinced that he should see Malvin's living face no more. His generous nature would fain have delayed him, at whatever risk, till the dying scene were past; but the desire of existence and the hope of happiness had strengthened in his heart, and he was unable to resist them.

"It is enough," said Roger Malvin, having listened to Reuben's promise. "Go, and God speed you!"

The youth pressed his hand in silence, turned, and was departing. His slow and faltering steps, however, had borne him but a little way before Malvin's voice recalled him.

"Reuben, Reuben," said he, faintly; and Reuben returned and knelt down by the dying man.

"Raise me, and let me lean against the rock," was his last request. "My face will be turned towards home, and I shall see you a moment longer as you pass among the trees."

Reuben, having made the desired alteration in his companion's posture, again began his solitary pilgrimage. He walked more hastily at first than was consistent with his strength; for a sort of guilty feeling, which sometimes torments men in their most justifiable acts, caused him to seek concealment from Malvin's eyes; but after he had trodden far upon the rustling forest leaves he crept back, impelled by a wild and painful curiosity, and, sheltered by the earthy roots

of an uptorn tree, gazed earnestly at the desolate man. The
morning sun was unclouded, and the trees and shrubs imbibed
the sweet air of the month of May; yet there seemed a gloom
on Nature's face, as if she sympathized with mortal pain and
sorrow. Roger Malvin's hands were uplifted in a fervent
prayer, some of the words of which stole through the stillness
of the woods and entered Reuben's heart, torturing it with
an unutterable pang. They were the broken accents of a petition for his own happiness and that of Dorcas; and, as the
youth listened, conscience, or something in its similitude,
pleaded strongly with him to return and lie down again by
the rock. He felt how hard was the doom of the kind and
generous being whom he had deserted in his extremity. Death
would come like the slow approach of a corpse, stealing
gradually towards him through the forest, and showing its
ghastly and motionless features from behind a nearer and yet
a nearer tree. But such must have been Reuben's own fate
had he tarried another sunset; and who shall impute blame
to him if he shrink from so useless a sacrifice? As he gave a
parting look, a breeze waved the little banner upon the sapling
oak and reminded Reuben of his vow.

Many circumstances combined to retard the wounded
traveller in his way to the frontiers. On the second day the
clouds, gathering densely over the sky, precluded the possibility
of regulating his course by the position of the sun; and he
knew not but that every effort of his almost exhausted strength
was removing him farther from the home he sought. His
scanty sustenance was supplied by the berries and other spontaneous products of the forest. Herds of deer, it is true, sometimes bounded past him, and partridges frequently whirred
up before his footsteps; but his ammunition had been expended in the fight, and he had no means of slaying them. His
wounds, irritated by the constant exertion in which lay the
only hope of life, wore away his strength and at intervals con-

fused his reason. But, even in the wanderings of intellect, Reuben's young heart clung strongly to existence; and it was only through absolute incapacity of motion that he at last sank down beneath a tree, compelled there to await death.

In this situation he was discovered by a party who, upon the first intelligence of the fight, had been despatched to the relief of the survivors. They conveyed him to the nearest settlement, which chanced to be that of his own residence.

Dorcas, in the simplicity of the olden time, watched by the bedside of her wounded lover, and administered all those comforts that are in the sole gift of woman's heart and hands. During several days Reuben's recollection strayed drowsily among the perils and hardships through which he had passed, and he was incapable of returning definite answers to the inquiries with which many were eager to harass him. No authentic particulars of the battle had yet been circulated; nor could mothers, wives, and children tell whether their loved ones were detained by captivity or by the stronger chain of death. Dorcas nourished her apprehensions in silence till one afternoon when Reuben awoke from an unquiet sleep, and seemed to recognize her more perfectly than at any previous time. She saw that his intellect had become composed, and she could no longer restrain her filial anxiety.

"My father, Reuben?" she began; but the change in her lover's countenance made her pause.

The youth shrank as if with a bitter pain, and the blood gushed vividly into his wan and hollow cheeks. His first impulse was to cover his face; but, apparently with a desperate effort, he half raised himself and spoke vehemently, defending himself against an imaginary accusation.

"Your father was sore wounded in the battle, Dorcas; and he bade me not burden myself with him, but only to lead him to the lakeside, that he might quench his thirst and die. But I would not desert the old man in his extremity, and, though bleeding myself, I supported him; I gave him half my strength, and led him away with me. For three days we journeyed on together, and your father was sustained beyond my hopes, but, awaking at sunrise on the fourth day, I found him faint and exhausted; he was unable to proceed; his life had ebbed away fast; and"—

"He died!" exclaimed Dorcas, faintly.

Reuben felt it impossible to acknowledge that his selfish love of life had hurried him away before her father's fate was decided. He spoke not; he only bowed his head; and between shame and exhaustion, sank back and hid his face in the pillow. Dorcas wept when her fears were thus confirmed; but the shock, as it had been long anticipated, was on that account the less violent.

"You dug a grave for my poor father in the wilderness, Reuben?" was the question by which her filial piety manifested itself.

"My hands were weak; but I did what I could," replied the youth in a smothered tone. "There stands a noble tombstone above his head; and I would to Heaven I slept as soundly as he!"

Dorcas, perceiving the wildness of his latter words, inquired no further at the time; but her heart found ease in the thought that Roger Malvin had not lacked such funeral rites as it was possible to bestow. The tale of Reuben's courage and fidelity lost nothing when she communicated it to her friends; and the poor youth, tottering from his sick chamber to breathe the sunny air, experienced from every tongue the miserable and humiliating torture of unmerited praise. All acknowledged that he might worthily demand the hand of the maiden to whose father he had been "faithful unto death;" and, as my tale is not of love, it shall suffice to say that in the space of a few months Reuben became the husband of Dorcas Malvin. During the marriage ceremony the bride was covered with blushes, but the bridegroom's face was pale.

There was now in the breast of Reuben Bourne an incommunicable thought—something which he was to conceal most heedfully from her whom he most loved and trusted. He regretted, deeply and bitterly, the moral cowardice that had restrained his words when he was about to disclose the truth to Dorcas; but pride, the fear of losing her affection, the dread of universal scorn, forbade him to rectify this falsehood. He felt that for leaving Roger Malvin he deserved no censure. His presence, the gratuitous sacrifice of his own life, would have added only another and a needless agony to the last moments of the dying man; but concealment had imparted to a justifiable act much of the secret effect of guilt; and Reuben, while reason told him that he had done right, experienced in no small degree the mental horrors which punish the perpetrator of undiscovered crime. By a certain association of ideas, he at times almost imagined himself a murderer. For years, also, a thought would occasionally recur, which, though he perceived all its folly and extravagance, he had not power to banish from his mind. It was a haunting and torturing fancy that his father-in-law was yet sitting at the foot of the rock, on the withered forest leaves, alive, and awaiting his pledged assistance. These mental deceptions, however, came and went, nor did he ever mistake them for realities, but in the calmest and clearest moods of his mind he was conscious that he had a deep vow unredeemed, and that an unburied corpse was calling to him out of the wilderness. Yet such was the consequence of his prevarication that he could not obey the call. It was now too late to require the assistance of Roger Malvin's friends in performing his long-deferred sepulture; and superstitious fears, of which none were more susceptible than the people of the outward settlements, forbade Reuben to go alone. Neither did he know where in the pathless and illimitable forest to seek that smooth and lettered rock at the base of which the body lay: his remembrance of every portion of his travel thence was indistinct, and the latter part had left no impression upon his mind. There was, however, a continual impulse, a voice audible only to himself, commanding him to go forth and redeem his vow; and he had a strange impression that, were he to make the trial, he would be led straight to Malvin's bones. But year after year that summons, unheard but felt, was disobeyed. His one secret thought became like a chain binding down his spirit and like a serpent gnawing into his heart; and he was transformed into a sad and downcast yet irritable man.

In the course of a few years after their marriage changes began to be visible in the external prosperity of Reuben and Dorcas. The only riches of the former had been his stout heart and strong arm; but the latter, her father's sole heiress, had made her husband master of a farm, under older cultivation, larger, and better stocked than most of the frontier establishments. Reuben Bourne, however, was a neglectful husbandman; and, while the lands of the other settlers became annually more fruitful, his deteriorated in the same proportion. The discouragements to agriculture were greatly lessened by the cessation of Indian war, during which men held the plough in one hand and the musket in the other, and were fortunate if the products of their dangerous labor were not destroyed, either in the field or in the barn, by the savage enemy. But Reuben did not profit by the altered condition of the country; nor can it be denied that his intervals of industrious attention to his affairs were but scantily rewarded with success. The irritability by which he had recently become distinguished was another cause of his declining prosperity, as it occasioned frequent quarrels in his unavoidable intercourse with the neighboring settlers. The results of these were innumerable lawsuits; for the people of New England, in the earliest stages and wildest circumstances of the country, adopted, whenever attainable, the legal mode of deciding their differences. To be brief, the world did not go well with Reuben Bourne; and, though not till many years after his marriage, he was finally a ruined man, with but one remaining expedient against the evil fate that had pursued him. He was to throw sunlight into some deep recess of the forest, and seek subsistence from the virgin bosom of the wilderness.

The only child of Reuben and Dorcas was a son, now arrived at the age of fifteen years, beautiful in youth, and giving promise of a glorious manhood. He was peculiarly qualified for, and already began to excel in, the wild accomplishments of frontier life. His foot was fleet, his aim true, his apprehension quick, his heart glad and high; and all who anticipated the return of Indian war spoke of Cyrus Bourne as a future leader in the land. The boy was loved by his father with a deep and silent strength, as if whatever was good and happy in his own nature had been transferred to his child, carrying his affections with it. Even Dorcas, though loving and beloved, was far less dear to him; for Reuben's secret thoughts and insulated emotions had gradually made him a selfish man, and he could no longer love deeply except where he saw or imagined some reflection or likeness of his own mind. In Cyrus he recognized what he had himself been in other days, and at intervals he seemed to partake of the boy's spirit, and to be revived with a fresh and happy life. Reuben was accompanied by his son in the expedition, for the purpose of selecting a tract of land and felling and burning the timber, which necessarily preceded the removal of the household goods. Two months of autumn were thus occupied, after which Reuben Bourne and his young hunter returned to spend their last winter in the settlements.

It was early in the month of May that the little family snapped asunder whatever tendrils of affections had clung to inanimate objects, and bade farewell to the few who, in the blight of fortune, called themselves their friends. The sadness of the parting moment had, to each of the pilgrims, its peculiar alleviations. Reuben, a moody man, and misanthropic because unhappy, strode onward with his usual stern brow and downcast eye, feeling few regrets and disdaining to acknowledge any. Dorcas, while she wept abundantly over the broken ties by which her simple and affectionate nature had bound itself to everything, felt that the inhabitants of her inmost heart moved on with her, and that all else would be supplied wherever she might go. And the boy dashed one teardrop from his eye, and thought of the adventurous pleasures of the untrodden forest.

Oh, who, in the enthusiasm of a daydream, has not wished

that he were a wanderer in a world of summer wilderness, with one fair and gentle being hanging lightly on his arm? In youth his free and exulting step would know no barrier but the rolling ocean or the snow-topped mountains; calmer manhood would choose a home where Nature had strewn a double wealth in the vale of some transparent stream; and when hoary age, after long, long years of that pure life, stole on and found him there, it would find him the father of a race, the patriarch of a people, the founder of a mighty nation yet to be. When death, like the sweet sleep which we welcome after a day of happiness, came over him, his far descendants would mourn over the venerated dust. Enveloped by tradition in mysterious attributes, the men of future generations would call him godlike; and remote posterity would see him standing, dimly glorious, far up the valley of a hundred centuries.

The tangled and gloomy forest through which the personages of my tale were wandering differed widely from the dreamer's land of fantasy; yet there was something in their way of life that Nature asserted as her own, and the gnawing cares which went with them from the world were all that now obstructed their happiness. One stout and shaggy steed, the bearer of all their wealth, did not shrink from the added weight of Dorcas, although her hardy breeding sustained her, during the latter part of each day's journey, by her husband's side. Reuben and his son, their muskets on their shoulders and their axes slung behind them, kept an unwearied pace, each watching with a hunter's eye for the game that supplied their food. When hunger bade, they halted and prepared their meal on the bank of some unpolluted forest brook, which, as they knelt down with thirsty lips to drink, murmured a sweet unwillingness, like a maiden at love's first kiss. They slept beneath a hut of branches, and awoke at peep of light refreshed for the toils of another day. Dorcas and the boy went on joyously, and even Reuben's spirit shone at intervals with an outward gladness; but inwardly there was a cold, cold sorrow, which he compared to the snowdrifts lying deep in the glens and hollows of the rivulets while the leaves were brightly green above.

Cyrus Bourne was sufficiently skilled in the travel of the woods to observe that his father did not adhere to the course they had pursued in their expedition of the preceding autumn. They were now keeping farther to the north, striking out more directly from the settlements, and into a region of which savage beasts and savage men were as yet the sole possessors. The boy sometimes hinted his opinions upon the subject, and Reuben listened attentively, and once or twice altered the direction of their march in accordance with his son's counsel; but, having so done, he seemed ill at ease. His quick and wandering glances were sent forward, apparently in search of enemies lurking behind the tree trunks; and, seeing nothing there, he would cast his eyes backwards as if in fear of some pursuer. Cyrus, perceiving that his father gradually resumed the old direction, forbore to interfere; nor, though something began to weigh upon his heart, did his adventurous nature permit him to regret the increased length and the mystery of their way.

On the afternoon of the fifth day they halted, and made their simple encampment nearly an hour before sunset. The face of the country, for the last few miles, had been diversified by swells of land resembling huge waves of a petrified sea; and in one of the corresponding hollows, a wild and romantic spot, had the family reared their hut and kindled their fire. There is something chilling, and yet heart-warming, in the thought of these three, united by strong bonds of love and insulated from all that breathe beside. The dark and gloomy pines looked down upon them, and, as the wind swept through their tops, a pitying sound was heard in the forest; or did those old trees groan in fear that men were come to lay the axe to their roots at last? Reuben and his son, while Dorcas made ready their meal, proposed to wander out in search of game, of which that day's march had afforded no supply. The boy, promising not to quit the vicinity of the encampment, bounded off with a step as light and elastic as that of the deer he hoped to slay; while his father, feeling a transient happiness as he gazed after him, was about to pursue an opposite direction. Dorcas, in the meanwhile, had

seated herself near their fire of fallen branches, upon the
mossgrown and mouldering trunk of a tree uprooted years
before. Her employment, diversified by an occasional glance
at the pot, now beginning to simmer over the blaze, was the
perusal of the current year's Massachusetts Almanac, which,
with the exception of an old black-letter Bible, comprised
all the literary wealth of the family. None pay a greater regard to arbitrary divisions of time than those who are excluded from society; and Dorcas mentioned, as if the information were of importance, that it was now the twelfth of May.
Her husband started.

"The twelfth of May! I should remember it well," muttered he, while many thoughts occasioned a momentary confusion in his mind. "Where am I? Whither am I wandering?
Where did I leave him?"

Dorcas, too well accustomed to her husband's wayward
moods to note any peculiarity of demeanor, now laid aside the
almanac and addressed him in that mournful tone which the
tender hearted appropriate to griefs long cold and dead.

"It was near this time of the month, eighteen years ago,
that my poor father left this world for a better. He had a
kind arm to hold his head and a kind voice to cheer him,
Reuben, in his last moments; and the thought of the faithful
care you took of him has comforted me many a time since. Oh,
death would have been awful to a solitary man in a wild
place like this!"

"Pray Heaven, Dorcas," said Reuben, in a broken voice,—
"pray Heaven that neither of us three dies solitary and lies
unburied in this howling wilderness!" And he hastened away,
leaving her to watch the fire beneath the gloomy pines.

Reuben Bourne's rapid pace gradually slackened as the
pang, unintentionally inflicted by the words of Dorcas, became
less acute. Many strange reflections, however, thronged upon
him; and, straying onward rather like a sleep walker than a
hunter, it was attributable to no care of his own that his
devious course kept him in the vicinity of the encampment.
His steps were imperceptibly led almost in a circle; nor did

[handwritten annotations:] Reuben Driven out of camp by anguish   you don't hunt near the encampment.

he observe that he was on the verge of a tract of land heavily timbered, but not with pine trees. The place of the latter was here supplied by oaks and other of the harder woods; and around their roots clustered a dense and bushy under-growth, leaving, however, barren spaces between the trees, thick strewn with withered leaves. Whenever the rustling of the branches or the creaking of the trunks made a sound, as if the forest were waking from slumber, Reuben instinctively raised the musket that rested on his arm, and cast a quick, sharp glance on every side; but, convinced by a partial observation that no animal was near, he would again give himself up to his thoughts. He was musing on the strange influence that had led him away from his premeditated course, and so far into the depths of the wilderness. Unable to penetrate to the secret place of his soul where his motives lay hidden, he believed that a supernatural voice had called him onward, and that a supernatural power had obstructed his retreat. He trusted that it was Heaven's intent to afford him an opportunity of expiating his sin; he hoped that he might find the bones so long unburied; and that, having laid the earth over them, peace would throw its sunlight into the sepulchre of his heart. From these thoughts he was aroused by a rustling in the forest at some distance from the spot to which he had wandered. Perceiving the motion of some object behind a thick veil of undergrowth, he fired, with the instinct of a hunter and the aim of a practised marksman. A low moan, which told his success, and by which even animals can express their dying agony, was unheeded by Reuben Bourne. What were the recollections now breaking upon him?

The thicket into which Reuben had fired was near the summit of a swell of land, and was clustered around the base of a rock, which, in the shape and smoothness of one of its surfaces, was not unlike a gigantic gravestone. As if reflected in a mirror, its likeness was in Reuben's memory. He even recognized the veins which seemed to form an inscription in forgotten characters: everything remained the same, except that a thick covert of bushes shrouded the lower part of the

you don't shoot at a rustling

rock, and would have hidden Roger Malvin had he still been
sitting there. Yet in the next moment Reuben's eye was
caught by another change that time had effected since he
last stood where he was now standing again behind the earthy
roots of the uptorn tree. The sapling to which he had bound
the bloodstained symbol of his vow had increased and
strengthened into an oak, far indeed from its maturity, but
with no mean spread of shadowy branches. There was one
singularity observable in this tree which made Reuben
tremble. The middle and lower branches were in luxuriant
life, and an excess of vegetation had fringed the trunk almost
to the ground; but a blight had apparently stricken the upper
part of the oak, and the very topmost bough was withered,
sapless, and utterly dead. Reuben remembered how the little
banner had fluttered on that topmost bough, when it was
green and lovely, eighteen years before. Whose guilt had
blasted it?

Dorcas, after the departure of the two hunters, continued
her preparations for their evening repast. Her sylvan table
was the moss-covered trunk of a large fallen tree, on the
broadest part of which she had spread a snow-white cloth and
arranged what were left of the bright pewter vessels that had
been her pride in the settlements. It had a strange aspect, that
one little spot of homely comfort in the desolate heart of
Nature. The sunshine yet lingered upon the higher branches
of the trees that grew on rising ground; but the shadows of
evening had deepened into the hollow where the encampment was made, and the firelight began to redden as it
gleamed up the tall trunks of the pines or hovered on the
dense and obscure mass of foliage that circled round the spot.
The heart of Dorcas was not sad; for she felt that it was better
to journey in the wilderness with two whom she loved than
to be a lonely woman in a crowd that cared not for her. As
she busied herself in arranging seats of mouldering wood,
covered with leaves, for Reuben and her son, her voice danced

through the gloomy forest in the measure of a song that she had learned in youth. The rude melody, the production of a bard who won no name, was descriptive of a winter evening in a frontier cottage, when, secured from savage inroad by the high-piled snow-drifts, the family rejoiced by their own fireside. The whole song possessed the nameless charm peculiar to unborrowed thought, but four continually-recurring lines shone out from the rest like the blaze of the hearth whose joys they celebrated. Into them, working magic with a few simple words, the poet had instilled the very essence of domestic love and household happiness, and they were poetry and picture joined in one. As Dorcas sang, the walls of her forsaken home seemed to encircle her; she no longer saw the gloomy pines, nor heard the wind which still, as she began each verse, sent a heavy breath through the branches, and died away in a hollow moan from the burden of the song. She was aroused by the report of a gun in the vicinity of the encampment; and either the sudden sound, or her loneliness by the glowing fire, caused her to tremble violently. The next moment she laughed in the pride of a mother's heart.

"My beautiful young hunter! My boy has slain a deer!" she exclaimed, recollecting that in the direction whence the shot proceeded Cyrus had gone to the chase.

She waited a reasonable time to hear her son's light step bounding over the rustling leaves to tell of his success. But he did not immediately appear; and she sent her cheerful voice among the trees in search of him.

"Cyrus! Cyrus!"

His coming was still delayed; and she determined, as the report had apparently been very near, to seek for him in person. Her assistance, also, might be necessary in bringing home the venison which she flattered herself he had obtained. She therefore set forward, directing her steps by the long-past sound, and singing as she went, in order that the boy might be aware of her approach and run to meet her. From behind the trunk of every tree, and from every hiding-place in the thick foliage of the undergrowth, she hoped to discover the

countenance of her son, laughing with the sportive mischief
that is born of affection. The sun was now beneath the horizon, and the light that came down among the leaves was
sufficiently dim to create many illusions in her expecting fancy.
Several times she seemed indistinctly to see his face gazing out
from among the leaves; and once she imagined that he stood
beckoning to her at the base of a craggy rock. Keeping her
eyes on this object, however, it proved to be no more than the
trunk of an oak fringed to the very ground with little
branches, one of which, thrust out farther than the rest, was
shaken by the breeze. Making her way round the foot of the
rock, she suddenly found herself close to her husband, who
had approached in another direction. Leaning upon the butt
of his gun, the muzzle of which rested upon the withered
leaves, he was apparently absorbed in the contemplation of
some object at his feet.

"How is this, Reuben? Have you slain the deer and fallen
asleep over him?" exclaimed Dorcas, laughing cheerfully, on
her first slight observation of his posture and appearance.

He stirred not, neither did he turn his eyes towards her;
and a cold, shuddering fear, indefinite in its source and object,
began to creep into her blood. She now perceived that her
husband's face was ghastly pale, and his features were rigid,
as if incapable of assuming any other expression than the
strong despair which had hardened upon them. He gave not
the slightest evidence that he was aware of her approach.

"For the love of Heaven, Reuben, speak to me!" cried
Dorcas; and the strange sound of her own voice affrighted
her even more than the dead silence.

Her husband started, stared into her face, drew her to the
front of the rock, and pointed with his finger.

Oh, there lay the boy, asleep, but dreamless, upon the fallen
forest leaves! His cheek rested upon his arm—his curled locks
were thrown back from his brow—his limbs were slightly
relaxed. Had a sudden weariness overcome the youthful
hunter? Would his mother's voice arouse him? She knew that
it was death.

"This broad rock is the gravestone of your near kindred, Dorcas," said her husband. "Your tears will fall at once over your father and your son."

She heard him not. With one wild shriek, that seemed to force its way from the sufferer's inmost soul, she sank insensible by the side of her dead boy. At that moment the withered topmost bough of the oak loosened itself in the still air, and fell in soft, light fragments upon the rock, upon the leaves, upon Reuben, upon his wife and child, and upon Roger Malvin's bones. Then Reuben's heart was stricken, and the tears gushed out like water from a rock. The vow that the wounded youth had made the blighted man had come to redeem. His sin was expiated,—the curse was gone from him; and in the hour when he had shed blood dearer to him than his own, a prayer, the first for years, went up to Heaven from the lips of Reuben Bourne.

Forces in human Beings no outside force of God or Devil but the fears of man him self.

THE
GENTLE BOY

In the course of the year 1656, several of the people called Quakers, led, as they professed, by the inward movement of the spirit, made their appearance in New England. Their reputation, as holders of mystic and pernicious principles, having spread before them, the Puritans early endeavored to banish, and to prevent the further intrusion of the rising sect. But the measures by which it was intended to purge the land of heresy, though more than sufficiently vigorous, were entirely unsuccessful. The Quakers, esteeming persecution as a divine call to the post of danger, laid claim to a holy courage, unknown to the Puritans themselves, who had shunned the cross, by providing for the peaceable exercise of their religion in a distant wilderness. Though it was the singular fact, that every nation of the earth rejected the wandering enthusiasts who practised peace towards all men, the place of greatest uneasiness and peril, and therefore, in their eyes the most eligible, was the province of Massachusetts Bay.

The fines, imprisonments, and stripes, liberally distributed by our pious forefathers; the popular antipathy, so strong that it endured nearly a hundred years after actual persecution had ceased, were attractions as powerful for the Quakers, as peace, honor, and reward, would have been for the worldly minded. Every European vessel brought new cargoes of the

First published in *The Token*, 1832.

68

sect, eager to testify against the oppression which they hoped to share; and when shipmasters were restrained by heavy fines from affording them passage, they made long and circuitous journeys through the Indian country, and appeared in the province as if conveyed by a supernatural power. Their enthusiasm, heightened almost to madness by the treatment which they received, produced actions contrary to the rules of decency, as well as of rational religion, and presented a singular contrast to the calm and staid deportment of their sectarian successors of the present day. The command of the spirit, inaudible except to the soul, and not to be controverted on grounds of human wisdom, was made a plea for most indecorous exhibitions, which, abstractedly considered, well deserved the moderate chastisement of the rod. These extravagances, and the persecution which was at once their cause and consequence, continued to increase, till, in the year 1659, the government of Massachusetts Bay indulged two members of the Quaker sect with the crown of martyrdom.

An indelible stain of blood is upon the hands of all who consented to this act, but a large share of the awful responsibility must rest upon the person then at the head of the government. He was a man of narrow mind and imperfect education, and his uncompromising bigotry was made hot and mischievous by violent and hasty passions; he exerted his influence indecorously and unjustifiably to compass the death of the enthusiasts; and his whole conduct, in respect to them, was marked by brutal cruelty. The Quakers, whose revengeful feelings were not less deep because they were inactive, remembered this man and his associates in after times. The historian of the sect affirms that, by the wrath of Heaven, a blight fell upon the land in the vicinity of the "bloody town" of Boston, so that no wheat would grow there; and he takes his stand, as it were, among the graves of the ancient persecutors, and triumphantly recounts the judgments that overtook them, in old age or at the parting hour. He tells us that they died suddenly and violently and in madness; but nothing can exceed the bitter mockery with which he records the loathsome disease, and "death by rottenness," of the fierce and cruel governor.

———————————

On the evening of the autumn day that had witnessed the martyrdom of two men of the Quaker persuasion, a Puritan settler was returning from the metropolis to the neighboring country town in which he resided. The air was cool, the sky clear, and the lingering twilight was made brighter by the rays of a young moon, which had now nearly reached the verge of the horizon. The traveller, a man of middle age, wrapped in a gray frieze cloak, quickened his pace when he had reached the outskirts of the town, for a gloomy extent of nearly four miles lay between him and his home. The low, straw-thatched houses were scattered at considerable intervals along the road, and the country having been settled but about thirty years, the tracts of original forest still bore no small proportion to the cultivated ground. The autumn wind wandered among the branches, whirling away the leaves from all except the pine-trees, and moaning as if it lamented the desolation of which it was the instrument. The road had penetrated the mass of woods that lay nearest to the town, and was just emerging into an open space, when the traveller's ears were saluted by a sound more mournful than even that of the wind. It was like the wailing of some one in distress, and it seemed to proceed from beneath a tall and lonely fir-tree, in the centre of a cleared but uninclosed and uncultivated field. The Puritan could not but remember that this was the very spot which had been made accursed a few hours before by the execution of the Quakers, whose bodies had been thrown together into one hasty grave, beneath the tree on which they suffered. He struggled, however, against the superstitious fears which belonged to the age, and compelled himself to pause and listen.

"The voice is most likely mortal, nor have I cause to tremble if it be otherwise," thought he, straining his eyes through the dim moonlight. "Methinks it is like the wailing of a child; some infant, it may be, which has strayed from its mother, and chanced upon this place of death. For the ease of mine own conscience I must search this matter out."

He therefore left the path, and walked somewhat fearfully across the field. Though now so desolate, its soil was pressed down and trampled by the thousand footsteps of those who had witnessed the spectacle of that day, all of whom had now retired, leaving the dead to their loneliness. The traveller at length reached the fir-tree, which from the middle upward was covered with living branches, although a scaffold had been erected beneath, and other preparations made for the work of death. Under this unhappy tree, which in after times was believed to drop poison with its dew, sat the one solitary mourner for innocent blood. It was a slender and light clad little boy, who leaned his face upon a hillock of fresh-turned and half-frozen earth, and wailed bitterly, yet in a suppressed tone, as if his grief might receive the punishment of crime. The Puritan, whose approach had been unperceived, laid his hand upon the child's shoulder, and addressed him compassionately.

"You have chosen a dreary lodging, my poor boy, and no wonder that you weep," said he. "But dry your eyes, and tell me where your mother dwells. I promise you, if the journey be not too far, I will leave you in her arms to-night."

The boy had hushed his wailing at once, and turned his face upward to the stranger. It was a pale, bright-eyed countenance, certainly not more than six years old, but sorrow, fear, and want had destroyed much of its infantile expression. The Puritan seeing the boy's frightened gaze, and feeling that he trembled under his hand, endeavored to reassure him.

"Nay, if I intended to do you harm, little lad, the readiest way were to leave you here. What! you do not fear to sit beneath the gallows on a new-made grave, and yet you tremble at a friend's touch. Take heart, child, and tell me what is your name and where is your home?"

"Friend," replied the little boy, in a sweet though faltering voice, "they call me Ilbrahim, and my home is here."

The pale, spiritual face, the eyes that seemed to mingle with the moonlight, the sweet, airy voice, and the outlandish name, almost made the Puritan believe that the boy was in truth a being which had sprung up out of the grave on which he sat. But perceiving that the apparition stood the test of a short mental prayer, and remembering that the arm which he had touched was lifelike, he adopted a more rational supposition. "The poor child is stricken in his intellect," thought he, "but verily his words are fearful in a place like this." He then spoke soothingly, intending to humor the boy's fantasy.

"Your home will scarce be comfortable, Ilbrahim, this cold autumn night, and I fear you are ill-provided with food. I am hastening to a warm supper and bed, and if you will go with me you shall share them!"

"I thank thee, friend, but though I be hungry, and shivering with cold, thou wilt not give me food nor lodging," replied the boy, in the quiet tone which despair had taught him, even so young. "My father was of the people whom all men hate. They have laid him under this heap of earth, and here is my home."

The Puritan, who had laid hold of little Ilbrahim's hand, relinquished it as if he were touching a loathsome reptile. But he possessed a compassionate heart, which not even religious prejudice could harden into stone.

"God forbid that I should leave this child to perish, though he comes of the accursed sect," said he to himself. "Do we not all spring from an evil root? Are we not all in darkness till the light doth shine upon us? He shall not perish, neither in body, nor, if prayer and instruction may avail for him, in soul." He then spoke aloud and kindly to Ilbrahim, who had again hid his face in the cold earth of the grave. "Was every door in the land shut against you, my child, that you have wandered to this unhallowed spot?"

"They drove me forth from the prison when they took my father thence," said the boy, "and I stood afar off watching the crowd of people, and when they were gone I came hither, and found only his grave. I knew that my father was sleeping here, and I said this shall be my home."

"No, child, no; not while I have a roof over my head, or a morsel to share with you!" exclaimed the Puritan, whose sympathies were now fully excited. "Rise up and come with me, and fear not any harm."

The boy wept afresh, and clung to the heap of earth as if the cold heart beneath it were warmer to him than any in a living breast. The traveller, however, continued to entreat him tenderly, and seeming to acquire some degree of confidence, he at length arose. But his slender limbs tottered with weakness, his little head grew dizzy, and he leaned against the tree of death for support.

"My poor boy, are you so feeble?" said the Puritan. "When did you taste food last?"

"I ate of bread and water with my father in the prison," replied Ilbrahim, "but they brought him none neither yesterday nor to-day, saying that he had eaten enough to bear him to his journey's end. Trouble not thyself for my hunger, kind friend, for I have lacked food many times ere now."

The traveller took the child in his arms and wrapped his cloak about him, while his heart stirred with shame and anger against the gratuitous cruelty of the instruments in this persecution. In the awakened warmth of his feelings he resolved that, at whatever risk, he would not forsake the poor little defenceless being whom Heaven had confided to his care. With this determination he left the accursed field, and resumed the homeward path from which the wailing of the boy had called him. The light and motionless burden scarcely impeded his progress, and he soon beheld the fire rays from the windows of the cottage which he, a native of a distant clime, had built in the western wilderness. It was surrounded by a considerable extent of cultivated ground, and the dwelling was situated in the nook of a wood-covered hill, whither it seemed to have crept for protection.

"Look up, child," said the Puritan to Ilbrahim, whose faint head had sunk upon his shoulder, "there is our home."

At the word "home," a thrill passed through the child's frame, but he continued silent. A few moments brought them to a cottage door, at which the owner knocked; for at that early period, when savages were wandering everywhere among the settlers, bolt and bar were indispensable to the security of a dwelling. The summons was answered by a bond-servant, a coarse-clad and dull-featured piece of humanity, who, after ascertaining that his master was the applicant, undid the door, and held a flaring pine-knot torch to light him in. Farther back in the passage-way, the red blaze discovered a matronly woman, but no little crowd of children came bounding forth to greet their father's return. As the Puritan entered, he thrust aside his cloak, and displayed Ilbrahim's face to the female.

"Dorothy, here is a little outcast, whom Providence hath put into our hands," observed he. "Be kind to him, even as if he were of those dear ones who have departed from us."

"What pale and bright-eyed little boy is this, Tobias?" she inquired. "Is he one whom the wilderness folk have ravished from some Christian mother?"

"No, Dorothy, this poor child is no captive from the wilderness," he replied. "The heathen savage would have given him to eat of his scanty morsel, and to drink of his birchen cup; but Christian men, alas! but cast him out to die."

Then he told her how he had found him beneath the gallows, upon his father's grave; and how his heart had prompted him, like the speaking of an inward voice, to take the little outcast home, and be kind unto him. He acknowledged his resolution to feed and clothe him, as if he were his own child, and to afford him the instruction which should counteract the pernicious errors hitherto instilled into his infant mind. Dorothy was gifted with even a quicker tenderness than her husband, and she approved of all his doings and intentions.

"Have you a mother, dear child?" she inquired.

The tears burst forth from his full heart, as he attempted to reply; but Dorothy at length understood that he had a mother, who, like the rest of her sect, was a persecuted wanderer. She had been taken from the prison a short time before, carried into the uninhabited wilderness, and left to perish there by hunger or wild beasts. This was no uncommon method of disposing of the Quakers, and they were accustomed to boast that the inhabitants of the desert were more hospitable to them than civilized man.

"Fear not, little boy, you shall not need a mother, and a kind one," said Dorothy, when she had gathered this information. "Dry your tears, Ilbrahim, and be my child, as I will be your mother."

The good woman prepared the little bed, from which her own children had successively been borne to another resting-place. Before Ilbrahim would consent to occupy it, he knelt down, and as Dorothy listened to his simple and affecting prayer, she marvelled how the parents that had taught it to him could have been judged worthy of death. When the boy had fallen asleep, she bent over his pale and spiritual countenance, pressed a kiss upon his white brow, drew the bed-clothes up about his neck, and went away with a pensive gladness in her heart.

Tobias Pearson was not among the earliest emigrants from the old country. He had remained in England during the first years of the civil war, in which he had borne some share as a cornet of dragoons, under Cromwell. But when the ambitious designs of his leader began to develop themselves, he quitted the army of the Parliament, and sought a refuge from the strife, which was no longer holy, among the people of his persuasion in the colony of Massachusetts. A more worldly consideration had perhaps an influence in drawing him thither; for New England offered advantages to men of unprosperous fortunes, as well as to dissatisfied religionists, and Pearson had hitherto found it difficult to provide for a wife and increasing family. To this supposed impurity of motive the more bigoted Puritans were inclined to impute the removal by death of all the children, for whose earthly good the father had been over-thoughtful. They had left their native country blooming like roses, and like roses they had perished in a foreign soil. Those expounders of the ways of Providence, who had thus judged their brother, and attributed his domestic sorrows to his sin, were not more charitable when they saw him and Dorothy endeavoring to fill up the void in their hearts by the adoption of an infant of the accursed sect. Nor did they fail to communicate their disapprobation to Tobias;

but the latter, in reply, merely pointed at the little, quiet, lovely boy, whose appearance and deportment were indeed as powerful arguments as could possibly have been adduced in his own favor. Even his beauty, however, and his winning manners, sometimes produced an effect ultimately unfavorable; for the bigots, when the outer surfaces of their iron hearts had been softened and again grew hard, affirmed that no merely natural cause could have so worked upon them.

Their antipathy to the poor infant was also increased by the ill success of divers theological discussions, in which it was attempted to convince him of the errors of his sect. Ilbrahim, it is true, was not a skilful controversialist; but the feeling of his religion was strong as instinct in him, and he could neither be enticed nor driven from the faith which his father had died for. The odium of this stubbornness was shared in a great measure by the child's protectors, insomuch that Tobias and Dorothy very shortly began to experience a most bitter species of persecution, in the cold regards of many a friend whom they had valued. The common people manifested their opinions more openly. Pearson was a man of some consideration, being a representative to the General Court, and an approved lieutenant in the trainbands, yet within a week after his adoption of Ilbrahim he had been both hissed and hooted. Once, also, when walking through a solitary piece of woods, he heard a loud voice from some invisible speaker; and it cried, "What shall be done to the backslider? Lo! the scourge is knotted for him, even the whip of nine cords, and every cord three knots!" These insults irritated Pearson's temper for the moment; they entered also into his heart, and became imperceptible but powerful workers towards an end which his most secret thought had not yet whispered.

On the second Sabbath after Ilbrahim became a member of their family, Pearson and his wife deemed it proper that he should appear with them at public worship. They had anticipated some opposition to this measure from the boy, but he prepared himself in silence, and at the appointed hour was clad in the new mourning suit which Dorothy had wrought for him. As the parish was then, and during many subsequent years, unprovided with a bell, the signal for the commencement of religious exercises was the beat of a drum. At the first sound of that martial call to the place of holy and quiet thoughts, Tobias and Dorothy set forth, each holding a hand of little Ilbrahim, like two parents linked together by the infant of their love. On their path through the leafless woods they were overtaken by many persons of their acquaintance, all of whom avoided them, and passed by on the other side; but a severer trial awaited their constancy when they had descended the hill, and drew near the pine-built and undecorated house of prayer. Around the door, from which the drummer still sent forth his thundering summons, was drawn up a formidable phalanx, including several of the oldest members of the congregation, many of the middle aged, and nearly all the younger males. Pearson found it difficult to sustain their united and disapproving gaze, but Dorothy, whose mind was differently circumstanced, merely drew the boy closer to her, and faltered not in her approach. As they entered the door, they overheard the muttered sentiments of the assemblage, and when the reviling voices of the little children smote Ilbrahim's ear, he wept.

The interior aspect of the meeting-house was rude. The low ceiling, the unplastered walls, the naked wood work, and the undraperied pulpit, offered nothing to excite the devotion, which, without such external aids, often remains latent in the heart. The floor of the building was occupied by rows of long, cushionless benches, supplying the place of pews, and the broad aisle formed a sexual division, impassable except by children beneath a certain age.

Pearson and Dorothy separated at the door of the meeting-house, and Ilbrahim, being within the years of infancy, was retained under the care of the latter. The wrinkled beldams involved themselves in their rusty cloaks as he passed by; even the mild-featured maidens seemed to dread contamination; and many a stern old man arose, and turned his repulsive and unheavenly countenance upon the gentle boy, as if the sanctuary were polluted by his presence. He was a sweet infant of the skies that had strayed away from his home, and all the inhabitants of this miserable world closed up their impure hearts against him, drew back their earth-soiled garments from his touch, and said, "We are holier than thou."

Ilbrahim, seated by the side of his adopted mother, and retaining fast hold of her hand, assumed a grave and decorous demeanor, such as might befit a person of matured taste and understanding, who should find himself in a temple dedicated to some worship which he did not recognize, but felt himself bound to respect. The exercises had not yet commenced, however, when the boy's attention was arrested by an event, apparently of trifling interest. A woman, having her face muffled in a hood, and a cloak drawn completely about her form, advanced slowly up the broad aisle and took a place upon the foremost bench. Ilbrahim's faint color varied, his nerves fluttered, he was unable to turn his eyes from the muffled female.

When the preliminary prayer and hymn were over, the minister arose, and having turned the hour-glass which stood by the great Bible, commenced his discourse. He was now well stricken in years, a man of pale, thin countenance, and his gray hairs were closely covered by a black velvet skullcap. In his younger days he had practically learned the meaning of persecution from Archbishop Laud, and he was not now disposed to forget the lesson against which he had murmured then. Introducing the often discussed subject of the Quakers, he gave a history of that sect, and a description of their tenets, in which error predominated, and prejudice distorted the aspect of what was true. He adverted to the recent measures in the province, and cautioned his hearers of weaker parts against calling in question the just severity which God-fearing magistrates had at length been compelled to exercise. He spoke of the danger of pity, in some cases a commendable and

Christian virtue, but inapplicable to this pernicious sect. He observed that such was their devilish obstinacy in error, that even the little children, the sucking babes, were hardened and desperate heretics. He affirmed that no man, without Heaven's especial warrant, should attempt their conversion, lest while he lent his hand to draw them from the slough, he should himself be precipitated into its lowest depths.

The sands of the second hour were principally in the lower half of the glass when the sermon concluded. An approving murmur followed, and the clergyman, having given out a hymn, took his seat with much self-congratulation, and endeavored to read the effect of his eloquence in the visages of the people. But while voices from all parts of the house were tuning themselves to sing, a scene occurred, which, though not very unusual at that period in the province, happened to be without precedent in this parish.

The muffled female, who had hitherto sat motionless in the front rank of the audience, now arose, and with slow, stately, and unwavering step, ascended the pulpit stairs. The quiverings of incipient harmony were hushed, and the divine sat in speechless and almost terrified astonishment, while she undid the door, and stood up in the sacred desk from which his maledictions had just been thundered. She then divested herself of the cloak and hood, and appeared in a most singular array. A shapeless robe of sackcloth was girded about her waist with a knotted cord; her raven hair fell down upon her shoulders, and its blackness was defiled by pale streaks of ashes, which she had strown upon her head. Her eyebrows, dark and strongly defined, added to the deathly whiteness of a countenance, which, emaciated with want, and wild with enthusiasm and strange sorrows, retained no trace of earlier beauty. This figure stood gazing earnestly on the audience, and there was no sound, nor any movement, except a faint shuddering which every man observed in his neighbor, but was scarcely conscious of in himself. At length, when her fit of inspiration came, she spoke, for the first few moments, in a low voice, and not invariably distinct utterance. Her discourse gave evidence of an imagination hopelessly entangled with her reason; it was a vague and incomprehensible rhapsody, which, however, seemed to spread its own atmosphere round the hearer's soul, and to move his feelings by some influence unconnected with the words. As she proceeded, beautiful but shadowy images would sometimes be seen, like bright things moving in a turbid river; or a strong and singularly-shaped idea leaped forth, and seized at once on the understanding or the heart. But the course of her unearthly eloquence soon led her to the persecutions of her sect, and from thence the step was short to her own peculiar sorrows. She was naturally a woman of mighty passions, and hatred and revenge now wrapped themselves in the garb of piety; the character of her speech was changed, her images became distinct though wild, and her denunciations had an almost hellish bitterness.

"The Governor and his mighty men," she said, "have gathered together, taking counsel among themselves and saying, 'What shall we do unto this people—even unto the people that have come into this land to put our inquity to the blush?' And lo! the devil entereth into the council chamber, like a lame man of low stature and gravely apparelled, with a dark and twisted countenance, and a bright, downcast eye. And he standeth up among the rulers; yea, he goeth to and fro, whispering to each; and every man lends his ear, for his word is 'Slay, slay!' But I say unto ye, Woe to them that slay! Woe to them that shed the blood of saints! Woe to them that have slain the husband, and cast forth the child, the tender infant, to wander homeless and hungry and cold, till he die; and have saved the mother alive, in the cruelty of their tender mercies! Woe to them in their lifetime! cursed are they in the delight and pleasure of their hearts! Woe to them in their death hour, whether it come swiftly with blood and violence, or after long and lingering pain! Woe, in the dark house, in the rottenness of the grave, when the children's children shall revile the ashes of the fathers! Woe, woe, woe, at the judgment, when all the persecuted and all the slain in this bloody land, and the father, the mother, and the child, shall await them in a day that they cannot escape! Seed of the faith, seed of the faith, ye whose hearts are moving with a power that ye know not, arise, wash your hands of this innocent blood! Lift your voices, chosen ones; cry aloud, and call down a woe and a judgment with me!"

Having thus given vent to the flood of malignity which she mistook for inspiration, the speaker was silent. Her voice was succeeded by the hysteric shrieks of several women, but the feelings of the audience generally had not been drawn onward in the current with her own. They remained stupefied, stranded as it were, in the midst of a torrent, which deafened them by its roaring, but might not move them by its violence. The clergyman, who could not hitherto have ejected the usurper of his pulpit otherwise than by bodily force, now addressed her in the tone of just indignation and legitimate authority.

"Get you down, woman, from the holy place which you profane," he said. "Is it to the Lord's house that you come to pour forth the foulness of your heart and the inspiration of the devil? Get you down, and remember that the sentence of death is on you; yea, and shall be executed, were it but for this day's work!"

"I go, friend, I go, for the voice hath had its utterance," replied she, in a depressed and even mild tone. "I have done my mission unto thee and to thy people. Reward me with stripes, imprisonment, or death, as ye shall be permitted."

The weakness of exhausted passion caused her steps to totter as she descended the pulpit stairs. The people, in the mean while, were stirring to and fro on the floor of the house, whispering among themselves, and glancing towards the intruder. Many of them now recognized her as the woman who had assaulted the Governor with frightful language as he passed by the window of her prison; they knew, also, that she was adjudged to suffer death, and had been preserved only by an involuntary banishment into the wilderness. The new outrage, by which she had provoked her fate, seemed to render further lenity impossible; and a gentleman in military dress, with a stout man of inferior rank, drew towards the door of the meeting-house, and awaited her approach.

Scarcely did her feet press the floor, however, when an unexpected scene occurred. In that moment of her peril, when every eye frowned with death, a little timid boy pressed forth, and threw his arms around his mother.

"I am here, mother; it is I, and I will go with thee to prison," he exclaimed.

She gazed at him with a doubtful and almost frightened expression, for she knew that the boy had been cast out to perish, and she had not hoped to see his face again. She feared, perhaps, that it was but one of the happy visions with which her excited fancy had often deceived her, in the solitude of the desert or in prison. But when she felt his hand warm within her own, and heard his little eloquence of childish love, she began to know that she was yet a mother.

"Blessed art thou, my son," she sobbed. "My heart was withered; yea, dead with thee and with thy father; and now it leaps as in the first moment when I pressed thee to my bosom."

She knelt down and embraced him again and again, while the joy that could find no words expressed itself in broken accents, like the bubbles gushing up to vanish at the surface of a deep fountain. The sorrows of past years, and the darker peril that was nigh, cast not a shadow on the brightness of that fleeting moment. Soon, however, the spectators saw a change upon her face, as the consciousness of her sad estate returned, and grief supplied the fount of tears which joy had opened. By the words she uttered, it would seem that the indulgence of natural love had given her mind a momentary sense of its errors, and made her know how far she had strayed from duty in following the dictates of a wild fanaticism.

"In a doleful hour art thou returned to me, poor boy," she said, "for thy mother's path has gone darkening onward, till now the end is death. Son, son, I have borne thee in my arms when my limbs were tottering, and I have fed thee with the food that I was fainting for; yet I have ill performed a mother's part by thee in life, and now I leave thee no inheritance but woe and shame. Thou wilt go seeking through the world, and find all hearts closed against thee and their sweet affections turned to bitterness for my sake. My child, my child, how many a pang awaits thy gentle spirit, and I the cause of all!"

She hid her face on Ilbrahim's head, and her long, raven hair, discolored with the ashes of her mourning, fell down about him like a veil. A low and interrupted moan was the voice of her heart's anguish, and it did not fail to move the sympathies of many who mistook their involuntary virtue for a sin. Sobs were audible in the female section of the house, and every man who was a father drew his hand across his eyes. Tobias Pearson was agitated and uneasy, but a certain feeling like the consciousness of guilt oppressed him, so that he could not go forth and offer himself as the protector of the child. Dorothy, however, had watched her husband's eye. Her mind was free from the influence that had begun to work on his, and she drew near the Quaker woman, and addressed her in the hearing of all the congregation.

"Stranger, trust this boy to me, and I will be his mother," she said, taking Ilbrahim's hand. "Providence has signally marked out my husband to protect him, and he has fed at our table and lodged under our roof now many days, till our hearts have grown very strongly unto him. Leave the tender child with us, and be at ease concerning his welfare."

The Quaker rose from the ground, but drew the boy closer to her, while she gazed earnestly in Dorothy's face. Her mild but saddened features, and neat matronly attire, harmonized together, and were like a verse of fireside poetry. Her very aspect proved that she was blameless, so far as mortal could be so, in respect to God and man; while the enthusiast, in her robe of sackcloth and girdle of knotted cord, had as evidently violated the duties of the present life and the future, by fixing her attention wholly on the latter. The two females, as they held each a hand of Ilbrahim, formed a practical allegory; it was rational piety and unbridled fanaticism contending for the empire of a young heart.

"Thou art not of our people," said the Quaker mournfully.

"No, we are not of your people," replied Dorothy, with mildness, "but we are Christians, looking upward to the same heaven with you. Doubt not that your boy shall meet you there, if there be a blessing on our tender and prayerful guidance of him. Thither, I trust, my own children have gone before me, for I also have been a mother; I am no longer so," she added, in a faltering tone, "and your son will have all my care."

"But will ye lead him in the path which his parents have trodden?" demanded the Quaker. "Can ye teach him the enlightened faith which his father has died for, and for which I, even I, am soon to become an unworthy martyr? The boy has been baptized in blood; will ye keep the mark fresh and ruddy upon his forehead?"

"I will not deceive you," answered Dorothy. "If your child become our child, we must breed him up in the instruction which Heaven has imparted to us; we must pray for him the prayers of our own faith; we must do towards him according to the dictates of our own consciences, and not of yours. Were we to act otherwise, we should abuse your trust, even in complying with your wishes."

The mother looked down upon her boy with a troubled countenance, and then turned her eyes upward to heaven. She seemed to pray internally, and the contention of her soul was evident.

"Friend," she said at length to Dorothy, "I doubt not that my son shall receive all earthly tenderness at thy hands. Nay, I will believe that even thy imperfect lights may guide him to a better world, for surely thou art on the path thither. But thou hast spoken of a husband. Doth he stand here among this multitude of people? Let him come forth, for I must know to whom I commit this most precious trust."

She turned her face upon the male auditors, and after a momentary delay, Tobias Pearson came forth from among them. The Quaker saw the dress which marked his military rank, and shook her head; but then she noted the hesitating air, the eyes that struggled with her own, and were vanquished; the color that went and came, and could find no resting-place. As she gazed, an unmirthful smile spread over her features, like sunshine that grows melancholy in some desolate spot. Her lips moved inaudibly, but at length she spake.

"I hear it, I hear it. The voice speaketh within me and saith, 'Leave thy child, Catherine, for his place is here, and go hence, for I have other work for thee. Break the bonds of natural affection, martyr thy love, and know that in all these things eternal wisdom hath its ends.' I go, friends; I go. Take ye my boy, my precious jewel. I go hence, trusting that all shall be well, and that even for his infant hands there is a labor in the vineyard."

She knelt down and whispered to Ilbrahim, who at first struggled and clung to his mother, with sobs and tears, but remained passive when she had kissed his cheek and arisen from the ground. Having held her hands over his head in mental prayer, she was ready to depart.

"Farewell, friends in mine extremity," she said to Pearson and his wife; "the good deed ye have done me is a treaure laid up in heaven, to be returned a thousand-fold hereafter. And farewell ye, mine enemies, to whom it is not permitted to harm so much as a hair of my head, nor to stay my footsteps even for a moment. The day is coming when ye shall call upon me to witness for ye to this one sin uncommitted, and I will rise up and answer."

She turned her steps towards the door, and the men, who had stationed themselves to guard it, withdrew, and suffered her to pass. A general sentiment of pity overcame the virulence of religious hatred. Sanctified by her love and her affliction, she went forth, and all the people gazed after her till she had journeyed up the hill, and was lost behind its brow. She went, the apostle of her own unquiet heart, to renew the wanderings of past years. For her voice had been already heard in many lands of Christendom; and she had pined in the cells of a Catholic Inquisition before she felt the lash and lay in the dungeons of the Puritans. Her mission had extended also to the followers of the Prophet, and from them she had received the courtesy and kindness which all the contending sects of our purer religion united to deny her. Her husband and herself had resided many months in Turkey, where even the Sultan's countenance was gracious to them; in that pagan land, too, was Ilbrahim's birthplace, and his oriental name was a mark of gratitude for the good deeds of an unbeliever.

When Pearson and his wife had thus acquired all the rights over Ilbrahim that could be delegated, their affection for him became like the memory of their native land, or their mild sorrow for the dead, a piece of the immovable furniture of their hearts. The boy, also, after a week or two of mental disquiet, began to gratify his protectors by many inadvertent proofs that he considered them as parents, and their house as home. Before the winter snows were melted, the persecuted infant, the little wanderer from a remote and heathen country, seemed native in the New England cottage, and inseparable from the warmth and security of its hearth. Under the influence of kind treatment, and in the consciousness that he was loved, Ilbrahim's demeanor lost a premature manliness, which had resulted from his earlier situation; he became more child-like, and his natural character displayed itself with freedom. It was in many respects a beautiful one, yet the disordered imaginations of both his father and mother had perhaps propagated a certain unhealthiness in the mind of the boy. In his general state, Ilbrahim would derive enjoyment from the most trifling events, and from every object about him; he seemed to discover rich treasures of happiness, by a faculty analogous to that of the witch hazel, which points to hidden gold where all is barren to the eye. His airy gayety, coming to him from a thousand sources, communicated itself to the family, and Ilbrahim was like a domesticated sunbeam, brightening moody countenances, and chasing away the gloom from the dark corners of the cottage.

On the other hand, as the susceptibility of pleasure is also that of pain, the exuberant cheerfulness of the boy's prevailing temper sometimes yielded to moments of deep depression. His sorrows could not always be followed up to their original source, but most frequently they appeared to flow, though Ilbrahim was young to be sad for such a cause, from wounded love. The flightiness of his mirth rendered him often guilty of offences against the decorum of a Puritan household, and on these occasions he did not invariably escape rebuke. But the slightest word of real bitterness, which he was infallible in distinguishing from pretended anger, seemed to sink into his heart and poison all his enjoyments, till he became sensible that he was entirely forgiven. Of the malice, which generally accompanies a superfluity of sensitiveness, Ilbrahim was altogether destitute: when trodden upon, he would not turn; when wounded, he could but die. His mind was wanting in the stamina for self-support; it was a plant that would twine beautifully round something stronger than itself, but if repulsed, or torn away, it had no choice but to wither on the ground. Dorothy's acuteness taught her that severity would crush the spirit of the child, and she nurtured him with the gentle care of one who handles a butterfly. Her husband manifested an equal affection, although it grew daily less productive of familiar caresses.

The feelings of the neighboring people, in regard to the Quaker infant and his protectors, had not undergone a favorable change, in spite of the momentary triumph which the desolate mother had obtained over their sympathies. The scorn and bitterness, of which he was the object, were very grievous to Ilbrahim, especially when any circumstance made him sensible that the children, his equals in age, partook of the enmity of their parents. His tender and social nature had already overflowed in attachments to everything about him, and still there was a residue of unappropriated love, which he yearned to bestow upon the little ones who were taught to hate him. As the warm days of spring came on, Ilbrahim was accustomed to remain for hours, silent and inactive, within hearing of the children's .voices at their play; yet, with his usual delicacy of feeling, he avoided their notice, and would flee and hide himself from the smallest individual among them. Chance, however, at length seemed to open a medium of communication between his heart and theirs; it was by means of a boy about two years older than Ilbrahim, who was injured by a fall from a tree in the vicinity of Pearson's habitation. As the sufferer's own home was at some distance, Dorothy willingly received him under her roof, and became his tender and careful nurse.

Ilbrahim was the unconscious possessor of much skill in physiognomy, and it would have deterred him, in other circumstances, from attempting to make a friend of this boy. The countenance of the latter immediately impressed a beholder disagreeably, but it required some examination to discover that the cause was a very slight distortion of the mouth, and the irregular, broken line, and near approach of the eyebrows. Analogous, perhaps, to these trifling deformities, was an almost imperceptible twist of every joint, and the uneven prominence of the breast; forming a body, regular in its general outline, but faulty in almost all its details. The disposition of the boy was sullen and reserved, and the village schoolmaster stigmatized him as obtuse in intellect; although, at a later period of life, he evinced ambition and very peculiar talents. But whatever might be his personal or moral irregularities, Ilbrahim's heart seized upon, and clung to him, from the moment that he was brought wounded into the cottage; the child of persecution seemed to compare his own fate with that of the sufferer, and to feel that even different modes of misfortune had created a sort of relationship between them. Food, rest, and the fresh air, for which he languished, were neglected; he nestled continually by the bedside of the little stranger, and, with a fond jealousy, endeavored to be the medium of all the cares that were bestowed upon him. As the boy became convalescent, Ilbrahim contrived games suitable to his situation, or amused him by a faculty which he had perhaps breathed

in with the air of his barbaric birthplace. It was that of reciting imaginary adventures, on the spur of the moment, and
apparently in inexhaustible succession. His tales were of
course monstrous, disjointed, and without aim; but they
were curious on account of a vein of human tenderness
which ran through them all, and was like a sweet, familiar
face, encountered in the midst of wild and unearthly scenery.
The auditor paid much attention to these romances, and
sometimes interrupted them by brief remarks upon the incidents, displaying shrewdness above his years, mingled with
a moral obliquity which grated very harshly against Ilbrahim's
instinctive rectitude. Nothing, however, could arrest the progress of the latter's affection, and there were many proofs that
it met with a response from the dark and stubborn nature on
which it was lavished. The boy's parents at length removed
him, to complete his cure under their own roof.

Ilbrahim did not visit his new friend after his departure;
but he made anxious and continual inquiries respecting
him, and informed himself of the day when he was to reappear among his playmates. On a pleasant summer afternoon,
the children of the neighborhood had assembled in the little
forest-crowned amphitheatre behind the meeting-house, and
the recovering invalid was there, leaning on a staff. The glee
of a score of untainted bosoms was heard in light and airy
voices, which danced among the trees like sunshine become
audible; the grown men of this weary world, as they journeyed
by the spot, marvelled why life, beginning in such brightness,
should proceed in gloom; and their hearts, or their imaginations, answered them and said, that the bliss of childhood
gushes from its innocence. But it happened that an unexpected addition was made to the heavenly little band. It was
Ilbrahim, who came towards the children with a look of sweet
confidence on his fair and spiritual face, as if, having manifested his love to one of them, he had no longer to fear a
repulse from their society. A hush came over their mirth the
moment they beheld him, and they stood whispering to each
other while he drew nigh; but, all at once, the devil of their

fathers entered into the unbreeched fanatics, and sending up a fierce, shrill cry, they rushed upon the poor Quaker child. In an instant, he was the centre of a brood of baby-fiends, who lifted sticks against him, pelted him with stones, and displayed an instinct of destruction far more loathsome than the bloodthirstiness of manhood.

The invalid, in the meanwhile, stood apart from the tumult, crying out with a loud voice, "Fear not, Ilbrahim, come hither and take my hand;" and his unhappy friend endeavored to obey him. After watching the victim's struggling approach with a calm smile and unabashed eye, the foul-hearted little villain lifted his staff and struck Ilbrahim on the mouth, so forcibly that the blood issued in a stream. The poor child's arms had been raised to guard his head from the storm of blows; but now he dropped them at once. His persecutors beat him down, trampled upon him, dragged him by his long, fair locks, and Ilbrahim was on the point of becoming as veritable a martyr as ever entered bleeding into heaven. The uproar, however, attracted the notice of a few neighbors, who put themselves to the trouble of rescuing the little heretic, and of conveying him to Pearson's door.

Ilbrahim's bodily harm was severe, but long and careful nursing accomplished his recovery; the injury done to his sensitive spirit was more serious, though not so visible. Its signs were principally of a negative character, and to be discovered only by those who had previously known him. His gait was thenceforth slow, even, and unvaried by the sudden bursts of sprightlier motion, which had once corresponded to his overflowing gladness; his countenance was heavier, and its former play of expression, the dance of sunshine reflected from moving water, was destroyed by the cloud over his existence; his notice was attracted in a far less degree by passing events, and he appeared to find greater difficulty in comprehending what was new to him than at a happier period. A stranger, founding his judgment upon these circumstances, would have said that the dulness of the child's intellect widely contradicted the promise of his features; but the secret was in the direction of Ilbrahim's thoughts, which were brooding within him when they should naturally have been wandering abroad. An attempt of Dorothy to revive his former sportiveness was the single occasion on which his quiet demeanor yielded to a violent display of grief; he burst into passionate weeping, and ran and hid himself, for his heart had become so miserably sore that even the hand of kindness tortured it like fire. Sometimes, at night and probably in his dreams, he was heard to cry "Mother! Mother!" as if her place, which a stranger had supplied while Ilbrahim was happy, admitted of no substitute in his extreme affliction. Perhaps, among the many life-weary wretches then upon the earth, there was not one who combined innocence and misery like this poor, broken-hearted infant, so soon the victim of his own heavenly nature.

While this melancholy change had taken place in Ilbrahim, one of an earlier origin and of different character had come to its perfection in his adopted father. The incident with which this tale commences found Pearson in a state of religious dulness, yet mentally disquieted, and longing for a more fervid faith than he possessed. The first effect of his kindness to Ilbrahim was to produce a softened feeling, and incipient love for the child's whole sect; but joined to this, and resulting perhaps from self-suspicion, was a proud and ostentatious contempt of all their tenets and practical extravagances. In the course of much thought, however, for the subject struggled irresistibly into his mind, the foolishness of the doctrine began to be less evident, and the points which had particularly offended his reason assumed another aspect, or vanished entirely away. The work within him appeared to go on even while he slept, and that which had been a doubt, when he laid down to rest, would often hold the place of a truth, confirmed by some forgotten demonstration, when he recalled his thoughts in the morning. But while he was thus becoming assimilated to the enthusiasts, his contempt, in nowise decreasing towards them, grew very fierce against himself; he imagined, also, that every face of his acquaintance wore a sneer, and that every word addressed to him was a gibe. Such was his state of mind at the period of Ilbrahim's misfortune; and the emotions consequent upon that event completed the change, of which the child had been the original instrument.

In the mean time, neither the fierceness of the persecutors, nor the infatuation of their victims, had decreased. The dungeons were never empty; the streets of almost every village echoed daily with the lash; the life of a woman, whose mild and Christian spirit no cruelty could embitter, had been sacrificed; and more innocent blood was yet to pollute the hands that were so often raised in prayer. Early after the Restoration, the English Quakers represented to Charles II. that a "vein of blood was open in his dominions;" but though the displeasure of the voluptuous king was roused, his interference was not prompt. And now the tale must stride forward over many months, leaving Pearson to encounter ignominy and misfortune; his wife to a firm endurance of a thousand sorrows; poor Ilbrahim to pine and droop like a cankered rosebud; his mother to wander on a mistaken errand, neglectful of the holiest trust which can be committed to a woman.

A winter evening, a night of storm, had darkened over Pearson's habitation, and there were no cheerful faces to drive the gloom from his broad hearth. The fire, it is true, sent forth a glowing heat and a ruddy light, and large logs, dripping with half-melted snow, lay ready to be cast upon the embers. But the apartment was saddened in its aspect by the absence of much of the homely wealth which had once adorned it; for the exaction of repeated fines, and his own neglect of temporal affairs, had greatly impoverished the owner. And with the furniture of peace, the implements of war had likewise disappeared; the sword was broken, the helm and cuirass were cast away forever; the soldier had done with battles, and might not lift so much as his naked hand to guard his head.

But the Holy Book remained, and the table on which it rested was drawn before the fire, while two of the persecuted sect sought comfort from its pages.

He who listened, while the other read, was the master of the house, now emaciated in form, and altered as to the expression and healthiness of his countenance; for his mind had dwelt too long among visionary thoughts, and his body had been worn by imprisonment and stripes. The hale and weather-beaten old man who sat beside him had sustained less injury from a far longer course of the same mode of life. In person he was tall and dignified, and, which alone would have made him hateful to the Puritans, his gray locks fell from beneath the broad-brimmed hat, and rested on his shoulders. As the old man read the sacred page the snow drifted against the windows, or eddied in at the crevices of the door, while a blast kept laughing in the chimney, and the blaze leaped fiercely up to seek it. And sometimes, when the wind struck the hill at a certain angle, and swept down by the cottage across the wintry plain, its voice was the most doleful that can be conceived; it came as if the Past were speaking, as if the Dead had contributed each a whisper, as if the Desolation of Ages were breathed in that one lamenting sound.

The Quaker at length closed the book, retaining however his hand between the pages which he had been reading, while he looked steadfastly at Pearson. The attitude and features of the latter might have indicated the endurance of bodily pain; he leaned his forehead on his hands, his teeth were firmly closed, and his frame was tremulous at intervals with a nervous agitation.

"Friend Tobias," inquired the old man, compassionately, "hast thou found no comfort in these many blessed passages of Scripture?"

"Thy voice has fallen on my ear like a sound afar off and indistinct," replied Pearson without lifting his eyes. "Yea, and when I have hearkened carefully the words seemed cold and lifeless, and intended for another and a lesser grief than

mine. Remove the book," he added, in a tone of sullen bitterness. "I have no part in its consolations, and they do but fret
my sorrow the more."

"Nay, feeble brother, be not as one who hath never known
the light," said the elder Quaker earnestly, but with mildness.
"Art thou he that wouldst be content to give all, and endure
all, for conscience' sake; desiring even peculiar trials, that
thy faith might be purified and thy heart weaned from worldly
desires? And wilt thou sink beneath an affliction which hap-
pens alike to them that have their portion here below, and
to them that lay up treasure in heaven? Faint not, for thy
burden is yet light."

"It is heavy! It is heavier than I can bear!" exclaimed
Pearson, with the impatience of a variable spirit. "From my
youth upward I have been a man marked out for wrath; and
year by year, yea, day after day, I have endured sorrows such
as others know not in their lifetime. And now I speak not of
the love that has been turned to hatred, the honor to ignominy, the ease and plentifulness of all things to danger, want,
and nakedness. All this I could have borne, and counted
myself blessed. But when my heart was desolate with many
losses I fixed it upon the child of a stranger, and he became
dearer to me than all my buried ones; and now he too must
die as if my love were poison. Verily, I am an accursed man,
and I will lay me down in the dust and lift up my head no
more."

"Thou sinnest, brother, but it is not for me to rebuke thee;
for I also have had my hours of darkness, wherein I have
murmured against the cross," said the old Quaker. He continued, perhaps in the hope of distracting his companion's
thoughts from his own sorrows. "Even of late was the light
obscured within me, when the men of blood had banished
me on pain of death, and the constables led me onward from
village to village towards the wilderness. A strong and cruel
hand was wielding the knotted cords; they sunk deep into the
flesh, and thou mightst have tracked every reel and totter of
my footsteps by the blood that followed. As we went on"—

"Have I not borne all this; and have I murmured?" interrupted Pearson impatiently.

"Nay, friend, but hear me," continued the other. "As we journeyed on, night darkened on our path, so that no man could see the rage of the persecutors or the constancy of my endurance, though Heaven forbid that I should glory therein. The lights began to glimmer in the cottage windows, and I could discern the inmates as they gathered in comfort and security, every man with his wife and children by their own evening hearth. At length we came to a tract of fertile land; in the dim light, the forest was not visible around it; and behold! there was a straw-thatched dwelling, which bore the very aspect of my home, far over the wild ocean, far in our own England. Then came bitter thoughts upon me; yea, remembrances that were like death to my soul. The happiness of my early days was painted to me; the disquiet of my manhood, the altered faith of my declining years. I remembered how I had been moved to go forth a wanderer when my daughter, the youngest, the dearest of my flock, lay on her dying bed, and"—

"Couldst thou obey the command at such a moment?" exclaimed Pearson, shuddering.

"Yea, yea," replied the old man hurriedly. "I was kneeling by her bedside when the voice spoke loud within me; but immediately I rose, and took my staff, and gat me gone. Oh! that it were permitted me to forget her woful look when I thus withdrew my arm, and left her journeying through the dark valley alone! for her soul was faint, and she had learned upon my prayers. Now in that night of horror I was assailed by the thought that I had been an erring Christian and a cruel parent; yea, even my daughter, with her pale, dying features, seemed to stand by me and whisper, 'Father, you are deceived; go home and shelter your gray head.' O Thou, to whom I have looked in my farthest wanderings," continued the Quaker, raising his agitated eyes to heaven, "inflict not upon the bloodiest of our persecutors the unmitigated agony of my soul, when I believed that all I had done and suffered for

Thee was at the instigation of a mocking fiend! But I yielded not; I knelt down and wrestled with the tempter, while the scourge bit more fiercely into the flesh. My prayer was heard, and I went on in peace and joy towards the wilderness."

The old man, though his fanaticism had generally all the calmness of reason, was deeply moved while reciting this tale; and his unwonted emotion seemed to rebuke and keep down that of his companion. They sat in silence, with their faces to the fire, imagining, perhaps, in its red embers new scenes of persecution yet to be encountered. The snow still drifted hard against the windows, and sometimes, as the blaze of the logs had gradually sunk, came down the spacious chimney and hissed upon the hearth. A cautious footstep might now and then be heard in a neighboring apartment, and the sound invariably drew the eyes of both Quakers to the door which led thither. When a fierce and riotous gust of wind had led his thoughts, by a natural association, to homeless travellers on such a night, Pearson resumed the conversation.

"I have well-nigh sunk under my own share of this trial," observed he, sighing heavily; "yet I would that it might be doubled to me, if so the child's mother could be spared. Her wounds have been deep and many, but this will be the sorest of all."

"Fear not for Catharine," replied the old Quaker, "for I know that valiant woman, and have seen how she can bear the cross. A mother's heart, indeed, is strong in her, and may seem to contend mightily with her faith; but soon she will stand up and give thanks that her son has been thus early an accepted sacrifice. The boy hath done his work, and she will feel that he is taken hence in kindness both to him and her. Blessed, blessed are they that with so little suffering can enter into peace!"

The fitful rush of the wind was now disturbed by a portentous sound; it was a quick and heavy knocking at the outer door. Pearson's wan countenance grew paler, for many a visit of persecution had taught him what to dread; the old man, on the other hand, stood up erect, and his glance was firm as that of the tried soldier who awaits his enemy.

"The men of blood have come to seek me," he observed with calmness. "They have heard how I was moved to return from banishment; and now am I to be led to prison, and thence to death. It is an end I have long looked for. I will open unto them, lest they say, 'Lo, he feareth!'"

"Nay, I will present myself before them," said Pearson, with recovered fortitude. "It may be that they seek me alone, and know not that thou abidest with me."

"Let us go boldly, both one and the other," rejoined his companion. "It is not fitting that thou or I should shrink."

They therefore proceeded through the entry to the door, which they opened, bidding the applicant "Come in, in God's name!" A furious blast of wind drove the storm into their faces, and extinguished the lamp; they had barely time to discern a figure, so white from head to foot with the drifted snow that it seemed like Winter's self, come in human shape, to seek refuge from its own desolation.

"Enter, friend, and do thy errand, be it what it may," said Pearson. "It must needs be pressing, since thou comest on such a bitter night."

"Peace be with this household," said the stranger, when they stood on the floor of the inner apartment.

Pearson started, the elder Quaker stirred the slumbering embers of the fire till they sent up a clear and lofty blaze; it was a female voice that had spoken; it was a female form that shone out, cold and wintry, in that comfortable light.

"Catharine, blessed woman!" exclaimed the old man, "art thou come to this darkened land again? art thou come to bear a valiant testimony as in former years? The scourge hath not prevailed against thee, and from the dungeon hast thou come forth triumphant; but strengthen, strengthen now thy heart, Catharine, for Heaven will prove thee yet this once, ere thou go to thy reward."

"Rejoice, friends!" she replied. "Thou who hast long been of our people, and thou whom a little child hath led to us, rejoice! Lo! I come, the messenger of glad tidings, for the day of persecution is overpast. The heart of the king, even Charles, hath been moved, in gentleness towards us, and he hath sent forth his letters to stay the hands of the men of blood. A ship's company of our friends hath arrived at yonder town, and I also sailed joyfully among them."

As Catharine spoke, her eyes were roaming about the room, in search of him for whose sake security was dear to her. Pearson made a silent appeal to the old man, nor did the latter shrink from the painful task assigned him.

"Sister," he began, in a softened yet perfectly calm tone, "thou tellest us of His love, manifested in temporal good; and now must we speak to thee of that selfsame love, displayed in chastenings. Hitherto, Catharine, thou hast been as one journeying in a darksome and difficult path, and leading an infant by the hand; fain wouldst thou have looked heavenward continually, but still the cares of that little child have drawn thine eyes and thy affections to the earth. Sister! go on rejoicing, for his tottering footsteps shall impede thine own no more."

But the unhappy mother was not thus to be consoled; she shook like a leaf, she turned white as the very snow that hung drifted into her hair. The firm old man extended his hand and held her up, keeping his eye upon hers, as if to repress any outbreak of passion.

"I am a woman, I am but a woman; will He try me above my strength?" said Catharine very quickly, and almost in a whisper. "I have been wounded sore: I have suffered much; many things in the body; many in the mind; crucified in myself, and in them that were dearest to me. Surely," added she, with a long shudder, "He hath spared me in this one thing." She broke forth with sudden and irrepressible violence. "Tell me, man of cold heart, what has God done to me? Hath He cast me down, never to rise again? Hath He crushed my very heart in his hand? And thou, to whom I committed my child, how hast thou fulfilled thy trust? Give me back the boy, well, sound, alive, alive; or earth and Heaven shall avenge me!"

The agonized shriek of Catharine was answered by the faint, the very faint, voice of a child.

On this day it had become evident to Pearson, to his aged

guest, and to Dorothy, that Ilbrahim's brief and troubled pilgrimage drew near its close. The two former would willingly have remained by him, to make use of the prayers and pious discourses which they deemed appropriate to the time, and which, if they be impotent as to the departing traveller's reception in the world whither it goes, may at least sustain him in bidding adieu to earth. But though Ilbrahim uttered no complaint, he was disturbed by the faces that looked upon him; so that Dorothy's entreaties, and their own conviction that the child's feet might tread heaven's pavement and not soil it, had induced the two Quakers to remove. Ilbrahim then closed his eyes and grew calm, and, except for now and then a kind and low word to his nurse, might have been thought to slumber. As nightfall came on, however, and the storm began to rise, something seemed to trouble the repose of the boy's mind, and to render his sense of hearing active and acute. If a passing wind lingered to shake the casement, he strove to turn his head towards it; if the door jarred to and fro upon its hinges, he looked long and anxiously thitherward; if the heavy voice of the old man, as he read the Scriptures, rose but a little higher, the child almost held his dying breath to listen; if a snow-drift swept by the cottage, with a sound like the trailing of a garment, Ilbrahim seemed to watch that some visitant should enter.

But, after a little time, he relinquished whatever secret hope had agitated him, and with one low, complaining whisper, turned his cheek upon the pillow. He then addressed Dorothy with his usual sweetness, and besought her to draw near him; she did so, and Ilbrahim took her hand in both of his, grasping it with a gentle pressure, as if to assure himself that he retained it. At intervals, and without disturbing the repose of his countenance, a very faint trembling passed over him from head to foot, as if a mild but somewhat cool wind had breathed upon him, and made him shiver. As the boy thus led her by the hand, in his quiet progress over the borders of eternity, Dorothy almost imagined that she could discern the near, though dim, delightfulness of the home he was about to reach; she would not have enticed the little wanderer back, though she bemoaned herself that she must leave him and return. But just when Ilbrahim's feet were pressing on the soil of Paradise he heard a voice behind him, and it recalled him a few, few paces of the weary path which he had travelled. As Dorothy looked upon his features, she perceived that their placid expression was again disturbed; her own thoughts had been so wrapped in him, that all sounds of the storm, and of human speech, were lost to her; but when Catharine's shriek pierced through the room, the boy strove to raise himself.

"Friend, she is come! Open unto her!" cried he.

In a moment his mother was kneeling by the bedside; she drew Ilbrahim to her bosom, and he nestled there, with no violence of joy, but contentedly, as if he were hushing himself to sleep. He looked into her face, and reading its agony, said, with feeble earnestness, "Mourn not, dearest mother. I am happy now." And with these words the gentle boy was dead.

The king's mandate to stay the New England persecutors was effectual in preventing further martyrdoms; but the colonial authorities, trusting in the remoteness of their situation, and perhaps in the supposed instability of the royal government, shortly renewed their severities in all other respects. Catharine's fanaticism had become wilder by the sundering of all human ties; and wherever a scourge was lifted there was she to receive the blow; and whenever a dungeon was unbarred thither she came, to cast herself upon the floor. But in process of time a more Christian spirit—a spirit of forbearance, though not of cordiality or approbation—began to pervade the land in regard to the persecuted sect. And then, when the rigid old Pilgrims eyed her rather in pity than in wrath; when the matrons fed her with the fragments of their children's food, and offered her a lodging on a hard and lowly bed; when no little crowd of schoolboys left their sports to cast stones after the roving enthusiast; then did Catharine return to Pearson's dwelling and made that her home.

As if Ilbrahim's sweetness yet lingered round his ashes; as if his gentle spirit came down from heaven to teach his parent a true religion, her fierce and vindictive nature was softened by the same griefs which had once irritated it. When the course of years had made the features of the unobtrusive mourner familiar in the settlement, she became a subject of not deep, but general, interest; a being on whom the otherwise superfluous sympathies of all might be bestowed. Every one spoke of her with that degree of pity which it is pleasant to experience; every one was ready to do her the little kindnesses which are not costly, yet manifest good will; and when at last she died, a long train of her once bitter persecutors followed her, with decent sadness and tears that were not painful, to her place by Ilbrahim's green and sunken grave.

THE CANTERBURY
PILGRIMS

The summer moon, which shines in so many a tale, was beaming over a broad extent of uneven country. Some of its brightest rays were flung into a spring of water, where no traveller, toiling, as the writer has, up the hilly road beside which it gushes, ever failed to quench his thirst. The work of neat hands and considerate art was visible about this blessed fountain. An open cistern, hewn and hollowed out of solid stone, was placed above the waters, which filled it to the brim, but by some invisible outlet were conveyed away without dripping down its sides. Though the basin had not room for another drop, and the continual gush of water made a tremor on the surface, there was a secret charm that forbade it to overflow. I remember, that when I had slaked my summer thirst, and sat panting by the cistern, it was my fanciful theory that Nature could not afford to lavish so pure a liquid, as she does the waters of all meaner fountains.

While the moon was hanging almost perpendicularly over this spot, two figures appeared on the summit of the hill, and came with noiseless footsteps down towards the spring. They were then in the first freshness of youth; nor is there a wrinkle now on either of their brows, and yet they wore a strange, old-fashioned garb. One, a young man with ruddy cheeks, walked beneath the canopy of a broad-brimmed gray hat; he seemed to have inherited his great-grandsire's square-skirted

First published in *The Token*, 1833.

coat, and a waistcoat that extended its immense flaps to his knees; his brown locks, also, hung down behind, in a mode unknown to our times. By his side was a sweet young damsel, her fair features sheltered by a prim little bonnet, within which appeared the vestal muslin of a cap; her close, long-waisted gown, and indeed her whole attire, might have been worn by some rustic beauty who had faded half a century before. But that there was something too warm and life-like in them, I would here have compared this couple to the ghosts of two young lovers who had died long since in the glow of passion, and now were straying out of their graves, to renew the old vows, and shadow forth the unforgotten kiss of their earthly lips, beside the moonlit spring.

"Thee and I will rest here a moment, Miriam," said the young man, as they drew near the stone cistern, "for there is no fear that the elders know what we have done; and this may be the last time we shall ever taste this water."

Thus speaking, with a little sadness in his face, which was also visible in that of his companion, he made her sit down on a stone, and was about to place himself very close to her side; she, however, repelled him, though not unkindly.

"Nay, Josiah," said she, giving him a timid push with her maiden hand, "thee must sit farther off, on that other stone, with the spring between us. What would the sisters say, if thee were to sit so close to me?"

"But we are of the world's people now, Miriam," answered Josiah.

The girl persisted in her prudery, nor did the youth, in fact, seem altogether free from a similar sort of shyness; so they sat apart from each other, gazing up the hill, where the moonlight discovered the tops of a group of buildings. While their attention was thus occupied, a party of travellers, who had come wearily up the long ascent, made a halt to refresh themselves at the spring. There were three men, a woman, and a little girl and boy. Their attire was mean, covered with the dust of the summer's day, and damp with the night-dew; they all looked woebegone, as if the cares and sorrows of the world had made their steps heavier as they climbed the hill; even the two little children appeared older in evil days than the young man and maiden who had first approached the spring.

"Good evening to you, young folks," was the salutation of the travellers; and "Good evening, friends," replied the youth and damsel.

"Is that white building the Shaker meeting-house?" asked one of the strangers. "And are those the red roofs of the Shaker village?"

"Friend, it is the Shaker village," answered Josiah, after some hesitation.

The travellers, who, from the first, had looked suspiciously at the garb of these young people, now taxed them with an intention which all the circumstances, indeed, rendered too obvious to be mistaken.

"It is true, friends," replied the young man, summoning up his courage. "Miriam and I have a gift to love each other, and we are going among the world's people, to live after their fashion. And ye know that we do not transgress the law of the land; and neither ye, nor the elders themselves, have a right to hinder us."

"Yet you think it expedient to depart without leave-taking," remarked one of the travellers.

"Yea, ye-a," said Josiah, reluctantly, "because father Job is a very awful man to speak with; and being aged himself, he has but little charity for what he calls the iniquities of the flesh."

"Well," said the stranger, "we will neither use force to bring you back to the village, nor will we betray you to the elders. But sit you here awhile, and when you have heard what we shall tell you of the world which we have left, and into which you are going, perhaps you will turn back with us of your own accord. What say you?" added he, turning to his companions. "We have travelled thus far without becoming known to each other. Shall we tell our stories, here by this pleasant spring, for our own pastime, and the benefit of these misguided young lovers?"

In accordance with this proposal, the whole party stationed themselves round the stone cistern; the two children, being very weary, fell asleep upon the damp earth, and the pretty Shaker girl, whose feelings were those of a nun or a Turkish lady, crept as close as possible to the female traveller, and as far as she well could from the unknown men. The same person who had hitherto been the chief spokesman now stood up, waving his hat in his hand, and suffered the moonlight to fall full upon his front.

"In me," said he, with a certain majesty of utterance,—"in me, you behold a poet."

Though a lithographic print of this gentleman is extant, it may be well to notice that he was now nearly forty, a thin and stooping figure, in a black coat, out at elbows; notwithstanding the ill condition of his attire, there were about him several tokens of a peculiar sort of foppery, unworthy of a mature man, particularly in the arrangement of his hair, which was so disposed as to give all possible loftiness and breadth to his forehead. However, he had an intelligent eye, and, on the whole, a marked countenance.

"A poet!" repeated the young Shaker, a little puzzled how to understand such a designation, seldom heard in the utilitarian community where he had spent his life. "Oh, ay, Miriam, he means a varse-maker, thee must know."

This remark jarred upon the susceptible nerves of the poet; nor could he help wondering what stronge fatality had put into this young man's mouth an epithet, which ill-natured people had affirmed to be more proper to his merit than the one assumed by himself.

"True, I am a verse-maker," he resumed, "but my verse is no more than the material body into which I breathe the celestial soul of thought. Alas! how many a pang has it cost me, this same insensibility to the ethereal essence of poetry, with which you have here tortured me again, at the moment when I am to relinquish my profession forever! O Fate! why hast thou warred with Nature, turning all her higher and more perfect gifts to the ruin of me, their possessor? What is the voice of song, when the world lacks the ear of taste? How can I rejoice in my strength and delicacy of feeling, when they have but made great sorrows out of little ones? Have I dreaded scorn like death, and yearned for fame as others pant for vital air, only to find myself in a middle state between obscurity and infamy? But I have my revenge! I could have given existence to a thousand bright creations. I crush them into my heart, and there let them putrefy! I shake off the dust of my feet against my countrymen! But posterity, tracing my footsteps up this weary hill, will cry shame upon the unworthy age that drove one of the fathers of American song to end his days in a Shaker village!"

During this harangue, the speaker gesticulated with great energy, and, as poetry is the natural language of passion, there appeared reason to apprehend his final explosion into an ode extempore. The reader must understand that, for all these bitter words, he was a kind, gentle, harmless, poor fellow enough, whom Nature, tossing her ingredients together without looking at her recipe, had sent into the world with too much of one sort of brain, and hardly any of another.

"Friend," said the young Shaker, in some perplexity, "thee seemest to have met with great troubles; and, doubtless, I should pity them, if—if I could but understand what they were."

"Happy in your ignorance!" replied the poet, with an air of sublime superiority. "To your coarser mind, perhaps, I may seem to speak of more important griefs when I add, what I had wellnigh forgotten, that I am out at elbows, and almost starved to death. At any rate, you have the advice and example of one individual to warn you back; for I am come hither, a disappointed man, flinging aside the fragments of my hopes, and seeking shelter in the calm retreat which you are so anxious to leave."

"I thank thee, friend," rejoined the youth, "but I do not mean to be a poet, nor, Heaven be praised! do I think Miriam ever made a varse in her life. So we need not fear thy disappointments. But, Miriam," he added, with real concern, "thee knowest that the elders admit nobody that has not a gift to be useful. Now, what under the sun can they do with this poor varse-maker?"

"Nay, Josiah, do not thee discourage the poor man," said the girl, in all simplicity and kindness. "Our hymns are very rough, and perhaps they may trust him to smooth them."

Without noticing this hint of professional employment, the poet turned away, and gave himself up to a sort of vague reverie, which he called thought. Sometimes he watched the moon, pouring a silvery liquid on the clouds, through which it slowly melted till they became all bright; then he saw the same sweet radiance dancing on the leafy trees which rustled as if to shake it off, or sleeping on the high tops of hills, or hovering down in distant valleys, like the material of un-shaped dreams; lastly, he looked into the spring, and there the light was mingling with the water. In its crystal bosom, too, beholding all heaven reflected there, he found an emblem of a pure and tranquil breast. He listened to that most ethereal of all sounds, the song of crickets, coming in full choir upon the wind, and fancied that, if moonlight could be heard, it would sound just like that. Finally, he took a draught at the Shaker spring, and, as if it were the true Castalia, was forthwith moved to compose a lyric, a Farewell to his Harp, which he swore should be its closing strain, the last verse that an ungrateful world should have from him. This effusion, with two or three other little pieces, subse-quently written, he took the first opportunity to send, by one of the Shaker brethren, to Concord, where they were pub-lished in the New Hampshire Patriot.

Meantime, another of the Canterbury pilgrims, one so dif-ferent from the poet that the delicate fancy of the latter could hardly have conceived of him, began to relate his sad experi-ence. He was a small man, of quick and unquiet gestures, about fifty years old, with a narrow forehead, all wrinkled and drawn together. He held in his hand a pencil, and a card of some commission-merchant in foreign parts, on the back of which, for there was light enough to read or write by, he seemed ready to figure out a calculation.

"Young man," said he, abruptly, "what quantity of land do the Shakers own here, in Canterbury?"

"That is more than I can tell thee, friend," answered Josiah, "but it is a very rich establishment, and for a long way by the roadside thee may guess the land to be ours, by the neatness of the fences."

"And what may be the value of the whole," continued the stranger, "with all the buildings and improvements, pretty nearly, in round numbers?"

"Oh, a monstrous sum,—more than I can reckon," replied the young Shaker.

"Well, sir," said the pilgrim, "there was a day, and not very long ago, neither, when I stood at my counting-room window, and watched the signal flags of three of my own ships entering the harbor, from the East Indies, from Liverpool, and from up the Straits, and I would not have given the invoice of the least of them for the title-deeds of this whole Shaker settlement. You stare. Perhaps, now, you won't believe that I could have put more value on a little piece of paper, no bigger than the palm of your hand, than all these solid acres of grain, grass, and pasture-land would sell for?"

"I won't dispute it, friend," answered Josiah, "but I know I had rather have fifty acres of this good land than a whole sheet of thy paper."

"You may say so now," said the ruined merchant, bitterly, "for my name would not be worth the paper I should write it on. Of course, you must have heard of my failure?"

And the stranger mentioned his name, which, however mighty it might have been in the commercial world, the young Shaker had never heard of among the Canterbury hills.

"Not heard of my failure!" exclaimed the merchant, considerably piqued. "Why, it was spoken of on 'Change in London, and from Boston to New Orleans men trembled in their shoes. At all events, I did fail, and you see me here on my road to the Shaker village, where, doubtless (for the Shakers are a shrewd sect), they will have a due respect for my experience, and give me the management of the trading part of the concern, in which case I think I can pledge myself to double their capital in four or five years. Turn back with me, young man; for though you will never meet with my good luck, you can hardly escape my bad."

"I will not turn back for this," replied Josiah, calmly, "any more than for the advice of the varse-maker, between whom and thee, friend, I see a sort of likeness, though I can't justly say where it lies. But Miriam and I can earn our daily bread among the world's people as well as in the Shaker village. And do we want anything more, Miriam?"

"Nothing more, Josiah," said the girl, quietly.

"Yea, Miriam, and daily bread for some other little mouths, if God send them," observed the simple Shaker lad.

Miriam did not reply, but looked down into the spring, where she encountered the image of her own pretty face, blushing within the prim little bonnet. The third pilgrim now took up the conversation. He was a sunburnt country-man, of tall frame and bony strength, on whose rude and manly face there appeared a darker, more sullen and obstinate despondency, than on those of either the poet or the merchant.

"Well, now, youngster," he began, "these folks have had their say, so I'll take my turn. My story will cut but a poor figure by the side of theirs; for I never supposed that I could have a right to meat and drink, and great praise besides, only for tagging rhymes together, as it seems this man does; nor ever tried to get the substance of hundreds into my own hands, like the trader there. When I was about of your years, I married me a wife,—just such a neat and pretty young woman as Miriam, if that's her name,—and all I asked of Providence was an ordinary blessing on the sweat of my brow, so that we might be decent and comfortable, and have daily bread for ourselves, and for some other little mouths that we soon had to feed. We had no very great prospects before us; but I never wanted to be idle; and I thought it a matter of course that the Lord would help me, because I was willing to help myself."

"And didn't He help thee, friend?" demanded Josiah, with some eagerness.

"No," said the yeoman, sullenly; "for then you would not

have seen me here. I have labored hard for years; and my means have been growing narrower, and my living poorer, and my heart colder and heavier, all the time; till at last I could bear it no longer. I set myself down to calculate whether I had best go on the Oregon expedition, or come here to the Shaker village; but I had not hope enough left in me to begin the world over again; and, to make my story short, here I am. And now, youngster, take my advice, and turn back; or else, some few years hence, you'll have to climb this hill, with as heavy a heart as mine."

This simple story had a strong effect on the young fugitives. The misfortunes of the poet and merchant had won little sympathy from their plain good sense and unworldly feelings, qualities which made them such unprejudiced and inflexible judges, that few men would have chosen to take the opinion of this youth and maiden as to the wisdom or folly of their pursuits. But here was one whose simple wishes had resembled their own, and who, after efforts which almost gave him a right to claim success from fate, had failed in accomplishing them.

"But thy wife, friend?" exclaimed the younger man. "What became of the pretty girl, like Miriam? Oh, I am afraid she is dead!"

"Yea, poor man, she must be dead,—she and the children, too," sobbed Miriam.

The female pilgrim had been leaning over the spring, wherein latterly a tear or two might have been seen to fall, and form its little circle on the surface of the water. She now looked up, disclosing features still comely, but which had acquired an expression of fretfulness, in the same long course of evil fortune that had thrown a sullen gloom over the temper of the unprosperous yeoman.

"I am his wife," said she, a shade of irritability just perceptible in the sadness of her tone. "These poor little things, asleep on the ground, are two of our children. We had two more, but God has provided better for them than we could, by taking them to Himself."

"And what would thee advise Josiah and me to do?" asked Miriam, this being the first question which she had put to either of the strangers.

" 'Tis a thing almost against nature for a woman to try to part true lovers," answered the yeoman's wife, after a pause; "but I'll speak as truly to you as if these were my dying words. Though my husband told you some of our troubles, he didn't mention the greatest, and that which makes all the rest so hard to bear. If you and your sweetheart marry, you'll be kind and pleasant to each other for a year or two, and while that's the case, you never will repent; but, by and by, he'll grow gloomy, rough, and hard to please, and you'll be peevish, and full of little angry fits, and apt to be complaining by the fireside, when he comes to rest himself from his troubles out of doors; so your love will wear away by little and little, and leave you miserable at last. It has been so with us; and yet my husband and I were true lovers once, if ever two young folks were."

As she ceased, the yeoman and his wife exchanged a glance, in which there was more and warmer affection than they had supposed to have escaped the frost of a wintry fate, in either of their breasts. At that moment, when they stood on the utmost verge of married life, one word fitly spoken, or perhaps one peculiar look, had they had mutual confidence enough to reciprocate it, might have renewed all their old feelings, and sent them back, resolved to sustain each other amid the struggles of the world. But the crisis passed and never came again. Just then, also, the children, roused by their mother's voice, looked up, and added their wailing accents to the testimony borne by all the Canterbury pilgrims against the world from which they fled.

"We are tired and hungry!" cried they. "Is it far to the Shaker village?"

The Shaker youth and maiden looked mournfully into each other's eyes. They had but stepped across the threshold of their homes, when lo! the dark array of cares and sorrows that rose up to warn them back. The varied narratives of the strangers had arranged themselves into a parable; they seemed not merely instances of woful fate that had befallen others, but shadowy omens of disappointed hope and unavailing toil, domestic grief and estranged affection, that would cloud the onward path of these poor fugitives. But after one instant's hesitation, they opened their arms, and sealed their resolve with as pure and fond an embrace as ever youthful love had hallowed.

"We will not go back," said they. "The world never can be dark to us, for we will always love one another."

Then the Canterbury pilgrims went up the hill, while the poet chanted a drear and desperate stanza of the Farewell to his Harp, fitting music for that melancholy band. They sought a home where all former ties of nature or society would be sundered, and all old distinctions levelled, and a cold and passionless security be substituted for mortal hope and fear, as in that other refuge of the world's weary outcasts, the grave. The lovers drank at the Shaker spring, and then, with chastened hopes, but more confiding affections, went on to mingle in an untried life.

MR. HIGGINBOTHAM'S
CATASTROPHE

A young fellow, a tobacco pedlar by trade, was on his way from Morristown, where he had dealt largely with the Deacon of the Shaker settlement, to the village of Parker's Falls, on Salmon River. He had a neat little cart, painted green, with a box of cigars depicted on each side panel, and an Indian chief, holding a pipe and a golden tobacco stalk, on the rear. The pedlar drove a smart little mare, and was a young man of excellent character, keen at a bargain, but none the worse liked by the Yankees; who, as I have heard them say, would rather be shaved with a sharp razor than a dull one. Especially was he beloved by the pretty girls along the Connecticut, whose favor he used to court by presents of the best smoking tobacco in his stock; knowing well that the country lasses of New England are generally great performers on pipes. Moreover, as will be seen in the course of my story, the pedlar was inquisitive, and something of a tattler, always itching to hear the news and anxious to tell it again.

After an early breakfast at Morristown, the tobacco pedlar, whose name was Dominicus Pike, had travelled seven miles through a solitary piece of woods, without speaking a word to anybody but himself and his little gray mare. It being nearly seven o'clock, he was as eager to hold a morning gossip as a city shopkeeper to read the morning paper. An op-

First published in *The New England Magazine,* December, 1834.

portunity seemed at hand when, after lighting a cigar with a
sun-glass, he looked up, and perceived a man coming over
the brow of the hill, at the foot of which the pedlar had
stopped his green cart. Dominicus watched him as he descended, and noticed that he carried a bundle over his
shoulder on the end of a stick, and travelled with a weary,
yet determined pace. He did not look as if he had started in
the freshness of the morning, but had footed it all night, and
meant to do the same all day.

"Good morning, mister," said Dominicus, when within
speaking distance. "You go a pretty good jog. What's the
latest news at Parker's Falls?"

The man pulled the broad brim of a gray hat over his eyes,
and answered, rather sullenly, that he did not come from
Parker's Falls, which, as being the limit of his own day's
journey, the pedlar had naturally mentioned in his inquiry.

"Well then," rejoined Dominicus Pike, "let's have the
latest news where you did come from. I'm not particular about
Parker's Falls. Any place will answer."

Being thus importuned, the traveller—who was as ill looking a fellow as one would desire to meet in a solitary piece
of woods—appeared to hesitate a little, as if he was either
searching his memory for news, or weighing the expediency
of telling it. At last, mounting on the step of the cart, he
whispered in the ear of Dominicus, though he might have
shouted aloud and no other mortal would have heard him.

"I do remember one little trifle of news," said he. "Old Mr.
Higginbotham, of Kimballton, was murdered in his orchard,
at eight o'clock last night, by an Irishman and a nigger. They
strung him up to the branch of a St. Michael's pear-tree,
where nobody would find him till the morning."

As soon as this horrible intelligence was communicated, the
stranger betook himself to his journey again, with more speed
than ever, not even turning his head when Dominicus invited
him to smoke a Spanish cigar and relate all the particulars.
The pedlar whistled to his mare and went up the hill, ponder-
ing on the doleful fate of Mr. Higginbotham whom he had

known in the way of trade, having sold him many a bunch of long nines, and a great deal of pigtail, lady's twist, and fig tobacco. He was rather astonished at the rapidity with which the news had spread. Kimballton was nearly sixty miles distant in a straight line; the murder had been perpetrated only at eight o'clock the preceding night; yet Dominicus had heard of it at seven in the morning, when, in all probability, poor Mr. Higginbotham's own family had but just discovered his corpse, hanging on the St. Michael's pear-tree. The stranger on foot must have worn seven-league boots to travel at such a rate.

"Ill news flies fast, they say," thought Dominicus Pike; "but this beats railroads. The fellow ought to be hired to go express with the President's Message."

The difficulty was solved by supposing that the narrator had made a mistake of one day in the date of the occurrence; so that our friend did not hesitate to introduce the story at every tavern and country store along the road, expending a whole bunch of Spanish wrappers among at least twenty horrified audiences. He found himself invariably the first bearer of the intelligence, and was so pestered with questions that he could not avoid filling up the outline, till it became quite a respectable narrative. He met with one piece of corroborative evidence. Mr. Higginbotham was a trader; and a former clerk of his, to whom Dominicus related the facts, testified that the old gentleman was accustomed to return home through the orchard about nightfall, with the money and valuable papers of the store in his pocket. The clerk manifested but little grief at Mr. Higginbotham's catastrophe, hinting, what the pedlar had discovered in his own dealings with him, that he was a crusty old fellow, as close as a vice. His property would descend to a pretty niece who was now keeping school in Kimballton.

What with telling the news for the public good, and driving bargains for his own, Dominicus was so much delayed on the road that he chose to put up at a tavern, about five miles short of Parker's Falls. After supper, lighting one of his prime cigars, he seated himself in the bar-room, and went through the story of the murder, which had grown so fast that it took him half an hour to tell. There were as many as twenty people in the room, nineteen of whom received it all for gospel. But the twentieth was an elderly farmer, who had arrived on horseback a short time before, and was now seated in a corner smoking his pipe. When the story was concluded, he rose up very deliberately, brought his chair right in front of Dominicus, and stared him full in the face, puffing out the vilest tobacco smoke the pedlar had ever smelt.

"Will you make affidavit," demanded he, in the tone of a country justice taking an examination, "that old Squire Higginbotham of Kimballton was murdered in his orchard the night before last, and found hanging on his great pear-tree yesterday morning?"

"I tell the story as I heard it, mister," answered Dominicus, dropping his half-burnt cigar; "I don't say that I saw the thing done. So I can't take my oath that he was murdered exactly in that way."

"But I can take mine," said the farmer, "that if Squire Higginbotham was murdered night before last, I drank a glass of bitters with his ghost this morning. Being a neighbor of mine, he called me into his store, as I was riding by, and treated me, and then asked me to do a little business for him on the road. He didn't seem to know any more about his own murder than I did."

"Why, then, it can't be a fact!" exclaimed Dominicus Pike.

"I guess he'd have mentioned, if it was," said the old farmer; and he removed his chair back to the corner, leaving Dominicus quite down in the mouth.

Here was a sad resurrection of old Mr. Higginbotham! The pedlar had no heart to mingle in the conversation any more, but comforted himself with a glass of gin and water, and went to bed where, all night long, he dreamed of hanging on the St. Michael's pear-tree. To avoid the old farmer (whom he so detested that his suspension would have pleased him better than Mr. Higginbotham's), Dominicus rose in the gray of the morning, put the little mare into the green cart, and trotted swiftly away towards Parker's Falls. The fresh breeze, the dewy road, and the pleasant summer dawn, revived his spirits, and might have encouraged him to repeat the old story had there been anybody awake to hear it. But he met neither ox team, light wagon chaise, horseman, nor foot traveller, till, just as he crossed Salmon River, a man came trudging down to the bridge with a bundle over his shoulder, on the end of a stick.

"Good morning, mister," said the pedlar, reining in his mare. "If you come from Kimballton or that neighborhood, may be you can tell me the real fact about this affair of old Mr. Higginbotham. Was the old fellow actually murdered two or three nights ago, by an Irishman and a nigger?"

Dominicus had spoken in too great a hurry to observe, at first, that the stranger himself had a deep tinge of negro blood. On hearing this sudden question, the Ethiopian appeared to change his skin, its yellow hue becoming a ghastly white, while, shaking and stammering, he thus replied:—

"No! no! There was no colored man! It was an Irishman that hanged him last night, at eight o'clock. I came away at seven! His folks can't have looked for him in the orchard yet."

Scarcely had the yellow man spoken, when he interrupted himself, and though he seemed weary enough before, continued his journey at a pace which would have kept the pedlar's mare on a smart trot. Dominicus stared after him in great perplexity. If the murder had not been committed till Tuesday night, who was the prophet that had foretold it, in all its circumstances, on Tuesday morning? If Mr. Higginbotham's corpse were not yet discovered by his own family, how came the mulatto, at above thirty miles' distance, to know that he was hanging in the orchard, especially as he had left Kimballton before the unfortunate man was hanged at all? These ambiguous circumstances, with the stranger's surprise and terror, made Dominicus think of raising a hue and cry after him, as an accomplice in the murder; since a murder, it seemed, had really been perpetrated.

"But let the poor devil go," thought the pedlar. "I don't want his black blood on my head; and hanging the nigger wouldn't unhang Mr. Higginbotham. Unhang the old gentleman! It's a sin, I know; but I should hate to have him come to life a second time, and give me the lie!"

With these meditations, Dominicus Pike drove into the street of Parker's Falls, which, as everybody knows, is as thriving a village as three cotton factories and a slitting mill can make it. The machinery was not in motion, and but a few of the shop doors unbarred, when he alighted in the stable yard of the tavern, and made it his first business to order the mare four quarts of oats. His second duty, of course, was to impart Mr. Higginbotham's catastrophe to the hostler. He deemed it advisable, however, not to be too positive as to the date of the direful fact, and also to be uncertain whether it were perpetrated by an Irishman and a mulatto, or by the son of Erin alone. Neither did he profess to relate it on his own authority, or that of any one person; but mentioned it as a report generally diffused.

The story ran through the town like fire among girdled trees, and became so much the universal talk that nobody could tell whence it had originated. Mr. Higginbotham was as well known at Parker's Falls as any citizen of the place, being part owner of the slitting mill, and a considerable stockholder in the cotton factories. The inhabitants felt their own prosperity interested in his fate. Such was the excitement, that the Parker's Falls Gazette anticipated its regular day of publication, and came out with half a form of blank paper and a column of double pica emphasized with capitals, and headed HORRID MURDER OF MR. HIGGINBOTHAM! Among other dreadful details, the printed account described the mark of the cord round the dead man's neck, and stated the number of thousand dollars of which he had been robbed; there was much pathos also about the affliction of his niece, who had gone from one fainting fit to another, ever since her uncle was found hanging on the St. Michael's pear-tree with his pockets inside out. The village poet likewise commemorated the young lady's grief in seventeen stanzas of a ballad. The selectmen held a meeting, and, in consideration of Mr. Higginbotham's claims on the town, determined to issue handbills, offering a reward of five hundred dollars for the apprehension of his murderers, and the recovery of the stolen property.

Meanwhile the whole population of Parker's Falls, consisting of shopkeepers, mistresses of boarding-houses, factory girls, mill men, and schoolboys, rushed into the street and kept up such a terrible loquacity as more than compensated for the silence of the cotton machines, which refrained from their usual din out of respect to the deceased. Had Mr. Higginbotham cared about posthumous renown, his untimely ghost would have exulted in this tumult. Our friend Dominicus, in his vanity of heart, forgot his intended precautions, and mounting on the town pump, announced himself as the bearer of the authentic intelligence which had caused so wonderful a sensation. He immediately became the great man of the moment, and had just begun a new edition of the narrative, with a voice like a field preacher, when the mail stage drove into the village street. It had travelled all night, and must have shifted horses at Kimballton, at three in the morning.

"Now we shall hear all the particulars," shouted the crowd.

The coach rumbled up to the piazza of the tavern, followed by a thousand people; for if any man had been minding his own business till then, he now left it at sixes and sevens, to hear the news. The pedlar, foremost in the race, discovered two passengers, both of whom had been startled from a comfortable nap to find themselves in the centre of a mob. Every man assailing them with separate questions, all propounded at once, the couple were struck speechless, though one was a lawyer and the other a young lady.

"Mr. Higginbotham! Mr. Higginbotham! Tell us the particulars about old Mr. Higginbotham!" bawled the mob. "What is the coroner's verdict? Are the murderers apprehended? Is Mr. Higginbotham's niece come out of her fainting fits? Mr. Higginbotham! Mr. Higginbotham!!"

The coachman said not a word, except to swear awfully at the hostler for not bringing him a fresh team of horses. The lawyer inside had generally his wits about him even when asleep; the first thing he did, after learning the cause of the excitement, was to produce a large, red pocketbook. Meantime Dominicus Pike, being an extremely polite young man, and also suspecting that a female tongue would tell the story as glibly as a lawyer's, had handed the lady out of the coach. She was a fine, smart girl, now wide awake and bright as a button, and had such a sweet pretty mouth, that Dominicus would almost as lief have heard a love tale from it as a tale of murder.

"Gentlemen and ladies," said the lawyer to the shopkeepers, the millmen, and the factory girls, "I can assure you that some unaccountable mistake, or, more probably, a wilful falsehood, maliciously contrived to injure Mr. Higginbotham's credit, has excited this singular uproar. We passed through Kimballton at three o'clock this morning, and most certainly should have been informed of the murder had any been perpetrated. But I have proof nearly as strong as Mr. Higginbotham's own oral testimony, in the negative. Here is a note relating to a suit of his in the Connecticut courts, which was delivered me from that gentleman himself. I find it dated at ten o'clock last evening."

So saying, the lawyer exhibited the date and signature of the note, which irrefragably proved, either that this perverse Mr. Higginbotham was alive when he wrote it, or—as some deemed the more probable case, of two doubtful ones—that he was so absorbed in worldly business as to continue to transact it even after his death. But unexpected evidence was forthcoming. The young lady, after listening to the pedlar's explanation, merely seized a moment to smooth her gown and put her curls in order, and then appeared at the tavern door, making a modest signal to be heard.

"Good people," said she, "I am Mr. Higginbotham's niece."

A wondering murmur passed through the crowd on beholding her so rosy and bright; that same unhappy niece, whom they had supposed, on the authority of the Parker's Falls Gazette, to be lying at death's door in a fainting fit. But some shrewd fellows had doubted, all along, whether a young lady would be quite so desperate at the hanging of a rich old uncle.

"You see," continued Miss Higginbotham, with a smile, "that this strange story is quite unfounded as to myself; and I believe I may affirm it to be equally so in regard to my dear uncle Higginbotham. He has the kindness to give me a home in his house, though I contribute to my own support by teaching a school. I left Kimballton this morning to spend the vacation of commencement week with a friend, about five miles from Parker's Falls. My generous uncle, when he heard me on the stairs, called me to his bedside, and gave me two dollars and fifty cents to pay my stage fare, and another dollar for my extra expenses. He then laid his pocketbook under his pillow, shook hands with me, and advised me to take some biscuit in my bag, instead of breakfasting on the road. I feel confident, therefore, that I left my beloved relative alive, and trust that I shall find him so on my return."

The young lady courtesied at the close of her speech, which was so sensible and well worded, and delivered with such grace and propriety, that everybody thought her fit to be preceptress of the best academy in the State. But a stranger would have supposed that Mr. Higginbotham was an object of abhorrence at Parker's Falls, and that a thanksgiving had been proclaimed for his murder; so excessive was the wrath of the inhabitants on learning their mistake. The millmen resolved to bestow public honors on Dominicus Pike, only hesitating whether to tar and feather him, ride him on a rail, or refresh him with an ablution at the town pump, on the top of which he had declared himself the bearer of the news. The selectmen, by advice of the lawyer, spoke of prosecuting him for a misdemeanor, in circulating unfounded reports, to the great disturbance of the peace of the Commonwealth. Nothing saved Dominicus, either from mob law or a court of justice, but an eloquent appeal made by the young lady in his behalf. Addressing a few words of heartfelt gratitude to his benefactress, he mounted the green cart and rode out of town, under a discharge of artillery from the school-boys, who found plenty of ammunition in the neighboring clay-pits and mud holes. As he turned his head to exchange a farewell glance with Mr. Higginbotham's niece, a ball, of the consistence of hasty pudding, hit him slap in the mouth, giving him a most grim aspect. His whole person was so bespattered with the like filthy missiles, that he had almost a mind to ride back, and supplicate for the threatened ablution at the town pump; for, though not meant in kindness, it would now have been a deed of charity.

However, the sun shone bright on poor Dominicus, and the mud, an emblem of all stains of undeserved opprobrium, was easily brushed off when dry. Being a funny rogue, his heart soon cheered up; nor could he refrain from a hearty laugh at the uproar which his story had excited. The handbills of the selectmen would cause the commitment of all the vagabonds in the State; the paragraph in the Parker's Falls Gazette would be reprinted from Maine to Florida, and perhaps form an item in the London newspapers; and many a miser would tremble for his money bags and life, on learning the catastrophe of Mr. Higginbotham. The pedlar meditated with much fervor on the charms of the young school-mistress, and swore that Daniel Webster never spoke nor looked so like an angel as Miss Higginbotham, while defending him from the wrathful populace at Parker's Falls.

Dominicus was now on the Kimballton turnpike, having all along determined to visit that place, though business had drawn him out of the most direct road from Morristown. As he approached the scene of the supposed murder, he continued to revolve the circumstances in his mind, and was astonished at the aspect which the whole case assumed. Had nothing occurred to corroborate the story of the first traveller, it might now have been considered as a hoax; but the yellow man was evidently acquainted either with the report or the fact; and there was a mystery in his dismayed and guilty look on being abruptly questioned. When, to this singular combination of incidents, it was added that the rumor tallied exactly with Mr. Higginbotham's character and habits of life; and that he had an orchard, and a St. Michael's pear-tree, near which he always passed at nightfall: the circumstantial evidence appeared so strong that Dominicus doubted whether the autograph produced by the lawyer, or even the niece's direct testimony, ought to be equivalent. Making cautious inquiries along the road, the pedlar further learned that Mr. Higginbotham had in his service an Irishman of doubtful character, whom he had hired without a recommendation, on the score of economy.

"May I be hanged myself," exclaimed Dominicus Pike aloud, on reaching the top of a lonely hill, "if I'll believe old Higginbotham is unhanged till I see him with my own eyes, and hear it from his own mouth! And as he's a real shaver, I'll have the minister or some other responsible man for an indorser."

It was growing dusk when he reached the toll-house on Kimballton turnpike, about a quarter of a mile from the village of this name. His little mare was fast bringing him up with a man on horseback, who trotted through the gate a few rods in advance of him, nodded to the toll-gatherer, and kept on towards the village. Dominicus was acquainted with the tollman, and, while making change, the usual remarks on the weather passed between them.

"I suppose," said the pedlar, throwing back his whiplash, to bring it down like a feather on the mare's flank, "you have not seen anything of old Mr. Higginbotham within a day or two?"

"Yes," answered the toll-gatherer. "He passed the gate just before you drove up, and yonder he rides now, if you can see him through the dusk. He's been to Woodfield this afternoon, attending a sheriff's sale there. The old man generally shakes hands and has a little chat with me; but to-night, he nodded, —as if to say, 'Charge my toll,' and jogged on; for wherever he goes, he must always be at home by eight o'clock."

"So they tell me," said Dominicus.

"I never saw a man look so yellow and thin as the squire does," continued the toll-gatherer. "Says I to myself, to-night, he's more like a ghost or an old mummy than good flesh and blood."

The pedlar strained his eyes through the twilight, and could just discern the horseman now far ahead on the village road. He seemed to recognize the rear of Mr. Higginbotham; but through the evening shadows, and amid the dust from the horse's feet, the figure appeared dim and unsubstantial; as if the shape of the mysterious old man were faintly moulded of darkness and gray light. Dominicus shivered.

"Mr. Higginbotham has come back from the other world, by way of the Kimballton turnpike," thought he.

He shook the reins and rode forward, keeping about the same distance in the rear of the gray old shadow, till the latter was concealed by a bend of the road. On reaching this point, the pedlar no longer saw the man on horseback, but found himself at the head of the village street, not far from a number of stores and two taverns, clustered round the meeting-house steeple. On his left were a stone wall and a gate, the boundary of a wood-lot, beyond which lay an orchard, farther still, a mowing field, and last of all, a house. These were the premises of Mr. Higginbotham, whose dwelling stood beside the old highway, but had been left in the background by the Kimballton turnpike. Dominicus knew the place; and the little mare stopped short by instinct; for he was not conscious of tightening the reins.

"For the soul of me, I cannot get by this gate!" said he, trembling. "I never shall be my own man again, till I see whether Mr. Higginbotham is hanging on the St. Michael's pear-tree!"

He leaped from the cart, gave the rein a turn round the gate post, and ran along the green path of the wood-lot as if Old Nick were chasing behind. Just then the village clock tolled eight, and as each deep stroke fell, Dominicus gave a fresh bound and flew faster than before, till, dim in the solitary centre of the orchard, he saw the fated pear-tree. One great branch stretched from the old contorted trunk across the path, and threw the darkest shadow on that one spot. But something seemed to struggle beneath the branch!

The pedlar had never pretended to more courage than befits a man of peaceful occupation, nor could he account for his valor on this awful emergency. Certain it is, however, that he rushed forward, prostrated a sturdy Irishman with the butt end of his whip, and found—not indeed hanging on the St. Michael's pear-tree, but trembling beneath it, with a halter round his neck—the old, identical Mr. Higginbotham!

"Mr. Higginbotham," said Dominicus tremulously, "you're an honest man, and I'll take your word for it. Have you been hanged or not?"

If the riddle be not already guessed, a few words will explain the simple machinery by which this "coming event" was made to "cast its shadow before." Three men had plotted the robbery and murder of Mr. Higginbotham; two of them, successively, lost courage and fled, each delaying the crime one night by their disappearance; the third was in the act of perpetration, when a champion, blindly obeying the call of fate, like the heroes of old romance, appeared in the person of Dominicus Pike.

It only remains to say, that Mr. Higginbotham took the pedlar into high favor, sanctioned his addresses to the pretty schoolmistress, and settled his whole property on their children, allowing themselves the interest. In due time, the old gentleman capped the climax of his favors, by dying a Christian death, in bed, since which melancholy event Dominicus Pike has removed from Kimballton, and established a large tobacco manufactory in my native village.

ALICE DOANE'S
APPEAL

BY THE AUTHOR OF THE GENTLE BOY.

O n a pleasant afternoon of June, it was my
good fortune to be the companion of two young ladies in a
walk. The direction of our course being left to me, I led
them neither to Legge's Hill, nor to the Cold Spring, nor to
the rude shores and old batteries of the Neck, nor yet to
Paradise; though if the latter place were rightly named, my
fair friends would have been at home there. We reached the
outskirts of the town, and turning aside from a street of tan-
ners and curriers, began to ascend a hill, which at a distance,
by its dark slope and the even line of its summit, resembled
a green rampart along the road. It was less steep than its
aspect threatened. The eminence formed part of an extensive
tract of pasture land, and was traversed by cow paths in various directions; but, strange to tell, though the whole slope
and summit were of a peculiarly deep green, scarce a blade of
grass was visible from the base upward. This deceitful verdure
was occasioned by a plentiful crop of "wood-wax," which
wears the same dark and glossy green throughout the summer,
except at one short period, when it puts forth a profusion of
yellow blossoms. At that season, to a distant spectator, the
hill appears absolutely overlaid with gold, or covered with a
glory of sunshine, even beneath a clouded sky. But the curious

First published in *The Token*, 1835.

wanderer on the hill will perceive that all the grass, and everything that should nourish man or beast, has been destroyed by this vile and ineradicable weed: its tufted roots make the soil their own, and permit nothing else to vegetate among them; so that a physical curse may be said to have blasted the spot, where guilt and frenzy consummated the most execrable scene that our history blushes to record. For this was the field where superstition won her darkest triumph; the high place where our fathers set up their shame, to the mournful gaze of generations far remote. The dust of martyrs was beneath our feet. We stood on Gallows Hill.

For my own part, I have often courted the historic influence of the spot. But it is singular how few come on pilgrimage to this famous hill; how many spend their lives almost at its base, and never once obey the summons of the shadowy past, as it beckons them to the summit. Till a year or two since, this portion of our history had been very imperfectly written, and, as we are not a people of legend or tradition, it was not every citizen of our ancient town that could tell, within half a century, so much as the date of the witchcraft delusion. Recently, indeed, an historian has treated the subject in a manner that will keep his name alive, in the only desirable connection with the errors of our ancestry, by converting the hill of their disgrace into an honorable monument of his own antiquarian lore, and of that better wisdom, which draws the moral while it tells the tale. But we are a people of the present, and have no heartfelt interest in the olden time. Every fifth of November, in commemoration of they know not what, or rather without an idea beyond the momentary blaze, the young men scare the town with bonfires on this haunted height, but never dream of paying funeral honors to those who died so wrongfully, and, without a coffin or a prayer, were buried here.

Though with feminine susceptibility, my companions caught all the melancholy associations of the scene, yet these could but imperfectly overcome the gayety of girlish spirits. Their emotions came and went with quick vicissitude, and sometimes combined to form a peculiar and delicious excitement, the mirth brightening the gloom into a sunny shower of feeling, and a rainbow in the mind. My own more sombre mood was tinged by theirs. With now a merry word and next a sad one, we trod among the tangled weeds, and almost hoped that our feet would sink into the hollow of a witch's grave. Such vestiges were to be found within the memory of man, but have vanished now, and with them, I believe, all traces of the precise spot of the executions. On the long and broad ridge of the eminence, there is no very decided elevation of any one point, nor other prominent marks, except the decayed stumps of two trees, standing near each other, and here and there the rocky substance of the hill, peeping just above the wood-wax.

There are few such prospects of town and village, woodland and cultivated field, steeples and country seats, as we beheld from this unhappy spot. No blight had fallen on old Essex; all was prosperity and riches, healthfully distributed. Before us lay our native town, extending from the foot of the hill to the harbor, level as a chess board, embraced by two arms of the sea, and filling the whole peninsula with a close assemblage of wooden roofs, overtopped by many a spire, and intermixed with frequent heaps of verdure, where trees threw up their shade from unseen trunks. Beyond was the bay and its islands, almost the only objects, in a country unmarked by strong natural features, on which time and human toil had produced no change. Retaining these portions of the scene, and also the peaceful glory and tender gloom of the declining sun, we threw, in imagination, a veil of deep forest over the land, and pictured a few scattered villages, and this old town itself a village, as when the prince of hell bore sway there. The idea thus gained of its former aspect, its quaint edifices standing far apart, with peaked roofs and projecting stories, and its single meeting-house pointing up a tall spire in the midst; the vision, in short, of the town in 1692, served to introduce a wondrous tale of those old times.

I had brought the manuscript in my pocket. It was one of

a series written years ago, when my pen, now sluggish and perhaps feeble, because I have not much to hope or fear, was driven by stronger external motives, and a more passionate impulse within, than I am fated to feel again. Three or four of these tales had appeared in the "Token," after a long time and various adventures, but had encumbered me with no troublesome notoriety, even in my birthplace. One great heap had met a brighter destiny: they had fed the flames; thoughts meant to delight the world and endure for ages had perished in a moment, and stirred not a single heart but mine. The story now to be introduced, and another, chanced to be in kinder custody at the time, and thus, by no conspicuous merits of their own, escaped destruction.

The ladies, in consideration that I had never before intruded my performances on them, by any but the legitimate medium, through the press, consented to hear me read. I made them sit down on a moss-grown rock, close by the spot where we chose to believe that the death tree had stood. After a little hesitation on my part, caused by a dread of renewing my acquaintance with fantasies that had lost their charm in the ceaseless flux of mind, I began the tale, which opened darkly with the discovery of a murder.

A hundred years, and nearly half that time, have elapsed since the body of a murdered man was found, at about the distance of three miles, on the old road to Boston. He lay in a solitary spot, on the bank of a small lake, which the severe frost of December had covered with a sheet of ice. Beneath this, it seemed to have been the intention of the murderer to conceal his victim in a chill and watery grave, the ice being deeply hacked, perhaps with the weapon that had slain him, though its solidity was too stubborn for the patience of a man with blood upon his hand. The corpse therefore reclined on the earth, but was separated from the road by a thick growth of dwarf pines. There had been a slight fall of snow during the night, and as if nature were shocked at the deed, and strove to hide it with her frozen tears, a little drifted heap had partly buried the body, and lay deepest over the pale dead face. An early traveller, whose dog had led him to the spot, ventured to uncover the features, but was affrighted by their expression. A look of evil and scornful triumph had hardened on them, and made death so life-like and so terrible, that the beholder at once took flight, as swiftly as if the stiffened corpse would rise up and follow.

I read on, and identified the body as that of a young man, a stranger in the country, but resident during several preceding months in the town which lay at our feet. The story described, at some length, the excitement caused by the murder, the unavailing quest after the perpetrator, the funeral ceremonies, and other commonplace matters, in the course of which, I brought forward the personages who were to move among the succeeding events. They were but three. A young man and his sister; the former characterized by a diseased imagination and morbid feelings; the latter, beautiful and virtuous, and instilling something of her own excellence into the wild heart of her brother, but not enough to cure the deep taint of his nature. The third person was a wizard; a small, gray, withered man, with fiendish ingenuity in devising evil, and superhuman power to execute it, but senseless as an idiot and feebler than a child to all better purposes. The central scene of the story was an interview between this wretch and Leonard Doane, in the wizard's hut, situated beneath a range of rocks at some distance from the town. They sat beside a mouldering fire, while a tempest of wintry rain was beating on the roof. The young man spoke of the closeness of the tie which united him and Alice, the consecrated fervor of their affection from childhood upwards, their sense of lonely sufficiency to each other, because they only of their race had escaped death, in a night attack by the Indians. He related his discovery or suspicion of a secret sympathy between his sister and Walter Brome, and told how a distempered jealousy had maddened him. In the following passage, I threw a glimmering light on the mystery of the tale.

"Searching," continued Leonard, "into the breast of Walter Brome, I at length found a cause why Alice must inevitably love him. For he was my very counterpart! I compared his mind by each individual portion, and as a whole, with mine. There was a resemblance from which I shrunk with sickness, and loathing, and horror, as if my own features had come and stared upon me in a solitary place, or had met me in struggling through a crowd. Nay! the very same thoughts would often express themselves in the same words from our lips, proving a hateful sympathy in our secret souls. His education, indeed, in the cities of the old world, and mine in this rude wilderness, had wrought a superficial difference. The evil of his character, also, had been strengthened and rendered prominent by a reckless and ungoverned life, while mine had been softened and purified by the gentle and holy nature of Alice. But my soul had been conscious of the germ of all the fierce and deep passions, and of all the many varieties of wickedness, which accident had brought to their full maturity in him. Nor will I deny that, in the accursed one, I could see the withered blossom of every virtue, which, by a happier culture, had been made to bring forth fruit in me. Now, here was a man whom Alice might love with all the strength of sisterly affection, added to that impure passion which alone engrosses all the heart. The stranger would have more than the love which had been gathered to me from the many graves of our household—and I be desolate!"

Leonard Doane went on to describe the insane hatred that had kindled his heart into a volume of hellish flame. It appeared, indeed, that his jealousy had grounds, so far as that Walter Brome had actually sought the love of Alice, who also had betrayed an undefinable, but powerful interest in the unknown youth. The latter, in spite of his passion for Alice, seemed to return the loathful antipathy of her brother; the similarity of their dispositions made them like joint possessors of an individual nature, which could not become

wholly the property of one, unless by the extinction of the
other. At last, with the same devil in each bosom, they
chanced to meet, they two on a lonely road. While Leonard
spoke, the wizard had sat listening to what he already knew,
yet with tokens of pleasurable interest, manifested by flashes
of expression across his vacant features, by grisly smiles and
by a word here and there, mysteriously filling up some void
in the narrative. But when the young man told how Walter
Brome had taunted him with indubitable proofs of the shame
of Alice, and, before the triumphant sneer could vanish from
his face, had died by her brother's hand, the wizard laughed
aloud. Leonard started, but just then a gust of wind came
down the chimney, forming itself into a close resemblance of
the slow, unvaried laughter, by which he had been interrupted. "I was deceived," thought he; and thus pursued his
fearful story.

"I trod out his accursed soul, and knew that he was dead;
for my spirit bounded as if a chain had fallen from it and
left me free. But the burst of exulting certainty soon fled,
and was succeeded by a torpor over my brain and a dimness
before my eyes, with the sensation of one who struggles
through a dream. So I bent down over the body of Walter
Brome, gazing into his face, and striving to make my soul glad
with the thought, that he, in very truth, lay dead before me.
I know not what space of time I had thus stood, nor how the
vision came. But it seemed to me that the irrevocable years
since childhood had rolled back, and a scene, that had long
been confused and broken in my memory, arrayed itself with
all its first distinctness. Methought I stood a weeping infant
by my father's hearth; by the cold and blood-stained hearth
where he lay dead. I heard the childish wail of Alice, and my
own cry arose with hers, as we beheld the features of our
parent, fierce with the strife and distorted with the pain, in
which his spirit had passed away. As I gazed, a cold wind
whistled by, and waved my father's hair. Immediately I stood

again in the lonesome road, no more a sinless child, but a man of blood, whose tears were falling fast over the face of his dead enemy. But the delusion was not wholly gone; that face still wore a likeness of my father; and because my soul shrank from the fixed glare of the eyes, I bore the body to the lake, and would have buried it there. But before his icy sepulchre was hewn, I heard the voices of two travellers and fled."

Such was the dreadful confession of Leonard Doane. And now tortured by the idea of his sister's guilt, yet sometimes yielding to a conviction of her purity; stung with remorse for the death of Walter Brome, and shuddering with a deeper sense of some unutterable crime, perpetrated, as he imagined, in madness or a dream; moved also by dark impulses, as if a field were whispering him to meditate violence against the life of Alice; he had sought this interview with the wizard, who, on certain conditions, had no power to withhold his aid in unravelling the mystery. The tale drew near its close.

The moon was bright on high; the blue firmament appeared to glow with an inherent brightness; the greater stars were burning in their spheres; the northern lights threw their mysterious glare far over the horizon; the few small clouds aloft were burdened with radiance; but the sky, with all its variety of light, was scarcely so brilliant as the earth. The rain of the preceding night had frozen as it fell, and, by that simple magic, had wrought wonders. The trees were hung with diamonds and many-colored gems; the houses were overlaid with silver, and the streets paved with slippery brightness; a frigid glory was flung over all familiar things, from the cottage chimney to the steeple of the meeting-house, that gleamed upward to the sky. This living world, where we sit by our firesides, or go forth to meet beings like ourselves, seemed rather the creation of wizard power, with so much of resemblance to known objects that a man might shudder at the ghostly shape of his old beloved dwelling, and the shadow of a ghostly tree before his door. One looked to behold inhabitants suited to such a town, glittering in icy garments, with motionless features, cold, sparkling eyes, and just sensation enough in their frozen hearts to shiver at each other's presence.

By this fantastic piece of description, and more in the same style, I intended to throw a ghostly glimmer round the reader, so that his imagination might view the town through a medium that should take off its every-day aspect, and make it a proper theatre for so wild a scene as the final one. Amid this unearthly show, the wretched brother and sister were represented as setting forth, at midnight, through the gleaming streets, and directing their steps to a graveyard, where all the dead had been laid, from the first corpse in that ancient town, to the murdered man who was buried three days before. As they went, they seemed to see the wizard gliding by their sides, or walking dimly on the path before them. But here I paused, and gazed into the faces of my two fair auditors, to judge whether, even on the hill where so many had been brought to death by wilder tales than this, I might venture to proceed. Their bright eyes were fixed on me; their lips apart. I took courage, and led the fated pair to a new made grave, where for a few moments, in the bright and silent midnight, they stood alone. But suddenly there was a multitude of people among the graves.

Each family tomb had given up its inhabitants, who, one by one, through distant years, had been borne to its dark chamber, but now came forth and stood in a pale group together. There was the gray ancestor, the aged mother, and all their descendants, some withered and full of years, like themselves, and others in their prime; there, too, were the children who went prattling to the tomb, and there the maiden who yielded her early beauty to death's embrace, before passion had polluted it. Husbands and wives arose, who had lain many years side by side, and young mothers who had forgotten to kiss their first babes, though pillowed so long on their bosoms. Many had been buried in the habiliments of life, and still wore their ancient garb; some were old defenders of the infant colony, and gleamed forth in their steel-caps and bright breastplates, as if starting up at an Indian warcry; other venerable shapes had been pastors of the church, famous among the New England clergy, and now leaned with hands clasped over their gravestones, ready to call the congregation to prayer. There stood the early settlers, those old illustrious ones, the heroes of tradition and fireside legends, the men of history whose features had been so long beneath the sod that few alive could have remembered them. There, too, were faces of former towns-people, dimly recollected from childhood, and others, whom Leonard and Alice had wept in later years, but who now were most terrible of all, by their ghastly smile of recognition. All, in short, were there; the dead of other generations, whose moss-grown names could scarce be read upon their tombstones, and their successors, whose graves were not yet green; all whom black funerals had followed slowly thither now reappeared where the mourners left them. Yet none but souls accursed were there, and fiends counterfeiting the likeness of departed saints.

The countenances of those venerable men, whose very features had been hallowed by lives of piety, were contorted now by intolerable pain or hellish passion, and now by an unearthly and derisive merriment. Had the pastors prayed, all saintlike as they seemed, it had been blasphemy. The chaste matrons, too, and the maidens with untasted lips, who had slept in their virgin graves apart from all other dust, now wore a look from which the two trembling mortals shrank, as if the unimaginable sin of twenty worlds were collected there. The faces of fond lovers, even of such as had pined into the tomb, because there their treasure was, were bent on one another with glances of hatred and smiles of bitter scorn, passions that are to devils what love is to the blest. At times, the features of those who had passed from a holy life to heaven would vary to and fro, between their assumed aspect and the fiendish lineaments whence they had been transformed. The whole miserable multitude, both sinful souls and false spectres of good men, groaned horribly and gnashed their teeth, as they looked upward to the calm loveliness of the midnight sky, and beheld those homes of bliss where they must never dwell. Such was the apparition, though too shadowy for language to portray; for here would be the moonbeams on the ice, glittering through a warrior's breastplate, and there the letters of a tombstone, on the form that stood before it; and whenever a breeze went by, it swept the old men's hoary heads, the women's fearful beauty, and all the unreal throng, into one indistinguishable cloud together.

I dare not give the remainder of the scene, except in a very brief epitome. This company of devils and condemned souls had come on a holiday, to revel in the discovery of a complicated crime; as foul a one as ever was imagined in their dreadful abode. In the course of the tale, the reader had been permitted to discover that all the incidents were results of the machinations of the wizard, who had cunningly devised that Walter Brome should tempt his unknown sister to guilt and shame, and himself perish by the hand of his twin-brother. I described the glee of the fiends at this hideous conception, and their eagerness to know if it were consummated. The story concluded with the Appeal of Alice to the spectre of Walter Brome; his reply, absolving her from every stain; and the trembling awe with which ghost and devil fled, as from the sinless presence of an angel.

The sun had gone down. While I held my page of wonders in the fading light, and read how Alice and her brother were left alone among the graves, my voice mingled with the sigh of a summer wind, which passed over the hill-top, with the

broad and hollow sound as of the flight of unseen spirits. Not
a word was spoken till I added that the wizard's grave was
close beside us, and that the wood-wax had sprouted originally
from his unhallowed bones. The ladies started; perhaps their
cheeks might have grown pale had not the crimson west been
blushing on them; but after a moment they began to laugh,
while the breeze took a livelier motion, as if responsive to
their mirth. I kept an awful solemnity of visage, being, indeed, a little piqued that a narrative which had good authority in our ancient superstitions, and would have brought
even a church deacon to Gallows Hill, in old witch times,
should now be considered too grotesque and extravagant for
timid maids to tremble at. Though it was past supper time, I
detained them a while longer on the hill, and made a trial
whether truth were more powerful than fiction.

We looked again towards the town, no longer arrayed in
that icy splendor of earth, tree, and edifice, beneath the glow
of a wintry midnight, which shining afar through the gloom
of a century had made it appear the very home of visions in
visionary streets. An indistinctness had begun to creep over
the mass of buildings and blend them with the intermingled
tree-tops, except where the roof of a statelier mansion, and
the steeples and brick towers of churches, caught the brightness of some cloud that yet floated in the sunshine. Twilight
over the landscape was congenial to the obscurity of time.
With such eloquence as my share of feeling and fancy could
supply, I called back hoar antiquity, and bade my companions imagine an ancient multitude of people, congregated on
the hillside, spreading far below, clustering on the steep old
roofs, and climbing the adjacent heights, wherever a glimpse
of this spot might be obtained. I strove to realize and faintly
communicate the deep, unutterable loathing and horror, the
indignation, the affrighted wonder, that wrinkled on every
brow, and filled the universal heart. See! the whole crowd
turns pale and shrinks within itself, as the virtuous emerge
from yonder street. Keeping pace with that devoted company,
I described them one by one; here tottered a woman in her

dotage, knowing neither the crime imputed her, nor its punishment; there another, distracted by the universal madness,
till feverish dreams were remembered as realities, and she
almost believed her guilt. One, a proud man once, was so
broken down by the intolerable hatred heaped upon him,
that he seemed to hasten his steps, eager to hide himself in
the grave hastily dug at the foot of the gallows. As they went
slowly on, a mother looked behind, and beheld her peaceful
dwelling; she cast her eyes elsewhere, and groaned inwardly
yet with bitterest anguish, for there was her little son among
the accusers. I watched the face of an ordained pastor, who
walked onward to the same death; his lips moved in prayer;
no narrow petition for himself alone, but embracing all his
fellow-sufferers and the frenzied multitude; he looked to
Heaven and trod lightly up the hill.

Behind their victims came the afflicted, a guilty and miserable band; villains who had thus avenged themselves on their
enemies, and viler wretches, whose cowardice had destroyed
their friends; lunatics, whose ravings had chimed in with the
madness of the land; and children, who had played a game
that the imps of darkness might have envied them, since it
disgraced an age, and dipped a people's hands in blood. In
the rear of the procession rode a figure on horseback, so darkly
conspicuous, so sternly triumphant, that my hearers mistook
him for the visible presence of the fiend himself; but it was
only his good friend, Cotton Mather, proud of his well-won
dignity, as the representative of all the hateful features of his
time; the one blood-thirsty man, in whom were concentrated
those vices of spirit and errors of opinion that sufficed to madden
the whole surrounding multitude. And thus I marshalled them
onward, the innocent who were to die, and the guilty who
were to grow old in long remorse—tracing their every step,
by rock, and shrub, and broken track, till their shadowy
visages had circled round the hill-top, where we stood. I
plunged into my imagination for a blacker horror, and a
deeper woe, and pictured the scaffold——

But here my companions seized an arm on each side; their

nerves were trembling; and, sweeter victory still, I had reached the seldom trodden places of their hearts, and found the well-spring of their tears. And now the past had done all it could. We slowly descended, watching the lights as they twinkled gradually through the town, and listening to the distant mirth of boys at play, and to the voice of a young girl warbling somewhere in the dusk, a pleasant sound to wanderers from old witch times. Yet, ere we left the hill, we could not but regret that there is nothing on its barren summit, no relic of old, nor lettered stone of later days, to assist the imagination in appealing to the heart. We build the memorial column on the height which our fathers made sacred with their blood, poured out in a holy cause. And here, in dark, funereal stone, should rise another monument, sadly commemorative of the errors of an earlier race, and not to be cast down, while the human heart has one infirmity that may result in crime.

THE GRAY
CHAMPION

There was once a time when New England groaned under the actual pressure of heavier wrongs than those threatened ones which brought on the Revolution. James II., the bigoted successor of Charles the Voluptuous, had annulled the charters of all the colonies, and sent a harsh and unprincipled soldier to take away our liberties and endanger our religion. The administration of Sir Edmund Andros lacked scarcely a single characteristic of tyranny: a Governor and Council, holding office from the King, and wholly independent of the country, laws made and taxes levied without concurrence of the people, immediate or by their representatives; the rights of private citizens violated, and the titles of all landed property declared void; the voice of complaint stifled by restrictions on the press; and, finally, disaffection overawed by the first band of mercenary troops that ever marched on our free soil. For two years our ancestors were kept in sullen submission by that filial love which had invariably secured their allegiance to the mother country, whether its head chanced to be a Parliament, Protector, or Popish Monarch. Till these evil times, however, such allegiance had been merely nominal, and the colonists had ruled themselves, enjoying far more freedom than is even yet the privilege of the native subjects of Great Britain.

First published in *The New England Magazine,* January, 1835.

At length a rumor reached our shores that the Prince of Orange had ventured on an enterprise, the success of which would be the triumph of civil and religious rights and the salvation of New England. It was but a doubtful whisper; it might be false, or the attempt might fail; and, in either case, the man that stirred against King James would lose his head. Still the intelligence produced a marked effect. The people smiled mysteriously in the streets, and threw bold glances at their oppressors; while far and wide there was a subdued and silent agitation, as if the slightest signal would rouse the whole land from its sluggish despondency. Aware of their danger, the rulers resolved to avert it by an imposing display of strength, and perhaps to confirm their despotism by yet harsher measures. One afternoon in April, 1689, Sir Edmund Andros and his favorite councillors, being warm with wine, assembled the redcoats of the Governor's Guard, and made their appearance in the streets of Boston. The sun was near setting when the march commenced.

The roll of the drum at that unquiet crisis seemed to go through the streets, less as the martial music of the soldiers, than as a muster-call to the inhabitants themselves. A multitude, by various avenues, assembled in King Street, which was destined to be the scene, nearly a century afterwards, of another encounter between the troops of Britain and a people struggling against her tyranny. Though more than sixty years had elapsed since the pilgrims came, this crowd of their descendants still showed the strong and sombre features of their character perhaps more strikingly in such a stern emergency than on happier occasions. There were the sober garb, the general severity of mien, the gloomy but undismayed expression, the scriptural forms of speech, and the confidence in Heaven's blessing on a righteous cause, which would have marked a band of the original Puritans, when threatened by some peril of the wilderness. Indeed, it was not yet time for the old spirit to be extinct; since there were men in the street that day who had worshipped there beneath the trees, before a house was reared to the God for whom they had become exiles. Old soldiers of the Parliament were here, too, smiling grimly at the thought that their aged arms might strike another blow against the house of Stuart. Here, also, were the veterans of King Philip's war, who had burned villages and slaughtered young and old, with pious fierceness, while the godly souls throughout the land were helping them with prayer. Several ministers were scattered among the crowd, which, unlike all other mobs, regarded them with such reverence, as if there were sanctity in their very garments. These holy men exerted their influence to quiet the people, but not to disperse them. Meantime, the purpose of the Governor, in disturbing the peace of the town at a period when the slightest commotion might throw the country into a ferment, was almost the universal subject of inquiry, and variously explained.

"Satan will strike his master-stroke presently," cried some, "because he knoweth that his time is short. All our godly pastors are to be dragged to prison! We shall see them at a Smithfield fire in King Street!"

Hereupon the people of each parish gathered closer round their minister, who looked calmly upwards and assumed a more apostolic dignity, as well befitted a candidate for the highest honor of his profession, the crown of martyrdom. It was actually fancied, at that period, that New England might have a John Rogers of her own to take the place of that worthy in the Primer.

"The Pope of Rome has given orders for a new St. Bartholomew!" cried others. "We are to be massacred, man and male child!"

Neither was this rumor wholly discredited, although the wiser class believed the Governor's object somewhat less atrocious. His predecessor under the old charter, Bradstreet, a venerable companion of the first settlers, was known to be in town. There were grounds for conjecturing that Sir Edmund Andros intended at once to strike terror by a parade of military force, and to confound the opposite faction by possessing himself of their chief.

"Stand firm for the old charter Governor!" shouted the

crowd, seizing upon the idea. "The good old Governor Bradstreet!"

While this cry was at the loudest, the people were surprised by the well-known figure of Governor Bradstreet himself, a patriarch of nearly ninety, who appeared on the elevated steps of a door, and, with characteristic mildness, besought them to submit to the constituted authorities.

"My children," concluded this venerable person, "do nothing rashly. Cry not aloud, but pray for the welfare of New England, and expect patiently what the Lord will do in this matter!"

The event was soon to be decided. All this time, the roll of the drum had been approaching through Cornhill, louder and deeper, till with reverberations from house to house, and the regular tramp of martial footsteps, it burst into the street. A double rank of soldiers made their appearance, occupying the whole breadth of the passage, with shouldered matchlocks, and matches burning, so as to present a row of fires in the dusk. Their steady march was like the progress of a machine, that would roll irresistibly over everything in its way. Next, moving slowly, with a confused clatter of hoofs on the pavement, rode a party of mounted gentlemen, the central figure being Sir Edmund Andros, elderly, but erect and soldier-like. Those around him were his favorite councillors, and the bitterest foes of New England. At his right hand rode Edward Randolph, our arch-enemy, that "blasted wretch," as Cotton Mather calls him, who achieved the downfall of our ancient government, and was followed with a sensible curse, through life and to his grave. On the other side was Bullivant, scattering jests and mockery as he rode along. Dudley came behind, with a downcast look, dreading, as well he might, to meet the indignant gaze of the people, who beheld him, their only countryman by birth, among the oppressors of his native land. The captain of a frigate in the harbor, and two or three civil officers under the Crown, were also there. But the figure which most attracted the public eye, and stirred up the deepest feeling, was the Episcopal clergyman of King's Chapel, riding haughtily among the magistrates in his priestly vestments, the fitting representative of prelacy and persecution, the union of church and state, and all those abominations which had driven the Puritans to the wilderness. Another guard of soldiers, in double rank, brought up the rear.

The whole scene was a picture of the condition of New England, and its moral, the deformity of any government that does not grow out of the nature of things and the character of the people. On one side the religious multitude, with their sad visages and dark attire, and on the other, the group of despotic rulers, with the high churchman in the midst, and here and there a crucifix at their bosoms, all magnificently clad, flushed with wine, proud of unjust authority, and scoffing at the universal groan. And the mercenary soldiers, waiting but the word to deluge the street with blood, showed the only means by which obedience could be secured.

"O Lord of Hosts," cried a voice among the crowd, "provide a Champion for thy people!"

This ejaculation was loudly uttered, and served as a herald's cry, to introduce a remarkable personage. The crowd had rolled back, and were now huddled together nearly at the extremity of the street, while the soldiers had advanced no more than a third of its length. The intervening space was empty—a paved solitude, between lofty edifices, which threw almost a twilight shadow over it. Suddenly, there was seen the figure of an ancient man, who seemed to have emerged from among the people, and was walking by himself along the centre of the street, to confront the armed band. He wore the old Puritan dress, a dark cloak and a steeple-crowned hat, in the fashion of at least fifty years before, with a heavy sword upon his thigh, but a staff in his hand to assist the tremulous gait of age.

When at some distance from the multitude, the old man turned slowly round, displaying a face of antique majesty, rendered doubly venerable by the hoary beard that descended on his breast. He made a gesture at once of encouragement and warning, then turned again, and resumed his way.

"Who is this gray patriarch?" asked the young men of their sires.

"Who is this venerable brother?" asked the old men among themselves.

But none could make reply. The fathers of the people, those of fourscore years and upwards, were disturbed, deeming it strange that they should forget one of such evident authority, whom they must have known in their early days, the associate of Winthrop, and all the old councillors, giving laws, and making prayers, and leading them against the savage. The elderly men ought to have remembered him, too, with locks as gray in their youth, as their own were now. And the young! How could he have passed so utterly from their memories— that hoary sire, the relic of long-departed times, whose awful benediction had surely been bestowed on their uncovered heads, in childhood?

"Whence did he come? What is his purpose? Who can this old man be?" whispered the wondering crowd.

Meanwhile, the venerable stranger, staff in hand, was pursuing his solitary walk along the centre of the street. As he drew near the advancing soldiers, and as the roll of their drum came full upon his ear, the old man raised himself to a loftier mien, while the decrepitude of age seemed to fall from his shoulders, leaving him in gray but unbroken dignity. Now, he marched onward with a warrior's step, keeping time to the military music. Thus the aged form advanced on one side, and the whole parade of soldiers and magistrates on the other, till, when scarcely twenty yards remained between, the old man grasped his staff by the middle, and held it before him like a leader's truncheon.

"Stand!" cried he.

The eye, the face, and attitude of command; the solemn, yet warlike peal of that voice, fit either to rule a host in the battlefield or be raised to God in prayer, were irresistible. At the old man's word and outstretched arm, the roll of the drum was hushed at once, and the advancing line stood still. A tremulous enthusiasm seized upon the multitude. That stately form, combining the leader and the saint, so gray, so dimly seen, in such an ancient garb, could only belong to some old champion of the righteous cause, whom the oppressor's drum had summoned from his grave. They raised a shout of awe and exultation, and looked for the deliverance of New England.

The Governor, and the gentlemen of his party, perceiving themselves brought to an unexpected stand, rode hastily forward, as if they would have pressed their snorting and affrighted horses right against the hoary apparition. He, however, blenched not a step, but glancing his severe eye round the group, which half encompassed him, at last bent it sternly on Sir Edmund Andros. One would have thought that the dark old man was chief ruler there, and that the Governor and Council, with soldiers at their back, representing the whole power and authority of the Crown, had no alternative but obedience.

"What does this old fellow here?" cried Edward Randolph, fiercely. "On, Sir Edmund! Bid the soldiers forward, and give the dotard the same choice that you give all his countrymen— to stand aside or be trampled on!"

"Nay, nay, let us show respect to the good grandsire," said Bullivant, laughing. "See you not, he is some old round-headed dignitary, who hath lain asleep these thirty years, and knows nothing of the change of time? Doubtless, he thinks to put us down with a proclamation in Old Noll's name!"

"Are you mad, old man?" demanded Sir Edmund Andros, in loud and harsh tones. "How dare you stay the march of King James's Governor?"

"I have stayed the march of a King himself, ere now," replied the gray figure, with stern composure. "I am here, Sir Governor, because the cry of an oppressed people hath disturbed me in my secret place; and beseeching this favor earnestly of the Lord, it was vouchsafed me to appear once again on earth, in the good old cause of his saints. And what speak ye of James? There is no longer a Popish tyrant on the throne of England, and by to-morrow noon, his name shall be a word of terror. Back, thou that wast a Governor, back! With this night thy power is ended—to-morrow, the prison!—back, lest I foretell the scaffold!"

The people had been drawing nearer and nearer, and drinking in the words of their champion, who spoke in accents long disused, like one unaccustomed to converse, except with the dead of many years ago. But his voice stirred their souls. They confronted the soldiers, not wholly without arms, and ready to convert the very stones of the street into deadly weapons. Sir Edmund Andros looked at the old man; then he cast his hard and cruel eye over the multitude, and beheld them burning with that lurid wrath, so difficult to kindle or to quench; and again he fixed his gaze on the aged form, which stood obscurely in an open space, where neither friend nor foe had thrust himself. What were his thoughts, he uttered no word which might discover. But whether the oppressor were overawed by the Gray Champion's look, or perceived his peril in the threatening attitude of the people, it is certain that he gave back, and ordered his soldiers to commence a slow and guarded retreat. Before another sunset, the Governor, and all that rode so proudly with him, were prisoners, and long ere it was known that James had abdicated, King William was proclaimed throughout New England.

But where was the Gray Champion? Some reported that, when the troops had gone from King Street, and the people were thronging tumultuously in their rear, Bradstreet, the aged Governor, was seen to embrace a form more aged than his own. Others soberly affirmed, that while they marvelled at the venerable grandeur of his aspect, the old man had faded from their eyes, melting slowly into the hues of twilight, till, where he stood, there was an empty space. But all agreed that the hoary shape was gone. The men of that generation watched for his reappearance, in sunshine and in twilight, but never saw him more, nor knew when his funeral passed, nor where his gravestone was.

And who was the Gray Champion? Perhaps his name might be found in the records of that stern Court of Justice, which

passed a sentence, too mighty for the age, but glorious in all
aftertimes, for its humbling lesson to the monarch and its high
example to the subject. I have heard, that whenever the descendants of the Puritans are to show the spirit of their sires,
the old man appears again. When eighty years had passed,
he walked once more in King Street. Five years later, in the
twilight of an April morning, he stood on the green, beside
the meeting-house, at Lexington, where now the obelisk of
granite, with a slab of slate inlaid, commemorates the first
fallen of the Revolution. And when our fathers were toiling
at the breastwork on Bunker's Hill, all through that night the
old warrior walked his rounds. Long, long may it be, ere he
comes again! His hour is one of darkness, and adversity, and
peril. But should domestic tyranny oppress us, or the invader's
step pollute our soil, still may the Gray Champion come, for
he is the type of New England's hereditary spirit; and his
shadowy march, on the eve of danger, must ever be the pledge,
that New England's sons will vindicate their ancestry.

YOUNG GOODMAN
BROWN

Young Goodman Brown came forth at sunset into the street at Salem village; but put his head back, after crossing the threshold, to exchange a parting kiss with his young wife. And Faith, as the wife was aptly named, thrust her own pretty head into the street, letting the wind play with the pink ribbons of her cap while she called to Goodman Brown.

"Dearest heart," whispered she, softly and rather sadly, when her lips were close to his ear, "prithee put off your journey until sunrise and sleep in your own bed to-night. A lone woman is troubled with such dreams and such thoughts that she's afeard of herself sometimes. Pray tarry with me this night, dear husband, of all nights in the year."

"My love and my Faith," replied young Goodman Brown, "of all nights in the year, this one night must I tarry away from thee. My journey, as thou callest it, forth and back again, must needs be done 'twixt now and sunrise. What, my sweet, pretty wife, dost thou doubt me already, and we but three months married?"

"Then God bless you!" said Faith, with the pink ribbons; "and may you find all well when you come back."

"Amen!" cried Goodman Brown. "Say thy prayers, dear Faith, and go to bed at dusk, and no harm will come to thee."

First published in *The New England Magazine*, April, 1835.

So they parted; and the young man pursued his way until, being about to turn the corner by the meeting-house, he looked back and saw the head of Faith still peeping after him with a melancholy air, in spite of her pink ribbons.

"Poor little Faith!" thought he, for his heart smote him. "What a wretch am I to leave her on such an errand! She talks of dreams, too. Methought as she spoke there was trouble in her face, as if a dream had warned her what work is to be done to-night. But no, no; 'twould kill her to think it. Well, she's a blessed angel on earth; and after this one night I'll cling to her skirts and follow her to heaven."

With this excellent resolve for the future, Goodman Brown felt himself justified in making more haste on his present evil purpose. He had taken a dreary road, darkened by all the gloomiest trees of the forest, which barely stood aside to let the narrow path creep through, and closed immediately behind. It was all as lonely as could be; and there is this peculiarity in such a solitude, that the traveller knows not who may be concealed by the innumerable trunks and the thick boughs overhead; so that with lonely footsteps he may yet be passing through an unseen multitude.

"There may be a devilish Indian behind every tree," said Goodman Brown to himself; and he glanced fearfully behind him as he added, "What if the devil himself should be at my very elbow!"

His head being turned back, he passed a crook of the road, and, looking forward again, beheld the figure of a man, in grave and decent attire, seated at the foot of an old tree. He arose at Goodman Brown's approach and walked onward side by side with him.

"You are late, Goodman Brown," said he. "The clock of the Old South was striking as I came through Boston, and that is full fifteen minutes agone."

"Faith kept me back a while," replied the young man, with a tremor in his voice, caused by the sudden appearance of his companion, though not wholly unexpected.

It was now deep dusk in the forest, and deepest in that part of it where these two were journeying. As nearly as could be discerned, the second traveller was about fifty years old, apparently in the same rank of life as Goodman Brown, and bearing a considerable resemblance to him, though perhaps more in expression than features. Still they might have been taken for father and son. And yet, though the elder person was as simply clad as the younger, and as simple in manner too, he had an indescribable air of one who knew the world, and who would not have felt abashed at the governor's dinner table or in King William's court, were it possible that his affairs should call him thither. But the only thing about him that could be fixed upon as remarkable was his staff, which bore the likeness of a great black snake, so curiously wrought that it might almost be seen to twist and wriggle itself like a living serpent. This, of course, must have been an ocular deception, assisted by the uncertain light.

"Come, Goodman Brown," cried his fellow-traveller, "this is a dull pace for the beginning of a journey. Take my staff, if you are so soon weary."

"Friend," said the other, exchanging his slow pace for a full stop, "having kept covenant by meeting thee here, it is my purpose now to return whence I came. I have scruples touching the matter thou wot'st of."

"Sayest thou so?" replied he of the serpent, smiling apart. "Let us walk on, nevertheless, reasoning as we go; and if I convince thee not thou shalt turn back. We are but a little way in the forest yet."

"Too far! too far!" exclaimed the goodman, unconsciously resuming his walk. "My father never went into the woods on such an errand, nor his father before him. We have been a race of honest men and good Christians since the days of the martyrs; and shall I be the first of the name of Brown that ever took this path and kept"—

"Such company, thou wouldst say," observed the elder person, interpreting his pause. "Well said, Goodman Brown! I have been as well acquainted with your family as with ever a one among the Puritans; and that's no trifle to say. I helped your grandfather, the constable, when he lashed the Quaker woman so smartly through the streets of Salem; and it was I that brought your father a pitch-pine knot, kindled at my own hearth, to set fire to an Indian village, in King Philip's war. They were my good friends, both; and many a pleasant walk have we had along this path, and returned merrily after midnight. I would fain be friends with you for their sake."

"If it be as thou sayest," replied Goodman Brown, "I marvel they never spoke of these matters; or, verily, I marvel not, seeing that the least rumor of the sort would have driven them from New England. We are a people of prayer, and good works to boot, and abide no such wickedness."

"Wickedness or not," said the traveller with the twisted staff, "I have a very general acquaintance here in New England. The deacons of many a church have drunk the communion wine with me; the selectmen of divers towns make me their chairman; and a majority of the Great and General Court are firm supporters of my interest. The governor and I, too—But these are state secrets."

"Can this be so?" cried Goodman Brown, with a stare of amazement at his undisturbed companion. "Howbeit, I have nothing to do with the governor and council; they have their own ways, and are no rule for a simple husbandman like me. But, were I to go on with thee, how should I meet the eye of that good old man, our minister, at Salem village? Oh, his voice would make me tremble both Sabbath day and lecture day."

Thus far the elder traveller had listened with due gravity; but now burst into a fit of irrepressible mirth, shaking himself so violently that his snake-like staff actually seemed to wriggle in sympathy.

"Ha! ha! ha!" shouted he again and again; then composing himself, "Well, go on, Goodman Brown, go on; but, prithee, don't kill me with laughing."

"Well, then, to end the matter at once," said Goodman Brown, considerably nettled, "there is my wife, Faith. It would break her dear little heart; and I'd rather break my own."

"Nay, if that be the case," answered the other, "e'en go thy ways, Goodman Brown. I would not for twenty old women like the one hobbling before us that Faith should come to any harm."

As he spoke he pointed his staff at a female figure on the path, in whom Goodman Brown recognized a very pious and exemplary dame, who had taught him his catechism in youth, and was still his moral and spiritual adviser, jointly with the minister and Deacon Gookin.

"A marvel, truly, that Goody Cloyse should be so far in the wilderness at nightfall," said he. "But with your leave, friend, I shall take a cut through the woods until we have left this Christian woman behind. Being a stranger to you, she might ask whom I was consorting with and whither I was going."

"Be it so," said his fellow-traveller. "Betake you to the woods, and let me keep the path."

Accordingly the young man turned aside, but took care to watch his companion, who advanced softly along the road until he had come within a staff's length of the old dame. She, meanwhile, was making the best of her way, with singular speed for so aged a woman, and mumbling some indistinct words—a prayer, doubtless—as she went. The traveller put forth his staff and touched her withered neck with what seemed the serpent's tail.

"The devil!" screamed the pious old lady.

"Then Goody Cloyse knows her old friend?" observed the traveller, confronting her and leaning on his writhing stick.

"Ah, forsooth, and is it your worship indeed?" cried the good dame. "Yes, truly is it, and in the very image of my old gossip, Goodman Brown, the grandfather of the silly fellow that now is. But—would your worship believe it?—my broomstick hath strangely disappeared, stolen, as I suspect, by that unhanged witch, Goody Cory, and that, too, when I was all anointed with the juice of smallage, and cinquefoil, and wolf's bane"—

"Mingled with fine wheat and the fat of a new-born babe," said the shape of old Goodman Brown.

"Ah, your worship knows the recipe," cried the old lady, cackling aloud. "So, as I was saying, being all ready for the meeting, and no horse to ride on, I made up my mind to foot it, for they tell me there is a nice young man to be taken into communion tonight. But now your good worship will lend me your arm, and we shall be there in a twinkling."

"That can hardly be," answered her friend. "I may not spare you my arm, Goody Cloyse; but here is my staff, if you will."

So saying, he threw it down at her feet, where, perhaps, it assumed life, being one of the rods which its owner had formerly lent to the Egyptian magi. Of this fact, however, Goodman Brown can not take cognizance. He had cast up his eyes in astonishment, and, looking down again, beheld neither Goody Cloyse nor the serpentine staff, but his fellow-traveller alone, who waited for him as calmly as if nothing had happened.

"That old woman taught me my catechism," said the young man; and there was a world of meaning in this simple comment.

They continued to walk onward, while the elder traveller exhorted his companion to make good speed and persevere in the path, discoursing so aptly that his arguments seemed rather to spring up in the bosom of his auditor than to be suggested by himself. As they went, he plucked a branch of maple to serve for a walking stick, and began to strip it of the twigs and little boughs, which were wet with evening dew. The moment his fingers touched them they became strangely withered and dried up as with a week's sunshine. Thus the pair proceeded, at a good free pace, until suddenly, in a gloomy hollow of the road, Goodman Brown sat himself down on the stump of a tree and refused to go any farther.

"Friend," said he, stubbornly, "my mind is made up. Not another step will I budge on this errand. What if a wretched old woman do choose to go to the devil when I thought she was going to heaven: is that any reason why I should quit my dear Faith and go after her?"

"You will think better of this by and by," said his acquaintance, composedly. "Sit here and rest yourself a while; and when you feel like moving again, there is my staff to help you along."

Without more words, he threw his companion the maple stick, and was as speedily out of sight as if he had vanished into the deepening gloom. The young man sat a few moments by the roadside, applauding himself greatly, and thinking with how clear a conscience he should meet the minister in his morning walk, nor shrink from the eye of good old Deacon Gookin. And what calm sleep would be his that very night, which was to have been spent so wickedly, but so purely and sweetly now, in the arms of Faith! Amidst these pleasant and praiseworthy meditations, Goodman Brown heard the tramp of horses along the road, and deemed it advisable to conceal himself within the verge of the forest, conscious of the guilty purpose that had bought him thither, though now so happily turned from it.

On came the hoof tramps and the voices of the riders, two grave old voices, conversing soberly as they drew near. These mingled sounds appeared to pass along the road, within a few yards of the young man's hiding-place; but, owing doubtless to the depth of the gloom at that particular spot, neither the travellers nor their steeds were visible. Though their figures brushed the small boughs by the wayside, it could not be seen that they intercepted, even for a moment; the faint gleam from the strip of bright sky athwart which they must have passed. Goodman Brown alternately crouched and stood on tiptoe, pulling aside the branches and thrusting forth his head as far as he durst without discerning so much as a shadow. It vexed him the more, because he could have sworn, were such a thing possible, that he recognized the voices of the minister and Deacon Gookin, jogging along quietly, as they were wont to do, when bound to some ordination or ecclesiastical council. While yet within hearing one of the riders stopped to pluck a switch.

"Of the two, reverend sir," said the voice like the deacon's,

"I had rather miss an ordination dinner than to-night's meeting. They tell me that some of our community are to be here from Falmouth and beyond, and others from Connecticut and Rhode Island besides several of Indian powwows, who, after their fashion, know almost as much deviltry as the best of us. Moreover, there is a goodly young woman to be taken into communion."

"Mighty well, Deacon Gookin!" replied the solemn old tones of the minister. "Spur up, or we shall be late. Nothing can be done you know until I get on the ground."

The hoofs clattered again; and the voices, talking so strangely in the empty air, passed on through the forest, where no church had ever been gathered or solitary Christian prayed. Whither, then, could these holy men be journeying so deep into the heathen wilderness? Young Goodman Brown caught hold of a tree for support, being ready to sink down on the ground, faint and overburdened with the heavy sickness of his heart. He looked up to the sky, doubting whether there really was a heaven above him. Yet there was the blue arch, and the stars brightening in it.

"With heaven above and Faith below, I will yet stand firm against the devil!" cried Goodman Brown.

While he still gazed upward into the deep arch of the firmament and had lifted his hands to pray, a cloud, though no wind was stirring, hurried across the zenith and hid the brightening stars. The blue sky was still visible, except directly overhead, where this black mass of cloud was sweeping swiftly northward. Aloft in the air, as if from the depths of the cloud, came a confused and doubtful sound of voices. Once the listener fancied that he could distinguish the accents of townspeople of his own, men, and women, both pious and ungodly, many of whom he had met at the communion table, and had seen others rioting at the tavern. The next moment, so indistinct were the sounds, he doubted whether he had heard aught but the murmur of the old forest, whispering without a wind. Then came a stronger swell of those familiar tones, heard daily in the sunshine at Salem village, but never until now from a

cloud of night. There was one voice of a young woman uttering lamentations, yet with an uncertain sorrow, and entreat-
ing for some favor, which perhaps, it would grieve her to obtain; and all the unseen multitude, both saints and sinners,
seemed to encourage her onward.

"Faith!" shouted Goodman Brown, in a voice of agony and
desperation; and the echoes of the forest mocked him, crying,
"Faith! Faith!" as if bewildered wretches were seeking her all
through the wilderness.

The cry of grief, rage, and terror was yet piercing the night,
when the unhappy husband held his breath for a response.
There was a scream, drowned immediately in a loud murmur
of voices, fading into far-off laughter, as the dark cloud swept
away, leaving the clear and silent sky above Goodman Brown.
But something fluttered lightly down through the air and
caught on the branch of a tree. The young man seized it, and
beheld a pink ribbon.

"My Faith is gone!" cried he, after one stupefied moment.
"There is no good on earth; and sin is but a name. Come,
devil; for to thee is this world given."

And, maddened with despair, so that he laughed loud and
long, did Goodman Brown grasp his staff and set forth again,
at such a rate that he seemed to fly along the forest path
rather than to walk or run. The road grew wilder and drearier
and more faintly traced, and vanished at length, leaving him
in the heart of the dark wilderness, still rushing onward with
the instinct that guides mortal man to evil. The whole forest
was peopled with frightful sounds—the creaking of the trees,
the howling of wild beasts, and the yell of Indians; while
sometimes the wind tolled like a distant church bell, and
sometimes gave a broad roar around the traveler, as if all
Nature were laughing him to scorn. But he was himself the
chief horror of the scene, and shrank not from its other
horrors.

"Ha! ha! ha!" roared Goodman Brown when the wind
laughed at him. "Let us hear which will laugh loudest. Think
not to frighten me with your deviltry. Come witch, come

wizard, come Indian powwow, come devil himself, and here comes Goodman Brown. You may as well fear him as he fear you."

In truth, all through the haunted forest there could be nothing more frightful than the figure of Goodman Brown. On he flew among the black pines, brandishing his staff with frenzied gestures, now giving vent to an inspiration of horrid blasphemy, and now shouting forth such laughter as set all the echoes of the forest laughing like demons around him. The fiend in his own shape is less hideous than when he rages in the breast of man. Thus sped the demoniac on his course, until, quivering among the trees, he saw a red light before him, as when the felled trunks and branches of a clearing have been set on fire, and throw up their lurid blaze against the sky, at the hour of midnight. He paused, in a lull of the tempest that had driven him onward, and heard the swell of what seemed a hymn, rolling solemnly from a distance with the weight of many voices. He knew the tune; it was a familiar one in the choir of the village meeting-house. The verse died heavily away, and was lengthened by a chorus, not of human voices, but of all the sounds of the benighted wilderness pealing in awful harmony together. Goodman Brown cried out, and his cry was lost to his own ear by its unison with the cry of the desert.

In the interval of silence he stole forward until the light glared full upon his eyes. At one extremity of an open space, hemmed in by the dark wall of the forest, arose a rock, bearing some rude, natural resemblance either to an altar or a pulpit, and surrounded by four blazing pines, their tops aflame, their stems untouched, like candles at an evening meeting. The mass of foliage that had overgrown the summit of the rock was all on fire, blazing into the night and fitfully illuminating the whole field. Each pendent twig and leafy festoon was in a blaze. As the red light arose and fell, a numerous congregation alternately shone forth, then disappeared in shadow, and again grew, as it were, out of the darkness, peopling the heart of the solitary woods at once.

"A grave and dark-clad company," quoth Goodman Brown.

In truth they were such. Among them, quivering to and fro between gloom and splendor, appeared faces that would be seen next day at the council board of the province, and others which, Sabbath after Sabbath, looked devoutly heavenward, and benignantly over the crowded pews, from the holiest pulpits in the land. Some affirm that the lady of the governor was there. At least there were high dames well known to her, and wives of honored husbands, and widows, a great multitude, and ancient maidens, all of excellent repute, and fair young girls, who trembled lest their mothers should espy them. Either the sudden gleams of light flashing over the obscure field bedazzled Goodman Brown, or he recognized a score of the church members of Salem village famous for their especial sanctity. Good old Deacon Gookin had arrived, and waited at the skirts of that venerable saint, his revered pastor. But, irreverently consorting with these grave, reputable, and pious people, these elders of the church, these chaste dames and dewy virgins, there were men of dissolute lives and women of spotted fame, wretches given over to all mean and filthy vice, and suspected even of horrid crimes. It was strange to see that the good shrank not from the wicked, nor were the sinners abashed by the saints. Scattered also among their pale-faced enemies were the Indian priests, or powwows, who had often scared their native forest with more hideous incantations than any known to English witchcraft.

"But where is Faith?" thought Goodman Brown; and, as hope came into his heart, he trembled.

Another verse of the hymn arose, a slow and mournful strain, such as the pious love, but joined to words which expressed all that our nature can conceive of sin, and darkly hinted at far more. Unfathomable to mere mortals is the lore of fiends. Verse after verse was sung; and still the chorus of the desert swelled between like the deepest tone of a mighty organ; and with the final peal of that dreadful anthem there came a sound, as if the roaring wind, the rushing streams, the howling beasts, and every other voice of the unconcerted wilderness were mingling and according with the voice of guilty man in homage to the prince of all. The four blazing pines threw up a loftier flame, and obscurely discovered shapes and visages of horror on the smoke wreaths above the impious assembly. At the same moment the fire on the rock shot redly forth and formed a glowing arch above its base, where now appeared a figure. With reverence be it spoken, the figure bore no slight similitude, both in garb and manner, to some grave divine of the New England churches.

"Bring forth the converts!" cried a voice that echoed through the field and rolled into the forest.

At the word, Goodman Brown stepped forth from the shadow of the trees and approached the congregation, with whom he felt a loathful brotherhood by the sympathy of all that was wicked in his heart. He could have well-nigh sworn that the shape of his own dead father beckoned him to advance, looking downward from a smoke wreath, while a woman, with dim features of despair, threw out her hand to warn him back. Was it his mother? But he had no power to retreat one step, nor to resist, even in thought, when the minister and good old Deacon Gookin seized his arms and led him to the blazing rock. Thither came also the slender form of a veiled female, led between Goody Cloyse, that pious teacher of the catechism, and Martha Carrier, who had received the devil's promise to be queen of hell. A rampant hag was she. And there stood the proselytes beneath the canopy of fire.

"Welcome, my children," said the dark figure, "to the communion of your race. Ye have found thus young your nature and your destiny. My children, look behind you!"

They turned; and flashing forth, as it were, in a sheet of flame, the fiend worshippers were seen; the smile of welcome gleamed darkly on every visage.

"There," resumed the sable form, "are all whom ye have reverenced from youth. Ye deemed them holier than yourself, and shrank from your own sin, contrasting it with their lives of righteousness and prayerful aspirations heavenward. Yet here are they all in my worshipping assembly. This night it shall be granted you to know their secret deeds: how hoary-bearded elders of the church have whispered wanton words to the young maids of their households; how many a woman, eager for widows' weeds, has given her husband a drink at bedtime and let him sleep his last sleep in her bosom; how beardless youths have made haste to inherit their fathers' wealth, and how fair damsels—blush not, sweet ones—have dug little graves in the garden, and bidden me, the sole guest to an infant's funeral. By the sympathy of your human hearts for sin ye shall scent out all the places—whether in church, bed-chamber, street, field, or forest—where crime has been committed, and shall exult to behold the whole earth one stain of guilt, one mighty blood spot. Far more than this. It shall be yours to penetrate, in every bosom, the deep mystery of sin, the fountain of all wicked arts, and which inexhaustibly supplies more evil impulses than human power—than my power at its utmost—can make manifest in deeds. And now, my children, look upon each other."

They did so; and, by the blaze of the hell-kindled torches, the wretched man beheld his Faith, and the wife her husband, trembling before that unhallowed altar.

"Lo, there ye stand, my children," said the figure, in a deep and solemn tone, almost sad with its despairing awfulness, as if his once angelic nature could yet mourn for our miserable race. "Depending upon one another's hearts, ye had still hoped that virtue were not all a dream. Now are ye unde-ceived. Evil is the nature of mankind. Evil must be your only happiness. Welcome again, my children, to the communion of your race."

"Welcome," repeated the fiend worshippers, in one cry of despair and triumph.

And there they stood, the only pair, as it seemed, who were yet hesitating on the verge of wickedness in this dark world. A basin was hollowed, naturally, in the rock. Did it contain water, reddened by the lurid light? or was it blood? or, per-chance, a liquid flame? Herein did the shape of evil dip his hand and prepare to lay the mark of baptism upon their foreheads, that they might be partakers of the mystery of sin, more conscious of the secret guilt of others, both in deed and thought, than they could now be of their own. The husband cast one look at his pale wife, and Faith at him. What polluted wretches would the next glance show them to each other, shuddering alike at what they disclosed and what they saw!

"Faith! Faith!" cried the husband, "look up to heaven, and resist the wicked one."

Whether Faith obeyed he knew not. Hardly had he spoken when he found himself amid calm night and solitude, listening to a roar of the wind which died heavily away through the forest. He staggered against the rock, and felt it chill and damp; while a hanging twig, that had been all on fire, besprinkled his cheek with the coldest dew.

The next morning young Goodman Brown came slowly into the street of Salem village, staring around him like a bewildered man. The good old minister was taking a walk along the graveyard to get an appetite for breakfast and meditate his sermon, and bestowed a blessing, as he passed, on Goodman Brown. He shrank from the venerable saint as if to avoid an anathema. Old Deacon Gookin was at domestic worship, and the holy words of his prayer were heard through the open window. "What God doth the wizard pray to?" quoth Goodman Brown. Goody Cloyse, that excellent old Christian, stood in the early sunshine at her own lattice, catechizing a little girl who had brought her a pint of morning's milk. Goodman Brown snatched away the child as from the grasp of the fiend himself. Turning the corner by the meeting-house, he spied the head of Faith, with the pink ribbons, gazing anxiously forth, and bursting into such joy at sight of him that she skipped along the street and almost kissed her husband before the whole village. But Goodman Brown looked sternly and sadly into her face, and passed on without a greeting.

Had Goodman Brown fallen asleep in the forest and only dreamed a wild dream of a witch-meeting?

Be it so if you will; but, alas! it was a dream of evil omen for young Goodman Brown. A stern, a sad, a darkly meditative, a distrustful, if not a desperate man did be become from the night of that fearful dream. On the Sabbath day, when the congregation were singing a holy psalm, he could not listen because an anthem of sin rushed loudly upon his ears and drowned all the blessed strain. When the minister spoke from the pulpit with power and fervid eloquence, and, with his hand on the open Bible, of the sacred truths of our religion, and of saint-like lives and triumphant death and of future bliss or misery unutterable, then did Goodman Brown turn pale, dreading lest the roof should thunder down upon the gray blasphemer and his hearers. Often, waking suddenly at midnight, he shrank from the bosom of Faith; and at morning or eventide, when the family knelt down at prayer, he scowled and muttered to himself, and gazed sternly at his wife, and turned away. And when he had lived long, and was borne to his grave a hoary corpse, followed by Faith, an aged woman, and children and grandchildren, a goodly procession, besides neighbors not a few, they carved no hopeful verse upon his tombstone, for his dying hour was gloom.

who is driving Goodman Brown that night further & further into the forest. Evil — it really does exist.

— Evil of forest — if a dream — Goodman Brown made up — Black Mass every one is there. Human community.

WAKEFIELD

In some old magazine or newspaper I recollect a story, told as truth, of a man—let us call him Wakefield—who absented himself for a long time from his wife. The fact, thus abstractedly stated, is not very uncommon, nor—without a proper distinction of circumstances—to be condemned either as naughty or nonsensical. Howbeit, this, though far from the most aggravated, is perhaps the strangest, instance on record, of marital delinquency; and, moreover, as remarkable a freak as may be found in the whole list of human oddities. The wedded couple lived in London. The man, under pretence of going a journey, took lodgings in the next street to his own house, and there, unheard of by his wife or friends, and without the shadow of a reason for such self-banishment, dwelt upwards of twenty years. During that period, he beheld his home every day, and frequently the forlorn Mrs. Wakefield. And after so great a gap in his matrimonial felicity—when his death was reckoned certain, his estate settled, his name dismissed from memory, and his wife, long, long ago, resigned to her autumnal widowhood—he entered the door one evening, quietly, as from a day's absence, and became a loving spouse till death.

This outline is all that I remember. But the incident,

First published in *The New England Magazine*, May, 1835.

though of the purest originality, unexampled, and probably never to be repeated, is one, I think, which appeals to the generous sympathies of mankind. We know, each for himself, that none of us would perpetrate such a folly, yet feel as if some other might. To my own contemplations, at least, it has often recurred, always exciting wonder, but with a sense that the story must be true, and a conception of its hero's character. Whenever any subject so forcibly affects the mind, time is well spent in thinking of it. If the reader choose, let him do his own meditation; or if he prefer to ramble with me through the twenty years of Wakefield's vagary, I bid him welcome; trusting that there will be a pervading spirit and a moral, even should we fail to find them, done up neatly, and condensed into the final sentence. Thought has always its efficacy, and every striking incident its moral.

What sort of a man was Wakefield? We are free to shape out our own idea, and call it by his name. He was now in the meridian of life; his matrimonial affections, never violent, were sobered into a calm, habitual sentiment; of all husbands, he was likely to be the most constant, because a certain sluggishness would keep his heart at rest, wherever it might be placed. He was intellectual, but not actively so; his mind occupied itself in long and lazy musings, that ended to no purpose, or had not vigor to attain it; his thoughts were seldom so energetic as to seize hold of words. Imagination, in the proper meaning of the term, made no part of Wakefield's gifts. With a cold but not depraved nor wandering heart, and a mind never feverish with riotous thoughts, nor perplexed with originality, who could have anticipated that our friend would entitle himself to a foremost place among the doers of eccentric deeds? Had his acquaintances been asked, who was the man in London the surest to perform nothing to-day which should be remembered on the morrow, they would have thought of Wakefield. Only the wife of his bosom might have hesitated. She, without having analyzed his character, was partly aware of a quiet selfishness, that had rusted into his inactive mind; of a peculiar sort of vanity, the most uneasy attribute about him; of a disposition to craft which had seldom produced more positive effects than the keeping of petty secrets, hardly worth revealing; and, lastly, of what she called a little strangeness, sometimes, in the good man. This latter quality is indefinable, and perhaps non-existent.

Let us now imagine Wakefield bidding adieu to his wife. It is the dusk of an October evening. His equipment is a drab greatcoat, a hat covered with an oilcloth, top-boots, an umbrella in one hand and a small portmanteau in the other. He has informed Mrs. Wakefield that he is to take the night coach into the country. She would fain inquire the length of his journey, its object, and the probable time of his return; but, indulgent to his harmless love of mystery, interrogates him only by a look. He tells her not to expect him positively by the return coach, nor to be alarmed should he tarry three or four days; but, at all events, to look for him at supper on Friday evening. Wakefield himself, be it considered, has no suspicion of what is before him. He holds out his hand, she gives her own, and meets his parting kiss in the matter-of-course way of a ten years' matrimony; and forth goes the middle-aged Mr. Wakefield, almost resolved to perplex his good lady by a whole week's absence. After the door has closed behind him, she perceives it thrust partly open, and a vision of her husband's face, through the aperture, smiling on her, and gone in a moment. For the time, this little incident is dismissed without a thought. But, long afterwards, when she has been more years a widow than a wife, that smile recurs, and flickers across all her reminiscences of Wakefield's visage. In her many musings, she surrounds the original smile with a multitude of fantasies, which make it strange and awful: as, for instance, if she imagines him in a coffin, that parting look is frozen on his pale features; or, if she dreams of him in heaven, still his blessed spirit wears a quiet and crafty smile. Yet, for its sake, when all others have given him up for dead, she sometimes doubts whether she is a widow.

But our business is with the husband. We must hurry after him along the street, ere he lose his individuality, and melt into the great mass of London life. It would be vain searching for him there. Let us follow close at his heels, therefore, until, after several superfluous turns and doublings, we find him comfortably established by the fireside of a small apartment, previously bespoken. He is in the next street to his own, and at his journey's end. He can scarcely trust his good fortune, in having got thither unperceived—recollecting that, at one time, he was delayed by the throng, in the very focus of a lighted lantern; and, again, there were footsteps that seemed to tread behind his own, distinct from the multitudinous tramp around him; and, anon, he heard a voice shouting afar, and fancied that it called his name. Doubtless, a dozen busybodies had been watching him, and told his wife the whole affair. Poor Wakefield! Little knowest thou thine own insignificance in this great world! No mortal eye but mine has traced thee. Go quietly to thy bed, foolish man; and, on the morrow, if thou wilt be wise, get thee home to good Mrs. Wakefield, and tell her the truth. Remove not thyself, even for a little week, from thy place in her chaste bosom. Were she, for a single moment, to deem thee dead, or lost, or lastingly divided from her, thou wouldst be wofully conscious of a change in thy true wife forever after. It is perilous to make a chasm in human affections; not that they gape so long and wide—but so quickly close again!

Almost repenting of his frolic, or whatever it may be termed, Wakefield lies down betimes, and starting from his first nap, spreads forth his arms into the wide and solitary waste of the unaccustomed bed. "No,"—thinks he, gathering the bedclothes about him,—"I will not sleep alone another night."

In the morning he rises earlier than usual, and set himself to consider what he really means to do. Such are his loose and rambling modes of thought that he has taken this very singular step with the consciousness of a purpose, indeed, but without being able to define it sufficiently for his own contemplation. The vagueness of the project, and the convulsive effort with which he plunges into the execution of it, are equally characteristic of a feeble-minded man. Wakefield sifts his ideas, however, as minutely as he may, and finds himself curious to know the progress of matters at home—how his exemplary wife will endure his widowhood of a week; and, briefly, how the little sphere of creatures and circumstances, in which he was a central object, will be affected by his removal. A morbid vanity, therefore, lies nearest the bottom of the affair. But, how is he to attain his ends? Not, certainly, by keeping close in this comfortable lodging, where, though he slept and awoke in the next street to his home, he is as effectually abroad as if the stage-coach had been whirling him away all night. Yet, should he reappear, the whole project is knocked in the head. His poor brains being hopelessly puzzled with this dilemma, he at length ventures out, partly resolving to cross the head of the street, and send one hasty glance towards his forsaken domicile. Habit—for he is a man of habits—takes him by the hand, and guides him, wholly unaware, to his own door, where, just at the critical moment, he is aroused by the scraping of his foot upon the step. Wakefield! whither are you going?

At that instant his fate was turning on the pivot. Little dreaming of the doom to which his first backward step devotes him, he hurries away, breathless with agitation hitherto unfelt, and hardly dares turn his head at the distant corner. Can it be that nobody caught sight of him? Will not the whole household—the decent Mrs. Wakefield, the smart maid servant, and the dirty little footboy—raise a hue and cry, through London streets, in pursuit of their fugitive lord and master? Wonderful escape! He gathers courage to pause and look homeward, but is perplexed with a sense of change about the familiar edifice, such as affects us all, when, after a separation of months or years, we again see some hill or lake, or work of art, with which we were friends of old. In ordinary cases, this indescribable impression is caused by the comparison and contrast between our imperfect reminiscences and the reality. In Wakefield, the magic of a single night was wrought a similar transformation, because, in that brief period, a great moral change has been effected. But this is a secret from himself. Before leaving the spot, he catches a far and momentary glimpse of his wife, passing athwart the front window, with her face turned towards the head of the street. The crafty nincompoop takes to his heels, scared with the idea that, among a thousand such atoms of mortality, her eye must have detected him. Right glad is his heart, though his brain be somewhat dizzy, when he finds himself by the coal fire of his lodgings.

So much for the commencement of this long whimwham. After the initial conception, and the stirring up of the man's sluggish temperament to put it in practice, the whole matter evolves itself in a natural train. We may suppose him, as the result of deep deliberation, buying a new wig, of reddish hair, and selecting sundry garments, in a fashion unlike his customary suit of brown, from a Jew's old-clothes bag. It is accomplished. Wakefield is another man. The new system being now established, a retrograde movement to the old would be almost as difficult as the step that placed him in his unparalleled position. Furthermore, he is rendered obstinate by a sulkiness occasionally incident to his temper, and brought on at present by the inadequate sensation which he conceives to have been produced in the bosom of Mrs. Wakefield. He will not go back until she be frightened half to death. Well; twice or thrice has she passed before his sight, each time with a heavier step, a paler cheek, and more anxious brow; and in the third week of his non-appearance he detects a portent of evil entering the house, in the guise of an apothecary. Next day the knocker is muffled. Towards nightfall comes the chariot of a physician, and deposits its big-wigged and solemn burden at Wakefield's door, whence, after a quarter of an hour's visit, he emerges, perchance the herald of a funeral. Dear woman! Will she die? By this time, Wakefield is excited to something like energy of feeling, but still lingers away from his wife's bedside, pleading with his conscience that she must not be disturbed at such a juncture. If aught else restrains him, he does not know it. In the course of a few weeks she gradually recovers; the crisis is over; her heart is sad, perhaps, but quiet; and let him return soon or late, it will never be feverish for him again. Such ideas glimmer through the midst of Wakefield's mind, and render him indistinctly conscious that an almost impassable gulf divides his hired apartment from his former home. "It is but in the next street!" he sometimes says. Fool! it is in another world. Hitherto, he has put off his return from one particular day to another; henceforward, he leaves the precise time undetermined. Not to-morrow—probably next week—pretty soon. Poor man! The dead have nearly as much chance of revisiting their earthly homes as the self-banished Wakefield.

Would that I had a folio to write, instead of an article of a dozen pages! Then might I exemplify how an influence beyond our control lays its strong hand on every deed which we do, and weaves its consequences into an iron tissue of necessity. Wakefield is spell-bound. We must leave him, for ten years or so, to haunt around his house, without once crossing the threshold, and to be faithful to his wife, with all the affection of which his heart is capable, while he is slowly fading out of hers. Long since, it must be remarked, he had lost the perception of singularity in his conduct.

Now for a scene! Amid the throng of a London street we distinguish a man, now waxing elderly, with few characteristics to attract careless observers, yet bearing, in his whole aspect, the handwriting of no common fate, for such as have the skill to read it. He is meagre; his low and narrow forehead is deeply wrinkled; his eyes, small and lustreless, sometimes wander apprehensively about him, but oftener seem to look inward. He bends his head, and moves with an indescribable obliquity of gait, as if unwilling to display his full front to the world. Watch him long enough to see what we have described, and you will allow that circumstances—which often produce remarkable men from nature's ordinary handiwork —have produced one such here. Next, leaving him to sidle along the footwalk, cast your eyes in the opposite direction, where a portly female, considerably in the wane of life, with a prayer-book in her hand, is proceeding to yonder church. She has the placid mien of settled widowhood. Her regrets have either died away, or have become so essential to her heart, that they would be poorly exchanged for joy. Just as the lean man and well-conditioned woman are passing, a slight obstruction occurs, and brings these two figures directly in contact. Their hands touch; the pressure of the crowd forces her bosom against his shoulder; they stand, face to face, staring into each other's eyes. After a ten years' separation, thus Wakefield meets his wife!

The throng eddies away, and carries them asunder. The sober widow, resuming her former pace, proceeds to church, but pauses in the portal, and throws a perplexed glance along the street. She passes in, however, opening her prayer-book as she goes. And the man! with so wild a face that busy and selfish London stands to gaze after him, he hurries to his lodgings, bolts the door, and throws himself upon the bed. The latent feelings of years break out; his feeble mind acquires a brief energy from their strength; all the miserable strangeness of his life is revealed to him at a glance: and he cries out, passionately, "Wakefield! Wakefield! You are mad!"

Perhaps he was so. The singularity of his situation must have so moulded him to himself, that, considered in regard to his fellow-creatures and the business of life, he could not be said to possess his right mind. He had contrived, or rather he had happened, to dissever himself from the world—to vanish—to give up his place and privileges with living men, without being admitted among the dead. The life of a hermit is nowise parallel to his. He was in the bustle of the city, as of old; but the crowd swept by and saw him not; he was, we may figuratively say, always beside his wife and at his hearth, yet must never feel the warmth of the one nor the affection of the other. It was Wakefield's unprecedented fate to retain his original share of human sympathies, and to be still involved in human interests, while he had lost his reciprocal influence on them. It would be a most curious speculation to trace out the effect of such circumstances on his heart and intellect, separately, and in unison. Yet, changed as he was, he would seldom be conscious of it, but deem himself the same man as ever; glimpses of the truth, indeed, would come, but only for the moment; and still he would keep saying, "I shall soon go back!"—nor reflect that he had been saying so for twenty years.

I conceive, also, that these twenty years would appear, in the retrospect, scarcely longer than the week to which Wakefield had at first limited his absence. He would look on the affair as no more than an interlude in the main business of his life. When, after a little while more, he should deem it time to reënter his parlor, his wife would clap her hands for joy, on beholding the middle-aged Mr. Wakefield. Alas, what a mistake! Would Time but await the close of our favorite follies, we should be young men, all of us, and till Doomsday.

One evening, in the twentieth year since he vanished, Wakefield is taking his customary walk towards the dwelling which he still calls his own. It is a gusty night of autumn, with frequent showers that patter down upon the pavement, and are gone before a man can put up his umbrella. Pausing near the house, Wakefield discerns, through the parlor windows of the second floor, the red glow and the glimmer and fitful flash of a comfortable fire. On the ceiling appears a grotesque shadow of good Mrs. Wakefield. The cap, the nose and chin, and the broad waist, form an admirable caricature, which dances, moreover, with the up-flickering and down-sinking blaze, almost too merrily for the shade of an elderly widow. At this instant a shower chances to fall, and is driven, by the unmannerly gust, full into Wakefield's face and bosom. He is quite penetrated with its autumnal chill. Shall he stand, wet and shivering here, when his own hearth has a good fire to warm him, and his own wife will run to fetch the gray coat and small-clothes, which doubtless, she has kept carefully in the closet of their bed chamber? No! Wakefield is no such fool. He ascends the steps—heavily!—for twenty years have stiffened his legs since he came down—but he knows it not. Stay, Wakefield! Would you go to the sole home that is left you? Then step into your grave! The door opens. As he passes in, we have a parting glimpse of his visage, and recognize the crafty smile, which was the precursor of the little joke that he has ever since been playing off at his wife's expense. How unmercifully has he quizzed the poor woman! Well, a good night's rest to Wakefield!

This happy event—supposing it to be such—could only have occurred at an unpremeditated moment. We will not follow our friend across the threshold. He has left us much food for thought, a portion of which shall lend its wisdom to a moral, and be shaped into a figure. Amid the seeming confusion of our mysterious world, individuals are so nicely adjusted to a system, and systems to one another and to a whole, that, by stepping aside for a moment, a man exposes himself to a fearful risk of losing his place forever. Like Wakefield, he may become, as it were, the Outcast of the Universe.

THE AMBITIOUS
GUEST

One September night a family had gathered round their hearth, and piled it high with the driftwood of mountain streams, the dry cones of the pine, and the splintered ruins of great trees that had come crashing down the precipice. Up the chimney roared the fire, and brightened the room with its broad blaze. The faces of the father and mother had a sober gladness; the children laughed; the eldest daughter was the image of Happiness at seventeen; and the aged grandmother, who sat knitting in the warmest place, was the image of Happiness grown old. They had found the "herb, heart's-ease," in the bleakest spot of all New England. This family were situated in the Notch of the White Hills, where the wind was sharp throughout the year, and pitilessly cold in the winter,—giving their cottage all its fresh inclemency before it descended on the valley of the Saco. They dwelt in a cold spot and a dangerous one; for a mountain towered above their heads, so steep, that the stones would often rumble down its sides and startle them at midnight.

The daughter had just uttered some simple jest that filled them all with mirth, when the wind came through the Notch and seemed to pause before their cottage—rattling the door, with a sound of wailing and lamentation, before it passed into the valley. For a moment it saddened them, though there

First published in *The New England Magazine*, June, 1835.

was nothing unusual in the tones. But the family were glad again when they perceived that the latch was lifted by some traveller, whose footsteps had been unheard amid the dreary blast which heralded his approach, and wailed as he was entering, and went moaning away from the door.

Though they dwelt in such a solitude, these people held daily converse with the world. The romantic pass of the Notch is a great artery, through which the life-blood of internal commerce is continually throbbing between Maine, on one side, and the Green Mountains and the shores of the St. Lawrence, on the other. The stage-coach always drew up before the door of the cottage. The wayfarer, with no companion but his staff, paused here to exchange a word, that the sense of loneliness might not utterly overcome him ere he could pass through the cleft of the mountain, or reach the first house in the valley. And here the teamster, on his way to Portland market, would put up the night; and, if a bachelor, might sit an hour beyond the usual bedtime, and steal a kiss from the mountain maid at parting. It was one of those primitive taverns where the traveller pays only for food and lodging, but meets with a homely kindness beyond all price. When the footsteps were heard, therefore, between the outer door and the inner one, the whole family rose up, grandmother, children, and all, as if about to welcome some one who belonged to them, and whose fate was linked with theirs.

The door was opened by a young man. His face at first wore the melancholy expression, almost despondency, of one who travels a wild and bleak road, at nightfall and alone, but soon brightened up when he saw the kindly warmth of his reception. He felt his heart spring forward to meet them all, from the old woman, who wiped a chair with her apron, to the little child that held out its arms to him. One glance and smile placed the stranger on a footing of innocent familiarity with the eldest daughter.

"Ah, this fire is the right thing!" cried he; "especially when there is such a pleasant circle round it. I am quite benumbed; for the Notch is just like the pipe of a great pair of bellows;

it has blown a terrible blast in my face all the way from Bartlett."

"Then you are going towards Vermont?" said the master of the house, as he helped to take a light knapsack off the young man's shoulders.

"Yes; to Burlington, and far enough beyond," replied he. "I meant to have been at Ethan Crawford's to-night; but a pedestrian lingers along such a road as this. It is no matter; for, when I saw the good fire, and all your cheerful faces, I felt as if you had kindled it on purpose for me, and were waiting my arrival. So I shall sit down among you, and make myself at home."

The frank-hearted stranger had just drawn his chair to the fire when something like a heavy footstep was heard without, rushing down the steep side of the mountain, as with long and rapid strides, and taking such a leap in passing the cottage as to strike the opposite precipice. The family held their breath, because they knew the sound, and their guest held his by instinct.

"The old mountain has thrown a stone at us, for fear we should forget him," said the landlord, recovering himself. "He sometimes nods his head and threatens to come down; but we are old neighbors, and agree together pretty well upon the whole. Besides we have a sure place of refuge hard by if he should be coming in good earnest."

Let us now suppose the stranger to have finished his supper of bear's meat; and, by his natural felicity of manner, to have placed himself on a footing of kindness with the whole family, so that they talked as freely together as if he belonged to their mountain brood. He was of a proud, yet gentle spirit— haughty and reserved among the rich and great; but ever ready to stoop his head to the lowly cottage door, and be like a brother or a son at the poor man's fireside. In the household of the Notch he found warmth and simplicity of feeling, the pervading intelligence of New England, and a poetry of native growth, which they had gathered when they little thought of it from the mountain peaks and chasms, and at the very threshold of their romantic and dangerous abode. He had travelled far and alone; his whole life, indeed, had been a solitary path; for, with the lofty caution of his nature, he had kept himself apart from those who might otherwise have been his companions. The family, too, though so kind and hospitable, had that consciousness of unity among themselves, and separation from the world at large, which, in every domestic circle, should still keep a holy place where no stranger may intrude. But this evening a prophetic sympathy impelled the refined and educated youth to pour out his heart before the simple mountaineers, and constrained them to answer him with the same free confidence. And thus it should have been. Is not the kindred of a common fate a closer tie than that of birth?

The secret of the young man's character was a high and abstracted ambition. He could have borne to live an undistinguished life, but not to be forgotten in the grave. Yearning desire had been transformed to hope; and hope, long cherished, had become like certainty, that, obscurely as he journeyed now, a glory was to beam on all his pathway,— though not, perhaps, while he was treading it. But when posterity should gaze back into the gloom of what was now the present, they would trace the brightness of his footsteps, brightening as meaner glories faded, and confess that a gifted one had passed from his cradle to his tomb with none to recognize him.

"As yet," cried the stranger—his cheek glowing and his eye flashing with enthusiasm—"as yet, I have done nothing. Were I to vanish from the earth to-morrow, none would know so much of me as you: that a nameless youth came up at nightfall from the valley of the Saco, and opened his heart to you in the evening, and passed through the Notch by sunrise, and was seen no more. Not a soul would ask, 'Who was he? Whither did the wanderer go?' But I cannot die till I have achieved my destiny. Then, let Death come! I shall have built my monument!"

There was a continual flow of natural emotion, gushing

forth amid abstracted reverie, which enabled the family to understand this young man's sentiments, though so foreign from their own. With quick sensibility of the ludicrous, he blushed at the ardor into which he had been betrayed.

"You laugh at me," said he, taking the eldest daughter's hand, and laughing himself. "You think my ambition as non-sensical as if I were to freeze myself to death on the top of Mount Washington, only that people might spy at me from the country round about. And, truly, that would be a. noble pedestal for a man's statue!"

"It is better to sit here by this fire," answered the girl, blushing, "and be comfortable and contented, though nobody thinks about us."

"I suppose," said her father, after a fit of musing, "there is something natural in what the young man says; and if my mind had been turned that way, I might have felt just the same. It is strange, wife, how his talk has set my head running on things that are pretty certain never to come to pass."

"Perhaps they may," observed the wife. "Is the man thinking what he will do when he is a widower?"

"No, no!" cried he, repelled the idea with reproachful kindness. "When I think of your death, Esther, I think of mine, too. But I was wishing we had a good farm in Bartlett, or Bethlehem, or Littleton, or some other township round the White Mountains; but not where they could tumble on our heads. I should want to stand well with my neighbors and be called Squire, and sent to General Court for a term or two; for a plain, honest man may do as much good there as a lawyer. And when I should be grown quite an old man, and you an old woman, so as not to be long apart, I might die happy enough in my bed, and leave you all crying around me. A slate gravestone would suit me as well as a marble one—with just my name and age, and a verse of a hymn, and something to let people know that I lived an honest man and died a Christian."

"There now!" exclaimed the stranger; "it is our nature to desire a monument, be it slate or marble, or a pillar of granite, or a glorious memory in the universal heart of man."

"We're in a strange way, to-night," said the wife, with tears in her eyes. "They say it's a sign of something, when folks' minds go a wandering so. Hark to the children!"

They listened accordingly. The young children had been put to bed in another room, but with an open door between, so that they could be heard talking busily among themselves. One and all seemed to have caught the infection from the fireside circle, and were outvying each other in wild wishes, and childish projects of what they would do when they came to be men and women. At length a little boy, instead of addressing his brothers and sisters, called out to his mother.

"I'll tell you what I wish, mother," cried he. "I want you and father and grandma'm, and all of us, and the stranger too, to start right away, and go and take a drink out of the basin of the Flume!"

Nobody could help laughing at the child's notion of leaving a warm bed, and dragging them from a cheerful fire, to visit the basin of the Flume,—a brook, which tumbles over the precipice, deep within the Notch. The boy had hardly spoken when a wagon rattled along the road, and stopped a moment before the door. It appeared to contain two or three men, who were cheering their hearts with the rough chorus of a song, which resounded, in broken notes, between the cliffs, while the singers hesitated whether to continue their journey or put up here for the night."

"Father," said the girl, "they are calling you by name."

But the good man doubted whether they had really called him, and was unwilling to show himself too solicitous of gain by inviting people to patronize his house. He therefore did not hurry to the door; and the lash being soon applied, the travellers plunged into the Notch, still singing and laughing, though their music and mirth came back drearily from the heart of the mountain.

"There, mother!" cried the boy, again. "They'd have given us a ride to the Flume."

Again they laughed at the child's pertinacious fancy for a night ramble. But it happened that a light cloud passed over the daughter's spirit; she looked gravely into the fire, and drew a breath that was almost a sigh. It forced its way, in spite of a little struggle to repress it. Then starting and blushing, she looked quickly round the circle as if they had caught a glimpse into her bosom. The stranger asked what she had been thinking of.

"Nothing," answered she, with a downcast smile. "Only I felt lonesome just then."

"Oh, I have always had a gift of feeling what is in other people's hearts," said he, half seriously. "Shall I tell the secrets of yours? For I know what to think when a young girl shivers by a warm hearth, and complains of lonesomeness at her mother's side. Shall I put these feelings into words?"

"They would not be a girl's feelings any longer if they could be put into words," replied the mountain nymph, laughing, but avoiding his eyes.

All this was said apart. Perhaps a germ of love was springing in their hearts, so pure that it might blossom in Paradise, since it could not be matured on earth; for women worship such gentle dignity as his; and the proud, contemplative, yet kindly soul is oftenest captivated by simplicity like hers. But while they spoke softly, and he was watching the happy sadness, the lightsome shadows, the shy yearnings of a maiden's nature, the wind through the Notch took a deeper and drearier sound. It seemed, as the fanciful stranger said, like the choral strain of the spirits of the blast, who in old Indian times had their dwelling among these mountains, and made their heights and recesses a sacred region. There was a wail along the road, as if a funeral were passing. To chase away the gloom, the family threw pine branches on their fire, till the dry leaves crackled and the flame arose, discovering once again a scene of peace and humble happiness. The light hovered about them fondly, and caressed them all. There were the little faces of the children, peeping from their bed apart, and here the father's frame of strength, the mother's subdued and careful mien, the high-browed youth, the budding girl, and the good old grandam, still knitting in the warmest place. The aged woman looked up from her task, and, with fingers ever busy, was the next to speak.

"Old folks have their notions," said she, "as well as young ones. You've been wishing and planning; and letting your heads run on one thing and another, till you've set my mind a wandering too. Now what should an old woman wish for, when she can go but a step or two before she comes to her grave? Children, it will haunt me night and day till I tell you."

"What is it, mother?" cried the husband and wife at once.

Then the old woman, with an air of mystery which drew the circle closer round the fire, informed them that she had provided her grave-clothes some years before,—a nice linen shroud, a cap with a muslin ruff, and everything of a finer sort than she had worn since her wedding day. But this evening an old superstition had strangely recurred to her. It used to be said, in her younger days, that if anything were amiss with a corpse, if only the ruff were not smooth, or the cap did not set right, the corpse in the coffin and beneath the clods would strive to put up its cold hands and arrange it. The bare thought made her nervous.

"Don't talk so, grandmother!" said the girl, shuddering.

"Now,"—continued the old woman, with singular earnestness, yet smiling strangely at her own folly,—"I want one of you to hold a looking-glass over my face. Who knows but I may take a glimpse at myself, and see whether all's right?"

"Old and young, we dream of graves and monuments," murmured the stranger youth. "I wonder how mariners feel when the ship is sinking, and they, unknown and undistinguished, are to be buried together in the ocean—that wide and nameless sepulchre?"

For a moment, the old woman's ghastly conception so engrossed the minds of her hearers that a sound abroad in the night, rising like the roar of a blast, had grown broad, deep, and terrible, before the fated group were conscious of it. The house and all within it trembled; the foundations of the earth seemed to be shaken, as if this awful sound were the peal of the last trump. Young and old exchanged one wild glance, and remained an instant, pale, affrighted, without utterance, or power to move. Then the same shriek burst simultaneously from all their lips.

"The Slide! The Slide!"

The simplest words must intimate, but not portray, the unutterable horror of the catastrophe. The victims rushed from their cottage, and sought refuge in what they deemed a safer spot—where, in contemplation of such an emergency, a sort of barrier had been reared. Alas! they had quitted their security, and fled right into the pathway of destruction. Down came the whole side of the mountain, in a cataract of ruin. Just before it reached the house, the stream broke into two branches—shivered not a window there, but overwhelmed the whole vicinity, blocked up the road, and annihilated everything in its dreadful course. Long ere the thunder of the great Slide had ceased to roar among the mountains, the mortal agony had been endured, and the victims were at peace. Their bodies were never found.

The next morning, the light smoke was seen stealing from the cottage chimney up the mountain side. Within, the fire was yet smouldering on the hearth, and the chairs in a circle round it, as if the inhabitants had but gone forth to view the devastation of the Slide, and would shortly return, to thank Heaven for their miraculous escape. All had left separate tokens, by which those who had known the family were made to shed a tear for each. Who has not heard their name? The story has been told far and wide, and will forever be a legend of these mountains. Poets have sung their fate.

There were circumstances which led some to suppose that a stranger had been received into the cottage on this awful night, and had shared the catastrophe of all its inmates. Others denied that there were sufficient grounds for such a conjecture. Woe for the high-souled youth, with his dream of Earthly Immortality! His name and person utterly unknown; his history, his way of life, his plans, a mystery never to be solved, his death and his existence equally a doubt! Whose was the agony of that death moment?

THE MINISTER'S BLACK VEIL

A PARABLE[1]

The sexton stood in the porch of Milford meeting-house, pulling busily at the bell-rope. The old people of the village came stooping along the street. Children, with bright faces, tripped merrily beside their parents, or mimicked a graver gait, in the conscious dignity of their Sunday clothes. Spruce bachelors looked sidelong at the pretty maidens, and fancied that the Sabbath sunshine made them prettier than on week days. When the throng had mostly streamed into the porch, the sexton began to toll the bell, keeping his eye on the Reverend Mr. Hooper's door. The first glimpse of the clergyman's figure was the signal for the bell to cease its summons.

"But what has good Parson Hooper got upon his face?" cried the sexton in astonishment.

All within hearing immediately turned about, and beheld the semblance of Mr. Hooper, pacing slowly his meditative way towards the meeting-house. With one accord they started, expressing more wonder than if some strange minister were coming to dust the cushions of Mr. Hooper's pulpit.

"Are you sure it is our parson?" inquired Goodman Gray of the sexton.

"Of a certainty it is good Mr. Hooper," replied the sexton.

First published in *The Token*, 1836.

"He was to have exchanged pulpits with Parson Shute, of Westbury; but Parson Shute sent to excuse himself yesterday, being to preach a funeral sermon."

The cause of so much amazement may appear sufficiently slight. Mr. Hooper, a gentlemanly person, of about thirty, though still a bachelor, was dressed with due clerical neatness, as if a careful wife had starched his band, and brushed the weekly dust from his Sunday's garb. There was but one thing remarkable in his appearance. Swathed about his forehead, and hanging down over his face, so low as to be shaken by his breath, Mr. Hooper had on a black veil. On a nearer view it seemed to consist of two folds of crape, which entirely concealed his features, except the mouth and chin, but probably did not intercept his sight, further than to give a darkened aspect of all living and inanimate things. With this gloomy shade before him, good Mr. Hooper walked onward, at a slow and quiet pace, stooping somewhat, and looking on the ground, as is customary with abstracted men, yet nodding kindly to those of his parishioners who still waited on the meeting-house steps. But so wonder-struck were they that his greeting hardly met with a return.

"I can't really feel as if good Mr. Hooper's face was behind that piece of crape," said the sexton.

"I don't like it," muttered an old woman, as she hobbled into the meeting-house. "He has changed himself into something awful, only by hiding his face."

"Our parson has gone mad!" cried Goodman Gray, following him across the threshold.

A rumor of some unaccountable phenomenon had preceded Mr. Hooper into the meeting-house, and set all the congregation astir. Few could refrain from twisting their heads towards the door; many stood upright, and turned directly about;

---

1 Another clergyman in New England, Mr. Joseph Moody, of York, Maine, who died about eighty years since, made himself remarkable by the same eccentricity that is here related of the Reverend Mr. Hooper. In his case, however, the symbol had a different import. In early life he had accidentally killed a beloved friend; and from that day till the hour of his own death, he hid his face from men. [Hawthorne's note]

while several little boys clambered upon the seats, and came down again with a terrible racket. There was a general bustle, a rustling of the women's gowns and shuffling of the men's feet, greatly at variance with that hushed repose which should attend the entrance of the minister. But Mr. Hooper appeared not to notice the perturbation of his people. He entered with an almost noiseless step, bent his head mildly to the pews on each side, and bowed as he passed his oldest parishioner, a white-haired great grandsire, who occupied an arm-chair in the centre of the aisle. It was strange to observe how slowly this venerable man became conscious of something singular in the appearance of his pastor. He seemed not fully to partake of the prevailing wonder, till Mr. Hooper had ascended the stairs, and showed himself in the pulpit, face to face with his congregation, except for the black veil. That mysterious emblem was never once withdrawn. It shook with his measured breath, as he gave out the psalm; it threw its obscurity between him and the holy page, as he read the Scriptures; and while he prayed, the veil lay heavily on his uplifted countenance. Did he seek to hide it from the dread Being whom he was addressing?

Such was the effect of this simple piece of crape, that more than one woman of delicate nerves was forced to leave the meeting-house. Yet perhaps the pale-faced congregation was almost as fearful a sight to the minister, as his black veil to them.

Mr. Hooper had the reputation of a good preacher, but not an energetic one: he strove to win his people heavenward by mild, persuasive influences, rather than to drive them thither by the thunders of the Word. The sermon which he now delivered was marked by the same characteristics of style and manner as the general series of his pulpit oratory. But there was something, either in the sentiment of the discourse itself, or in the imagination of the auditors, which made it greatly the most powerful effort that they had ever heard from their pastor's lips. It was tinged, rather more darkly than usual, with the gentle gloom of Mr. Hooper's temperament. The subject had reference to secret sin, and those sad mysteries which we hide from our nearest and dearest, and would fain conceal from our own consciousness, even forgetting that the Omniscient can detect them. A subtle power was breathed into his words. Each member of the congregation, the most innocent girl, and the man of hardened breast, felt as if the preacher had crept upon them, behind his awful veil, and discovered their hoarded iniquity of deed or thought. Many spread their clasped hands on their bosoms. There was nothing terrible in what Mr. Hooper said, at least, no violence; and yet, with every tremor of his melancholy voice, the hearers quaked. An unsought pathos came hand in hand with awe. So sensible were the audience of some unwonted attribute in their minister, that they longed for a breath of wind to blow aside the veil, almost believing that a stranger's visage would be discovered, though the form, gesture, and voice were those of Mr. Hooper.

At the close of the services, the people hurried out with indecorous confusion, eager to communicate their pent-up amazement, and conscious of lighter spirits the moment they lost sight of the black veil. Some gathered in little circles, huddled closely together, with their mouths all whispering in the centre; some went homeward alone, wrapt in silent meditation; some talked loudly, and profaned the Sabbath day with ostentatious laughter. A few shook their sagacious heads, intimating that they could penetrate the mystery; while one or two affirmed that there was no mystery at all, but only that Mr. Hooper's eyes were so weakened by the midnight lamp, as to require a shade. After a brief interval, forth came good Mr. Hooper also, in the rear of his flock. Turning his veiled face from one group to another, he paid due reverence to the hoary heads, saluted the middle aged with kind dignity as their friend and spiritual guide, greeted the young with mingled authority and love, and laid his hands on the little children's heads to bless them. Such was always his custom on the Sabbath day. Strange and bewildered looks repaid him for his courtesy. None, as on former occasions, aspired to the honor of walking by their pastor's side. Old Squire Saunders, doubtless by an accidental lapse of memory, neglected to invite Mr. Hooper to his table, where the good clergyman had been wont to bless the food, almost every Sunday since his settlement. He returned, therefore, to the parsonage, and, at the moment of closing the door, was observed to look back upon the people, all of whom had their eyes fixed upon the minister. A sad smile gleamed faintly from beneath the black veil, and flickered about his mouth, glimmering as he disappeared.

"How strange," said a lady, "that a simple black veil, such as any woman might wear on her bonnet, should become such a terrible thing on Mr. Hooper's face!"

"Something must surely be amiss with Mr. Hooper's intellects," observed her husband, the physician of the village. "But the strangest part of the affair is the effect of this vagary, even on a sober-minded man like myself. The black veil, though it covers only our pastor's face, throws its influence over his whole person, and makes him ghostlike from head to foot. Do you not feel it so?"

"Truly do I," replied the lady; "and I would not be alone with him for the world. I wonder he is not afraid to be alone with himself!"

"Men sometimes are so," said her husband.

The afternoon service was attended with similar circumstances. At its conclusion, the bell tolled for the funeral of a young lady. The relatives and friends were assembled in the house, and the more distant acquaintances stood about the door, speaking of the good qualities of the deceased, when their talk was interrupted by the appearance of Mr. Hooper, still covered with his black veil. It was now an appropriate emblem. The clergyman stepped into the room where the corpse was laid, and bent over the coffin, to take a last farewell of his deceased parishioner. As he stooped, the veil hung straight down from his forehead, so that, if her eyelids had not been closed forever, the dead maiden might have seen his face. Could Mr. Hooper be fearful of her glance, that he

so hastily caught back the black veil? A person who watched
the interview between the dead and living, scrupled not to
affirm, that, at the instant when the clergyman's features were
disclosed, the corpse had slightly shuddered, rustling the
shroud and muslin cap, though the countenance retained the
composure of death. A superstitious old woman was the only
witness of this prodigy. From the coffin Mr. Hooper passed
into the chamber of the mourners, and thence to the head of
the staircase, to make the funeral prayer. It was a tender and
heart-dissolving prayer, full of sorrow, yet so imbued with
celestial hopes, that the music of a heavenly harp, swept by
the fingers of the dead, seemed faintly to be heard among the
saddest accents of the minister. The people trembled, though
they but darkly understood him when he prayed that they,
and himself, and all of mortal race, might be ready, as he
trusted this young maiden had been, for the dreadful hour
that should snatch the veil from their faces. The bearers went
heavily forth, and the mourners followed, saddening all the
street, with the dead before them, and Mr. Hooper in his
black veil behind.

"Why do you look back?" said one in the procession to his
partner.

"I had a fancy," replied she, "that the minister and the
maiden's spirit were walking hand in hand."

"And so had I, at the same moment," said the other.

That night, the handsomest couple in Milford village were
to be joined in wedlock. Though reckoned a melancholy man,
Mr. Hooper had a placid cheerfulness for such occasions,
which often excited a sympathetic smile where livelier merriment would have been thrown away. There was no quality
of his disposition which made him more beloved than this.
The company at the wedding awaited his arrival with impatience, trusting that the strange awe, which had gathered
over him throughout the day, would now be dispelled. But
such was not the result. When Mr. Hooper came, the first
thing that their eyes rested on was the same horrible black
veil, which had added deeper gloom to the funeral, and could

portend nothing but evil to the wedding. Such was its immediate effect on the guests that a cloud seemed to have rolled duskily from beneath the black crape, and dimmed the light of the candles. The bridal pair stood up before the minister. But the bride's cold fingers quivered in the tremulous hand of the bridegroom, and her deathlike paleness caused a whisper that the maiden who had been buried a few hours before was come from her grave to be married. If ever another wedding were so dismal, it was that famous one where they tolled the wedding knell. After performing the ceremony, Mr. Hooper raised a glass of wine to his lips, wishing happiness to the new-married couple in a strain of mild pleasantry that ought to have brightened the features of the guests, like a cheerful gleam from the hearth. At that instant, catching a glimpse of his figure in the looking-glass, the black veil involved his own spirit in the horror with which it overwhelmed all others. His frame shuddered, his lips grew white, he spilt the untasted wine upon the carpet, and rushed forth into the darkness. For the Earth, too, had on her Black Veil.

The next day, the whole village of Milford talked of little else than Parson Hooper's black veil. That, and the mystery concealed behind it, supplied a topic for discussion between acquaintances meeting in the street, and good women gossiping at their open windows. It was the first item of news that the tavern-keeper told to his guests. The children babbled of it on their way to school. One imitative little imp covered his face with an old black handkerchief, thereby so affrighting his playmates that the panic seized himself, and he well-nigh lost his wits by his own waggery.

It was remarkable that all of the busybodies and impertinent people in the parish, not one ventured to put the plain question to Mr. Hooper, wherefore he did this thing. Hitherto, whenever there appeared the slightest call for such interference, he had never lacked advisers, nor shown himself averse to be guided by their judgment. If he erred at all, it was by so painful a degree of self-distrust, that even the mildest censure would lead him to consider an indifferent action as a crime. Yet, though so well acquainted with this amiable weakness, no individual among his parishioners chose to make the black veil a subject of friendly remonstrance. There was a feeling of dread, neither plainly confessed nor carefully concealed, which caused each to shift the responsibility upon another, till at length it was found expedient to send a deputation of the church, in order to deal with Mr. Hooper about the mystery, before it should grow into a scandal. Never did an embassy so ill discharge its duties. The minister received them with friendly courtesy, but became silent, after they were seated, leaving to his visitors the whole burden of introducing their important business. The topic, it might be supposed, was obvious enough. There was the black veil swathed round Mr. Hooper's forehead, and concealing every feature above his placid mouth, on which, at times, they could perceive the glimmering of a melancholy smile. But that piece of crape, to their imagination, seemed to hang down before his heart, the symbol of a fearful secret between him and them. Were the veil but cast aside, they might speak freely of it, but not till then. Thus they sat a considerable time, speechless, confused, and shrinking uneasily from Mr. Hooper's eye, which they felt to be fixed upon them with an invisible glance. Finally, the deputies returned abashed to their constituents, pronouncing the matter too weighty to be handled, except by a council of the churches, if, indeed, it might not require a general synod.

But there was one person in the village unappalled by the awe with which the black veil had impressed all beside herself. When the deputies returned without an explanation, or even venturing to demand one, she, with the calm energy of her character, determined to chase away the strange cloud that appeared to be settling round Mr. Hooper, every moment more darkly than before. As his plighted wife, it should be her privilege to know what the black veil concealed. At the minister's first visit, therefore, she entered upon the subject with a direct simplicity, which made the task easier both for him and her. After he had seated himself, she fixed her eyes steadfastly upon the veil, but could discern nothing of the dreadful gloom that had so overawed the multitude: it was but a double fold of crape, hanging down from his forehead to his mouth, and slightly stirring with his breath.

"No," said she aloud, and smiling, "there is nothing terrible in this piece of crape, except that it hides a face which I am always glad to look upon. Come, good sir, let the sun shine from behind the cloud. First lay aside your black veil: then tell me why you put it on."

Mr. Hooper's smile glimmered faintly.

"There is an hour to come," said he, "when all of us shall cast aside our veils. Take it not amiss, beloved friend, if I wear this piece of crape till then."

"Your words are a mystery, too," returned the young lady. "Take away the veil from them, at least."

"Elizabeth, I will," said he, "so far as my vow may suffer me. Know, then, this veil is a type and a symbol, and I am bound to wear it ever, both in light and darkness, in solitude and before the gaze of multitudes, and as with strangers, so with my familiar friends. No mortal eye will see it withdrawn. This dismal shade must separate me from the world: even you, Elizabeth, can never come behind it!"

"What grievous affliction hath befallen you," she earnestly inquired, "that you should thus darken your eyes forever?"

"If it be a sign of mourning," replied Mr. Hooper, "I, perhaps, like most other mortals, have sorrows dark enough to be typified by a black veil."

"But what if the world will not believe that it is the type of an innocent sorrow?" urged Elizabeth. "Beloved and respected as you are, there may be whispers that you hide your face under the consciousness of secret sin. For the sake of your holy office, do away this scandal!"

The color rose into her cheeks as she intimated the nature of the rumors that were already abroad in the village. But Mr. Hooper's mildness did not forsake him. He even smiled again—that same sad smile, which always appeared like a faint glimmering of light, proceeding from the obscurity beneath the veil.

"If I hide my face for sorrow, there is cause enough," he

merely replied; "and if I cover it for secret sin, what mortal might not do the same?"

And with this gentle, but unconquerable obstinacy did he resist all her entreaties. At length Elizabeth sat silent. For a few moments she appeared lost in thought, considering, probably, what new methods might be tried to withdraw her lover from so dark a fantasy, which, if it had no other meaning, was perhaps a symptom of mental disease. Though of a firmer character than his own, the tears rolled down her cheeks. But, in an instant, as it were, a new feeling took the place of sorrow: her eyes were fixed insensibly on the black veil, when, like a sudden twilight in the air, its terrors fell around her. She arose, and stood trembling before him.

"And do you feel it then, at last?" said he mournfully.

She made no reply, but covered her eyes with her hand, and turned to leave the room. He rushed forward and caught her arm.

"Have patience with me, Elizabeth!" cried he, passionately. "Do not desert me, though this veil must be between us here on earth. Be mine, and hereafter there shall be no veil over my face, no darkness between our souls! It is but a mortal veil—it is not for eternity! O! you know now how lonely I am, and how frightened, to be alone behind my black veil. Do not leave me in this miserable obscurity forever!"

"Lift the veil but once, and look me in the face," said she.

"Never! It cannot be!" replied Mr. Hooper.

"Then farewell!" said Elizabeth.

She withdrew her arm from his grasp, and slowly departed, pausing at the door, to give one long shuddering gaze, that seemed almost to penetrate the mystery of the black veil. But, even amid his grief, Mr. Hooper smiled to think that only a material emblem had separated him from happiness, though the horrors, which it shadowed forth, must be drawn darkly between the fondest of lovers.

From that time no attempts were made to remove Mr. Hooper's black veil, or, by a direct appeal, to discover the secret which it was supposed to hide. By persons who claimed a superiority to popular prejudice, it was reckoned merely an eccentric whim, such as often mingles with the sober actions of men otherwise rational, and tinges them all with its own semblance of insanity. But with the multitude, good Mr. Hooper was irreparably a bugbear. He could not walk the street with any peace of mind, so conscious was he that the gentle and timid would turn aside to avoid him, and that others would make it a point of hardihood to throw themselves in his way. The impertinence of the latter class compelled him to give up his customary walk at sunset to the burial ground; for when he leaned pensively over the gate, there would always be faces behind the gravestones, peeping at his black veil. A fable went the rounds that the stare of the dead people drove him thence. It grieved him, to the very depth of his kind heart, to observe how the children fled from his approach, breaking up their merriest sports, while his melancholy figure was yet afar off. Their instinctive dread caused him to feel more strongly than aught else, that a preternatural horror was interwoven with the threads of the black crape. In truth, his own antipathy to the veil was known to be so great, that he never willingly passed before a mirror, nor stopped to drink at a still fountain, lest, in its peaceful bosom, he should be affrighted by himself. This was what gave plausibility to the whispers, that Mr. Hooper's conscience tortured him for some great crime too horrible to be entirely concealed, or otherwise than so obscurely intimated. Thus, from beneath the black veil, there rolled a cloud into the sunshine, an ambiguity of sin or sorrow, which enveloped the poor minister, so that love or sympathy could never reach him. It was said that ghost and fiend consorted with him there. With self-shudderings and outward terrors, he walked continually in its shadow, groping darkly within his own soul, or gazing through a medium that saddened the whole world. Even the lawless wind, it was believed, respected his dreadful secret, and never blew aside the veil. But still good Mr. Hooper sadly smiled at the pale visages of the worldly throng as he passed by.

Among all its bad influences, the black veil had the one desirable effect, of making its wearer a very efficient clergyman. By the aid of his mysterious emblem—for there was no other apparent cause—he became a man of awful power over souls that were in agony for sin. His converts always regarded him with a dread peculiar to themselves, affirming, though but figuratively, that, before he brought them to celestial light, they had been with him behind the black veil. Its gloom, indeed, enabled him to sympathize with all dark affections. Dying sinners cried aloud for Mr. Hooper, and would not yield their breath till he appeared; though ever, as he stooped to whisper consolation, they shuddered at the veiled face so near their own. Such were the terrors of the black veil, even when Death had bared his visage! Strangers came long distances to attend service at his church, with the mere idle purpose of gazing at his figure, because it was forbidden them to behold his face. But many were made to quake ere they departed! Once, during Governor Belcher's administration, Mr. Hooper was appointed to preach the election sermon. Covered with his black veil, he stood before the chief magistrate, the council, and the representatives, and wrought so deep an impression, that the legislative measures of that year were characterized by all the gloom and piety of our earliest ancestral sway.

In this manner Mr. Hooper spent a long life, irreproachable in outward act, yet shrouded in dismal suspicions; kind and loving, though unloved, and dimly feared; a man apart from men, shunned in their health and joy, but ever summoned to their aid in mortal anguish. As years wore on, shedding their snows above his sable veil, he acquired a name throughout the New England churches, and they called him Father Hooper. Nearly all his parishioners, who were of mature age when he was settled, had been borne away by many a funeral: he had one congregation in the church, and a more crowded one in the churchyard; and having wrought so late into the evening, and done his work so well, it was now good Father Hooper's turn to rest.

Several persons were visible by the shaded candlelight, in the death chamber of the old clergyman. Natural connections he had none. But there was the decorously grave, though unmoved physician, seeking only to mitigate the last pangs of the patient whom he could not save. There were the deacons, and other eminently pious members of his church. There, also, was the Reverend Mr. Clark, of Westbury, a young and zealous divine, who had ridden in haste to pray by the bedside of the expiring minister. There was the nurse, no hired handmaiden of death, but one whose calm affection had endured thus long in secrecy, in solitude, amid the chill of age, and would not perish, even at the dying hour. Who, but Elizabeth! And there lay the hoary head of good Father Hooper upon the death pillow, with the black veil still swathed about his brow, and reaching down over his face, so that each more difficult gasp of his faint breath caused it to stir. All through life that piece of crape had hung between him and the world: it had separated him from cheerful brotherhood and woman's love, and kept him in that saddest of all prisons, his own heart; and still it lay upon his face, as if to deepen the gloom of his darksome chamber, and shade him from the sunshine of eternity.

For some time previous, his mind had been confused, wavering doubtfully between the past and the present, and hovering forward, as it were, at intervals, into the indistinctness of the world to come. There had been feverish turns, which tossed him from side to side, and wore away what little strength he had. But in his most convulsive struggles, and in the wildest vagaries of his intellect, when no other thought retained its sober influence, he still showed an awful solicitude lest the black veil should slip aside. Even if his bewildered soul could have forgotten, there was a faithful woman at this pillow, who, with averted eyes, would have covered that aged face, which she had last beheld in the comeliness of manhood. At length the death-stricken old man lay quietly in the torpor of mental and bodily exhaustion, with an imperceptible pulse, and breath that grew fainter and fainter, except when a long, deep, and irregular inspiration seemed to prelude the flight of his spirit.

The minister of Westbury approached the bedside.

"Venerable Father Hooper," said he, "the moment of your release is at hand. Are you ready for the lifting of the veil that shuts in time from eternity?"

Father Hooper at first replied merely by a feeble motion of his head; then, apprehensive, perhaps, that his meaning might be doubted, he exerted himself to speak.

"Yea," said he, in faint accents, "my soul hath a patient weariness until that veil be lifted."

"And is it fitting," resumed the Reverend Mr. Clark, "that a man so given to prayer, of such a blameless example, holy in deed and thought, so far as mortal judgment may pronounce; is it fitting that a father in the church should leave a shadow on his memory, that may seem to blacken a life so pure? I pray you, my venerable brother, let not this thing be! Suffer us to be gladdened by your triumphant aspect as you go to your reward. Before the veil of eternity be lifted, let me cast aside this black veil from your face!"

And thus speaking, the Reverend Mr. Clark bent forward to reveal the mystery of so many years. But, exerting a sudden energy, that made all the beholders stand aghast, Father Hooper snatched both his hands from beneath the bedclothes, and pressed them strongly on the black veil, resolute to struggle, if the minister of Westbury would contend with a dying man.

"Never!" cried the veiled clergyman. "On earth, never!"

"Dark old man!" exclaimed the affrighted minister, "with what horrible crime upon your soul are you now passing to the judgment?"

Father Hooper's breath heaved; it rattled in his throat; but, with a mighty effort, grasping forward with his hands, he caught hold of life, and held it back till he should speak. He even raised himself in bed; and there he sat, shivering with the arms of death around him, while the black veil hung down, awful, at that last moment, in the gathered terrors of a lifetime. And yet the faint, sad smile, so often there, now seemed to glimmer from its obscurity, and linger on Father Hooper's lips.

"Why do you tremble at me alone?" cried he, turning his veiled face round the circle of pale spectators. "Tremble also at each other! Have men avoided me, and women shown no pity, and children screamed and fled, only for my black veil? What, but the mystery which it obscurely typifies, has made this piece of crape so awful? When the friend shows his inmost heart to his friend; the lover to his best beloved; when man does not vainly shrink from the eye of his Creator, loathsomely treasuring up the secret of his sin; then deem me a monster, for the symbol beneath which I have lived, and die! I look around me, and, lo! on every visage a Black Veil!"

While his auditors shrank from one another, in mutual affright, Father Hooper fell back upon his pillow, a veiled corpse, with a faint smile lingering on the lips. Still veiled, they laid him in his coffin, and a veiled corpse they bore him to the grave. The grass of many years has sprung up and withered on that grave, the burial stone is moss-grown, and good Mr. Hooper's face is dust; but awful is still the thought that it mouldered beneath the Black Veil!

THE MAYPOLE
OF MERRY MOUNT

There is an admirable foundation for a philosophic romance in the curious history of the early settlement of Mount Wollaston, or Merry Mount. In the slight sketch here attempted, the facts, recorded on the grave pages of our New England annalists, have wrought themselves, almost spontaneously, into a sort of allegory. The masques, mummeries, and festive customs, described in the text, are in accordance with the manners of the age. Authority on these points may be found in Strutt's Book of English Sports and Pastimes.

Bright were the days at Merry Mount, when the Maypole was the banner staff of that gay colony! They who reared it, should their banner be triumphant, were to pour sunshine over New England's rugged hills, and scatter flower seeds throughout the soil. Jollity and gloom were contending for an empire. Midsummer eve had come, bringing deep verdure to the forest, and roses in her lap, of a more vivid hue than the tender buds of Spring. But May, or her mirthful spirit, dwelt all the year round at Merry Mount,

First published in *The Token,* 1836.

sporting with the Summer months, and revelling with Autumn, and basking in the glow of Winter's fireside. Through a world of toil and care she flitted with a dreamlike smile, and came hither to find a home among the lightsome hearts of Merry Mount.

Never had the Maypole been so gayly decked as at sunset on midsummer eve. This venerated emblem was a pine-tree, which had preserved the slender grace of youth, while it equalled the loftiest height of the old wood monarchs. From its top streamed a silken banner, colored like the rainbow. Down nearly to the ground the pole was dressed with birchen boughs, and others of the liveliest green, and some with silvery leaves, fastened by ribbons that fluttered in fantastic knots of twenty different colors, but no sad ones. Garden flowers, and blossoms of the wilderness, laughed gladly forth amid the verdure, so fresh and dewy that they must have grown by magic on that happy pine-tree. Where this green and flowery splendor terminated, the shaft of the Maypole was stained with the seven brilliant hues of the banner at its top. On the lowest green bough hung an abundant wreath of roses, some that had been gathered in the sunniest spots of the forest, and others, of still richer blush, which the colonists had reared from English seed. O, people of the Golden Age, the chief of your husbandry was to raise flowers!

But what was the wild throng that stood hand in hand about the Maypole? It could not be that the fauns and nymphs, when driven from their classic groves and homes of ancient fable, had sought refuge, as all the persecuted did, in the fresh woods of the West. These were Gothic monsters, though perhaps of Grecian ancestry. On the shoulders of a comely youth uprose the head and branching antlers of a stag; a second, human in all other points, had the grim visage of a wolf; a third, still with the trunk and limbs of a mortal man, showed the beard and horns of a venerable he-goat. There was the likeness of a bear erect, brute in all but his hind legs, which were adorned with pink silk stockings. And here again, almost as wondrous, stood a real bear of the dark

forest, lending each of his fore paws to the grasp of a human
hand, and as ready for the dance as any in that circle. His
inferior nature rose half way, to meet his companions as they
stooped. Other faces wore the similitude of man or woman,
but distorted or extravagant, with red noses pendulous before
their mouths, which seemed of awful depth, and stretched
from ear to ear in an eternal fit of laughter. Here might be
seen the Savage Man, well known in heraldry, hairy as a
baboon, and girdled with green leaves. By his side, a noble
figure, but still a counterfeit, appeared an Indian hunter,
with feathery crest and wampum belt. Many of this strange
company wore foolscaps, and had little bells appended to
their garments, tinkling with a silvery sound, responsive to
the inaudible music of their gleesome spirits. Some youths
and maidens were of soberer garb, yet well maintained their
places in the irregular throng by the expression of wild revelry
upon their features. Such were the colonists of Merry Mount,
as they stood in the broad smile of sunset round their venerated Maypole.

Had a wanderer, bewildered in the melancholy forest, heard
their mirth, and stolen a half-affrighted glance, he might have
fancied them the crew of Comus, some already transformed to
brutes, some midway between man and beast, and the others
rioting in the flow of tipsy jollity that foreran the change.
But a band of Puritans, who watched the scene, invisible
themselves, compared the masques to those devils and ruined
souls with whom their superstition peopled the black wilderness.

Within the ring of monsters appeared the two airiest forms
that had ever trodden on any more solid footing than a
purple and golden cloud. One was a youth in glistening apparel, with a scarf of the rainbow pattern crosswise on his
breast. His right hand held a gilded staff, the ensign of high
dignity among the revellers, and his left grasped the slender
fingers of a fair maiden, not less gayly decorated than himself.
Bright roses glowed in contrast with the dark and glossy curls
of each, and were scattered round their feet, or had sprung

up spontaneously there. Behind this lightsome couple, so close to the Maypole that its boughs shaded his jovial face, stood the figure of an English priest, canonically dressed, yet decked with flowers, in heathen fashion, and wearing a chaplet of the native vine leaves. By the riot of his rolling eye, and the pagan decorations of his holy garb, he seemed the wildest monster there, and the very Comus of the crew.

"Votaries of the Maypole," cried the flower-decked priest, "merrily, all day long, have the woods echoed to your mirth. But be this your merriest hour, my hearts! Lo, here stand the Lord and Lady of the May, whom I, a clerk of Oxford, and high priest of Merry Mount, am presently to join in holy matrimony. Up with your nimble spirits, ye morris-dancers, green men, and glee maidens, bears and wolves, and horned gentlemen! Come; a chorus now, rich with the old mirth of Merry England, and the wilder glee of this fresh forest; and then a dance, to show the youthful pair what life is made of, and how airily they should go through it! All ye that love the Maypole, lend your voices to the nuptial song of the Lord and Lady of the May!"

This wedlock was more serious than most affairs of Merry Mount, where jest and delusion, trick and fantasy, kept up a continual carnival. The Lord and Lady of the May, though their titles must be laid down at sunset, were really and truly to be partners for the dance of life, beginning the measure that same bright eve. The wreath of roses, that hung from the lowest green bough of the Maypole, had been twined for them, and would be thrown over both their heads, in symbol of their flowery union. When the priest had spoken, therefore, a riotous uproar burst from the rout of monstrous figures.

"Begin you the stave, reverend Sir," cried they all; "and never did the woods ring to such a merry peal as we of the Maypole shall send up!"

Immediately a prelude of pipe, cithern, and viol, touched with practised minstrelsy, began to play from a neighboring thicket, in such a mirthful cadence that the boughs of the Maypole quivered to the sound. But the May Lord, he of the gilded staff, chancing to look into his Lady's eyes, was wonder struck at the almost pensive glance that met his own.

"Edith, sweet Lady of the May," whispered he reproachfully, "is yon wreath of roses a garland to hang above our graves, that you look so sad? O, Edith, this is our golden time! Tarnish it not by any pensive shadow of the mind; for it may be that nothing of futurity will be brighter than the mere remembrance of what is now passing."

"That was the very thought that saddened me! How came it in your mind too?" said Edith, in a still lower tone than he, for it was high treason to be sad at Merry Mount. "Therefore do I sigh amid the festive music. And besides, dear Edgar, I struggle as with a dream, and fancy that these shapes of our jovial friends are visionary, and their mirth unreal, and that we are no true Lord and Lady of the May. What is the mystery in my heart?"

Just then, as if a spell had loosened them, down came a little shower of withering rose leaves from the Maypole. Alas, for the young lovers! No sooner had their hearts glowed with real passion than they were sensible of something vague and unsubstantial in their former pleasures, and felt a dreary presentiment of inevitable change. From the moment that they truly loved, they had subjected themselves to earth's doom of care and sorrow, and troubled joy, and had no more a home at Merry Mount. That was Edith's mystery. Now leave we the priest to marry them, and the masquers to sport round the Maypole, till the last sunbeam be withdrawn from its summit, and the shadows of the forest mingle gloomily in the dance. Meanwhile, we may discover who these gay people were.

Two hundred years ago, and more, the old world and its inhabitants became mutually weary of each other. Men voyaged by thousands to the West: some to barter glass beads, and such like jewels, for the furs of the Indian hunter; some to conquer virgin empires; and one stern band to pray. But none of these motives had much weight with the colonists of Merry Mount. Their leaders were men who had sported so long with life, that when Thought and Wisdom came, even these unwelcome guests were led astray by the crowd of vanities which they should have put to flight. Erring Thought and perverted Wisdom were made to put on masques, and play the fool. The men of whom we speak, after losing the heart's fresh gayety, imagined a wild philosophy of pleasure, and came hither to act out their latest day-dream. They gathered followers from all that giddy tribe whose whole life is like the festal days of soberer men. In their train were minstrels, not unknown in London streets; wandering players, whose theatres had been the halls of noblemen; mummers, rope-dancers, and mountebanks, who would long be missed at wakes, church ales, and fairs; in a word, mirth makers of every sort, such as abounded in that age, but now began to be discountenanced by the rapid growth of Puritanism. Light had their footsteps been on land, and as lightly they came across the sea. Many had been maddened by their previous troubles into a gay despair; others were as madly gay in the flush of youth, like the May Lord and his Lady; but whatever might be the quality of their mirth, old and young were gay at Merry Mount. The young deemed themselves happy. The elder spirits, if they knew that mirth was but the counterfeit of happiness, yet followed the false shadow wilfully, because at least her garments glittered brightest. Sworn triflers of a lifetime, they would not venture among the sober truths of life not even to be truly blest.

All the hereditary pastimes of Old England were transplanted hither. The King of Christmas was duly crowned, and the Lord of Misrule bore potent sway. On the Eve of St. John, they felled whole acres of the forest to make bonfires, and danced by the blaze all night, crowned with garlands, and throwing flowers into the flame. At harvest time, though their crop was of the smallest, they made an image with the sheaves of Indian corn, and wreathed it with autumnal garlands, and bore it home triumphantly. But what chiefly characterized the colonists of Merry Mount was their veneration for the Maypole. It has made their true history a poet's tale. Spring decked the hallowed emblem with young blossoms and fresh green boughs; Summer brought roses of the deepest blush, and the perfected foliage of the forest; Autumn enriched it with that red and yellow gorgeousness which converts each wildwood leaf into a painted flower; and Winter silvered it with sleet, and hung it round with icicles, till it flashed in the cold sunshine, itself a frozen sunbeam. Thus each alternate season did homage to the Maypole, and paid it a tribute of its own richest splendor. Its votaries danced round it, once, at least, in every month; sometimes they called it their religion, or their altar; but always, it was the banner staff of Merry Mount.

Unfortunately, there were men in the new world of a sterner faith than those Maypole worshippers. Not far from Merry Mount was a settlement of Puritans, most dismal wretches, who said their prayers before daylight, and then wrought in the forest or the cornfield till evening made it prayer time again. Their weapons were always at hand to shoot down the straggling savage. When they met in conclave, it was never to keep up the old English mirth, but to hear sermons three hours long, or to proclaim bounties on the heads of wolves and the scalps of Indians. Their festivals were fast days, and their chief pastime the singing of psalms. Woe to the youth or maiden who did but dream of a dance! The selectman nodded to the constable; and there sat the light-heeled reprobate in the stocks; or if he danced, it was round the whipping-post, which might be termed the Puritan May-pole.

A party of these grim Puritans, toiling through the difficult woods, each with a horseload of iron armor to burden his footsteps, would sometimes draw near the sunny precincts of Merry Mount. There were the silken colonists, sporting round their Maypole; perhaps teaching a bear to dance, or striving to communicate their mirth to the grave Indian; or masquerading in the skins of deer and wolves, which they had hunted for that especial purpose. Often, the whole colony were playing at blindman's buff, magistrates and all, with their eyes bandaged, except a single scapegoat, whom the blinded sinners pursued by the tinkling of the bells at his garments. Once, it is said, they were seen following a flower-decked corpse, with merriment and festive music, to his grave. But did the dead man laugh? In their quietest times, they sang ballads and told tales, for the edification of their pious visitors; or perplexed them with juggling tricks; or grinned at them through horse collars; and when sport itself grew wearisome, they made game of their own stupidity, and began a yawning match. At the very least of these enormities, the men of iron shook their heads and frowned so darkly that the revellers looked up imagining that a momentary cloud had overcast the sunshine, which was to be perpetual there. On the other hand, the Puritans affirmed that, when a psalm was pealing from their place of worship, the echo which the forest sent them back seemed often like the chorus of a jolly catch, closing with a roar of laughter. Who but the fiend, and his bond slaves, the crew of Merry Mount, had thus disturbed them? In due time, a feud arose, stern and bitter on one side, and as serious on the other as anything could be among such light spirits as had sworn allegiance to the Maypole. The future complexion of New England was involved in this important quarrel. Should the grizzly saints establish their jurisdiction over the gay sinners, then would their spirits darken all the clime, and make it a land of clouded visages, of hard toil, of sermon and psalm forever. But should the banner staff of Merry Mount be fortunate, sunshine would break upon the hills, and flowers would beautify the forest, and late posterity do homage to the Maypole.

After these authentic passages from history, we return to the nuptials of the Lord and Lady of the May. Alas! we have delayed too long, and must darken our tale too suddenly. As we glance again at the Maypole, a solitary sunbeam is fading from the summit, and leaves only a faint, golden tinge blended with the hues of the rainbow banner. Even that dim light is now withdrawn, relinquishing the whole domain of Merry Mount to the evening gloom, which has rushed so instantaneously from the black surrounding woods. But some of these black shadows have rushed forth in human shape.

Yes, with the setting sun, the last day of mirth had passed from Merry Mount. The ring of gay masquers was disordered and broken; the stag lowered his antlers in dismay; the wolf grew weaker than a lamb; the bells of the morris-dancers tinkled with tremulous affright. The Puritans had played a characteristic part in the Maypole mummeries. Their darksome figures were intermixed with the wild shapes of their foes, and made the scene a picture of the moment, when waking thoughts start up amid the scattered fantasies of a dream. The leader of the hostile party stood in the centre of the circle, while the route of monsters cowered around him, like evil spirits in the presence of a dread magician. No fantastic foolery could look him in the face. So stern was the energy of his aspect, that the whole man, visage, frame, and soul, seemed wrought of iron, gifted with life and thought, yet all of one substance with his headpiece and breastplate. It was the Puritan of Puritans; it was Endicott himself!

"Stand off, priest of Baal!" said he, with a grim frown, and laying no reverent hand upon the surplice. "I know thee, Blackstone![1] Thou art the man who couldst not abide the rule even of thine own corrupted church, and hast come hither to preach iniquity, and to give example of it in thy life. But now shall it be seen that the Lord hath sanctified this wilderness for his peculiar people. Woe unto them that would defile it! And first, for this flower-decked abomination, the altar of thy worship!"

And with his keen sword Endicott assaulted the hallowed Maypole. Nor long did it resist his arm. It groaned with a dismal sound; it showered leaves and rosebuds upon the remorseless enthusiast; and finally, with all its green boughs and ribbons and flowers, symbolic of departed pleasures, down

---

[1] Did Governor Endicott speak less positively, we should suspect a mistake here. The Rev. Mr. Blackstone, though an eccentric, is not known to have been an immoral man. We rather doubt his identity with the priest of Merry Mount. [Hawthorne's note.]

fell the banner staff of Merry Mount. As it sank, tradition says, the evening sky grew darker, and the woods threw forth a more sombre shadow.

"There," cried Endicott, looking triumphantly on his work, "there lies the only Maypole in New England! The thought is strong within me that, by its fall, is shadowed forth the fate of light and idle mirth makers, amongst us and our posterity. Amen, saith John Endicott."

"Amen!" echoed his followers.

But the votaries of the Maypole gave one groan for their idol. At the sound, the Puritan leader glanced at the crew of Comus, each a figure of broad mirth, yet, at this moment, strangely expressive of sorrow and dismay.

"Valiant captain," quoth Peter Palfrey, the Ancient of the band, "what order shall be taken with the prisoners?"

"I thought not to repent me of cutting down a Maypole," replied Endicott, "yet now I could find in my heart to plant it again, and give each of these bestial pagans one other dance round their idol. It would have served rarely for a whipping-post!"

"But there are pine-trees enow," suggested the lieutenant.

"True, good Ancient," said the leader. "Wherefore, bind the heathen crew, and bestow on them a small matter of stripes apiece, as earnest of our future justice. Set some of the rogues in the stocks to rest themselves, so soon as Providence shall bring us to one of our own well-ordered settlements where such accommodations may be found. Further penalties, such as branding and cropping of ears, shall be thought of hereafter."

"How many stripes for the priest?" inquired Ancient Palfrey.

"None as yet," answered Endicott, bending his iron frown upon the culprit. "It must be for the Great and General Court to determine, whether stripes and long imprisonment, and other grievous penalty, may atone for his transgressions. Let him look to himself! For such as violate our civil order, it may be permitted us to show mercy. But woe to the wretch that troubleth our religion."

"And this dancing bear," resumed the officer. "Must he share the stripes of his fellows?"

"Shoot him through the head!" said the energetic Puritan. "I suspect witchcraft in the beast."

"Here be a couple of shining ones," continued Peter Palfrey, pointing his weapon at the Lord and Lady of the May. "They seem to be of high station among these misdoers. Methinks their dignity will not be fitted with less than a double share of stripes."

Endicott rested on his sword, and closely surveyed the dress and aspect of the hapless pair. There they stood, pale, downcast, and apprehensive. Yet there was an air of mutual support and of pure affection, seeking aid and giving it, that showed them to be man and wife, with the sanction of a priest upon their love. The youth, in the peril of the moment, had dropped his gilded staff, and thrown his arm about the Lady of the May, who leaned against his breast, too lightly to burden him, but with weight enough to express that their destinies were linked together, for good or evil. They looked first at each other, and then into the grim captain's face. There they stood, in the first hour of wedlock, while the idle pleasures, of which their companions were the emblems, had given place to the sternest cares of life, personified by the dark Puritans. But never had their youthful beauty seemed so pure and high as when its glow was chastened by adversity.

"Youth," said Endicott, "ye stand in an evil case, thou and thy maiden wife. Make ready presently, for I am minded that ye shall both have a token to remember your wedding day!"

"Stern man," cried the May Lord, "how can I move thee? Were the means at hand, I would resist to the death. Being powerless, I entreat! Do with me as thou wilt, but let Edith go untouched!"

"Not so," replied the immitigable zealot. "We are not wont to show an idle courtesy to that sex, which requireth the stricter discipline. What sayest thou, maid? Shall thy silken bridegroom suffer thy share of the penalty, besides his own?"

"Be it death," said Edith, "and lay it all on me!"

Truly, as Endicott had said, the poor lovers stood in a woful case. Their foes were triumphant, their friends captive and abased, their home desolate, the benighted wilderness around them, and a rigorous destiny, in the shape of the Puritan leader, their only guide. Yet the deepening twilight could not altogether conceal that the iron man was softened; he smiled at the fair spectacle of early love; he almost sighed for the inevitable blight of early hopes.

"The troubles of life have come hastily on this young couple," observed Endicott. "We will see how they comport themselves under their present trials ere we burden them with greater. If, among the spoil, there be any garments of a more decent fashion, let them be put upon this May Lord and his Lady, instead of their glistening vanities. Look to it, some of you."

"And shall not the youth's hair be cut?" asked Peter Palfrey, looking with abhorrence at the lovelock and long glossy curls of the young man.

"Crop it forthwith, and that in the true pumpkin-shell fashion," answered the captain. "Then bring them along with us, but more gently than their fellows. There be qualities in the youth, which may make him valiant to fight, and sober to toil, and pious to pray; and in the maiden, that may fit her to become a mother in our Israel, bringing up babes in better nurture than her own hath been. Nor think ye, young ones, that they are the happiest, even in our lifetime of a moment, who misspend it in dancing round a Maypole!"

And Endicott, the severest Puritan of all who laid the rock foundation of New England, lifted the wreath of roses from the ruin of the Maypole, and threw it, with his own gauntleted hand, over the heads of the Lord and Lady of the May. It was a deed of prophecy. As the moral gloom of the world overpowers all systematic gayety, even so was their home of wild mirth made desolate amid the sad forest. They returned to it no more. But as their flowery garland was wreathed of the brightest roses that had grown there, so, in the tie that united them, were intertwined all the purest and best of their early joys. They went heavenward, supporting each other along the difficult path which it was their lot to tread, and never wasted one regretful thought on the vanities of Merry Mount.

THE GREAT CARBUNCLE[1]

A MYSTERY OF THE WHITE MOUNTAINS

At nightfall, once in the olden time, on the rugged side of one of the Crystal Hills, a party of adventurers were refreshing themselves, after a toilsome and fruitless quest for the Great Carbuncle. They had come thither, not as friends nor partners in the enterprise, but each, save one youthful pair, impelled by his own selfish and solitary longing for this wondrous gem. Their feeling of brotherhood, however, was strong enough to induce them to contribute a mutual aid in building a rude hut of branches, and kindling a great fire of shattered pines, that had drifted down the headlong current of the Amonoosuck, on the lower bank of which they were to pass the night. There was but one of their number, perhaps, who had become so estranged from natural sympathies, by the absorbing spell of the pursuit, as to acknowledge no satisfaction at the sight of human faces, in the remote and solitary region whither they had ascended. A vast extent of wilderness lay between them and the nearest settlement, while a scant mile above their heads was that black verge where the hills throw off their shaggy mantle of forest

First published in *The Token*, 1837.

[1] The Indian tradition, on which this somewhat extravagant tale is founded, is both too wild and too beautiful to be adequately wrought up in prose. Sullivan, in his History of Maine, written since the Revolution, remarks, that even then the existence of the Great Carbuncle was not entirely discredited. [Hawthorne's note]

trees, and either robe themselves in clouds or tower naked into the sky. The roar of the Amonoosuck would have been too awful for endurance if only a solitary man had listened, while the mountain stream talked with the wind.

The adventurers, therefore, exchanged hospitable greetings, and welcomed one another to the hut, where each man was the host, and all were the guests of the whole company. They spread their individual supplies of food on the flat surface of a rock, and partook of a general repast; at the close of which, a sentiment of good fellowship was perceptible among the party, though repressed by the idea, that the renewed search for the Great Carbuncle must make them strangers again in the morning. Seven men and one young woman, they warmed themselves together at the fire, which extended its bright wall along the whole front of their wigwam. As they observed the various and contrasted figures that made up the assemblage, each man looking like a caricature of himself, in the unsteady light that flickered over him, they came mutually to the conclusion, that an odder society had never met, in city or wilderness, on mountain or plain.

The eldest of the group, a tall, lean, weather-beaten man, some sixty years of age, was clad in the skins of wild animals, whose fashion of dress he did well to imitate, since the deer, the wolf, and the bear, had long been his most intimate companions. He was one of those ill-fated mortals, such as the Indians told of, whom, in their early youth, the Great Carbuncle smote with a peculiar madness, and became the passionate dream of their existence. All who visited that region knew him as the Seeker, and by no other name. As none could remember when he first took up the search, there went a fable in the valley of the Saco, that for his inordinate lust after the Great Carbuncle, he had been condemned to wander among the mountains till the end of time, still with the same feverish hopes at sunrise—the same despair at eve. Near this miserable Seeker sat a little elderly personage, wearing a high-crowned hat, shaped somewhat like a crucible. He was from beyond the sea, a Doctor Cacaphodel, who had wilted and dried himself into a mummy by continually stooping over charcoal furnaces, and inhaling unwholesome fumes during his researches in chemistry and alchemy. It was told of him, whether truly or not, that, at the commencement of his studies, he had drained his body of all its richest blood, and wasted it, with other inestimable ingredients, in an unsuccessful experiment—and had never been a well man since. Another of the adventurers was Master Ichabod Pigsnort, a weighty merchant and selectman of Boston, and an elder of the famous Mr. Norton's church. His enemies had a ridiculous story that Master Pigsnort was accustomed to spend a whole hour after prayer time, every morning and evening, in wallowing naked among an immense quantity of pine-tree shillings, which were the earliest silver coinage of Massachusetts. The fourth whom we shall notice had no name that his companions knew of, and was chiefly distinguished by a sneer that always contorted his thin visage, and by a prodigious pair of spectacles, which were supposed to deform and discolor the whole face of nature, to this gentleman's perception. The fifth adventurer likewise lacked a name, which was the greater pity, as he appeared to be a poet. He was a bright-eyed man, but wofully pined away, which was no more than natural, if, as some people affirmed, his ordinary diet was fog, morning mist, and a slice of the densest cloud within his reach, sauced with moonshine, whenever he could get it. Certain it is, that the poetry which flowed from him had a smack of all these dainties. The sixth of the party was a young man of haughty mien, and sat somewhat apart from the rest, wearing his plumed hat loftily among his elders, while the fire glittered on the rich embroidery of his dress, and gleamed intensely on the jewelled pommel of his sword. This was the Lord de Vere, who, when at home, was said to spend much of his time in the burial vault of his dead progenitors, rummaging their mouldy coffins in search of all the earthly pride and vainglory that was hidden among bones and dust; so that, besides his own share, he had the collected haughtiness of his whole line of ancestry.

Lastly, there was a handsome youth in rustic garb, and by his side a blooming little person, in whom a delicate shade of maiden reserve was just melting into the rich glow of a young wife's affection. Her name was Hannah, and her husband's Matthew; two homely names, yet well enough adapted to the simple pair, who seemed strangely out of place among the whimsical fraternity whose wits had been set agog by the Great Carbuncle.

Beneath the shelter of one hut, in the bright blaze of the same fire, sat this varied group of adventurers, all so intent upon a single object, that, of whatever else they began to speak, their closing words were sure to be illuminated with the Great Carbuncle. Several related the circumstances that brought them thither. One had listened to a traveller's tale of this marvellous stone in his own distant country, and had immediately been seized with such a thirst for beholding it as could only be quenched in its intensest lustre. Another, so long ago as when the famous Captain Smith visited these coasts, had seen it blazing far at sea, and had felt no rest in all the intervening years till now that he took up the search. A third, being encamped on a hunting expedition full forty miles south of the White Mountains, awoke at midnight, and beheld the Great Carbuncle gleaming like a meteor, so that the shadows of the trees fell backward from it. They spoke of the innumerable attempts which had been made to reach the spot, and of the singular fatality which had hitherto withheld success from all adventurers, though it might seem so easy to follow to its source a light that overpowered the moon, and almost matched the sun. It was observable that each smiled scornfully at the madness of every other in anticipating better fortune than the past, yet nourished a scarcely hidden conviction that he would himself be the favored one. As if to allay their too sanguine hopes, they recurred to the Indian traditions that a spirit kept watch about the gem, and bewildered those who sought it either by removing it from peak to peak of the higher hills, or by calling up a mist from the enchanted lake over which it hung. But these tales were deemed unworthy of credit, all professing to believe that the search had been baffled by want of sagacity or perseverance in the adventurers, or such other causes as might naturally obstruct the passage to any given point among the intricacies of forest, valley, and mountain.

In a pause of the conversation the wearer of the prodigious spectacles looked round upon the party, making each individual, in turn, the object of the sneer which invariably dwelt upon his countenance.

"So, fellow-pilgrims," said he, "here we are, seven wise men, and one fair damsel—who, doubtless, is as wise as any graybeard of the company: here we are, I say, all bound on the same goodly enterprise. Methinks, now, it were not amiss that each of us declare what he proposes to do with the Great Carbuncle, provided he have the good hap to clutch it. What says our friend in the bear skin? How mean you, good sir, to enjoy the prize which you have been seeking, the Lord knows how long, among the Crystal Hills?"

"How enjoy it!" exclaimed the aged Seeker, bitterly. "I hope for no enjoyment from it; that folly has passed long ago! I keep up the search for this accursed stone because the vain ambition of my youth has become a fate upon me in old age. The pursuit alone is my strength,—the energy of my soul,—the warmth of my blood,—and the pith and marrow of my bones! Were I to turn my back upon it I should fall down dead on the hither side of the Notch, which is the gateway of this mountain region. Yet not to have my wasted lifetime back again would I give up my hopes of the Great Carbuncle! Having found it, I shall bear it to a certain cavern that I wot of, and there, grasping it in my arms, lie down and die, and keep it buried with me forever."

"O wretch, regardless of the interests of science!" cried Doctor Cacaphodel, with philosophic indignation. "Thou art not worthy to behold, even from afar off, the lustre of this most precious gem that ever was concocted in the laboratory of Nature. Mine is the sole purpose for which a wise man may desire the possession of the Great Carbuncle. Immediately on obtaining it—for I have a presentiment, good people, that the prize is reserved to crown my scientific reputation—I shall return to Europe, and employ my remaining years in reducing it to its first elements. A portion of the stone will I grind to impalpable powder; other parts shall be dissolved in acids, or whatever solvents will act upon so admirable a composition; and the remainder I design to melt in the crucible, or set on fire with the blow-pipe. By these various methods I shall gain an accurate analysis, and finally bestow the result of my labors upon the world in a folio volume."

"Excellent!" quoth the man with the spectacles. "Nor need you hesitate, learned sir, on account of the necessary destruction of the gem; since the perusal of your folio may teach every mother's son of us to concoct a Great Carbuncle of his own."

"But, verily," said Master Ichabod Pigsnort, "for mine own part I object to the making of these counterfeits, as being calculated to reduce the marketable value of the true gem. I tell ye frankly, sirs, I have an interest in keeping up the price. Here have I quitted my regular traffic, leaving my warehouse in the care of my clerks, and putting my credit to great hazard, and, furthermore, have put myself in peril of death or captivity by the accursed heathen savages—and all this without daring to ask the prayers of the congregation, because the quest for the Great Carbuncle is deemed little better than a traffic with the Evil One. Now think ye that I would have done this grievous wrong to my soul, body, reputation, and estate, without a reasonable chance of profit?"

"Not I, pious Master Pigsnort," said the man with the spectacles. "I never laid such a great folly to thy charge."

"Truly, I hope not," said the merchant. "Now, as touching this Great Carbuncle, I am free to own that I have never had a glimpse of it; but be it only the hundredth part so bright as people tell, it will surely outvalue the Great Mogul's best diamond, which he holds at an incalculable sum. Wherefore, I am minded to put the Great Carbuncle on shipboard, and voyage with it to England, France, Spain, Italy, or into Heathendom, if Providence should send me thither, and, in a word, dispose of the gem to the best bidder among the potentates of the earth, that he may place it among his crown jewels. If any of ye have a wiser plan, let him expound it."

"That have I, thou sordid man!" exclaimed the poet. "Dost thou desire nothing brighter than gold that thou wouldst transmute all this ethereal lustre into such dross as thou wallowest in already? For myself, hiding the jewel under my cloak, I shall hie me back to my attic chamber, in one of the darksome alleys of London. There, night and day, will I gaze upon it; my soul shall drink its radiance; it shall be diffused throughout my intellectual powers, and gleam brightly in every line of poesy that I indite. Thus, long ages after I am gone, the splendor of the Great Carbuncle will blaze around my name!"

"Well said, Master Poet!" cried he of the spectacles. "Hide it under thy cloak, sayest thou? Why, it will gleam through the holes, and make thee look like a jack-o'-lantern!"

"To think!" ejaculated the Lord de Vere, rather to himself than his companions, the best of whom he held utterly unworthy of his intercourse—"to think that a fellow in a tattered cloak should talk of conveying the Great Carbuncle to a garret in Grub Street! Have not I resolved within myself that the whole earth contains no fitter ornament for the great hall of my ancestral castle? There shall it flame for ages, making a noonday of midnight, glittering on the suits of armor, the banners, and escutcheons, that hang around the wall, and keeping bright the memory of heroes. Wherefore have all other adventurers sought the prize in vain but that I might win it, and make it a symbol of the glories of our lofty line? And never, on the diadem of the White Mountains, did the Great Carbuncle hold a place half so honored as is reserved for it in the hall of the De Veres!"

"It is a noble thought," said the Cynic, with an obsequious sneer. "Yet, might I presume to say so, the gem would make a rare sepulchral lamp, and would display the glories of your lordship's progenitors more truly in the ancestral vault than in the castle hall."

"Nay, forsooth," observed Matthew, the young rustic, who

sat hand in hand with his bride, "the gentleman has bethought himself of a profitable use for this bright stone. Hannah here and I are seeking it for a like purpose."

"How, fellow!" exclaimed his lordship, in surprise. "What castle hall hast thou to hang it in?"

"No castle," replied Matthew, "but as neat a cottage as any within sight of the Crystal Hills. Ye must know, friends, that Hannah and I, being wedded the last week, have taken up the search of the Great Carbuncle, because we shall need its light in the long winter evenings; and it will be such a pretty thing to show the neighbors when they visit us. It will shine through the house so that we may pick up a pin in any corner, and will set all the windows aglowing as if there were a great fire of pine knots in the chimney. And then how pleasant, when we awake in the night, to be able to see one another's faces!"

There was a general smile among the adventurers at the simplicity of the young couple's project in regard to this wondrous and invaluable stone, with which the greatest monarch on earth might have been proud to adorn his palace. Especially the man with spectacles, who had sneered at all the company in turn, now twisted his visage into such an expression of ill-natured mirth, that Matthew asked him, rather peevishly, what he himself meant to do with the Great Carbuncle.

"The Great Carbuncle!" answered the Cynic, with ineffable scorn. "Why, you blockhead, there is no such thing in *rerum natura*. I have come three thousand miles, and am resolved to set my foot on every peak of these mountains, and poke my head into every chasm, for the sole purpose of demonstrating to the satisfaction of any man one whit less an ass than thyself that the Great Carbuncle is all a humbug!"

Vain and foolish were the motives that had brought most of the adventurers to the Crystal Hills; but none so vain, so foolish, and so impious too, as that of the scoffer with the prodigious spectacles. He was one of those wretched and evil men whose yearnings are downward to the darkness, instead of heavenward, and who, could they but extinguish the lights which God hath kindled for us, would count the midnight gloom their chiefest glory. As the Cynic spoke, several of the party were startled by a gleam of red splendor, that showed the huge shapes of the surrounding mountains and the rock-bestrewn bed of the turbulent river with an illumination unlike that of their fire on the trunks and black boughs of the forest trees. They listened for the roll of thunder, but heard nothing, and were glad that the tempest came not near them. The stars, those dial points of heaven, now warned the adventurers to close their eyes on the blazing logs, and open them, in dreams, to the glow of the Great Carbuncle.

The young married couple had taken their lodgings in the farthest corner of the wigwam, and were separated from the rest of the party by a curtain of curiously-woven twigs, such as might have hung, in deep festoons, around the bridal-bower of Eve. The modest little wife had wrought this piece of tapestry while the other guests were talking. She and her husband fell asleep with hands tenderly clasped, and awoke from visions of unearthly radiance to meet the more blessed light of one another's eyes. They awoke at the same instant, and with one happy smile beaming over their two faces, which grew brighter with their consciousness of the reality of life and love. But no sooner did she recollect where they were, than the bride peeped through the interstices of the leafy curtain, and saw that the outer room of the hut was deserted.

"Up, dear Matthew!" cried she, in haste. "The strange folk are all gone! Up, this very minute, or we shall lose the Great Carbuncle!"

In truth, so little did these poor young people deserve the mighty prize which had lured them thither, that they had slept peacefully all night, and till the summits of the hills were glittering with sunshine; while the other adventurers had tossed their limbs in feverish wakefulness, or dreamed of climbing precipices, and set off to realize their dreams with the earliest peep of dawn. But Matthew and Hannah, after their calm rest, were as light as two young deer, and merely stopped to say their prayers and wash themselves in a cold pool of the Amonoosuck, and then to taste a morsel of food, ere they turned their faces to the mountain-side. It was a sweet emblem of conjugal affection, as they toiled up the difficult ascent, gathering strength from the mutual aid which they afforded. After several little accidents, such as a torn robe, a lost shoe, and the entanglement of Hannah's hair in a bough, they reached the upper verge of the forest, and were now to pursue a more adventurous course. The innumerable trunks and heavy foliage of the trees had hitherto shut in their thoughts, which now shrank affrighted from the region of wind and cloud and naked rocks and desolate sunshine, that rose immeasurably above them. They gazed back at the obscure wilderness which they had traversed, and longed to be buried again in its depths rather than trust themselves to so vast and visible a solitude.

"Shall we go on?" said Matthew, throwing his arm round Hannah's waist, both to protect her and to comfort his heart by drawing her close to it.

But the little bride, simple as she was, had a woman's love of jewels, and could not forego the hope of possessing the very brightest in the world, in spite of the perils with which it must be won.

"Let us climb a little higher," whispered she, yet tremulously, as she turned her face upward to the lonely sky.

"Come, then," said Matthew, mustering his manly courage and drawing her along with him, for she became timid again the moment that he grew bold.

And upward, accordingly, went the pilgrims of the Great Carbuncle, now treading upon the tops and thickly-interwoven branches of dwarf pines, which, by the growth of centuries, though mossy with age, had barely reached three feet in altitude. Next, they came to masses and fragments of naked rock heaped confusedly together, like a cairn reared by giants in memory of a giant chief. In this bleak realm of upper air nothing breathed, nothing grew; there was no life but what was concentrated in their two hearts; they had climbed so high that Nature herself seemed no longer to keep them company. She lingered beneath them, within the verge of the forest trees, and sent a farewell glance after her children as they strayed where her own green footprints had never been. But soon they were to be hidden from her eye. Densely and dark the mists began to gather below, casting black spots of shadow on the vast landscape, and sailing heavily to one centre, as if the loftiest mountain peak had summoned a council of its kindred clouds. Finally, the vapors welded themselves, as it were, into a mass, presenting the appearance of a pavement over which the wanderers might have trodden, but where they would vainly have sought an avenue to the blessed earth which they had lost. And the lovers yearned to behold that green earth again, more intensely, alas! than, beneath a clouded sky, they had ever desired a glimpse of heaven. They even felt it a relief to their desolation when the mists, creeping gradually up the mountain, concealed its lonely peak, and thus annihilated, at least for them, the whole region of visible space. But they drew closer together, with a fond and melancholy gaze, dreading lest the universal cloud should snatch them from each other's sight.

Still, perhaps, they would have been resolute to climb as far and as high, between earth and heaven, as they could find foothold, if Hannah's strength had not begun to fail, and with that, her courage also. Her breath grew short. She refused to burden her husband with her weight, but often tottered against his side, and recovered herself each time by a feebler effort. At last, she sank down on one of the rocky steps of the acclivity.

"We are lost, dear Matthew," said she, mournfully. "We shall never find our way to the earth again. And oh how happy we might have been in our cottage!"

"Dear heart!—we will yet be happy there," answered Matthew. "Look! In this direction, the sunshine penetrates the dismal mist. By its aid, I can direct our course to the passage of the Notch. Let us go back, love, and dream no more of the Great Carbuncle!"

"The sun cannot be yonder," said Hannah, with despond-ence. "By this time it must be noon. If there could ever be any sunshine here, it would come from above our heads."

"But look!" repeated Matthew, in a somewhat altered tone. "It is brightening every moment. If not sunshine, what can it be?"

Nor could the young bride any longer deny that a radiance was breaking through the mist, and changing its dim hue to a dusky red, which continually grew more vivid, as if brilliant particles were interfused with the gloom. Now, also, the cloud began to roll away from the mountain, while, as it heavily withdrew, one object after another started out of its impenetrable obscurity into sight, with precisely the effect of a new creation, before the indistinctness of the old chaos had been completely swallowed up. As the process went on, they saw the gleaming of water close at their feet, and found themselves on the very border of a mountain lake, deep, bright, clear, and calmly beautiful, spreading from brim to brim of a basin that had been scooped out of the solid rock. A ray of glory flashed across its surface. The pilgrims looked whence it should proceed, but closed their eyes with a thrill of awful admiration, to exclude the fervid splendor that glowed from the brow of a cliff impending over the enchanted lake. For the simple pair had reached that lake of mystery, and found the long-sought shrine of the Great Carbuncle!

They threw their arms around each other, and trembled at their own success; for, as the legends of this wondrous gem rushed thick upon their memory, they felt themselves marked out by fate—and the consciousness was fearful. Often, from childhood upward, they had seen it shining like a distant star. And now that star was throwing its intensest lustre on their hearts. They seemed changed to one another's eyes, in the red brilliancy that flamed upon their cheeks, while it lent the same fire to the lake, the rocks, and sky, and to the mists which had rolled back before its power. But, with their next glance, they beheld an object that drew their attention even from the mighty stone. At the base of the cliff, directly beneath the Great Carbuncle, appeared the figure of a man, with his arms extended in the act of climbing, and his face turned upward, as if to drink the full gush of splendor. But he stirred not, no more than if changed to marble.

"It is the Seeker," whispered Hannah, convulsively grasping her husband's arm. "Matthew, he is dead."

"The joy of success has killed him," replied Matthew, trembling violently. "Or, perhaps, the very light of the Great Carbuncle was death!"

"The Great Carbuncle," cried a peevish voice behind them. "The Great Humbug! If you have found it, prithee point it out to me."

They turned their heads, and there was the Cynic, with his prodigious spectacles set carefully on his nose, staring now at the lake, now at the rocks, now at the distant masses of vapor, now right at the Great Carbuncle itself, yet seemingly as unconscious of its light as if all the scattered clouds were condensed about his person. Though its radiance actually threw the shadow of the unbeliever at his own feet, as he turned his back upon the glorious jewel, he would not be convinced that there was the least glimmer there.

"Where is your Great Humbug?" he repeated. "I challenge you to make me see it!"

"There," said Matthew, incensed at such perverse blindness, and turning the Cynic round towards the illuminated cliff. "Take off those abominable spectacles, and you cannot help seeing it!"

Now these colored spectacles probably darkened the Cynic's sight, in at least as great a degree as the smoked glasses through which people gaze at an eclipse. With resolute bravado, however, he snatched them from his nose, and fixed a bold stare full upon the ruddy blaze of the Great Carbuncle. But scarcely had he encountered it, when, with a deep, shuddering groan, he dropped his head, and pressed both hands across his miserable eyes. Thenceforth there was, in very truth, no light of the Great Carbuncle, nor any other light on earth, nor light of heaven itself, for the poor Cynic. So long accustomed to view all objects through a medium that deprived them of every glimpse of brightness, a single flash of so glorious a phenomenon, striking upon his naked vision, had blinded him forever.

"Matthew," said Hannah, clinging to him, "let us go hence!"

Matthew saw that she was faint, and kneeling down, supported her in his arms, while he threw some of the thrillingly cold water of the enchanted lake upon her face and bosom. It revived her, but could not renovate her courage.

"Yes, dearest!" cried Matthew, pressing her tremulous form to his breast,—"we will go hence, and return to our humble cottage. The blessed sunshine and the quiet moonlight shall come through our window. We will kindle the cheerful glow of our hearth, at eventide, and be happy in its light. But never again will we desire more light than all the world may share with us."

"No," said his bride, "for how could we live by day, or sleep by night in this awful blaze of the Great Carbuncle!"

Out of the hollow of their hands, they drank each a draught from the lake, which presented them its waters uncontaminated by an earthly lip. Then, lending their guidance to the blinded Cynic, who uttered not a word, and even stifled his groans in his own most wretched heart, they began to descend the mountain. Yet, as they left the shore, till then untrodden, of the spirit's lake, they threw a farewell glance towards the cliff, and beheld the vapors gathering in dense volumes, through which the gem burned duskily.

As touching the other pilgrims of the Great Carbuncle, the legend goes on to tell, that the worshipful Master Ichabod Pigsnort soon gave up the quest as a desperate speculation, and wisely resolved to betake himself again to his warehouse, near the town dock, in Boston. But, as he passed through the Notch of the mountains, a war party of Indians captured our unlucky merchant, and carried him to Montreal, there holding him in bondage, till, by the payment of a heavy ransom, he had woefully subtracted from his hoard of pine-tree shillings. By his long absence, moreover, his affairs had become so disordered that, for the rest of his life, instead of wallowing in silver, he had seldom a sixpence worth of copper. Doctor Cacaphodel, the alchemist, returned to his laboratory with a prodigious fragment of granite, which he ground to powder, dissolved in acids, melted in the crucible, and burned with the blow-pipe, and published the result of his experiments in one of the heaviest folios of the day. And, for all these purposes, the gem itself could not have answered better than the granite. The poet, by a somewhat similar mistake, made prize of a great piece of ice, which he found in a sunless chasm of the mountains, and swore that it corresponded, in all points, with his idea of the Great Carbuncle. The critics say, that, if his poetry lacked the splendor of the gem, it retained all the coldness of the ice. The Lord de Vere went back to his ancestral hall, where he contented himself with a wax-lighted chandelier, and filled, in due course of time, another coffin in the ancestral vault. As the funeral torches gleamed within that dark receptacle, there was no need of the Great Carbuncle to show the vanity of earthly pomp.

The Cynic, having cast aside his spectacles, wandered about the world, a miserable object, and was punished with an agonizing desire of light, for the wilful blindness of his former life. The whole night long, he would lift his splendor-blasted orbs to the moon and stars; he turned his face eastward, at sunrise, as duly as a Persian idolater; he made a pilgrimage to Rome, to witness the magnificent illumination of St. Peter's Church; and finally perished in the great fire of London, into the midst of which he had thrust himself, with the desperate idea of catching one feeble ray from the blaze that was kindling earth and heaven.

Matthew and his bride spent many peaceful years, and were fond of telling the legend of the Great Carbuncle. The tale, however, towards the close of their lengthened lives, did not meet with the full credence that had been accorded to it by those who remembered the ancient lustre of the gem. For it is affirmed that, from the hour when two mortals had shown themselves so simply wise as to reject a jewel which would have dimmed all earthly things, its splendor waned. When other pilgrims reached the cliff, they found only an opaque stone, with particles of mica glittering on its surface. There is also a tradition that, as the youthful pair departed, the gem was loosened from the forehead of the cliff, and fell into the enchanted lake, and that, at noontide, the Seeker's form may still be seen to bend over its quenchless gleam.

Some few believe that this inestimable stone is blazing as of old, and say that they have caught its radiance, like a flash of summer lightning, far down the valley of the Saco. And be it owned that, many a mile from the Crystal Hills, I saw a wondrous light around their summits, and was lured, by the faith of poesy, to be the latest pilgrim of the GREAT CARBUNCLE.

THE MAN
OF ADAMANT

AN APOLOGUE

In the old times of religious gloom and intolerance, lived Richard Digby, the gloomiest and most intolerant of a stern brotherhood. His plan of salvation was so narrow, that, like a plank in a tempestuous sea, it could avail no sinner but himself, who bestrode it triumphantly, and hurled anathemas against the wretches whom he saw struggling with the billows of eternal death. In his view of the matter, it was a most abominable crime—as, indeed, it is a great folly—for men to trust to their own strength, or even to grapple to any other fragment of the wreck, save this narrow plank, which, moreover, he took special care to keep out of their reach. In other words, as his creed was like no man's else, and being well pleased that Providence had intrusted him alone, of mortals, with the treasure of a true faith, Richard Digby determined to seclude himself to the sole and constant enjoyment of his happy fortune.

"And verily," thought he, "I deem it a chief condition of Heaven's mercy to myself, that I hold no communion with those abominable myriads which it hath cast off to perish. Peradventure, were I to tarry longer in the tents of Kedar, the gracious boon would be revoked, and I also be swallowed up in the deluge of wrath, or consumed in the storm of fire and brimstone, or involved in whatever new kind of ruin is ordained for the horrible perversity of this generation."

So Richard Digby took an axe, to hew space enough for a tabernacle in the wilderness, and some few other necessaries, especially a sword and gun, to smite and slay any intruder upon his hallowed seclusion; and plunged into the dreariest depths of the forest. On its verge, however, he paused a moment, to shake off the dust of his feet against the village where he had dwelt, and to invoke a curse on the meeting-house, which he regarded as a temple of heathen idolatry. He felt a curiosity, also, to see whether the fire and brimstone would not rush down from Heaven at once, now that the one righteous man had provided for his own safety. But, as the sunshine continued to fall peacefully on the cottages and fields, and the husbandmen labored and children played, and as there were many tokens of present happiness, and nothing ominous of a speedy judgment, he turned away, somewhat disappointed. The further he went, however, and the lonelier he felt himself, and the thicker the trees stood along his path, and the darker the shadow overhead, so much the more did Richard Digby exult. He talked to himself, as he strode onward; he read his Bible to himself, as he sat beneath the trees; and, as the gloom of the forest hid the blessed sky, I had almost added, that, at morning, noon, and eventide, he prayed to himself. So congenial was this mode of life to his disposition, that he often laughed to himself, but was displeased when an echo tossed him back the long, loud roar.

In this manner, he journeyed onward three days and two nights, and came, on the third evening, to the mouth of a cave, which, at first sight, reminded him of Elijah's cave at Horeb, though perhaps it more resembled Abraham's sepulchral cave, at Machpelah. It entered into the heart of a rocky hill. There was so dense a veil of tangled foliage about it, that none but a sworn lover of gloomy recesses would have discovered the low arch of its entrance, or have dared to step within its vaulted chamber, where the burning eyes of a panther might encounter him. If Nature meant this remote and dismal cavern for the use of man, it could only be to bury in its gloom the victims of a pestilence, and then to block up its mouth with stones, and avoid the spot forever after. There was nothing bright nor cheerful near it, except a bubbling fountain, some twenty paces off, at which Richard Digby hardly threw away a glance. But he thrust his head into the cave, shivered, and congratulated himself.

"The finger of Providence hath pointed my way!" cried he, aloud, while the tomb-like den returned a strange echo, as if some one within were mocking him. "Here my soul will be at peace; for the wicked will not find me. Here I can read the Scriptures and be no more provoked with lying interpretations. Here I can offer up acceptable prayers because my voice will not be mingled with the sinful supplications of the multitude. Of a truth, the only way to heaven leadeth through the narrow entrance of this cave,—and I alone have found it!"

In regard to this cave, it was observable that the roof, so far as the imperfect light permitted it to be seen, was hung with substances resembling opaque icicles; for the damps of unknown centuries, dripping down continually, had become as hard as adamant; and wherever that moisture fell, it seemed to possess the power of converting what it bathed to stone. The fallen leaves and sprigs of foliage, which the wind had swept into the cave, and the little feathery shrubs, rooted near the threshold, were not wet with a natural dew, but had been embalmed by this wondrous process. And here I am put in mind that Richard Digby, before he withdrew himself from the world, was supposed by skilful physicians to have contracted a disease for which no remedy was written in their medical books. It was a deposition of calculous particles within his heart, caused by an obstructed circulation of the blood; and, unless a miracle should be wrought for him, there was danger that the malady might act on the entire substance of the organ, and change his fleshy heart to stone. Many, indeed, affirmed that the process was already near its consummation. Richard Digby, however, could never be convinced that any such direful work was going on within him; nor when he saw the sprigs of marble foliage, did his heart even throb the quicker, at the similitude suggested by these once tender herbs. It may be that this same insensibility was a symptom of the disease.

Be that as it might, Richard Digby was well contented with his sepulchral cave. So dearly did he love this congenial spot, that, instead of going a few paces to the bubbling spring for water, he allayed his thirst with now and then a drop of moisture from the roof, which, had it fallen anywhere but on his tongue, would have been congealed into a pebble. For a man predisposed to stoniness of the heart, this surely was unwholesome liquor. But there he dwelt, for three days more, eating herbs and roots, drinking his own destruction, sleeping, as it were, in a tomb, and awaking to the solitude of death, yet esteeming this horrible mode of life as hardly inferior to celestial bliss. Perhaps superior; for, above the sky, there would be angels to disturb him. At the close of the third day he sat in the portal of his mansion, reading the Bible aloud, because no other ear could profit by it, and reading it amiss, because the rays of the setting sun did not penetrate the dismal depth of shadow round about him, nor fall upon the sacred page. Suddenly, however, a faint gleam of light was thrown over the volume, and, raising his eyes, Richard Digby saw that a young woman stood before the mouth of the cave, and that the sunbeams bathed her white garment, which thus seemed to possess a radiance of its own.

"Good-evening, Richard," said the girl; "I have come from afar to find thee."

The slender grace and gentle loveliness of this young woman were at once recognized by Richard Digby. Her name was Mary Goffe. She had been a convert to his preaching of the word in England, before he yielded himself to that exclusive bigotry which now enfolded him with such an iron grasp that no other sentiment could reach his bosom. When he came a pilgrim to America, she had remained in her father's hall; but now, as it appeared, had crossed the ocean after him, impelled by the same faith that led other exiles hither, and perhaps by love almost as holy. What else but faith and love united could have sustained so delicate a creature, wandering thus far into the forest, with her golden hair dishevelled by the boughs, and her feet wounded by the thorns? Yet, weary and faint though she must have been, and affrighted at the dreariness of the cave, she looked on the lonely man with a mild and pitying expression, such as might beam from an angel's eyes, towards an afflicted mortal. But the recluse, frowning sternly upon her, and keeping his finger between the leaves of his half-closed Bible, motioned her away with his hand.

"Off!" cried he. "I am sanctified, and thou art sinful. Away!"

"O, Richard," said she, earnestly, "I have come this weary way because I heard that a grievous distemper had seized upon thy heart; and a great Physician hath given me the skill to cure it. There is no other remedy than this which I have brought thee. Turn me not away, therefore, nor refuse my medicine; for then must this dismal cave be thy sepulchre."

"Away!" replied Richard Digby, still with a dark frown. "My heart is in better condition than thine own. Leave me, earthly one; for the sun is almost set; and when no light reaches the door of the cave, then is my prayer-time."

Now, great as was her need, Mary Goffe did not plead with this stony-hearted man for shelter and protection, nor ask anything whatever for her own sake. All her zeal was for his welfare.

"Come back with me!" she exclaimed, clasping her hands,— "come back to thy fellow-men; for they need thee, Richard, and thou hast ten-fold need of them. Stay not in this evil den; for the air is chill, and the damps are fatal; nor will any that perish within it ever find the path to heaven. Hasten hence, I entreat thee, for thine own soul's sake; for either the roof will fall upon thy head, or some other speedy destruction is at hand."

"Perverse woman!" answered Richard Digby, laughing aloud,—for he was moved to bitter mirth by her foolish vehemence,—"I tell thee that the path to heaven leadeth straight through this narrow portal where I sit. And, moreover, the destruction thou speakest of is ordained, not for this blessed cave, but for all other habitations of mankind, throughout the earth. Get thee hence speedily, that thou mayst have thy share!"

So saying, he opened his Bible again, and fixed his eyes intently on the page, being resolved to withdraw his thoughts from this child of sin and wrath, and to waste no more of his holy breath upon her. The shadow had now grown so deep, where he was sitting, that he made continual mistakes in what he read, converting all that was gracious and merciful to denunciations of vengeance and unutterable woe on every created being but himself. Mary Goffe, meanwhile, was leaning against a tree, beside the sepulchral cave, very sad, yet with something heavenly and ethereal in her unselfish sorrow. The light from the setting sun still glorified her form and was reflected a little way within the darksome den, discovering so terrible a gloom that the maiden shuddered for its self-doomed inhabitants. Espying the bright fountain near at hand, she hastened thither, and scooped up a portion of its water in a cup of birchen bark. A few tears mingled with the draught, and perhaps gave it all its efficacy. She then returned to the mouth of the cave, and knelt down at Richard Digby's feet.

"Richard," she said, with passionate fervor, yet a gentleness in all her passion, "I pray thee, by thy hope of heaven, and as thou wouldst not dwell in this tomb forever, drink of this hallowed water, be it but a single drop! Then, make room for me by thy side, and let us read together one page of that blessed volume,—and, lastly, kneel down with me and pray! Do this, and thy stony heart shall become softer than a babe's, and all be well."

But Richard Digby, in utter abhorrence of the proposal, cast the Bible at his feet, and eyed her with such a fixed and evil frown, that he looked less like a living man than a marble statue, wrought by some dark-imagined sculptor to express the most repulsive mood that human features could assume. And, as his look grew even devilish, so, with an equal change, did Mary Goffe become more sad, more mild, more pitiful, more like a sorrowing angel. But, the more heavenly she was, the more hateful did she seem to Richard Digby, who at length raised his hand, and smote down the cup of hallowed water upon the threshold of the cave, thus rejecting the only medicine that could have cured his stony heart. A sweet perfume lingered in the air for a moment, and then was gone.

"Tempt me no more, accursed woman," exclaimed he, still with his marble frown, "lest I smite thee down also! What hast thou to do with my prayers?—what with my heaven?"

No sooner had he spoken these dreadful words, than Richard Digby's heart ceased to beat; while—so the legend says—the form of Mary Goffe melted into the last sunbeams, and returned from the sepulchral cave to heaven. For Mary Goffe had been buried in an English church-yard, months before; and either it was her ghost that haunted the wild forest, or else a dreamlike spirit, typifying pure Religion.

Above a century afterward, when the trackless forest of Richard Digby's day had long been interspersed with settlements, the children of a neighboring farmer were playing at the foot of a hill. The trees, on account of the rude and broken surface of this acclivity, had never been felled, and were crowded so densely together as to hide all but a few rocky prominences, wherever their roots could grapple with the soil. A little boy and girl, to conceal themselves from their playmates, had crept into the deepest shade, where not only the darksome pines, but a thick veil of creeping plants suspended from an overhanging rock, combined to make a twilight at noonday, and almost a midnight at all other seasons. There the children hid themselves, and shouted, repeating the cry at intervals, till the whole party of pursuers were drawn thither, and pulling aside the matted foliage, let in a doubtful glimpse of daylight. But scarcely was this accomplished, when the little group uttered a simultaneous shriek, and tumbled headlong down the hill, making the best of their way homeward, without a second glance into the gloomy recess. Their father, unable to comprehend what had so startled them, took his axe, and, by felling one or two trees, and tearing away the creeping plants, laid the mystery open to the day. He had discovered the entrance of a cave, closely resembling the mouth of a sepulchre, within which sat the figure of a man, whose gesture and attitude warned the father and children to stand back, while his visage wore a most forbidding frown. This repulsive personage seemed to have been carved in the same gray stone that formed the walls and portal of the cave. On minuter inspection, indeed, such blemishes were observed, as made it doubtful whether the figure were really a statue, chiselled by human art, and somewhat worn and defaced by the lapse of ages, or a freak of Nature, who might have chosen to imitate, in stone, her usual handiwork of flesh. Perhaps it was the least unreasonable idea, suggested by this strange spectacle, that the moisture of the cave possessed a petrifying quality, which had thus awfully embalmed a human corpse.

There was something so frightful in the aspect of this Man of Adamant, that the farmer, the moment that he recovered from the fascination of his first gaze, began to heap stones into the mouth of the cavern. His wife, who had followed him to the hill, assisted her husband's efforts. The children, also, approached as near as they durst, with their little hands full of pebbles, and cast them on the pile. Earth was then thrown into the crevices, and the whole fabric overlaid with sods. Thus all traces of the discovery were obliterated, leaving only a marvellous legend, which grew wilder from one generation to another, as the children told it to their grandchildren, and they to their posterity, till few believed that there had ever been a cavern or a statue, where now they saw but a grassy path on the shadowy hill-side. Yet, grown people avoid the spot, nor do children play there. Friendship, and Love, and Piety, all human and celestial sympathies, should keep aloof from that hidden cave; for there still sits, and, unless an earthquake crumble down the roof upon his head, shall sit forever, the shape of Richard Digby, in the attitude of repelling the whole race of mortals—not from heaven—but from the horrible loneliness of his dark, cold sepulchre!

LADY ELEANORE'S
MANTLE

Not long after Colonel Shute had assumed the government of Massachusetts Bay, now nearly a hundred and twenty years ago, a young lady of rank and fortune arrived from England, to claim his protection as her guardian. He was her distant relative, but the nearest who had survived the gradual extinction of her family; so that no more eligible shelter could be found for the rich and highborn Lady Eleanore Rochcliffe than within the Province House of a transatlantic colony. The consort of Governor Shute, moreover, had been as a mother to her childhood, and was now anxious to receive her, in the hope that a beautiful young woman would be exposed to infinitely less peril from the primitive society of New England than amid the artifices and corruptions of a court. If either the Governor or his lady had especially consulted their own comfort, they would probably have sought to devolve the responsibility on other hands; since, with some noble and splendid traits of character, Lady Eleanore was remarkable for a harsh, unyielding pride, a haughty consciousness of her hereditary and personal advantages, which made her almost incapable of control. Judging from many traditionary anecdotes, this peculiar temper was hardly less than a monomania; or, if the acts which it inspired were those of a sane person, it seemed due from Providence

First published in *The Democratic Review*, December, 1838.

that pride so sinful should be followed by as severe a retribution. That tinge of the marvellous, which is thrown over so many of these half-forgotten legends, has probably imparted an additional wildness to the strange story of Lady Eleanore Rochcliffe.

The ship in which she came passenger had arrived at Newport, whence Lady Eleanore was conveyed to Boston in the Governor's coach, attended by a small escort of gentlemen on horseback. The ponderous equipage, with its four black horses, attracted much notice as it rumbled through Cornhill, surrounded by the prancing steeds of half a dozen cavaliers, with swords dangling to their stirrups and pistols at their holsters. Through the large glass windows of the coach, as it rolled along, the people could discern the figure of Lady Eleanore, strangely combining an almost queenly stateliness with the grace and beauty of a maiden in her teens. A singular tale had gone abroad among the ladies of the province, that their fair rival was indebted for much of the irresistible charm of her appearance to a certain article of dress—an embroidered mantle—which had been wrought by the most skillful artist in London, and possessed even magical properties of adornment. On the present occasion, however, she owed nothing to the witchery of dress, being clad in a riding habit of velvet, which would have appeared stiff and ungraceful on any other form.

The coachman reined in his four black steeds, and the whole cavalcade came to a pause in front of the contorted iron balustrade that fenced the Province House from the public street. It was an awkward coincidence that the bell of the Old South was just then tolling for a funeral; so that, instead of gladsome peal with which it was customary to announce the arrival of distinguished strangers, Lady Eleanore Rochcliffe was ushered by a doleful clang, as if calamity had come embodied in her beautiful person.

"A very great disrespect!" exclaimed Captain Langford, an English officer, who had recently brought dispatches to Governor Shute. "The funeral should have been deferred, lest Lady Eleanore's spirits be affected by such a dismal welcome."

"With your pardon, sir," replied Doctor Clarke, a physician, and a famous champion of the popular party, "whatever the heralds may pretend, a dead beggar must have precedence of a living queen. King Death confers high privileges."

These remarks were interchanged while the speakers waited a passage through the crowd, which had gathered on each side of the gateway, leaving an open avenue to the portal of the Province House. A black slave in livery now leaped from behind the coach, and threw open the door; while at the same moment Governor Shute descended the flight of steps from his mansion, to assist Lady Eleanore in alighting. But the Governor's stately approach was anticipated in a manner that excited general astonishment. A pale young man, with his black hair all in disorder, rushed from the throng, and prostrated himself beside the coach, thus offering his person as a footstool for Lady Eleanore Rochcliffe to tread upon. She held back an instant, yet with an expression as if doubting whether the young man were worthy to bear the weight of her footstep, rather than dissatisfied to receive such awful reverence from a fellow-mortal.

"Up, sir," said the Governor, sternly, at the same time lifting his cane over the intruder. "What means the Bedlamite by this freak?"

"Nay," answered Lady Eleanore playfully, but with more scorn than pity in her tone, "your Excellency shall not strike him. When men seek only to be trampled upon, it were a pity to deny them a favor so easily granted—and so well deserved!"

Then, though as lightly as a sunbeam on a cloud, she placed her foot upon the cowering form, and extended her hand to meet that of the Governor. There was a brief interval, during which Lady Eleanore retained this attitude; and never, surely, was there an apter emblem of aristocracy and hereditary pride trampling on human sympathies and the kindred of nature, than these two figures presented at that moment. Yet the spectators were so smitten with her beauty, and so essential did pride seem to the existence of such a creature, that they gave a simultaneous acclamation of applause.

"Who is this insolent young fellow?" inquired Captain Langford, who still remained beside Doctor Clarke. "If he be in his senses, his impertinence demands the bastinado. If mad, Lady Eleanore should be secured from further inconvenience, by his confinement."

"His name is Jervase Helwyse," answered the Doctor; "a youth of no birth or fortune, or other advantages, save the mind and soul that nature gave him; and being secretary to our colonial agent in London, it was his misfortune to meet this Lady Eleanore Rochcliffe. He loved her—and her scorn has driven him mad."

"He was mad so to aspire," observed the English officer.

"It may be so," said Doctor Clarke, frowning as he spoke. "But I tell you, sir, I could well-nigh doubt the justice of the Heaven above us if no signal humiliation overtake this lady, who now treads so haughtily into yonder mansion. She seeks to place herself above the sympathies of our common nature, which envelops all human souls. See, if that nature do not assert its claim over her in some mode that shall bring her level with the lowest!"

"Never!" cried Captain Langford indignantly—"neither in life, nor when they lay her with her ancestors."

Not many days afterwards the Governor gave a ball in honor of Lady Eleanore Rochcliffe. The principal gentry of the colony received invitations, which were distributed to their residents, far and near, by messengers on horseback, bearing missives sealed with all the formality of official dispatches. In obedience to the summons, there was a general gathering of rank, wealth, and beauty; and the wide door of the Province House had seldom given admittance to more numerous and honorable guests than on the evening of Lady Eleanore's ball. Without much extravagance of eulogy, the spectacle might even be termed splendid; for, according to the fashion of the times, the ladies shone in rich silks and satins, outspread over wide-projecting hoops; and the gentlemen glittered in gold embroidery laid unsparingly upon the purple, or scarlet, or sky-blue velvet, which was the material of their coats and waistcoats. The latter article of dress was of great importance, since it enveloped the wearer's body nearly to the knees, and was perhaps bedizened with the amount of his whole year's income, in golden flowers and foliage. The altered taste of the present day—a taste symbolic of a deep change in the whole system of society—would look upon almost any of those gorgeous figures as ridiculous; although that evening the guests sought their reflections in the pierglasses, and rejoiced to catch their own glitter amid the glittering crowd. What a pity that one of the stately mirrors has not preserved a picture of the scene, which, by the very traits that were so transitory, might have taught as much that would be worth knowing and remembering!

Would, at least, that either painter or mirror could convey to us some faint idea of a garment, already noticed in this legend,—the Lady Eleanore's embroidered mantle,—which the gossips whispered was invested with magic properties, so as to lend a new and untried grace to her figure each time that she put it on! Idle fancy as it is, this mysterious mantle has thrown an awe around my image of her, partly from its fabled virtues, and partly because it was the handiwork of a dying woman, and, perchance, owed the fantastic grace of its conception to the delirium of approaching death.

After the ceremonial greetings had been paid, Lady Eleanore Rochcliffe stood apart from the mob of guests, insulating herself within a small and distinguished circle, to whom she accorded a more cordial favor than to the general throng. The waxen torches threw their radiance vividly over the scene, bringing out its brilliant points in strong relief; but she gazed carelessly, and with now and then an expression of weariness or scorn, tempered with such feminine grace that her auditors scarcely perceived the moral deformity of which it was the utterance. She beheld the spectacle not with vulgar ridicule, as disdaining to be pleased with the provincial mockery of a court festival, but with the deeper scorn of one whose spirit held itself too high to participate in the enjoyment of other human souls. Whether or no the recollections

of those who saw her that evening were influenced by the
strange events with which she was subsequently connected,
so it was that her figure ever after recurred to them as marked
by something wild and unnatural,—although, at the time, the
general whisper was of her exceeding beauty, and of the
indescribable charm which her mantle threw around her.
Some close observers, indeed, detected a feverish flush and
alternate paleness of countenance, with corresponding flow
and revulsion of spirits, and once or twice a painful and
helpless betrayal of lassitude, as if she were on the point of
sinking to the ground. Then, with a nervous shudder, she
seemed to arouse her energies and threw some bright and
playful yet half-wicked sarcasm into the conversation. There
was so strange a characteristic in her manners and sentiments
that it astonished every right-minded listener; till looking in
her face, a lurking and incomprehensible glance and smile
perplexed them with doubts both as to her seriousness and
sanity. Gradually, Lady Eleanor Rochcliffe's circle grew
smaller, till only four gentlemen remained in it. These were
Captain Langford, the English officer before mentioned; a
Virginian planter, who had come to Massachusetts on some
political errand; a young Episcopal clergyman, the grandson
of a British earl; and, lastly, the private secretary of Governor
Shute, whose obsequiousness had won a sort of tolerance from
Lady Eleanore.

At different periods of the evening the liveried servants of
the Province House passed among the guests, bearing huge
trays of refreshments and French and Spanish wines. Lady
Eleanore Rochcliffe, who refused to wet her beautiful lips
with a bubble of Champagne, had sunk back into a large
damask chair, apparently overwearied either with the excitement of the scene or its tedium, and while, for an instant, she
was unconscious of voices, laughter and music, a young man
strode forward, and knelt down at her feet. He bore a salver
in his hand, on which was a chased silver goblet, filled to the
brim with wine, which he offered as reverentially as to a
crowned queen, or rather with the awful devotion of a priest

doing sacrifice to his idol. Conscious that some one touched her robe, Lady Eleanore started, and unclosed her eyes upon the pale, wild features and dishevelled hair of Jervase Helwyse.

"Why do you haunt me thus?" said she, in a languid tone, but with a kindlier feeling than she ordinarily permitted herself to express. "They tell me that I have done you harm."

"Heaven knows if that be so," replied the young man solemnly. "But, Lady Eleanore, in requital of that harm, if such there be, and for your own earthly and heavenly welfare, I pray you to take one sip of this holy wine, and then to pass the goblet round among the guests. And this shall be a symbol that you have not sought to withdraw yourself from the chain of human sympathies—which whoso would shake off must keep company with fallen angels."

"Where has this mad fellow stolen that sacramental vessel?" exclaimed the Episcopal clergyman.

This question drew the notice of the guests to the silver cup, which was recognized as appertaining to the communion plate of the Old South Church; and, for aught that could be known, it was brimming over with the consecrated wine.

"Perhaps it is poisoned," half whispered the Governor's secretary.

"Pour it down the villain's throat!" cried the Virginian fiercely.

"Turn him out of the house!" cried Captain Langford, seizing Jervase Helwyse so roughly by the shoulders that the sacramental cup was overturned, and its contents sprinkled upon Lady Eleanore's mantle. "Whether knave, fool, or Bedlamite, it is intolerable that the fellow should go at large."

"Pray, gentlemen, do my poor admirer no harm," said Lady Eleanore, with a faint and weary smile. "Take him out of my sight, if such be your pleasure; for I can find in my heart to do nothing but laugh at him; whereas, in all decency and conscience, it would become me to weep for the mischief I have wrought!"

But while the by-standers were attempting to lead away the

unfortunate young man, he broke from them, and with a wild impassioned earnestness, offered a new and equally strange petition to Lady Eleanore. It was no other than that she should throw off the mantle, which, while he pressed the silver cup of wine upon her, she had drawn more closely around her form, so as almost to shroud herself within it.

"Cast it from you!" exclaimed Jervase Helwyse, clasping his hands in an agony of entreaty. "It may not yet be too late! Give the accursed garment to the flames!"

But Lady Eleanore, with a laugh of scorn, drew the rich folds of the embroidered mantle over her head, in such a fashion as to give a completely new aspect to her beautiful face, which—half hidden, half revealed—seemed to belong to some being of mysterious character and purposes.

"Farewell, Jervase Helwyse!" said she. "Keep my image in your remembrance, as you behold it now."

"Alas, lady!" he replied, in a tone no longer wild, but sad as a funeral bell. "We must meet shortly, when your face may wear another aspect—and that shall be the image that must abide within me."

He made no more resistance to the violent efforts of the gentlemen and servants, who almost dragged him out of the apartment, and dismissed him roughly from the iron gate of the Province House. Captain Langford, who had been very active in this affair, was returning to the presence of Lady Eleanore Rochcliffe, when he encountered the physician, Doctor Clarke, with whom he had held some casual talk on the day of her arrival. The Doctor stood apart, separated from Lady Eleanore by the width of the room, but eying her with such keen sagacity that Captain Langford involuntarily gave him credit for the discovery of some deep secret.

"You appear to be smitten, after all, with the charms of this queenly maiden," said he, hoping thus to draw forth the physician's hidden knowledge.

"God forbid!" answered Doctor Clarke, with a grave smile; "and if you be wise you will put up the same prayer for yourself. Woe to those who shall be smitten by this beautiful Lady

Eleanore! But yonder stands the Governor—and I have a word or two for his private ear. Good night!"

He accordingly advanced to Governor Shute, and addressed him in so low a tone that none of the by-standers could catch a word of what he said, although the sudden change of his Excellency's hitherto cheerful visage betokened that the communication could be of no agreeable import. A very few moments afterwards it was announced to the guests that an unforeseen circumstance rendered it necessary to put a premature close to the festival.

The ball at the Province House supplied a topic of conversation for the colonial metropolis for some days after its occurrence, and might still longer have been the general theme, only that a subject of all-engrossing interest thrust it, for a time, from the public recollection. This was the appearance of a dreadful epidemic, which, in that age and long before and afterwards, was wont to slay its hundreds and thousands on both sides of the Atlantic. On the occasion of which we speak, it was distinguished by a peculiar virulence, insomuch that it has left its traces—its pit-marks, to use an appropriate figure—on the history of the country, the affairs of which were thrown into confusion by its ravages. At first, unlike its ordinary course, the disease seemed to confine itself to the higher circles of society, selecting its victims from among the proud, the well-born, and the wealthy, entering unabashed into stately chambers, and lying down with the slumberers in silken beds. Some of the most distinguished guests of the Province House—even those whom the haughty Lady Eleanore Rochcliffe had deemed not unworthy of her favor—were stricken by this fatal scourge. It was noticed, with an ungenerous bitterness of feeling, that the four gentlemen —the Virginian, the British officer, the young clergyman, and the Governor's secretary—who had been her most devoted attendants on the evening of the ball, were the foremost on whom the plague stroke fell. But the disease, pursuing its onward progress, soon ceased to be exclusively a prerogative of aristocracy. Its red brand was no longer conferred like a

noble's star, or an order of knighthood. It threaded its way
through the narrow and crooked streets, and entered the low,
mean, darksome dwellings, and laid its hand of death upon the
artisans and laboring classes of the town. It compelled rich
and poor to feel themselves brethren then; and stalking to
and fro across the Three Hills, with a fierceness which made it
almost a new pestilence, there was that mighty conqueror—
that scourge and horror of our forefathers—the Small-Pox!

We cannot estimate the affright which this plague inspired
of yore, by contemplating it as the fangless monster of the
present day. We must remember, rather, with what awe we
watched the gigantic footsteps of the Asiatic cholera, striding
from shore to shore of the Atlantic, and marching like destiny
upon cities far remote which flight had already half depopu-
lated. There is no other fear so horrible and unhumanizing as
that which makes man dread to breathe heaven's vital air
lest it be poison, or to grasp the hand of a brother or friend
lest the gripe of the pestilence should clutch him. Such was
the dismay that now followed in the track of the disease, or
ran before it throughout the town. Graves were hastily dug,
and the pestilential relics as hastily covered, because the
dead were enemies of the living, and strove to draw them
headlong, as it were, into their own dismal pit. The public
councils were suspended, as if mortal wisdom might relinquish
its devices, now that an unearthly usurper had found his
way into the ruler's mansion. Had an enemy's fleet been
hovering on the coast, or his armies trampling on our soil,
the people would probably have committed their defence to
that same direful conqueror who had wrought their own
calamity, and would permit no interference with his sway.
This conquerer had a symbol of his triumphs. It was a blood-
red flag, that fluttered in the tainted air, over the door of
every dwelling into which the Small-Pox had entered.

Such a banner was long since waving over the portal of the
Province House; for thence, as was proved by tracking its
footsteps back, had all this dreadful mischief issued. It had
been traced back to a lady's luxurious chamber—to the proud-

est of the proud—to her that was so delicate, and hardly owned herself of earthly mould—to the haughty one, who took her stand above human sympathies—to Lady Eleanore! There remained no room for doubt that the contagion had lurked in that gorgeous mantle, which threw so strange a grace around her at the festival. Its fantastic splendor had been conceived in the delirious brain of a woman on her death-bed, and was the last toil of her stiffening fingers, which had interwoven fate and misery with its golden threads. This dark tale, whispered at first, was now bruited far and wide. The people raved against the Lady Eleanore, and cried out that her pride and scorn had evoked a fiend, and that, between them both, this monstrous evil had been born. At times, their rage and despair took the semblance of grinning mirth; and whenever the red flag of the pestilence was hoisted over another and yet another door, they clapped their hands and shouted through the streets, in bitter mockery: "Behold a new triumph for the Lady Eleanore!"

One day, in the midst of these dismal times, a wild figure approached the portal of the Province House, and folding his arms, stood contemplating the scarlet banner which a passing breeze shook fitfully, as if to fling abroad the contagion that it typified. At length, climbing one of the pillars by means of the iron balustrade, he took down the flag and entered the mansion, waving it above his head. At the foot of the staircase he met the Governor, booted and spurred, with his cloak drawn around him, evidently on the point of setting forth upon a journey.

"Wretched lunatic, what do you seek here?" exclaimed Shute, extending his cane to guard himself from contact. "There is nothing here but Death. Back—or you will meet him!"

"Death will not touch me, the banner-bearer of the pestilence!" cried Jervase Helwyse, shaking the red flag aloft. "Death, and the Pestilence, who wears the aspect of the Lady Eleanore, will walk through the streets to-night, and I must march before them with this banner!"

"Why do I waste words on the fellow?" muttered the Governor, drawing his cloak across his mouth. "What matters his miserable life, when none of us are sure of twelve hours' breath? On, fool, to your own destruction!"

He made way for Jervase Helwyse, who immediately ascended the staircase, but, on the first landing place, was arrested by the firm grasp of a hand upon his shoulder. Looking fiercely up, with a madman's impulse to struggle with and rend asunder his opponent, he found himself powerless beneath a calm, stern eye, which possessed the mysterious property of quelling frenzy at its height. The person whom he had now encountered was the physician, Doctor Clarke, the duties of whose sad profession had led him to the Province House, where he was an infrequent guest in more prosperous times.

"Young man, what is your purpose?" demanded he.

"I seek the Lady Eleanore," answered Jervase Helwyse, submissively.

"All have fled from her," said the physician. "Why do you seek her now? I tell you, youth, her nurse fell death-stricken on the threshold of that fatal chamber. Know ye not, that never came such a curse to our shores as this lovely Lady Eleanore?—that her breath has filled the air with poison?— that she has shaken pestilence and death upon the land, from the folds of her accursed mantle?"

"Let me look upon her!" rejoined the mad youth, more wildly. "Let me behold her, in her awful beauty, clad in the regal garments of the pestilence! She and Death sit on a throne together. Let me kneel down before them!"

"Poor youth!" said Doctor Clarke; and, moved by a deep sense of human weakness, a smile of caustic humor curled his lip even then. "Wilt thou still worship the destroyer and surround her image with fantasies the more magnificent, the more evil she has wrought? Thus man doth ever to his tyrants. Approach, then! Madness, as I have noted, has that good efficacy, that it will guard you from contagion—and perchance its own cure may be found in yonder chamber."

Ascending another flight of stairs, he threw open a door

and signed to Jervase Helwyse that he should enter. The poor lunatic, it seems probable, had cherished a delusion that his haughty mistress sat in state, unharmed herself by the pestilential influence, which, as by enchantment, she scattered round about her. He dreamed, no doubt, that her beauty was not dimmed, but brightened into superhuman splendor. With such anticipations, he stole reverentially to the door at which the physician stood, but paused upon the threshold, gazing fearfully into the gloom of the darkened chamber.

"Where is the Lady Eleanore?" whispered he.

"Call her," replied the physician.

"Lady Eleanore!—Princess!—Queen of Death!" cried Jervase Helwyse, advancing three steps into the chamber. "She is not here! There, on yonder table, I behold the sparkle of a diamond which once she wore upon her bosom. There"— and he shuddered—"there hangs her mantle, on which a dead woman embroidered a spell of dreadful potency. But where is the Lady Eleanore?"

Something stirred within the silken curtains of a canopied bed; and a low moan was uttered, which, listening intently, Jervase Helwyse began to distinguish as a woman's voice, complaining dolefully of thirst. He fancied, even, that he recognized its tones.

"My throat!—my throat is scorched," murmured the voice. "A drop of water!"

"What thing art thou?" said the brain-stricken youth, drawing near the bed and tearing asunder its curtains. "Whose voice hast thou stolen for thy murmurs and miserable petitions, as if Lady Eleanore could be conscious of mortal infirmity? Fie! Heap of diseased mortality, why lurkest thou in my lady's chamber?"

"O Jervase Helwyse," said the voice—and as it spoke the figure contorted itself, struggling to hide its blasted face— "look not now on the woman you once loved! The curse of Heaven hath stricken me, because I would not call man my brother, nor woman sister. I wrapped myself in PRIDE as in a MANTLE, and scorned the sympathies of nature; and therefore has nature made this wretched body the medium of a dreadful sympathy. You are avenged—they are all avenged—Nature is avenged—for I am Eleanore Rochcliffe!"

The malice of his mental disease, the bitterness lurking at the bottom of his heart, mad as he was, for a blighted and ruined life, and love that had been paid with cruel scorn, awoke within the breast of Jervase Helwyse. He shook his finger at the wretched girl, and the chamber echoed, the curtains of the bed were shaken, with his outburst of insane merriment.

"Another triumph for the Lady Eleanore!" he cried. "All have been her victims! Who so worthy to be the final victim as herself?"

Impelled by some new fantasy of his crazed intellect, he snatched the fatal mantle and rushed from the chamber and the house. That night a procession passed, by torchlight, through the streets, bearing in the midst the figure of a woman, enveloped with a richly embroidered mantle; while in advance stalked Jervase Helwyse, waving the red flag of the pestilence. Arriving opposite the Province House, the mob burned the effigy, and a strong wind came and swept away the ashes. It was said that, from that very hour, the pestilence abated, as if its sway had some mysterious connection, from the first plague stroke to the last, with Lady Eleanore's Mantle. A remarkable uncertainty broods over that unhappy lady's fate. There is a belief, however, that in a certain chamber of this mansion a female form may sometimes be duskily discerned, shrinking into the darkest corner and muffling her face within an embroidered mantle. Supposing the legend true, can this be other than the once proud Lady Eleanore?

EGOTISM;[1]
OR, THE BOSOM SERPENT

[FROM THE UNPUBLISHED
"ALLEGORIES OF THE HEART"]

"Here he comes!" shouted the boys along the street. "Here comes the man with a snake in his bosom!"

This outcry, saluting Herkimer's ears as he was about to enter the iron gate of the Elliston mansion, made him pause. It was not without a shudder that he found himself on the point of meeting his former acquaintance, whom he had known in the glory of youth, and whom now after an interval of five years, he was to find the victim either of a diseased fancy or a horrible physical misfortune.

"A snake in his bosom!" repeated the young sculptor to himself. "It must be he. No second man on earth has such a bosom friend. And now, my poor Rosina, Heaven grant me wisdom to discharge my errand aright! Woman's faith must be strong indeed since thine has not yet failed."

Thus musing, he took his stand at the entrance of the gate and waited until the personage so singularly announced should make his appearance. After an instant or two he beheld the figure of a lean man, of unwholesome look, with glittering eyes and long black hair, who seemed to imitate

First published in *The Democratic Review*, March, 1843.

[1] The physical fact, to which it is here attempted to give a moral signification, has been known to occur in more than one instance. [Hawthorne's note]

the motion of a snake; for, instead of walking straight forward with open front, he undulated along the pavement in a curved line. It may be too fanciful to say that something, either in his moral or material aspect, suggests the idea that a miracle had been wrought by transforming a serpent into a man, but so imperfectly that the snaky nature was yet hidden, and scarcely hidden, under the mere outward guise of humanity. Herkimer remarked that his complexion had a greenish tinge over its sickly white, reminding him of a species of marble out of which he had once wrought a head of Envy, with her snaky locks.

The wretched being approached the gate, but, instead of entering, stopped short and fixed the glitter of his eye full upon the compassionate yet steady countenance of the sculptor.

"It gnaws me! It gnaws me!" he exclaimed.

And then there was an audible hiss, but whether it came from the apparent lunatic's own lips, or was the real hiss of a serpent, might admit of a discussion. At all events, it made Herkimer shudder to his heart's core.

"Do you know me, George Herkimer?" asked the snake-possessed.

Herkimer did know him; but it demanded all the intimate and practical acquaintance with the human face, acquired by modelling actual likenesses in clay, to recognize the features of Roderick Elliston in the visage that now met the sculptor's gaze. Yet it was he. It added nothing to the wonder to reflect that the once brilliant young man had undergone this odious and fearful change during the no more than five brief years of Herkimer's abode at Florence. The possibility of such a transformation being granted, it was as easy to conceive it effected in a moment as in an age. Inexpressibly shocked and startled, it was still the keenest pang when Herkimer remembered that the fate of his cousin Rosina, the ideal of gentle womanhood, was indissolubly interwoven with that of a being whom Providence seemed to have unhumanized.

"Elliston! Roderick!" cried he, "I had heard of this; but my

conception came far short of the truth. What has befallen you?
Why do I find you thus?"

"Oh, 'tis a mere nothing! A snake! A snake! the commonest
thing in the world. A snake in the bosom—that's all," answered Roderick Elliston. "But how is your own breast?"
continued he, looking the sculptor in the eye with the most
acute and penetrating glance that it had ever been his fortune
to encounter. "All pure and wholesome? No reptile there? By
my faith and conscience, and by the devil within me, here is
a wonder! A man without a serpent in his bosom!"

"Be calm, Elliston," whispered George Herkimer, laying
his hand upon the shoulder of the snake-possessed. "I have
crossed the ocean to meet you. Listen! Let us be private. I
bring a message from Rosina—from your wife!"

"It gnaws me! It gnaws me!" muttered Roderick.

With this exclamation, the most frequent in his mouth, the
unfortunate man clutched both hands upon his breast as if
an intolerable sting or torture impelled him to rend it open
and let out the living mischief, even should it be intertwined
with his own life. He then freed himself from Herkimer's
grasp by a subtle motion, and, gliding through the gate, took
refuge in his antiquated family residence. The sculptor did
not pursue him. He saw that no available intercourse could
be expected at such a moment, and was desirous, before another meeting, to inquire closely into the nature of Roderick's
disease and the circumstances that had reduced him to so
lamentable a condition. He succeeded in obtaining the necessary information from an eminent medical gentleman.

Shortly after Elliston's separation from his wife—now nearly
four years ago—his associates had observed a singular gloom
spreading over his daily life, like those chill, gray mists that
sometimes steal away the sunshine from a summer's morning.
The symptoms caused them endless perplexity. They knew not
whether ill health were robbing his spirits of elasticity, or
whether a canker of the mind was gradually eating, as such
cankers do, from his moral system into the physical frame,
which is but the shadow of the former. They looked for the

root of this trouble in his shattered schemes of domestic bliss,
—wilfully shattered by himself,—but could not be satisfied
of its existence there. Some thought that their once brilliant
friend was in an incipient stage of insanity, of which his passionate impulses had perhaps been the forerunners; others
prognosticated a general blight and gradual decline. From
Roderick's own lips they could learn nothing. More than once,
it is true, he had been heard to say, clutching his hands convulsively upon his breast,—"It gnaws me! It gnaws me!"—but,
by different auditors, a great diversity of explanation was
assigned to this ominous expression. What could it be that
gnawed the breast of Roderick Elliston? Was it sorrow? Was
it merely the tooth of physical disease? Or, in his reckless
course, often verging upon profligacy, if not plunging into
its depths, had he been guilty of some deed which made his
bosom a prey to the deadlier fangs of remorse? There was
plausible ground for each of these conjectures; but it must
not be concealed that more than one elderly gentleman, the
victim of good cheer and slothful habits, magisterially pronounced the secret of the whole matter to be Dyspepsia!

Meanwhile, Roderick seemed aware how generally he had
become the subject of curiosity and conjecture, and, with a
morbid repugnance to such notice, or to any notice whatso-
ever, estranged himself from all companionship. Not merely
the eye of man was a horror to him; not merely the light of a
friend's countenance; but even the blessed sunshine, likewise,
which in its universal beneficence typifies the radiance of the
Creator's face, expressing his love for all the creatures of his
hand. The dusky twilight was now too transparent for Roderick Elliston; the blackest midnight was his chosen hour to
steal abroad; and if ever he were seen, it was when the watchman's lantern gleamed upon his figure, gliding along the
street, with his hands clutched upon his bosom, still muttering, "It gnaws me! It gnaws me!" What could it be that
gnawed him?

After a time, it became known that Elliston was in the habit
of resorting to all the noted quacks that infested the city, or

whom money would tempt to journey thither from a distance. By one of these persons, in the exultation of a supposed cure, it was proclaimed far and wide, by dint of handbills and little pamphlets on dingy paper, that a distinguished gentleman, Roderick Elliston, Esq., had been relieved of a SNAKE in his stomach! So here was the monstrous secret, ejected from its lurking place into public view, in all its horrible deformity. The mystery was out; but not so the bosom serpent. He, if it were anything but a delusion, still lay coiled in his living den. The empiric's cure had been a sham, the effect, it was supposed, of some stupefying drug which more nearly caused the death of the patient than of the odious reptile that possessed him. When Roderick Elliston regained entire sensibility, it was to find his misfortune the town talk—the more than nine days' wonder and horror—while, at his bosom, he felt the sickening motion of a thing alive, the gnawing of that restless fang which seemed to gratify at once a physical appetite and a fiendish spite.

He summoned the old black servant, who had been bred up in his father's house, and was a middle-aged man while Roderick lay in his cradle.

"Scipio!" he began; and then paused, with his arms folded over his heart. "What do people say of me, Scipio."

"Sir! my poor master! that you had a serpent in your bosom," answered the servant with hesitation.

"And what else?" asked Roderick, with a ghastly look at the man.

"Nothing else, dear master," replied Scipio, "only that the doctor gave you a powder, and that the snake leaped out upon the floor."

"No, no!" muttered Roderick to himself, as he shook his head, and pressed his hands with a more convulsive force upon his breast, "I feel him still. It gnaws me! It gnaws me!"

From this time the miserable sufferer ceased to shun the world, but rather solicited and forced himself upon the notice of acquaintances and strangers. It was partly the result of desperation on finding that the cavern of his own bosom had not proved deep and dark enough to hide the secret, even while it was so secure a fortress for the loathsome fiend that had crept into it. But still more, this craving for notoriety was a symptom of the intense morbidness which now pervaded his nature. All persons chronically diseased are egotists, whether the disease be of the mind or body; whether it be sin, sorrow, or merely the more tolerable calamity of some endless pain, or mischief among the cords of mortal life. Such individuals are made acutely conscious of a self, by the torture in which it dwells. Self, therefore, grows to be so prominent an object with them that they cannot but present it to the face of every casual passer-by. There is a pleasure—perhaps the greatest of which the sufferer is susceptible—in displaying the wasted or ulcerated limb, or the cancer in the breast; and the fouler the crime, with so much the more difficulty does the perpetrator prevent it from thrusting up its snake-like head to frighten the world; for it is that cancer, or that crime, which constitutes their respective individuality. Roderick Elliston, who, a little while before, had held himself so scornfully above the common lot of men, now paid full allegiance to this humiliating law. The snake in his bosom seemed the symbol of a monstrous egotism to which everything was referred, and which he pampered, night and day, with a continual and exclusive sacrifice of devil worship.

He soon exhibited what most people considered indubitable tokens of insanity. In some of his moods, strange to say, he prided and gloried himself on being marked out from the ordinary experience of mankind, by the possession of a double nature, and a life within a life. He appeared to imagine that the snake was a divinity,—not celestial, it is true, but darkly infernal,—and that he thence derived an eminence and a sanctity, horrid, indeed, yet more desirable than whatever ambition aims at. Thus he drew his misery around him like a regal mantle, and looked down triumphantly upon those whose vitals nourished no deadly monster. Oftener, however, his human nature asserted its empire over him in the shape of a yearning for fellowship. It grew to be his custom to spend the whole day in wandering about the streets, aimlessly, unless it might be called an aim to establish a species of brotherhood between himself and the world. With cankered ingenuity, he sought out his own disease in every breast. Whether insane or not, he showed so keen a perception of frailty, error, and vice, that many persons gave him credit for being possessed not merely with a serpent, but with an actual fiend, who imparted this evil faculty of recognizing whatever was ugliest in man's heart.

For instance, he met an individual, who, for thirty years, had cherished a hatred against his own brother. Roderick, amidst the throng of the street, laid his hand on this man's chest, and looking full into his forbidding face,—

"How is the snake to-day?" he inquired, with a mock expression of sympathy.

"The snake!" exclaimed the brother hater—"what do you mean?"

"The snake! The snake! Does it gnaw you?" persisted Roderick. "Did you take counsel with him this morning when you should have been saying your prayers? Did he sting, when you thought of your brother's health, wealth, and good repute? Did he caper for joy, when you remembered the profligacy of his only son? And whether he stung or whether he frolicked, did you feel his poison throughout your body and soul, converting everything to sourness and bitterness? That is the way of such serpents. I have learned the whole nature of them from my own!"

"Where is the police?" roared the object of Roderick's persecution, at the same time giving an instinctive clutch to his breast. "Why is this lunatic allowed to go at large?"

"Ha, ha!" chuckled Roderick, releasing his grasp of the man. "His bosom serpent has stung him then!"

Often it pleased the unfortunate young man to vex people with a lighter satire, yet still characterized by somewhat of snake-like virulence. One day he encountered an ambitious statesman, and gravely inquired after the welfare of his boa constrictor; for of that species, Roderick affirmed, this gentleman's serpent must needs be, since its appetite was enormous enough to devour the whole country and constitution. At another time, he stopped a close-fisted old fellow, of great wealth, but who skulked about the city in the guise of a scarecrow, with a patched blue surtout, brown hat, and mouldy boots, scraping pence together, and picking up rusty nails. Pretending to look earnestly at this respectable person's stomach, Roderick assured him that his snake was a copper-head, and had been generated by the immense quantities of that base metal, with which he daily defiled his fingers. Again, he assaulted a man of rubicund visage, and told him that few bosom serpents had more of the devil in them than those that breed in the vats of a distillery. The next whom Roderick honored with his attention was a distinguished clergyman, who happened just then to be engaged in a theological controversy, where human wrath was more perceptible than divine inspiration.

"You have swallowed a snake in a cup of sacramental wine," quoth he.

"Profane wretch!" exclaimed the divine; but, nevertheless, his hand stole to his breast.

He met a person of sickly sensibility, who, on some early disappointment, had retired from the world, and thereafter held no intercourse with his fellow-men, but brooded sullenly or passionately over the irrevocable past. This man's very heart, if Roderick might be believed, had been changed into a serpent, which would finally torment both him and itself to death. Observing a married couple, whose domestic troubles were a matter of notoriety, he condoled with both on having mutually taken a house adder to their bosoms. To an envious author, who depreciated works which he could never equal, he said that his snake was the slimiest and filthiest of all the reptile tribe, but was fortunately without a sting. A man of impure life, and a brazen face, asking Roderick if there were any serpent in his breast, he told him that there was, and of the same species that once tortured Don Rodrigo, the Goth. He took a fair young girl by the hand, and gazing sadly into her eyes, warned her that she cherished a serpent of the deadliest kind within her gentle breast; and the world found the truth of those ominous words, when, a few months afterwards, the poor girl died of love and shame. Two ladies, rivals in fashionable life, who tormented one another with a thousand little stings of womanish spite, were given to understand that each of their hearts was a nest of diminutive snakes, which did quite as much mischief as one great one.

But nothing seemed to please Roderick better than to lay hold of a person infected with jealousy, which he represented as an enormous green reptile, with an ice-cold length of body, and the sharpest sting of any snake save one.

"And what one is that?" asked a by-stander, overhearing him.

It was a dark-browed man who put the question; he had an evasive eye, which in the course of a dozen years had looked no mortal directly in the face. There was an ambiguity about this person's character,—a stain upon his reputation,—yet none could tell precisely of what nature, although the city gossips, male and female, whispered the most atrocious surmises. Until a recent period he had followed the sea, and was, in fact, the very shipmaster whom George Herkimer had encountered, under such singular circumstances, in the Grecian Archipelago.

"What bosom serpent has the sharpest sting?" repeated this man; but he put the question as if by a reluctant necessity, and grew pale while he was uttering it.

"Why need you ask?" replied Roderick, with a look of dark intelligence. "Look into your own breast. Hark! my serpent bestirs himself! He acknowledges the presence of a master fiend!"

And then, as the by-standers afterwards affirmed, a hissing sound was heard, apparently in Roderick Elliston's breast. It was said, too, that an answering hiss came from the vitals of the shipmaster, as if a snake were actually lurking there and had been aroused by the call of its brother reptile. If there were in fact any such sound, it might have been caused by a malicious exercise of ventriloquism on the part of Roderick.

Thus making his own actual serpent—if a serpent there actually was in his bosom—the type of each man's fatal error, or hoarded sin, or unquiet conscience, and striking his sting so unremorsefully into the sorest spot, we may well imagine that Roderick became the pest of the city. Nobody could elude him—none could withstand him. He grappled with the ugliest truth that he could lay his hand on, and compelled his adversary to do the same. Strange spectacle in human life where it is the instinctive effort of one and all to hide those sad realities, and leave them undisturbed beneath a heap of superficial topics which constitute the materials of intercourse between man and man! It was not to be tolerated that Roderick Elliston should break through the tacit compact by which the world has done its best to secure repose without relinquishing evil. The victims of his malicious remarks, it is true, had brothers enough to keep them in countenance; for, by Roderick's theory, every mortal bosom harbored either a brood of small serpents or one overgrown monster that had devoured all the rest. Still the city could not bear this new apostle. It was demanded by nearly all, and particularly by the most respectable inhabitants, that Roderick should no longer be permitted to violate the received rules of decorum by obtruding his own bosom serpent to the public gaze, and dragging those of decent people from their lurking places.

Accordingly, his relatives interfered and placed him in a private asylum for the insane. When the news was noised abroad, it was observed that many persons walked the streets with freer countenances and covered their breasts less carefully with their hands.

His confinement, however, although it contributed not a little to the peace of the town, operated unfavorably upon Roderick himself. In solitude his melancholy grew more black and sullen. He spent whole days—indeed, it was his sole occupation—in communing with the serpent. A conversation was sustained, in which, as it seemed, the hidden monster bore a part, though unintelligibly to the listeners, and inaudible except in a hiss. Singular as it may appear, the sufferer had now contracted a sort of affection for his tormentor, mingled, however, with the intensest loathing and horror. Nor were such discordant emotions incompatible. Each, on the contrary, imparted strength and poignancy to its opposite. Horrible love—horrible antipathy—embracing one another in his bosom, and both concentrating themselves upon a being that had crept into his vitals or been engendered there, and which was nourished with his food, and lived upon his life, and was as intimate with him as his own heart, and yet was the foulest of all created things! But not the less was it the true type of a morbid nature.

Sometimes, in his moments of rage and bitter hatred against the snake and himself, Roderick determined to be the death of him, even at the expense of his own life. Once he attempted it by starvation; but, while the wretched man was on the point of famishing, the monster seemed to feed upon his heart, and to thrive and wax gamesome, as if it were his sweetest and most congenial diet. Then he privily took a dose of active poison, imagining that it would not fail to kill either himself or the devil that possessed him, or both together. Another mistake; for if Roderick had not yet been destroyed by his own poisoned heart nor the snake by gnawing it, they had little to fear from arsenic or corrosive sublimate. Indeed, the venomous pest appeared to operate as an antidote against all other poisons. The physicians tried to suffocate the fiend with tobacco smoke. He breathed it as freely as if it were his native atmosphere. Again, they drugged their patient with opium and drenched him with intoxicating liquors, hoping that the snake might thus be reduced to stupor and perhaps be ejected from the stomach. They succeeded in rendering Roderick insensible; but, placing their hands upon his breast, they were inexpressibly horror stricken to feel the monster wriggling, twining, and darting to and fro within his narrow limits, evidently enlivened by the opium or alcohol, and incited to unusual feats of activity. Thenceforth they gave up all attempts at cure or palliation. The doomed sufferer sub-

mitted to his fate, resumed his former loathsome affection
for the bosom fiend, and spent whole miserable days before a
looking-glass, with his mouth wide open, watching, in hope
and horror, to catch a glimpse of the snake's head far down
within his throat. It is supposed that he succeeded; for the
attendants once heard a frenzied shout, and, rushing into the
room, found Roderick lifeless upon the floor.

He was kept but little longer under restraint. After minute
investigation, the medical directors of the asylum decided that
his mental disease did not amount to insanity, nor would
warrant his confinement, especially as its influence upon his
spirits was unfavorable, and might produce the evil which
it was meant to remedy. His eccentricities were doubtless
great; he had habitually violated many of the customs and
prejudices of society; but the world was not, without surer
ground, entitled to treat him as a madman. On this decision
of such competent authority Roderick was released, and had
returned to his native city the very day before his encounter
with George Herkimer.

As soon as possible after learning these particulars the
sculptor, together with a sad and tremulous companion,
sought Elliston at his own house. It was a large, sombre edifice
of wood, with pilasters and a balcony, and was divided from
one of the principal streets by a terrace of three elevations,
which was ascended by successive flights of stone steps. Some
immense old elms almost concealed the front of the mansion.
This spacious and once magnificent family residence was built
by a grandee of the race early in the past century, at which
epoch, land being of small comparative value, the garden and
other grounds had formed quite an extensive domain. Although a portion of the ancestral heritage had been alienated,
there was still a shadowy enclosure in the rear of the mansion
where a student, or a dreamer, or a man of stricken heart
might lie all day upon the grass, amid the solitude of murmuring boughs, and forget that a city had grown up around
him.

Into this retirement the sculptor and his companion were

ushered by Scipio, the old black servant, whose wrinkled visage grew almost sunny with intelligence and joy as he paid his humble greetings to one of the two visitors.

"Remain in the arbor," whispered the sculptor to the figure that leaned upon his arm. "You will know whether, and when, to make your appearance."

"God will teach me," was the reply. "May He support me too!"

Roderick was reclining on the margin of a fountain which gushed into the fleckered sunshine with the same clear sparkle and the same voice of airy quietude as when trees of primeval growth flung their shadows across its bosom. How strange is the life of a fountain!—born at every moment, yet of an age coeval with the rocks, and far surpassing the venerable antiquity of a forest.

"You are come! I have expected you," said Elliston, when he became aware of the sculptor's presence.

His manner was very different from that of the preceding day—quiet, courteous, and, as Herkimer thought, watchful both over his guest and himself. This unnatural restraint was almost the only trait that betokened anything amiss. He had just thrown a book upon the grass, where it lay half opened, thus disclosing itself to be a natural history of the serpent tribe, illustrated by lifelike plates. Near it lay that bulky volume, the Ductor Dubitantium of Jeremy Taylor, full of cases of conscience, and in which most men, possessed of a conscience, may find something applicable to their purpose.

"You see," observed Elliston, pointing to the book of serpents, while a smile gleamed upon his lips, "I am making an effort to become better acquainted with my bosom friend; but I find nothing satisfactory in this volume. If I mistake not, he will prove to be *sui generis,* and akin to no other reptile in creation."

"Whence came this strange calamity?" inquired the sculptor.

"My sable friend Scipio has a story," replied Roderick, "of a snake that had lurked in this fountain—pure and innocent as it looks—ever since it was known to the first settlers. This insinuating personage once crept into the vitals of my great grandfather and dwelt there many years, tormenting the old gentleman beyond mortal endurance. In short it is a family peculiarity. But, to tell you the truth, I have no faith in this idea of the snake's being an heirloom. He is my own snake, and no man's else."

"But what was his origin?" demanded Herkimer.

"Oh, there is poisonous stuff in any man's heart sufficient to generate a brood of serpents," said Elliston with a hollow laugh. "You should have heard my homilies to the good town's-people. Positively, I deem myself fortunate in having bred but a single serpent. You, however, have none in your bosom, and therefore cannot sympathize with the rest of the world. It gnaws me! It gnaws me!"

With this exclamation Roderick lost his self-control and threw himself upon the grass, testifying his agony by intricate writhings, in which Herkimer could not but fancy a resemblance to the motions of a snake. Then, likewise, was heard that frightful hiss, which often ran through the sufferer's speech, and crept between the words and syllables without interrupting their succession.

"This is awful indeed!" exclaimed the sculptor—"an awful infliction, whether it be actual or imaginary. Tell me, Roderick Elliston, is there any remedy for this loathsome evil?"

"Yes, but an impossible one," muttered Roderick, as he lay wallowing with his face in the grass. "Could I for one moment forget myself, the serpent might not abide within me. It is my diseased self-contemplation that has engendered and nourished him."

"Then forget yourself, my husband," said a gentle voice above him; "forget yourself in the idea of another!"

Rosina had emerged from the arbor, and was bending over him with the shadow of his anguish reflected in her countenance, yet so mingled with hope and unselfish love that all anguish seemed but an earthly shadow and a dream. She touched Roderick with her hand. A tremor shivered through his frame. At that moment, if report be trustworthy, the sculptor beheld a waving motion through the grass, and heard a tinkling sound, as if something had plunged into the fountain. Be the truth as it might, it is certain that Roderick Elliston sat up like a man renewed, restored to his right mind, and rescued from the fiend which had so miserably overcome him in the battle-field of his own breast.

"Rosina!" cried he, in broken and passionate tones, but with nothing of the wild wail that had haunted his voice so long, "forgive! forgive!"

Her happy tears bedewed his face.

"The punishment has been severe," observed the sculptor. "Even Justice might now forgive; how much more a woman's tenderness! Roderick Elliston, whether the serpent was a physical reptile, or whether the morbidness of your nature suggested that symbol to your fancy, the moral of the story is not the less true and strong. A tremendous Egotism, manifesting itself in your case in the form of jealousy, is as fearful a fiend as ever stole into the human heart. Can a breast, where it has dwelt so long, be purified?"

"Oh yes," said Rosina with a heavenly smile. "The serpent was but a dark fantasy, and what it typified was as shadowy as itself. The past, dismal as it seems, shall fling no gloom upon the future. To give it its due importance we must think of it but as an anecdote in our Eternity."

THE
BIRTHMARK

In the latter part of the last century there lived a man of science, an eminent proficient in every branch of natural philosophy, who not long before our story opens had made experience of a spiritual affinity more attractive than any chemical one. He had left his laboratory to the care of an assistant, cleared his fine countenance from the furnace smoke, washed the stain of acids from his fingers, and persuaded a beautiful woman to become his wife. In those days when the comparatively recent discovery of electricity and other kindred mysteries of Nature seemed to open paths into the region of miracle, it was not unusual for the love of science to rival the love of woman in its depth and absorbing energy. The higher intellect, the imagination, the spirit, and even the heart might all find their congenial aliment in pursuits which, as some of their ardent votaries believed, would ascend from one step of powerful intelligence to another, until the philosopher should lay his hand on the secret of creative force and perhaps make new worlds for himself. We know not whether Aylmer possessed this degree of faith in man's ultimate control over Nature. He had devoted himself, however, too unreservedly to scientific studies ever to be weaned from them by any second passion. His love for his young wife might prove the stronger of the two; but it could

First published in *The Pioneer*, March, 1843.

264

mostly religious terms.

only be by intertwining itself with his love of science, and uniting the strength of the latter to his own.

Such a union accordingly took place, and was attended with truly remarkable consequences and a deeply impressive moral. One day, very soon after their marriage, Aylmer sat gazing at his wife with a trouble in his countenance that grew stronger until he spoke.

"Georgiana," said he, "has it never occurred to you that the mark upon your cheek might be removed?"

"No, indeed," said she, smiling; but perceiving the seriousness of his manner, she blushed deeply. "To tell you the truth it has been so often called a charm that I was simple enough to imagine it might be so."

"Ah, upon another face perhaps it might," replied her husband; "but never on yours. No, dearest Georgiana, you came so nearly perfect from the hand of Nature that this slightest possible defect, which we hesitate whether to term a defect or a beauty, shocks me, as being the visible mark of earthly imperfection."

"Shocks you, my husband!" cried Georgiana, deeply hurt; at first reddening with momentary anger, but then bursting into tears. "Then why did you take me from my mother's side? You cannot love what shocks you!"

To explain this conversation it must be mentioned that in the centre of Georgiana's left cheek there was a singular mark, deeply interwoven, as it were, with the texture and substance of her face. In the usual state of her complexion—a healthy though delicate bloom—the mark wore a tint of deeper crimson, which imperfectly defined its shape amid the surrounding rosiness. When she blushed it gradually became more indistinct, and finally vanished amid the triumphant rush of blood that bathed the whole cheek with its brilliant glow. But if any shifting motion caused her to turn pale there was the mark again, a crimson stain upon the snow, in what Aylmer sometimes deemed an almost fearful distinctness. Its shape bore not a little similarity to the human hand, though of the smallest pygmy size. Georgiana's lovers were wont to say that some fairy at her birth hour had laid her tiny hand upon the infant's cheek, and left this impress there in token of the magic endowments that were to give her such sway over all hearts. Many a desperate swain would have risked life for the privilege of pressing his lips to the mysterious hand. It must not be concealed, however, that the impression wrought by this fairy sign manual varied exceedingly, according to the difference of temperament in the beholders. Some fastidious persons—but they were exclusively of her own sex—affirmed that the bloody hand, as they chose to call it, quite destroyed the effect of Georgiana's beauty, and rendered her countenance even hideous. But it would be as reasonable to say that one of those small blue stains which sometimes occur in the purest statuary marble would convert the Eve of Powers to a monster. Masculine observers, if the birthmark did not heighten their admiration, contented themselves with wishing it away, that the world might possess one living specimen of ideal loveliness without the semblance of a flaw. After his marriage,—for he thought little or nothing of the matter before,—Aylmer discovered that this was the case with himself.

Had she been less beautiful,—if Envy's self could have found aught else to sneer at,—he might have felt his affection heightened by the prettiness of this mimic hand, now vaguely portrayed, now lost, now stealing forth again and glimmering to and fro with every pulse of emotion that throbbed within her heart; but seeing her otherwise so perfect, he found this one defect grow more and more intolerable with every moment of their united lives. It was the fatal flaw of humanity which Nature, in one shape or another, stamps ineffaceably on all her productions, either to imply that they are temporary and finite, or that their perfection must be wrought by toil and pain. The crimson hand expressed the ineludible gripe in which mortality clutches the highest and purest of earthly mould, degrading them into kindred with the lowest, and even with the very brutes, like whom their visible frames return to dust. In this manner, selecting it as the symbol of his wife's liability to sin, sorrow, decay, and death, Aylmer's sombre imagination was not long in rendering the birthmark a frightful object, causing him more trouble and horror than ever Georgiana's beauty, whether of soul or sense, had given him delight.

At all the seasons which should have been their happiest, he invariably and without intending it, nay, in spite of a purpose to the contrary, reverted to this one disastrous topic. Trifling as it at first appeared, it so connected itself with innumerable trains of thought and modes of feeling that it became the central point of all. With the morning twilight Aylmer opened his eyes upon his wife's face and recognized the symbol of imperfection; and when they sat together at the evening hearth his eyes wandered stealthily to her cheek, and beheld, flickering with the blaze of the wood fire, the spectral hand that wrote mortality where he would fain have worshipped. Georgiana soon learned to shudder at his gaze. It needed but a glance with the peculiar expression that his face often wore to change the roses of her cheek into a deathlike paleness, amid which the crimson hand was brought strongly out, like a bas-relief of ruby on the whitest marble.

Late one night when the lights were growing dim, so as hardly to betray the stain on the poor wife's cheek, she herself, for the first time, voluntarily took up the subject.

"Do you remember, my dear Aylmer," said she, with a feeble attempt at a smile, "have you any recollection of a dream last night about this odious hand?"

"None! none whatever!" replied Aylmer, starting; but then he added, in a dry, cold tone, affected for the sake of concealing the real depth of his emotion, "I might well dream of it; for before I fell asleep it had taken a pretty firm hold of my fancy."

"And you did dream of it?" continued Georgiana, hastily; for she dreaded lest a gush of tears should interrupt what she had to say. "A terrible dream! I wonder that you can forget it. Is it possible to forget this one expression?—'It is in her heart now; we must have it out!' Reflect, my husband; for by all means I would have you recall that dream."

The mind is in a sad state when Sleep, the all-involving,

cannot confine her spectres within the dim region of her sway, but suffers them to break forth, affrighting this actual life with secrets that perchance belong to a deeper one. Aylmer now remembered his dream. He had fancied himself with his servant Aminadab, attempting an operation for the removal of the birthmark; but the deeper went the knife, the deeper sank the hand, until at length its tiny grasp appeared to have caught hold of Georgiana's heart; whence, however, her husband was inexorably resolved to cut or wrench it away.

When the dream had shaped itself perfectly in his memory, Aylmer sat in his wife's presence with a guilty feeling. Truth often finds its way to the mind close muffled in robes of sleep, and then speaks with uncompromising directness of matters in regard to which we practice an unconscious self-deception during our waking moments. Until now he had not been aware of the tyrannizing influence acquired by one idea over his mind, and of the lengths which he might find in his heart to go for the sake of giving himself peace.

"Aylmer," resumed Georgiana, solemnly, "I know not what may be the cost to both of us to rid me of this fatal birthmark. Perhaps its removal may cause cureless deformity; or it may be the stain goes as deep as life itself. Again: do we know that there is a possibility, on any terms, of unclasping the firm gripe of this little hand which was laid upon me before I came into the world?"

"Dearest Georgiana, I have spent much thought upon the subject," hastily interrupted Aylmer. "I am convinced of the perfect practicability of its removal."

"If there be the remotest possibility of it," continued Georgiana, "let the attempt be made at whatever risk. Danger is nothing to me; for life, while this hateful mark makes me the object of your horror and disgust,—life is a burden which I would fling down with joy. Either remove this dreadful hand, or take my wretched life! You have deep science. All the world bears witness of it. You have achieved great wonders. Cannot you remove this little, little mark, which I cover with the tips of two small fingers? Is this beyond your power, for the sake of your own peace, and to save your poor wife from madness?"

"Noblest, dearest, tenderest wife," cried Aylmer, rapturously, "doubt not my power. I have already given this matter the deepest thought—thought which might almost have enlightened me to create a being less perfect than yourself. Georgiana, you have led deeper than ever into the heart of science. I feel myself fully competent to render this dear cheek as faultless as its fellow; and then, most beloved, what will be my triumph when I shall have corrected what Nature left imperfect in her fairest work! Even Pygmalion, when his sculptured woman assumed life, felt not greater ecstasy than mine will be."

"Is it resolved, then," said Georgiana, faintly smiling. "And, Aylmer, spare me not, though you should find the birthmark take refuge in my heart at last."

Her husband tenderly kissed her cheek—her right cheek— not that which bore the impress of the crimson hand.

The next day Aylmer apprised his wife of a plan that he had formed whereby he might have opportunity for the intense thought and constant watchfulness which the proposed operation would require; while Georgiana, likewise, would enjoy the perfect repose essential to its success. They were to seclude themselves in the extensive apartments occupied by Aylmer as a laboratory, and where, during his toilsome youth, he had made discoveries in the elemental powers of Nature that had roused the admiration of all the learned societies in Europe. Seated calmly in this laboratory, the pale philosopher had investigated the secrets of the highest cloud region and of the profoundest mines; he had satisfied himself of the causes that kindled and kept alive the fires of the volcano; and had explained the mystery of the fountains, and how it is that they gush forth, some so bright and pure, and others with such rich medicinal virtues, from the dark bosom of the earth. Here, too, at an earlier period, he had studied the wonders of the human frame, and attempted to fathom the very process by which Nature assimilates all her precious influences from earth and air, and from the spiritual world, to create and foster man, her masterpiece. The latter pursuit, however, Aylmer had long laid aside in unwilling recognition of the truth—against which all seekers sooner or later stumble—that our great creative Mother, while she amuses us with apparently working in the broadest sunshine, is yet severely careful to keep her own secrets, and, in spite of her pretended openness, shows us nothing but results. She permits us, indeed, to mar, but seldom to mend, and, like a jealous patentee, on no account to make. Now, however, Aylmer resumed these half-forgotten investigations; not, of course, with such hopes or wishes as first suggested them; but because they involved much physiological truth and lay in the path of his proposed scheme for the treatment of Georgiana.

As he led her over the threshold of the laboratory, Georgiana was cold and tremulous. Aylmer looked cheerfully into her face, with intent to reassure her, but was so startled with the intense glow of the birthmark upon the whiteness of her cheek that he could not restrain a strong convulsive shudder. His wife fainted.

"Aminadab! Aminadab!" shouted Aylmer, stamping violently on the floor.

Forthwith there issued from an inner apartment a man of low stature, but bulky frame, with shaggy hair hanging about his visage, which was grimed with the vapors of the furnace. This personage had been Aylmer's underworker during his whole scientific career, and was admirably fitted for that office by his great mechanical readiness, and the skill with which, while incapable of comprehending a single principle, he executed all the details of his master's experiments. With his vast strength, his shaggy hair, his smoky aspect, and the indescribable earthiness that incrusted him, he seemed to represent man's physical nature; while Aylmer's slender figure, and pale, intellectual face, were no less apt a type of the spiritual element.

"Throw open the door of the boudoir, Aminadab," said Aylmer, "and burn a pastil."

"Yes, master," answered Aminadab, looking intently at the lifeless form of Georgiana; and then he muttered to himself, "If she were my wife, I'd never part with that birthmark."

When Georgiana recovered consciousness she found herself breathing an atmosphere of penetrating fragrance, the gentle potency of which had recalled her from her deathlike faintness. The scene around her looked like enchantment. Aylmer had converted those smoky, dingy, sombre rooms, where he had spent his brightest years in recondite pursuits, into a series of beautiful apartments not unfit to be the secluded abode of a lovely woman. The walls were hung with gorgeous curtains, which imparted the combination of grandeur and grace that no other species of adornment can achieve; and as they fell from the ceiling to the floor, their rich and ponderous folds, concealing all angles and straight lines, appeared to shut in the scene from infinite space. For aught Georgiana knew, it might be a pavilion among the clouds. And Aylmer, excluding the sunshine, which would have interfered with his chemical processes, had supplied its place with perfumed lamps, emitting flames of various hue, but all uniting a soft, impurpled radiance. He now knelt by his wife's side, watching her earnestly, but without alarm; for he was confident in his science, and felt that he could draw a magic circle round her within which no evil might intrude.

"Where am I? Ah, I remember," said Georgiana, faintly; and she placed her hand over her cheek to hide the terrible mark from her husband's eyes.

"Fear not, dearest!" exclaimed he. "Do not shrink from me! Believe me, Georgiana, I even rejoice in this single imperfection, since it will be such a rapture to remove it."

"Oh, spare me!" sadly replied his wife. "Pray do not look at it again. I never can forget that convulsive shudder."

In order to soothe Georgiana, and, as it were, to release her mind from the burden of actual things, Aylmer now put in practice some of the light and playful secrets which science had taught him among its profounder lore. Airy figures, absolutely bodiless ideas, and forms of unsubstantial beauty came and danced before her, imprinting their momentary footsteps on beams of light. Though she had some indistinct idea of the method of these optical phenomena, still the illusion was almost perfect enough to warrant the belief that her husband possessed sway over the spiritual world. Then again, when she felt a wish to look forth from her seclusion, immediately, as if her thoughts were answered, the procession of external existence flitted across a screen. The scenery and the figures of actual life were perfectly represented, but with that bewitching, yet indescribable difference which always makes a picture, an image, or a shadow so much more attractive than the original. When wearied of this Aylmer bade her cast her eyes upon a vessel containing a quantity of earth. She did so, with little interest at first; but was soon startled to perceive the germ of a plant shooting upward from the soil. Then came the slender stalk; the leaves gradually unfolded themselves; and amid them was a perfect and lovely flower.

"It is magical!" cried Georgiana. "I dare not touch it."

"Nay, pluck it," answered Aylmer,—"pluck it, and inhale its brief perfume while you may. The flower will wither in a few moments and leave nothing save its brown seed vessels; but thence may be perpetuated a race as ephemeral as itself."

But Georgiana had no sooner touched the flower than the whole plant suffered a blight, its leaves turning coal-black as if by the agency of fire.

"There was too powerful a stimulus," said Aylmer, thoughtfully.

To make up for this abortive experiment, he proposed to take her portrait by a scientific process of his own invention. It was to be effected by rays of light striking upon a polished plate of metal. Georgiana assented; but, on looking at the result, was affrighted to find the features of the portrait blurred and indefinable; while the minute figure of a hand appeared where the cheek should have been. Aylmer snatched the metallic plate and threw it into a jar of corrosive acid.

Soon, however, he forgot these mortifying failures. In the intervals of study and chemical experiment he came to her flushed and exhausted, but seemed invigorated by her presence, and spoke in glowing language of the resources of his art. He gave a history of the long dynasty of the alchemists, who spent so many ages in quest of the universal solvent by which the golden principle might be elicited from all things vile and base. Aylmer appeared to believe that, by the plainest scientific logic, it was altogether within the limits of possibility to discover this long-sought medium; "but," he added, "a philosopher who should go deep enough to acquire the power would attain too lofty a wisdom to stoop to the exercise of it." Not less singular were his opinions in regard to the elixir vitæ. He more than intimated that it was at his option to concoct a liquid that should prolong life for years, perhaps interminably; but that it would produce a discord in Nature which all the world, and chiefly the quaffer of the immortal nostrum, would find cause to curse.

"Aylmer, are you in earnest?" asked Georgiana, looking at him with amazement and fear. "It is terrible to possess such power, or even to dream of possessing it."

"Oh, do not tremble, my love," said her husband. "I would not wrong either you or myself by working such inharmonious effects upon our lives; but I would have you consider how trifling, in comparison, is the skill requisite to remove this little hand."

At the mention of the birthmark, Georgiana, as usual, shrank as if a redhot iron had touched her cheek.

Again Aylmer applied himself to his labors. She could hear his voice in the distant furnace room giving directions to Aminadab, whose harsh, uncouth, misshapen tones were audible in response, more like the grunt or growl of a brute than human speech. After hours of absence, Aylmer reappeared and proposed that she should now examine his cabinet of chemical products and natural treasures of the earth. Among the former he showed her a small vial, in which, he remarked, was contained a gentle yet most powerful fragrance, capable of impregnating all the breezes that blow across a kingdom. They were of inestimable value, the contents of that little vial; and, as he said so, he threw some of the perfume into the air and filled the room with piercing and invigorating delight.

"And what is this?" asked Georgiana, pointing to a small crystal globe containing a gold-colored liquid. "It is so beautiful to the eye that I could imagine it the elixir of life."

"In one sense it is," replied Aylmer; "or, rather, the elixir of immortality. It is the most precious poison that ever was concocted in this world. By its aid I could apportion the lifetime of any mortal of whom you might point your finger. The strength of the dose would determine whether he were to linger out years, or drop dead in the midst of a breath. No king on his guarded throne could keep his life if I, in my private station, should deem that the welfare of millions justified me in depriving him of it."

"Why do you keep such a terrific drug?" inquired Georgiana in horror.

"Do not mistrust me, dearest," said her husband, smiling; "its virtuous potency is yet greater than its harmful one. But see! here is a powerful cosmetic. With a few drops of this in a vase of water, freckles may be washed away as easily as the hands are cleansed. A stronger infusion would take the blood out of the cheek, and leave the rosiest beauty a pale ghost."

"Is it with this lotion that you intend to bathe my cheek?" asked Georgiana, anxiously.

"Oh, no," hastily replied her husband; "this is merely superficial. Your case demands a remedy that shall go deeper."

In his interviews with Georgiana, Aylmer generally made minute inquiries as to her sensations and whether the confinement of the rooms and the temperature of the atmosphere agreed with her. These questions had such a particular drift that Georgiana began to conjecture that she was already subjected to certain physical influences, either breathed in with the fragrant air or taken with her food. She fancied likewise, but it might be altogether fancy, that there was a stirring up of her system—a strange, indefinite sensation creeping through her veins, and tingling, half painfully, half pleasurably, at her heart. Still, whenever she dared to look into the mirror, there she beheld herself pale as a white rose and with the crimson birthmark stamped upon her cheek. Not even Aylmer now hated it so much as she.

To dispel the tedium of the hours which her husband found it necessary to devote to the processes of combination and analysis, Georgiana turned over the volumes of his scientific library. In many dark old tomes she met with chapters full of romance and poetry. They were the works of philosophers of the middle ages, such as Albertus Magnus, Cornelius Agrippa, Paracelsus, and the famous friar who created the prophetic Brazen Head. All these antique naturalists stood in advance of their centuries, yet were imbued with some of their credulity, and therefore were believed, and perhaps imagined themselves to have acquired from the investigation of Nature a power above Nature, and from physics a sway over the spiritual world. Hardly less curious and imaginative were the early volumes of the Transactions of the Royal Society, in which the members, knowing little of the limits of natural possibility, were continually recording wonders or proposing methods whereby wonders might be wrought.

But to Georgiana the most engrossing volume was a large folio from her husband's own hand, in which he had recorded every experiment of his scientific career, its original aim, the methods adopted for its development, and its final success or failure, with the circumstances to which either event was attributable. The book, in truth, was both the history and emblem of his ardent, ambitious, imaginative, yet practical and laborious life. He handled physical details as if there were nothing beyond them; yet spiritualized them all, and redeemed himself from materialism by his strong and eager aspiration towards the infinite. In his grasp the veriest clod of earth assumed a soul. Georgiana, as she read, reverenced Aylmer and loved him more profoundly than ever, but with a less entire dependence on his judgment than heretofore. Much as he had accomplished, she could not but observe that his most splendid successes were almost invariably failures, if compared with the ideal at which he aimed. His brightest diamonds were the merest pebbles, and felt to be so by himself, in comparison with the inestimable gems which lay hidden beyond his reach. The volume, rich with achievements that had won renown for its author, was yet as melancholy a record as ever mortal hand had penned. It was the sad confession and continual exemplification of the shortcomings of the composite man, the spirit burdened with clay and working in matter, and of the despair that assails the higher nature at finding itself so miserably thwarted by the earthly part. Perhaps every man of genius in whatever sphere might recognize the image of his own experience in Aylmer's journal.

So deeply did these reflections affect Georgiana that she laid her face upon the open volume and burst into tears. In this situation she was found by her husband.

"It is dangerous to read in a sorcerer's books," said he with a smile, though his countenance was uneasy and displeased. "Georgiana, there are pages in that volume which I can scarcely glance over and keep my senses. Take heed lest it prove as detrimental to you."

"It has made me worship you more than ever," said she.

"Ah, wait for this one success," rejoined he, "then worship me if you will. I shall deem myself hardly unworthy of it. But come, I have sought you for the luxury of your voice. Sing to me, dearest."

So she poured out the liquid music of her voice to quench the thirst of his spirit. He then took his leave with a boyish exuberance of gayety, assuring her that her seclusion would endure but a little longer, and that the result was already certain. Scarcely had he departed when Georgiana felt irresistibly impelled to follow him. She had forgotten to inform Aylmer of a symptom which for two or three hours past had begun to excite her attention. It was a sensation in the fatal birthmark, not painful, but which induced a restlessness throughout her system. Hastening after her husband, she intruded for the first time into the laboratory.

The first thing that struck her eye was the furnace, that hot and feverish worker, with the intense glow of its fire, which by the quantities of soot clustered above it seemed to have been burning for ages. There was a distilling apparatus in full operation. Around the room were retorts, tubes, cylinders, crucibles, and other apparatus of chemical research. An electrical machine stood ready for immediate use. The atmosphere felt oppressively close, and was tainted with gaseous odors which had been tormented forth by the processes of science. The severe and homely simplicity of the apartment, with its naked walls and brick pavement, looked strange, accustomed as Georgiana had become to the fantastic elegance of her boudoir. But what chiefly, indeed almost solely, drew her attention, was the aspect of Aylmer himself.

He was pale as death, anxious and absorbed, and hung over the furnace as if it depended upon his utmost watchfulness whether the liquid which it was distilling should be the draught of immortal happiness or misery. How different from the sanguine and joyous mien that he had assumed for Georgiana's encouragement!

"Carefully now, Aminadab; carefully, thou human machine; carefully, thou man of clay!" muttered Aylmer, more to himself than his assistant. "Now if there be a thought too much or too little, it is all over."

"Ho! ho!" mumbled Aminadab. "Look, master! look!"

Aylmer raised his eyes hastily, and at first reddened, then grew paler than ever, on beholding Georgiana. He rushed towards her and seized her arm with a gripe that left the print of his fingers upon it.

"Why do you come hither? Have you no trust in your husband?" cried he, impetuously. "Would you throw the blight of that fatal birthmark over my labors? It is not well done. Go, prying woman, go!"

"Nay, Aylmer," said Georgiana with the firmness of which she possessed no stinted endowment, "it is not you that have a right to complain. You mistrust your wife; you have concealed the anxiety with which you watch the development of this experiment. Think not so unworthily of me, my husband. Tell me all the risk we run, and fear not that I shall shrink; for my share in it is far less than your own."

"No, no, Georgiana!" said Aylmer, impatiently; "it must not be."

"I submit," replied she calmly. "And, Aylmer, I shall quaff

whatever draught you bring me; but it will be on the same principle that would induce me to take a dose of poison if offered by your hand."

"My noble wife," said Aylmer, deeply moved, "I knew not the height and depth of your nature until now. Nothing shall be concealed. Know, then, that this crimson hand, superficial as it seems, has clutched its grasp into your being with a strength of which I had no previous conception. I have already administered agents powerful enough to do aught except to change your entire physical system. Only one thing remains to be tried. If that fail us we are ruined."

"Why did you hesitate to tell me this?" asked she.

"Because, Georgiana," said Aylmer, in a low voice, "there is danger."

"Danger? There is but one danger—that this horrible stigma shall be left upon my cheek!" cried Georgiana. "Remove it, remove it, whatever be the cost, or we shall both go mad!"

"Heaven knows your words are too true," said Aylmer, sadly. "And now, dearest, return to your boudoir. In a little while all will be tested."

He conducted her back and took leave of her with a solemn tenderness which spoke far more than his words how much was now at stake. After his departure, Georgiana became rapt in musings. She considered the character of Aylmer, and did it completer justice than at any previous moment. Her heart exulted, while it trembled, at his honorable love—so pure and lofty that it would accept nothing less than perfection nor miserably make itself contented with an earthlier nature than he had dreamed of. She felt how much more precious was such a sentiment than that meaner kind which would have borne with the imperfection for her sake, and have been guilty of treason to holy love by degrading its perfect idea to the level of the actual; and with her whole spirit she prayed that, for a single moment, she might satisfy his highest and deepest conception. Longer than one moment she well knew it could not be; for his spirit was ever on the march, ever ascending, and each instant required something that was beyond the scope of the instant before.

The sound of her husband's footsteps aroused her. He bore a crystal goblet containing a liquor colorless as water, but bright enough to be the draught of immortality. Aylmer was pale; but it seemed rather the consequence of a highly-wrought state of mind and tension of spirit than of fear or doubt.

"The concoction of the draught has been perfect," said he, in answer to Georgiana's look. "Unless all my science have deceived me, it cannot fail."

"Save on your account, my dearest Aylmer," observed his wife, "I might wish to put off this birthmark of mortality by relinquishing mortality itself in preference to any other mode. Life is but a sad possession to those who have attained precisely the degree of moral advancement at which I stand. Were I weaker and blinder it might be happiness. Were I stronger, it might be endured hopefully. But being what I find myself, methinks I am of all mortals the most fit to die."

"You are fit for heaven without tasting death!" replied her husband. "But why do we speak of dying? The draught cannot fail. Behold its effect upon this plant."

On the window seat there stood a geranium diseased with yellow blotches, which had overspread all its leaves. Aylmer poured a small quantity of the liquid upon the soil in which it grew. In a little time, when the roots of the plant had taken up the moisture, the unsightly blotches began to be extinguished in a living verdure.

"There needed no proof," said Georgiana, quietly. "Give me the goblet. I joyfully stake all upon your word."

"Drink, then, thou lofty creature!" exclaimed Aylmer, with fervid admiration. "There is no taint of imperfection on thy spirit. Thy sensible frame, too, shall soon be all perfect."

She quaffed the liquid and returned the goblet to his hand.

"It is grateful," said she with a placid smile. "Methinks it is like water from a heavenly fountain; for it contains I know not what of unobtrusive fragrance and deliciousness. It allays a feverish thirst that had parched me for many days. Now, dearest, let me sleep. My earthly senses are closing over my spirit like the leaves around the heart of a rose at sunset."

She spoke the last words with a gentle reluctance, as if it

almost a communa

required almost more energy than she could command to pronounce the faint and lingering syllables. Scarcely had they loitered through her lips ere she was lost in slumber. Aylmer sat by her side, watching her aspect with the emotions proper to a man the whole value of whose existence was involved in the process now to be tested. Mingled with this mood, however, was the philosophic investigation characteristic of the man of science. Not the minutest symptom escaped him. A heightened flush of the cheek, a slight irregularity of breath, a quiver of the eyelid, a hardly perceptible tremor through the frame,—such were the details which, as the moments passed, he wrote down in his folio volume. Intense thought had set its stamp upon every previous page of that volume, but the thoughts of years were all concentrated upon the last.

While thus employed, he failed not to gaze often at the fatal hand, and not without a shudder. Yet once, by a strange and unaccountable impulse, he pressed it with his lips. His spirit recoiled, however, in the very act; and Georgiana, out of the midst of her deep sleep, moved uneasily and murmured as if in remonstrance. Again Aylmer resumed his watch. Nor was it without avail. The crimson hand, which at first had been strongly visible upon the marble paleness of Georgiana's cheek, now grew more faintly outlined. She remained not less pale than ever; but the birthmark, with every breath that came and went, lost somewhat of its former distinctness. Its presence had been awful; its departure was more awful still. Watch the stain of the rainbow fading out the sky, and you will know how that mysterious symbol passed away.

"By Heaven! it is well-nigh gone!" said Aylmer to himself, in almost irrepressible ecstasy. "I can scarcely trace it now. Success! success! And now it is like the faintest rose color. The lightest flush of blood across her cheek would overcome it. But she is so pale!"

He drew aside the window curtain and suffered the light of natural day to fall into the room and rest upon her cheek. At the same time he heard a gross, hoarse chuckle, which he had long known as his servant Aminadab's expression of delight.

"Ah, clod! ah, earthly mass!" cried Aylmer, laughing in a sort of frenzy, "you have served me well! Matter and spirit—earth and heaven—have both done their part in this! Laugh, thing of the senses! You have earned the right to laugh."

These exclamations broke Georgiana's sleep. She slowly unclosed her eyes and gazed into the mirror which her husband had arranged for that purpose. A faint smile flitted over her lips when she recognized how barely perceptible was now that crimson hand which had once blazed forth with such disastrous brilliancy as to scare away all their happiness. But then her eyes sought Aylmer's face with a trouble and anxiety that he could by no means account for.

"My poor Aylmer!" murmured she.

"Poor? Nay, richest, happiest, most favored!" exclaimed he. "My peerless bride, it is successful! You are perfect!"

"My poor Aylmer," she repeated, with a more than human tenderness, "you have aimed loftily; you have done nobly. Do not repent that with so high and pure a feeling, you have rejected the best the earth could offer. Aylmer, dearest Aylmer, I am dying!"

Alas! it was too true! the fatal hand had grappled with the mystery of life, and was the bond by which an angelic spirit kept itself in union with a mortal frame. As the last crimson tint of the birthmark—that sole token of human imperfection—faded from her cheek, the parting breath of the now perfect woman passed into the atmosphere, and her soul, lingering a moment near her husband, took its heavenward flight. Then a hoarse, chuckling laugh was heard again! Thus ever does the gross fatality of earth exult in its invariable triumph over the immortal essence which, in this dim sphere of half development, demands the completeness of a higher state. Yet, had Aylmer reached a profounder wisdom, he need not thus have flung away the happiness which would have woven his mortal life of the selfsame texture with the celestial. The momentary circumstance was too strong for him; he failed to look beyond the shadowy scope of time, and, living once for all in eternity, to find the perfect future in the present.

THE CHRISTMAS
BANQUET

[FROM THE UNPUBLISHED
"ALLEGORIES OF THE HEART"]

"I have here attempted," said Roderick, unfolding a few sheets of manuscript, as he sat with Rosina and the sculptor in the summer-house,—"I have attempted to seize hold of a personage who glides past me occasionally, in my walk through life. My former sad experience, as you know, has gifted me with some degree of insight into the gloomy mysteries of the human heart, through which I have wandered like one astray in a dark cavern, with his torch fast flickering to extinction. But this man, this class of men, is a hopeless puzzle."

"Well, but propound him," said the sculptor. "Let us have an idea of him, to begin with."

"Why, indeed," replied Roderick, "he is such a being as I could conceive you to carve out of marble, and some yet unrealized perfection of human science to endow with an exquisite mockery of intellect; but still there lacks the last inestimable touch of a divine Creator. He looks like a man; and, perchance, like a better specimen of man than you ordinarily meet. You might esteem him wise; he is capable of cultivation and refinement, and has at least an external conscience, but the demands that spirit makes upon spirit are precisely those

First published in *The Democratic Review*, January, 1844.

to which he cannot respond. When at last you come close to him you find him chill and unsubstantial—a mere vapor."

"I believe," said Rosina, "I have a glimmering idea of what you mean."

"Then be thankful," answered her husband smiling; "but do not anticipate any further illumination from what I am about to read. I have here imagined such a man to be—what, probably, he never is—conscious of the deficiency in his spiritual organization. Methinks the result would be a sense of cold unreality wherewith he would go shivering through the world, longing to exchange his load of ice for any burden of real grief that fate could fling upon a human being."

Contenting himself with this preface, Roderick began to read.

In a certain old gentleman's last will and testament there appeared a bequest, which, as his final thought and deed, was singularly in keeping with a long life of melancholy eccentricity. He devised a considerable sum for establishing a fund, the interest of which was to be expended, annually forever, in preparing a Christmas Banquet for ten of the most miserable persons that could be found. It seemed not to be the testator's purpose to make these half a score of sad hearts merry, but to provide that the stern or fierce expression of human discontent should not be drowned, even for that one holy and joyful day, amid the acclamations of festal gratitude which all Christendom sends up. And he desired, likewise, to perpetuate his own remonstrance against the earthly course of Providence, and his sad and sour dissent from those systems of religion or philosophy which either find sunshine in the world or draw it down from heaven.

The task of inviting the guests, or of selecting among such as might advance their claims to partake of this dismal hospitality, was confided to the two trustees or stewards of the fund. These gentlemen, like their deceased friend, were sombre humorists, who made it their principal occupation to

number the sable threads in the web of human life, and drop
all the golden ones out of the reckoning. They performed
their present office with integrity and judgment. The aspect
of the assembled company on the day of the first festival might
not, it is true, have satisfied every beholder that these were
especially the individuals, chosen forth from all the world,
whose griefs were worthy to stand as indicators of the mass
of human suffering. Yet, after due consideration, it could
not be disputed that here was a variety of hopeless discomfort, which, if it sometimes arose from causes apparently
inadequate, was thereby only the shrewder imputation against
the nature and mechanism of life.

The arrangements and decorations of the banquet were
probably intended to signify that death in life which had
been the testator's definition of existence. The hall, illuminated by torches, was hung round with curtains of deep and
dusky purple, and adorned with branches of cypress and
wreaths of artificial flowers imitative of such as used to be
strown over the dead. A sprig of parsley was laid by every
plate. The main reservoir of wine was a sepulchral urn of
silver, whence the liquor was distributed around the table
in small vases, accurately copied from those that held the tears
of ancient mourners. Neither had the stewards—if it were
their taste that arranged these details—forgotten the fantasy
of the old Egyptians, who seated a skeleton at every festive
board, and mocked their own merriment with the imperturbable grin of a death's head. Such a fearful guest, shrouded in
a black mantle, sat now at the head of the table. It was whispered, I know not with what truth, that the testator himself
had once walked the visible world with the machinery of that
same skeleton, and that it was one of the stipulations of his
will that he should thus be permitted to sit, from year to year,
at the banquet which he had instituted. If so, it was perhaps
covertly implied that he had cherished no hopes of bliss beyond the grave to compensate for the evils which he felt or
imagined here. And if, in their bewildered conjectures as to
the purpose of earthly existence, the banqueters should throw

aside the veil, and cast an inquiring glance at this figure of
death, as seeking thence the solution otherwise unattainable,
the only reply would be a stare of the vacant eye caverns and
a grin of the skeleton jaws. Such was the response that the
dead man had fancied himself to receive when he asked of
Death to solve the riddle of his life; and it was his desire to
repeat it when the guests of his dismal hospitality should find
themselves perplexed with the same question.

"What means that wreath?" asked several of the company,
while viewing the decorations of the table.

They alluded to a wreath of cypress which was held on high
by a skeleton arm, protruding from within the black mantle.

"It is a crown," said one of the stewards, "not for the
worthiest, but for the wofulest, when he shall prove his claim
to it."

The guest earliest bidden to the festival was a man of soft
and gentle character, who had not energy to struggle against
the heavy despondency to which his temperament rendered
him liable; and therefore with nothing outwardly to excuse
him from happiness, he had spent a life of quiet misery that
made his blood torpid, and weighed upon his breath, and sat
like a ponderous night fiend upon every throb of his unresist-
ing heart. His wretchedness seemed as deep as his original
nature, if not identical with it. It was the misfortune of a
second guest to cherish within his bosom a diseased heart,
which had become so wretchedly sore that the continual and
unavoidable rubs of the world, the blow of an enemy, the
careless jostle of a stranger, and even the faithful and loving
touch of a friend, alike made ulcers in it. As is the habit of
people thus afflicted, he found his chief employment in exhibiting these miserable sores to any who would give themselves the pain of viewing them. A third guest was a hypochondriac, whose imagination wrought necromancy in its
outward and inward world, and caused him to see monstrous
faces in the household fire, and dragons in the clouds of sunset, and fiends in the guise of beautiful women, and something ugly or wicked beneath all the pleasant surfaces of

nature. His neighbor at table was one who, in his early youth, had trusted mankind too much, and hoped too highly in their behalf, and, in meeting with many disappointments, had become desperately soured. For several years back this misanthrope had employed himself in accumulating motives for hating and despising his race—such as murder, lust, treachery, ingratitude, faithlessness of trusted friends, instinctive vices of children, impurity of women, hidden guilt in men of saintlike aspect—and, in short, all manner of black realities that sought to decorate themselves with outward grace or glory. But at every atrocious fact that was added to his catalogue, at every increase of the sad knowledge which he spent his life to collect, the native impulses of the poor man's loving and confiding heart made him groan with anguish. Next, with his heavy brow bent downward, there stole into the hall a man naturally earnest and impassioned, who, from his immemorial infancy, had felt the consciousness of a high message to the world; but, essaying to deliver it, had found either no voice or form of speech, or else no ears to listen. Therefore his whole life was a bitter questioning of himself—"Why have not men acknowledged my mission? Am I not a self-deluding fool? What business have I on earth? Where is my grave?" Throughout the festival, he quaffed frequent draughts from the sepulchral urn of wine, hoping thus to quench the celestial fire that tortured his own breast and could not benefit his race.

Then there entered, having flung away a ticket for a ball, a gay gallant of yesterday, who had found four or five wrinkles in his brow, and more gray hairs than he could well number on his head. Endowed with sense and feeling, he had nevertheless spent his youth in folly, but had reached at last that dreary point in life where Folly quits us of her own accord, leaving us to make friends with Wisdom if we can. Thus, cold and desolate, he had come to seek Wisdom at the banquet, and wondered if the skeleton were she. To eke out the company, the stewards had invited a distressed poet from his home in the almshouse, and a melancholy idiot from the street corner. The latter had just the glimmering of sense that was sufficient to make him conscious of a vacancy, which the poor fellow, all his life long, had mistily sought to fill up with intelligence, wandering up and down the streets, and groaning miserably because his attempts were ineffectual. The only lady in the hall was one who had fallen short of absolute and perfect beauty, merely by the trifling defect of a slight cast in her left eye. But this blemish, minute as it was, so shocked the pure ideal of her soul, rather than her vanity, that she passed her life in solitude, and veiled her countenance even from her own gaze. So the skeleton sat shrouded at one end of the table and this poor lady at the other.

One other guest remains to be described. He was a young man of smooth brow, fair cheek, and fashionable mien. So far as his exterior developed him, he might much more suitably have found a place at some merry Christmas table, than have been numbered among the blighted, fate-stricken, fancy-tortured set of ill-starred banqueters. Murmurs arose among the guests as they noted the glance of general scrutiny which the intruder threw over his companions. What had he to do among them? Why did not the skeleton of the dead founder of the feast unbend its rattling joints, arise, and motion the unwelcome stranger from the board?

"Shameful!" said the morbid man, while a new ulcer broke out in his heart. "He comes to mock us,—we shall be the jest of his tavern friends!—he will make a farce of our miseries, and bring it out upon the stage!"

"Oh, never mind him!" said the hypochondriac, smiling sourly. "He shall feast from yonder tureen of viper soup; and if there is a fricassee of scorpions on the table, pray let him have his share of it. For the dessert, he shall taste the apples of Sodom. Then, if he like our Christmas fare, let him return again next year!"

"Trouble him not," murmured the melancholy man, with gentleness. "What matters it whether the consciousness of misery come a few years sooner or later? If this youth deem himself happy now, yet let him sit with us for the sake of the wretchedness to come."

The poor idiot approached the young man with that

mournful aspect of vacant inquiry which his face continually
wore, and which caused people to say that he was always in
search of his missing wits. After no little examination he
touched the stranger's hand, but immediately drew back his
own, shaking his head and shivering.

"Cold, cold, cold!" muttered the idiot.

The young man shivered too, and smiled.

"Gentlemen,—and you, madam,"—said one of the stewards
of the festival, "do not conceive so ill either of our caution
or judgment as to imagine that we have admitted this young
stranger—Gervayse Hastings by name—without a full investigation and thoughtful balance of his claims. Trust me, not a
guest at the table is better entitled to his seat."

The steward's guaranty was perforce satisfactory. The company, therefore, took their places and addressed themselves
to the serious business of the feast, but were soon disturbed
by the hypochondriac, who thrust back his chair complaining
that a dish of stewed toads and vipers was set before him, and
that there was green ditch water in his cup of wine. This
mistake being amended, he quietly resumed his seat. The wine,
as it flowed freely from the sepulchral urn, seemed to come
imbued with all gloomy inspirations; so that its influence
was not to cheer, but either to sink the revellers into a deeper
melancholy or elevate their spirits to an enthusiasm of wretchedness. The conversation was various. They told sad stories
about people who might have been worthy guests at such a
festival as the present. They talked of grisly incidents in
human history; of strange crimes, which, if truly considered,
were but convulsions of agony; of some lives that had been
altogether wretched, and of others, which, wearing a general
semblance of happiness, had yet been deformed sooner or
later by misfortune, as by the intrusion of a grim face at a
banquet; of death-bed scenes, and what dark intimations
might be gathered from the words of dying men; of suicide,
and whether the more eligible mode were by halter, knife,
poison, drowning, gradual starvation, or the fumes of charcoal. The majority of the guests, as is the custom with people

thoroughly and profoundly sick at heart, were anxious to make their own woes the theme of discussion, and prove themselves most excellent in anguish. The misanthropist went deep into the philosophy of evil, and wandered about in the darkness, with now and then a gleam of discolored light hovering on ghastly shapes and horrid scenery. Many a miserable thought, such as men have stumbled upon from age to age, did he now rake up again, and gloat over it as an inestimable gem, a diamond, a treasure far preferable to those bright, spiritual revelations of a better world, which are like precious stones from heaven's pavement. And then, amid his lore of wretchedness, he hid his face and wept.

It was a festival at which the woful man of Uz might suitably have been a guest, together with all, in each succeeding age, who have tasted deepest of the bitterness of life. And be it said, too, that every son or daughter of woman, however favored with happy fortune, might, at one sad moment or another, have claimed the privilege of a stricken heart, to sit down at this table. But, throughout the feast, it was remarked that the young stranger, Gervayse Hastings, was unsuccessful in his attempts to catch its pervading spirit. At any deep, strong thought that found utterance, and which was torn out, as it were, from the saddest recesses of human consciousness, he looked mystified and bewildered; even more than the poor idiot, who seemed to grasp at such things with his earnest heart, and thus occasionally to comprehend them. The young man's conversation was of a colder and lighter kind, often brilliant, but lacking the powerful characteristics of a nature that had been developed by suffering.

"Sir," said the misanthropist, bluntly, in reply to some observation by Gervayse Hastings, "pray do not address me again. We have no right to talk together. Our minds have nothing in common. By what claim you appear at this banquet I cannot guess; but methinks, to a man who could say what you have just now said, my companions and myself must seem no more than shadows flickering on the wall. And precisely such a shadow are you to us."

The young man smiled and bowed, but drawing himself back in his chair, he buttoned his coat over his breast, as if the banqueting hall were growing chill. Again the idiot fixed his melancholy stare upon the youth and murmured, "Cold, cold, cold!"

The banquet drew to its conclusion, and the guests departed. Scarcely had they stepped across the threshold of the hall, when the scene that had there passed seemed like the vision of a sick fancy, or an exhalation from a stagnant heart. Now and then, however, during the year that ensued, these melancholy people caught glimpses of one another, transient, indeed, but enough to prove that they walked the earth with the ordinary allotment of reality. Sometimes a pair of them came face to face, while stealing through the evening twilight, enveloped in their sable cloaks. Sometimes they casually met in churchyards. Once, also, it happened that two of the dismal banqueters mutually started at recognizing each other in the noonday sunshine of a crowded street, stalking there like ghosts astray. Doubtless they wondered why the skeleton did not come abroad at noonday too.

But whenever the necessity of their affairs compelled these Christmas guests into the bustling world, they were sure to encounter the young man who had so unaccountably been admitted to the festival. They saw him among the gay and fortunate; they caught the sunny sparkle of his eye; they heard the light and careless tones of his voice, and muttered to themselves with such indignation as only the aristocracy of wretchedness could kindle—"The traitor! The vile impostor! Providence, in its own good time, may give him a right to feast among us!" But the young man's unabashed eye dwelt upon their gloomy figures as they passed him, seeming to say, perchance with somewhat of a sneer, "First know my secret!—then, measure your claims with mine!"

The step of Time stole onward, and soon brought merry Christmas round again, with glad and solemn worship in the churches, and sports, games, festivals, and everywhere the bright face of Joy beside the household fire. Again likewise the hall, with its curtains of dusky purple, was illuminated by the death torches gleaming on the sepulchral decorations of the banquet. The veiled skeleton sat in state, lifting the cypress wreath above its head, as the guerdon of some guest illustrious in the qualifications which there claimed precedence. As the stewards deemed the world inexhaustible in misery, and were desirous of recognizing it in all its forms, they had not seen fit to reassemble the company of the former year. New faces now threw their gloom across the table.

There was a man of nice conscience, who bore a blood stain in his heart—the death of a fellow-creature—which, for his more exquisite torture, had chanced with such a peculiarity of circumstances, that he could not absolutely determine whether his will had entered into the deed or not. Therefore, his whole life was spent in the agony of an inward trial for murder, with a continual sifting of the details of his terrible calamity, until his mind had no longer any thought, nor his soul any emotion, disconnected with it. There was a mother, too—a mother once, but a desolation now—who, many years before, had gone out on a pleasure party, and, returning, found her infant smothered in its little bed. And ever since she had been tortured with the fantasy that her buried baby lay smothering in its coffin. Then there was an aged lady, who had lived from time immemorial with a constant tremor quivering through her frame. It was terrible to discern her dark shadow tremulous upon the wall; her lips, likewise, were tremulous; and the expression of her eye seemed to indicate that her soul was trembling too. Owing to the bewilderment and confusion which made almost a chaos of her intellect, it was impossible to discover what dire misfortune had thus shaken her nature to its depths; so that the stewards had admitted her to the table, not from any acquaintance with her history, but on the safe testimony of her miserable aspect. Some surprise was expressed at the presence of a bluff, red-faced gentleman, a certain Mr. Smith, who had evidently the fat of many a rich feast within him, and the habitual twinkle of whose eye betrayed a disposition to break forth into up-

roarious laughter for little cause or none. It turned out, however, that with the best possible flow of spirits, our poor friend
was afflicted with a physical disease of the heart, which threatened instant death on the slightest cachinnatory indulgence,
or even that titillation of the bodily frame produced by merry
thoughts. In this dilemma he had sought admittance to the
banquet, on the ostensible plea of his irksome and miserable
state, but, in reality, with the hope of imbibing a life-preserv-
ing melancholy.

A married couple had been invited from a motive of bitter
humor, it being well understood that they rendered each
other unutterably miserable whenever they chanced to meet,
and therefore must necessarily be fit associates at the festival.
In contrast with these was another couple, still unmarried,
who had interchanged their hearts in early life, but had been
divided by circumstances as impalpable as morning mist, and
kept apart so long that their spirits now found it impossible
to meet. Therefore yearning for communion, yet shrinking
from one another and choosing none beside, they felt themselves companionless in life, and looked upon eternity as a
boundless desert. Next to the skeleton sat a mere son of
earth—a hunter of the Exchange—a gatherer of shining dust
—a man whose life's record was in his ledger, and whose soul's
prison house the vaults of the bank where he kept his deposits. This person had been greatly perplexed at his invitation, deeming himself one of the most fortunate men in the
city; but the stewards persisted in demanding his presence,
assuring him that he had no conception how miserable he was.

And now appeared a figure which we must acknowledge as
our acquaintance of the former festival. It was Gervayse
Hastings, whose presence had then caused so much question
and criticism, and who now took his place with the composure
of one whose claims were satisfactory to himself and must
needs be allowed by others. Yet his easy and unruffled face
betrayed no sorrow. The well-skilled beholders gazed a moment into his eyes and shook their heads, to miss the unuttered
sympathy—the countersign, never to be falsified—of those

whose hearts are cavern mouths, through which they descend into a region of illimitable woe and recognize other wanderers there.

"Who is this youth?" asked the man with a blood stain on his conscience. "Surely he has never gone down into the depths! I know all the aspects of those who have passed through the dark valley. By what right is he among us?"

"Ah, it is a sinful thing to come hither without a sorrow," murmured the aged lady, in accents that partook of the eternal tremor which pervaded her whole being. "Depart, young man! Your soul has never been shaken, and, therefore, I tremble so much the more to look at you."

"His soul shaken! No; I'll answer for it," said bluff Mr. Smith, pressing his hand upon his heart and making himself as melancholy as he could, for fear of a fatal explosion of laughter. "I know the lad well; he has as fair prospects as any young man about town, and has no more right among us miserable creatures than the child unborn. He never was miserable and probably never will be!"

"Our honored guests," interposed the stewards, "pray have patience with us, and believe, at least, that our deep veneration for the sacredness of this solemnity would preclude any wilful violation of it. Receive this young man to your table. It may not be too much to say that no guest here would exchange his own heart for the one that beats within that youthful bosom!"

"I'd call it a bargain, and gladly too," muttered Mr. Smith, with a perplexing mixture of sadness and mirthful conceit. "A plague upon their nonsense! My own heart is the only really miserable one in the company; it will certainly be the death of me at last!"

Nevertheless, as on the former occasion, the judgment of the stewards being without appeal, the company sat down. The obnoxious guest made no more attempt to obtrude his conversation on those about him, but appeared to listen to the table talk with peculiar assiduity, as if some inestimable secret, otherwise beyond his reach, might be conveyed in a casual word. And in truth, to those who could understand and value it, there was rich matter in the upgushings and outpourings of these initiated souls to whom sorrow had been a talisman, admitting them into spiritual depths which no other spell can open. Sometimes out of the midst of densest gloom there flashed a momentary radiance, pure as crystal, bright as the flame of stars, and shedding such a glow upon the mysteries of life that the guests were ready to exclaim, "Surely the riddle is on the point of being solved!" At such illuminated intervals the saddest mourners felt it to be revealed that mortal griefs are but shadowy and external; no more than the sable robes voluminously shrouding a certain divine reality, and thus indicating what might otherwise be altogether invisible to mortal eye.

"Just now," remarked the trembling old woman, "I seemed to see beyond the outside. And then my everlasting tremor passed away!"

"Would that I could dwell always in these momentary gleams of light!" said the man of stricken conscience. "Then the blood stain in my heart would be washed clean away."

This strain of conversation appeared so unintelligibly absurd to good Mr. Smith, that he burst into precisely the fit of laughter which his physicians had warned him against, as likely to prove instantaneously fatal. In effect, he fell back in his chair a corpse, with a broad grin upon his face, while his ghost, perchance, remained beside it bewildered at its unpremeditated exit. This catastrophe of course broke up the festival.

"How is this? You do not tremble?" observed the tremulous old woman to Gervayse Hastings, who was gazing at the dead man with singular intentness. "Is it not awful to see him so suddenly vanish out of the midst of life—this man of flesh and blood, whose earthly nature was so warm and strong? There is a never-ending tremor in my soul, but it trembles afresh at this! And you are calm!"

"Would that he could teach me somewhat!" said Gervayse Hastings, drawing a long breath. "Men pass before me like shadows on the wall; their actions, passions, feelings, are flickerings of the light, and then they vanish! Neither the corpse, nor yonder skeleton, nor this old woman's everlasting tremor, can give me what I seek."

And then the company departed.

We cannot linger to narrate, in such detail, more circumstances of these singular festivals, which, in accordance with the founder's will, continued to be kept with the regularity of an established institution. In process of time the stewards adopted the custom of inviting, from far and near, those individuals whose misfortunes were prominent above other men's, and whose mental and moral development might, therefore, be supposed to possess a corresponding interest. The exiled noble of the French Revolution, and the broken soldier of the Empire, were alike represented at the table. Fallen monarchs, wandering about the earth, have found places at that forlorn and miserable feast. The statesman, when his party flung him off, might, if he chose it, be once more a great man for the space of a single banquet. Aaron Burr's name appears on the record at a period when his ruin—the profoundest and most striking, with more of moral circumstance in it than that of almost any other man—was complete in his lonely age. Stephen Girard, when his wealth weighed upon him like a mountain, once sought admittance of his own accord. It is not probable, however, that these men had any lesson to teach in the lore of discontent and misery which might not equally well have been studied in the common walks of life. Illustrious unfortunates attract a wider sympathy, not because their griefs are more intense, but because, being set on lofty pedestals, they the better serve mankind as instances and by-words of calamity.

It concerns our present purpose to say that, at each successive festival, Gervayse Hastings showed his face, gradually changing from the smooth beauty of his youth to the thoughtful comeliness of manhood, and thence to the bald impressive dignity of age. He was the only individual invariably present. Yet on every occasion there were murmurs, both from those

who knew his character and position, and from them whose
hearts shrank back as denying his companionship in their
mystic fraternity.

"Who is this impassive man?" had been asked a hundred
times. "Has he suffered? Has he sinned? There are no traces
of either. Then wherefore is he here?"

"You must inquire of the stewards, or of himself," was the
constant reply. "We seem to know him well here in our city,
and know nothing of him but what is creditable and fortunate. Yet hither he comes, year after year, to this gloomy
banquet, and sits among the guests like a marble statue. Ask
yonder skeleton; perhaps that may solve the riddle."

It was in truth a wonder. The life of Gervayse Hastings was
not merely a prosperous, but a brilliant one. Everything had
gone well with him. He was wealthy, far beyond the expendi-
ture that was required by habits of magnificence, a taste of
rare purity and cultivation, a love of travel, a scholar's instinct to collect a splendid library, and, moreover, what seemed
a magnificent liberality to the distressed. He had sought happiness, and not vainly, if a lovely and tender wife and children of fair promise could insure it. He had, besides, ascended
above the limit which separates the obscure from the distinguished, and had won a stainless reputation in affairs of the
widest public importance. Not that he was a popular character, or had within him the mysterious attributes which are
essential to that species of success. To the public he was a
cold abstraction, wholly destitute of those rich hues of personality, that living warmth, and the peculiar faculty of stamping his own heart's impression on a multitude of hearts by
which the people recognize their favorites. And it must be
owned that, after his most intimate associates had done their
best to know him thoroughly and love him warmly, they were
startled to find how little hold he had upon their affections.
They approved, they admired, but still in those moments
when the human spirit most craves reality they shrank back
from Gervayse Hastings, as powerless to give them what they
sought. It was the feeling of distrustful regret with which we

should draw back the hand after extending it, in an illusive twilight, to grasp the hand of a shadow upon the wall.

As the superficial fervency of youth decayed, this peculiar effect of Gervayse Hastings's character grew more perceptible. His children, when he extended his arms, came coldly to his knees, but never climbed them of their own accord. His wife wept secretly, and almost adjudged herself a criminal, because she shivered in the chill of his bosom. He, too, occasionally appeared not unconscious of the chillness of his moral atmosphere, and willing, if it might be so, to warm himself at a kindly fire. But age stole onward and benumbed him more and more. As the hoarfrost began to gather on him his wife went to her grave, and was doubtless warmer there; his children either died or were scattered to different homes of their own; and old Gervayse Hastings, unscathed by grief—alone, but needing no companionship, continued his steady walk through life, and still on every Christmas day attended at the dismal banquet. His privilege as a guest had become prescriptive now. Had he claimed the head of the table, even the skeleton would have been ejected from its seat.

Finally, at the merry Christmas tide, when he had numbered fourscore years complete, this pale, high-browed, marble-featured old man once more entered the long-frequented hall, with the same impassive aspect that had called forth so much dissatisfied remark at his first attendance. Time, except in matters merely external, had done nothing for him, either of good or evil. As he took his place he threw a calm, inquiring glance around the table, as if to ascertain whether any guest had yet appeared, after so many unsuccessful banquets, who might impart to him the mystery—the deep, warm secret—the life within the life—which, whether manifested in joy or sorrow, is what gives substance to a world of shadows.

"My friends," said Gervayse Hastings, assuming a position which his long conversance with the festival caused to appear natural, "you are welcome! I drink to you all in this cup of sepulchral wine."

The guests replied courteously, but still in a manner that

proved them unable to receive the old man as a member of their sad fraternity. It may be well to give the reader an idea of the present company at the banquet.

One was formerly a clergyman, enthusiastic in his profession, and apparently of the genuine dynasty of those old Puritan divines whose faith in their calling, and stern exercise of it, had placed them among the mighty of the earth. But, yielding to the speculative tendency of the age, he had gone astray from the firm foundation of an ancient faith, and wandered into a cloud region, where everything was misty and deceptive, ever mocking him with a semblance of reality, but still dissolving when he flung himself upon it for support and rest. His instinct and early training demanded something steadfast; but, looking forward, he beheld vapors piled on vapors, and behind him an impassable gulf between the man of yesterday and to-day, on the borders of which he paced to and fro, sometimes wringing his hands in agony, and often making his own woe a theme of scornful merriment. This surely was a miserable man. Next there was a theorist—one of a numerous tribe, although he deemed himself unique since the creation—a theorist who had conceived a plan, by which all the wretchedness of earth, moral and physical, might be done away, and the bliss of the millennium at once accomplished. But, the incredulity of mankind debarring him from action, he was smitten with as much grief as if the whole mass of woe which he was denied the opportunity to remedy were crowded into his own bosom. A plain old man in black attracted much of the company's notice, on the supposition that he was no other than Father Miller, who, it seemed, had given himself up to despair at the tedious delay of the final conflagration. Then there was a man distinguished for native pride and obstinacy, who, a little while before, had possessed immense wealth, and held the control of a vast moneyed interest which he had wielded in the same spirit as a despotic monarch would wield the power of his empire, carrying on a tremendous moral warfare, the roar and tremor of which was felt at every fireside in the land. At length came a crushing ruin—a total overthrow of fortune, power, and character—

the effect of which on his imperious, and, in many respects, noble and lofty nature, might have entitled him to a place, not merely at our festival, but among the peers of Pandemonium.

There was a modern philanthropist, who had become so deeply sensible of the calamities of thousands and millions of his fellow-creatures, and of the impracticableness of any general measures for their relief, that he had no heart to do what little good lay immediately within his power, but contented himself with being miserable for sympathy. Near him sat a gentleman in a predicament hitherto unprecedented, but of which the present epoch probably affords numerous examples. Ever since he was of capacity to read a newspaper, this person had prided himself on his consistent adherence to one political party, but, in the confusion of these latter days, had got bewildered and knew not whereabouts his party was. This wretched condition, so morally desolate and disheartening to a man who has long accustomed himself to merge his individuality in the mass of a great body, can only be conceived by such as have experienced it. His next companion was a popular orator who had lost his voice, and—as it was pretty much all that he had to lose—had fallen into a state of hopeless melancholy. The table was likewise graced by two of the gentler sex: one, a half-starved, consumptive seamstress, the representative of thousands just as wretched; the other, a woman of unemployed energy, who found herself in the world with nothing to achieve, nothing to enjoy, and nothing even to suffer. She had, therefore, driven herself to the verge of madness by dark broodings over the wrongs of her sex, and its exclusion from a proper field of action. The roll of guests being thus complete, a side table had been set for three or four disappointed office seekers, with hearts as sick as death, whom the stewards had admitted partly because their calamities really entitled them to entrance here, and partly that they were in especial need of a good dinner. There was likewise a homeless dog, with his tail between his legs, licking up the crumbs and gnawing the fragments of the feast,—such a melancholy cur as one sometimes sees about the streets without a master, and willing to follow the first that will accept his service.

In their own way, these were as wretched a set of people as ever had assembled at the festival. There they sat, with the veiled skeleton of the founder holding aloft the cypress wreath at one end of the table, and at the other, wrapped in furs, the withered figure of Gervayse Hastings, stately, calm, and cold, impressing the company with awe, yet so little interesting their sympathy that he might have vanished into thin air without their once exclaiming, "Whither is he gone?"

"Sir," said the philanthropist, addressing the old man, "you have been so long a guest at this annual festival, and have thus been conversant with so many varieties of human afflic-tion, that, not improbably, you have thence derived some great and important lessons. How blessed were your lot could you reveal a secret by which all this mass of woe might be removed!"

"I know of but one misfortune," answered Gervayse Hast-ings, quietly, "and that is my own."

"Your own!" rejoined the philanthropist. "And looking back on your serene and prosperous life, how can you claim to be the sole unfortunate of the human race?"

"You will not understand it," replied Gervayse Hastings, feebly, and with a singular inefficiency of pronunciation, and sometimes putting one word for another. "None have under-stood it—not even those who experience the like. It is a chilliness—a want of earnestness—a feeling as if what should be my heart were a thing of vapor—a haunting perception of unreality! Thus seeming to possess all that other men have—all that men aim at—I have really possessed nothing, neither joy nor griefs. All things, all persons—as was truly said to me at this table long and long ago—have been like shadows flickering on the wall. It was so with my wife and children—with those who seemed my friends: it is so with yourselves, whom I see now before me. Neither have I myself any real existence, but am a shadow like the rest."

"And how is it with your views of a future life?" inquired the speculative clergyman.

"Worse than with you," said the old man, in a hollow and feeble tone; "for I cannot conceive it earnestly enough to feel either hope or fear. Mine—mine is the wretchedness! This cold heart—this unreal life! Ah! it grows colder still."

It so chanced that at this juncture the decayed ligaments of the skeleton gave way, and the dry bones fell together in a heap, thus causing the dusty wreath of cypress to drop upon the table. The attention of the company being thus diverted for a single instant from Gervayse Hastings, they perceived, on turning again towards him, that the old man had undergone a change. His shadow had ceased to flicker on the wall.

"Well, Rosina, what is your criticism?" asked Roderick as he rolled up the manuscript.

"Frankly, your success is by no means complete," replied she. "It is true, I have an idea of the character you endeavor to describe; but it is rather by dint of my own thought than your expression."

"That is unavoidable," observed the sculptor, "because the characteristics are all negative. If Gervayse Hastings could have imbibed one human grief at the gloomy banquet, the task of describing him would have been infinitely easier. Of such persons—and we do meet with these moral monsters now and then—it is difficult to conceive how they came to exist here, or what there is in them capable of existence hereafter. They seem to be on the outside of everything; and nothing wearies the soul more than an attempt to comprehend them within its grasp."

THE ARTIST
OF THE BEAUTIFUL

An elderly man, with his pretty daughter on his arm, was passing along the street, and emerged from the gloom of the cloudy evening into the light that fell across the pavement from the window of a small shop. It was a projecting window; and on the inside were suspended a variety of watches, pinchbeck, silver, and one or two of gold, all with their faces turned from the streets, as if churlishly disinclined to inform the wayfarers what o'clock it was. Seated within the shop, sidelong to the window, with his pale face bent earnestly over some delicate piece of mechanism on which was thrown the concentrated lustre of a shade lamp, appeared a young man.

"What can Owen Warland be about?" muttered old Peter Hovenden, himself a retired watchmaker, and the former master of this same young man whose occupation he was now wondering at. "What can the fellow be about? These six months past I have never come by his shop without seeing him just as steadily at work as now. It would be a flight beyond his usual foolery to seek for the perpetual motion; and yet I know enough of my old business to be certain that what he is now so busy with is no part of the machinery of a watch."

"Perhaps, father," said Annie, without showing much interest in the question, "Owen is inventing a new kind of timekeeper. I am sure he has ingenuity enough."

First published in *The Democratic Review*, June, 1844.

"Poh, child! He has not the sort of ingenuity to invent anything better than a Dutch toy," answered her father, who had formerly been put to much vexation by Owen Warland's irregular genius. "A plague on such ingenuity! All the effect that ever I knew of it was to spoil the accuracy of some of the best watches in my shop. He would turn the sun out of its orbit and derange the whole course of time, if, as I said before, his ingenuity could grasp anything bigger than a child's toy!"

"Hush, father! He hears you!" whispered Annie, pressing the old man's arm. "His ears are as delicate as his feelings; and you know how easily disturbed they are. Do let us move on."

So Peter Hovenden and his daughter Annie plodded on without further conversation, until in a by-street of the town they found themselves passing the open door of a blacksmith's shop. Within was seen the forge, now blazing up and illuminating the high and dusky roof, and now confining its lustre to a narrow precinct of the coal-strewn floor, according as the breath of the bellows was puffed forth or again inhaled into its vast leathern lungs. In the intervals of brightness it was easy to distinguish objects in remote corners of the shop and the horseshoes that hung upon the wall; in the momentary gloom the fire seemed to be glimmering amidst the vagueness of unenclosed space. Moving about in this red glare and alternate dusk was the figure of the blacksmith, well worthy to be viewed in so picturesque an aspect of light and shade, where the bright blaze struggled with the black night, as if each would have snatched his comely strength from the other. Anon he drew a white-hot bar of iron from the coals, laid it on the anvil, uplifted his arm of might, and was soon enveloped in the myriads of sparks which the strokes of his hammer scattered into the surrounding gloom.

"Now, that is a pleasant sight," said the old watchmaker. "I know what it is to work in gold; but give me the worker in iron after all is said and done. He spends his labor upon a reality. What say you, daughter Annie?"

"Pray don't speak so loud, father," whispered Annie, "Robert Danforth will hear you."

"And what if he should hear me?" said Peter Hovenden. "I say again, it is a good and a wholesome thing to depend upon main strength and reality, and to earn one's bread with the bare and brawny arm of a blacksmith. A watchmaker gets his brain puzzled by his wheels within a wheel, or loses his health or the nicety of his eyesight, as was my case, and finds himself at middle age, or a little after, past labor at his own trade and fit for nothing else, yet too poor to live at his ease. So I say once again, give me main strength for my money. And then, how it takes the nonsense out of a man! Did you ever hear of a blacksmith being such a fool as Owen Warland yonder?"

"Well said, uncle Hovenden!" shouted Robert Danforth from the forge, in a full, deep, merry voice, that made the roof reëcho. "And what says Miss Annie to that doctrine? She, I suppose, will think it a genteeler business to tinker up a lady's watch than to forge a horseshoe or make a gridiron."

Annie drew her father onward without giving him time for reply.

But we must return to Owen Warland's shop, and spend more meditation upon his history and character than either Peter Hovenden, or probably his daughter Annie, or Owen's old school-fellow, Robert Danforth, would have thought due to so slight a subject. From the time that his little fingers could grasp a pen-knife, Owen had been remarkable for a delicate ingenuity, which sometimes produced pretty shapes in wood, principally figures of flowers and birds, and sometimes seemed to aim at the hidden mysteries of mechanism. But it was always for purposes of grace, and never with any mockery of the useful. He did not, like the crowd of schoolboy artisans, construct little windmills on the angle of a barn or watermills across the neighboring brook. Those who discovered such peculiarity in the boy as to think it worth their while to observe him closely, sometimes saw reason to suppose that he was attempting to imitate the beautiful movements of Nature as exemplified in the flight of birds or the activity of little animals. It seemed, in fact, a new development of the love of the beautiful, such as might have made him a poet, a painter, or a sculptor, and which was as completely refined from all utilitarian coarseness as it could have been in either of the fine arts. He looked with singular distaste at the stiff and regular processes of ordinary machinery. Being once carried to see a steam-engine, in the expectation that his intuitive comprehension of mechanical principles would be gratified, he turned pale and grew sick, as if something monstrous and unnatural had been presented to him. This horror was partly owing to the size and terrible energy of the iron laborer; for the character of Owen's mind was microscopic, and tended naturally to the minute, in accordance with his diminutive frame and the marvellous smallness and delicate power of his fingers. Not that his sense of beauty was thereby diminished into a sense of prettiness. The beautiful idea has no relation to size, and may be as perfectly developed in a space too minute for any but microscopic investigation as within the ample verge that is measured by the arc of the rainbow. But, at all events, this characteristic minuteness in his objects and accomplishments made the world even more incapable than it might otherwise have been of appreciating Owen Warland's genius. The boy's relatives saw nothing better to be done—as perhaps there was not—than to bind him apprentice to a watchmaker, hoping that his strange ingenuity might thus be regulated and put to utilitarian purposes.

Peter Hovenden's opinion of his apprentice has already been expressed. He could make nothing of the lad. Owen's apprehension of the professional mysteries, it is true, was inconceivably quick; but he altogether forgot or despised the grand object of a watchmaker's business, and cared no more for the measurement of time than if it had been merged into eternity. So long, however, as he remained under his old master's care, Owen's lack of sturdiness made it possible, by strict injunctions and sharp oversight, to restrain his creative eccentricity within bounds; but when his apprenticeship was served out, and he had taken the little shop which Peter Hovenden's failing eyesight compelled him to relinquish, then did people recognize how unfit a person was Owen Warland to lead old blind Father Time along his daily course. One of his most rational projects was to connect a musical operation with the machinery of his watches, so that all the harsh dissonances of life might be rendered tuneful, and each flitting moment fall into the abyss of the past in golden drops of harmony. If a family clock was intrusted to him for repair, —one of those tall, ancient clocks that have grown nearly allied to human nature by measuring out the lifetime of many generations,—he would take upon himself to arrange a dance or funeral procession of figures across its venerable face, repre- senting twelve mirthful or melancholy hours. Several freaks of this kind quite destroyed the young watchmaker's credit with that steady and matter-of-fact class of people who hold the opinion that time is not to be trifled with, whether considered as the medium of advancement and prosperity in this world or preparation for the next. His custom rapidly diminished— a misfortune, however, that was probably reckoned among his better accidents by Owen Warland, who was becoming more and more absorbed in a secret occupation which drew all his science and manual dexterity into itself, and likewise gave full employment to the characteristic tendencies of his genius. This pursuit had already consumed many months.

After the old watchmaker and his pretty daughter had gazed at him out of the obscurity of the street, Owen Warland was seized with a fluttering of the nerves, which made his hand tremble too violently to proceed with such delicate labor as he was now engaged upon.

"It was Annie herself!" murmured he. "I should have known it, by this throbbing of my heart, before I heard her father's voice. Ah, how it throbs! I shall scarcely be able to work again on this exquisite mechanism to-night. Annie! dearest Annie! thou shouldst give firmness to my heart and hand, and not shake them thus; for if I strive to put the very spirit of beauty into form and give it motion, it is for thy sake alone. O throbbing heart, be quiet! If my labor be thus thwarted, there will come vague and unsatisfied dreams which will leave me spiritless to-morrow."

As he was endeavoring to settle himself again to his task, the shop door opened and gave admittance to no other than the stalwart figure which Peter Hovenden had paused to admire, as seen amid the light and shadow of the blacksmith's shop. Robert Danforth had brought a little anvil of his own manufacture, and peculiarly constructed, which the young artist had recently bespoken. Owen examined the article and pronounced it fashioned according to his wish.

"Why, yes," said Robert Danforth, his strong voice filling the shop as with the sound of a bass viol, "I consider myself equal to anything in the way of my own trade; though I should have made but a poor figure at yours with such a fist as this," added he, laughing, as he laid his vast hand beside the delicate one of Owen. "But what then? I put more main strength into one blow of my sledge hammer than all that you have expended since you were a 'prentice. Is not that the truth?"

"Very probably," answered the low and slender voice of Owen. "Strength is an earthly monster. I make no pretensions to it. My force, whatever there may be of it, is altogether spiritual."

"Well, but, Owen, what are you about?" asked his old school-fellow, still in such a hearty volume of tone that it made the artist shrink, especially as the question related to a subject so sacred as the absorbing dream of his imagination. "Folks do say that you are trying to discover the perpetual motion."

"The perpetual motion? Nonsense!" replied Owen Warland, with a movement of disgust; for he was full of little petulances. "It can never be discovered. It is a dream that may delude men whose brains are mystified with matter, but not me. Besides, if such a discovery were possible, it would not be worth my while to make it only to have the secret turned to such purposes as are now effected by steam and water power. I am not ambitious to be honored with the paternity of a new kind of cotton machine."

"That would be droll enough!" cried the blacksmith, breaking out into such an uproar of laughter that Owen himself and the bell glasses on his work-board quivered in unison. "No, no, Owen! No child of yours will have iron joints and sinews. Well, I won't hinder you any more. Good night, Owen, and success, and if you need any assistance, so far as a downright blow of hammer upon anvil will answer the purpose, I'm your man."

And with another laugh the man of main strength left the shop.

"How strange it is," whispered Owen Warland to himself, leaning his head upon his hand, "that all my musings, my purposes, my passion for the beautiful, my consciousness of power to create it,—a finer, more ethereal power, of which this earthly giant can have no conception,—all, all, look so vain and idle whenever my path is crossed by Robert Danforth! He would drive me mad were I to meet him often. His hard, brute force darkens and confuses the spiritual element within me; but I, too, will be strong in my own way. I will not yield to him."

He took from beneath a glass a piece of minute machinery, which he set in the condensed light of his lamp, and, looking intently at it through a magnifying glass, proceeded to operate with a delicate instrument of steel. In an instant, however, he fell back in his chair and clasped his hands, with a look of horror on his face that made its small features as impressive as those of a giant would have been.

"Heaven! What have I done?" exclaimed he. "The vapor, the influence of that brute force,—it has bewildered me and obscured my perception. I have made the very stroke—the fatal stroke—that I have dreaded from the first. It is all over —the toil of months, the object of my life. I am ruined!"

And there he sat, in strange despair, until his lamp flickered in the socket and left the Artist of the Beautiful in darkness.

Thus it is that ideas, which grow up within the imagination and appear so lovely to it and of a value beyond whatever men call valuable, are exposed to be shattered and annihilated by contact with the practical. It is requisite for the ideal artist to possess a force of character that seems hardly compatible with its delicacy; he must keep his faith in himself while the incredulous world assails him with its utter disbelief; he must stand up against mankind and be his own sole disciple, both as respects his genius and the objects to which it is directed.

For a time Owen Warland succumbed to this severe but inevitable test. He spent a few sluggish weeks with his head so continually resting in his hands that the towns-people had scarcely an opportunity to see his countenance. When at last it was again uplifted to the light of day, a cold, dull, nameless change was perceptible upon it. In the opinion of Peter Hovenden, however, and that order of sagacious understandings who think that life should be regulated, like clockwork, with leaden weights, the alteration was entirely for the better. Owen now, indeed, applied himself to business with dogged industry. It was marvellous to witness the obtuse gravity with which he would inspect the wheels of a great old silver watch; thereby delighting the owner, in whose fob it had been worn till he deemed it a portion of his own life, and was accordingly jealous of its treatment. In consequence of the good report thus acquired, Owen Warland was invited by the proper authorities to regulate the clock in the church steeple. He succeeded so admirably in this matter of public interest that the merchants gruffly acknowledged his merits on 'Change; the nurse whispered his praises as she gave the potion in the sick-chamber; the lover blessed him at the hour of appointed interview; and the town in general thanked Owen for the punctuality of dinner time. In a word, the heavy weight upon his spirits kept everything in order, not merely within his own system, but wheresoever the iron accents of the church clock were audible. It was a circumstance, though minute, yet characteristic of his present state, that, when employed to engrave names or initials on silver spoons, he now wrote the requisite letters in the plainest possible style, omitting a variety of fanciful flourishes that had heretofore distinguished his work in this kind.

One day, during the era of this happy transformation, old Peter Hovenden came to visit his former apprentice.

"Well, Owen," said he, "I am glad to hear such good accounts of you from all quarters, and especially from the town clock yonder, which speaks in your commendation every hour of the twenty-four. Only get rid altogether of your nonsensical trash about the beautiful, which I nor nobody else, nor yourself to boot, could ever understand,—only free yourself of that, and your success in life is as sure as daylight. Why, if you go on in this way, I should even venture to let you doctor this precious old watch of mine; though, except my daughter Annie, I have nothing else so valuable in the world."

"I should hardly dare touch it, sir," replied Owen, in a depressed tone; for he was weighed down by his old master's presence.

"In time," said the latter,—"in time, you will be capable of it."

The old watchmaker, with the freedom naturally consequent on his former authority, went on inspecting the work which Owen had in hand at the moment, together with other matters that were in progress. The artist, meanwhile, could scarcely lift his head. There was nothing so antipodal to his nature as this man's cold, unimaginative sagacity, by contact with which everything was converted into a dream except the densest matter of the physical world. Owen groaned in spirit and prayed fervently to be delivered from him.

"But what is this?" cried Peter Hovenden abruptly, taking up a dusty bell glass, beneath which appeared a mechanical something, as delicate and minute as the system of a butterfly's anatomy. "What have we here? Owen! Owen! there is witchcraft in these little chains, and wheels, and paddles. See! with one pinch of my finger and thumb I am going to deliver you from all future peril."

"For Heaven's sake," screamed Owen Warland, springing up with wonderful energy, "as you would not drive me mad, do not touch it. The slightest pressure of your finger would ruin me forever."

"Aha, young man! And is it so?" said the old watchmaker, looking at him with just enough penetration to torture Owen's soul with the bitterness of worldly criticism. "Well, take your own course; but I warn you again that in this small piece of mechanism lives your evil spirit. Shall I exorcise him?"

"You are my evil spirit," answered Owen, much excited,— "you and the hard, coarse world! The leaden thoughts and the despondency that you fling upon me are my clogs, else I should long ago have achieved the task that I was created for."

Peter Hovenden shook his head, with the mixture of contempt and indignation which mankind, of whom he was partly a representative, deem themselves entitled to feel towards all simpletons who seek other prizes than the dusty one along the highway. He then took his leave, with an uplifted finger and a sneer upon his face that haunted the artist's dreams for many a night afterwards. At the time of his old master's visit, Owen was probably on the point of taking up the relinquished task; but, by this sinister event, he was thrown back into the state whence he had been slowly emerging.

But the innate tendency of his soul had only been accumulating fresh vigor during its apparent sluggishness. As the summer advanced he almost totally relinquished his business and permitted Father Time, so far as the old gentleman was represented by the clocks and watches under his control, to stray at random through human life, making infinite confusion among the train of bewildered hours. He wasted the sunshine, as people said, in wandering through the woods and fields and along the banks of streams. There, like a child, he found amusement in chasing butterflies or watching the motions of water insects. There was something truly mysterious in the intentness with which he contemplated these living playthings as they sported on the breeze or examined the structure of an imperial insect whom he had imprisoned. The chase of butterflies was an apt emblem of the ideal pursuit in which he had spent so many golden hours, but would the beautiful idea ever be yielded to his hand like the butterfly that symbolized it? Sweet, doubtless, were these days, and congenial to the artist's soul. They were full of bright conceptions, which gleamed through his intellectual world as the butterflies gleamed through the outward atmosphere, and were real to him, for the instant, without the toil, and perplexity, and many disappointments of attempting to make them visible to the sensual eye. Alas that the artist, whether in poetry, or whatever other material, may not content himself with the inward enjoyment of the beautiful, but must chase the fitting mystery beyond the verge of his ethereal domain, and crush its frail being in seizing it with a material grasp. Owen Warland felt the impulse to give external reality to his ideas as irresistibly as any of the poets or painters who have arrayed the world in a dimmer and fainter beauty, imperfectly copied from the richness of their visions.

The night was now his time for the slow progress of re-creating the one idea to which all his intellectual activity referred itself. Always at the approach of dusk he stole into the town, locked himself within his shop, and wrought with patient delicacy of touch for many hours. Sometimes he was startled by the rap of the watchman, who, when all the world should be asleep, had caught the gleam of lamplight through the crevices of Owen Warland's shutters. Daylight, to the morbid sensibility of his mind, seemed to have an intrusiveness that interfered with his pursuits. On cloudy and inclement days, therefore, he sat with his head upon his hands, muffling, as it were, his sensitive brain in a mist of indefinite musings; for it was a relief to escape from the sharp distinctness with which he was compelled to shape out his thoughts during his nightly toil.

From one of these fits of torpor he was aroused by the entrance of Annie Hovenden, who came into the shop with the freedom of a customer, and also with something of the familiarity of a childish friend. She had worn a hole through her silver thimble, and wanted Owen to repair it.

"But I don't know whether you will condescend to such a task," said she, laughing, "now that you are so taken up with the notion of putting spirit into machinery."

"Where did you get that idea, Annie?" said Owen, staring in surprise.

"Oh, out of my own head," answered she, "and from something that I heard you say, long ago, when you were but a boy and I a little child. But come; will you mend this poor thimble of mine?"

"Anything for your sake, Annie," said Owen Warland,— "anything, even were it to work at Robert Danforth's forge."

"And that would be a pretty sight!" recorded Annie, glancing with imperceptible slightness at the artist's small and slender frame. "Well; here is the thimble."

"But that is a strange idea of yours," said Owen, "about the spiritualization of matter."

And then the thought stole into his mind that this young girl possessed the gift to comprehend him better than all the world besides. And what a help and strength would it be to him in his lonely toil if he could gain the sympathy of the only being whom he loved! To persons whose pursuits are insulated from the common business of life—who are either in advance of mankind or apart from it—there often comes a sensation of moral cold that makes the spirit shiver as if it had reached the frozen solitudes around the pole. What the prophet, the poet, the reformer, the criminal, or any other man with human yearnings, but separated from the multitude by a peculiar lot, might feel, poor Owen felt.

"Annie," cried he, growing pale as death at the thought, "how gladly would I tell you the secret of my pursuit! You, methinks, would estimate it rightly. You, I know, would hear it with a reverence that I must not expect from the harsh, material world."

"Would I not? to be sure I would!" replied Annie Hovenden, lightly laughing. "Come; explain to me quickly what is the meaning of this little whirligig, so delicately wrought that it might be a plaything for Queen Mab. See! I will put it in motion."

"Hold!" exclaimed Owen, "hold!"

Annie had but given the slightest possible touch, with the point of a needle, to the same minute portion of complicated machinery which has been more than once mentioned, when the artist seized her by the wrist with a force that made her scream aloud. She was affrighted at the convulsion of intense rage and anguish that writhed across his features. The next instant he let his head sink upon his hands.

"Go, Annie," murmured he; "I have deceived myself, and must suffer for it. I yearned for sympathy, and thought, and fancied, and dreamed that you might give it me; but you lack the talisman, Annie, that should admit you into my secrets. That touch has undone the toil of months and the thought of a lifetime! It was not your fault, Annie; but you have ruined me!"

Poor Owen Warland! He had indeed erred, yet pardonably; for if any human spirit could have sufficiently reverenced the processes so sacred in his eyes; it must have been a woman's. Even Annie Hovenden, possibly, might not have disappointed him had she been enlightened by the deep intelligence of love.

The artist spent the ensuing winter in a way that satisfied any persons who had hitherto retained a hopeful opinion of him that he was, in truth, irrevocably doomed to unutility as regarded the world, and to an evil destiny on his own part. The decease of a relative had put him in possession of a small inheritance. Thus freed from the necessity of toil, and having lost the steadfast influence of a great purpose,—great, at least, to him,—he abandoned himself to habits from which it might have been supposed the mere delicacy of his organization would have availed to secure him. But when the ethereal portion of a man of genius is obscured, the earthly part assumes an influence the more uncontrollable, because the character is now thrown off the balance to which Providence had so nicely adjusted it, and which, in coarser natures, is adjusted by some other method. Owen Warland made proof of whatever show of bliss may be found in riot. He looked at the world through the golden medium of wine, and contemplated the visions that bubble up so gayly around the brim of the glass, and that people the air with shapes of pleasant madness, which so soon grow ghostly and forlorn. Even when this dismal and inevitable change had taken place, the young man might still have continued to quaff the cup of enchantments, though its vapor did but shroud life in gloom and fill the gloom with spectres that mocked at him. There was a certain irksomeness the artist was now conscious, was more intolerable than any fantastic miseries and horrors that the abuse of wine could summon up. In the latter case he could remember, even out of the midst of his trouble, that all was but a delusion; in the former, the heavy anguish was his actual life.

From this perilous state he was redeemed by an incident which more than one person witnessed, but of which the shrewdest could not explain or conjecture the operation on Owen Warland's mind. It was very simple. On a warm afternoon of spring, as the artist sat among his riotous companions with a glass of wine before him, a splendid butterfly flew in at the open window and fluttered about his head.

"Ah," exclaimed Owen, who had drank freely, "are you alive again, child of the sun and playmate of the summer breeze, after your dismal winter's nap? Then it is time for me to be at work!"

And, leaving his unemptied glass upon the table, he departed and was never known to sip another drop of wine.

And now, again, he resumed his wanderings in the woods and fields. It might be fancied that the bright butterfly, which had come so spirit-like into the window as Owen sat with the rude revellers, was indeed a spirit commissioned to recall him to the pure, ideal life that had so etherealized him among men. It might be fancied that he went forth to seek this spirit in its sunny haunts; for still, as in the summer time gone by, he was seen to steal gently up wherever a butterfly had alighted, and lose himself in contemplation of it. When it took flight his eyes followed the winged vision, as if its airy track would show the path to heaven. But what could be the purpose of the unseasonable toil, which was again resumed, as the watchman knew by the lines of lamplight through the crevices of Owen Warland's shutters? The towns-people had one comprehensive explanation of all these singularities. Owen Warland had gone mad! How universally efficacious— how satisfactory, too, and soothing to the injured sensibility of narrowness and dulness—is this easy method of accounting for whatever lies beyond the world's most ordinary scope! From St. Paul's days down to our poor little Artist of the Beautiful, the same talisman had been applied to the elucidation of all mysteries in the words or deeds of men who spoke or acted too wisely or too well. In Owen Warland's case the judgment of his towns-people may have been correct. Perhaps he was mad. The lack of sympathy—that contrast between himself and his neighbors which took away the restraint of example—was enough to make him so. Or possibly he had caught just so much ethereal radiance as served to bewilder him, in an earthly sense, by its intermixture with the common daylight.

One evening, when the artist had returned from a customary ramble and had just thrown the lustre of his lamp on the delicate piece of work so often interrupted, but still taken up again, as if his fate were embodied in its mechanism, he was surprised by the entrance of old Peter Hovenden. Owen never met this man without a shrinking of the heart. Of all the world he was most terrible, by reason of a keen understanding which saw so distinctly what it did see, and disbelieved so uncompromisingly in what it could not see. On this occasion the old watchmaker had merely a gracious word or two to say.

"Owen, my lad," said he, "we must see you at my house to-morrow night."

The artist began to mutter some excuse.

"Oh, but it must be so," quoth Peter Hovenden, "for the sake of the days when you were one of the household. What, my boy! don't you know that my daughter Annie is engaged to Robert Danforth? We are making an entertainment, in our humble way, to celebrate the event."

"Ah!" said Owen.

That little monosyllable was all he uttered; its tone seemed cold and unconcerned to an ear like Peter Hovenden's, and yet there was in it the stifled outcry of the poor artist's heart, which he compressed within him like a man holding down an evil spirit. One slight outbreak, however, imperceptible to the old watchmaker, he allowed himself. Raising the instrument with which he was about to begin his work, he let it fall upon the little system of machinery that had, anew, cost him months of thought and toil. It was shattered by the stroke!

Owen Warland's story would have been no tolerable representation of the troubled life of those who strive to create the beautiful, if, amid all other thwarting influences, love had not interposed to steal the cunning from his hand. Outwardly he had been no ardent or enterprising lover; the career of his passion had confined its tumults and vicissitudes so entirely within the artist's imagination that Annie herself had scarcely more than a woman's intuitive perception of it; but, in Owen's view, it covered the whole field of his life. Forgetful of the time when she had shown herself incapable of any deep response, he had persisted in connecting all his dreams of artistical success with Annie's image; she was the visible shape in which the spiritual power that he worshipped, and on whose altar he hoped to lay a not unworthy offering, was made manifest to him. Of course he had deceived himself; there were no such attributes in Annie Hovenden as his imagination had endowed her with. She, in the aspect which she wore to his inward vision, was as much a creature of his own as the mysterious piece of mechanism would be were it ever realized. Had he become convinced of his mistake through the medium of successful love,—had he won Annie to his bosom, and there beheld her fade from angel into ordinary woman,—the disappointment might have driven him back, with concentrated energy, upon his one remaining object. On the other hand, had he found Annie what he fancied, his lot would have been so rich in beauty that out of its mere redundancy he might have wrought the beautiful into many a worthier type than he had toiled for; but the guise in which his sorrow came to him, the sense that the angel of his life had been snatched away and given to a rude man of earth and iron, who could neither need nor appreciate her ministrations, —this was the very perversity of fate that makes human existence appear too absurd and contradictory to be the scene of one other hope or one other fear. There was nothing left for Owen Warland but to sit down like a man that had been stunned.

He went through a fit of illness. After his recovery his small and slender frame assumed an obtuser garniture of flesh than it had ever before worn. His thin cheeks became round; his delicate little hand, so spiritually fashioned to achieve fairy task-work, grew plumper than the hand of a thriving infant. His aspect had a childishness such as might have induced a stranger to pat him on the head—pausing, however, in the act, to wonder what manner of child was here. It was as if the spirit had gone out of him, leaving the body to flourish in a sort of vegetable existence. Not that Owen Warland was idiotic. He could talk, and not irrationally. Somewhat of a babbler, indeed, did people begin to think him; for he was apt to discourse at wearisome length of marvels of mechanism that he had read about in books, but which he had learned to consider as absolutely fabulous. Among them he enumerated the Man of Brass, constructed by Albertus Magnus, and the Brazen Head of Friar Bacon; and, coming down to later times, the automata of a little coach and horses, which it was pretended had been manufactured for the Dauphin of France; together with an insect that buzzed about the ear like a living fly, and yet was but a contrivance of minute steel springs. There was a story, too, of a duck that waddled, and quacked, and ate; though, had any honest citizen purchased it for dinner, he would have found himself cheated with the mere mechanical apparition of a duck.

"But all these accounts," said Owen Warland, "I am now satisfied are mere impositions."

Then, in a mysterious way, he would confess that he once thought differently. In his idle and dreamy days he had considered it possible, in a certain sense, to spiritualize machinery, and to combine with the new species of life and motion thus produced a beauty that should attain to the ideal which Nature has proposed to herself in all her creatures, but has never taken pains to realize. He seemed, however, to retain no very distinct perception either of the process of achieving this object or of the design itself.

"I have thrown it all aside now," he would say. "It was a dream such as young men are always mystifying themselves with. Now that I have acquired a little common sense, it makes me laugh to think of it."

Poor, poor and fallen Owen Warland! These were the symptoms that he had ceased to be an inhabitant of the better sphere that lies unseen around us. He lost his faith in the invisible, and now prided himself, as such unfortunates invariably do, in the wisdom which rejected much that even his eye could see, and trusted confidently in nothing but what his hand could touch. This is the calamity of men whose spiritual part dies out of them and leaves the grosser understanding to assimilate them more and more to the things of which alone it can take cognizance; but in Owen Warland the spirit was not dead nor passed away; it only slept.

How it awoke again is not recorded. Perhaps the torpid slumber was broken by a convulsive pain. Perhaps, as in a former instance, the butterfly came and hovered about his head and reinspired him,—as indeed this creature of the sunshine had always a mysterious mission for the artist,—reinspired him with the former purpose of his life. Whether it were pain or happiness that thrilled through his veins, his first impulse was to thank Heaven for rendering him again the being of thought, imagination, and keenest sensibility that he had long ceased to be.

"Now for my task," said he. "Never did I feel such strength for it as now."

Yet, strong as he felt himself, he was incited to toil the more diligently by an anxiety lest death should surprise him in the midst of his labors. This anxiety, perhaps, is common to all men who set their hearts upon anything so high, in their own view of it, that life becomes of importance only as conditional to its accomplishment. So long as we love life for itself, we seldom dread the losing it. When we desire life for the attainment of an object, we recognize the frailty of its texture. But, side by side with this sense of insecurity, there is a vital faith in our invulnerability to the shaft of death while engaged in any task that seems assigned by Providence as our proper thing to do, and which the world would have cause to mourn for should we leave it unaccomplished. Can the philosopher, big with the inspiration of an idea that is to reform mankind, believe that he is to be beckoned from this sensible existence at the very instant when he is mustering his breath to speak the word of light? Should he perish so, the weary ages may pass away—the world's, whose life sand may fall, drop by drop—before another intellect is prepared to develop the truth that might have been uttered then. But history affords many an example where the most precious spirit, at any particular epoch manifested in human shape, has gone hence untimely, without space allowed him, so far as mortal judgment could discern, to perform his mission on the earth. The prophet dies, and the man of torpid heart and sluggish brain lives on. The poet leaves his song half sung, or finishes it, beyond the scope of mortal ears, in a celestial choir. The painter—as Allston did—leaves half his conception on the canvas to sadden us with its imperfect beauty, and goes to picture forth the whole, if it be no irreverence to say, in the hues of heaven. But rather such incomplete designs of this life will be perfected nowhere. This so frequent abortion of man's dearest projects must be taken as a proof that the deeds of earth, however etherealized by piety or genius, are without value, except as exercises and manifestations of the spirit. In heaven, all ordinary thought is higher and more melodious than Milton's song. Then, would he add another verse to any strain that he had left unfinished here?

But to return to Owen Warland. It was his fortune, good or ill, to achieve the purpose of his life. Pass we over a long space of intense thought, yearning effort, minute toil, and wasting anxiety, succeeded by an instant of solitary triumph: let all this be imagined; and then behold the artist, on a winter evening, seeking admittance to Robert Danforth's fireside circle. There he found the man of iron, with his massive substance thoroughly warmed and attempered by domestic influences. And there was Annie, too, now transformed into a matron, with much of her husband's plain and sturdy nature, but imbued, as Owen Warland still believed, with a finer grace, that might enable her to be the interpreter between strength and beauty. It happened, likewise, that old Peter Hovenden was a guest this evening at his daughter's fireside, and it was his well-remembered expression of keen, cold criticism that first encountered the artist's glance.

"My old friend Owen!" cried Robert Danforth, starting up, and compressing the artist's delicate fingers within a hand that was accustomed to gripe bars of iron. "This is kind and neighborly to come to us at last. I was afraid your perpetual motion had bewitched you out of the remembrance of old times."

"We are glad to see you," said Annie, while a blush reddened her matronly cheek. "It was not like a friend to stay from us so long."

"Well, Owen," inquired the old watchmaker, as his first greeting, "how comes on the beautiful? Have you created it at last?"

The artist did not immediately reply, being startled by the apparition of a young child of strength that was tumbling about on the carpet,—a little personage who had come mysteriously out of the infinite, but with something so sturdy and real in his composition that he seemed moulded out of the densest substance which earth could supply. This hopeful infant crawled towards the new-comer, and setting himself on end, as Robert Danforth expressed the posture, stared at Owen with a look of such sagacious observation that the mother could not help exchanging a proud glance with her husband. But the artist was disturbed by the child's look, as imaging a resemblance between it and Peter Hovenden's habitual expression. He could have fancied that the old watchmaker was compressed into this baby shape, and looking out of those baby eyes, and repeating, as he now did, the malicious question:—

"The beautiful, Owen! How comes on the beautiful? Have you succeeded in creating the beautiful?"

"I have succeeded," replied the artist, with a momentary light of triumph in his eyes and a smile of sunshine, yet steeped in such depth of thought that it was almost sadness. "Yes, my friends, it is the truth. I have succeeded."

"Indeed!" cried Annie, a look of maiden mirthfulness peeping out of her face again. "And it is lawful, now, to inquire what the secret is?"

"Surely; it is to disclose it that I have come," answered Owen Warland. "You shall know, and see, and touch, and possess the secret! For, Annie,—if by that name I may still address the friend of my boyish years,—Annie, it is for your bridal gift that I have wrought this spiritualized mechanism, this harmony of motion, this mystery of beauty. It comes late, indeed; but it is as we go onward in life, when objects begin to lose their freshness of hue and our souls their delicacy of perception, that the spirit of beauty is most needed. If,— forgive me, Annie,—if you know how to value this gift, it can never come too late."

He produced, as he spoke, what seemed a jewel box. It was carved richly out of ebony by his own hand, and inlaid with a fanciful tracery of pearl, representing a boy in pursuit of a butterfly, which, elsewhere, had become a winged spirit, and was flying heavenward; while the boy, or youth, had found such efficacy in his strong desire that he ascended from earth to cloud, and from cloud to celestial atmosphere, to win the beautiful. This case of ebony the artist opened, and bade Annie place her fingers on its edge. She did so, but almost screamed as a butterfly fluttered forth, and, alighting on her finger's tip, sat waving the ample magnificence of its purple and gold-speckled wings, as if in prelude to a flight. It is impossible to express by words the glory, the splendor, the delicate gorgeousness which were softened into the beauty of this object. Nature's ideal butterfly was here realized in all its perfection; not in the pattern of such faded insects as flit among earthly flowers, but of those which hover across the meads of paradise for child-angels and the spirits of departed infants to disport themselves with. The rich down was visible upon its wings; the lustre of its eyes seemed instinct with spirit. The firelight glimmered around this wonder— the candles gleamed upon it; but it glistened apparently by its own radiance, and illuminated the finger and outstretched hand on which it rested with a white gleam like that of precious stones. In its perfect beauty, the consideration of size was entirely lost. Had its wings overreached the firmament, the mind could not have been more filled or satisfied.

"Beautiful! beautiful!" exclaimed Annie. "Is it alive? Is it alive?"

"Alive? To be sure it is," answered her husband. "Do you suppose any mortal has skill enough to make a butterfly, or would put himself to the trouble of making one, when any child may catch a score of them in a summer's afternoon? Alive? Certainly! But this pretty box is undoubtedly of our friend Owen's manufacture; and really it does him credit."

At this moment the butterfly waved it swings anew, with a motion so absolutely lifelike that Annie was startled, and even awe-stricken; for, in spite of her husband's opinion, she could not satisfy herself whether it was indeed a living creature or a piece of wondrous mechanism.

"Is it alive?" she repeated, more earnestly than before.

"Judge for yourself," said Owen Warland, who stood gazing in her face with fixed attention.

The butterfly now flung itself upon the air, fluttered round Annie's head, and soared into a distant region of the parlor, still making itself perceptible to sight by the starry gleam in which the motion of its wings enveloped it. The infant on the floor followed its course with his sagacious little eyes. After flying about the room, it returned in a spiral curve and settled again on Annie's finger.

"But is it alive?" exclaimed she again; and the finger on which the gorgeous mystery had alighted was so tremulous that the butterfly was forced to balance himself with his wings. "Tell me if it be alive, or whether you created it."

"Wherefore ask who created it, so it be beautiful?" replied Owen Warland. "Alive? Yes, Annie; it may well be said to possess life, for it had absorbed my own being into itself; and in the secret of that butterfly, and in its beauty,—which is not merely outward, but deep as its whole system,—is represented the intellect, the imagination, the sensibility, the soul of an Artist of the Beautiful! Yes; I created it. But"—and here his countenance somewhat changed—"this butterfly is not now to me what it was when I beheld it afar off in the daydreams of my youth."

"Be it what it may, it is a pretty plaything," said the blacksmith, grinning with childlike delight. "I wonder whether it would condescend to alight on such a great clumsy finger as mine? Hold it hither, Annie."

By the artist's direction, Annie touched her finger's tip to that of her husband; and, after a momentary delay, the butterfly fluttered from one to the other. It preluded a second flight by a similar, yet not precisely the same, waving of wings as in the first experiment; then, ascending from the blacksmith's stalwart finger, it rose in a gradually enlarging curve to the ceiling, made one wide sweep around the room, and returned with an undulating movement to the point whence it had started.

"Well, that does beat all nature!" cried Robert Danforth,

bestowing the heartiest praise that he could find expression for; and, indeed, had he paused there, a man of finer words and nicer perception could not easily have said more. "That goes beyond me, I confess. But what then? There is more real use in one downright blow of my sledge hammer than in the whole five years' labor that our friend Owen has wasted on this butterfly."

Here the child clapped his hands and made a great babble of indistinct utterance, apparently demanding that the butterfly should be given him for a plaything.

Owen Warland, meanwhile, glanced sidelong at Annie, to discover whether she sympathized in her husband's estimate of the comparative value of the beautiful and the practical. There was, amid all her kindness towards himself, amid all the wonder and admiration with which she contemplated the marvellous work of his hands and incarnation of his idea, a secret scorn—too secret, perhaps, for her own consciousness, and perceptible only to such intuitive discernment as that of the artist. But Owen, in the latter stages of his pursuit, had risen out of the region in which such a discovery might have been torture. He knew that the world, and Annie as the representative of the world, whatever praise might be bestowed, could never say the fitting word nor feel the fitting sentiment which should be the perfect recompense of an artist who, symbolizing a lofty moral by a material trifle,—converting what was earthly to spiritual gold,—had won the beautiful into his handiwork. Not at this latest moment was he to learn that the reward of all high performance must be sought within itself, or sought in vain. There was, however, a view of the matter which Annie and her husband, and even Peter Hovenden, might fully have understood, and which would have satisfied them that the toil of years had here been worthily bestowed. Owen Warland might have told them that this butterfly, this plaything, this bridal gift of a poor watchmaker to a blacksmith's wife, was, in truth, a gem of art that a monarch would have purchased with honors and abundant wealth, and have treasured it among the jewels of his kingdom as the most unique and wondrous of them all. But the artist smiled and kept the secret to himself.

"Father," said Annie, thinking that a word of praise from the old watchmaker might gratify his former apprentice, "do come and admire this pretty butterfly."

"Let us see," said Peter Hovenden, rising from his chair, with a sneer upon his face that always made people doubt, as he himself did, in everything but a material existence. "Here is my finger for it to alight upon. I shall understand it better when once I have touched it."

But, to the increased astonishment of Annie, when the tip of her father's finger was pressed against that of her husband, on which the butterfly still rested, the insect drooped its wings and seemed on the point of falling to the floor. Even the bright spots of gold upon its wings and body, unless her eyes deceived her, grew dim, and the glowing purple took a dusky hue, and the starry lustre that gleamed around the blacksmith's hand became faint and vanished.

"It is dying! it is dying!" cried Annie, in alarm.

"It has been delicately wrought," said the artist, calmly. "As I told you, it has imbibed a spiritual essence—call it magnetism, or what you will. In an atmosphere of doubt and mockery its exquisite susceptibility suffers torture, as does the soul of him who instilled his own life into it. It has already lost its beauty; in a few moments more its mechanism would be irreparably injured."

"Take away your hand, father!" entreated Annie turning pale. "Here is my child; let it rest on his innocent hand. There, perhaps, its life will revive and its colors grow brighter than ever."

Her father, with an acrid smile, withdrew his finger. The butterfly then appeared to recover the power of voluntary motion, while its hues assumed much of their original lustre, and the gleam of starlight, which was its most ethereal attribute, again formed a halo round about it. At first, when transferred from Robert Danforth's hand to the small finger of the child, this radiance grew so powerful that it positively threw the little fellow's shadow back against the wall. He, meanwhile, extended his plump hand as he had seen his father and mother do, and watched the waving of the insect's wings with infantine delight. Nevertheless, there was a certain odd expression of sagacity that made Owen Warland feel as if here were old Peter Hovenden, partially, and but partially, redeemed from his hard scepticism into childish faith.

"How wise the little monkey looks!" whispered Robert Danforth to his wife.

"I never saw such a look on a child's face," answered Annie, admiring her own infant, and with good reason, far more than the artistic butterfly. "The darling knows more of the mystery than we do."

As if the butterfly, like the artist, were conscious of something not entirely congenial in the child's nature, it alternately sparkled and grew dim. At length it arose from the small hand of the infant with an airy motion that seemed to bear it upward without an effort, as if the ethereal instincts with which its master's spirit had endowed it impelled this fair vision involuntarily to a higher sphere. Had there been no obstruction, it might have soared into the sky and grown immortal. But its lustre gleamed upon the ceiling; the exquisite texture of its wings brushed against that earthly medium; and a sparkle or two, as of stardust, floated downward and lay glimmering on the carpet. Then the butterfly came fluttering down, and, instead of returning to the infant, was apparently attracted towards the artist's hand.

"Not so! not so!" murmured Owen Warland, as if his handiwork could have understood him. "Thou hast gone forth out of thy master's heart. There is no return for thee."

With a wavering movement, and emitting a tremulous radiance, the butterfly struggled, as it were, towards the infant, and was about to alight upon his finger; but while it still hovered in the air, the little child of strength, with his grandsire's sharp and shrewd expression in his face, made a snatch at the marvellous insect and compressed it in his hand. Annie screamed. Old Peter Hovenden burst into a cold and scornful laugh. The blacksmith, by main force, unclosed the infant's hand, and found within the palm a small heap of glittering fragments, whence the mystery of beauty had fled forever. And as for Owen Warland, he looked placidly at what seemed the ruin of his life's labor, and which was yet no ruin. He had caught a far other butterfly than this. When the artist rose high enough to achieve the beautiful, the symbol by which he made it perceptible to mortal senses became of little value in his eyes while his spirit possessed itself in the enjoyment of the reality.

RAPPACCINI'S
DAUGHTER

A young man, named Giovanni Guasconti, came, very long ago, from the more southern region of Italy, to pursue his studies at the University of Padua. Giovanni, who had but a scanty supply of gold ducats in his pocket, took lodgings in a high and gloomy chamber of an old edifice which looked not unworthy to have been the palace of a Paduan noble, and which, in fact, exhibited over its entrance the armorial bearings of a family long since extinct. The young stranger, who was not unstudied in the great poem of his country, recollected that one of the ancestors of this family, and perhaps an occupant of this very mansion, had been pictured by Dante as a partaker of the immortal agonies of his Inferno. These reminiscences and associations, together with the tendency to heartbreak natural to a young man for the first time out of his native sphere, caused Giovanni to sigh heavily as he looked around the desolate and ill-furnished apartment.

"Holy Virgin, signor!" cried old Dame Lisabetta, who, won by the youth's remarkable beauty of person, was kindly endeavoring to give the chamber a habitable air, "what a sigh was that to come out of a young man's heart! Do you find this old mansion gloomy? For the love of Heaven, then, put your head out of the window, and you will see as bright sunshine as you have left in Naples."

First published in *The Democratic Review*, December, 1844.

Guasconti mechanically did as the old woman advised, but could not quite agree with her that the Paduan sunshine was as cheerful as that of southern Italy. Such as it was, however, it fell upon a garden beneath the window and expended its fostering influences on a variety of plants, which seemed to have been cultivated with exceeding care.

"Does this garden belong to the house?" asked Giovanni.

"Heaven forbid, signor, unless it were fruitful of better pot herbs than any that grow there now," answered old Lisabetta. "No; that garden is cultivated by the own hands of Signor Giacomo Rappaccini, the famous doctor, who, I warrant him, has been heard of as far as Naples. It is said that he distils these plants into medicines that are as potent as a charm. Oftentimes you may see the signor doctor at work, and perchance the signora, his daughter, too, gathering the strange flowers that grow in the garden."

The old woman had now done what she could for the aspect of the chamber; and, commending the young man to the protection of the saints, took her departure.

Giovanni still found no better occupation than to look down into the garden beneath his window. From its appearance, he judged it to be one of those botanic gardens which were of earlier date in Padua than elsewhere in Italy or in the world. Or, not improbably, it might once have been the pleasure-place of an opulent family; for there was the ruin of a marble fountain in the centre, sculptured with rare art, but so wofully shattered that it was impossible to trace the original design from the chaos of remaining fragments. The water, however, continued to gush and sparkle into the sunbeams as cheerfully as ever. A little gurgling sound ascended to the young man's window, and made him feel as if the fountain were an immortal spirit that sung its song unceasingly and without heeding the vicissitudes around it, while one century imbodied it in marble and another scattered the perishable garniture on the soil. All about the pool into which the water subsided grew various plants, that seemed to require a plentiful supply of moisture for the nourishment of gigantic leaves, and in some instances, flowers gorgeously magnificent. There was one shrub in particular, set in a marble vase in the midst of the pool, that bore a profusion of purple blossoms, each of which had the lustre and richness of a gem; and the whole together made a show so resplendent that it seemed enough to illuminate the garden, even had there been no sunshine. Every portion of the soil was peopled with plants and herbs, which, if less beautiful, still bore tokens of assiduous care, as if all had their individual virtues, known to the scientific mind that fostered them. Some were placed in urns, rich with old carving, and others in common garden pots; some crept serpent-like along the ground or climbed on high, using whatever means of ascent was offered them. One plant had wreathed itself round a statue of Vertumnus, which was thus quite veiled and shrouded in a drapery of hanging foliage, so happily arranged that it might have served a sculptor for a study.

While Giovanni stood at the window he heard a rustling behind a screen of leaves, and became aware that a person was at work in the garden. His figure soon emerged into view, and showed itself to be that of no common laborer, but a tall, emaciated, sallow, and sickly-looking man, dressed in a scholar's garb of black. He was beyond the middle term of life, with gray hair, a thin, gray beard, and a face singularly marked with intellect and cultivation, but which could never, even in his more youthful days, have expressed much warmth of heart.

Nothing could exceed the intentness with which this scientific gardener examined every shrub which grew in his path: it seemed as if he was looking into their inmost nature, making observations in regard to their creative essence, and discovering why one leaf grew in this shape and another in that, and wherefore such and such flowers differed among themselves in hue and perfume. Nevertheless, in spite of this deep intelligence on his part, there was no approach to intimacy between himself and these vegetable existences. On the contrary, he avoided their actual touch or the direct inhaling of their odors with a caution that impressed Giovanni most disagreeably; for the man's demeanor was that of one walking among malignant influences, such as savage beasts, or deadly snakes, or evil spirits, which, should he allow them one moment of license, would wreak upon him some terrible fatality. It was strangely frightful to the young man's imagination to see this air of insecurity in a person cultivating a garden, that most simple and innocent of human toils, and which had been alike the joy and labor of the unfallen parents of the race. Was this garden, then, the Eden of the present world? And this man, with such a perception of harm in what his own hands caused to grow,—was he the Adam?

The distrustful gardener, while plucking away the dead leaves or pruning the too luxuriant growth of the shrubs, defended his hands with a pair of thick gloves. Nor were these his only armor. When, in his walk through the garden, he came to the magnificent plant that hung its purple gems beside the marble fountain, he placed a kind of mask over his mouth and nostrils, as if all this beauty did but conceal a deadlier malice; but, finding his task still too dangerous, he drew back, removed the mask, and called loudly, but in the infirm voice of a person affected with inward disease,—

"Beatrice! Beatrice!"

"Here am I, my father. What would you?" cried a rich and youthful voice from the window of the opposite house—a voice as rich as a tropical sunset, and which made Giovanni, though he knew not why, think of deep hues of purple or crimson and of perfumes heavily delectable. "Are you in the garden?"

"Yes, Beatrice," answered the gardener, "and I need your help."

Soon there emerged from under a sculptured portal the figure of a young girl, arrayed with as much richness of taste as the most splendid of the flowers, beautiful as the day, and with a bloom so deep and vivid that one shade more would have been too much. She looked redundant with life, health, and energy; all of which attributes were bound down and compressed, as it were, and girdled tensely, in their luxuriance, by her virgin zone. Yet Giovanni's fancy must have grown morbid while he looked down into the garden; for the impression which the fair stranger made upon him was as if here were another flower, the human sister of those vegetable ones, as beautiful as they, more beautiful than the richest of them, but still to be touched only with a glove, nor to be approached without a mask. As Beatrice came down the garden path, it was observable that she handled and inhaled the odor of several of the plants which her father had most sedulously avoided.

"Here, Beatrice," said the latter, "see how many needful offices require to be done to our chief treasure. Yet, shattered as I am, my life might pay the penalty of approaching it so closely as circumstances demand. Henceforth, I fear, this plant must be consigned to your sole charge."

"And gladly will I undertake it," cried again the rich tones of the young lady, as she bent towards the magnificent plant and opened her arms as if to embrace it. "Yes, my sister, my splendor, it shall be Beatrice's task to nurse and serve thee; and thou shalt reward her with thy kisses and perfumed breath, which to her is as the breath of life."

Then, with all the tenderness in her manner that was so strikingly expressed in her words, she busied herself with such attentions as the plant seemed to require; and Giovanni, at his lofty window, rubbed his eyes and almost doubted whether it were a girl tending her favorite flower, or one sister performing the duties of affection to another. The scene soon terminated. Whether Dr. Rappaccini had finished his labors in the garden, or that his watchful eye had caught the stranger's face, he now took his daughter's arm and retired. Night was already closing in; oppressive exhalations seemed to proceed from the plants and steal upward past the open window; and Giovanni, closing the lattice, went to his couch and dreamed of a rich flower and beautiful girl. Flower and maiden were different, and yet the same, and fraught with some strange peril in either shape.

But there is an influence in the light of morning that tends to rectify whatever errors of fancy, or even of judgment, we may have incurred during the sun's decline, or among the shadows of the night, or in the less wholesome glow of moon-shine. Giovanni's first movement, on starting from sleep, was to throw open the window and gaze down into the garden which his dreams had made so fertile of mysteries. He was surprised and a little ashamed to find how real and matter-of-fact an affair it proved to be, in the first rays of the sun which gilded the dew-drops that hung upon leaf and blossom, and, while giving a brighter beauty to each rare flower, brought everything within the limits of ordinary experience. The young man rejoiced that, in the heart of the barren city, he had the privilege of overlooking this spot of lovely and luxuriant vegetation. It would serve, he said to himself, as a symbolic language to keep him in communion with Nature. Neither the sickly and thoughtworn Dr. Giacomo Rappaccini, it is true, nor his brilliant daughter, were now visible; so that Giovanni could not determine how much of the singularity which he attributed to both was due to their own qualities and how much to his wonder-working fancy; but he was inclined to take a most rational view of the whole matter.

In the course of the day he paid his respects to Signor Pietro Baglioni, professor of medicine in the university, a physician of eminent repute to whom Giovanni had brought a letter of introduction. The professor was an elderly personage, apparently of genial nature, and habits that might almost be called jovial. He kept the young man to dinner, and made himself very agreeable by the freedom and liveliness of his conversation, especially when warmed by a flask or two of Tuscan wine. Giovanni, conceiving that men of science, inhabitants of the same city, must needs be on familiar terms with one another, took an opportunity to mention the name of Dr. Rappaccini. But the professor did not respond with so much cordiality as he had anticipated.

"Ill would it become a teacher of the divine art of medicine," said Professor Pietro Baglioni, in answer to a question

of Giovanni, "to withhold due and well-considered praise of
a physician so eminently skilled as Rappaccini; but, on the
other hand, I should answer it but scantily to my conscience
were I to permit a worthy youth like yourself, Signor
Giovanni, the son of an ancient friend, to imbibe erroneous
ideas respecting a man who might hereafter chance to hold
your life and death in his hands. The truth is, our worshipful
Dr. Rappaccini has as much science as any member of the
faculty—with perhaps one single exception—in Padua, or
all Italy; but there are certain grave objections to his professional character."

"And what are they?" asked the young man.

"Has my friend Giovanni any disease of body or heart, that
he is so inquisitive about physicians?" said the professor, with
a smile. "But as for Rappaccini, it is said of him—and I, who
know the man well, can answer for its truth—that he cares
infinitely more for science than for mankind. His patients are
interesting to him only as subjects for some new experiment.
He would sacrifice human life, his own among the rest, or
whatever else was dearest to him, for the sake of adding so
much as a grain of mustard seed to the great heap of his
accumulated knowledge."

"Methinks he is an awful man indeed," remarked Guasconti,
mentally recalling the cold and purely intellectual aspect of
Rappaccini. "And yet, worshipful professor, is it not a noble
spirit? Are there many men capable of so spiritual a love of
science?"

"God forbid," answered the professor, somewhat testily; "at
least, unless they take sounder views of the healing art than
those adopted by Rappaccini. It is his theory that all medicinal
virtues are comprised within those substances which we term
vegetable poisons. These he cultivates with his own hands,
and is said even to have produced new varieties of poison,
more horribly deleterious than Nature, without the assistance
of this learned person, would ever have plagued the world
withal. That the signor doctor does less mischief than might
be expected with such dangerous substances is undeniable.

Now and then, it must be owned, he has effected, or seemed to effect, a marvellous cure; but, to tell you my private mind, Signor Giovanni, he should receive little credit for such instances of success,—they being probably the work of chance, —but should be held strictly accountable for his failures, which may justly be considered his own work."

The youth might have taken Baglioni's opinions with many grains of allowance had he known that there was a professional warfare of long continuance between him and Dr. Rappaccini, in which the latter was generally thought to have gained the advantage. If the reader be inclined to judge for himself, we refer him to certain black-letter tracts on both sides, preserved in the medical department of the University of Padua.

"I know not, most learned professor," returned Giovanni, after musing on what had been said of Rappaccini's exclusive zeal for science,—"I know not how dearly this physician may love his art; but surely there is one object more dear to him. He has a daughter."

"Aha!" cried the professor, with a laugh. "So now our friend Giovanni's secret is out. You have heard of this daughter, whom all the young men in Padua are wild about, though not half a dozen have ever had the good hap to see her face. I know little of the Signora Beatrice save that Rappaccini is said to have instructed her deeply in his science, and that, young and beautiful as fame reports her, she is already qualified to fill a professor's chair. Perchance her father destines her for mine! Other absurd rumors there be, not worth talking about or listening to. So now, Signor Giovanni, drink off your glass of lachryma."

Guasconti returned to his lodgings somewhat heated with the wine he had quaffed, and which caused his brain to swim with strange fantasies in reference to Dr. Rappaccini and the beautiful Beatrice. On his way, happening to pass by a florist's, he bought a fresh bouquet of flowers.

Ascending to his chamber, he seated himself near the window, but within the shadow thrown by the depth of the wall, so that he could look down into the garden with little risk of being discovered. All beneath his eye was a solitude. The strange plants were basking in the sunshine, and now and then nodding gently to one another, as if in acknowledgment of sympathy and kindred. In the midst, by the shattered fountain, grew the magnificent shrub, with its purple gems clustering all over it; they glowed in the air, and gleamed back again out of the depths of the pool, which thus seemed to overflow with colored radiance from the rich reflection that was steeped in it. At first, as we have said, the garden was a solitude. Soon, however,—as Giovanni had half hoped, half feared, would be the case,—a figure appeared beneath the antique sculptured portal, and came down between the rows of plants, inhaling their various perfumes as if she were one of those beings of old classic fable that lived upon sweet odors. On again beholding Beatrice, the young man was even startled to perceive how much her beauty exceeded his recollection of it; so brilliant, so vivid, was its character, that she glowed amid the sunlight, and, as Giovanni whispered to himself, positively illuminated the more shadowy intervals of the garden path. Her face being now more revealed than on the former occasion, he was struck by its expression of simplicity and sweetness,—qualities that had not entered into his idea of her character, and which made him ask anew what manner of mortal she might be. Nor did he fail again to observe, or imagine, an analogy between the beautiful girl and the gorgeous shrub that hung its gemlike flowers over the fountain, —a resemblance which Beatrice seemed to have indulged a fantastic humor in heightening, both by the arrangement of her dress and the selection of its hues.

Approaching the shrub, she threw open her arms, as with a passionate ardor, and drew its branches into an intimate embrace—so intimate that her features were hidden in its leafy bosom and her glistening ringlets all intermingled with the flowers.

"Give me thy breath, my sister," exclaimed Beatrice; "for I am faint with common air. And give me this flower of thine, which I separate with gentlest fingers from the stem and place it close beside my heart."

With these words the beautiful daughter of Rappaccini plucked one of the richest blossoms of the shrub, and was about to fasten it in her bosom. But now, unless Giovanni's draughts of wine had bewildered his senses, a singular accident occurred. A small orange-colored reptile, of the lizard or chameleon species, chanced to be creeping along the path, just at the feet of Beatrice. It appeared to Giovanni,—but, at the distance from which he gazed, he could scarcely have seen anything so minute,—it appeared to him, however, that a drop or two of moisture from the broken stem of the flower descended upon the lizard's head. For an instant the reptile contorted itself violently, and then lay motionless in the sunshine. Beatrice observed this remarkable phenomenon, and crossed herself, sadly, but without surprise; nor did she therefore hesitate to arrange the fatal flower in her bosom. There it blushed, and almost glimmered with the dazzling effect of a precious stone, adding to her dress and aspect the one appropriate charm which nothing else in the world could have supplied. But Giovanni, out of the shadow of his window, bent forward and shrank back, and murmured and trembled.

"Am I awake? Have I my senses" said he to himself. "What is this being? Beautiful shall I call her, or inexpressibly terrible?"

Beatrice now strayed carelessly through the garden, approaching closer beneath Giovanni's window, so that he was compelled to thrust his head quite out of its concealment in order to gratify the intense and painful curiosity which she excited. At this moment there came a beautiful insect over the garden wall; it had, perhaps, wandered through the city, and found no flowers or verdure among those antique haunts of men until the heavy perfumes of Dr. Rappaccini's shrubs had lured it from afar. Without alighting on the flowers, this winged brightness seemed to be attracted by Beatrice, and lingered in the air and fluttered about her head. Now, here it could not be but that Giovanni Guasconti's eyes deceived him. Be that as it might, he fancied that, while Beatrice was gazing at the insect with childish delight, it grew faint and fell at her feet; its bright wings shivered; it was dead—from no cause that he could discern, unless it were the atmosphere of her breath. Again Beatrice crossed herself and sighed heavily as she bent over the dead insect.

An impulsive movement of Giovanni drew her eyes to the window. There she beheld the beautiful head of the young man—rather a Grecian than an Italian head, with fair, regular features, and a glistening of gold among his ringlets—gazing down upon her like a being that hovered in mid air. Scarcely knowing what he did, Giovanni threw down the bouquet which he had hitherto held in his hand.

"Signora," said he, "there are pure and healthful flowers. Wear them for the sake of Giovanni Guasconti."

"Thanks, signor," replied Beatrice, with her rich voice, that came forth as it were like a gush of music, and with a mirthful expression half childish and half woman-like. "I accept your gift, and would fain recompense it with this precious purple flower; but if I toss it into the air it will not reach you. So Signor Guasconti must even content himself with my thanks."

She lifted the bouquet from the ground, and then, as if inwardly ashamed at having stepped aside from her maidenly reserve to respond to a stranger's greeting, passed swiftly homeward through the garden. But few as the moments were, it seemed to Giovanni, when she was on the point of vanishing beneath the sculptured portal, that his beautiful bouquet was already beginning to wither in her grasp. It was an idle thought; there could be no possibility of distinguishing a faded flower from a fresh one at so great a distance.

For many days after this incident the young man avoided the window that looked into Dr. Rappaccini's garden, as if something ugly and monstrous would have blasted his eyesight had he been betrayed into a glance. He felt conscious of having put himself, to a certain extent, within the influence of an unintelligible power by the communication which he had opened with Beatrice. The wisest course would have been,

if his heart were in any real danger, to quit his lodgings and
Padua itself at once; the next wiser, to have accustomed himself, as far as possible, to the familiar and daylight view of
Beatrice—thus bringing her rigidly and systematically within
the limits of ordinary experience. Least of all, while avoiding
her sight, ought Giovanni to have remained so near this
extraordinary being that the proximity and possibility even
of intercourse should give a kind of substance and reality to
the wild vagaries which his imagination ran riot continually
in producing. Guasconti had not a deep heart—or, at all
events, its depths were not sounded now; but he had a quick
fancy, and an ardent southern temperament, which rose every
instant to a higher fever pitch. Whether or no Beatrice possessed those terrible attributes, that fatal breath, the affinity
with those so beautiful and deadly flowers which were indicated by what Giovanni had witnessed, she had at least instilled a fierce and subtle poison into his system. It was not
love, although her rich beauty was a madness to him; nor
horror, even while he fancied her spirit to be imbued with the
same baneful essence that seemed to pervade her physical
frame; but a wild offspring of both love and horror that had
each parent in it, and burned like one and shivered like the
other. Giovanni knew not what to dread; still less did he know
what to hope; yet hope and dread kept a continual warfare in
his breast, alternately vanquishing one another and starting
up afresh to renew the contest. Blessed are all simple emotions, be they dark or bright! It is the lurid intermixture of
the two that produces the illuminating blaze of the infernal
regions.

Sometimes he endeavored to assuage the fever of his spirit
by a rapid walk through the streets of Padua or beyond its
gates: his footsteps kept time with the throbbings of his brain,
so that the walk was apt to accelerate itself to a race. One day
he found himself arrested; his arm was seized by a portly
personage, who had turned back on recognizing the young
man and expended much breath in overtaking him.

"Signor Giovanni! Stay, my young friend!" cried he. "Have

you forgotten me? That might well be the case if I were as much altered as yourself."

It was Baglioni, whom Giovanni had avoided ever since their first meeting, from a doubt that the professor's sagacity would look too deeply into his secrets. Endeavoring to recover himself, he stared forth wildly from his inner world into the outer one and spoke like a man in a dream.

"Yes; I am Giovanni Guasconti. You are Professor Pietro Baglioni. Now let me pass!"

"Not yet, not yet, Signor Giovanni Guasconti," said the professor, smiling, but at the same time scrutinizing the youth with an earnest glance. "What! did I grow up side by side with your father? and shall his son pass me like a stranger in these old streets of Padua? Stand still, Signor Giovanni; for we must have a word or two before we part."

"Speedily, then, most worshipful professor, speedily," said Giovanni with feverish impatience. "Does not your worship see that I am in haste?"

Now, while he was speaking there came a man in black along the street, stooping and moving feebly like a person in inferior health. His face was all overspread with a most sickly and sallow hue, but yet so pervaded with an expression of piercing and active intellect that an observer might easily have overlooked the merely physical attributes and have seen only this wonderful energy. As he passed, this person exchanged a cold and distant salutation with Baglioni, but fixed his eyes upon Giovanni with an intentness that seemed to bring out whatever was within him worthy of notice. Nevertheless, there was a peculiar quietness in the look, as if taking merely a speculative, not a human interest, in the young man.

"It is Dr. Rappaccini!" whispered the professor when the stranger had passed. "Has he ever seen your face before?"

"Not that I know," answered Giovanni, starting at the name.

"He *has* seen you! he must have seen you!" said Baglioni, hastily. "For some purpose or other, this man of science is making a study of you. I know that look of his! It is the same that coldly illuminates his face as he bends over a bird, a mouse, or a butterfly, which, in pursuance of some experiment, he has killed by the perfume of a flower; a look as deep as Nature itself, but without Nature's warmth of love. Signor Giovanni, I will stake my life upon it, you are the subject of one of Rappaccini's experiments!"

"Will you make a fool of me?" cried Giovanni passionately. "*That,* signor professor, were an untoward experiment."

"Patience! patience!" replied the imperturbable professor. "I tell thee, my poor Giovanni, that Rappaccini has a scientific interest in thee. Thou hast fallen into fearful hands! And the Signora Beatrice,—what part does she act in this mystery?"

But Guasconti, finding Baglioni's pertinacity intolerable, here broke away, and was gone before the professor could again seize his arm. He looked after the young man intently and shook his head.

"This must not be," said Baglioni to himself. "The youth is the son of my old friend, and shall not come to any harm from which the arcana of medical science can preserve him. Besides, it is too insufferable an impertinence in Rappaccini, thus to snatch the lad out of my own hands, as I may say, and make use of him for his infernal experiments. This daughter of his! It shall be looked to. Perchance, most learned Rappaccini, I may foil you where you little dream of it!"

Meanwhile Giovanni had pursued a circuitious route, and at length found himself at the door of his lodgings. As he crossed the threshold he was met by old Lisabetta, who smirked and smiled, and was evidently desirous to attract his attention; vainly, however, as the ebullition of his feelings had momentarily subsided into a cold and dull vacuity. He turned his eyes full upon the withered face that was puckering itself into a smile, but seemed to behold it not. The old dame, therefore, laid her grasp upon his cloak.

"Signor! signor!" whispered she, still with a smile over the whole breadth of her visage, so that it looked not unlike a grotesque carving in wood, darkened by centuries. "Listen, signor! There is a private entrance into the garden!"

"What do you say?" exclaimed Giovanni, turning quickly about, as if an inanimate thing should start into feverish life. "A private entrance into Dr. Rappaccini's garden?"

"Hush! hush! not so loud!" whispered Lisabetta, putting her hand over his mouth. "Yes; into the worshipful doctor's garden, where you may see all his fine shrubbery. Many a young man in Padua would give gold to be admitted among those flowers."

Giovanni put a piece of gold into her hand.

"Show me the way," said he.

A surmise, probably excited by his conversation with Baglioni, crossed his mind, that this interposition of old Lisabetta might perchance be connected with the intrigue, whatever were its nature, in which the professor seemed to suppose that Dr. Rappaccini was involving him. But such a suspicion, though it disturbed Giovanni, was inadequate to restrain him. The instant that he was aware of the possibility of approaching Beatrice, it seemed an absolute necessity of his existence to do so. It mattered not whether she were angel or demon; he was irrevocably within her sphere, and must obey the law that whirled him onward, in ever-lessening circles, towards a result which he did not attempt to foreshadow; and yet, strange to say, there came across him a sudden doubt whether this intense interest on his part were not delusory; whether it were really of so deep and positive a nature as to justify him in now thrusting himself into an incalculable position; whether it were not merely the fantasy of a young man's brain, only slightly or not at all connected with his heart.

He paused, hesitated, turned half about, but again went on. His withered guide led him along several obscure passages, and finally undid a door, through which, as it was opened, there came the sight and sound of rustling leaves, with the broken sunshine glimmering among them. Giovanni stepped forth, and, forcing himself through the entanglement of a shrub that wreathed its tendrils over the hidden entrance, stood beneath his own window in the open area of Dr. Rappaccini's garden.

How often is it the case that, when impossibilities have come to pass and dreams have condensed their misty substance into tangible realities, we find ourselves calm, and even coldly self-possessed, amid circumstances which it would have been a delirium of joy or agony to anticipate! Fate delights to thwart us thus. Passion will choose his own time to rush upon the scene, and lingers sluggishly behind when an appropriate adjustment of events would seem to summon his appearance. So was it now with Giovanni. Day after day his pulses had throbbed with feverish blood at the improbable idea of an interview with Beatrice, and of standing with her, face to face, in this very garden, basking in the Oriental sunshine of her beauty, and snatching from her full gaze the mystery which he deemed the riddle of his own existence. But now there was a singular and untimely equanimity within his breast. He threw a glance around the garden to discover if Beatrice or her father were present, and, perceiving that he was alone, began a critical observation of the plants.

The aspect of one and all of them dissatisfied him; their gorgeousness seemed fierce, passionate, and even unnatural. There was hardly an individual shrub which a wanderer, straying by himself through a forest, would not have been startled to find growing wild, as if an unearthly face had glared at him out of the thicket. Several also would have shocked a delicate instinct by an appearance of artificialness indicating that there had been such commixture, and, as it were, adultery, of various vegetable species, that the production was no longer of God's making, but the monstrous offspring of man's depraved fancy, glowing with only an evil mockery of beauty. They were probably the result of experiment, which in one or two cases had succeeded in mingling plants individually lovely into a compound possessing the questionable and ominous character that distinguished the whole growth of the garden. In fine, Giovanni recognized but two or three plants in the collection, and those of a kind that he well knew to be poisonous. While busy with these contemplations he heard the rustling of a silken garment, and, turning, beheld Beatrice emerging from beneath the sculptured portal.

Giovanni had not considered with himself what should be his deportment; whether he should apologize for his intrusion into the garden, or assume that he was there with the privity at least, if not by the desire, of Dr. Rappaccini or his daughter; but Beatrice's manner placed him at his ease, though leaving him still in doubt by what agency he had gained admittance. She came lightly along the path and met him near the broken fountain. There was surprise in her face, but brightened by a simple and kind expression of pleasure.

"You are a connoisseur in flowers, signor," said Beatrice, with a smile, alluding to the bouquet which he had flung her from the window. "It is no marvel, therefore, if the sight of my father's rare collection has tempted you to take a nearer view. If he were here, he could tell you many strange and interesting facts as to the nature and habits of these shrubs; for he has spent a lifetime in such studies, and this garden is his world."

"And yourself, lady," observed Giovanni, "if fame says true, —you likewise are deeply skilled in the virtues indicated by these rich blossoms and these spicy perfumes. Would you deign to be my instructress, I should prove an apter scholar than if taught by Signor Rappaccini himself."

"Are there such idle rumors?" asked Beatrice, with the music of a pleasant laugh. "Do people say that I am skilled in my father's science of plants? What a jest is there! No; though I have grown up among these flowers, I know no more of them than their hues and perfume; and sometimes methinks I would fain rid myself of even that small knowledge. There are many flowers here, and those not the least brilliant, that shock and offend me when they meet my eye. But pray, signor, do not believe these stories about my science. Believe nothing of me save what you see with your own eyes."

"And must I believe all that I have seen with my own eyes?" asked Giovanni, pointedly, while the recollection of former scenes make him shrink. "No, signora; you demand too little of me. Bid me believe nothing save what comes from your own lips."

It would appear that Beatrice understood him. There came a deep flush to her cheek; but she looked full into Giovanni's eyes, and responded to his gaze of uneasy suspicion with a queenlike haughtiness.

"I do so bid you, signor," she replied. "Forget whatever you may have fancied in regard to me. If true to the outward senses, still it may be false in its essence; but the words of Beatrice Rappaccini's lips are true from the depths of the heart outward. Those you may believe."

A fervor glowed in her whole aspect and beamed upon Giovanni's consciousness like the light of truth itself; but while she spoke there was a fragrance in the atmosphere around her, rich and delightful, though evanescent, yet which the young man, from an indefinable reluctance, scarcely dared to draw into his lungs. It might be the odor of the flowers. Could it be Beatrice's breath which thus embalmed her words with a strange richness, as if by steeping them in her heart? A faintness passed like a shadow over Giovanni and flitted away; he seemed to gaze through the beautiful girl's eyes into her transparent soul, and felt no more doubt or fear.

The tinge of passion that had colored Beatrice's manner vanished; she became gay, and appeared to derive a pure delight from her communion with the youth not unlike what the maiden of a lonely island might have felt conversing with a voyager from the civilized world. Evidently her experience of life had been confined within the limits of that garden. She talked now about matters as simple as the daylight or summer clouds, and now asked questions in reference to the city, or Giovanni's distant home, his friends, his mother, and his sisters—questions indicating such seclusion, and such lack of familiarity with modes and forms, that Giovanni responded as if to an infant. Her spirit gushed out before him like a fresh rill that was just catching its first glimpse of the sunlight and wondering at the reflections of earth and sky which were flung into its bosom. There came thoughts, too, from a deep source, and fantasies of a gemlike brilliancy, as if diamonds and rubies sparkled upward among the bubbles of the fountain. Ever and anon there gleamed across the young man's mind a sense of wonder that he should be walking side by side with the being who had so wrought upon his imagination, whom he had idealized in such hues of terror, in whom he had positively witnessed such manifestations of dreadful attributes, —that he should be conversing with Beatrice like a brother, and should find her so human and so maidenlike. But such reflections were only momentary; the effect of her character was too real not to make itself familiar at once.

In this free intercourse they had strayed through the garden, and now, after many turns among its avenues, were come to the shattered fountain, beside which grew the magnificent shrub, with its treasury of glowing blossoms. A fragrance was diffused from it which Giovanni recognized as identical with that which he had attributed to Beatrice's breath, but incomparably more powerful. As her eyes fell upon it, Giovanni beheld her press her hand to her bosom as if her heart were throbbing suddenly and painfully.

"For the first time in my life," murmured she, addressing the shrub, "I had forgotten thee."

"I remember, signora" said Giovanni "that you once promised to reward me with one of these living gems for the bouquet which I had the happy boldness to fling to your feet. Permit me now to pluck it as a memorial of this interview."

He made a step towards the shrub with extended hand; but Beatrice darted forward uttering a shriek that went through his heart like a dagger. She caught his hand and drew it back with the whole force of her slender figure. Giovanni felt her touch thrilling through his fibres.

"Touch it not!" exclaimed she in a voice of agony. "Not for thy life! It is fatal!"

Then hiding her face she fled from him and vanished beneath the sculptured portal. As Giovanni followed her with his eyes he beheld the emaciated figure and pale intelligence of Dr. Rappaccini, who had been watching the scene he knew not how long, within the shadow of the entrance.

No sooner was Guasconti alone in his chamber than the image of Beatrice came back to his passionate musings, invested with all the witchery that had been gathering around it ever since his first glimpse of her, and now likewise imbued with a tender warmth of girlish womanhood. She was human; her nature was endowed with all gentle and feminine qualities; she was worthiest to be worshipped; she was capable, surely, on her part, of the height and heroism of love. Those tokens which he had hitherto considered as proofs of a frightful peculiarity in her physical and moral system were now either forgotten, or, by the subtle sophistry of passion transmitted into a golden crown of enchantment, rendering Beatrice the more admirable by so much as she was the more unique. Whatever had looked ugly was now beautiful; or, if incapable of such a change, it stole away and hid itself among those shapeless half ideas which throng the dim region beyond the daylight of our perfect consciousness. Thus did he spend the night, nor fell asleep until the dawn had begun to awaken the slumbering flowers in Dr. Rappaccini's garden, whither Giovanni's dreams doubtless led him. Up rose the sun in his due season, and, flinging his beams upon the young man's eyelids, awoke him to a sense of pain. When thoroughly aroused, he became sensible of a burning and tingling agony in his hand—in his right hand—the very hand which Beatrice had grasped in her own when he was on the point of plucking one of the gemlike flowers. On the back of that hand there was now a purple print like that of four small fingers, and the likeness of a slender thumb upon his wrist.

Oh, how stubbornly does love,—or even that cunning semblance of love which flourishes in the imagination, but strikes no depth of root into the heart,—how stubbornly does it hold its faith until the moment comes when it is doomed to vanish into thin mist! Giovanni wrapped a handkerchief about his hand and wondered what evil thing had stung him, and soon forgot his pain in a reverie of Beatrice.

After the first interview, a second was in the inevitable course of what we call fate. A third; a fourth; and a meeting with Beatrice in the garden was no longer an incident in Giovanni's daily life, but the whole space in which he might be said to live; for the anticipation and memory of that ecstatic hour made up the remainder. Nor was it otherwise with the daughter of Rappaccini. She watched for the youth's appearance, and flew to his side with confidence as unreserved as if they had been playmates from early infancy—as if they were such playmates still. If, by any unwonted chance, he failed to come at the appointed moment, she stood beneath the window and sent up the rich sweetness of her tones to float around him in his chamber and echo and reverberate throughout his heart: "Giovanni! Giovanni! Why tarriest thou? Come down!" And down he hastened into that Eden of poisonous flowers.

But, with all this intimate familiarity, there was still a reserve in Beatrice's demeanor, so rigidly and invariably sustained that the idea of infringing it scarcely occurred to his imagination. By all appreciable signs, they loved; they had looked love with eyes that conveyed the holy secret from the depths of one soul into the depths of the other, as if it were too sacred to be whispered by the way; they had even spoken love in those gushes of passion when their spirits darted forth in articulated breath like tongues of long-hidden flame; and yet there had been no seal of lips, no clasp of hands, nor any slightest caress such as love claims and hallows. He had never touched one of the gleaming ringlets of her hair; her garment—so marked was the physical barrier between them—had never been waved against him by a breeze. On the few occasions when Giovanni had seemed tempted to overstep the limit, Beatrice grew so sad, so stern, and withal wore such a look of desolate separation, shuddering at itself, that not a spoken word was requisite to repel him. At such times he was startled at the horrible suspicions that rose, monster-like, out of the caverns of his heart and stared him in the face; his love grew thin and faint as the morning mist, his doubts alone had substance. But, when Beatrice's face brightened again after the momentary shadow, she was transformed at once from the mysterious, questionable being whom he had watched with so much awe and horror; she was now the beautiful and unsophisticated girl whom he felt that his spirit knew with a certainty beyond all other knowledge.

A considerable time had now passed since Giovanni's last meeting with Baglioni. One morning, however, he was disagreeably surprised by a visit from the professor, whom he had scarcely thought of for whole weeks, and would willingly have forgotten still longer. Given up as he had long been to a pervading excitement, he could tolerate no companions except upon condition of their perfect sympathy with his present state of feeling. Such sympathy was not to be expected from Professor Baglioni.

The visitor chatted carelessly for a few moments about the gossip of the city and the university, and then took up another topic.

"I have been reading an old classic author lately," said he, "and met with a story that strangely interested me. Possibly you may remember it. It is of an Indian prince, who sent a beautiful woman as a present to Alexander the Great. She was as lovely as the dawn and gorgeous as the sunset; but what especially distinguished her was a certain rich perfume in her breath—richer than a garden of Persian roses. Alexander, as was natural to a youthful conqueror, fell in love at first sight with this magnificent stranger; but a certain sage physician, happening to be present, discovered a terrible secret in regard to her."

"And what was that?" asked Giovanni, turning his eyes downward to avoid those of the professor.

"That this lovely woman," continued Baglioni, with emphasis, "had been nourished with poisons from her birth upward, until her whole nature was so imbued with them that she herself had become the deadliest poison in existence. Poison was her element of life. With that rich perfume of her breath she blasted the very air. Her love would have been poison—her embrace death. Is not this a marvellous tale?"

"A childish fable," answered Giovanni, nervously starting from his chair. "I marvel how your worship finds time to read such nonsense among your graver studies."

"By the by," said the professor, looking uneasily about him, "what singular fragrance is this in your apartment? Is it the perfume of your gloves? It is faint, but delicious; and yet, after all, by no means agreeable. Were I to breathe it long, methinks it would make me ill. It is like the breath of a flower; but I see no flowers in the chamber."

"Nor are there any," replied Giovanni, who had turned pale as the professor spoke; "nor, I think, is there any fragrance except in your worship's imagination. Odors, being a sort of element combined of the sensual and the spiritual, are apt to deceive us in this manner. The recollection of a perfume, the bare idea of it, may easily be mistaken for a present reality."

"Ay; but my sober imagination does not often play such tricks," said Baglioni; "and, were I to fancy any kind of odor, it would be that of some vile apothecary drug, wherewith my fingers are likely enough to be imbued. Our worshipful friend Rappaccini, as I have heard, tinctures his medicaments with odors richer than those of Araby. Doubtless, likewise, the fair and learned Signora Beatrice would minister to her patients with draughts as sweet as a maiden's breath; but woe to him that sips them!"

Giovanni's face evinced many contending emotions. The tone in which the professor alluded to the pure and lovely daughter of Rappaccini was a torture to his soul; and yet the intimation of a view of her character, opposite to his own, gave instantaneous distinctness to a thousand dim suspicions, which now grinned at him like so many demons. But he strove hard to quell them and to respond to Baglioni with a true lover's perfect faith.

"Signor professor," said he, "you were my father's friend; perchance, too, it is your purpose to act a friendly part towards his son. I would fain feel nothing towards you save respect and deference; but I pray you to observe, signor, that there is one subject on which we must not speak. You know not the Signora

Beatrice. You cannot, therefore, estimate the wrong—the blasphemy, I may even say—that is offered to her character by a light or injurious word."

"Giovanni! my poor Giovanni!" answered the professor, with calm expression of pity, "I know this wretched girl far better than yourself. You shall hear the truth in respect to the poisoner Rappaccini and his poisonous daughter; yes, poisonous as she is beautiful. Listen; for, even should you do violence to my gray hairs, it shall not silence me. That old fable of the Indian woman has become a truth by the deep and deadly science of Rappaccini and in the person of the lovely Beatrice."

Giovanni groaned and hid his face.

"Her father," continued Baglioni, "was not restrained by natural affection from offering up his child in this horrible manner as the victim of his insane zeal for science; for, let us do him justice, he is as true a man of science as ever distilled his own heart in an alembic. What, then, will be your fate? Beyond a doubt you are selected as the material of some new experiment. Perhaps the result is to be death; perhaps a fate more awful still. Rappaccini, with what he calls the interest of science before his eyes, will hesitate at nothing."

"It is a dream," muttered Giovanni to himself; "surely it is a dream."

"But," resumed the professor, "be of good cheer, son of my friend. It is not yet too late for the rescue. Possibly we may even succeed in bringing back this miserable child within the limits of ordinary nature, from which her father's madness has estranged her. Behold this little silver vase! It was wrought by the hands of the renowned Benvenuto Cellini, and is well worthy to be a love gift to the fairest dame in Italy. But its contents are invaluable. One little sip of this antidote would have rendered the most virulent poisons of the Borgias innocuous. Doubt not that it will be as efficacious against those of Rappaccini. Bestow the vase, and the precious liquid within it, on your Beatrice, and hopefully await the result."

Baglioni laid a small, exquisitely wrought silver vial on the table and withdrew, leaving what he had said to produce its effect upon the young man's mind.

"We will thwart Rappaccini yet," thought he, chuckling to himself, as he descended the stairs; "but, let us confess the truth of him, he is a wonderful man—a wonderful man indeed; a vile empiric, however, in his practice, and therefore not to be tolerated by those who respect the good old rules of the medical profession."

Throughout Giovanni's whole acquaintance with Beatrice, he had occasionally, as we have said, been haunted by dark surmises as to her character; yet so thoroughly had she made herself felt by him as a simple, natural, most affectionate, and guileless creature, that the image now held up by Professor Baglioni looked as strange and incredible as if it were not in accordance with his own original conception. True, there were ugly recollections connected with his first glimpses of the beautiful girl; he could not quite forget the bouquet that withered in her grasp, and the insect that perished amid the sunny air, by no ostensible agency save the fragrance of her breath. These incidents, however, dissolving in the pure light of her character, had no longer the efficacy of facts, but were acknowledged as mistaken fantasies, by whatever testimony of the senses they might appear to be substantiated. There is something truer and more real than what we can see with the eyes and touch with the finger. On such better evidence had Giovanni founded his confidence in Beatrice, though rather by the necessary force of her high attributes than by any deep and generous faith on his part. But now his spirit was incapable of sustaining itself at the height to which the early enthusiasm of passion had exalted it; he fell down, grovelling among earthly doubts, and defiled therewith the pure whiteness of Beatrice's image. Not that he gave her up; he did but distrust. He resolved to institute some decisive test that should satisfy him, once for all, whether there were those dreadful peculiarities in her physical nature which could not be supposed to exist without some corresponding monstrosity of soul. His eyes, gazing down afar, might have deceived him as to the lizard, the insect, and the flowers; but if he could witness, at the distance of a few paces, the sudden blight of one fresh and healthful flower in Beatrice's hand, there would

be room for no further 'question. With this idea he hastened
to the florist's and purchased a bouquet that was still gemmed
with the morning dew-drops.

It was now the customary hour of his daily interview with
Beatrice. Before descending into the garden, Giovanni failed
not to look at his figure in the mirror,—a vanity to be expected
in a beautiful young man, yet, as displaying itself at that
troubled and feverish moment, the token of a certain shallow-
ness of feeling and insincerity of character. He did gaze, however, and said to himself that his features had never before
possessed so rich a grace, nor his eyes such vivacity, nor his
cheeks so warm a hue of superabundant life.

"At least," thought he, "her poison has not yet insinuated
itself into my system. I am no flower to perish in her grasp."

With that thought he turned his eyes on the bouquet,
which he had never once laid aside from his hand. A thrill
of indefinable horror shot through his frame on perceiving
that those dewy flowers were already beginning to droop; they
wore the aspect of things that had been fresh and lovely
yesterday. Giovanni grew white as marble, and stood motionless before the mirror, staring at his own reflection there as at
the likeness of something frightful. He remembered Baglioni's
remark about the fragrance that seemed to pervade the
chamber. It must have been the poison in his breath! Then he
shuddered—shuddered at himself. Recovering from his stupor,
he began to watch with curious eye a spider that was busily
at work hanging its web from the antique cornice of the
apartment, crossing and recrossing the artful system of interwoven lines—as vigorous and active a spider as ever dangled
from an old ceiling. Giovanni bent towards the insect, and
emitted a deep, long breath. The spider suddenly ceased its
toil; the web vibrated with a tremor originating in the body
of the small artisan. Again Giovanni sent forth a breath,
deeper, longer, and imbued with a venomous feeling out of
his heart: he knew not whether he were wicked, or only
desperate. The spider made a convulsive gripe with his limbs
and hung dead across the window.

"Accursed! accursed!" muttered Giovanni, addressing himself. "Hast thou grown so poisonous that this deadly insect perishes by thy breath?"

At that moment a rich, sweet voice came floating up from the garden.

"Giovanni! Giovanni! It is past the hour! Why tarriest thou? Come down!"

"Yes," muttered Giovanni again. "She is the only being whom my breath may not slay! Would that it might!"

He rushed down, and in an instant was standing before the bright and loving eyes of Beatrice. A moment ago his wrath and despair had been so fierce that he could have desired nothing so much as to wither her by a glance; but with her actual presence there came influences which had too real an existence to be at once shaken off: recollections of the delicate and benign power of her feminine nature, which had so often enveloped him in a religious calm; recollections of many a holy and passionate outgush of her heart, when the pure fountain had been unsealed from its depths and made visible in its transparency to his mental eye; recollections which, had Giovanni known how to estimate them, would have assured him that all this ugly mystery was but an earthly illusion, and that, whatever mist of evil might seem to have gathered over her, the real Beatrice was a heavenly angel. Incapable as he was of such high faith, still her presence had not utterly lost its magic. Giovanni's rage was quelled into an aspect of sullen insensibility. Beatrice, with a quick spiritual sense, immediately felt that there was a gulf of blackness between them which neither he nor she could pass. They walked on together, sad and silent, and came thus to the marble fountain and to its pool of water on the ground, in the midst of which grew the shrub that bore gem-like blossoms. Giovanni was affrighted at the eager enjoyment—the appetite, as it were—with which he found himself inhaling the fragrance of the flowers.

"Beatrice," asked he, abruptly, "whence came this shrub?"

"My father created it," answered she, with simplicity.

"Created it! created it!" repeated Giovanni. "What mean you, Beatrice?"

"He is a man fearfully acquainted with the secrets of Nature," replied Beatrice; "and, at the hour when I first drew breath, this plant sprang from the soil, the offspring of his science, of his intellect, while I was but his earthly child. Approach it not!" continued she, observing with terror that Giovanni was drawing nearer to the shrub. "It has qualities that you little dream of. But I, dearest Giovanni,—I grew up and blossomed with the plant and was nourished with its breath. It was my sister, and I loved it with a human affection; for, alas!—hast thou not suspected it?—there was an awful doom."

Here Giovanni frowned so darkly upon her that Beatrice paused and trembled. But her faith in his tenderness reassured her, and made her blush that she had doubted for an instant.

"There was an awful doom," she continued, "the effect of my father's fatal love of science, which estranged me from all society of my kind. Until Heaven sent thee, dearest Giovanni, oh, how lonely was thy poor Beatrice!"

"Was it a hard doom?" asked Giovanni, fixing his eyes upon her.

"Only of late have I known how hard it was," answered she, tenderly. "Oh, yes; but my heart was torpid, and therefore quiet."

Giovanni's rage broke forth from his sullen gloom like a lightning flash out of a dark cloud.

"Accursed one!" cried he, with venomous scorn and anger. "And, finding thy solitude wearisome, thou hast severed me likewise from all the warmth of life and enticed me into the region of unspeakable horror!"

"Giovanni!" exclaimed Beatrice, turning her large bright eyes upon his face. The force of his words had not found its way into her mind; she was merely thunderstruck.

"Yes, poisonous thing!" repeated Giovanni, beside himself with passion. "Thou hast done it! Thou has blasted me! Thou hast filled my veins with poison! Thou hast made me as hateful, as ugly, as loathsome and deadly a creature as thyself—a world's wonder of hideous monstrosity! Now, if our breath be happily as fatal to ourselves as to all others, let us join our lips in one kiss of unutterable hatred, and so die!"

"What has befallen me?" murmured Beatrice, with a low moan out of her heart. "Holy Virgin, pity me, a poor heart-broken child!"

"Thou,—dost thou pray?" cried Giovanni, still with the same fiendish scorn. "Thy very prayers, as they come from thy lips, taint the atmosphere with death. Yes, yes; let us pray! Let us to church and dip our fingers in the holy water at the portal! They that come after us will perish as by a pestilence! Let us sign crosses in the air! It will be scattering curses abroad in the likeness of holy symbols!"

"Giovanni," said Beatrice, calmly, for her grief was beyond passion, "why dost thou join thyself with me thus in those terrible words? I, it is true, am the horrible thing thou namest me. But thou,—what hast thou to do, save with one other shudder at my hideous misery to go forth out of the garden and mingle with thy race, and forget there ever crawled on earth such a monster as poor Beatrice?"

"Dost thou pretend ignorance?" asked Giovanni, scowling upon her. "Behold this power have I gained from the pure daughter of Rappaccini."

There was a swarm of summer insects flitting through the air in search of the food promised by the flower odors of the fatal garden. They circled round Giovanni's head, and were evidently attracted towards him by the same influence which had drawn them for an instant within the sphere of several of the shrubs. He sent forth a breath among them, and smiled bitterly at Beatrice as at least a score of the insects fell dead upon the ground.

"I see it! I see it!" shrieked Beatrice. "It is my father's fatal science! No, no, Giovanni; it was not I! Never! never! I dreamed only to love thee and be with thee a little time, and so to let thee pass away, leaving but thine image in mine heart; for, Giovanni, believe it, though my body be nourished with poison, my spirit is God's creature, and craves love as its daily food. But my father,—he has united us in this fearful sympathy. Yes; spurn me, tread upon me, kill me! Oh, what is death after such words as thine? But it was not I. Not for a world of bliss would I have done it."

Giovanni's passion had exhausted itself in its outburst from his lips. There now came across him a sense, mournful, and not without tenderness, of the intimate and peculiar relationship between Beatrice and himself. They stood, as it were, in an utter solitude, which would be made none the less solitary by the densest throng of human life. Ought not, then, the desert of humanity around them to press this insulated pair closer together? If they should be cruel to one another, who was there to be kind to them? Besides, thought Giovanni, might there not still be a hope of his returning within the limits of ordinary nature, and leading Beatrice, the redeemed Beatrice, by the hand? O, weak, and selfish, and unworthy spirit, that could dream of an earthly union and earthly happiness as possible, after such deep love had been so bitterly wronged as was Beatrice's love by Giovanni's blighting words! No, no; there could be no such hope. She must pass heavily, with that broken heart, across the borders of Time—she must bathe her hurts in some fount of paradise, and forget her grief in the light of immortality, and *there* be well.

But Giovanni did not know it.

"Dear Beatrice," said he, approaching her, while she shrank away as always at his approach, but now with a different impulse, "dearest Beatrice our fate is not yet so desperate. Behold! there is a medicine, potent, as a wise physician has assured me, and almost divine in its efficacy. It is composed of ingredients the most opposite to those by which thy awful father has brought this calamity upon thee and me. It is distilled of blessed herbs. Shall we not quaff it together, and thus be purified from evil?"

"Give it me!" said Beatrice, extending her hand to receive the little silver vial which Giovanni took from his
bosom. She added, with a peculiar emphasis, "I will drink;
but do thou await the result."

She put Baglioni's antidote to her lips; and, at the same moment, the figure of Rappaccini emerged from the portal and
came slowly towards the marble fountain. As he drew near,
the pale man of science seemed to gaze with a triumphant expression at the beautiful youth and maiden, as might an
artist who should spend his life in achieving a picture or a
group of statuary and finally be satisfied with his success.
He paused; his bent form grew erect with conscious power; he
spread out his hands over them in the attitude of a father im-
ploring a blessing upon his children; but those were the same
hands that had thrown poison into the stream of their lives.
Giovanni trembled. Beatrice shuddered nervously, and pressed
her hand upon her heart.

"My daughter," said Rappaccini, "thou art no longer lonely
in the world. Pluck one of those precious gems from thy
sister shrub and bid thy bridegroom wear it in his bosom. It
will not harm him now. My science and the sympathy between
thee and him have so wrought within his system that he now
stands apart from common men, as thou dost, daughter of my
pride and triumph, from ordinary women. Pass on, then,
through the world, most dear to one another and dreadful
to all besides!"

"My father," said Beatrice, feebly,—and still as she spoke
she kept her hand upon her heart,—"wherefore didst thou
inflict this miserable doom upon thy child?"

"Miserable!" exclaimed Rappaccini. "What mean you, foolish girl? Dost thou deem it misery to be endowed with
marvellous gifts against which no power nor strength could
avail an enemy—misery, to be able to quell the mightiest with
a breath—misery, to be as terrible as thou art beautiful?
Wouldst thou, then, have preferred the condition of a weak
woman, exposed to all evil and capable of none?"

"I would fain have been loved, not feared," murmured

Beatrice, sinking down upon the ground. "But now it matters not. I am going, father, where the evil which thou hast striven to mingle with my being will pass away like a dream—like the fragrance of these poisonous flowers, which will no longer taint my breath among the flowers of Eden. Farewell, Giovanni! Thy words of hatred are like lead within my heart; but they, too, will fall away as I ascend. Oh, was there not, from the first, more poison in thy nature than in mine?"

To Beatrice,—so radically had her earthly part been wrought upon by Rappaccini's skill,—as poison had been life, so the powerful antidote was death; and thus the poor victim of man's ingenuity and of thwarted nature, and of the fatality that attends all such efforts of perverted wisdom, perished there, at the feet of her father and Giovanni. Just at that moment Professor Pietro Baglioni looked forth from the window, and called loudly, in a tone of triumph mixed with horror, to the thunderstricken man of science,—

"Rappaccini! Rappaccini! and is *this* the upshot of your experiment!"

ETHAN
BRAND

A CHAPTER FROM AN ABORTIVE ROMANCE

Bartram the lime-burner, a rough, heavy-looking man, begrimed with charcoal, sat watching his kiln at nightfall, while his little son played at building houses with the scattered fragments of marble, when, on the hill-side below them, they heard a roar of laughter, not mirthful, but slow, and even solemn, like a wind shaking the boughs of the forest.

"Father, what is that?" asked the little boy, leaving his play, and pressing betwixt his father's knees.

"Oh, some drunken man, I suppose," answered the lime-burner; "some merry fellow from the bar-room in the village, who dared not laugh loud enough within doors lest he should blow the roof of the house off. So here he is, shaking his jolly sides at the foot of Graylock."

"But, father," said the child, more sensitive than the obtuse, middle-aged clown, "he does not laugh like a man that is glad. So the noise frightens me!"

"Don't be a fool, child!" cried his father, gruffly. "You will never make a man, I do believe; there is too much of your mother in you. I have known the rustling of a leaf startle you. Hark! Here comes the merry fellow now. You shall see that there is no harm in him."

Bartram and his little son, while they were talking thus, sat

First published in *The Dollar Magazine,* May, 1851.

watching the same lime-kiln that had been the scene of Ethan Brand's solitary and meditative life, before he began his search for the Unpardonable Sin. Many years, as we have seen, had now elapsed, since that portentous night when the IDEA was first developed. The kiln, however, on the mountain-side, stood unimpaired, and was in nothing changed since he had thrown his dark thoughts into the intense glow of its furnace, and melted them, as it were, into the one thought that took possession of his life. It was a rude, round, tower-like structure about twenty feet high, heavily built of rough stones, and with a hillock of earth heaped about the larger part of its circumference; so that the blocks and fragments of marble might be drawn by cart-loads, and thrown in at the top. There was an opening at the bottom of the tower, like an oven-mouth, but large enough to admit a man in a stooping pos-ture, and provided with a massive iron door. With the smoke and jets of flame issuing from the chinks and crevices of this door, which seemed to give admittance into the hill-side, it resembled nothing so much as the private entrance to the in-fernal regions, which the shepherds of the Delectable Moun-tains were accustomed to show to pilgrims.

There are many such lime-kilns in that tract of country, for the purpose of burning the white marble which composes a large part of the substance of the hills. Some of them, built years ago, and long deserted, with weeds growing in the vacant round of the interior, which is open to the sky, and grass and wild-flowers rooting themselves into the chinks of the stones, look already like relics of antiquity, and may yet be over-spread with the lichens of centuries to come. Others, where the lime-burner still feeds his daily and night-long fire, afford points of interest to the wanderer among the hills, who seats himself on a log of wood or a fragment of marble, to hold a chat with the solitary man. It is a lonesome, and, when the character is inclined to thought, may be an intensely thought-ful occupation; as it proved in the case of Ethan Brand, who had mused to such strange purpose, in days gone by, while the fire in this very kiln was burning.

The man who now watched the fire was of a different order, and troubled himself with no thoughts save the very few that were requisite to his business. At frequent intervals, he flung back the clashing weight of the iron door, and, turning his face from the insufferable glare, thrust in huge logs of oak, or stirred the immense brands with a long pole. Within the furnace were seen the curling and riotous flames, and the burning marble, almost molten with the intensity of heat; while without, the reflection of the fire quivered on the dark intricacy of the surrounding forest, and showed in the foreground a bright and ruddy little picture of the hut, the spring beside its door, the athletic and coal-begrimed figure of the lime-burner, and the half-frightened child, shrinking into the protection of his father's shadow. And when, again, the iron door was closed, then reappeared the tender light of the half-full moon, which vainly strove to trace out the indistinct shapes of the neighboring mountains; and, in the upper sky, there was a flitting congregation of clouds, still faintly tinged with the rosy sunset, though thus far down into the valley the sunshine had vanished long and long ago.

The little boy now crept still closer to his father, as footsteps were heard ascending the hill-side, and a human form thrust aside the bushes that clustered beneath the trees.

"Halloo! who is it?" cried the lime-burner, vexed at his son's timidity, yet half infected by it. "Come forward, and show yourself, like a man, or I'll fling this chunk of marble at your head!"

"You offer me a rough welcome," said a gloomy voice, as the unknown man drew nigh. "Yet I neither claim nor desire a kinder one, even at my own fireside."

To obtain a distincter view, Bartram threw open the iron door of the kiln, whence immediately issued a gush of fierce light, that smote full upon the stranger's face and figure. To a careless eye there appeared nothing very remarkable in his aspect, which was that of a man in a coarse, brown, country-made suit of clothes, tall and thin, with the staff and heavy shoes of a wayfarer. As he advanced, he fixed his eyes—

which were very bright—intently upon the brightness of the furnace, as if he beheld, or expected to behold, some object worthy of note within it.

"Good evening, stranger," said the lime-burner; "whence come you, so late in the day?"

"I come from my search," answered the wayfarer; "for, at last, it is finished."

"Drunk!—or crazy!" muttered Bartram to himself. "I shall have trouble with the fellow. The sooner I drive him away, the better."

The little boy, all in a tremble, whispered to his father, and begged him to shut the door of the kiln, so that there might not be so much light; for that there was something in the man's face which he was afraid to look at, yet could not look away from. And, indeed, even the lime-burner's dull and torpid sense began to be impressed by an indescribable something in that thin, rugged, thoughtful visage, with the grizzled hair hanging wildly about it, and those deeply sunken eyes, which gleamed like fires within the entrance of a mysterious cavern. But, as he closed the door, the stranger turned towards him, and spoke in a quiet, familiar way, that made Bartram feel as if he were a sane and sensible man, after all.

"Your task draws to an end, I see," said he. "This marble has already been burning three days. A few hours more will convert the stone to lime."

"Why, who are you?" exclaimed the lime-burner. "You seem as well acquainted with my business as I am myself."

"And well I may be," said the stranger; "for I followed the same craft many a long year, and here, too, on this very spot. But you are a new-comer in these parts. Did you never hear of Ethan Brand?"

"The man that went in search of the Unpardonable Sin?" asked Bartram, with a laugh.

"The same," answered the stranger. "He has found what he sought, and therefore he comes back again."

"What! then you are Ethan Brand himself?" cried the lime-burner, in amazement. "I am a new-comer here, as you say, and they call it eighteen years since you left the foot of Gray-lock. But, I can tell you, the good folks still talk about Ethan Brand, in the village yonder, and what a strange errand took him away from his lime-kiln. Well, and so you found the Unpardonable Sin?"

"Even so!" said the stranger, calmly.

"If the question is a fair one," proceeded Bartram, "where might it be?"

Ethan Brand laid his finger on his own heart.

"Here!" replied he.

And then, without mirth in his countenance, but as if moved by an involuntary recognition of the infinite absurdity of seeking throughout the world for what was the closest of all things to himself, and looking into every heart, save his own, for what was hidden in no other breast, he broke into a laugh of scorn. It was the same slow, heavy laugh, that had almost appalled the lime-burner when it heralded the way-farer's approach.

The solitary mountain-side was made dismal by it. Laugh-ter, when out of place, mistimed, or bursting forth from a disordered state of feeling, may be the most terrible modula-tion of the human voice. The laughter of one asleep, even if it be a little child,—the madman's laugh,—the wild, scream-ing laugh of a born idiot,—are sounds that we sometimes tremble to hear, and would always willingly forget. Poets have imagined no utterance of fiends or hobgoblins so fear-fully appropriate as a laugh. And even the obtuse lime-burner felt his nerves shaken, as this strange man looked inward at his own heart, and burst into laughter that rolled away into the night, and was indistinctly reverberated among the hills.

"Joe," said he to his little son, "scamper down to the tavern in the village, and tell the jolly fellows there that Ethan Brand has come back, and that he has found the Un-pardonable Sin!"

The boy darted away on his errand, to which Ethan Brand made no objection, nor seemed hardly to notice it. He sat on a log of wood, looking steadfastly at the iron door of the kiln.

When the child was out of sight, and his swift and light foot-steps ceased to be heard treading first on the fallen leaves and then on the rocky mountain-path, the lime-burner began to regret his departure. He felt that the little fellow's presence had been a barrier between his guest and himself, and that he must now deal, heart to heart, with a man who, on his own confession, had committed the one only crime for which Heaven could afford no mercy. That crime, in its indistinct blackness, seemed to overshadow him, and made his memory riotous with a throng of evil shapes that asserted their kindred with the Master Sin, whatever it might be, which it was within the scope of man's corrupted nature to conceive and cherish. They were all of one family; they went to and fro between his breast and Ethan Brand's, and carried dark greetings from one to the other.

Then Bartram remembered the stories which had grown traditionary in reference to this strange man, who had come upon him like a shadow of the night, and was making him-self at home in his old place, after so long absence, that the dead people, dead and buried for years, would have had more right to be at home, in any familiar spot, than he. Ethan Brand, it was said, had conversed with Satan himself in the lurid blaze of this very kiln. The legend had been matter of mirth heretofore, but looked grisly now. According to this tale, before Ethan Brand departed on his search, he had been accustomed to evoke a fiend from the hot furnace of the lime-kiln, night after night, in order to confer with him about the Unpardonable Sin; the man and the fiend each laboring to frame the image of some mode of guilt which could neither be atoned for nor forgiven. And, with the first gleam of light upon the mountain-top, the fiend crept in at the iron door, there to abide the intensest element of fire until again sum-moned forth to share in the dreadful task of extending man's possible guilt beyond the scope of Heaven's else infinite mercy.

While the lime-burner was struggling with the horror of these thoughts, Ethan Brand rose from the log, and flung open the door of the kiln. The action was in such accordance with the idea in Bartram's mind, that he almost expected to see the Evil One issue forth, red-hot, from the raging furnace.

"Hold! hold!" cried he, with a tremulous attempt to laugh; for he was ashamed of his fears, although they overmastered him. "Don't, for mercy's sake, bring out your Devil now!"

"Man!" sternly replied Ethan Brand, "what need have I of the Devil? I have left him behind me, on my track. It is with such half-way sinners as you that he busies himself. Fear not, because I open the door. I do but act by old custom, and am going to trim your fire, like a lime-burner, as I was once."

He stirred the vast coals, thrust in more wood, and bent forward to gaze into the hollow prison-house of the fire, regardless of the fierce glow that reddened upon his face. The lime-burner sat watching him, and half suspected this strange guest of a purpose, if not to evoke a fiend, at least to plunge into the flames, and thus vanish from the sight of man. Ethan Brand, however, drew quietly back, and closed the door of the kiln.

"I have looked," said he, "into many a human heart that was seven times hotter with sinful passions than yonder furnace is with fire. But I found not there what I sought. No, not the Unpardonable Sin!"

"What is the Unpardonable Sin?" asked the lime-burner; and then he shrank farther from his companion, trembling lest his question should be answered.

"It is a sin that grew within my own breast," replied Ethan Brand, standing erect with a pride that distinguishes all enthusiasts of his stamp. "A sin that grew nowhere else! The sin of an intellect that triumphed over the sense of brotherhood with man and reverence for God, and sacrificed everything to its own mighty claims! The only sin that deserves a recompense of immortal agony! Freely, were it to do again, would I incur the guilt. Unshrinkingly I accept the retribution!"

"The man's head is turned," muttered the lime-burner to himself. "He may be a sinner like the rest of us,—nothing more likely,—but, I'll be sworn, he is a madman too."

Nevertheless, he felt uncomfortable at his situation, alone

with Ethan Brand on the wild mountain-side, and was right
glad to hear the rough murmur of tongues, and the footsteps
of what seemed a pretty numerous party, stumbling over the
stones and rustling through the underbrush. Soon appeared
the whole lazy regiment that was wont to infest the village
tavern, comprehending three or four individuals who had
drunk flip beside the bar-room fire through all the winters,
and smoked their pipes beneath the stoop through all the
summers, since Ethan Brand's departure. Laughing boister-
ously, and mingling all their voices together in unceremonious
talk, they now burst into the moonshine and narrow streaks
of firelight that illuminated the open space before the lime-
kiln. Bartram set the door ajar again, flooding the spot with
light, that the whole company might get a fair view of Ethan
Brand, and he of them.

There, among other old acquaintances, was a once ubiqui-
tous man, now almost extinct, but whom we were formerly
sure to encounter at the hotel of every thriving village
throughout the country. It was the stage-agent. The present
specimen of the genus was a wilted and smoke-dried man,
wrinkled and red-nosed, in a smartly cut, brown, bobtailed
coat, with brass buttons, who, for a length of time unknown,
had kept his desk and corner in the bar-room, and was still
puffing what seemed to be the same cigar that he had lighted
twenty years before. He had great fame as a dry joker, though,
perhaps, less on account of any intrinsic humor than from a
certain flavor of brandy-toddy and tobacco-smoke, which impregnated all his ideas and expressions, as well as his person.
Another well-remembered, though strangely altered, face was
that of Lawyer Giles, as people still called him in courtesy;
an elderly ragamuffin, in his soiled shirtsleeves and tow-cloth
trousers. This poor fellow had been an attorney, in what he
called his better days, a sharp practitioner, and in great vogue
among the village litigants; but flip, and sling, and toddy,
and cocktails, imbibed at all hours, morning, noon, and
night, had caused him to slide from intellectual to various
kinds and degrees of bodily labor, till at last, to adopt his own

phrase, he slid into a soap-vat. In other words, Giles was now a soap-boiler, in a small way. He had come to be but the fragment of a human being, a part of one foot having been chopped off by an axe, and an entire hand torn away by the devilish grip of a steam-engine. Yet, though the corporeal hand was gone, a spiritual member remained; for, stretching forth the stump, Giles steadfastly averred that he felt an invisible thumb and fingers with as vivid a sensation as before the real ones were amputated. A maimed and miserable wretch he was; but one, nevertheless, whom the world could not trample on, and had no right to scorn, either in this or any previous stage of his misfortunes, since he had still kept up the courage and spirit of a man, asked nothing in charity, and with his one hand—and that the left one— fought a stern battle against want and hostile circumstances.

Among the throng, too, came another personage, who with certain points of similarity to Lawyer Giles, had many more of difference. It was the village doctor; a man of some fifty years, whom, at an earlier period of his life, we introduced as paying a professional visit to Ethan Brand during the latter's supposed insanity. He was now a purple-visaged, rude, and brutal, yet half-gentlemanly figure, with something wild, ruined, and desperate in his talk, and in all the details of his gesture and manners. Brandy possessed this man like an evil spirit, and made him as surly and savage as a wild beast, and as miserable as a lost soul; but there was supposed to be in him such wonderful skill, such native gifts of healing, beyond any which medical science could impart, that society caught hold of him, and would not let him sink out of its reach. So, swaying to and fro upon his horse, and grumbling thick accents at the bedside, he visited all the sick-chambers for miles about among the mountain towns, and sometimes raised a dying man, as it were, by miracle, or quite as often, no doubt, sent his patient to a grave that was dug many a year too soon. The doctor had an everlasting pipe in his mouth, and, as somebody said, in allusion to his habit of swearing, it was always alight with hell-fire.

These three worthies pressed forward, and greeted Ethan Brand each after his own fashion, earnestly inviting him to partake of the contents of a certain black bottle, in which, as they averred, he would find something far better worth seeking than the Unpardonable Sin. No mind, which has wrought itself by intense and solitary meditation into a high state of enthusiasm, can endure the kind of contact with low and vulgar modes of thought and feeling to which Ethan Brand was now subjected. It made him doubt—and, strange to say, it was a painful doubt—whether he had indeed found the Unpardonable Sin, and found it within himself. The whole question on which he had exhausted life, and more than life, looked like a delusion.

"Leave me," he said bitterly, "ye brute beasts, that have made yourselves so, shrivelling up your souls with fiery liquors! I have done with you. Years and years ago, I groped into your hearts and found nothing there for my purpose. Get ye gone!"

"Why, you uncivil scoundrel," cried the fierce doctor, "is that the way you respond to the kindness of your best friends? Then let me tell you the truth. You have no more found the Unpardonable Sin than yonder boy Joe has. You are but a crazy fellow,—I told you so twenty years ago,—neither better nor worse than a crazy fellow, and the fit companion of old Humphrey, here!"

He pointed to an old man, shabbily dressed, with long white hair, thin visage, and unsteady eyes. For some years past this aged person had been wandering about among the hills, inquiring of all travellers whom he met for his daughter. The girl, it seemed, had gone off with a company of circus-performers, and occasionally tidings of her came to the village, and fine stories were told of her glittering appearance as she rode on horseback in the ring, or performed marvellous feats on the tight-rope.

The white-haired father now approached Ethan Brand, and gazed unsteadily into his face.

"They tell me you have been all over the earth," said he,

wringing his hands with earnestness. "You must have seen my daughter, for she makes a grand figure in the world, and everybody goes to see her. Did she send any word to her old father, or say when she was coming back?"

Ethan Brand's eye quailed beneath the old man's. That daughter, from whom he so earnestly desired a word of greeting, was the Esther of our tale, the very girl whom, with such cold and remorseless purpose, Ethan Brand had made the subject of a psychological experiment, and wasted, absorbed, and perhaps annihilated her soul, in the process.

"Yes," he murmured, turning away from the hoary wanderer, "it is no delusion. There is an Unpardonable Sin!"

While these things were passing, a merry scene was going forward in the area of cheerful light, beside the spring and before the door of the hut. A number of the youth of the village, young men and girls, had hurried up the hill-side, impelled by curiosity to see Ethan Brand, the hero of so many a legend familiar to their childhood. Finding nothing, however, very remarkable in his aspect,—nothing but a sunburnt wayfarer, in plain garb and dusty shoes, who sat looking into the fire as if he fancied pictures among the coals,—these young people speedily grew tired of observing him. As it happened, there was other amusement at hand. An old German Jew, travelling with a diorama on his back, was passing down the mountain-road towards the village just as the party turned aside from it, and, in hopes of eking out the profits of the day, the showman had kept them company to the lime-kiln.

"Come, old Dutchman," cried one of the young men, "let us see your pictures, if you can swear they are worth looking at!"

"Oh yes, Captain," answered the Jew,—whether as a matter of courtesy or craft, he styled everybody Captain,—"I shall show you, indeed, some very superb pictures!"

So, placing his box in a proper position, he invited the young men and girls to look through the glass orifices of the machine, and proceeded to exhibit a series of the most outrageous scratchings and daubings, as specimens of the fine arts, that ever an itinerant showman had the face to impose upon his circle of spectators. The pictures were worn out, moreover, tattered, full of cracks and wrinkles, dingy with tobacco-smoke, and otherwise in a most pitiable condition. Some purported to be cities, public edifices, and ruined castles in Europe; others represented Napoleon's battles and Nelson's sea-fights; and in the midst of these would be seen a gigantic, brown, hairy hand,—which might have been mistaken for the Hand of Destiny, though, in truth, it was only the showman's, —pointing its forefinger to various scenes of the conflict, which its owner gave historical illustrations. When, with much merriment at its abominable deficiency of merit, the exhibition was concluded, the German bade little Joe put his head into the box. Viewed through the magnifying-glasses, the boy's round, rosy visage assumed the strangest imaginable aspect of an immense Titanic child, the mouth grinning broadly, and the eyes and every other feature overflowing with fun at the joke. Suddenly, however, that merry face turned pale, and its expression changed to horror, for this easily impressed and excitable child had become sensible that the eye of Ethan Brand was fixed upon him through the glass.

"You make the little man to be afraid, Captain," said the German Jew, turning up the dark and strong outline of his visage from his stooping posture. "But look again, and, by chance, I shall cause you to see somewhat that is very fine, upon my word!"

Ethan Brand gazed into the box for an instant, and then starting back, looked fixedly at the German. What had he seen? Nothing, apparently; for a curious youth, who had peeped in almost at the same moment, beheld only a vacant space of canvas.

"I remember you now," muttered Ethan Brand to the showman.

"Ah, Captain," whispered the Jew of Nuremberg, with a dark smile, "I find it to be a heavy matter in my show-box, —this Unpardonable Sin! By my faith, Captain, it has wearied my shoulders, this long day, to carry it over the mountain."

"Peace," answered Ethan Brand, sternly, "or get thee into the furnace yonder!"

The Jew's exhibition had scarcely concluded, when a great, elderly dog—who seemed to be his own master, as no person in the company laid claim to him—saw fit to render himself the object of public notice. Hitherto, he had shown himself a very quiet, well-disposed old dog, going round from one to another, and, by way of being sociable, offering his rough head to be patted by any kindly hand that would take so much trouble. But now, all of a sudden, this grave and venerable quadruped, of his own mere notion, and without the slightest suggestion from anybody else, began to run round after his tail, which, to heighten the absurdity of the proceeding, was a great deal shorter than it should have been. Never was seen such headlong eagerness in pursuit of an object that could not possibly be attained; never was heard such a tremendous outbreak of growling, snarling, barking, and snapping,— as if one end of the ridiculous brute's body were at deadly and most unforgivable enmity with the other. Faster and faster, round about went the cur; and faster and still faster fled the unapproachable brevity of his tail; and louder and fiercer grew his yells of rage and animosity; until, utterly exhausted, and as far from the goal as ever, the foolish old dog ceased his performance as suddenly as he had begun it. The next moment he was as mild, quiet, sensible, and respectable in his deportment, as when he first scraped acquaintance with the company.

As may be supposed, the exhibition was greeted with universal laughter, clapping of hands, and shouts of encore, to which the canine performer responded by wagging all that there was to wag of his tail, but appeared totally unable to repeat his very successful effort to amuse the spectators.

Meanwhile, Ethan Brand had resumed his seat upon the log, and moved, as it might be, by a perception of some remote analogy between his own case and that of this self-pursuing cur, he broke into the awful laugh, which, more than any other token, expressed the condition of his inward being. From that moment, the merriment of the party was at an end; they stood aghast, dreading lest the inauspicious sound should be reverberated around the horizon, and that mountain would thunder it to mountain, and so the horror be prolonged upon their ears. Then, whispering one to another that it was late,—that the moon was almost down,—that the August night was growing chill,—they hurried homewards, leaving the lime-burner and little Joe to deal as they might with their unwelcome guest. Save for these three human beings, the open space on the hill-side was a solitude, set in a vast gloom of forest. Beyond that darksome verge, the firelight glimmered on the stately trunks and almost black foliage of pines, intermixed with the lighter verdure of sapling oaks, maples, and poplars, while here and there lay the gigantic corpses of dead trees, decaying on the leaf-strewn soil. And it seemed to little Joe—a timorous and imaginative child—that the silent forest was holding its breath until some fearful thing should happen.

Ethan Brand thrust more wood into the fire, and closed the door of the kiln; then looking over his shoulder at the lime-burner and his son, he bade, rather than advised, them to retire to rest.

"For myself, I cannot sleep," said he. "I have matters that it concerns me to meditate upon. I will watch the fire, as I used to do in the old time."

"And call the Devil out of the furnace to keep you company, I suppose," muttered Bartram, who had been making intimate acquaintance with the black bottle above mentioned. "But watch, if you like, and call as many devils as you like! For my part, I shall be all the better for a snooze. Come, Joe!"

As the boy followed his father into the hut, he looked back at the wayfarer, and the tears came into his eyes, for his tender spirit had an intuition of the bleak and terrible loneliness in which this man had enveloped himself.

When they had gone, Ethan Brand sat listening to the crackling of the kindled wood, and looking at the little spirts of fire that issued through the chinks of the door. These trifles, however, once so familiar, had but the slightest hold of his attention, while deep within his mind he was reviewing the gradual but marvellous change that had been wrought upon him by the search to which he had devoted himself. He remembered how the night dew had fallen upon him,—how the dark forest had whispered to him,—how the stars had gleamed upon him,—a simple and loving man, watching his fire in the years gone by, and ever musing as it burned. He remembered with what tenderness, with what love and sympathy for mankind, and what pity for human guilt and woe, he had first begun to contemplate those ideas which afterwards became the inspiration of his life; with what reverence he had then looked into the heart of man, viewing it as a temple originally divine, and, however desecrated, still to be held sacred by a brother; with what awful fear he had deprecated the success of his pursuit, and prayed that the Unpardonable Sin might never be revealed to him. Then ensued that vast intellectual development, which, in its progress, disturbed the counterpoise between his mind and heart. The Idea that possessed his life had operated as a means of education; it had gone on cultivating his powers to the highest point of which they were susceptible; it had raised him from the level of an unlettered laborer to stand on a star-lit eminence, whither the philosophers of the earth, laden with the lore of universities, might vainly strive to clamber after him. So much for the intellect! But where was the heart? That, indeed, had withered,—had contracted,—had hardened, —had perished! It had ceased to partake of the universal throb. He had lost his hold of the magnetic chain of humanity. He was no longer a brother-man, opening the chambers or the dungeons of our common nature by the key of holy sympathy, which gave him a right to share in all its secrets; he was now a cold observer, looking on mankind as the subject of his experiment, and, at length, converting man and woman to be his puppets, and pulling the wires that moved them to such degrees of crime as were demanded for his study.

Thus Ethan Brand became a fiend. He began to be so from

the moment that his moral nature had ceased to keep the pace of improvement with his intellect. And now, as his highest effort and inevitable development,—as the bright and gorgeous flower, and rich, delicious fruit of his life's labor,— he had produced the Unpardonable Sin!

"What more have I to seek? what more to achieve?" said Ethan Brand to himself. "My task is done, and well done!"

Starting from the log with a certain alacrity in his gait and ascending the hillock of earth that was raised against the stone circumference of the lime-kiln, he thus reached the top of the structure. It was a space of perhaps ten feet across, from edge to edge, presenting a view of the upper surface of the immense mass of broken marble with which the kiln was heaped. All these innumerable blocks and fragments of marble were red-hot and vividly on fire, sending up great spouts of blue flame, which quivered aloft and danced madly, as within a magic circle, and sank and rose again, with continual and multitudinous activity. As the lonely man bent forward over this terrible body of fire, the blasting heat smote up against his person with a breath that, it might be supposed, would have scorched and shrivelled him up in a moment.

Ethan Brand stood erect, and raised his arms on high. The blue flames played upon his face, and imparted the wild and ghastly light which alone could have suited its expression; it was that of a fiend on the verge of plunging into his gulf of intensest torment.

"O Mother Earth," cried he, "who art no more my Mother, and into whose bosom this frame shall never be resolved! O mankind, whose brotherhood I have cast off, and trampled thy great heart beneath my feet! O stars of heaven, that shone on me of old, as if to light me onward and upward!— farewell all, and forever. Come, deadly element of Fire,— henceforth my familiar friend! Embrace me, as I do thee!"

That night the sound of a fearful peal of laughter rolled heavily through the sleep of the lime-burner and his little son; dim shapes of horror and anguish haunted their dreams, and seemed still present in the rude hovel, when they opened their eyes to the daylight.

"Up, boy, up!" cried the lime-burner, staring about him. "Thank Heaven, the night is gone, at last; and rather than pass such another, I would watch my lime-kiln, wide awake, for a twelve-month. This Ethan Brand, with his humbug of an Unpardonable Sin, has done me no such mighty favor, in taking my place!"

He issued from the hut, followed by little Joe, who kept fast hold of his father's hand. The early sunshine was already pouring its gold upon the mountain-tops, and though the valleys were still in shadow, they smiled cheerfully in the promise of the bright day that was hastening onward. The village, completely shut in by hills, which swelled away gently about it, looked as if it had rested peacefully in the hollow of the great hand of Providence. Every dwelling was distinctly visible; the little spires of the two churches pointed upwards, and caught a fore-glimmering of brightness from the sun-gilt skies upon their gilded weather-cocks. The tavern was astir, and the figure of the old, smoke-dried stage-agent, cigar in mouth, was seen beneath the stoop. Old Graylock was glorified with a golden cloud upon his head. Scattered likewise over the breasts of the surrounding mountains, there were heaps of hoary mist, in fantastic shapes, some of them far down into the valley, others high up towards the summits, and still others, of the same family of mist or cloud, hovering in the gold radiance of the upper atmosphere. Stepping from one to another of the clouds that rested on the hills, and thence to the loftier brotherhood that sailed in air, it seemed almost as if a mortal man might thus ascend into the heavenly regions. Earth was so mingled with sky that it was a daydream to look at it.

To supply that charm of the familiar and homely, which Nature so readily adopts into a scene like this, the stage-coach was rattling down the mountain-road, and the driver sounded his horn, while Echo caught up the notes, and intertwined them into a rich and varied and elaborate harmony, of which the original performer could lay claim to little share. The great hills played a concert among themselves, each contributing a strain of airy sweetness.

Little Joe's face brightened at once.

"Dear father," cried he, skipping cheerily to and fro, "that strange man is gone, and the sky and the mountains all seem glad of it!"

"Yes," growled the lime-burner, with an oath, "but he has let the fire go down, and no thanks to him if five hundred bushels of lime are not spoiled. If I catch the fellow hereabouts again, I shall feel like tossing him into the furnace!"

With his long pole in his hand, he ascended to the top of the kiln. After a moment's pause, he called to his son.

"Come up here, Joe!" said he.

So little Joe ran up the hillock, and stood by his father's side. The marble was all burnt into perfect, snow-white lime. But on its surface, in the midst of the circle,—snow-white too, and thoroughly converted into lime,—lay a human skeleton, in the attitude of a person who, after long toil, lies down to long repose. Within the ribs—strange to say—was the shape of a human heart.

"Was the fellow's heart made of marble?" cried Bartram, in some perplexity at this phenomenon. "At any rate, it is burnt into what looks like special good lime; and, taking all the bones together, my kiln is half a bushel the richer for him."

So saying, the rude lime-burner lifted his pole, and, letting it fall upon the skeleton, the relics of Ethan Brand were crumbled into fragments.

FEATHERTOP:
A MORALIZED LEGEND

"Dickon," cried Mother Rigby, "a coal for my pipe!"

The pipe was in the old dame's mouth when she said these words. She had thrust it there after filling it with tobacco, but without stooping to light it at the hearth, where indeed there was no appearance of a fire having been kindled that morning. Forthwith, however, as soon as the order was given, there was an intense red glow out the bowl of the pipe, and a whiff of smoke from Mother Rigby's lips. Whence the coal came, and how brought thither by an invisible hand, I have never been able to discover.

"Good!" quoth Mother Rigby, with a nod of her head. "Thank ye, Dickon! And now for making this scarecrow. Be within call, Dickon, in case I need you again."

The good woman had risen thus early (for as yet it was scarcely sunrise) in order to set about making a scarecrow, which she intended to put in the middle of her corn-patch. It was now the latter week of May, and the crows and blackbirds had already discovered the little, green, rolled-up leaf of the Indian corn just peeping out of the soil. She was determined, therefore, to contrive as lifelike a scarecrow as ever was seen, and to finish it immediately, from top to toe, so that it should begin its sentinel's duty that very morning. Now Mother Rigby (as everybody must have heard) was one

First published in *The International Magazine,* 1852.

of the most cunning and potent witches in New England, and might, with very little trouble, have made a scarecrow ugly enough to frighten the minister himself. But on this occasion, as she had awakened in an uncommonly pleasant humor, and was further dulcified by her pipe of tobacco, she resolved to produce something fine, beautiful, and splendid, rather than hideous and horrible.

"I don't want to set up a hobgoblin in my own corn-patch, and almost at my own doorstep," said Mother Rigby to herself, puffing out a whiff of smoke; "I could do it if I pleased, but I'm tired of doing marvellous things, and so I'll keep within the bounds of every-day business just for variety's sake. Besides, there is no use in scaring the little children for a mile roundabout, though 't is true I'm a witch."

It was settled, therefore, in her own mind, that the scarecrow should represent a fine gentleman of the period, so far as the materials at hand would allow. Perhaps it may be as well to enumerate the chief of the articles that went to the composition of this figure.

The most important item of all, probably, although it made so little show, was a certain broomstick, on which Mother Rigby had taken many an airy gallop at mid-night, and which now served the scarecrow by way of a spinal column, or, as the unlearned phrase it, a backbone. One of its arms was a disabled flail which used to be wielded by Goodman Rigby, before his spouse worried him out of this trouble-some world; the other, if I mistake not, was composed of the pudding stick and a broken rung of a chair, tied loosely to-gether at the elbow. As for its legs, the right was a hoe handle, and the left an undistinguished and miscellaneous stick from the woodpile. Its lungs, stomach, and other affairs of that kind were nothing better than a meal bag stuffed with straw. Thus we have made out the skeleton and entire corporosity of the scarecrow, with the exception of its head; and this was admirably supplied by a somewhat withered and shrivelled pumpkin, in which Mother Rigby cut two holes for the eyes, and a slit for the mouth, leaving a bluish-colored knob in the middle to pass for a nose. It was really quite a respectable face.

"I've seen worse ones on human shoulders, at any rate," said Mother Rigby. "And many a fine gentleman has a pumpkin head, as well as my scarecrow."

But the clothes, in this case, were to be the making of the man. So the good old woman took down from a peg an ancient plum-colored coat of London make, and with relics of embroidery on its seams, cuffs, pocket-flaps, and button-holes, but lamentably worn and faded, patched at the elbows, tattered at the skirts, and threadbare all over. On the left breast was a round hole, whence either a star of nobility had been rent away, or else the hot heart of some former wearer had scorched it through and through. The neighbors said that this rich garment belonged to the Black Man's wardrobe, and that he kept it at Mother Rigby's cottage for the convenience of slipping it on whenever he wished to make a grand appearance at the governor's table. To match the coat there was a velvet waistcoat of very ample size, and formerly embroidered with foliage that had been as brightly golden as the maple leaves in October, but which had now quite vanished out of the substance of the velvet. Next came a pair of scarlet breeches, once worn by the French governor of Louisbourg, and the knees of which had touched the lower step of the throne of Louis le Grand. The Frenchman had given these smallclothes to an Indian powwow, who parted with them to the old witch for a gill of strong waters, at one of their dances in the forest. Furthermore, Mother Rigby produced a pair of silk stockings and put them on the figure's legs, where they showed as unsubstantial as a dream, with the wooden reality of the two sticks making itself miserably apparent through the holes. Lastly, she put her dead husband's wig on the bare scalp of the pumpkin, and surmounted the whole with a dusty three-cornered hat, in which was stuck the longest tail feather of a rooster.

Then the old dame stood the figure up in a corner of her cottage and chuckled to behold its yellow semblance of a visage, with its nobby little nose thrust into the air. It had a strangely self-satisfied aspect, and seemed to say, "Come look at me!"

"And you are well worth looking at, that's a fact!" quoth Mother Rigby, in admiration at her own handiwork. "I've made many a puppet since I've been a witch, but methinks this is the finest of them all. 'Tis almost too good for a scare-crow. And, by the by, I'll just fill a fresh pipe of tobacco and then take him out to the corn-patch."

While filling her pipe the old woman continued to gaze with almost motherly affection at the figure in the corner. To say the truth, whether it were chance, or skill, or downright witchcraft, there was something wonderfully human in this ridiculous shape, bedizened with its tattered finery; and as for the countenance, it appeared to shrivel its yellow surface into a grin—a funny kind of expression betwixt scorn and merriment, as if it understood itself to be a jest at mankind. The more Mother Rigby looked the better she was pleased.

"Dickon," cried she sharply, "another coal for my pipe!"

Hardly had she spoken, than, just as before, there was a red-glowing coal on the top of the tobacco. She drew in a long whiff and puffed it forth again into the bar of morning sunshine which struggled through the one dusty pane of her cottage window. Mother Rigby always liked to flavor her pipe with a coal of fire from the particular chimney corner whence this had been brought. But where that chimney corner might be, or who brought the coal from it,—further than that the invisible messenger seemed to respond to the name of Dickon,—I cannot tell.

"That puppet yonder," thought Mother Rigby, still with her eyes fixed on the scarecrow, "is too good a piece of work to stand all summer in a corn-patch, frightening away the crows and blackbirds. He's capable of better things. Why, I've danced with a worse one, when partners happened to be scarce, at our witch meetings in the forest! What if I should let him take his chance among the other men of straw and empty fellows who go bustling about the world?"

The old witch took three or four more whiffs of her pipe and smiled.

"He'll meet plenty of his brethren at every street corner!" continued she. "Well; I didn't mean to dabble in witchcraft to-day, further than the lighting of my pipe, but a witch I am, and a witch I'm likely to be, and there's no use trying to shirk it. I'll make a man of my scarecrow, were it only for the joke's sake!"

While muttering these words, Mother Rigby took the pipe from her own mouth and thrust it into the crevice which represented the same feature in the pumpkin visage of the scarecrow.

"Puff, darling, puff!" said she. "Puff away, my fine fellow! your life depends on it!"

This was a strange exhortation, undoubtedly, to be addressed to a mere thing of sticks, straw, and old clothes, with nothing better than a shrivelled pumpkin for a head,—as we know to have been the scarecrow's case. Nevertheless, as we must carefully hold in remembrance, Mother Rigby was a witch of singular power and dexterity; and, keeping this fact duly before our minds, we shall see nothing beyond credibility in the remarkable incidents of our story. Indeed, the great difficulty will be at once got over, if we can only bring ourselves to believe that, as soon as the old dame bade him puff, there came a whiff of smoke from the scarecrow's mouth. It was the very feeblest of whiffs, to be sure; but it was followed by another and another, each more decided than the preceding one.

"Puff away, my pet! puff away, my pretty one!" Mother Rigby kept repeating, with her pleasantest smile. "It is the breath of life to ye; and that you may take my word for."

Beyond all question the pipe was bewitched. There must have been a spell either in the tobacco or in the fiercely-glowing coal that so mysteriously burned on top of it, or in the pungently-aromatic smoke which exhaled from the kindled weed. The figure, after a few doubtful attempts, at length blew forth a volley of smoke extending all the way from the obscure corner into the bar of sunshine. There it eddied and melted away among the motes of dust. It seemed a convulsive effort; for the two or three next whiffs were fainter, although the coal still glowed and threw a gleam over the scarecrow's visage. The old witch clapped her skinny hands together, and smiled encouragingly upon her handiwork. She saw that the charm worked well. The shrivelled, yellow face, which heretofore had been no face at all, had already a thin, fantastic haze as it were of human likeness, shifting to and fro across it; sometimes vanishing entirely, but growing more perceptible than ever with the next whiff from the pipe. The whole figure, in like manner, assumed a show of life, such as we impart to ill-defined shapes among the clouds, and half deceive ourselves with the pastime of our own fancy.

If we must needs pry closely into the matter, it may be doubted whether there was any real change, after all, in the sordid, wornout, worthless, and ill-jointed substance of the scarecrow; but merely a spectral illusion, and a cunning effect of light and shade so colored and contrived as to delude the eyes of most men. The miracles of witchcraft seem always to have had a very shallow subtlety; and, at least, if the above explanation do not hit the truth of the process, I can suggest no better.

"Well puffed, my pretty lad!" still cried old Mother Rigby. "Come, another good stout whiff, and let it be with might and main. Puff for thy life, I tell thee! Puff out of the very bottom of thy heart, if any heart thou hast, or any bottom to it! Well done, again! Thou didst suck in that mouthful as if for the pure love of it."

And then the witch beckoned to the scarecrow, throwing so much magnetic potency into her gesture that it seemed as if it must inevitably be obeyed, like the mystic call of the loadstone when it summons the iron.

"Why lurkest thou in the corner, lazy one?" said she. "Step forth! Thou hast the world before thee!"

Upon my word, if the legend were not one which I heard

on my grandmother's knee, and which had established its
place among things credible before my childish judgment
could analyze its probability, I question whether I should
have the face to tell it now.

In obedience to Mother Rigby's word, and extending its
arm as if to reach her outstretched hand, the figure made a
step forward—a kind of hitch and jerk, however, rather than
a step—then tottered and almost lost its balance. What could
the witch expect? It was nothing, after all, but a scarecrow
stuck upon two sticks. But the strong-willed old beldam
scowled, and beckoned, and flung the energy of her purpose
so forcibly at this poor combination of rotten wood, and
musty straw, and ragged garments, that it was compelled to
show itself a man, in spite of the reality of things. So it stepped
into the bar of sunshine. There it stood—poor devil of a
contrivance that it was!—with only the thinnest vesture of
human similitude about it, through which was evident the
stiff, rickety, incongruous, faded, tattered, good-for-nothing
patch-work of its substance, ready to sink in a heap upon the
floor, as conscious of its own unworthiness to be erect. Shall
I confess the truth? At its present point of vivification, the
scarecrow reminds me of some of the lukewarm and abortive
characters, composed of heterogeneous materials, used for the
thousandth time, and never worth using, with which romance
writers (and myself, no doubt, among the rest) have so over-
peopled the world of fiction.

But the fierce old hag began to get angry and show a
glimpse of her diabolic nature (like a snake's head, peeping
with a hiss out of her bosom), at this pusillanimous behavior
of the thing which she had taken the trouble to put together.

"Puff away, wretch!" cried she, wrathfully. "Puff, puff, puff,
thou thing of straw and emptiness! thou rag or two! thou meal
bag! thou pumpkin head! thou nothing! Where shall I find
a name vile enough to call thee by? Puff, I say, and suck in thy
fantastic life along with the smoke! else I snatch the pipe from
thy mouth and hurl thee where that red coal came from."

Thus threatened, the unhappy scarecrow had nothing for

it but to puff away for dear life. As need was, therefore, it
applied itself lustily to the pipe, and sent forth such abundant
volleys of tobacco smoke that the small cottage kitchen became all vaporous. The one sunbeam struggled mistily
through, and could but imperfectly define the image of the
cracked and dusty window pane on the opposite wall. Mother
Rigby, meanwhile, with one brown arm akimbo and the
other stretched towards the figure, loomed grimly amid the
obscurity with such port and expression as when she was
wont to heave a ponderous nightmare on her victims and
stand at the bedside to enjoy their agony. In fear and trembling did this poor scarecrow puff. But its efforts, it must be
acknowledged, served an excellent purpose; for, with each
successive whiff, the figure lost more and more of its dizzy
and perplexing tenuity and seemed to take denser substance.
Its very garments, moreover, partook of the magical change,
and shone with the gloss of novelty and glistened with the
skilfully embroidered gold that had long ago been rent away.
And, half revealed among the smoke, a yellow visage bent
its lustreless eyes on Mother Rigby.

At last the old witch clinched her fist and shook it at the
figure. Not that she was positively angry, but merely acting
on the principle—perhaps untrue, or not the only truth,
though as high a one as Mother Rigby could be expected to
attain—that feeble and torpid natures, being incapable of
better inspiration, must be stirred up by fear. But here was
the crisis. Should she fail in what she now sought to effect,
it was her ruthless purpose to scatter the miserable simulacre
into its original elements.

"Thou hast a man's aspect," said she, sternly. "Have also
the echo and mockery of a voice! I bid thee speak!"

The scarecrow gasped, struggled, and at length emitted a
murmur, which was so incorporated with its smoky breath
that you could scarcely tell whether it were indeed a voice or
only a whiff of tobacco. Some narrators of this legend hold
the opinion that Mother Rigby's conjurations and the fierceness of her will had compelled a familiar spirit into the figure,
and that the voice was his.

"Mother," mumbled the poor stifled voice, "be not so awful with me! I would fain speak; but being without wits, what can I say?"

"Thou canst speak, darling, canst thou?" cried Mother Rigby, relaxing her grim countenance into a smile. "And what shalt thou say, quotha! Say, indeed! Art thou of the brotherhood of the empty skull, and demandest of me what thou shalt say? Thou shalt say a thousand things, and saying them a thousand times over, thou shalt still have said nothing! Be not afraid, I tell thee! When thou comest into the world (whither I purpose sending thee forthwith) thou shalt not lack the wherewithal to talk. Talk! Why, thou shall babble like a mid-stream, if thou wilt. Thou hast brains enough for that, I trow!"

"At your service, mother," responded the figure.

"And that was well said, my pretty one," answered Mother Rigby. "Then thou speakest like thyself, and meant nothing. Thou shalt have a hundred such set phrases, and five hundred to the boot of them. And now, darling, I have taken so much pains with thee and thou art so beautiful, that, by my troth, I love thee better than any witch's puppet in the world; and I've made them of all sorts—clay, wax, straw, sticks, night fog, morning mist, sea foam, and chimney smoke. But thou art the very best. So give heed to what I say."

"Yes, kind mother," said the figure, "with all my heart!"

"With all thy heart!" cried the old witch, setting her hands to her sides and laughing loudly. "Thou hast such a pretty way of speaking. With all thy heart! And thou didst put thy hand to the left side of thy waistcoat as if thou really hadst one!"

So now, in high good humor with this fantastic contrivance of hers, Mother Rigby told the scarecrow that it must go and play its part in the great world, where not one man in a hundred, she affirmed, was gifted with more real substance than itself. And, that he might hold up his head with the best of them, she endowed him, on the spot, with an un-reckonable amount of wealth. It consisted partly of a gold mine in Eldorado, and of ten thousand shares in a broken bubble, and a half a million acres of vineyard at the North Pole, and of a castle in the air, and a chateau in Spain, together with all the rents and income therefrom accruing. She further made over to him the cargo of a certain ship, laden with salt of Cadiz, which she herself, by her necromantic arts, had caused to founder, ten years before, in the deepest part of mid-ocean. If the salt were not dissolved, and could be brought to market, it would fetch a pretty penny among the fishermen. That he might not lack ready money, she gave him a copper farthing of Birmingham manufacture, being all the coin she had about her, and likewise a great deal of brass, which she applied to her forehead, thus making it yellower than ever.

"With that brass alone," quoth Mother Rigby, "thou canst pay thy way all over the earth. Kiss me, pretty darling! I have done my best for thee."

Furthermore, that the adventurer might lack no possible advantage towards a fair start in life, this excellent old dame gave him a token by which he was to introduce himself to a certain magistrate, member of the council, merchant, and elder of the church (the four capacities constituting but one man), who stood at the head of society in the neighboring metropolis. The token was neither more nor less than a single word, which Mother Rigby whispered to the scarecrow, and which the scarecrow was to whisper to the merchant.

"Gouty as the old fellow is, he'll run thy errands for thee, when once thou hast given him that word in his ear," said the old witch. "Mother Rigby knows the worshipful Justice Gookin, and the worshipful Justice knows Mother Rigby!"

Here the witch thrust her wrinkled face close to the puppet's, chuckling irrepressibly, and fidgeting all through her system, with delight at the idea which she meant to communicate.

"The worshipful Master Gookin," whispered she, "hath a comely maiden to his daughter. And hark ye, my pet! Thou hast a fair outside, and a pretty wit enough of thine own. Yea, a pretty wit enough! Thou wilt think better of it when thou hast seen more of other people's wits. Now, with thy outside and thy inside, thou art the very man to win a young girl's heart. Never doubt it! I tell thee it shall be so. Put but a bold face on the matter, sigh, smile, flourish thy hat, thrust forth thy leg like a dancing-master, put thy right hand to the left side of thy waistcoat, and pretty Polly Gookin is thine own!"

All this while the new creature had been sucking in and exhaling the vapory fragrance of his pipe, and seemed now to continue this occupation as much for the enjoyment it afforded as because it was an essential condition of his existence. It was wonderful to see how exceedingly like a human being it behaved. Its eyes (for it appeared to possess a pair) were bent on Mother Rigby, and at suitable junctions it nodded or shook its head. Neither did it lack words proper for the occasion: "Really! Indeed! Pray tell me! Is it possible! Upon my word! By no means! Oh! Ah! Hem!" and other such weighty utterances as imply attention, inquiry, acquiescence, or dissent on the part of the auditor. Even had you stood by and seen the scarecrow made, you could scarcely have resisted the conviction that it perfectly understood the cunning counsels which the old witch poured into its counterfeit of an ear. The more earnestly it applied its lips to the pipe, the more distinctly was its human likeness stamped among visible realities, the more sagacious grew its expression, the more lifelike its gestures and movements, and the more intelligibly audible its voice. Its garments, too, glistened so much the brighter with an illusory magnificence. The very pipe, in which burned the spell of all this wonderwork, ceased to appear as a smoke-blackened earthen stump, and became a meerschaum, with painted bowl and amber mouthpiece.

It might be apprehended, however, that as the life of the illusion seemed identical with the vapor of the pipe, it would terminate simultaneously with the reduction of the tobacco to ashes. But the beldam foresaw the difficulty.

"Hold thou the pipe, my precious one," said she, "while I fill it for thee again."

It was sorrowful to behold how the fine gentleman began

to fade back into a scarecrow while Mother Rigby shook the ashes out of the pipe and proceeded to replenish it from her tobacco-box.

"Dickon," cried she, in her high, sharp tone, "another coal for this pipe!"

No sooner said than the intensely red speck of fire was glowing within the pipe-bowl; and the scarecrow, without waiting for the witch's bidding, applied the tube to his lips and drew in a few short, convulsive whiffs, which soon, however, became regular and equable.

"Now, mine own heart's darling," quoth Mother Rigby, "whatever may happen to thee, thou must stick to thy pipe. Thy life is in it; and that, at least, thou knowest well, if thou knowest nought besides. Stick to thy pipe, I say! Smoke, puff, blow thy cloud; and tell the people, if any question be made, that it is for thy health, and that so the physician orders thee to do. And, sweet one, when thou shalt find thy pipe getting low, go apart into some corner, and (first filling thyself with smoke) cry sharply, 'Dickon, a fresh pipe of tobacco!' and, 'Dickon, another coal for my pipe!' and have it into thy pretty mouth as speedily as may be. Else, instead of a gallant gentleman in a gold-laced coat, thou wilt be a jumble of sticks and tattered clothes, and a bag of straw, and a withered pumpkin! Now depart, my treasure, and good luck go with thee!"

"Never fear, mother!" said the figure, in a stout voice, and sending forth a courageous whiff of smoke, "I will thrive, if an honest man and a gentleman may!"

"Oh, thou wilt be the death of me!" cried the old witch, convulsed with laughter. "That was well said. If an honest man and a gentleman may! Thou playest thy part to perfection. Get along with thee for a smart fellow; and I will wager on thy head, as a man of pith and substance, with a brain and what they call a heart, and all else that a man should have, against any other thing on two legs. I hold myself a better witch than yesterday, for thy sake. Did not I make thee? And I defy any witch in New England to make such another! Here; take my staff along with thee!"

The staff, though it was but a plain oaken stick, immediately took the aspect of a gold-headed cane.

"That gold head has as much sense in it as thine own," said Mother Rigby, "and it will guide thee straight to worshipful Master Gookin's door. Get thee gone, my pretty pet, my darling, my precious one, my treasure; and if any ask thy name, it is Feathertop. For thou hast a feather in thy hat, and I have thrust a handful of feathers into the hollow of thy head, and thy wig, too, is of the fashion they call Feathertop, —so be Feathertop thy name!"

And, issuing from the cottage, Feathertop strode manfully towards town. Mother Rigby stood at the threshold, well pleased to see how the sunbeams glistened on him, as if all his magnificence were real, and how diligently and lovingly he smoked his pipe, and how handsomely he walked, in spite of a little stiffness of his legs. She watched him until out of sight, and threw a witch benediction after her darling, when a turn of the road snatched him from her view.

Betimes in the forenoon, when the principal street of the neighboring town was just at its acme of life and bustle, a stranger of very distinguished figure was seen on the sidewalk. His port as well as his garments betokened nothing short of nobility. He wore a richly-embroidered plum-colored coat, a waistcoat of costly velvet, magnificently adorned with golden foliage, a pair of splendid scarlet breeches, and the finest and glossiest of white silk stockings. His head was covered with a peruke, so daintily powdered and adjusted that it would have been sacrilege to disorder it with a hat; which, therefore (and it was a gold-laced hat, set off with a snowy feather), he carried beneath his arm. On the breast of his coat glistened a star. He managed his gold-headed cane with an airy grace, peculiar to the fine gentlemen of the period; and, to give the highest possible finish to his equipment, he had lace ruffles at his wrist, of a most ethereal delicacy, sufficiently avouching how idle and aristocratic must be the hands which they half concealed.

It was a remarkable point in the accoutrement of this bril-

liant personage that he held in his left hand a fantastic kind
of a pipe, with an exquisitely painted bowl and an amber
mouthpiece. This he applied to his lips as often as every five
or six paces, and inhaled a deep whiff of smoke, which, after
being retained a moment in his lungs, might be seen to eddy
gracefully from his mouth and nostrils.

As may well be supposed, the street was all astir to find out
the stranger's name.

"It is some great nobleman, beyond question," said one of
the towns-people. "Do you see the star at his breast?"

"Nay; it is too bright to be seen," said another. "Yes; he
must needs be a nobleman, as you say. But by what conveyance, think you, can his lordship have voyaged or travelled
hither? There has been no vessel from the old country for a
month past; and if he have arrived overland from the south-
ward, pray where are his attendants and equipage?"

"He needs no equipage to set off his rank," remarked a
third. "If he came among us in rags, nobility would shine
through a hole in his elbow. I never saw such dignity of
aspect. He has the old Norman blood in his veins, I warrant
him."

"I rather take him to be a Dutchman, or one of your high
Germans," said another citizen. "The men of those countries
have always the pipe at their mouths."

"And so has a Turk," answered his companion. "But, in my
judgment, this stranger hath been bred at the French court,
and hath there learned politeness and grace of manner, which
none understand so well as the nobility of France. That gait,
now! A vulgar spectator might deem it stiff—he might call
it a hitch and jerk—but, to my eye, it hath an unspeakable
majesty, and must have been acquired by constant observation of the deportment of the Grand Monarque. The stranger's
character and office are evident enough. He is a French ambas-
sador, come to treat with our rulers about the cession of
Canada."

"More probably a Spaniard," said another, "and hence his
yellow complexion; or, most likely, he is from the Havana,

or from some port on the Spanish main, and comes to make investigation about the piracies which our government is thought to connive at. Those settlers in Peru and Mexico have skins as yellow as the gold which they dig out of their mines."

"Yellow or not," cried a lady, "he is a beautiful man!—so tall, so slender! such a fine, noble face, with so well-shaped a nose, and all that delicacy of expression about the mouth! And, bless me, how bright his star is! It positively shoots out flames!"

"So do your eyes, fair lady," said the stranger, with a bow and a flourish of his pipe; for he was just passing at the instant. "Upon my honor, they have quite dazzled me."

"Was ever so original and exquisite a compliment?" murmured the lady, in an ecstasy of delight.

Amid the general admiration excited by the stranger's appearance, there were only two dissenting voices. One was that of an impertinent cur, which, after snuffing at the heels of the glistening figure, put its tail between its legs and skulked into its master's back yard, vociferating an execrable howl. The other dissentient was a young child, who squalled at the fullest stretch of his lungs, and babbled some unintelligible nonsense about a pumpkin.

Feathertop meanwhile pursued his way along the street. Except for the few complimentary words to the lady, and now and then a slight inclination of the head in requital of the profound reverences of the bystanders, he seemed wholly absorbed in his pipe. There needed no other proof of his rank and consequence than the perfect equanimity with which he comported himself, while the curiosity and admiration of the town swelled almost into clamor around him. With a crowd gathering behind his footsteps, he finally reached the mansion-house of the worshipful Justice Gookin, entered the gate, ascended the steps of the front door, and knocked. In the interim, before his summons was answered, the stranger was observed to shake the ashes out of his pipe.

"What did he say in that sharp voice?" inquired one of the spectators.

"Nay, I know not," answered his friend. "But the sun dazzles my eyes strangely. How dim and faded his lordship looks all of a sudden! Bless my wits, what is the matter with me?"

"The wonder is," said the other, "that his pipe, which was out only an instant ago, should be all alight again, and with the reddest coal I ever saw. There is something mysterious about this stranger. What a whiff of smoke was that! Dim and faded did you call him? Why, as he turns about the star on his breast is all ablaze."

"It is, indeed," said his companion; "and it will go near to dazzle pretty Polly Gookin, whom I see peeping at it out of the chamber window."

The door being now opened, Feathertop turned to the crowd, made a stately bend of his body like a great man acknowledging the reverence of the meaner sort, and vanished into the house. There was a mysterious kind of a smile, if it might not better be called a grin or grimace, upon his visage; but, of all the throng that beheld him, not an individual appears to have possessed insight enough to detect the illusive character of the stranger except a little child and a cur dog.

Our legend here loses somewhat of its continuity, and, passing over the preliminary explanation between Feathertop and the merchant, goes in quest of the pretty Polly Gookin. She was a damsel of a soft, round figure, with light hair and blue eyes, and a fair, rosy face, which seemed neither very shrewd nor very simple. This young lady had caught a glimpse of the glistening stranger while standing at the threshold, and had forthwith put on a laced cap, a string of beads, her finest kerchief, and her stiffest damask petticoat in preparation for the interview. Hurrying from her chamber to the parlor, she had ever since been viewing herself in the large looking-glass and practising pretty airs—now a smile, now a ceremonious dignity of aspect, and now a softer smile than the former, kissing her hand likewise, tossing her head, and managing her fan; while within the mirror an unsubstantial little maid repeated every gesture and did all the foolish things that

Polly did, but without making her ashamed of them. In short, it was the fault of pretty Polly's ability rather than her will if she failed to be as complete an artifice as the illustrious Feathertop himself; and, when she thus tampered with her own simplicity, the witch's phantom might well hope to win her.

No sooner did Polly hear her father's gouty footsteps approaching the parlor door, accompanied with the stiff clatter of Feathertop's high-heeled shoes, than she seated herself bolt upright and innocently began warbling a song.

"Polly! daughter Polly!" cried the old merchant. "Come hither, child."

Master Gookin's aspect, as he opened the door, was doubtful and troubled.

"This gentleman," continued he, presenting the stranger, "is the Chevalier Feathertop,—nay, I beg his pardon, my Lord Feathertop,—who hath brought me a token of remembrance from an ancient friend of mine. Pay your duty to his lordship, child, and honor him as his quality deserves."

After these few words of introduction, the worshipful magistrate immediately quitted the room. But, even in that brief moment, had the fair Polly glanced aside at her father instead of devoting herself wholly to the brilliant guest, she might have taken warning of some mischief nigh at hand. The old man was nervous, fidgety, and very pale. Purposing a smile of courtesy, he had deformed his face with a sort of galvanic grin, which, when Feathertop's back was turned, he exchanged for a scowl, at the same time shaking his fist and stamping his gouty foot—an incivility which brought its retribution along with it. The truth appears to have been that Mother Rigby's word of introduction, whatever it might be, had operated far more on the rich merchant's fears than on his good will. Moreover, being a man of wonderfully acute observation, he had noticed that these painted figures on the bowl of Feathertop's pipe were in motion. Looking more closely, he became convinced that these figures were a party of little demons, each duly provided with horns and a tail, and dancing hand in hand, with gestures of diabolical merriment, round the circumference of the pipe bowl. As if to confirm his suspicions, while Master Gookin ushered his guest along a dusky passage from his private room to the parlor, the star on Feathertop's breast had scintillated actual flames, and threw a flickering gleam upon the wall, the ceiling, and the floor.

With such sinister prognostics manifesting themselves on all hands, it is not to be marvelled at that the merchant should have felt that he was committing his daughter to a very questionable acquaintance. He cursed, in his secret soul, the insinuating elegance of Feathertop's manners, as this brilliant personage bowed, smiled, put his hand on his heart, inhaled a long whiff from his pipe, and enriched the atmosphere with the smoky vapor of a fragrant and visible sigh. Gladly would poor Master Gookin have thrust his dangerous guest into the street; but there was a constraint and terror within him. This respectable old gentleman, we fear, at an earlier period of life, had given some pledge or other to the evil principle, and perhaps was now to redeem it by the sacrifice of his daughter.

It so happened that the parlor door was partly of glass, shaded by a silken curtain, the folds of which hung a little awry. So strong was the merchant's interest in witnessing what was to ensue between the fair Polly and the gallant Feathertop that, after quitting the room, he could by no means refrain from peeping through the crevice of the curtain.

But there was nothing very miraculous to be seen; nothing —except the trifles previously noticed—to confirm the idea of a supernatural peril environing the pretty Polly. The stranger it is true was evidently a thorough and practised man of the world, systematic and self-possessed, and therefore the sort of a person to whom a parent ought not to confide a simple, young girl without due watchfulness for the result. The worthy magistrate, who had been conversant with all degrees and qualities of mankind, could not but perceive every motion and gesture of the distinguished Feathertop came in its proper place; nothing had been left rude or native in him;

a well-digested conventionalism had incorporated itself thoroughly with his substance and transformed him into a work of art. Perhaps it was this peculiarity that invested him with a species of ghastliness and awe. It is the effect of anything completely and consummately artificial, in human shape, that the person impresses us as an unreality and as having hardly pith enough to cast a shadow upon the floor. As regarded Feathertop, all this resulted in a wild, extravagant, and fantastical impression, as if his life and being were akin to the smoke that curled upward from his pipe.

But pretty Polly Gookin felt not thus. The pair were now promenading the room: Feathertop with his dainty stride and no less dainty grimace; the girl with a native maidenly grace, just touched, not spoiled, by a slightly affected manner, which seemed caught from the perfect artifice of her companion. The longer the interview continued, the more charmed was pretty Polly, until, within the first quarter of an hour (as the old magistrate noted by his watch), she was evidently beginning to be in love. Nor need it have been witchcraft that subdued her in such a hurry; the poor child's heart, it may be, was so very fervent that it melted her with its own warmth as reflected from the hollow semblance of a lover. No matter what Feathertop said, his words found depth and reverberation in her ear; no matter what he did, his action was heroic to her eye. And by this time it is to be supposed there was a blush on Polly's cheek, a tender smile about her mouth, and a liquid softness in her glance; while the star kept coruscating on Feathertop's breast, and the little demons careered with more frantic merriment than ever about the circumference of his pipe bowl. O pretty Polly Gookin, why should these imps rejoice so madly that a silly maiden's heart was about to be given to a shadow! Is it so unusual a misfortune, so rare a triumph?

By and by Feathertop paused, and throwing himself into an imposing attitude, seemed to summon the fair girl to survey his figure and resist him longer if she could. His star, his embroidery, his buckles glowed at that instant with unutterable splendor; the picturesque hues of his attire took a richer depth of coloring; there was a gleam and polish over his whole presence betokening the perfect witchery of well-ordered manners. The maiden raised her eyes and suffered them to linger upon her companion with a bashful and admiring gaze. Then, as if desirous of judging what value her own simple comeliness might have side by side with so much brilliancy, she cast a glance towards the full-length looking-glass in front of which they happened to be standing. It was one of the truest plates in the world and incapable of flattery. No sooner did the images therein reflected meet Polly's eye than she shrieked, shrank from the stranger's side, gazed at him for a moment in the wildest dismay, and sank insensible upon the floor. Feathertop likewise had looked towards the mirror, and there beheld, not the glittering mockery of his outside show, but a picture of the sordid patchwork of his real composition, stripped of all witchcraft.

The wretched simulacrum! We almost pity him, He threw up his arms with an expression of despair that went further than any of his previous manifestations towards vindicating his claims to be reckoned human; for, perchance the only time since this so often empty and deceptive life of mortals began its course, an illusion had seen and fully recognized itself.

Mother Rigby was seated by her kitchen hearth in the twilight of this eventful day, and had just shaken the ashes out of a new pipe, when she heard a hurried tramp along the road. Yet it did not seem so much the tramp of human footsteps as the clatter of sticks or the rattling of dry bones.

"Ha!" thought the old witch, "what step is that? Whose skeleton is out of its grave now, I wonder?"

A figure burst headlong into the cottage door. It was Feathertop! His pipe was still alight; the star still flamed upon his breast; the embroidery still glowed upon his garments; nor had he lost, in any degree or manner that could be estimated, the aspect that assimilated him with our mortal brotherhood. But yet, in some indescribable way (as is the case with all that has deluded us when once found out), the poor reality was felt beneath the cunning artifice.

"What has gone wrong?" demanded the witch. "Did yonder sniffling hypocrite thrust my darling from his door? The villain! I'll set twenty fiends to torment him till he offer thee his daughter on his bended knees!"

"No, mother," said Feathertop despondingly; "it was not that."

"Did the girl scorn my precious one?" asked Mother Rigby, her fierce eyes glowing like two coals of Tophet. "I'll cover her face with pimples! Her nose shall be as red as the coal in thy pipe! Her front teeth shall drop out! In a week hence she shall not be worth thy having!"

"Let her alone, mother," answered poor Feathertop; "the girl was half won; and methinks a kiss from her sweet lips might have made me altogether human. But," he added, after a brief pause and then a howl of self-contempt, "I've seen myself, mother! I've seen myself for the wretched, ragged, empty thing I am! I'll exist no longer!"

Snatching the pipe from his mouth, he flung it with all his might against the chimney, and at the same instant sank upon the floor, a medley of straw and tattered garments, with some sticks protruding from the heap, and a shrivelled pumpkin in the midst. The eyeholes were now lustreless; but the rudely-carved gap, that just before had been a mouth, still seemed to twist itself into a despairing grin, and was so far human.

"Poor fellow!" quoth Mother Rigby, with a rueful glance at the relics of her ill-fated contrivance. "My poor, dear, pretty Feathertop! There are thousands upon thousands of coxcombs and charlatans in the world, made up of just such a jumble of wornout, forgotten, and good-for-nothing trash as he was! Yet they live in fair repute, and never see themselves for what they are. And why should my poor puppet be the only one to know himself and perish for it?"

While thus muttering, the witch had filled a fresh pipe of tobacco, and held the stem between her fingers, as doubtful whether to thrust it into her own mouth or Feathertop's.

"Poor Feathertop!" she continued. "I could easily give him another chance and send him forth again tomorrow. But no; his feelings are too tender, his sensibilities too deep. He seems to have too much heart to bustle for his own advantage in such an empty and heartless world. Well! well! I'll make a scarecrow of him after all. 'Tis an innocent and useful vocation, and will suit my darling well; and, if each of his human brethren had as fit a one, 'twould be the better for mankind; and as for this pipe of tobacco, I need it more than he."

So saying Mother Rigby put the stem between her lips. "Dickon!" cried she, in her high, sharp tone, "another coal for my pipe!"

Sketches

SIGHTS FROM
A STEEPLE

So! I have climbed high, and my reward is small. Here I stand, with wearied knees, earth, indeed, at a dizzy depth below, but heaven far, far beyond me still. Oh that I could soar up into the very zenith, where man never breathed, nor eagle ever flew, and where the ethereal azure melts away from the eye, and appears only a deepened shade of nothingness! And yet I shiver at that cold and solitary thought. What clouds are gathering in the golden west, with direful intent against the brightness and the warmth of this summer afternoon! They are ponderous air ships, black as death, and freighted with the tempest; and at intervals their thunder, the signal guns of that unearthly squadron, rolls distant along the deep of heaven. These nearer heaps of fleecy vapor—methinks I could roll and toss upon them the whole day long!—seem scattered here and there for the repose of tired pilgrims through the sky. Perhaps—for who can tell?—beautiful spirits are disporting themselves there, and will bless my mortal eye with the brief appearance of their curly locks of golden light, and laughing faces, fair and faint as the people of a rosy dream. Or, where the floating mass so imperfectly obstructs the color of the firmament, a slender foot and fairy limb, resting too heavily upon the frail support, may be thrust through, and suddenly withdrawn, while longing fancy fol-

First published in *The Token,* 1831.

lows them in vain. Yonder again is an airy archipelago, where
the sunbeams love to linger in their journeyings through
space. Every one of those little clouds has been dipped and
steeped in radiance, which the slightest pressure might dis-
engage in silvery profusion, like water wrung from a sea-
maid's hair. Bright they are as a young man's visions, and,
like them, would be realized in chillness, obscurity, and tears.
I will look on them no more.

In three parts of the visible circle, whose centre is this spire,
I discern cultivated fields, villages, white country seats, the
waving lines of rivulets, little placid lakes, and here and there
a rising ground, that would fain be termed a hill. On the
fourth side is the sea, stretching away towards a viewless
boundary, blue and calm, except where the passing anger of
a shadow flits across its surface, and is gone. Hitherward, a
broad inlet penetrates far into the land; on the verge of the
harbor, formed by its extremity, is a town; and over it am I,
a watchman, all-heeding and unheeded. Oh that the multitude
of chimneys could speak, like those of Madrid, and betray,
in smoky whispers, the secrets of all who, since their first
foundation, have assembled at the hearths within! Oh that the
the Limping Devil of Le Sage would perch beside me here,
extend his wand over this contiguity of roofs, uncover every
chamber, and make me familiar with their inhabitants! The
most desirable mode of existence might be that of a spiritualized Paul Pry, hovering invisible round man and woman, witnessing their deeds, searching into their hearts, borrowing
brightness from their felicity and shade from their sorrow, and
retaining no emotion peculiar to himself. But none of these
things are possible; and if I would know the interior of brick
walls, or the mystery of human bosoms, I can but guess.

Yonder is a fair street, extending north and south. The
stately mansions are placed each on its carpet of verdant
grass, and a long flight of steps descends from every door to
the pavement. Ornamental trees—the broad-leafed horse-
chestnut, the elm so lofty and bending, the graceful but
infrequent willow, and others whereof I know not the names

—grow thrivingly among brick and stone. The oblique rays
of the sun are intercepted by these green citizens, and by the
houses, so that one side of the street is a shaded and pleasant
walk. On its whole extent there is now but a single passenger,
advancing from the upper end; and he, unless distance and
the medium of a pocket spyglass do him more than justice,
is a fine young man of twenty. He saunters slowly forward,
slapping his left hand with his folded gloves, bending his eyes
upon the pavement, and sometimes raising them to throw a
glance before him. Certainly, he has a pensive air. Is he in
doubt, or in debt? Is he, if the question be allowable, in love?
Does he strive to be melancholy and gentleman-like? Or, is he
merely overcome by the heat? But I bid him farewell for the
present. The door of one of the houses—an aristocratic edifice,
with curtains of purple and gold waving from the windows,
is now opened, and down the steps come two ladies, swinging
their parasols, and lightly arrayed for a summer ramble. Both
are young, both are pretty, but methinks the left-hand lass is
the fairer of the twain; and, though she be so serious at this
moment, I could swear that there is a treasure of gentle fun
within her. They stand talking a little while upon the steps,
and finally proceed up the street. Meantime, as their faces
are now turned from me, I may look elsewhere.

Upon that wharf, and down the corresponding street, is a
busy contrast to the quiet scene which I have just noticed.
Business evidently has its centre there, and many a man is
wasting the summer afternoon in labor and anxiety, in losing
riches or in gaining them, when he would be wiser to flee away
to some pleasant country village, or shaded lake in the forest,
or wild and cool sea-beach. I see vessels unlading at the wharf,
and precious merchandise strewn upon the ground, abundantly as at the bottom of the sea, that market whence no
goods return, and where there is no captain nor supercargo
to render an account of sales. Here, the clerks are diligent
with their paper and pencils, and sailors ply the block and
tackle that hang over the hold, accompanying their toil with
cries, long drawn and roughly melodious, till the bales and

puncheons ascend to upper air. At a little distance a group of gentlemen are assembled round the door of a warehouse. Grave seniors be they, and I would wager—if it were safe in these times to be responsible for any one—that the least eminent among them might vie with old Vicentio, that incomparable trafficker of Pisa. I can even select the wealthiest of the company. It is the elderly personage, in somewhat rusty black, with powdered hair, the superfluous whiteness of which is visible upon the cape of his coat. His twenty ships are wafted on some of their many courses by every breeze that blows, and his name—I will venture to say, though I know it not—is a familiar sound among the far separated merchants of Europe and the Indies.

But I bestow too much of my attention in this quarter. On looking again to the long and shady walk, I perceive that the two fair girls have encountered the young man. After a sort of shyness in the recognition, he turns back with them. Moreover, he has sanctioned my taste in regard to his companions by placing himself on the inner side of the pavement, nearest the Venus to whom I—enacting, on a steeple top, the part of Paris on the top of Ida—adjudged the golden apple.

In two streets, converging at right angles towards my watchtower, I distinguish three different processions. One is a proud array of voluntary soldiers, in bright uniform, resembling, from the height whence I look down, the painted veterans that garrison the windows of a toyshop. And yet, it stirs my heart; their regular advance, their nodding plumes, the sun-flash on their bayonets and musket barrels, the roll of their drums ascending past me, and the fife ever and anon piercing through—these things have wakened a warlike fire, peaceful though I be. Close to their rear marches a battalion of schoolboys, ranged in crooked and irregular platoons, shouldering sticks, thumping a harsh and unripe clatter from an instrument of tin, and ridiculously aping the intricate manœuvres of the foremost band. Nevertheless, as slight differences are scarcely perceptible from a church spire, one might be tempted to ask, "Which are the boys?"—or rather, "Which the men?"

But, leaving these, let us turn to the third procession, which, though sadder in outward show, may excite identical reflections in the thoughtful mind. It is a funeral. A hearse, drawn by a black and bony steed, and covered by a dusty pall; two or three coaches rumbling over the stones, their drivers half asleep; a dozen couple of careless mourners in their everyday attire; such was not the fashion of our fathers, when they carried a friend to his grave. There is now no doleful clang of the bell to proclaim sorrow to the town. Was the King of Terrors more awful in those days than in our own, that wisdom and philosophy have been able to produce this change? Not so. Here is a proof that he retains his proper majesty. The military men and the military boys are wheeling round the corner, and meet the funeral full in the face. Immediately the drum is silent, all but the tap that regulates each simultaneous footfall. The soldiers yield the path to the dusty hearse and unpretending train, and the children quit their ranks, and cluster on the sidewalks, with timorous and instinctive curiosity. The mourners enter the churchyard at the base of the steeple, and pause by an open grave among the burial stones; the lightning glimmers on them as they lower down the coffin, and the thunder rattles heavily while they throw the earth upon its lid. Verily, the shower is near, and I tremble for the young man and the girls, who have now disappeared from the long and shady street.

How various are the situations of the people covered by the roofs beneath me, and how diversified are the events at this moment befalling them! The new born, the aged, the dying, the strong in life, and the recent dead, are in the chambers of these many mansions. The full of hope, the happy, the miserable, and the desperate, dwell together within the circle of my glance. In some of the houses over which my eyes roam so coldly, guilt is entering into hearts that are still tenanted by a debased and trodden virtue,—guilt is on the very edge of commission, and the impending deed might be averted; guilt is done, and the criminal wonders if it be irrevocable. There are broad thoughts struggling in my mind, and, were I able to give them distinctness, they would make their way in eloquence. Lo! the raindrops are descending.

The clouds, within a little time, have gathered over all the sky, hanging heavily, as if about to drop in one unbroken mass upon the earth. At intervals, the lightning flashes from their brooding hearts, quivers, disappears, and then comes the thunder, travelling slowly after its twin-born flame. A strong wind has sprung up, howls through the darkened streets, and raises the dust in dense bodies, to rebel against the approaching storm. The disbanded soldiers fly, the funeral has already vanished like its dead, and all people hurry homeward—all that have a home; while a few lounge by the corners, or trudge on desperately, at their leisure. In a narrow lane, which communicates with the shady street, I discern the rich old merchant, putting himself to the top of his speed, lest the rain should convert his hair powder to a paste. Unhappy gentleman! By the slow vehemence and painful moderation wherewith he journeys, it is but too evident that Podagra has left its thrilling tenderness in his great toe. But yonder, at a far more rapid pace, come three other of my acquaintance, the two pretty girls and the young man, unseasonably interrupted in their walk. Their footsteps are supported by the risen dust,—the wind lends them its velocity,—they fly like three sea-birds driven landward by the tempestuous breeze. The ladies would not thus rival Atalanta if they but knew that any one were at leisure to observe them. Ah! as they hasten onward, laughing in the angry face of nature, a sudden catastrophe has chanced. At the corner where the narrow lane enters into the street, they come plump against the old merchant, whose tortoise motion has just brought him to that point. He likes not the sweet encounter; the darkness of the whole air gathers speedily upon his visage, and there is a pause on both sides. Finally, he thrusts aside the youth with little courtesy, seizes an arm of each of the two girls, and plods onward like a magician with a prize of captive fairies. All this is easy to be understood. How disconsolate the poor lover stands! regardless of the rain that threatens an exceeding damage to his well-fashioned habiliments, till he catches a backward glance of mirth from a bright eye, and turns away with whatever comfort it conveys.

The old man and his daughters are safely housed, and now the storm lets loose its fury. In every dwelling I perceive the faces of the chambermaids as they shut down the windows, excluding the impetuous shower, and shrinking away from the quick fiery glare. The large drops descend with force upon the slated roofs, and rise again in smoke. There is a rush and roar, as of a river through the air, and muddy streams bubble majestically along the pavement, whirl their dusky foam into the kennel, and disappear beneath iron grates. Thus did Arethusa sink. I love not my station here aloft, in the midst of the tumult which I am powerless to direct or quell, with the blue lightning wrinkling on my brow, and the thunder muttering its first awful syllables in my ear. I will descend. Yet let me give another glance to the sea, where the foam breaks out in long white lines upon a broad expanse of blackness, or boils up in far distant points, like snowy mountain tops in the eddies of a flood; and let me look once more at the green plain, and little hills of the country, over which the giant of the storm is striding in robes of mist, and at the town, whose obscured and desolate streets might beseem a city of the dead; and turning a single moment to the sky, now gloomy as an author's prospects, I prepare to resume my station on lower earth. But stay! A little speck of azure has widened in the western heavens; the sunbeams find a passage, and go rejoicing through the tempest; and on yonder darkest cloud, born, like hallowed hopes, of the glory of another world and the trouble and tears of this, brightens forth the Rainbow!

THE HAUNTED
MIND

What a singular moment is the first one, when you have hardly begun to recollect yourself, after starting from midnight slumber? By unclosing your eyes so suddenly, you seem to have surprised the personages of your dream in full convocation round your bed, and catch one broad glance at them before they can flit into obscurity. Or, to vary the metaphor, you find yourself, for a single instant, wide awake in that realm of illusions, whither sleep has been the passport, and behold its ghostly inhabitants and wondrous scenery, with a perception of their strangeness such as you never attain while the dream is undisturbed. The distant sound of a church clock is borne faintly on the wind. You question with yourself, half seriously, whether it has stolen to your waking ear from some gray tower that stood within the precincts of your dream. While yet in suspense, another clock flings its heavy clang over the slumbering town, with so full and distinct a sound, and such a long murmur in the neighboring air, that you are certain it must proceed from the steeple at the nearest corner. You count the strokes—one—two, and there they cease, with a booming sound, like the gathering of a third stroke within the bell.

If you could choose an hour of wakefulness out of the whole night, it would be this. Since your sober bedtime, at eleven,

First published in *The Token,* 1835.

you have had rest enough to take off the pressure of yesterday's fatigue; while before you, till the sun comes from "far
Cathay" to brighten your window, there is almost the space
of a summer night; one hour to be spent in thought, with the
mind's eye half shut, and two in pleasant dreams, and two
in that strangest of enjoyments, the forgetfulness alike of joy
and woe. The moment of rising belongs to another period of
time, and appears so distant that the plunge out of a warm
bed into the frosty air cannot yet be anticipated with dismay.
Yesterday 'has already vanished among the shadows of the
past; to-morrow has not yet emerged from the future. You
have found an intermediate space, where the business of life
does not intrude; where the passing moment lingers, and
becomes truly the present; a spot where Father Time, when
he thinks nobody is watching him, sits down by the wayside
to take breath. Oh, that he would fall asleep, and let mortals
live on without growing older!

Hitherto you have lain perfectly still, because the slightest
motion would dissipate the fragments of your slumber. Now,
being irrevocably awake, you peep through the half-drawn
window curtain, and observe that the glass is ornamented with
fanciful devices in frostwork, and that each pane presents
something like a frozen dream. There will be time enough to
trace out the analogy while waiting the summons to breakfast.
Seen through the clear portion of the glass, where the silvery
mountain peaks of the frost scenery do not ascend, the most
conspicuous object is the steeple; the white spire of which
directs you to the wintry lustre of the firmament. You may
almost distinguish the figures on the clock that has just told
the hour. Such a frosty sky, and the snow-covered roofs, and
the long vista of the frozen street, all white, and the distant
water hardened into rock, might make you shiver, even under
four blankets and a woollen comforter. Yet look at that one
glorious star! Its beams are distinguishable from all the rest,
and actually cast the shadow of the casement on the bed, with
a radiance of deeper hue than moonlight, though not so accurate an outline.

You sink down and muffle your head in the clothes, shivering all the while, but less from bodily chill than the bare idea of a polar atmosphere. It is too cold even for the thoughts to venture abroad. You speculate on the luxury of wearing out a whole existence in bed, like an oyster in its shell, content with the sluggish ecstasy of inaction, and drowsily conscious of nothing but delicious warmth, such as you now feel again. Ah! that idea has brought a hideous one in its train. You think how the dead are lying in their cold shrouds and narrow coffins, through the drear winter of the grave, and cannot persuade your fancy that they neither shrink nor shiver, when the snow is drifting over their little hillocks, and the bitter blast howls against the door of the tomb. That gloomy thought will collect a gloomy multitude, and throw its complexion over your wakeful hour.

In the depths of every heart there is a tomb and a dungeon, though the lights, the music, and revelry above may cause us to forget their existence, and the buried ones, or prisoners, whom they hide. But sometimes, and oftenest at midnight, these dark receptacles are flung wide open. In an hour like this, when the mind has a passive sensibility, but no active strength; when the imagination is a mirror, imparting vividness to all ideas, without the power of selecting or controlling them; then pray that your griefs may slumber, and the brotherhood of remorse not break their chain. It is too late! A funeral train comes gliding by your bed, in which Passion and Feeling assume bodily shape, and things of the mind become dim spectres to the eye. There is your earliest Sorrow, a pale young mourner, wearing a sister's likeness to first love, sadly beautiful, with a hallowed sweetness in her melancholy features, and grace in the flow of her sable robe. Next appears a shade of ruined loveliness, with dust among her golden hair, and her bright garments all faded and defaced, stealing from your glance with drooping head, as fearful of reproach; she was your fondest Hope, but a delusive one; so call her Disappointment now. A sterner form succeeds, with a brow of wrinkles, a look and gesture of iron authority; there is no name for him unless it be Fatality, an emblem of the evil influence that rules your fortunes; a demon to whom you subjected yourself by some error at the outset of life, and were bound his slave forever, by once obeying him. See! those fiendish lineaments graven on the darkness, the writhed lip of scorn, the mockery of that living eye, the pointed finger, touching the sore place in your heart! Do you remember any act of enormous folly at which you would blush, even in the remotest cavern of the earth? Then recognize your Shame.

Pass, wretched band! Well for the wakeful one, if, riotously miserable, a fiercer tribe do not surround him, the devils of a guilty heart, that holds its hell within itself. What if Remorse should assume the features of an injured friend? What if the fiend should come in woman's garments, with a pale beauty amid sin and desolation, and lie down by your side? What if he should stand at your bed's foot, in the likeness of a corpse, with a bloody stain upon the shroud? Sufficient, without such guilt, is this nightmare of the soul; this heavy, heavy sinking of the spirits; this wintry gloom about the heart; this indistinct horror of the mind, blending itself with the darkness of the chamber.

By a desperate effort you start upright, breaking from a sort of conscious sleep, and gazing wildly round the bed, as if the fiends were anywhere but in your haunted mind. At the same moment, the slumbering embers on the hearth send forth a gleam which palely illuminates the whole outer room, and flickers through the door of the bed-chamber, but cannot quite dispel its obscurity. Your eye searches for whatever may remind you of the living world. With eager minuteness you take note of the table near the fireplace, the book with an ivory knife between its leaves, the unfolded letter, the hat, and the fallen glove. Soon the flame vanishes, and with it the whole scene is gone, though its image remains an instant in your mind's eye, when darkness has swallowed the reality. Throughout the chamber there is the same obscurity as before, but not the same gloom within your breast. As your head falls back upon the pillow, you think—in a whisper be it spoken—how pleasant, in these night solitudes, would be the rise and fall of a softer breathing than your own, the slight pressure of a tenderer bosom, the quiet throb of a purer heart, imparting its peacefulness to your troubled one, as if the fond sleeper were involving you in her dream.

Her influence is over you, though she have no existence but in that momentary image. You sink down in a flowery spot, on the borders of sleep and wakefulness, while your thoughts rise before you in pictures, all disconnected, yet all assimilated by a pervading gladsomeness and beauty. The wheeling of gorgeous squadrons that glitter in the sun is succeeded by the merriment of children round the door of a school-house, beneath the glimmering shadow of old trees, at the corner of a rustic lane. You stand in the sunny rain of a summer shower, and wander among the sunny trees of an autumnal wood, and look upward at the brightest of all rainbows, overarching the unbroken sheet of snow, on the American side of Niagara. Your mind struggles pleasantly between the dancing radiance round the hearth of a young man and his recent bride, and the twittering flight of birds in spring about their new-made nest. You feel the merry bounding of a ship before the breeze, and watch the tuneful feet of rosy girls as they twine their last and merriest dance in a splendid ball-room, and find yourself in the brilliant circle of a crowded theatre as the curtain falls over a light and airy scene.

With an involuntary start you seize hold on consciousness, and prove yourself but half awake, by running a doubtful parallel between human life and the hour which has now elapsed. In both you emerge from mystery, pass through a vicissitude that you can but imperfectly control, and are borne onward to another mystery. Now comes the peal of the distant clock, with fainter and fainter strokes as you plunge farther into the wilderness of sleep. It is the knell of a temporary death. Your spirit has departed, and strays, like a free citizen, among the people of a shadowy world, beholding strange sights, yet without wonder or dismay. So calm, perhaps, will be the final change; so undisturbed, as if among familiar things the entrance of the soul to its Eternal home!

SUNDAY
AT HOME

Every Sabbath morning in the summer time, I thrust back the curtain, to watch the sunrise stealing down a steeple which stands opposite my chamber window. First, the weather-cock begins to flash; then, a fainter lustre gives the spire an airy aspect; next, it encroaches on the tower, and causes the index of the dial to glisten like gold as it points to the gilded figure of the hour. Now, the loftiest window gleams, and now the lower. The carved frame-work of the portal is marked strongly out. At length, the morning glory, in its descent from heaven, comes down the stone steps, one by one; and there stands the steeple, glowing with fresh radiance, while the shades of twilight still hide themselves among the nooks of the adjacent buildings. Methinks, though the same sun brightens it every fair morning, yet the steeple has a peculiar robe of brightness for the Sabbath.

By dwelling near a church, a person soon contracts an attachment for the edifice. We naturally personify it, and conceive its massy walls, and its dim emptiness, to be instinct with a calm, and meditative, and somewhat melancholy spirit. But the steeple stands foremost, in our thoughts, as well as locally. It impresses us as a giant, with a mind comprehensive and discriminating enough to care for the great and small concerns of all the town. Hourly, while it speaks a moral to

First published in *The Token*, 1837.

the few that think, it reminds thousands of busy individuals of their separate and most secret affairs. It is the steeple, too, that flings abroad the hurried and irregular accents of general alarm; neither have gladness and festivity found a better utterance than by its tongue; and when the dead are slowly passing to their home, the steeple has a melancholy voice to bid them welcome. Yet, in spite of this connection with human interests, what a moral loneliness, on week days, broods round about its stately height! It has no kindred with the houses above which it towers; it looks down into the narrow thoroughfare, the lonelier, because the crowd are elbowing their passage at its base. A glance at the body of the church deepens this impression. Within, by the light of distant windows, amid refracted shadows, we discern the vacant pews and empty galleries, the silent organ, the voiceless pulpit, and the clock, which tells to solitude how time is passing. Time—where man lives not—what is it but eternity? And in the church, we might suppose, are garnered up, throughout the week, all thoughts and feelings that have reference to eternity, until the holy day comes round again, to let them forth. Might not, then, its more appropriate site be in the outskirts of the town, with space for old trees to wave around it, and throw their solemn shadows over a quiet green? We will say more of this, hereafter.

But, on the Sabbath, I watch the earliest sunshine, and fancy that a holier brightness marks the day, when there shall be no buzz of voices on the exchange, nor traffic in the shops, nor crowd, nor business, anywhere but at church. Many have fancied so. For my own part, whether I see it scattered down among tangled woods, or beaming broad across the fields, or hemmed in between brick buildings, or tracing out the figure of the casement on my chamber floor, still I recognize the Sabbath sunshine. And ever let me recognize it! Some illusions, and this among them, are the shadows of great truths. Doubts may flit around me, or seem to close their evil wings, and settle down; but, so long as I imagine that the earth is hallowed, and the light of heaven retains its sanctity, on the

Sabbath—while that blessed sunshine lives within me—never can my soul have lost the instinct of its faith. If it have gone astray, it will return again.

I love to spend such pleasant Sabbaths, from morning till night, behind the curtain of my open window. Are they spent amiss? Every spot, so near the church as to be visited by the circling shadow of the steeple, should be deemed consecrated ground, to-day. With stronger truth be it said, that a devout heart may consecrate a den of thieves, as an evil one may convert a temple to the same. My heart, perhaps, has not such holy, nor, I would fain trust, such impious potency. It must suffice, that, though my form be absent, my inner man goes constantly to church, while many, whose bodily presence fills the accustomed seats, have left their souls at home. But I am there, even before my friend, the sexton. At length, he comes —a man of kindly, but sombre aspect, in dark gray clothes, and hair of the same mixture—he comes and applies his key to the wide portal. Now, my thoughts may go in among the dusty pews, or ascend the pulpit, without sacrilege, but soon come forth again to enjoy the music of the bell. How glad, yet solemn too! All the steeples in town are talking together, aloft in the sunny air, and rejoicing among themselves, while their spires point heavenward. Meantime, here are the children assembling to the Sabbath-school, which is kept somewhere within the church. Often, while looking at the arched portal, I have been gladdened by the sight of a score of these little girls and boys, in pink, blue, yellow, and crimson frocks, bursting suddenly forth into the sunshine, like a swarm of gay butterflies that had been shut up in the solemn gloom. Or I might compare them to cherubs, haunting that holy place.

About a quarter of an hour before the second ringing of the bell, individuals of the congregation begin to appear. The earliest is invariably an old woman in black, whose bent frame and rounded shoulders are evidently laden with some heavy affliction, which she is eager to rest upon the altar. Would that the Sabbath come twice as often, for the sake of that sorrowful old soul! There is an elderly man, also, who arrives in good season, and leans against the corner of the tower, just within the line of its shadow, looking downward with a darksome brow. I sometimes fancy that the old woman is the happier of the two. After these, others drop in singly, and by twos and threes, either disappearing through the doorway, or taking their stand in its vicinity. At last, and always with an unexpected sensation, the bell turns in the steeple overhead, and throws out an irregular clangor, jarring the tower to its foundation. As if there were magic in the sound, the sidewalks of the street, both up and down along, are immediately thronged with two long lines of people, all converging hitherward, and streaming into the church. Perhaps the far-off roar of a coach draws nearer—a deeper thunder by its contrast with the surrounding stillness—until it sets down the wealthy worshippers at the portal, among their humblest brethren. Beyond that entrance, in theory at least, there are no distinctions of earthly rank; nor, indeed, by the goodly apparel which is flaunting in the sun, would there seem to be such, on the hither side. Those pretty girls! Why will they disturb my pious meditations! Of all days in the week, they should strive to look least fascinating on the Sabbath, instead of heightening their mortal loveliness, as if to rival the blessed angels, and keep our thoughts from heaven. Were I the minister himself, I must needs look. One girl is white muslin from the waist upwards, and black silk downwards to her slippers; a second blushes from topknot to shoetie, one universal scarlet; another shines of a pervading yellow, as if she had made a garment of the sunshine. The greater part, however, have adopted a milder cheerfulness of hue. Their veils, especially when the wind raises them, give a lightness to the general effect, and make them appear like airy phantoms, as they flit up the steps, and vanish into the sombre doorway. Nearly all —though it is very strange that I should know it—wear white stockings, white as snow, and neat slippers, laced crosswise with black ribbon, pretty high above the ankles. A white stocking is infinitely more effective than a black one.

Here comes the clergyman, slow and solemn, in severe simplicity, needing no black silk gown to denote his office. His aspect claims my reverence, but cannot win my love. Were I to picture Saint Peter keeping fast the gate of heaven, and frowning, more stern than pitiful, on the wretched applicants, that face should be my study. By middle age, or sooner, the creed has generally wrought upon the heart, or been attempered by it. As the minister passes into the church the bell holds its iron tongue, and all the low murmur of the congregation dies away. The gray sexton looks up and down the street, and then at my window curtain, where, through the small peephole, I half fancy that he has caught my eye. Now every loiterer has gone in, and the street lies asleep in the quiet sun, while a feeling of loneliness comes over me, and brings also an uneasy sense of neglected privileges and duties. O, I ought to have gone to church! The bustle of the rising congregation reaches my ears. They are standing up to pray. Could I bring my heart into unison with those who are praying in yonder church, and lift it heavenward, with a fervor of supplication, but no distinct request, would not that be the safest kind of prayer? "Lord, look down upon me in mercy!" With that sentiment gushing from my soul, might I not leave all the rest to Him?

Hark! the hymn. This, at least, is a portion of the service which I can enjoy better than if I sat within the walls, where the full choir and the massive melody of the organ would fall with a weight upon me. At this distance it thrills through my frame and plays upon my heartstrings with a pleasure both of the sense and spirit. Heaven be praised, I know nothing of music as a science; and the most elaborate harmonies, if they please me, please as simply as a nurse's lullaby. The strain has ceased, but prolongs itself in my mind with fanciful echoes till I start from my reverie, and find that the sermon has commenced. It is my misfortune seldom to fructify, in a regular way, by any but printed sermons. The first strong idea which the preacher utters gives birth to a train of thought, and leads me onward, step by step, quite out of hearing of the good man's voice, unless he be indeed a son of thunder. At

my open window, catching now and then a sentence of the
"parson's saw," I am as well situated as at the foot of the
pulpit stairs. The broken and scattered fragments of this one
discourse will be the texts of many sermons, preached by
those colleague pastors—colleagues, but often disputants—
my Mind and Heart. The former pretends to be a scholar,
and perplexes me with doctrinal points; the latter takes me
on the score of feeling; and both, like several other preachers,
spend their strength to very little purpose. I, their sole auditor,
cannot always understand them.

Suppose that a few hours have passed, and behold me still
behind my curtain, just before the close of the afternoon
service. The hour hand on the dial has passed beyond four
o'clock. The declining sun is hidden behind the steeple, and
throws its shadow straight across the street, so that my chamber is darkened as with a cloud. Around the church-door all
is solitude, and an impenetrable obscurity beyond the threshold. A commotion is heard. The seats are slammed down, and
the pew-doors thrown back—a multitude of feet are trampling
along the unseen aisles—and the congregation bursts suddenly through the portal. Foremost, scampers a rabble of boys,
behind whom moves a dense and dark phalanx of grown men,
and lastly, a crowd of females, with young children, and a few
scattered husbands. This instantaneous outbreak of life into
loneliness is one of the pleasantest scenes of the day. Some of
the good people are rubbing their eyes, thereby intimating
that they have been wrapped, as it were, in a sort of holy
trance by the fervor of their devotion. There is a young man,
a third rate coxcomb, whose first care is always to flourish a
white handkerchief, and brush the seat of a tight pair of black
silk pantaloons, which shine as if varnished. They must have
been made of the stuff called "everlasting," or perhaps of the
same piece as Christian's garments in the "Pilgrim's Progress,"
for he put them on two summers ago, and has not yet worn
the gloss off. I have taken a great liking to those black silk
pantaloons. But now, with nods and greetings among friends,
each matron takes her husband's arm and paces gravely home-

ward, while the girls also flutter away after arranging sunset walks with their favored bachelors. The Sabbath eve is the eve of love. At length the whole congregation is dispersed. No; here, with faces as glossy as black satin, come two sable ladies and a sable gentleman, and close in their rear the minister, who softens his severe visage, and bestows a kind word on each. Poor souls! To them the most captivating picture of bliss in heaven is—"There we shall be white!"

All is solitude again. But, hark!—a broken warbling of voices, and now, attuning its grandeur to their sweetness, a stately peal of the organ. Who are the choristers? Let me dream that the angels, who came down from heaven, this blessed morn, to blend themselves with the worship of the truly good, are playing and singing their farewell to the earth. On the wings of that rich melody they were borne upward.

This, gentle reader, is merely a flight of poetry. A few of the singing men and singing women had lingered behind their fellows, and raised their voices fitfully, and blew a careless note upon the organ. Yet, it lifted my soul higher than all their former strains. They are gone—the sons and daughters of music—and the gray sexton is just closing the portal. For six days more, there will be no face of man in the pews, and aisles, and galleries, nor a voice in the pulpit, nor music in the choir. Was it worth while to rear this massive edifice, to be a desert in the heart of the town, and populous only for a few hours of each seventh day? O, but the church is a symbol of religion. May its site, which was consecrated on the day when the first tree was felled, be kept holy forever, a spot of solitude and peace, amid the trouble and vanity of our week-day world! There is a moral, and a religion too, even in the silent walls. And may the steeple still point heavenward, and be decked with the hallowed sunshine of the Sabbath morn!

FANCY'S
SHOW BOX

A MORALITY

What is Guilt? A stain upon the soul. And it is a point of vast interest whether the soul may contract such stains, in all their depth and flagrancy, from deeds which may have been plotted and resolved upon, but which, physically, have never had existence. Must the fleshly hand and visible frame of man set its seal to the evil designs of the soul, in order to give them their entire validity against the sinner? Or, while none but crimes perpetrated are cognizable before an earthly tribunal, will guilty thoughts—of which guilty deeds are no more than shadows—will these draw down the full weight of a condemning sentence, in the supreme court of eternity? In the solitude of a midnight chamber or in a desert, afar from men or in a church, while the body is kneeling, the soul may pollute itself even with those crimes which we are accustomed to deem altogether carnal. If this be true, it is a fearful truth.

Let us illustrate the subject by an imaginary example. A venerable gentleman, one Mr. Smith, who had long been regarded as a pattern of moral excellence, was warming his aged blood with a glass or two of generous wine. His children being gone forth about their worldly business, and his grandchildren at school, he sat alone, in a deep, luxurious arm-chair, with

First published in *The Token,* 1837.

his feet beneath a richly-carved mahogany table. Some old people have a dread of solitude, and when better company may not be had, rejoice even to hear the quiet breathing of a babe, asleep upon the carpet. But Mr. Smith, whose silver hair was the bright symbol of a life unstained, except by such spots as are inseparable from human nature, had no need of a babe to protect him by its purity, nor of a grown person to stand between him and his own soul. Nevertheless, either Manhood must converse with Age, or Womanhood must soothe him with gentle cares, or Infancy must sport around his chair, or his thoughts will stray into the misty region of the past, and the old man be chill and sad. Wine will not always cheer him. Such might have been the case with Mr. Smith, when, through the brilliant medium of his glass of old Madeira, he beheld three figures entering the room. These were Fancy, who had assumed the garb and aspect of an itinerant showman, with a box of pictures on her back; and Memory, in the likeness of a clerk, with a pen behind her ear, an inkhorn at her buttonhole, and a huge manuscript volume beneath her arm; and lastly, behind the other two, a person shrouded in a dusky mantle, which concealed both face and form. But Mr. Smith had a shrewd idea that it was Conscience.

How kind of Fancy, Memory, and Conscience to visit the old gentleman, just as he was beginning to imagine that the wine had neither so bright a sparkle nor so excellent a flavor as when himself and the liquor were less aged! Through the dim length of the apartment, where crimson curtains muffled the glare of sunshine and created a rich obscurity, the three guests drew near the silver-haired old man. Memory, with a finger between the leaves of her huge volume, placed herself at his right hand. Conscience, with her face still hidden in the dusky mantle, took her station on the left, so as to be next his heart; while Fancy set down her picture box upon the table, with the magnifying glass convenient to his eye. We can sketch merely the outlines of two or three out of the many pictures which, at the pulling of a string, successively peopled the box with the semblances of living scenes.

One was a moonlight picture: in the background, a lowly dwelling; and in front, partly shadowed by a tree, yet besprinkled with flakes of radiance, two youthful figures, male and female. The young man stood with folded arms, a haughty smile upon his lip, and a gleam of triumph in his eye, as he glanced downward at the kneeling girl. She was almost prostrate at his feet, evidently sinking under a weight of shame and anguish, which hardly allowed her to lift her clasped hands in supplication. Her eyes she could not lift. But neither her agony, nor the lovely features on which it was depicted, nor the slender grace of the form which it convulsed, appeared to soften the obduracy of the young man. He was the personification of triumphant scorn. Now, strange to say, as old Mr. Smith peeped through the magnifying glass, which made the objects start out from the canvas with magical deception, he began to recognize the farm-house, the tree, and both the figures of the picture. The young man, in times long past, had often met his gaze within the looking-glass; the girl was the very image of his first love—his cottage love—his Martha Burroughs! Mr. Smith was scandalized. "O vile and slanderous picture!" he exclaims. "When have I triumphed over ruined innocence? Was not Martha wedded, in her teens, to David Tomkins, who won her girlish love, and long enjoyed her affection as a wife? And ever since his death she has lived a reputable widow!" Meantime, Memory was turning over the leaves of her volume, rustling them to and fro with uncertain fingers, until, among the earlier pages, she found one which had reference to this picture. She reads it, close to the old gentleman's ear; it is a record merely of sinful thought, which never was embodied in an act; but while Memory is reading, Conscience unveils her face, and strikes a dagger to the heart of Mr. Smith. Though not a death-blow, the torture was extreme.

The exhibition proceeded. One after another, Fancy displayed her pictures, all of which appeared to have been painted by some malicious artist on purpose to vex Mr. Smith. Not a shadow of proof could have been adduced, in any earthly court, that he was guilty of the slightest of those sins which were thus made to stare him in the face. In one scene there was a table set out, with several bottles, and glasses half filled with wine, which threw back the dull ray of an expiring lamp. There had been mirth and revelry, until the hand of the clock stood just at midnight, when murder stepped between the boon companions. A young man had fallen on the floor, and lay stone dead, with a ghastly wound crushed into his temple, while over him, with a delirium of mingled rage and horror in his countenance, stood the youthful likeness of Mr. Smith. The murdered youth wore the features of Edward Spencer! "What does this rascal of a painter mean?" cries Mr. Smith, provoked beyond all patience. "Edward Spencer was my earliest and dearest friend, true to me as I to him, through more than half a century. Neither I, nor any other, ever murdered him. Was he not alive within five years, and did he not, in token of our long friendship, bequeath me his gold-headed cane and a mourning ring?" Again had Memory been turning over her volume, and fixed at length upon so confused a page that she surely must have scribbled it when she was tipsy. The purport was, however, that while Mr. Smith and Edward Spencer were heating their young blood with wine, a quarrel had flashed up between them, and Mr. Smith, in deadly wrath, had flung a bottle at Spencer's head. True, it missed its aim, and merely smashed a looking-glass; and the next morning, when the incident was imperfectly remembered, they had shaken hands with a hearty laugh. Yet, again, while Memory was reading, Conscience unveiled her face, struck a dagger to the heart of Mr. Smith, and quelled his remonstrance with her iron frown. The pain was quite excruciating.

Some of the pictures had been painted with so doubtful a touch, and in colors so faint and pale, that the subjects could barely be conjectured. A dull, semi-transparent mist had been thrown over the surface of the canvas, into which the figures seemed to vanish, while the eye sought most earnestly to fix them. But in every scene, however dubiously portrayed, Mr.

Smith was invariably haunted by his own lineaments, at various ages, as in a dusty mirror. After poring several minutes over one of these blurred and almost indistinguishable pictures, he began to see that the painter had intended to represent him, now in the decline of life, as stripping the clothes from the backs of three half-starved children. "Really, this puzzles me!" quoth Mr. Smith, with the irony of conscious rectitude. "Asking pardon of the painter, I pronounce him a fool, as well as a scandalous knave. A man of my standing in the world to be robbing little children of their clothes! Ridiculous!" But while he spoke, Memory had searched her fatal volume, and found a page, which, with her sad, calm voice, she poured into his ear. It was not altogether inapplicable to the misty scene. It told how Mr. Smith had been grievously tempted by many devilish sophistries, on the ground of a legal quibble, to commence a lawsuit against three orphan children, joint heirs to a considerable estate. Fortunately, before he was quite decided, his claims had turned out nearly as devoid of law as justice. As Memory ceased to read, Conscience again thrust aside her mantle, and would have struck her victim with the envenomed dagger, only that he struggled and clasped his hands before his heart. Even then, however, he sustained an ugly gash.

Why should we follow Fancy through the whole series of those awful pictures? Painted by an artist of wondrous power, and terrible acquaintance with the secret soul, they embodied the ghosts of all the never perpetrated sins that had glided through the lifetime of Mr. Smith. And could such beings of cloudy fantasy, so near akin to nothingness, give valid evidence against him at the day of judgment? Be that the case or not, there is reason to believe that one truly penitential tear would have washed away each hateful picture, and left the canvas white as snow. But Mr. Smith, at a prick of Conscience too keen to be endured, bellowed aloud, with impatient agony, and suddenly discovered that his three guests were gone. There he sat alone, a silver-haired and highly-venerated old man, in the rich gloom of the crimson-curtained room, with no box of pictures on the table, but only a decanter of most excellent Madeira. Yet his heart still seemed to fester with the venom of the dagger.

Nevertheless, the unfortunate old gentleman might have argued the matter with Conscience, and alleged many reasons wherefore she should not smite him so pitilessly. Were we to take up his cause, it should be somewhat in the following fashion: A scheme of guilt, till it be put in execution, greatly resembles a train of incidents in a projected tale. The latter, in order to produce a sense of reality in the reader's mind, must be conceived with such proportionate strength by the author as to seem, in the glow of fancy, more like truth, past, present, or to come, than purely fiction. The prospective sinner, on the other hand, weaves his plot of crime, but seldom or never feels a perfect certainty that it will be executed. There is a dreaminess diffused about his thoughts; in a dream, as it were, he strikes the death-blow into his victim's heart, and starts to find an indelible blood-stain on his hand. Thus a novel writer or a dramatist, in creating a villain of romance and fitting him with evil deeds, and the villain of actual life, in projecting crimes that will be perpetrated, may almost meet each other half-way between reality and fancy. It is not until the crime is accomplished that guilt clinches its gripe upon the guilty heart, and claims it for its own. Then, and not before, sin is actually felt and acknowledged, and, if unaccompanied by repentance, grows a thousand-fold more virulent by its self-consciousness. Be it considered, also, that men often over-estimate their capacity for evil. At a distance, while its attendant circumstances do not press upon their notice, and its results are dimly seen, they can bear to contemplate it. They may take the steps which lead to crime, impelled by the same sort of mental action as in working out a mathematical problem, yet be powerless with compunction at the final moment. They knew not what deed it was that they deemed themselves resolved to do. In truth, there is no such thing in man's nature as a settled and full resolve, either for good or evil, except at the very moment of execution. Let us hope, therefore, that all the dreadful consequences of sin will not be incurred, unless the act have set its seal upon the thought.

Yet, with the slight fancy work which we have framed, some sad and awful truths are interwoven. Man must not disclaim his brotherhood, even with the guiltiest, since, though his hand be clean, his heart has surely been polluted by the flitting phantoms of iniquity. He must feel that, when he shall knock at the gate of heaven, no semblance of an unspotted life can entitle him to entrance there. Penitence must kneel, and Mercy come from the footstool of the throne, or that golden gate will never open!

NIGHT
SKETCHES
BENEATH AN UMBRELLA

Pleasant is a rainy winter's day, within doors! The best study for such a day, or the best amusement,—call it which you will,—is a book of travels, describing scenes the most unlike that sombre one which is mistily presented through the windows. I have experienced that fancy is then most successful in imparting distinct shapes and vivid colors to the objects which the author has spread upon his page, and that his words become magic spells to summon up a thousand varied pictures. Strange landscapes glimmer through the familiar walls of the room, and outlandish figures thrust themselves almost within the sacred precincts of the hearth. Small as my chamber is, it has space enough to contain the ocean-like circumference of an Arabian desert, its parched sands tracked by the long line of a caravan, with the camels patiently journeying through the heavy sunshine. Though my ceiling be not lofty, yet I can pile up the mountains of Central Asia beneath it, till their summits shine far above the clouds of the middle atmosphere. And with my humble means, a wealth that is not taxable, I can transport hither the magnificent merchandise of an Oriental bazaar, and call a crowd of purchasers from distant countries to pay a fair profit for the precious articles which are displayed on all sides. True it is,

First published in *The Token*, 1838.

however, that amid the bustle of traffic, or whatever else may seem to be going on around me, the rain-drops will occasionally be heard to patter against my window panes, which look forth upon one of the quietest streets in a New England town. After a time, too, the visions vanish, and will not appear again at my bidding. Then, it being nightfall, a gloomy sense of unreality depresses my spirits, and impels me to venture out, before the clock shall strike bedtime, to satisfy myself that the world is not entirely made up of such shadowy materials as have busied me throughout the day. A dreamer may dwell so long among fantasies, that the things without him will seem as unreal as those within.

When eve has fairly set in, therefore, I sally forth, tightly buttoning my shaggy overcoat, and hoisting my umbrella, the silken dome of which immediately resounds with the heavy drumming of the invisible rain-drops. Pausing on the lowest doorstep, I contrast the warmth and cheerfulness of my deserted fireside with the drear obscurity and chill discomfort into which I am about to plunge. Now come fearful auguries, innumerable as the drops of rain. Did not my manhood cry shame upon me I should turn back within doors, resume my elbow-chair, my slippers, and my book, pass such an evening of sluggish enjoyment as the day has been, and go to bed inglorious. The same shivering reluctance, no doubt, has quelled, for a moment, the adventurous spirit of many a traveller, when his feet, which were destined to measure the earth around, were leaving their last tracks in the home paths.

In my own case poor human nature may be allowed a few misgivings. I look upward, and discern no sky, not even an unfathomable void, but only a black, impenetrable nothingness, as though heaven and all its lights were blotted from the system of the universe. It is as if Nature were dead, and the world had put on black, and the clouds were weeping for her. With their tears upon my cheek, I turn my eyes earthward, but find little consolation here below. A lamp is burning dimly at the distant corner, and throws just enough of light along the street to show and exaggerate by so faintly showing the perils and difficulties which beset my path. Yonder dingily white remnant of a huge snow-bank,—which will yet cumber the sidewalk till the latter days of March,—over or through that wintry waste must I stride onward. Beyond lies a certain Slough of Despond, a concoction of mud and liquid filth, ankle-deep, leg-deep, neck-deep,—in a word, of unknown bottom,—on which the lamplight does not even glimmer, but which I have occasionally watched in the gradual growth of its horrors from morn till nightfall. Should I flounder into its depths, farewell to upper earth! And hark! how roughly resounds the roaring of a stream, the turbulent career of which is partially reddened by the gleam of the lamp, but elsewhere brawls noisily through the densest gloom. Oh, should I be swept away in fording that impetuous and unclean torrent, the coroner will have a job with an unfortunate gentleman who would fain end his troubles anywhere but in a mud puddle!

Pshaw! I will linger not another instant at arm's-length from these dim terrors, which grow more obscurely formidable the longer I delay to grapple with them. Now for the onset! And lo! with little damage, save a dash of rain in the face and breast, a splash of mud high up the pantaloons, and the left boot full of ice-cold water, behold me at the corner of the street. The lamp throws down a circle of red light around me: and twinkling onward from corner to corner I discern other beacons marshalling my way to a brighter scene. But this is a lonesome and dreary spot. The tall edifices bid gloomy defiance to the storm, with their blinds all closed, even as a man winks when he faces a spattering gust. How loudly tinkles the collected rain down the tin spouts! The puffs of wind are boisterous, and seem to assail me from various quarters at once. I have often observed that this corner is a haunt and loitering-place for those winds which have no work to do upon the deep, dashing ships against our iron-bound shores; nor in the forest, tearing up the sylvan giants with half a rood of soil at their vast roots. Here they amuse themselves with lesser freaks of mischief. See, at this moment, how they assail yonder poor woman, who is passing just within the verge of the lamplight! One blast struggles for her umbrella, and turns it wrong side outward; another whisks the cape of her cloak across her eyes; while a third takes most unwarrantable liberties with the lower part of her attire. Happily the good dame is no gossamer, but a figure of rotundity and fleshly substance; else would these aerial tormentors whirl her aloft, like a witch upon a broomstick, and set her down, doubtless, in the filthiest kennel hereabout.

From hence I tread upon firm pavements into the centre of the town. Here there is almost as brilliant an illumination as when some great victory has been won, either on the battlefield or at the polls. Two rows of shops, with windows down nearly to the ground, cast a glow from side to side, while the black night hangs overhead like a canopy, and thus keeps the splendor from diffusing itself away. The wet sidewalks gleam with a broad sheet of red light. The rain-drops glitter, as if the sky were pouring down rubies. The spouts gush with fire. Methinks the scene is an emblem of the deceptive glare which mortals throw around their footsteps in the moral world, thus bedazzling themselves till they forget the impenetrable obscurity that hems them in, and that can be dispelled only by radiance from above. And after all it is a cheerless scene, and cheerless are the wanderers in it. Here comes one who has so long been familiar with tempestuous weather that he takes the bluster of the storm for a friendly greeting, as if it should say, "How fare ye, brother?" He is a retired sea-captain, wrapped in some nameless garment of the pea-jacket order, and is now laying his course towards the Marine Insurance Office, there to spin yarns of gale and shipwreck with a crew of old sea-dogs like himself. The blast will put in its word among their hoarse voices, and be understood by all of them. Next I meet an unhappy slipshod gentleman, with a cloak flung hastily over his shoulders, running a race with boisterous winds, and striving to glide between the drops of rain. Some domestic emergency or other has blown this miserable man from his warm fireside in quest of a doctor! See that little vagabond—

how carelessly he has taken his stand right underneath a spout, while staring at some object of curiosity in a shop-window! Surely the rain is his native element; he must have fallen with it from the clouds, as frogs are supposed to do.

Here is a picture, and a pretty one. A young man and a girl, both enveloped in cloaks, and huddled beneath the scanty protection of a cotton umbrella. She wears rubber overshoes, but he is in his dancing pumps; and they are on their way, no doubt, to some cotillion party, or subscription ball at a dollar a head, refreshments included. Thus they struggle against the gloomy tempest, lured onward by a vision of festal splendor. But, ah! a most lamentable disaster. Bewildered by the red, blue, and yellow meteors, in an apothecary's window, they have stepped upon a slippery remnant of ice, and are precipitated into a confluence of swollen floods, at the corner of two streets. Luckless lovers! Were it my nature to be other than a looker-on in life, I would attempt your rescue. Since that may not be, I vow, should you be drowned, to weave such a pathetic story of your fate as shall call forth tears enough to drown you both anew. Do ye touch bottom, my young friends? Yes; they emerge like a water nymph and a river deity, and paddle hand in hand out of the depths of the dark pool. They hurry homeward, dripping, disconsolate, abashed, but with love too warm to be chilled by the cold water. They have stood a test which proves too strong for many. Faithful, though over head and ears in trouble!

Onward I go, deriving a sympathetic joy or sorrow from the varied aspect of mortal affairs, even as my figure catches a gleam from the lighted windows, or is blackened by an interval of darkness. Not that mine is altogether a chameleon spirit, with no hue of its own. Now I pass into a more retired street, where the dwellings of wealth and poverty are intermingled, presenting a range of strongly contrasted pictures. Here, too, may be found the golden mean. Through yonder casement I discern a family circle,—the grandmother, the parents, and the children,—all flickering, shadow-like, in the glow of a wood fire. Bluster, fierce blast, and beat, thou win-

try rain, against the window panes! Ye cannot damp the enjoyment of that fireside. Surely my fate is hard that I should
be wandering homeless here, taking to my bosom night and
storm and solitude, instead of wife and children. Peace, mur-
murer! Doubt not that darker guests are sitting round the
hearth, though the warm blaze hides all but blissful images.
Well; here is still a brighter scene. A stately mansion illuminated for a ball, with cut-glass chandeliers and alabaster
lamps in every room, and sunny landscapes hanging round
the walls. See! a coach has stopped, whence emerges a slender
beauty, who, canopied by two umbrellas, glides within the
portal, and vanishes amid lightsome thrills of music. Will she
ever feel the night wind and the rain? Perhaps,—perhaps!
And will Death and Sorrow ever enter that proud mansion?
As surely as the dancers will be gay within its halls to-night.
Such thoughts sadden, yet satisfy my heart; for they teach me
that the poor man in this mean, weather-beaten hovel, without a fire to cheer him, may call the rich his brother,—
brethren by Sorrow, who must be an inmate of both their
households,—brethren by Death, who will lead them both to
other homes.

Onward, still onward, I plunge into the night. Now have I
reached the utmost limits of the town, where the last lamp
struggles feebly with the darkness, like the farthest star that
stands sentinel on the borders of uncreated space. It is strange
what sensations of sublimity may spring from a very humble
source. Such are suggested by this hollow roar of a subter-
ranean cataract, where the mighty stream of a kennel precipi-
tates itself beneath an iron grate, and is seen no more on
earth. Listen awhile to its voice of mystery, and fancy will
magnify it till you start and smile at the illusion. And now
another sound,—the rumbling of wheels,—as the mail-coach,
outward bound, rolls heavily off the pavement, and splashes
through the mud and water of the road. All night long the
poor passengers will be tossed to and fro between drowsy
watch and troubled sleep, and will dream of their own quiet
beds, and awake to find themselves still jolting onward.

Happier my lot, who will straightway hie me to my familiar room, and toast myself comfortably before the fire, musing and fitfully dozing, and fancying a strangeness in such sights as all may see. But first let me gaze at this solitary figure who comes hitherward with a tin lantern, which throws the circular pattern of its punched holes on the ground about him. He passes fearlessly into the unknown gloom, whither I will not follow him.

This figure shall supply me with a moral, wherewith, for lack of a more appropriate one, I may wind up my sketch. He fears not to tread the dreary path before him, because his lantern, which was kindled at the fireside of his home, will light him back to that same fireside again. And thus we, night wanderers through a stormy and dismal world, if we bear the lamp of Faith, enkindled at a celestial fire, it will surely lead us home to that heaven whence its radiance was borrowed.

A VIRTUOSO'S
COLLECTION

The other day, having a leisure hour at my disposal, I stepped into a new museum, to which my notice was casually drawn by a small and unobtrusive sign: "To BE SEEN HERE, A VIRTUOSO'S COLLECTION." Such was the simple, yet not altogether unpromising, announcement that turned my steps aside for a little while from the sunny sidewalk of our principal thoroughfare. Mounting a sombre staircase, I pushed open a door at its summit, and found myself in the presence of a person, who mentioned the moderate sum that would entitle me to admittance.

"Three shillings, Massachusetts tenor," said he. "No, I mean half a dollar, as you reckon in these days."

While searching my pocket for the coin I glanced at the doorkeeper, the marked character and individuality of whose aspect encouraged me to expect something not quite in the ordinary way. He wore an old-fashioned greatcoat, much faded, within which his meagre person was so completely enveloped that the rest of his attire was undistinguishable. But his visage was remarkably wind-flushed, sunburnt, and weather-worn, and had a most unquiet, nervous, and apprehensive expression. It seemed as if this man had some all-important object in view, some point of deepest interest to be decided, some momentous question to ask, might he but hope for a reply. As it was evident, however, that I could

First published in *The Boston Miscellany*, May, 1842.

have nothing to do with his private affairs, I passed through an open doorway, which admitted me into the extensive hall of the museum.

Directly in front of the portal was the bronze statue of a youth with winged feet. He was represented in the act of flitting away from earth, yet wore such a look of earnest invitation that it impressed me like a summons to enter the hall.

"It is the original statue of Opportunity, by the ancient sculptor Lysippus," said a gentleman who now approached me. "I place it at the entrance of my museum, because it is not at all times that one can gain admittance to such a collection."

The speaker was a middle-aged person, of whom it was not easy to determine whether he had spent his life as a scholar or as a man of action; in truth, all outward and obvious peculiarities had been worn away by an extensive and promiscuous intercourse with the world. There was no mark about him of profession, individual habits, or scarcely of country; although his dark complexion and high features made me conjecture that he was a native of some southern clime of Europe. At all events, he was evidently the virtuoso in person.

"With your permission," said he, "as we have no descriptive catalogue, I will accompany you through the museum and point out whatever may be most worthy of attention. In the first place, here is a choice collection of stuffed animals."

Nearest the door stood the outward semblance of a wolf, exquisitely prepared, it is true, and showing a very wolfish fierceness in the large glass eyes which were inserted into its wild and crafty head. Still it was merely the skin of a wolf, with nothing to distinguish it from other individuals of that unlovely breed.

"How does this animal deserve a place in your collection?" inquired I.

"It is the wolf that devoured Little Red Riding-Hood," answered the virtuoso; "and by his side—with a milder and more matronly look, as you perceive—stands the she-wolf that suckled Romulus and Remus."

"Ah, indeed!" exclaimed I. "And what lovely lamb is this with the snow-white fleece, which seems to be of as delicate a texture as innocence itself?"

"Methinks you have but carelessly read Spenser," replied my guide, "or you would at once recognize the 'milk-white lamb' which Una led. But I set no great value upon the lamb. The next specimen is better worth our notice."

"What!" cried I, "this strange animal, with the black head of an ox upon the body of a white horse? Were it possible to suppose it, I should say that this was Alexander's steed Bucephalus."

"The same," said the virtuoso. "And can you likewise give a name to the famous charger that stands beside him?"

Next to the renowned Bucephalus stood the mere skeleton of a horse, with the white bones peeping through his ill-conditioned hide; but, if my heart had not warmed towards that pitiful anatomy, I might as well have quitted the museum at once. Its rarities had not been collected with pain and torn from the four quarters of the earth, and from the depths of the sea, and from the palaces and sepulchres of ages, for those who could mistake this illustrious steed.

"It is Rosinante!" exclaimed I, with enthusiasm.

And so it proved. My admiration for the noble and gallant horse caused me to glance with less interest at the other animals, although many of them might have deserved the notice of Cuvier himself. There was the donkey which Peter Bell cudgelled so soundly, and a brother of the same species who had suffered a similar infliction from the ancient prophet Balaam. Some doubts were entertained, however, as to the authenticity of the latter beast. My guide pointed out the venerable Argus, that faithful dog of Ulysses, and also another dog (for so the skin bespoke it), which, though imperfectly preserved, seemed once to have had three heads. It was Cerberus. I was considerably amused at detecting in an obscure corner the fox that became so famous by the loss of his tail. There were several stuffed cats, which, as a dear lover of that comfortable beast, attracted my affectionate regards. One was

Dr. Johnson's cat Hodge; and in the same row stood the favorite cats of Mahomet, Gray, and Walter Scott, together with Puss in Boots, and a cat of very noble aspect who had once been a deity of ancient Egypt. Byron's tame bear came next. I must not forget to mention the Erymanthean boar, the skin of St. George's dragon, and that of the serpent Python; and another skin with beautifully variegated hues, supposed to have been the garment of the "spirited sly snake" which tempted Eve. Against the walls were suspended the horns of the stag that Shakespeare shot; and on the floor lay the ponderous shell of the tortoise which fell upon the head of Æschylus. In one row, as natural as life, stood the sacred bull Apis, the "cow with the crumpled horn," and a very wild-looking young heifer, which I guessed to be the cow that jumped over the moon. She was probably killed by the rapidity of her descent. As I turned away, my eyes fell upon an indescribable monster, which proved to be a griffin.

"I look in vain," observed I, "for the skin of an animal which might well deserve the closest study of a naturalist— the winged horse, Pegasus."

"He is not yet dead," replied the virtuoso; "but he is so hard ridden by many young gentlemen of the day that I hope soon to add his skin and skeleton to my collection."

We now passed to the next alcove of the hall, in which was a multitude of stuffed birds. They were very prettily arranged, some upon the branches of trees, others brooding upon nests, and others suspended by wires so artificially that they seemed in the very act of flight. Among them was a white dove, with a withered branch of olive leaves in her mouth.

"Can this be the very dove," inquired I, "that brought the message of peace and hope to the tempest-beaten passengers of the ark?"

"Even so," said my companion.

"And this raven, I suppose," continued I, "is the same that fed Elijah in the wilderness."

"The raven? No," said the virtuoso; "it is a bird of modern date. He belonged to one Barnaby Rudge; and many people fancied that the devil himself was disguised under his sable plumage. But poor Grip has drawn his last cork, and has been forced to 'say die' at last. This other raven, hardly less curious, is that in which the soul of King George I. revisited his lady love, the Duchess of Kendall."

My guide next pointed out Minerva's owl and the vulture that preyed upon the liver of Prometheus. There was likewise the sacred ibis of Egypt, and one of the Stymphalides which Hercules shot in his sixth labor. Shelley's skylark, Bryant's water-fowl, and a pigeon from the belfry of the Old South Church, preserved by N. P. Willis, were placed on the same perch. I could not but shudder on beholding Coleridge's albatross, transfixed with the Ancient Mariner's cross-bow shaft. Beside this bird of awful poesy stood a gray goose of very ordinary aspect.

"Stuffed goose is no such rarity," observed I. "Why do you preserve such a specimen in your museum?"

"It is one of the flock whose cackling saved the Roman Capitol," answered the virtuoso. "Many geese have cackled and hissed both before and since; but none, like these, have clamored themselves into immortality."

There seemed to be little else that demanded notice in this department of the museum, unless we except Robinson Crusoe's parrot, a live phœnix, a footless bird of paradise, and a splendid peacock, supposed to be the same that once contained the soul of Pythagoras. I therefore passed to the next alcove, the shelves of which were covered with a miscellaneous collection of curiosities such as are usually found in similar establishments. One of the first things that took my eye was a strange-looking cap, woven of some substance that appeared to be neither woollen, cotton, nor linen.

"Is this a magician's cap?" I asked.

"No," replied the virtuoso; "it is merely Dr. Franklin's cap of asbestos. But here is one which, perhaps, may suit you better. It is the wishing cap of Fortunatus. Will you try it on?"

"By no means," answered I, putting it aside with my hand. "The day of wild wishes is past with me. I desire nothing that may not come in the ordinary course of Providence."

"Then probably," returned the virtuoso, "you will not be tempted to rub this lamp?"

While speaking, he took from the shelf an antique brass-lamp, curiously wrought with embossed figures, but so covered with verdigris that the sculpture was almost eaten away.

"It is a thousand years," said he, "since the genius of this lamp constructed Aladdin's palace in a single night. But he still retains his power; and the man who rubs Aladdin's lamp has but to desire either a palace or a cottage."

"I might desire a cottage," replied I; "but I would have it founded on sure and stable truth, not on dreams and fantasies. I have learned to look for the real and the true."

My guide next showed me Prospero's magic wand, broken into three fragments by the hand of its mighty master. On the same shelf lay the gold ring of ancient Gyges, which enabled the wearer to walk invisible. On the other side of the alcove was a tall looking-glass in a frame of ebony, but veiled with a curtain of purple silk, through the rents of which the gleam of the mirror was perceptible.

"This is Cornelius Agrippa's magic glass," observed the virtuoso. "Draw aside the curtain, and picture any human form within your mind, and it will be reflected in the mirror."

"It is enough, if I can picture it within my mind," answered I. "Why should I wish it to be repeated in the mirror? But, indeed, these works of magic have grown wearisome to me. There are so many greater wonders in the world, to those who keep their eyes open and their sight undimmed by custom, that all the delusions of the old sorcerers seem flat and stale. Unless you can show me something really curious, I care not to look farther into your museum."

"Ah, well, then," said the virtuoso, composedly, "perhaps you may deem some of my antiquarian rarities deserving of a glance."

He pointed out the iron mask, now corroded with rust; and my heart grew sick at the sight of this dreadful relic, which had shut out a human being from sympathy with his race. There was nothing half so terrible in the axe that beheaded King Charles, nor in the dagger that slew Henry of Navarre, nor in the arrow that pierced the heart of William Rufus—all of which were shown to me. Many of the articles derived their interest, such as it was, from having been formerly in the possession of royalty. For instance, here was Charlemagne's sheepskin cloak, the flowing wig of Louis Quatorze, the spinning-wheel of Sardanapalus, and King Stephen's famous breeches which cost him but a crown. The heart of the Bloody Mary, with the word "Calais" worn into its diseased substance, was preserved in a bottle of spirits; and near it lay the golden case in which the queen of Gustavus Adolphus treasured up that hero's heart. Among these relics and heirlooms of kings I must not forget the long, hairy ears of Midas, and a piece of bread which had been changed to gold by the touch of that unlucky monarch. And as Grecian Helen was a queen, it may here be mentioned that I was permitted to take into my hand a lock of her golden hair and the bowl which a sculptor modelled from the curve of her perfect breast. Here, likewise, was the robe that smothered Agamemnon, Nero's fiddle, the Czar Peter's brandy bottle, the crown of Semiramis, and Canute's sceptre which he extended over the sea. That my own land may not deem itself neglected, let me add that I was favored with a sight of the skull of King Philip, the famous Indian chief, whose head the Puritans smote off and exhibited upon a pole.

"Show me something else," said I to the virtuoso. "Kings are in such an artificial position that people in the ordinary walks of life cannot feel an interest in their relics. If you could show me the straw hat of sweet little Nell, I would far rather see it than a king's golden crown."

"There it is," said my guide, pointing carelessly with his staff to the straw hat in question. "But, indeed, you are hard to please. Here are the seven-league boots. Will you try them on?"

"Our modern railroads have superseded their use," answered I; "and as to these cowhide boots, I could show you quite as curious a pair at the Transcendental community in Roxbury."

We next examined a collection of swords and other

weapons, belonging to different epochs, but thrown together without much attempt at arrangement. Here was Arthur's sword Excalibar, and that of the Cid Campeador, and the sword of Brutus rusted with Cæsar's blood and his own, and the sword of Joan of Arc, and that of Horatius, and that with which Virginius slew his daughter, and the one which Dionysius suspended over the head of Damocles. Here also was Arria's sword, which she plunged into her own breast, in order to taste of death before her husband. The crooked blade of Saladin's cimeter next attracted my notice. I know not by what chance, but so it happened, that the sword of one of our own militia generals was suspended between Don Quixote's lance and the brown blade of Hudibras. My heart throbbed high at the sight of the helmet of Miltiades and the spear that was broken in the breast of Epaminondas. I recognized the shield of Achilles by its resembiance to the admirable cast in the possession of Professor Felton. Nothing in this apartment interested me more than Major Pitcairn's pistol, the discharge of which, at Lexington, began the War of the Revolution, and was reverberated in thunder around the land for seven long years. The bow of Ulysses, though unstrung for ages, was placed against the wall, together with a sheaf of Robin Hood's arrows and the rifle of Daniel Boone.

"Enough of weapons," said I, at length; "although I would gladly have seen the sacred shield which fell from heaven in the time of Numa. And surely you should obtain the sword which Washington unsheathed at Cambridge. But the collection does you much credit. Let us pass on."

In the next alcove we saw the golden thigh of Pythagoras, which had so divine a meaning; and, by one of the queer analogies to which the virtuoso seemed to be addicted, this ancient emblem lay on the same shelf with Peter Stuyvesant's wooden leg, that was fabled to be of silver. Here was a remnant of the Golden Fleece, and a sprig of yellow leaves that resembled the foliage of a frost-bitten elm, but was duly authenticated as a portion of the golden branch by which Æneas gained admittance to the realm of Pluto. Atalanta's golden apple and one of the apples of discord were wrapped in the napkin of gold which Rampsinitus brought from Hades; and the whole were deposited in the golden vase of Bias, with its inscription: "To the wisest."

"And how did you obtain this vase?" said I to the virtuoso.

"It was given me long ago," replied he, with a scornful expression in his eye, "because I had learned to despise all things."

It had not escaped me that, though the virtuoso was evidently a man of high cultivation, yet he seemed to lack sympathy with the spiritual, the sublime, and the tender. Apart from the whim that had led him to devote so much time, pains, and expense to the collection of this museum, he impressed me as one of the hardest and coldest men of the world whom I had ever met.

"To despise all things!" repeated I. "This, at best, is the wisdom of the understanding. It is the creed of a man whose soul, whose better and diviner part, has never been awakened, or has died out of him."

"I did not think that you were still so young," said the virtuoso. "Should you live to my years, you will acknowledge that the vase of Bias was not ill bestowed."

Without further discussion of the point, he directed my attention to other curiosities. I examined Cinderella's little glass slipper, and compared it with one of Diana's sandals, and with Fanny Elssler's shoe, which bore testimony to the muscular character of her illustrious foot. On the same shelf were Thomas the Rhymer's green velvet shoes, and the brazen shoe of Empedocles which was thrown out of Mount Ætna. Anacreon's drinking-cup was placed in apt juxtaposition with one of Tom Moore's wineglasses and Circe's magic bowl. Those were symbols of luxury and riot; but near them stood the cup whence Socrates drank his hemlock, and that which Sir Philip Sidney put from his death-parched lips to bestow the draught upon a dying soldier. Next appeared a cluster of tobacco-pipes, consisting of Sir Walter Raleigh's, the earliest on record, Dr. Parr's, Charles Lamb's, and the first calumet of peace which was ever smoked between a European and an Indian. Among other musical instruments, I noticed the lyre of Orpheus and those of Homer and Sappho, Dr. Franklin's famous whistle, the trumpet of Anthony Van Corlear, and the flute which Goldsmith played upon in his rambles through the French provinces. The staff of Peter the Hermit stood in a corner with that of good old Bishop Jewel, and one of ivory, which had belonged to Papirius, the Roman senator. The ponderous club of Hercules was close at hand. The virtuoso showed me the chisel of Phidias, Claude's palette, and the brush of Apelles, observing that he intended to bestow the former either on Greenough, Crawford, or Powers, and the two latter upon Washington Allston. There was a small vase of oracular gas from Delphos, which I trust will be submitted to the scientific analysis of Professor Silliman. I was deeply moved on beholding a vial of the tears into which Niobe was dissolved; nor less so on learning that a shapeless fragment of salt was a relic of that victim of despondency and sinful regrets—Lot's wife. My companion appeared to set great value upon some Egyptian darkness in a blacking jug. Several of the shelves were covered by a collection of coins, among which, however, I remember none but the Splendid Shilling, celebrated by Phillips, and a dollar's worth of the iron money of Lycurgus, weighing about fifty pounds.

Walking carelessly onward, I had nearly fallen over a huge bundle, like a pedlar's pack, done up in sackcloth and very securely strapped and corded.

"It is Christian's burden of sin," said the virtuoso.

"Oh, pray let us open it!" cried I. "For many a year I have longed to know its contents."

"Look into your own consciousness and memory," replied the virtuoso. "You will there find a list of whatever it contains."

As this was an undeniable truth, I threw a melancholy look at the burden and passed on. A collection of old garments, hanging on pegs, was worthy of some attention, especially the shirt of Nessus, Cæsar's mantle, Joseph's coat of many colors, the Vicar of Bray's cassock, Goldsmith's peach-bloom suit, a pair of President Jefferson's scarlet breeches, John Randolph's red baize hunting shirt, the drab smallclothes of the Stout Gentleman, and the rags of the "man all tattered and torn." George Fox's hat impressed me with deep reverence as a relic of perhaps the truest apostle that has appeared on earth for these eighteen hundred years. My eye was next attracted by an old pair of shears, which I should have taken for a memorial of some famous tailor, only that the virtuoso pledged his veracity that they were the identical scissors of Atropes. He also showed me a broken hour-glass which had been thrown aside by Father Time, together with the old gentleman's gray forelock, tastefully braided into a brooch. In the hour-glass was the handful of sand, the grains of which had numbered the years of the Cumæan sibyl. I think it was in this alcove that I saw the inkstand which Luther threw at the devil, and the ring which Essex, while under sentence of death, sent to Queen Elizabeth. And here was the blood-incrusted pen of steel with which Faust signed away his salvation.

The virtuoso now opened the door of a closet and showed me a lamp burning, while three others stood unlighted by its side. One of the three was the lamp of Diogenes, another that of Guy Fawkes, and the third that which Hero set forth to the midnight breeze in the high tower of Abydos.

"See!" said the virtuoso, blowing with all his force at the lighted lamp.

The flame quivered and shrank away from his breath, but clung to the wick, and resumed its brilliancy as soon as the blast was exhausted.

"It is an undying lamp from the tomb of Charlemagne," observed my guide. "That flame was kindled a thousand years ago."

"How ridiculous to kindle an unnatural light in tombs!" exclaimed I. "We should seek to behold the dead in the light of heaven. But what is the meaning of this chafing-dish of glowing coals?"

"That," answered the virtuoso, "is the original fire which Prometheus stole from heaven. Look steadfastly into it, and you will discern another curiosity."

I gazed into that fire,—which, symbolically, was the origin of all that was bright and glorious in the soul of man,—and in the midst of it, behold, a little reptile, sporting with evident enjoyment of the fervid heat! It was a salamander.

"What a sacrilege!" cried I, with inexpressible disgust. "Can you find no better use for this ethereal fire than to cherish a loathsome reptile in it? Yet there are men who abuse the sacred fire of their own souls to as foul and guilty a purpose."

The virtuoso made no answer except by a dry laugh and an assurance that the salamander was the very same which Benvenuto Cellini had seen in his father's household fire. He then proceeded to show me other rarities; for this closet appeared to be the receptacle of what he considered most valuable in his collection.

"There," said he, "is the Great Carbuncle of the White Mountains."

I gazed with no little interest at this mighty gem, which it had been one of the wild projects of my youth to discover. Possibly it might have looked brighter to me in those days than now; at all events, it had not such brilliancy as to detain me long from the other articles of the museum. The virtuoso pointed out to me a crystalline stone which hung by a gold chain against the wall.

"That is the philosopher's stone," said he.

"And have you the elixir vitæ which generally accompanies it?" inquired I.

"Even so; this urn is filled with it," he replied. "A draught would refresh you. Here is Hebe's cup; will you quaff a health from it?"

My heart thrilled within me at the idea of such a reviving draught; for methought I had great need of it after traveling so far on the dusty road of life. But I know not whether it were a peculiar glance in the virtuoso's eye, or the circumstance that this most precious liquid was contained in an antique sepulchral urn, that made me pause. Then came many a thought with which, in the calmer and better hours of life, I had strengthened myself to feel that Death is the very friend whom, in his due season, even the happiest mortal should be willing to embrace.

"No; I desire not an earthly immortality," said I. "Were man to live longer on the earth, the spiritual would die out of him. The spark of ethereal fire would be choked by the material, the sensual. There is a celestial something within us that requires, after a certain time, the atmosphere of heaven to preserve it from decay and ruin. I will have none of this liquid. You do well to keep it in a sepulchral urn; for it would produce death while bestowing the shadow of life."

"All this is unintelligible to me," responded my guide, with indifference. "Life—earthly life—is the only good. But you refuse the draught? Well, it is not likely to be offered twice within one man's experience. Probably you have griefs which you seek to forget in death. I can enable you to forget them in life. Will you take a draught of Lethe?"

As he spoke, the virtuoso took from the shelf a crystal vase containing a sable liquor, which caught no reflected image from the objects around.

"Not for the world!" exclaimed I, shrinking back. "I can spare none of my recollections, not even those of error or sorrow. They are all alike the food of my spirit. As well never to have lived as to lose them now."

Without further parley we passed to the next alcove, the shelves of which were burdened with ancient volumes and with those rolls of papyrus in which was treasured up the eldest wisdom of the earth. Perhaps the most valuable work in the collection, to a bibliomaniac, was the Book of Hermes. For my part, however, I would have given a higher price for those six of the Sibyl's books which Tarquin refused to purchase, and which, the virtuoso informed me, he had himself found in the cave of Trophonius. Doubtless these old volumes contain prophecies of the fate of Rome, both as respects the decline and fall of her temporal empire and the rise of her spiritual one. Not without value, likewise, was the work of Anaxagoras on Nature, hitherto supposed to be irrecoverably lost, and the missing treatises of Longinus, by which modern criticism might profit, and those books of Livy for which the classic student has so long sorrowed without hope. Among these precious tomes I observed the original manuscript of the Koran, and also that of the Mormon Bible in Joe Smith's authentic autograph. Alexander's copy of the Iliad was also there, enclosed in the jewelled casket of Darius, still fragrant of the perfumes which the Persian kept in it.

Opening an iron-clasped volume, bound in black leather, I discovered it to be Cornelius Agrippa's book of magic; and it was rendered still more interesting by the fact that many flowers, ancient and modern, were pressed between its leaves. Here was a rose from Eve's bridal bower, and all those red and white roses which were plucked in the garden of the Temple by the partisans of York and Lancaster. Here was Halleck's Wild Rose of Alloway. Cowper had contributed a Sensitive Plant, and Wordsworth an Eglantine, and Burns a Mountain Daisy, and Kirke White a Star of Bethlehem, and Longfellow a Spring of Fennel, with its yellow flowers. James Russell Lowell had given a Pressed Flower, but fragrant still, which had been shadowed in the Rhine. There was also a sprig from Southey's Holly-Tree. One of the most beautiful specimens was a Fringed Gentian, which had been plucked and preserved for immortality by Bryant. From Jones Very, a poet whose voice is scarcely heard among us by reason of its depth, there was a Wind Flower and a Columbine.

As I closed Cornelius Agrippa's magic volume, an old, mildewed letter fell upon the floor. It proved to be an autograph from the Flying Dutchman to his wife. I could linger no longer among books; for the afternoon was waning, and there was yet much to see. The bare mention of a few more curiosities must suffice. The immense skull of Polyphemus was recognizable by the cavernous hollow in the centre of the forehead where once had blazed the giant's single eye. The tub of Diogenes, Medea's caldron, and Psyche's vase of beauty were placed one within another. Pandora's box, without the lid, stood next, containing nothing but the girdle of Venus, which had been carelessly flung into it. A bundle of birch rods which had been used by Shenstone's schoolmistress were tied up with the Countess of Salisbury's garter. I knew

not which to value most, a roc's egg as big as an ordinary
hogshead, or the shell of the egg which Columbus set upon
its end. Perhaps the most delicate article in the whole museum
was Queen Mab's chariot, which, to guard it from the touch
of meddlesome fingers, was placed under a glass tumbler.

Several of the shelves were occupied by specimens of en-
tomology. Feeling but little interest in the science I noticed
only Anacreon's grasshopper, and a humble bee which had
been presented to the virtuoso by Ralph Waldo Emerson.

In the part of the hall which we had now reached I observed a curtain that descended from the ceiling to the floor
in voluminous folds, of a depth, richness, and magnificence
which I had never seen equalled. It was not to be doubted
that this splendid though dark and solemn veil concealed a
portion of the museum even richer in wonders than that
through which I had already passed; but, on my attempting to
grasp the edge of the curtain and draw it aside, it proved to
be an illusive picture.

"You need not blush," remarked the virtuoso; "for that
same curtain deceived Zeuxis. It is the celebrated painting
of Parrhasius."

In a range with the curtain there were a number of other
choice pictures by artists of ancient days. Here was the famous
cluster of grapes by Zeuxis, so admirably depicted that it
seemed as if the ripe juice were bursting forth. As to the
picture of the old woman by the same illustrious painter, and
which was so ludicrous that he himself died with laughing
at it, I cannot say that it particularly moved my risibility.
Ancient humor seems to have little power over modern
muscles. Here, also, was the horse painted by Apelles which
living horses neighed at; his first portrait of Alexander the
Great, and his last unfinished picture of Venus asleep. Each
of these works of art, together with others by Parrhasius,
Timanthes, Polygnotus, Apollodorus, Pausias, and Pamphilus,
required more time and study than I could bestow for the
adequate perception of their merits. I shall therefore leave
them undescribed and uncriticised, nor attempt to settle the
question of superiority between ancient and modern art.

For the same reason I shall pass lightly over the specimens of antique sculpture which this indefatigable and fortunate virtuoso had dug out of the dust of fallen empires. Here was Ætion's cedar statue of Æsculapius, much decayed, and Alcon's iron statue of Hercules, lamentably rusted. Here was the statue of Victory, six feet high, which the Jupiter Olympus of Phidias had held in his hand. Here was a forefinger of the Colossus of Rhodes, seven feet in length. Here was the Venus Urania of Phidias, and other images of male and female beauty or grandeur, wrought by sculptors who appear never to have debased their souls by the sight of any meaner forms than those of gods or godlike mortals. But the deep simplicity of these great works was not to be comprehended by a mind excited and disturbed, as mine was, by the various objects that had recently been presented to it. I therefore turned away with merely a passing glance, resolving on some future occasion to brood over each individual statue and picture until my inmost spirit should feel their excellence. In this department, again, I noticed the tendency to whimsical combinations and ludicrous analogies which seemed to influence many of the arrangements of the museum. The wooden statue so well known as the Palladium of Troy was placed in close apposition with the wooden head of General Jackson which was stolen a few years since from the bows of the frigate Constitution.

We had now completed the circuit of the spacious hall, and found ourselves again near the door. Feeling somewhat wearied with the survey of so many novelties and antiquities, I sat down upon Cowper's sofa, while the virtuoso threw himself carelessly into Rabelais' easy chair. Casting my eyes upon the opposite wall, I was surprised to perceive the shadow of a man flickering unsteadily across the wainscot, and looking as if it were stirred by some breath of air that found its way through the door or windows. No substantial figure was visible from which this shadow might be thrown; nor, had there been such, was there any sunshine that would have caused it to darken upon the wall.

"It is Peter Schlemihl's shadow," observed the virtuoso, "and one of the most valuable articles in my collection."

"Methinks a shadow would have made a fitting door-keeper to such a museum," said I; "although, indeed, yonder figure has something strange and fantastic about him, which suits well enough with many of the impressions which I have received here. Pray, who is he?"

While speaking, I gazed more scrutinizingly than before at the antiquated presence of the person who had admitted me, and who still sat on his bench with the same restless aspect, and dim, confused questioning anxiety that I had noticed on my first entrance. At this moment he looked eagerly towards us, and, half starting from his seat, addressed me.

"I beseech you, kind sir," said he, in a cracked, melancholy tone, "have pity on the most unfortunate man in the world. For Heaven's sake, answer me a single question! Is this the town of Boston?"

"You have recognized him now," said the virtuoso. "It is Peter Rugg, the missing man. I chanced to meet him the other day still in search of Boston, and conducted him hither; and, as he could not succeed in finding his friends, I have taken him into my service as door-keeper. He is somewhat too apt to ramble, but otherwise a man of trust and integrity."

"And might I venture to ask," continued I, "to whom am I indebted for this afternoon's gratification?"

The virtuoso, before replying, laid his hand upon an antique dart, or javelin, the rusty steel head of which seemed to have been blunted, as if it had encountered the resistance of a tempered shield, or breastplate.

"My name has not been without its distinction in the world for a longer period than that of any other man alive," answered he. "Yet many doubt of my existence; perhaps you will do so to-morrow. This dart which I hold in my hand was once grim Death's own weapon. It served him well for the space of four thousand years; but it fell blunted, as you see, when he directed it against my breast."

These words were spoken with the calm and cold courtesy of manner that had characterized this singular personage throughout our interview. I fancied, it is true, that there was a bitterness indefinably mingled with his tone, as of one cut off from natural sympathies and blasted with a doom that had been inflicted on no other human being, and by the results of which he had ceased to be human. Yet, withal, it seemed one of the most terrible consequences of that doom that the victim no longer regarded it as a calamity, but had finally accepted it as the greatest good that could have befallen him.

"You are the Wandering Jew!" exclaimed I.

The virtuoso bowed without emotion of any kind; for, by centuries of custom, he had almost lost the sense of strangeness in his fate, and was but imperfectly conscious of the astonishment and awe with which it affected such as are capable of death.

"Your doom is indeed a fearful one!" said I, with irrepressible feeling and a frankness that afterwards startled me; "yet perhaps the ethereal spirit is not entirely extinct under all this corrupted or frozen mass of earthly life. Perhaps the immortal spark may yet be rekindled by a breath of Heaven. Perhaps you may yet be permitted to die before it is too late to live eternally. You have my prayers for such a consummation. Farewell."

"Your prayers will be in vain," replied he, with a smile of cold triumph. "My destiny is linked with the realities of earth. You are welcome to your visions and shadows of a future state; but give me what I can see, and touch, and understand, and I ask no more."

"It is indeed too late," thought I. "The soul is dead within him."

Struggling between pity and horror, I extended my hand, to which the virtuoso gave his own, still with the habitual courtesy of a man of the world, but without a single heart throb of human brotherhood. The touch seemed like ice, yet I know not whether morally or physically. As I departed, he bade me observe that the inner door of the hall was constructed with the ivory leaves of the gateway through which Æneas and the Sibyl had been dismissed from Hades.

THE OLD
APPLE DEALER

The lover of the moral picturesque may some-
times find what he seeks in a character which is nevertheless
of too negative a description to be seized upon and represented to the imaginative vision by word painting. As an
instance, I remember an old man who carries on a little trade
of gingerbread and apples at the depot of one of our railroads.
While awaiting the department of the cars, my observation,
flitting to and fro among the livelier characteristics of the
scene, has often settled insensibly upon this almost hueless
object. Thus, unconsciously to myself and unsuspected by
him, I have studied the old apple dealer until he has become
a naturalized citizen of my inner world. How little would he
imagine—poor, neglected, friendless, unappreciated, and with
little that demands appreciation—that the mental eye of an
utter stranger has so often reverted to his figure! Many a
noble form, many a beautiful face, has flitted before me and
vanished like a shadow. It is a strange witchcraft whereby this
faded and featureless old apple dealer has gained a settlement
in my memory.

He is a small man, with gray hair and gray stubble beard,
and is invariably clad in a shabby surtout of snuff color, closely
buttoned, and half concealing a pair of gray pantaloons; the
whole dress, though clean and entire, being evidently flimsy

First published in *Sargent's New Monthly Magazine*, January, 1843.

with much wear. His face, thin, withered, furrowed, and with features which even age has failed to render impressive, has a frost-bitten aspect. It is a moral frost which no physical warmth or comfortableness could counteract. The summer sunshine may fling its white heat upon him, or the good fire of the depot room may make him the focus of its blaze on a winter's day; but all in vain; for still the old man looks as if he were in a frosty atmosphere, with scarcely warmth enough to keep life in the region about his heart. It is a patient, long-suffering, quiet, hopeless, shivering aspect. He is not desperate,—that, though its etymology implies no more, would be too positive an expression,—but merely devoid of hope. As all his past life, probably, offers no spots of brightness to his memory, so he takes his present poverty and discomfort as entirely a matter of course: he thinks it the definition of existence, so far as himself is concerned, to be poor, cold, and uncomfortable. It may be added, that time has not thrown dignity as a mantle over the old man's figure: there is nothing venerable about him: you pity him without a scruple.

He sits on a bench in the deport room; and before him, on the floor, are deposited two baskets of a capacity to contain his whole stock in trade. Across from one basket to the other extends a board, on which is displayed a plate of cakes and gingerbread, some russet and red-cheeked apples, and a box containing variegated sticks of candy, together with that delectable condiment known by children as Gibraltar rock, neatly done up in white paper. There is likewise a half-peck measure of cracked walnuts and two or three tin half pints or gills filled with the nut kernels, ready for purchasers. Such are the small commodities with which our old friend comes daily before the world, ministering to its petty needs and little freaks of appetite, and seeking thence the solid subsistence —so far as he may subsist—of his life.

A slight observer would speak of the old man's quietude; but, on closer scrutiny, you discover that there is a continual unrest within him, which somewhat resembles the fluttering action of the nerves in a corpse from which life has recently departed. Though he never exhibits any violent action, and, indeed, might appear to be sitting quite still, yet you perceive, when his minuter peculiarities began to be detected, that he is always making some little movement or other. He looks anxiously at his plate of the cakes or pyramid of apples and slightly alters their arrangement, with an evident idea that a great deal depends on their being disposed exactly thus and so. Then for a moment he gazes out of the window; then he shivers quietly and folds his arms across his breast, as if to draw himself closer within himself, and thus keep a flicker of warmth in his lonesome heart. Now he turns again to his merchandise of cakes, apples, and candy, and discovers that this cake or that apple, or yonder stick of red and white candy, has somehow got out of its proper position. And is there not a walnut kernel too many or too few in one of those small tin measures? Again the whole arrangement appears to be settled to his mind; but, in the course of a minute or two, there will assuredly be something to set right. At times, by an indescribable shadow upon his features, too quiet, however, to be noticed until you are familiar with his ordinary aspect, the expression of frost-bitten, patient despondency becomes very touching. It seems as if just at that instant the suspicion occurred to him that, in his chill decline of life, earning scanty bread by selling cakes, apples, and candy, he is a very miserable old fellow.

But, if he think so, it is a mistake. He can never suffer the extreme of misery, because the tone of his whole being is too much subdued for him to feel anything acutely.

Occasionally one of the passengers, to while away a tedious interval, approaches the old man, inspects the articles upon his board, and even peeps curiously into the two baskets. Another, striding to and fro along the room, throws a look at the apples and gingerbread at every turn. A third, it may be of a more sensitive and delicate texture of being, glances shyly thitherward, cautious not to excite expectations of a purchaser while yet undetermined whether to buy. But there appears to be no need of such a scrupulous regard to our old friend's feelings. True, he is conscious of the remote possibility to sell a cake or an apple; but innumerable disappointments have rendered him so far a philosopher, that, even if the purchased article should be returned, he will consider it altogether in the ordinary train of events. He speaks to none, and makes no sign of offering his wares to the public: not that he is deterred by pride, but by the certain conviction that such demonstrations would not increase his custom. Besides, this activity in business would require an energy that never could have been a characteristic of his almost passive disposition even in youth. Whenever an actual customer appears the old man looks up with a patient eye: if the price and the article are approved, he is ready to make change; otherwise his eyelids droop again sadly enough, but with no heavier despondency than before. He shivers, perhaps folds his lean arms around his lean body, and resumes the lifelong, frozen patience in which consists his strength. Once in a while a school-boy comes hastily up, places a cent or two upon the board, and takes up a cake, or stick of candy, or a measure of walnuts, or an apple as red cheeked as himself. There are no words as to price, that being as well known to the buyer as to the seller. The old apple dealer never speaks an unnecessary word: not that he is sullen and morose; but there is none of the cheeriness and briskness in him that stirs up people to talk.

Not seldom he is greeted by some old neighbor, a man well to do in the world, who makes a civil, patronizing observation about the weather; and then, by way of performing a charitable deed, begins to chaffer for an apple. Our friend presumes not on any past acquaintance; he makes the briefest possible response to all general remarks, and shrinks quietly into himself again. After every diminution of his stock he takes care to produce from the basket another cake, another stick of candy, another apple, or another measure of walnuts, to supply the place of the article sold. Two or three attempts—or, perchance, half a dozen—are requisite before the board can be rearranged to his satisfaction. If he have received a silver coin, he waits till the purchaser is out of sight, then he examines

it closely, and tries to bend it with his finger and thumb:
finally he puts it into his waistcoat pocket with seemingly a
gentle sigh. This sigh, so faint as to be hardly perceptible, and
not expressive of any definite emotion, is the accompaniment
and conclusion of all his actions. It is the symbol of the
chillness and torpid melancholy of his old age, which only
make themselves felt sensibly when his repose is slightly disturbed.

Our man of gingerbread and apples is not a specimen of
the "needy man who has seen better days." Doubtless there
have been better and brighter days in the far-off time of his
youth; but none with so much sunshine of prosperity in
them that the chill, the depression, the narrowness of means,
in his declining years, can have come upon him by surprise.
His life has all been of a piece. His subdued and nerveless
boyhood prefigured his abortive prime, which likewise contained within itself the prophecy and image of his lean and
torpid age. He was perhaps a mechanic, who never came to be
a master in his craft, or a petty tradesman, rubbing onward
between passably to do and poverty. Possibly he may look back
to some brilliant epoch of his career when there were a hundred or two of dollars to his credit in the Savings Bank. Such
must have been the extent of his better fortune—his little
measure of this world's triumphs—all that he has known of
success. A meek, downcast, humble, uncomplaining creature,
he probably has never felt himself entitled to more than so
much of the gifts of Providence. Is it not still something that
he has never held out his hand for charity, nor has yet been
driven to that sad home and household of Earth's forlorn
and broken-spirited children, the almshouse? He cherishes
no quarrel, therefore, with his destiny, nor with the Author
of it. All is as it should be.

If, indeed, he have been bereaved of a son, a bold, energetic,
vigorous young man, on whom the father's feeble nature
leaned as on a staff of strength, in that case he may have felt
a bitterness that could not otherwise have been generated
in his heart. But methinks the joy of possessing such a son,

and the agony of losing him would have developed the old man's moral and intellectual nature to a much greater degree than we now find it. Intense grief appears to be as much out of keeping with his life as fervid happiness.

To confess the truth, it is not the easiest matter in the world to define and individualize a character like this which we are now handling. The portrait must be so generally negative that the most delicate pencil is likely to spoil it by introducing some too positive tint. Every touch must be kept down, or else you destroy the subdued tone which is absolutely essential to the whole effect. Perhaps more may be done by contrast than by direct description. For this purpose I make use of another cake and candy merchant, who likewise infests the railroad depot. This latter worthy is a very smart and well-dressed boy of ten years old or thereabouts, who skips briskly hither and thither, addressing the passengers in a pert voice, yet with somewhat of good breeding in his tone and pronunciation. Now he has caught my eye, and skips across the room with a pretty pertness which I should like to correct with a box on the ear. "Any cake, sir? any candy?"

No, none for me, my lad. I did but glance at your brisk figure in order to catch a reflected light and throw it upon your old rival yonder.

Again, in order to invest my conception of the old man with a more decided sense of reality, I look at him in the very moment of intensest bustle, on the arrival of the cars. The shriek of the engine as it rushes into the car-house is the utterance of the steam fiend, whom man has subdued by magic spells and compels to serve as a beast of burden. He has skimmed rivers in his headlong rush, dashed through forests, plunged into the hearts of mountains, and glanced from the city to the desert-place, and again to a far-off city, with a meteoric progress, seen and out of sight, while his reverberating roar still fills the ear. The travellers swarm forth from the cars. All are full of the momentum which they have caught from their mode of conveyance. It seems as if the whole world, both morally and physically, were detached from its old standfasts and set in rapid motion. And, in the midst of this terrible activity, there sits the old man of gingerbread; so subdued, so hopeless, so without a stake in life, and yet not positively miserable,—there he sits, the forlorn old creature, one chill and sombre day after another, gathering scanty coppers for his cakes, apples, and candy,—there sits the old apple dealer, in his threadbare suit of snuff color and gray and his grizzly stubble beard. See! he folds his lean arms around his lean figure with that quiet sigh and that scarcely perceptible shiver which are the tokens of his inward state. I have him now. He and the steam fiend are each other's antipodes; the latter's the type of all that go ahead, and the old man the representative of that melancholy class who, by some sad witchcraft, are doomed never to share in the world's exulting progress. Thus the contrast between mankind and this desolate brother becomes picturesque, and even sublime.

And now farewell, old friend! Little do you suspect that a student of human life had made your character the theme of more than one solitary and thoughtful hour. Many would say that you have hardly individuality enough to be the object of your own self-love. How, then, can a stranger's eye detect anything in your mind and heart to study and to wonder at? Yet, could I read but a tithe of what is written there, it would be a volume of deeper and more comprehensive import than all that the wisest mortals have given to the world; for the soundless depths of the human soul and of eternity have an opening through your breast. God be praised, were it only for your sake, that the present shapes of human existence are not cast in iron nor hewn in everlasting adamant, but moulded of the vapors that vanish away while the essence flits upward to the Infinite. There is a spiritual essence in this gray and lean old shape that shall flit upward too. Yes; doubtless there is a region where the lifelong shiver will pass away from his being, and that quiet sigh, which it has taken him so many years to breathe, will be brought to a close for good and all.

THE HALL
OF FANTASY

It has happened to me, on various occasions, to find myself in a certain edifice which would appear to have some of the characteristics of a public exchange. Its interior is a spacious hall, with a pavement of white marble. Overhead is a lofty dome, supported by long rows of pillars of fantastic architecture, the idea of which was probably taken from the Moorish ruins of the Alhambra, or perhaps from some enchanted edifice in the Arabian tales. The windows of this hall have a breadth and grandeur of design and an elaborateness of workmanship that have nowhere been equalled except in the Gothic cathedrals of the old world. Like their prototypes, too, they admit the light of heaven only through stained and pictured glass, thus filling the hall with many-colored radiance and painting its marble floor with beautiful or grotesque designs; so that its inmates breathe, as it were, a visionary atmosphere, and tread upon the fantasies of poetic minds. These peculiarities, combining a wilder mixture of styles than even an American architect usually recognizes as allowable,—Grecian, Gothic, Oriental, and nondescript,—cause the whole edifice to give the impression of a dream, which might be dissipated and shattered to fragments by merely stamping the foot upon the pavement. Yet, with such modifications and repairs as successive ages demand, the Hall of Fantasy is likely

First published in *The Pioneer*, February, 1843.

to endure longer than the most substantial structure that ever cumbered the earth.

It is not at all times that one can gain admittance into this edifice, although most persons enter it at some period or other of their lives; if not in their making moments, then by the universal passport of a dream. At my last visit I wandered thither unawares while my mind was busy with an idle tale, and was startled by the throng of people who seemed suddenly to rise up around me.

"Bless me! Where am I?" cried I, with but a dim recognition of the place.

"You are in a spot," said a friend who chanced to be near at hand, "which occupies in the world of fancy the same position which the Bourse, the Rialto, and the Exchange do in the commercial world. All who have affairs in that mystic region, which lies above, below, or beyond the actual, may have meet and talk over the business of their dreams."

"It is a noble hall," observed I.

"Yes," he replied. "Yet we see but a small portion of the edifice. In its upper stories are said to be apartments where the inhabitants of earth may hold converse with those of the moon; and beneath our feet are gloomy cells, which communicate with the infernal regions, and where monsters and chimeras are kept in confinement and fed with all unwholesomeness."

In niches and on pedestals around about the hall stood the statues or busts of men who in every age have been rulers and demigods in the realms of imagination and its kindred regions. The grand old countenance of Homer; the shrunken and decrepit form but vivid face of Æsop; the dark presence of Dante; the wild Ariosto, Rabelais' smile of deep-wrought mirth; the profound, pathetic humor of Cervantes; the all-glorious Shakespeare; Spenser, meet guest for an allegoric structure; the severe divinity of Milton; and Bunyan, moulded of homeliest clay, but instinct with celestial fire,—were those that chiefly attracted my eye. Fielding, Richardson, and Scott occupied conspicuous pedestals. In an obscure and shadowy niche was deposited the bust of our countryman, the author of Arthur Mervyn.

"Besides these indestructible memorials of real genius," remarked my companion, "each century has erected statues of its own ephemeral favorites in wood."

"I observe a few crumbling relics of such," said I. "But ever and anon, I suppose, Oblivion comes with her huge broom and sweeps them all from the marble floor. But such will never be the fate of this fine statue of Goethe."

"Nor of that next to it—Emanuel Swedenborg," said he. "Were ever two men of transcendent imagination more unlike?"

In the centre of the hall springs an ornamental fountain, the water of which continually throws itself into new shapes and snatches the most diversified hues from the stained atmosphere around. It is impossible to conceive what a strange vivacity is imparted to the scene by the magic dance of this fountain, with its endless transformations, in which the imaginative beholder may discern what form he will. The water is supposed by some to flow from the same source as the Castalian spring, and is extolled by others as uniting the virtues of the Fountain of Youth with those of many other enchanted wells long celebrated in tale and song. Having never tasted it, I can bear no testimony to its quality.

"Did you ever drink this water?" I inquired of my friend.

"A few sips now and then," answered he. "But there are men here who make it their constant beverage—or, at least, have the credit of doing so. In some instances it is known to have intoxicating qualities."

"Pray let us look at these water drinkers," said I.

So we passed among the fantastic pillars till we came to a spot where a number of persons were clustered together in the light of one of the great stained windows, which seemed to glorify the whole group as well as the marble that they trod on. Most of them were men of broad foreheads, meditative countenances, and thoughtful, inward eyes; yet it required but a trifle to summon up mirth, peeping out from the very midst of grave and lofty musings. Some strode about, or leaned against the pillars of the hall, alone and in silence; their faces wore a rapt expression, as if sweet music were in the air around them or as if their inmost souls were about to float away in song. One or two, perhaps, stole a glance at the by-standers, to watch if their poetic absorption were observed. Others stood talking in groups, with a liveliness of expression, a ready smile, and a light, intellectual laughter, which showed how rapidly the shafts of wit were glancing to and fro among them.

A few held higher converse, which caused their calm and melancholy souls to beam moonlight from their eyes. As I lingered near them,—for I felt an inward attraction towards these men, as if the sympathy of feeling, if not of genius, had united me to their order,—my friend mentioned several of their names. The world has likewise heard those names; with some it has been familiar for years; and others are daily making their way deeper into the universal heart.

"Thank Heaven," observed I to my companion, as we passed to another part of the hall, "we have done with this techy, wayward, shy, proud, unreasonable set of laurel gatherers. I love them in their works, but have little desire to meet them elsewhere."

"You have adopted an old prejudice, I see," replied my friend, who was familiar with most of these worthies, being himself a student of poetry, and not without the poetic flame. "But, so far as my experience goes, men of genius are fairly gifted with the social qualities; and in this age there appears to be a fellow-feeling among them which had not heretofore been developed. As men, they ask nothing better than to be on equal terms with their fellow-men; and as authors, they have thrown aside their proverbial jealousy, and acknowledge a generous brotherhood."

"The world does not think so," answered I. "An author is received in general society pretty much as we honest citizens are in the Hall of Fantasy. We gaze at him as if he had no business among us, and question whether he is fit for any of our pursuits."

"Then it is a very foolish question," said he. "Now here are a class of men whom we may daily meet on Change. Yet what poet in the hall is more a fool of fancy than the sagest of them?"

He pointed to a number of persons, who, manifest as the fact was, would have deemed it an insult to be told that they stood in the Hall of Fantasy. Their visages were traced into wrinkles and furrows, each of which seemed the record of some actual experience in life. Their eyes had the shrewd, calculating glance which detects so quickly and so surely all that it concerns a man of business to know about the characters and purposes of his fellow-men. Judging them as they stood, they might be honored and trusted members of the Chamber of Commerce, who had found the genuine secret of wealth, and whose sagacity gave them the command of fortune. There was a character of detail and matter of fact in their talk which concealed the extravagance of its purport, insomuch that the wildest schemes had the aspect of everyday realities. Thus the listener was not startled at the idea of cities to be built, as if by magic, in the heart of pathless forests; and of streets to be laid out where now the sea was tossing; and of mighty rivers to be stayed in their courses in order to turn the machinery of a cotton mill. It was only by an effort, and scarcely then, that the mind convinced itself that such speculations were as much matter of fantasy as the old dream of Eldorado, or as Mammon's Cave, or any other vision of gold ever conjured up by the imagination of needy poet or romantic adventurer.

"Upon my word," said I, "it is dangerous to listen to such dreamers as these. Their madness is contagious."

"Yes," said my friend, "because they mistake the Hall of Fantasy for actual brick and mortar, and its purple atmosphere for unsophisticated sunshine. But the poet knows his whereabout, and therefore is less likely to make a fool of himself in real life."

"Here again," observed I, as we advanced a little farther, "we see another order of dreamers, peculiarly characteristic, too, of the genius of our country."

These were the inventors of fantastic machines. Models of their contrivances were placed against some of the pillars of the hall, and afforded good emblems of the result generally to be anticipated from an attempt to reduce daydreams to practice. The analogy may hold in morals as well as physics; for instance, here was the model of a railroad through the air and a tunnel under the sea. Here was a machine—stolen, I believe—for the distillation of heat from moonshine; and another for the condensation of morning mist into square blocks of granite, wherewith it was proposed to rebuild the entire Hall of Fantasy. One man exhibited a sort of lens whereby he had suceeded in making sunshine out of a lady's smile; and it was his purpose wholly to irradiate the earth by means of this wonderful invention.

"It is nothing new," said I; "for most of our sunshine comes from woman's smile already."

"True," answered the inventor; "but any machine will secure a constant supply for domestic use; whereas hitherto it has been very precarious."

Another person had a scheme for fixing the reflections of objects in a pool of water, and thus taking the most lifelike portraits imaginable; and the same gentleman demonstrated the practicability of giving a permanent dye to ladies' dresses, in the gorgeous clouds of sunset. There were at least fifty kinds of perpetual motion, one of which was applicable to the wits of newspaper editors and writers of every description. Professor Espy was here, with a tremendous storm in a gum-elastic bag. I could enumerate many more of these Utopian inventions; but, after all, a more imaginative collection is to be found in the patent office at Washington.

Turning from the inventors we took a more general survey of the inmates of the hall. Many persons were present whose right of entrance appeared to consist in some crotchet of the brain, which, so long as it might operate, produced a change in their relation to the actual world. It is singular how very few there are who do not occasionally gain admittance on such a score, either in abstracted musings, or momentary thoughts, or bright anticipations, or vivid remembrances; for even the actual becomes ideal, whether in hope or memory, and beguiles the dreamer into the Hall of Fantasy. Some unfortunates make their whole abode and business here, and contract habits which unfit them for all the real employments of life. Others—but these are few—possess the faculty, in their occasional visits, of discovering a purer truth than the world can impart among the lights and shadows of these pictured windows.

And with all its dangerous influences, we have reason to thank God that there is such a place of refuge from the gloom and chillness of actual life. Hither may come the prisoner, escaping from his dark and narrow cell and cankerous chain, to breathe free air in this enchanted atmosphere. The sick man leaves his weary pillow, and finds strength to wander hither, though his wasted limbs might not support him even to the threshold of his chamber. The exile passes through the Hall of Fantasy to revisit his native soil. The burden of years rolls down from the old man's shoulders the moment that the door uncloses. Mourners leave their heavy sorrows at the entrance, and here rejoin the lost ones whose faces would else be seen no more, until thought shall have become the only fact. It may be said, in truth, that there is but half a life— the meaner and earthlier half—for those who never find their way into the hall. Nor must I fail to mention that in the observatory of the edifice is kept that wonderful perspective glass, through which the shepherds of the Delectable Mountains showed Christian the far-off gleam of the Celestial City. The eye of Faith still loves to gaze through it.

"I observe some men here," said I to my friend, "who might set up a strong claim to be reckoned among the most real personages of the day."

"Certainly," he replied. "If a man be in advance of his age, he must be content to make his abode in this hall until the lingering generations of his fellowmen come up with him. He can find no other shelter in the universe. But the fantasies of one day are the deepest realities of a future one."

"It is difficult to distinguish them apart amid the gorgeous and bewildering light of this hall," rejoined I. "The white sunshine of actual life is necessary in order to test them. I am rather apt to doubt both men and their reasonings till I meet them in that truthful medium."

"Perhaps your faith in the ideal is deeper than you are aware," said my friend. "You are at least a democrat; and methinks no scanty share of such faith is essential to the adoption of that creed."

Among the characters who had elicited these remarks were most of the noted reformers of the day, whether in physics, politics, morals, or religion. There is no surer method of arriving at the Hall of Fantasy than to throw one's self into the current of a theory; for, whatever landmarks of fact may be set up along the stream, there is a law of nature that impels it thither. And let it be so; for here the wise head and capacious heart may do their work; and what is good and true becomes gradually hardened into fact, while error melts away and vanishes among the shadows of the hall. Therefore may none who believe and rejoice in the progress of mankind be angry with me because I recognized their apostles and leaders amid the fantastic radiance of those pictured windows. I love and honor such men as well as they.

It would be endless to describe the herd of real or self-styled reformers that peopled this place of refuge. They were the representatives of an unquiet period, when mankind is seeking to cast off the whole tissue of ancient custom like a tattered garment. Many of them had got possession of some crystal fragment of truth, the brightness of which so dazzled them that they could see nothing else in the wide universe. Here were men whose faith had embodied itself in the form of a potato; and others whose long beards had a deep spiritual significance. Here was the abolitionist, brandishing his one idea like an iron flail. In a word, there were a thousand shapes

of good and evil, faith and infidelity, wisdom and nonsense—
a most incongruous throng.

Yet, withal, the heart of the stanchest conservative, unless
he abjured his fellowship with man, could hardly have helped
throbbing in sympathy with the spirit that pervaded these
innumerable theorists. It was good for the man of unquickened
heart to listen even to their folly. Far down beyond the fathom
of the intellect the soul acknowledged that all these varying
and conflicting developments of humanity were united in one
sentiment. Be the individual theory as wild as fancy could
make it, still the wiser spirit would recognize the struggle of
the race after a better and purer life than had yet been realized
on earth. My faith revived even while I rejected all their
schemes. It could not be that the world should continue forever what it has been; a soil where Happiness is so rare a
flower and Virtue so often a blighted fruit; a battlefield where
the good principle, with its shield flung above its head, can
hardly save itself amid the rush of adverse influences. In the
enthusiasm of such thoughts I gazed through one of the
pictured windows, and, behold! the whole external world
was tinged with the dimly glorious aspect that is peculiar to
the Hall of Fantasy, insomuch that it seemed practicable at
that very instant to realize some plan for the perfection of
mankind. But, alas! if reformers would understand the sphere
in which their lot is cast they must cease to look through
pictured windows. Yet they not only use their medium, but
mistake it for the whitest sunshine.

"Come," said I to my friend, starting from a deep reverie,
"let us hasten hence or I shall be tempted to make a theory,
after which there is little hope of any man."

"Come hither, then," answered he. "Here is one theory
that swallows up and annihilates all others."

He led me to a distant part of the hall where a crowd
of deeply attentive auditors were assembled round an elderly
man of plain, honest, trustworthy aspect. With an earnestness
that betokened the sincerest faith in his own doctrine, he an-

nounced that the destruction of the world was close at hand.

"It is Father Miller himself!" exclaimed I.

"No less a man," said my friend; "and observe how picturesque a contrast between his dogma and those of the reformers whom we have just glanced at. They look for the earthly perfection of mankind, and are forming schemes which imply that the immortal spirit will be connected with a physical nature for innumerable ages of futurity. On the other hand, here comes good Father Miller, and with one puff of his relentless theory scatters all their dreams like so many withered leaves upon the blast."

"It is, perhaps, the only method of getting mankind out of the various perplexities into which they have fallen," I replied. "Yet I could wish that the world might be permitted to endure until some great moral shall have been evolved. A riddle is propounded. Where is the solution? The sphinx did not slay herself until her riddle had been guessed. Will it not be so with the world? Now, if it should be burned tomorrow morning, I am at a loss to know what purpose will have been accomplished, or how the universe will be wiser or better for our existence and destruction."

"We cannot tell what mighty truths may have been embodied in act through the existence of the globe and its inhabitants," rejoined my companion. "Perhaps it may be revealed to us after the fall of the curtain over our catastrophe; or not impossibly, the whole drama, in which we are involuntary actors, may have been performed for the instruction of another set of spectators. I cannot perceive that our own comprehension of it is at all essential to the matter. At any rate, while our view is so ridiculously narrow and superficial it would be absurd to argue the continuance of the world from the fact that it seems to have existed hitherto in vain."

"The poor old earth," murmured I. "She has faults enough, in all conscience, but I cannot bear to have her perish."

"It is no great matter," said my friend. "The happiest of us has been weary of her many a time and oft."

"I doubt it," answered I, pertinaciously; "the root of human nature strikes down deep into this earthly soil, and it is but reluctantly that we submit to be transplanted, even for a higher cultivation in heaven. I query whether the destruction of the earth would gratify any one individual, except perhaps some embarrassed man of business whose notes fall due a day after the day of doom."

Then methought I heard the expostulating cry of a multitude against the consummation prophesied by Father Miller. The lover wrestled with Providence for his foreshadowed bliss. Parents entreated that the earth's span of endurance might be prolonged by some seventy years, so that their newborn infant should not be defrauded of his lifetime. A youthful poet murmured because there would be no posterity to recognize the inspiration of his song. The reformers, one and all, demanded a few thousand years to test their theories, after which the universe might go to wreck. A mechanician, who was busied with an improvement of the steam-engine, asked merely time to perfect his model. A miser insisted that the world's destruction would be a personal wrong to himself, unless he should first be permitted to add a specified sum to his enormous heap of gold. A little boy made dolorous inquiry whether the last day would come before Christmas, and thus deprive him of his anticipated dainties. In short, nobody seemed satisfied that this mortal scene of things should have its close just now. Yet, it must be confessed, the motives of the crowd for desiring its continuance were mostly so absurd that unless infinite Wisdom had been aware of much better reasons, the solid earth must have melted away at once.

For my own part, not to speak of a few private and personal ends, I really desired our old mother's prolonged existence for her own dear sake.

"The poor old earth!" I repeated. "What I should chiefly regret in her destruction would be that very earthliness which no other sphere or state of existence can renew or compensate. The fragrance of flowers and of new-mown hay; the genial warmth of sunshine and the beauty of a sunset among clouds; the comfort and cheerful glow of the fireside; the deliciousness of fruits and of all good cheer; the magnificence of mountains and seas and cataracts, and the softer charm of rural scenery; even the fast falling snow and the gray atmosphere through which it descends,—all these and innumerable other enjoyable things of earth must perish with her. Then the country frolics; the homely humor; the broad, open-mouthed roar of laughter, in which body and soul conjoin so heartily! I fear that no other world can show us anything just like this. As for purely moral enjoyments, the good will find them in every state of being. But where the material and the moral exist together, what is to happen then? And then our mute four-footed friends and the winged songsters of our woods! Might it not be lawful to regret them, even in the hallowed groves of paradise?"

"You speak like the very spirit of earth, imbued with a scent of freshly turned soil," exclaimed my friend.

"It is not that I so much object to giving up these enjoyments on my own account," continued I, "but I hate to think that they will have been eternally annihilated from the list of joys."

"Nor need they be," he replied. "I see no real force in what you say. Standing in this Hall of Fantasy, we perceive what even the earth-clogged intellect of man can do in creating circumstances which, though we call them shadowy and visionary, are scarcely more so than those that surround us in actual life. Doubt not then that man's disembodied spirit may recreate time and the world for itself, with all their peculiar enjoyments, should there still be human yearnings amid life eternal and infinite. But I doubt whether we shall be inclined to play such a poor scene over again."

"Oh, you are ungrateful to our mother earth!" rejoined I. "Come what may, I never will forget her! Neither will it satisfy me to have her exist merely in idea. I want her great, round, solid self to endure interminably, and still to be peopled with the kindly race of man, whom I uphold to be much better than he thinks himself. Nevertheless, I confide the whole matter to Providence, and shall endeavor so to live that the world may come to an end at any moment without leaving me at a loss to find foothold somewhere else."

"It is an excellent resolve," said my companion, looking at his watch. "But come; it is the dinner hour. Will you partake of my vegetable diet?"

A thing so matter-of-fact as an invitation to dinner, even when the fare was to be nothing more substantial than vegetables and fruit, compelled us forthwith to remove from the Hall of Fantasy. As we passed out of the portal we met the spirits of several persons who had been sent thither in magnetic sleep. I looked back among the sculptured pillars and at the transformations of the gleaming fountain, and almost desired that the whole of life might be spent in that visionary scene where the actual world, with its hard angles, should never rub against me, and only be viewed through the medium of pictured windows. But for those who waste all their days in the Hall of Fantasy, good Father Miller's prophecy is already accomplished, and the solid earth has come to an untimely end. Let us be content, therefore, with merely an occasional visit, for the sake of spiritualizing the grossness of this actual life, and prefiguring to ourselves a state in which the Idea shall be all in all.

THE CELESTIAL
RAILROAD

Not a great while ago, passing through the gate of dreams, I visited that region of the earth in which lies the famous City of Destruction. It interested me much to learn that by the public spirit of some of the inhabitants a railroad has recently been established between this populous and flourishing town and the Celestial City. Having a little time upon my hands, I resolved to gratify a liberal curiosity by making a trip thither. Accordingly, one fine morning after paying my bill at the hotel, and directing the porter to stow my luggage behind a coach, I took my seat in the vehicle and set out for the station-house. It was my good fortune to enjoy the company of a gentleman—one Mr. Smooth-it-away —who, though he had never actually visited the Celestial City, yet seemed as well acquainted with its laws, customs, policy, and statistics, as with those of the City of Destruction, of which he was a native townsman. Being, moreover, a director of the railroad corporation and one of its largest stockholders, he had it in his power to give me all desirable information respecting that praiseworthy enterprise.

Our coach rattled out of the city, and at a short distance from its outskirts passed over a bridge of elegant construction, but somewhat too slight, as I imagined, to sustain any considerable weight. On both sides lay an extensive quagmire,

First published in *The Democratic Review*, May, 1843.

which could not have been more disagreeable, either to sight
or smell, had all the kennels of the earth emptied their pol-
lution there.

"This," remarked Mr. Smoth-it-away, "is the famous Slough
of Despond—a disgrace to all the neighborhood; and the
greater that it might so easily be converted into firm ground."

"I have understood," said I, "that efforts have been made
for that purpose from time immemorial. Bunyan mentions
that above twenty thousand cartloads of wholesome instructions had been thrown in here without effect."

"Very probably! And what effect could be anticipated from
such unsubstantial stuff?" cried Mr. Smooth-it-away. "You
observe this convenient bridge. We obtained a sufficient
foundation for it by throwing into the slough some editions
of books of morality; volumes of French philosophy and German rationalism; tracts, sermons, and essays of modern clergy-
men; extracts from Plato, Confucius, and various Hindoo
sages, together with a few ingenious commentaries upon texts
of Scripture,—all of which by some scientific process, have
been converted into a mass like granite. The whole bog might
be filled up with similar matter."

It really seemed to me, however, that the bridge vibrated
and heaved up and down in a very formidable manner; and,
spite of Mr. Smooth-it-away's testimony to the solidity of its
foundation, I should be loath to cross it in a crowded omnibus,
especially if each passenger were encumbered with as heavy
luggage as that gentleman and myself. Nevertheless we got
over without accident, and soon found ourselves at the station-
house. This very neat and spacious edifice is erected on the site
of the little wicket game, which formerly, as all old pilgrims
will recollect, stood directly across the highway, and, by its
inconvenient narrowness, was a great obstruction to the
traveller of liberal mind and expansive stomach. The reader
of John Bunyan will be glad to know that Christian's old
friend Evangelist, who was accustomed to supply each pilgrim
with a mystic roll, now presides at the ticket office. Some
malicious persons it is true deny the identity of this reputable

character with the Evangelist of old times, and even pretend to bring competent evidence of an imposture. Without involving myself in a dispute I shall merely observe that, so far as my experience goes, the square pieces of pasteboard now delivered to passengers are much more convenient and useful along the road than the antique roll of parchment. Whether they will be as readily received at the gate of the Celestial City I decline giving an opinion.

A large number of passengers were already at the station-house awaiting the departure of the cars. By the aspect and demeanor of these persons it was easy to judge that the feelings of the community had undergone a very favorable change in reference to the celestial pilgrimage. It would have done Bunyan's heart good to see it. Instead of a lonely and ragged man with a huge burden on his back, plodding along sorrowfully on foot while the whole city hooted after him, here were parties of the first gentry and most respectable people in the neighborhood setting forth towards the Celestial City as cheerfully as if the pilgrimage were merely a summer tour. Among the gentlemen were characters of deserved eminence—magistrates, politicians, and men of wealth, by whose example religion could not but be greatly recommended to their meaner brethren. In the ladies' apartment, too, I rejoiced to distinguish some of those flowers of fashionable society who are so well fitted to adorn the most elevated circles of the Celestial City. There was much pleasant conversation about the news of the day, topics of business and politics, or the lighter matters of amusement; while religion, though indubitably the main thing at heart, was thrown tastefully into the background. Even an infidel would have heard little or nothing to shock his sensibility.

One great convenience of the new method of going on pilgrimage I must not forget to mention. Our enormous burdens, instead of being carried on our shoulders as had been the custom of old, were all snugly deposited in the baggage car, and, as I was assured, would be delivered to their respective owners at the journey's end. Another thing, likewise, the benevolent reader will be delighted to understand. It may be remembered that there was an ancient feud between Prince Beelzebub and the keeper of the wicket gate, and that the adherents of the former distinguished personage were accustomed to shoot deadly arrows at honest pilgrims while knocking at the door. This dispute, much to the credit as well of the illustrious potentate above mentioned as of the worthy and enlightened directors of the railroad, has been pacifically arranged on the principle of mutual compromise. The prince's subjects are now pretty numerously employed about the station-house, some in taking care of the baggage, others in collecting fuel, feeding the engines, and such congenial occupations; and I can conscientiously affirm that persons more attentive to their business, more willing to accommodate, or more generally agreeable to the passengers, are not to be found on any railroad. Every good heart must surely exult at so satisfactory an arrangement of an immemorial difficulty.

"Where is Mr. Greatheart?" inquired I. "Beyond a doubt the directors have engaged that famous old champion to be chief conductor on the railroad?"

"Why, no," said Mr. Smooth-it-away, with a dry cough. "He was offered the situation of brakeman; but, to tell you the truth, our friend Greatheart has grown preposterously stiff and narrow in his old age. He has so often guided pilgrims over the road on foot that he considers it a sin to travel in any other fashion. Besides, the old fellow had entered so heartily into the ancient feud with Prince Beelzebub that he would have been perpetually at blows or ill language with some of the prince's subjects, and thus have embroiled us anew. So, on the whole, we were not sorry when honest Greatheart went off to the Celestial City in a huff and left us at liberty to choose a more suitable and accommodating man. Yonder comes the engineer of the train. You will probably recognize him at once."

The engine at this moment took its station in advance of the cars, looking, I must confess, much more like a sort of mechanical demon that would hurry us to the infernal regions than a laudable contrivance for smoothing our way to the Celestial City. On its top sat a personage almost enveloped in smoke and flame, which, not to startle the reader, appeared to gush from his own mouth and stomach as well as from the engine's brazen abdomen.

"Do my eyes deceive me?" cried I. "What on earth is this! A living creature? If so, he is own brother to the engine he rides upon!"

"Poh, poh, you are obtuse!" said Mr. Smooth-it-away, with a hearty laugh. "Don't you know Apollyon, Christian's old enemy, with whom he fought so fierce a battle in the Valley of Humiliation? He was the very fellow to manage the engine; and so we have reconciled him to the custom of going on pilgrimage, and engaged him as chief engineer."

"Bravo, bravo!" exclaimed I, with irrepressible enthusiasm; "this shows the liberality of the age; this proves, if anything can, that all musty prejudices are in a fair way to be obliterated. And how will Christian rejoice to hear of this happy transformation of his old antagonist! I promise myself great pleasure in informing him of it when we reach the Celestial City."

The passengers being all comfortably seated, we now rattled away merrily, accomplishing a greater distance in ten minutes than Christian probably trudged over in a day. It was laughable, while we glanced along, as it were, at the tail of a thunderbolt, to observe two dusty foot travellers in the old pilgrim guise, with cockle shell and staff, their mystic rolls of parchment in their hands and their intolerable burdens on their backs. The preposterous obstinacy of these honest people in persisting to groan and stumble along the difficult pathway rather than take advantage of modern improvements, excited great mirth among our wiser brotherhood. We greeted the two pilgrims with many pleasant gibes and a roar of laughter; whereupon they gazed at us with such woful and absurdly compassionate visages that our merriment grew tenfold more obstreperous. Apollyon also entered heartily into the fun, and contrived to flirt the smoke and flame of the engine, or of his own breath, into their faces, and envelop them in an atmosphere of scalding steam. These little practical jokes amused us mightily, and doubtless afforded the pilgrims the gratification of considering themselves martyrs.

At some distance from the railroad Mr. Smooth-it-away pointed to a large, antique edifice, which, he observed, was a tavern of long standing, and had formerly been a noted stopping-place for pilgrims. In Bunyan's road-book it is mentioned as the Interpreter's House.

"I have long had a curiosity to visit that old mansion," remarked I.

"It is not one of our stations, as you perceive," said my companion. "The keeper was violently opposed to the railroad; and well he might be, as the track left his house of entertainment on one side, and thus was pretty certain to deprive him of all his reputable customers. But the footpath still passes his door, and the old gentleman now and then receives a call from some simple traveller, and entertains him with fare as old-fashioned as himself."

Before our talk on this subject came to a conclusion we were rushing by the place where Christian's burden fell from his shoulders at the sight of the Cross. This served as a theme for Mr. Smooth-it-away, Mr. Live-for-the-world, Mr. Hide-sin-in-the-heart, Mr. Scaly-conscience, and a knot of gentlemen from the town of Shun-repentance, to descant upon the inestimable advantages resulting from the safety of our baggage. Myself, and all the passengers indeed, joined with great unanimity in this view of the matter; for our burdens were rich in many things esteemed precious throughout the world; and, especially, we each of us possessed a great variety of favorite Habits, which we trusted would not be out of fashion even in the polite circles of the Celestial City. It would have been a sad spectacle to see such an assortment of valuable articles tumbling into the sepulchre. Thus pleasantly conversing on the favorable circumstances of our position as compared with those of past pilgrims and of narrow-minded ones at the present day, we soon found ourselves at the foot of the Hill of

Difficulty. Through the very heart of this rocky mountain a tunnel has been constructed of most admirable architecture, with a lofty arch and a spacious double track; so that, unless the earth and rocks should chance to crumble down, it will remain an eternal monument of the builder's skill and enterprise. It is a great though incidental advantage that the materials from the heart of the Hill Difficulty have been employed in filling up the Valley of Humiliation, thus obviating the necessity of descending into that disagreeable and unwholesome hollow.

"This is a wonderful improvement, indeed," said I. "Yet I should have been glad of an opportunity to visit the Palace Beautiful and be introduced to the charming young ladies— Miss Prudence, Miss Piety, Miss Charity, and the rest—who have the kindness to entertain pilgrims there."

"Young ladies!" cried Mr. Smooth-it-away, as soon as he could speak for laughing. "And charming young ladies! Why, my dear fellow, they are old maids, every soul of them—prim, starched, dry, and angular; and not one of them, I will venture to say, has altered so much as the fashion of her gown since the days of Christian's pilgrimage."

"Ah, well," said I, much comforted, "then I can very readily dispense with their acquaintance."

The respectable Apollyon was now putting on the steam at a prodigious rate, anxious, perhaps, to get rid of the unpleasant reminiscences connected with the spot where he had so disastrously encountered Christian. Consulting Mr. Bunyan's road-book, I perceived that we must now be within a few miles of the Valley of the Shadow of Death, into which doleful region, at our present speed, we should plunge much sooner than seemed at all desirable. In truth, I expected nothing better than to find myself in the ditch on one side or the quag on the other; but on communicating my apprehensions to Mr. Smooth-it-away, he assured me that the difficulties of this passage, even in its worst condition, had been vastly exaggerated, and that, in its present state of improvement, I might consider myself as safe as on any railroad in Christendom.

Even while we were speaking the train shot into the entrance of this dreaded Valley. Though I plead guilty to some foolish palpitations of the heart during our headlong rush over the causeway here constructed, yet it were unjust to withhold the highest encomiums on the boldness of its original conception and the ingenuity of those who executed it. It was gratifying, likewise, to observe how much care had been taken to dispel the everlasting gloom and supply the defect of cheerful sunshine, not a ray of which has ever penetrated among these awful shadows. For this purpose, the inflammable gas which exudes plentifully from the soil is collected by means of pipes, and thence communicated to a quadruple row of lamps along the whole extent of the passage. Thus a radiance has been created even out of the fiery and sulphurous curse that rests forever upon the valley—a radiance hurtful, however, to the eyes, and somewhat bewildering, as I discovered by the changes which it wrought in the visages of my companions. In this respect, as compared with natural daylight, there is the same difference as between truth and falsehood; but if the reader have ever travelled through the dark Valley, he will have learned to be thankful for any light that he could get—if not from the sky above, then from the blasted soil beneath. Such was the red brilliancy of these lamps that they appeared to build walls of fire on both sides of the track, between which we held our course at lightning speed, while a reverberating thunder filled the Valley with its echoes. Had the engine run off the track,—a catastrophe, it is whispered, by no means unprecedented,—the bottomless pit, if there be any such place, would undoubtedly have received us. Just as some dismal fooleries of this nature had made my heart quake there came a tremendous shriek, careering along the valley as if a thousand devils had burst their lungs to utter it, but which proved to be merely the whistle of the engine on arriving at a stopping-place.

The spot where we had now paused is the same that our friend Bunyan—a truthful man, but infected with many fantastic notions—has designated, in terms plainer than I like to repeat, as the mouth of the infernal region. This, however, must be a mistake, inasmuch as Mr. Smooth-it-away, while we remained in the smoky and lurid cavern, took occasion to prove that Tophet has not even a metaphorical existence. The place, he assured us, is no other than the crater of a half-extinct volcano, in which the directors had caused forges to be set up for the manufacture of railroad iron. Hence, also, is obtained a plentiful supply of fuel for the use of the engines. Whoever had gazed into the dismal obscurity of the broad cavern mouth, whence ever and anon darted huge tongues of dusky flame, and had seen the strange, half-shaped monsters, and visions of faces horribly grotesque, into which the smoke seemed to wreathe itself, and had heard the awful murmurs, and shrieks, and deep shuddering whispers of the blast, sometimes forming themselves into words almost articulate, would have seized upon Mr. Smooth-it-away's comfortable explanation as greedily as we did. The inhabitants of the cavern, moreover, were unlovely personages, dark, smoke-begrimed, generally deformed, with misshapen feet, and a glow of dusky redness in their eyes as if their hearts had caught fire and were blazing out of the upper windows. It struck me as a peculiarity that the laborers at the forge and those who brought fuel to the engine, when they began to draw short breath, positively emitted smoke from their mouth and nostrils.

Among the idlers about the train, most of whom were puffing cigars which they had lighted at the flame of the crater, I was perplexed to notice several who, to my certain knowledge, had heretofore set forth by railroad for the Celestial City. They looked dark, wild, and smoky, with a singular resemblance, indeed, to the native inhabitants, like whom, also, they had a disagreeable propensity to ill-natured gibes and sneers, the habit of which had wrought a settled contortion of their visages. Having been on speaking terms with one of these persons,—an indolent, good-for-nothing fellow, who went by the name of Take-it-easy,—I called him, and inquired what was his business there.

"Did you not start," said I, "for the Celestial City?"

"That's a fact," said Mr. Take-it-easy, carelessly puffing some smoke into my eyes. "But I heard such bad accounts that I never took pains to climb the hill on which the city stands. No business doing, no fun going on, nothing to drink, and no smoking allowed, and a thrumming of church music from morning till night. I would not stay in such a place if they offered me house room and living free."

"But, my good Mr. Take-it-easy," cried I, "why take up your residence here, of all places in the world?"

"Oh," said the loafer, with a grin, "it is very warm hereabouts, and I meet with plenty of old acquaintants, and altogether the place suits me. I hope to see you back again some day soon. A pleasant journey to you."

While he was speaking the bell of the engine rang, and we dashed away after dropping a few passengers, but receiving no new ones. Rattling onward through the Valley, we were dazzled with the fiercely gleaming gas lamps, as before. But sometimes, in the dark of intense brightness, grim faces, that bore the aspect and expression of individual sins, or evil passions, seemed to thrust themselves through the veil of light, glaring upon us, and stretching forth a great, dusky hand, as if to impede our progress. I almost thought that they were my own sins that appalled me there. These were freaks of imagination—nothing more, certainly—mere delusions, which I ought to be heartily ashamed of; but all through the Dark Valley I was tormented, and pestered, and dolefully bewildered with the same kind of waking dreams. The mephitic gases of that region intoxicate the brain. As the light of natural day, however, began to struggle with the glow of the lanterns, these vain imaginations lost their vividness, and finally vanished with the first ray of sunshine that greeted our escape from the Valley of the Shadow of Death. Ere we had gone a mile beyond it I could well-nigh have taken my oath that this whole gloomy passage was a dream.

At the end of the valley, as John Bunyan mentions, is a cavern, where, in his days, dwelt two cruel giants, Pope and

Pagan, who had strown the ground about their residence with the bones of slaughtered pilgrims. These vile old troglodytes are no longer there; but into their deserted cave another terrible giant has thrust himself, and makes it his business to seize upon honest travellers and fatten them for his table with plentiful meals of smoke, mist, moonshine, raw potatoes, and sawdust. He is a German by birth, and is called Giant Transcendentalist; but as to his form, his features, his substance, and his nature generally, it is the chief peculiarity of this huge miscreant that neither he for himself, nor anybody for him, has ever been able to describe them. As we rushed by the cavern's mouth we caught a hasty glimpse of him, looking somewhat like an ill-proportioned figure, but considerably more like a heap of fog and duskiness. He shouted after us, but in so strange a phraseology that we knew not what he meant, nor whether to be encouraged or affrighted.

It was late in the day when the train thundered into the ancient city of Vanity, where Vanity Fair is still at the height of prosperity, and exhibits an epitome of whatever is brilliant, gay, and fascinating beneath the sun. As I purposed to make a considerable stay here, it gratified me to learn that there is no longer the want of harmony between the town's-people and pilgrims, which impelled the former to such lamentably mistaken measures as the persecution of Christian and the fiery martyrdom of Faithful. On the contrary, as the new railroad brings with it great trade and a constant influx of strangers, the lord of Vanity Fair is its chief patron, and the capitalists of the city are among the largest stockholders. Many passengers stop to take their pleasure or make their profit in the Fair, instead of going onward to the Celestial City. Indeed, such are the charms of the place that people often affirm it to be the true and only heaven; stoutly contending that there is no other, that those who seek further are mere dreamers, and that, if the fabled brightness of the Celestial City lay but a bare mile beyond the gates of Vanity, they would not be fools enough to go thither. Without subscribing to these perhaps exaggerated encomiums, I can truly say that my abode in the city was mainly agreeable, and my intercourse with the inhabitants productive of much amusement and instruction.

Being naturally of a serious turn, my attention was directed to the solid advantages derivable from a residence here, rather than to the effervescent pleasures which are the grand object with too many visitants. The Christian reader, if he have had no accounts of the city later than Bunyan's time, will be surprised to hear that almost every street has its church, and that the reverend clergy are nowhere held in higher respect than at Vanity Fair. And well do they deserve such honorable estimation; for the maxims of wisdom and virtue which fall from their lips comes from as deep a spiritual source, and tend to as lofty a religious aim, as those of the sagest philosophers of old. In justification of this high praise I need only mention the names of the Rev. Mr. Shallow-deep, the Rev. Mr. Stumble-at-truth, that fine old clerical character the Rev. Mr. This-to-day, who expects shortly to resign his pulpit to the Rev. Mr. That-to-morrow; together with the Rev. Mr. Bewilderment, the Rev. Mr. Clog-the-spirit, and, last and greatest, the Rev. Dr. Wind-of-doctrine. The labors of these eminent divines are aided by those of innumerable lecturers, who diffuse such a various profundity, in all subjects of human or celestial science, that any man may acquire an omnigenous erudition without the trouble of even learning to read. Thus literature is etherealized by assuming for its medium the human voice; and knowledge, depositing all its heavier particles, except, doubtless, its gold, becomes exhaled into a sound, which forthwith steals into the ever-open ear of the community. These ingenious methods constitute a sort of machinery, by which thought and study are done to every person's hand without his putting himself to the slightest inconvenience in the matter. There is another species of machine for the wholesale manufacture of individual morality. This excellent result is effected by societies for all manner of virtuous purposes, with which a man has merely to connect himself, throwing, as it were, his quota of virtue into the common stock, and the president and directors will take care that the aggregate amount be well applied. All these, and other wonderful improvements in ethics, religion, and literature, being made plain to my comprehension by the ingenious Mr. Smooth-it-away, inspired me with a vast admiration of Vanity Fair.

It would fill a volume, in an age of pamphlets, were I to record all my observations in this great capital of human business and pleasure. There was an unlimited range of society— the powerful, the wise, the witty, and the famous in every walk of life; princes, presidents, poets, generals, artists, actors, and philanthropists,—all making their own market at the fair, and deeming no price too exorbitant for such commodities as hit their fancy. It was well worth one's while, even if he had no idea of buying or selling, to loiter through the bazaars and observe the various sorts of traffic that were going forward.

Some of the purchasers, I thought, made very foolish bargains. For instance, a young man having inherited a splendid fortune, laid out a considerable portion of it in the purchase of diseases, and finally spent all the rest for a heavy lot of repentance and a suit of rags. A very pretty girl bartered a heart as clear as crystal, and which seemed her most valuable possession, for another jewel of the same kind, but so worn and defaced as to be utterly worthless. In one shop there were a great many crowns of laurel and myrtle, which soldiers, authors, statesmen, and various other people pressed eagerly to buy; some purchased these paltry wreaths with their lives, others by a toilsome servitude of years, and many sacrificed whatever was most valuable, yet finally slunk away without the crown. There was a sort of stock or scrip, called Conscience, which seemed to be in great demand, and would purchase almost anything. Indeed, few rich commodities were to be obtained without paying a heavy sum in this particular stock, and a man's business was seldom very lucrative unless he knew precisely when and how to throw his hoard of conscience into the market. Yet as this stock was the only thing of permanent value, whoever parted with it was sure to find himself a loser in the long run. Several of the speculations were of a questionable character. Occasionally a member of Congress recruited his pocket by the sale of his constituents; and I was assured that public officers have often sold their country at very moderate prices. Thousands sold their happiness for a whim. Gilded chains were in great demand, and purchased with almost any sacrifice. In truth, those who desired, according to the old adage, to sell anything valuable for a song, might find customers all over the Fair; and there were innumerable messes of pottage, piping hot, for such as chose to buy them with their birthrights. A few articles, however, could not be found genuine at Vanity Fair. If a customer wished to renew his stock of youth the dealers offered him a set of false teeth and an auburn wig; if he demanded peace of mind, they recommended opium or a brandy bottle.

Tracts of land and golden mansions, situated in the Celestial City, were often exchanged, at very disadvantageous rates, for a few years' lease of small, dismal, inconvenient tenements in Vanity Fair. Prince Beelzebub himself took great interest in this sort of traffic, and sometimes condescended to meddle with smaller matters. I once had the pleasure to see him bargaining with a miser for his soul, which, after much ingenious skirmishing on both sides, his highness succeeded in obtaining at about the value of six-pence. The prince remarked with a smile, that he was a loser by the transaction.

Day after day, as I walked the streets of Vanity, my manners and deportment became more and more like those of the inhabitants. The place began to seem like home; the idea of pursuing my travels to the Celestial City was almost obliterated from my mind. I was reminded of it, however, by the sight of the same pair of simple pilgrims at whom we had laughed so heartily when Apollyon puffed smoke and steam into their faces at the commencement of our journey. There they stood amidst the densest bustle of Vanity; the dealers offering them their purple and fine linen and jewels, the men of wit and humor gibing at them, a pair of buxom ladies ogling them askance, while the benevolent Mr. Smooth-it-away whispered some of his wisdom at their elbows, and pointed to a newly-erected temple; but there were these worthy simpletons, making the scene look wild and monstrous, merely by their sturdy repudiation of all part in its business or pleasures.

One of them—his name was Stick-to-the-right—perceived in my face, I suppose, a species of sympathy and almost admiration, which, to my own great surprise, I could not help feeling for this pragmatic couple. It prompted him to address me.

"Sir," inquired he, with a sad, yet mild and kindly voice, "do you call yourself a pilgrim?"

"Yes," I replied, "my right to that appellation is indubitable. I am merely a sojourner here in Vanity Fair, being bound to the Celestial City by the new railroad."

"Alas, friend," rejoined Mr. Stick-to-the-right, "I do assure you, and beseech you to receive the truth of my words, that that whole concern is a bubble. You may travel on it all your lifetime, were you to live thousands of years, and yet never get beyond the limits of Vanity Fair. Yea, though you should deem yourself entering the gates of the blessed city, it will be nothing but a miserable delusion."

"The Lord of the Celestial City," began the other pilgrim, whose name was Mr. Foot-it-to-heaven, "has refused, and will ever refuse, to grant an act of incorporation for this railroad; and unless that be obtained, no passenger can ever hope to enter his dominions. Wherefore every man who buys a ticket must lay his account with losing the purchase money, which is the value of his own soul."

"Poh, nonsense!" said Mr. Smooth-it-away, taking my arm and leading me off, "these fellows ought to be indicted for a libel. If the law stood as it once did in Vanity Fair we should see them grinning through the iron bars of the prison window."

This incident made a considerable impression on my mind, and contributed with other circumstances to indispose me to a permanent residence in the city of Vanity; although, of course, I was not simple enough to give up my original plan of gliding along easily and commodiously by railroad. Still, I grew anxious to be gone. There was one strange thing that troubled me. Amid the occupations or amusements of the Fair, nothing was more common than for a person—whether at feast, theatre, or church, or trafficking for wealth and honors, or whatever he might be doing, and however unseasonable the interruption—suddenly to vanish like a soap bubble, and be never more seen of his fellows; and so accustomed were the latter to such little accidents that they went on with their business as quietly as if nothing had happened. But it was otherwise with me.

Finally, after a pretty long residence at the Fair, I resumed my journey towards the Celestial City, still with Mr. Smooth-it-away at my side. At a short distance beyond the suburbs of Vanity we passed the ancient silver mine, of which Demas was the first discoverer, and which is now wrought to great advantage, supplying nearly all the coined currency of the world. A little further onward was the spot where Lot's wife had stood forever under the semblance of a pillar of salt. Curious travellers have long since carried it away piecemeal. Had all regrets been punished as rigorously as this poor dame's were, my yearning for the relinquished delights of Vanity Fair might have produced a similar change in my own corporeal substance, and left me a warning to future pilgrims.

The next remarkable object was a large edifice, constructed of mossgrown stone, but in a modern and airy style of architecture. The engine came to a pause in its vicinity, with the usual tremendous shriek.

"This was formerly the castle of the redoubted giant Despair," observed Mr. Smooth-it-away; "but since his death Mr. Flimsy-faith has repaired it, and keeps an excellent house of entertainment here. It is one of our stopping-places."

"It seems but slightly put together," remarked I, looking at the frail yet ponderous walls. "I do not envy Mr. Flimsy-faith his habitation. Some day it will thunder down upon the heads of the occupants."

"We shall escape at all events," said Mr. Smooth-it-away, "for Apollyon is putting on the steam again."

The road now plunged into a gorge of the Delectable Mountains, and traversed the field where in former ages the blind men wandered and stumbled among the tombs. One of these ancient tombstones had been thrust across the track by some malicious person, and gave the train of cars a terrible jolt. Far up the rugged side of a mountain I perceived a rusty iron door, half overgrown with bushes and creeping plants, but with smoke issuing from its crevices.

"Is that," inquired I, "the very door in the hill-side which the shepherds assured Christian was a by-way to hell?"

"That was a joke on the part of the shepherds," said Mr. Smooth-it-away, with a smile. "It is neither more nor less than the door of a cavern which they use as a smoke-house for the preparation of mutton hams."

My recollections of the journey are now, for a little space, dim and confused, inasmuch as a singular drowsiness here overcame me, owing to the fact that we were passing over the enchanted ground, the air of which encourages a disposition to sleep. I awoke, however, as soon as we crossed the borders of the pleasant land of Beulah. All the passengers were rubbing their eyes, comparing watches, and congratulating one another on the prospect of arriving so seasonably at the journey's end. The sweet breezes of this happy clime came refreshingly to our nostrils; we beheld the glimmering gush of silver fountains, overhung by trees of beautiful foliage and delicious fruit, which were propagated by grafts from the celestial gardens. Once, as we dashed onward like a hurricane, there was a flutter of wings and the bright appearance of an angel in the air, speeding forth on some heavenly mission. The engine now announced the close vicinity of the final station-house by one last and horrible scream, in which there seemed to be distinguishable every kind of wailing and woe, and bitter fierceness of wrath, all mixed up with the wild laughter of a devil or a madman. Throughout our journey, at every stopping-place, Apollyon had exercised his ingenuity in screwing the most abominable sounds out of the whistle of the steam-engine; but in this closing effort he outdid himself and created an infernal uproar, which, besides disturbing the peaceful inhabitants of Beulah, must have sent its discord even through the celestial gates.

While the horrid clamor was still ringing in our ears we heard an exulting strain, as if a thousand instruments of music, with height and depth and sweetness in their tones, at once tender and triumphant, were struck in unison, to greet the approach of some illustrious hero, who had fought the good fight and won a glorious victory, and was come to lay aside his battered arms forever. Looking to ascertain what might be the occasion of this glad harmony, I perceived, on alighting from the cars, that a multitude of shining ones had assembled on the other side of the river, to welcome two poor pilgrims, who were just emerging from its depths. They were the same whom Apollyon and ourselves had persecuted with taunts, and gibes, and scalding steam, at the commencement of our journey—the same whose unworldly aspect and impressive words had stirred my conscience amid the wild revelers of Vanity Fair.

"How amazingly well those men have got on," cried I to Mr. Smooth-it-away. "I wish we were secure of as good a reception."

"Never fear, never fear!" answered my friend. "Come, make haste; the ferry boat will be off directly, and in three minutes you will be on the other side of the river. No doubt you will find coaches to carry you up to the city gates."

A steam ferry boat, the last improvement on this important route, lay at the river side, puffing, snorting, and emitting all those other disagreeable utterances which betoken the departure to be immediate. I hurried on board with the rest of the passengers, most of whom were in great perturbation: some bawling out for their baggage; some tearing their hair and exclaiming that the boat would explode or sink; some already pale with the heaving of the stream; some gazing affrighted at the ugly aspect of the steersman; and some still dizzy with the slumberous influences of the Enchanted Ground. Looking back to the shore, I was amazed to discern Mr. Smooth-it-away waving his hand in token of farewell.

"Don't you go over to the Celestial City?" exclaimed I.

"Oh, no!" answered he with a queer smile, and that same disagreeable contortion of visage which I had remarked in the inhabitants of the Dark Valley. "Oh, no! I have come thus far only for the sake of your pleasant company. Good-by! We shall meet again."

And then did my excellent friend Mr. Smooth-it-away laugh outright, in the midst of which cachinnation a smoke-wreath issued from his mouth and nostrils, while a twinkle of lurid flame darted out of either eye, proving indubitably that his heart was all of a red blaze. The impudent fiend! To deny the existence of Tophet, when he felt its fiery tortures raging within his breast. I rushed to the side of the boat, intending to fling myself on shore; but the wheels, as they began their revolutions, threw a dash of spray over me so cold—so deadly cold, with the chill that will never leave those waters until Death be drowned in his own river—that with a shiver and a heartquake I awoke. Thank Heaven it was a Dream!

FIRE
WORSHIP

It is a great revolution in social and domestic life, and no less so in the life of a secluded student, this almost universal exchange of the open fireplace for the cheerless and ungenial stove. On such a morning as now lowers around our old gray parsonage I miss the bright face of my ancient friend, who was wont to dance upon the hearth and play the part of more familiar sunshine. It is sad to turn from the cloudy sky and sombre landscape; from yonder hill, with its crown of rusty, black pines, the foliage of which is so dismal in the absence of the sun; that bleak pasture land, and the broken surface of the potato field, with the brown clods partly concealed by the snow fall of last night; the swollen and sluggish river, with ice-incrusted borders, dragging its bluish-gray stream along the verge of our orchard like a snake half torpid with the cold,—it is sad to turn from an outward scene of so little comfort and find the same sullen influences brooding within the precincts of my study. Where is that brilliant guest, that quick and subtle spirit, whom Prometheus lured from heaven to civilize mankind and cheer them in their wintry desolation—that comfortable inmate, whose smile, during eight months of the year, was our sufficient consolation for summer's lingering advance and early flight? Alas! blindly inhospitable, grudging the food that kept him cheery and

First published in *The Democratic Review,* December, 1843.

mercurial, we have thrust him into an iron prison, and compel him to smoulder away his life on a daily pittance which once would have been too scanty for his breakfast. Without a metaphor, we now make our fire in an air-tight stove, and supply it with some half a dozen sticks of wood between dawn and nightfall.

I never shall be reconciled to this enormity. Truly may it be said that the world looks darker for it. In one way or another, here and there and all around us, the inventions of mankind are fast blotting the picturesque, the poetic, and the beautiful out of human life. The domestic fire was a type of all these attributes, and seemed to bring might and majesty, and wild Nature and a spiritual essence into our inmost home, and yet to dwell with us in such friendliness that its mysteries and marvels excited no dismay. The same mild companion that smiled so placidly in our faces was he that comes roaring out of Ætna and rushes madly up the sky like a fiend breaking loose from torment and fighting for a place among the upper angels. He it is, too, that leaps from cloud to cloud amid the crashing thunder storm. It was he whom the Gheber worshipped with no unnatural idolatry; and it was he who devoured London and Moscow and many another famous city; and who loves to riot through our own dark forests and sweep across our prairies, and to whose ravenous maw, it is said, the universe shall one day be given as a final feast. Meanwhile he is the great artisan and laborer by whose aid men are enabled to build a world within a world, or, at least, to smooth down the rough creation which Nature flung to us. He forges the mighty anchor and every lesser instrument; he drives the steamboat and drags the rail-car; and it was he—this creature of terrible might, and so many-sided utility and all-comprehensive destructiveness—that used to be the cheerful, homely friend of our wintry days, and whom we have made the prisoner of this iron cage.

How kindly he was! and, though the tremendous agent of change, yet bearing himself with such gentleness, so rendering himself a part of all lifelong and age-coeval associations, that it seemed as if he were the great conservative of Nature. While a man was true to the fireside, so long would he be true to country and law, to the God whom his fathers worshipped, to the wife of his youth, and to all things else which instinct or religion has taught us to consider sacred. With how sweet humility did this elemental spirit perform all needful offices for the household in which he was domesticated! He was equal to the concoction of a grand dinner, yet scorned not to roast a potato or toast a bit of cheese. How humanely did he cherish the school-boy's icy fingers, and thaw the old man's joints with a genial warmth which almost equalled the glow of youth! And how carefully did he dry the cow-hide boots that had trudged through mud and snow, and the shaggy outside garment stiff with frozen sleet! taking heed, likewise, to the comfort of the faithful dog who had followed his master through the storm. When did he refuse a coal to light a pipe, or even a part of his own substance to kindle a neighbor's fire? And then at twilight, when laborer, or scholar, or mortal of whatever age, sex, or degree, drew a chair beside him and looked into his glowing face, how acute, how profound, how comprehensive was his sympathy with the mood of each and all! He pictured forth their very thoughts. To the youthful he showed the scenes of the adventurous life before them; to the aged the shadows of departed love and hope; and if all earthly things had grown distasteful, he could gladden the fireside muser with golden glimpses of a better world. And, amid this varied communion with the human soul, how busily would the sympathizer, the deep moralist, the painter of magic pictures be causing the teakettle to boil!

Nor did it lessen the charm of his soft, familiar courtesy and helpfulness that the mighty spirit, were opportunity offered him, would run riot through the peaceful house, wrap its inmates in his terrible embrace, and leave nothing of them save their whitened bones. This possibility of mad destruction only made his domestic kindness the more beautiful and touching. It was so sweet of him, being endowed with such power, to dwell day after day, and one long lonesome night after another, on the dusky hearth, only now and then betraying his wild nature by thrusting his red tongue out of the chimney top! True, he had done much mischief in the world, and was pretty certain to do more; but his warm heart atoned for all. He was kindly to the race of man; and they pardoned his characteristic imperfections.

The good old clergyman, my predecessor in this mansion, was well acquainted with the comforts of the fireside. His yearly allowance of wood, according to the terms of his settlement, was no less than sixty cords. Almost an annual forest was converted from sound oak logs into ashes, in the kitchen, the parlor, and this little study, where now an unworthy successor, not in the pastoral office, but merely in his earthly abode, sits scribbling beside an air-tight stove. I love to fancy one of those fireside days while the good man, a contemporary of the Revolution, was in his early prime, some five and sixty years ago. Before sunrise, doubtless, the blaze hovered upon the gray skirts of night and dissolved the frostwork that had gathered like a curtain over the small window panes. There is something peculiar in the aspect of the morning fireside: a fresher, brisker glare; the absence of that mellowness which can be produced only by half-consumed logs, and shapeless brands with the white ashes on them, and mighty coals, the remnant of tree trunks that the hungry elements have gnawed for hours. The morning hearth, too, is newly swept, and the brazen andirons well brightened, so that the cheerful fire may see its face in them. Surely it was happiness, when the pastor, fortified with a substantial breakfast, sat down in his armchair and slippers and opened the Whole Body of Divinity, or the Commentary on Job, or whichever of his old folios or quartos might fall within the range of his weekly sermons. It must have been his own fault if the warmth and glow of this abundant hearth did not permeate the discourse and keep his audience comfortable in spite of the bitterest northern blast that ever wrestled with the church steeple. He reads while the heat warps the stiff covers of the volume; he writes without numbness either in his heart or fingers; and, with unstinted hand, he throws fresh sticks of wood upon the fire.

A parishioner comes in. With what warmth of benevolence

—how should he be otherwise than warm in any of his attributes?—does the minister bid him welcome, and set a chair
for him in so close proximity to the hearth that soon the guest
finds it needful to rub his scorched shins with his great red
hands! The melted snow drips from his steaming boots and
bubbles upon the hearth. His puckered forehead unravels its
entanglement of criss-cross wrinkles. We lose much of the enjoyment of fireside heat without such an opportunity of marking its genial effect upon those who have been looking the
inclement weather in the face. In the course of the day our
clergyman himself strides forth, perchance to pay a round of
pastoral visits; or, it may be, to visit his mountain of a woodpile and cleave the monstrous logs into billets suitable for
the fire. He returns with fresher life to his beloved hearth.
During the short afternoon the western sunshine comes into
the study and strives to stare the ruddy blaze out of countenance, but with only a brief triumph, soon to be succeeded
by brighter glories of its rival. Beautiful it is to see the
strengthening gleam, the deepening light that gradually casts
distinct shadows of the human figure, the table, and the high-
backed chairs upon the opposite wall, and at length, as twilight comes on, replenishes the room with living radiance and
makes life all rose color. Afar the wayfarer discerns the flickering flame as it dances upon the windows, and hails it as a
beacon light of humanity, reminding him, in his cold and
lonely path, that the world is not all snow and solitude and
desolation. At eventide, probably, the study was peopled with
the clergyman's wife and family, and children tumbled themselves upon the hearth rug, and grave puss sat with her back
to the fire, or gazed, with a semblance of human meditation,
into its fervid depths. Seasonably the plenteous ashes of the
day were raked over the mouldering brands, and from the
heap came jets of flame, and an incense of nightlong smoke
creeping quietly up the chimney.

Heaven forgive the old clergyman! In his later life, when
for almost ninety winters he had been gladdened by the firelight,—when it had gleamed upon him from infancy to ex-

treme age, and never without brightening his spirits as well
as his visage, and perhaps keeping him alive so long,—he had
the heart to brick up his chimney-place and bid farewell to
the face of his old friend forever, why did he not take an
eternal leave of the sunshine too? His sixty cords of wood
had probably dwindled to a far less ample supply in modern
times; and it is certain that the parsonage had grown crazy
with time and tempest and pervious to the cold; but still it
was one of the saddest tokens of the decline and fall of open
fireplaces that the gray patriarch should have deigned to
warm himself at an air-tight stove.

And I, likewise,—who have found a home in this ancient
owl's nest since its former occupant took his heavenward
flight,—I, to my shame, have put up stoves in kitchen and
parlor and chamber. Wander where you will about the house,
not a glimpse of the earth-born, heaven-aspiring fiend of
Ætna,—him that sports in the thunder storm, the idol of the
Ghebers, the devourer of cities, the forest rioter and prairie
sweeper, the future destroyer of our earth, the old chimney-
corner companion who mingled himself so sociably with household joys and sorrows,—not a glimpse of this mighty and
kindly one will greet your eyes. He is now an invisible presence. There is his iron cage. Touch it and he scorches your
fingers. He delights to singe a garment or perpetrate any
other little unworthy mischief; for his temper is ruined by the
ingratitude of mankind, for whom he cherished such warmth
of feeling, and to whom he taught all their arts, even that of
making his own prison house. In his fits of rage he puffs volumes of smoke and noisome gas through the crevices of the
door, and shakes the iron walls of his dungeon so as to overthrow the ornamental urn upon its summit. We tremble lest
he should break forth amongst us. Much of his time is spent
in sighs, burdened with unutterable grief, and long drawn
through the funnel. He amuses himself, too, with repeating
all the whispers, the moans, and the louder utterances or tempestuous howls of the wind; so that the stove becomes a micro-
cosm of the aerial world. Occasionally there are strange com-

binations of sounds,—voices talking almost articulately within
the hollow chest of iron,—insomuch that fancy beguiles me
with the idea that my firewood must have grown in that infernal forest of lamentable trees which breathed their com-
plaints to Dante. When the listener is half asleep he may
readily take these voices for the conversation of spirits and
assign them an intelligible meaning. Anon there is a pattering
noise,—drip, drip, drip,—as if a summer shower were falling
within the narrow circumference of the stove.

These barren and tedious eccentricities are all that the air-
tight stove can bestow in exchange for the invaluable moral
influences which we have lost by our desertion of the open
fireplace. Alas! is this world so very bright that we can afford
to choke up such a domestic fountain of gladsomeness, and
sit down by its darkened source without being conscious of a
gloom?

It is my belief that social intercourse cannot long continue
what it has been, now that we have subtracted from it so important and vivifying an element as firelight. The effects will
be more perceptible on our children and the generations that
shall succeed them than on ourselves, the mechanism of whose
life may remain unchanged, though its spirit be far other
than it was. The sacred trust of the household fire has been
transmitted in unbroken succession from the earliest ages and
faithfully cherished in spite of every discouragement, such as
the curfew law of the Norman conquerors, until in these evil
days physical science has nearly succeeded in extinguishing it.
But we at least have our youthful recollections tinged with
the glow of the hearth, and our lifelong habits and associations
arranged on the principle of a mutual bond in the domestic
fire. Therefore, though the sociable friend be forever departed,
yet in a degree he will be spiritually present with us; and still
more will the empty forms which were once full of his rejoicing presence continue to rule our manners. We shall draw
our chairs together as we and our forefathers have been wont
for thousands of years back, and sit around some blank and
empty corner of the room, babbling with unreal cheerfulness

of topics suitable to the homely fireside. A warmth from the past—from the ashes of by-gone years and the raked-up embers of long ago—will sometimes thaw the ice about our hearth; but it must be otherwise with our successors. On the most favorable supposition, they will be acquainted with the fireside in no better shape than that of the sullen stove; and more probably they will have grown up amid furnace heat in houses which might be fancied to have their foundation over the infernal pit, whence sulphurous steams and unbreathable exhalations ascend through the apertures of the floor. There will be nothing to attract these poor children to one centre. They will never behold one another through that peculiar medium of vision—the ruddy gleam of blazing wood or bituminous coal—which gives the human spirit so deep an insight into its fellows and melts all humanity into one cordial heart of hearts. Domestic life, if it may still be termed domestic, will seek its separate corners, and never gather itself into groups. The easy gossip; the merry yet unambitious jest; the lifelike, practical discussion of real matters in a casual way; the soul of truth which is so often incarnated in a simple fireside word,—will disappear from earth. Conversation will contract the air of debate and all mortal intercourse be chilled with a fatal frost.

In classic times, the exhortation to fight "pro aris et focis," for the altars and the hearths, was considered the strongest appeal that could be made to patriotism. And it seemed an immortal utterance; for all subsequent ages and people have acknowledged its force and responded to it with the full portion of manhood that Nature had assigned to each. Wisely were the altar and the hearth conjoined in one mighty sentence; for the hearth, too, had its kindred sanctity. Religion sat down beside it, not in the priestly robes which decorated and perhaps disguised her at the altar, but arrayed in a simple matron's garb, and uttering her lessons with the tenderness of a mother's voice and heart. The holy hearth! If any earthly and material thing, or rather a divine idea embodied in brick and mortar, might be supposed to possess the permanence of moral truth, it was this. All revered it. The man who did not put off his shoes upon this holy ground would have deemed it pastime to trample upon the altar. It has been our task to uproot the hearth. What further reform is left for our children to achieve, unless they overthrow the altar too? And by what appeal hereafter, when the breath of hostile armies may mingle with the poor, cold breezes of our country, shall we attempt to rouse up native valor? Fight for your hearths? There will be none throughout the land. Fight for your stoves! Not I, in faith. If in such a cause I strike a blow, it shall be on the invader's part; and Heaven grant that it may shatter the abomination all to pieces.

EARTH'S
HOLOCAUST

Once upon a time—but whether in the time past or time to come is a matter of little or no moment—this wide world had become so overburdened with an accumulation of wornout trumpery that the inhabitants determined to rid themselves of it by a general bonfire. The site fixed upon at the representation of the insurance companies, and as being as central a spot as any other on the globe, was one of the broadest prairies of the West, where no human habitation would be endangered by the flames, and where a vast assemblage of spectators might commodiously admire the show. Having a taste for sights of this kind, and imagining, likewise, that the illumination of the bonfire might reveal some profundity of moral truth heretofore hidden in mist or darkness, I made it convenient to journey thither and be present. At my arrival, although the heap of condemned rubbish was as yet comparatively small, the torch had already been applied. Amid that boundless plain, in the dusk of the evening, like a far off star alone in the firmament, there was merely visible one tremulous gleam, whence none could have anticipated so fierce a blaze as was destined to ensue. With every moment, however, there came foot travellers, women holding up their aprons, men on horseback, wheelbarrows, lumbering baggage wagons, and other vehicles, great and small, and from far and

First published in *Graham's Magazine*, May, 1844.

near laden with articles that were judged fit for nothing but to be burned.

"What materials have been used to kindle the flame?" inquired I of a by-stander; for I was desirous of knowing the whole process of the affair from beginning to end.

The person whom I addressed was a grave man, fifty years old or thereabout, who had evidently come thither as a looker on. He struck me immediately as having weighed for himself the true value of life and its circumstances, and therefore as feeling little personal interest in whatever judgment the world might form of them. Before answering my question, he looked me in the face by the kindling light of the fire.

"Oh, some very dry combustibles," replied he, "and extremely suitable to the purpose—no other, in fact, than yesterday's newspapers, last month's magazines, and last year's withered leaves. Here now comes some antiquated trash that will take fire like a handful of shavings."

As he spoke some rough-looking men advanced to the verge of the bonfire, and threw in, as it appeared, all the rubbish of the herald's office—the blazonry of coat armor, the crests and devices of illustrious families, pedigrees that extended back, like lines of light, into the mist of the dark ages, together with stars, garters, and embroidered collars, each of which, as paltry a bawble as it might appear to the uninstructed eye, had once possessed vast significance, and was still, in truth, reckoned among the most precious of moral or material facts by the worshippers of the gorgeous past. Mingled with this confused heap, which was tossed into the flames by armfuls at once, were innumerable badges of knighthood, comprising those of all the European sovereignties, and Napoleon's decoration of the Legion of Honor, the ribbons of which were entangled with those of the ancient order of St. Louis. There, too, were the medals of our own society of Cincinnati, by means of which, as history tells us, an order of hereditary knights came near being constituted out of the king quellers of the revolution. And besides, there were the patents of nobility of German counts and barons, Spanish grandees, and English peers, from the worm-eaten instruments signed by William the Conqueror down to the brand new parchment of the latest lord who has received his honors from the fair hand of Victoria.

At sight of the dense volumes of smoke, mingled with vivid jets of flame, that gushed and eddied forth from this immense pile of earthly distinctions, the multitude of plebeian spectators set up a joyous shout, and clapped their hands with an emphasis that made the welkin echo. That was their moment of triumph, achieved, after long ages, over creatures of the same clay and the same spiritual infirmities, who had dared to assume the privileges due only to Heaven's better workmanship. But now there rushed towards the blazing heap a grayhaired man, of stately presence, wearing a coat, from the breast of which a star, or other badge of rank, seemed to have been forcibly wrenched away. He had not the tokens of intellectual power in his face; but still there was the demeanor, the habitual and almost native dignity, of one who had been born to the idea of his own social superiority, and had never felt it questioned till that moment.

"People," cried he, gazing at the ruin of what was dearest to his eyes with grief and wonder, but nevertheless with a degree of stateliness,—"people, what have you done? This fire is consuming all that marked your advance from barbarism, or that could have prevented your relapse thither. We, the men of the privileged orders, were those who kept alive from age to age the old chivalrous spirit; the gentle and generous thought; the higher, the purer, the more refined and delicate life. With the nobles, too, you cast off the poet, the painter, the sculptor—all the beautiful arts; for we were their patrons, and created the atmosphere in which they flourish. In abolishing the majestic distinctions of rank, society loses not only its grace, but its steadfastness"—

More he would doubtless have spoken; but here there arose an outcry, sportive, contemptuous, and indignant, that altogether drowned the appeal of the fallen nobleman, insomuch that, casting one look of despair at his own half-burned pedigree, he shrunk back into the crowd, glad to shelter himself under his new-found insignificance.

"Let him thank his stars that we have not flung him into the same fire!" shouted a rude figure, spurning the embers with his foot. "And henceforth let no man dare to show a piece of musty parchment as his warrant for lording it over his fellows. If he have strength of arm, well and good; it is one species of superiority. If he have wit, wisdom, courage, force of character, let these attributes do for him what they may; but from this day forward no mortal must hope for place and consideration by reckoning up the mouldy bones of his ancestors. That nonsense is done away."

"And in good time," remarked the grave observer by my side, in a low voice, however, "if no worse nonsense comes in its place; but, at all events, this species of nonsense has fairly lived out its life."

There was little space to muse or moralize over the embers of this time-honored rubbish; for, before it was half burned out, there came another multitude from beyond the sea, bearing the purple robes of royalty, and the crowns, globes, and sceptres of emperors and kings. All these had been condemned as useless bawbles, playthings at best, fit only for the infancy of the world or rods to govern and chastise it in its nonage, but with which universal manhood at its full-grown stature could no longer brook to be insulted. Into such contempt had these regal insignia now fallen that the gilded crown and tinselled robes of the player king from Drury Lane Theatre had been thrown in among the rest, doubtless as a mockery of his brother monarchs on the great stage of the world. It was a strange sight to discern the crown jewels of England glowing and flashing in the midst of the fire. Some of them had been delivered from the time of the Saxon princes; others were purchased with vast revenues, or perchance ravished from the dead brows of the native potentates of Hindostan; and the whole now blazed with a dazzling lustre, as if a star had fallen in that spot and been shattered into fragments. The splendor of the ruined monarchy had no reflection save in those inestimable precious stones. But enough on this subject. It were but tedious to describe how the Emperor of Austria's mantle was converted to tinder, and how the posts and pillars of the French throne became a heap of coals, which it was impossible to distinguish from those of any other wood. Let me add, however, that I noticed one of the exiled Poles stirring up the bonfire with the Czar of Russia's sceptre, which he afterwards flung into the flames.

"The smell of singed garments is quite intolerable here," observed my new acquaintance, as the breeze enveloped us in the smoke of a royal wardrobe. "Let us get to windward and see what they are doing on the other side of the bonfire."

We accordingly passed around, and were just in time to witness the arrival of a vast procession of Washingtonians,—as the votaries of temperance call themselves nowadays,—accompanied by thousands of the Irish disciples of Father Mathew, with that great apostle at their head. They brought a rich contribution to the bonfire—being nothing less than all the hogsheads and barrels of liquor in the world, which they rolled before them across the prairie.

"Now, my children," cried Father Mathew, when they reached the verge of the fire, "one shove more, and the work is done. And now let us stand off and see Satan deal with his own liquor."

Accordingly, having placed their wooden vessels within reach of the flames, the procession stood off at a safe distance, and soon beheld them burst into a blaze that reached the clouds and threatened to set the sky itself on fire. And well it might; for here was the whole world's stock of spirituous liquors, which, instead of kindling a frenzied light in the eyes of individual topers as of yore, soared upwards with a bewildering gleam that startled all mankind. It was the aggregate of that fierce fire which would otherwise have scorched the hearts of millions. Meantime numberless bottles of precious wine were flung into the blaze, which lapped up the contents as if it loved them, and grew, like other drunkards, the merrier and fiercer for what it quaffed. Never again will the insatiable thirst of the fire fiend be so pampered. Here were the treasures of famous bon vivants—liquors that had been tossed on ocean, and mellowed in the sun, and hoarded long in the recesses of the earth—the pale, the gold, the ruddy juice of whatever vineyards were most delicate—the entire vintage of Tokay—all mingled in one stream with the vile fluids of the common pothouse, and contributing to heighten the selfsame blaze. And while it rose in a gigantic spire that seemed to wave against the arch of the firmament and combine itself with the light of stars, the multitude gave a shout as if the broad earth were exulting in its deliverance from the curse of ages.

But the joy was not universal. Many deemed that human life would be gloomier than ever when that brief illumination should sink down. While the reformers were at work, I overheard muttered expostulations from several respectable gentlemen with red noses and wearing gouty shoes; and a ragged worthy, whose face looked like a hearth where the fire is burned out, now expressed his discontent more openly and boldly.

"What is this world good for," said the last toper, "now that we can never be jolly any more? What is to comfort the poor man in sorrow and perplexity? How is he to keep his heart warm against the cold winds of this cheerless earth? And what do you propose to give him in exchange for the solace that you take away? How are old friends to sit together by the fireside without a cheerful glass between them? A plague upon your reformation! It is a sad world, a cold world, a selfish world, a low world not worth an honest fellow's living in, now that good fellowship is gone forever!"

This harangue excited great mirth among the bystanders; but, preposterous as was the sentiment, I could not help commiserating the forlorn condition of the last toper, whose boon companions had dwindled away from his side, leaving the poor fellow without a soul to countenance him in sipping his liquor, nor indeed any liquor to sip. Not that this was quite the true state of the case; for I had observed him at a critical moment filch a bottle of fourth-proof brandy that fell beside the bonfire and hide it in his pocket.

The spirituous and fermented liquors being thus disposed of, the zeal of the reformers next induced them to replenish the fire with all the boxes of tea and bags of coffee in the world. And now came the planters of Virginia, bringing their crops and tobacco. These, being cast upon the heap of inutility, aggregated it to the size of a mountain, and incensed the atmosphere with such potent fragrance that methought we should never draw pure breath again. The present sacrifice seemed to startle the lovers of the weed more than any that they had hitherto witnessed.

"Well, they've put my pipe out," said an old gentleman flinging it into the flames in a pet. "What is this world coming to? Everything rich and racy—all the spice of life—is to be condemned as useless. Now that they have kindled the bonfire, if these nonsensical reformers would fling themselves into it, all would be well enough!"

"Be patient," responded a stanch conservative; "it will come to that in the end. They will first fling us in, and finally themselves."

From the general and systematic measures of reform I now turned to consider the individual contributions to this memorable bonfire. In many instances these were of a very amusing character. One poor fellow threw in his empty purse, and another a bundle of counterfeit or insolvable bank notes. Fashionable ladies threw in their last season's bonnets, together with heaps of ribbons, yellow lace, and much other half-worn milliner's ware, all of which proved even more evanescent in the fire than it had been in the fashion. A multitude of lovers of both sexes—discarded maids or bachelors and couples mutually weary of one another—tossed in bundles of perfumed letters and enamored sonnets. A hack politician, being deprived of bread by the loss of office, threw in his teeth, which happened to be false ones. The Rev. Sydney Smith—having voyaged across the Atlantic for that sole purpose—came up to the bonfire with a bitter grin and threw in certain repudiated bonds, fortified though they were with the broad seal of a sovereign state. A little boy of five years old, in the premature manliness of the present epoch, threw in his playthings; a college graduate his diploma; an apothecary, ruined by the spread of homœopathy, his whole stock of drugs and medicines; a physician his library; a parson his old sermons; and a fine gentleman of the old school his code of manners, which he had formerly written down for the benefit of the next generation. A widow, resolving on a second marriage, slyly threw in her dead husband's miniature. A young man, jilted by his mistress, would willingly have flung his own desperate heart into the flames, but could find no means to wrench it out of his bosom. An American author, whose words were neglected by the public, threw his pen and paper into the bonfire, and betook himself to some less discouraging occupation. It somewhat startled me to overhear a number of ladies, highly respectable in appearance, proposing to fling their gowns and petticoats into the flames, and assume the garb, together with the manners, duties, offices, and responsibilities, of the opposite sex.

What favor was accorded to this scheme I am unable to say, my attention being suddenly drawn to a poor, deceived, and half-delirious girl, who, exclaiming that she was the most worthless thing alive or dead, attempted to cast herself into the fire amid all that wrecked and broken trumpery of the world. A good man, however, ran to her rescue.

"Patience, my poor girl!" said he, as he drew her back from the fierce embrace of the destroying angel. "Be patient, and abide Heaven's will. So long as you possess a living soul, all may be restored to its first freshness. These things of matter and creations of human fantasy are fit for nothing but to be burned when once they have had their day; but your day is eternity!"

"Yes," said the wretched girl, whose frenzy seemed now to have sunk down into deep despondency,—"yes and the sunshine is blotted out of it!"

It was now rumored among the spectators that all the

weapons and munitions of war were to be thrown into the
bonfire, with the exception of the world's stock of gunpowder,
which, as the safest mode of disposing of it, had already been
drowned in the sea. This intelligence seemed to awaken great
diversity of opinion. The hopeful philanthropist esteemed it
a token that the millennium was already come, while persons
of another stamp, in whose view mankind was a breed of bull-
dogs, prophesied that all the old stoutness, fervor, nobleness,
generosity, and magnanimity of the race would disappear,—
these qualities, as they affirmed, requiring blood for their
nourishment. They comforted themselves, however, in the
belief that the proposed abolition of war was impracticable
for any length of time together.

Be that as it might, numberless great guns, whose thunder
had long been the voice of battle,—the artillery of the Ar-
mada, the battering trains of Marlborough, and the adverse
cannon of Napoleon and Wellington,—were trundled into the
midst of the fire. By the continual addition of dry combustibles, it had now waxed so intense that neither brass nor iron
could withstand it. It was wonderful to behold how these
terrible instruments of slaughter melted away like playthings
of wax. Then the armies of the earth wheeled around the
mighty furnace, with their military music playing triumphant
marches, and flung in their muskets and swords. The standard-
bearers, likewise, cast one look upward at their banners, all
tattered with shot holes and inscribed with the names of
victorious fields; and, giving them a last flourish on the
breeze, they lowered them into the flame, which snatched them
upward in its rush towards the clouds. This ceremony being
over, the world was left without a single weapon in its hands,
except possibly a few old king's arms and rusty swords and
other trophies of the Revolution in some of our state armories.
And now the drums were beaten and the trumpets brayed all
together, as a prelude to the proclamation of universal and
eternal peace and the announcement that glory was no longer
to be won by blood, but that it would henceforth be the contention of the human race to work out the greatest mutual

good, and that beneficence, in the future annals of the earth, would claim the praise of valor. The blessed tidings were accordingly promulgated, and caused infinite rejoicing among those who had stood aghast at the horror and absurdity of war.

But I saw a grim smile pass over the seared visage of a stately old commander,—by his warworn figure and rich military dress, he might have been one of Napoleon's famous marshals,—who, with the rest of the world's soldiery, had just flung away the sword that had been familiar to his right hand for half a century.

"Ay! ay!" grumbled he. "Let them proclaim what they please; but, in the end, we shall find that all this foolery has only made more work for the armorers and cannon founders."

"Why, sir," exclaimed I, in astonishment, "do you imagine that the human race will ever so far return on the steps of its past madness as to weld another sword or cast another cannon?"

"There will be no need," observed, with a sneer, one who neither felt benevolence nor had faith in it. "When Cain wished to slap his brother, he was at no loss for a weapon."

"We shall see," replied the veteran commander. "If I am mistaken, so much the better; but in my opinion, without pretending to philosophize about the matter, the necessity of war lies far deeper than these honest gentlemen suppose. What! is there a field for all the petty disputes of individuals? and shall there be no great law court for the settlement of national difficulties? The battle field is the only court where such suits can be tried."

"You forget, general," rejoined I, "that, in this advanced stage of civilization, Reason and Philanthropy combined will constitute just such a tribunal as is requisite."

"Ah, I had forgotten that, indeed!" said the old warrior, as he limped away.

The fire was now to be replenished with materials that had hitherto been considered of even greater importance to the well being of society than the warlike munitions which we had already seen consumed. A body of reformers had travelled all over the earth in quest of the machinery by which the different nations were accustomed to inflict the punishment of death. A shudder passed through the multitude as these ghastly emblems were dragged forward. Even the flames seemed at first to shrink away, displaying the shape and murderous contrivance of each in a full blaze of light, which of itself was sufficient to convince mankind of the long and deadly error of human law. Those old implements of cruelty; those horrible monsters of mechanism; those inventions which seemed to demand something worse than man's natural heart to contrive, and which had lurked in the dusky nooks of ancient prisons, the subject of terror-stricken legend,—were now brought forth to view. Headsmen's axes, with the rust of noble and royal blood upon them, and a vast collection of halters that had choked the breath of plebeian victims, were thrown in together. A shout greeted the arrival of the guillotine, which was thrust forward on the same wheels that had borne it from one to another of the blood-stained streets of Paris. But the loudest roar of applause went up, telling the distant sky of the triumph of the earth's redemption, when the gallows made its appearance. An ill-looking fellow, however, rushed forward, and, putting himself in the path of the reformers, bellowed hoarsely, and fought with brute fury to stay their progress.

It was little matter of surprise, perhaps, that the executioner should thus do his best to vindicate and uphold the machinery by which he himself had his livelihood and worthier individuals their death; but it deserved special note that men of a far different sphere—even of that consecrated class in whose guardianship the world is apt to trust its benevolence—were found to take the hangman's view of the question.

"Stay, my brethren!" cried one of them. "You are misled by a false philanthropy; you know not what you do. The gallows is a Heaven-ordained instrument. Bear it back, then, reverently, and set it up in its old place, else the world will fall to speedy ruin and desolation!"

"Onward! onward!" shouted a leader in the reform. "Into the flames with the accursed instrument of man's blood policy! How can human law inculcate benevolence and love while it persists in setting up the gallows as its chief symbol? One heave more, good friends, and the world will be redeemed from its greatest error."

A thousand hands, that nevertheless loathed the touch, now lent their assistance, and thrust the ominous burden far, far into the centre of the raging furnace. There its fatal and abhorred image was beheld, first black, then a red coal, then ashes.

"That was well done!" exclaimed I.

"Yes, it was well done," replied, but with less enthusiasm than I expected, the thoughtful observer who was still at my side; "well done, if the world be good enough for the measure. Death, however, is an idea that cannot easily be dispensed with in any condition between the primal innocence and that other purity and perfection which perchance we are destined to attain after travelling round the full circle; but, at all events, it is well that the experiment should now be tried."

"Too cold! too cold!" impatiently exclaimed the young and ardent leader in this triumph. "Let the heart have its voice here as well as the intellect. And as for ripeness, and as for progress, let mankind always do the highest, kindest, noblest thing that, at any given period, it has attained the perception of; and surely that thing cannot be wrong nor wrongly timed."

I know not whether it were the excitement of the scene, or whether the good people around the bonfire were really growing more enlightened every instant; but they now proceeded to measures in the full length of which I was hardly prepared to keep them company. For instance, some threw their marriage certificates into the flames, and declared themselves candidates for a higher, holier, and more comprehensive union than that which had subsisted from the birth of time under the form of the connubial tie. Others hastened to the vaults of banks and to the coffers of the rich,—all of which were open to the first comer on this fated occasion,—and brought entire bales of paper money to enliven the blaze, and tons of coin to be melted down by its intensity. Henceforth, they said, universal benevolence, uncoined and exhaustless, was to be the golden currency of the world. At this intelligence the bankers and speculators in the stocks grew pale, and a pickpocket, who had reaped a rich harvest among the crowd, fell down in a deadly fainting fit. A few men of business burned their daybooks and ledgers, the notes and obligations of their creditors, and all other evidence of debts due to themselves; while perhaps a somewhat larger number satisfied their zeal for reform with the sacrifice of any uncomfortable recollection of their own indebtment. There was then a cry that the period was arrived when the title deeds of landed property should be given to the flames, and the whole soil of the earth revert to the public, from whom it had been wrongfully abstracted and most unequally distributed among individuals. Another party demanded that all written constitutions, set forms of government, legislative acts, statute books, and everything else on which human invention had endeavored to stamp its arbitrary laws, should at once be destroyed, leaving the consummated world as free as the man first created.

Whether any ultimate action was taken with regard to these propositions is beyond my knowledge; for, just then, some matters were in progress that concerned my sympathies more nearly.

"See! see! What heaps of books and pamphlets!" cried a fellow, who did not seem to be a lover of literature. "Now we shall have a glorious blaze!"

"That's just the thing!" said a modern philosopher. "Now we shall get rid of the weight of dead men's thought, which has hitherto pressed so heavily on the living intellect that it has been incompetent to any effectual self-exertion. Well done, my lads! Into the fire with them! Now you are enlightening the world indeed!"

"But what is to become of the trade?" cried a frantic bookseller.

"Oh, by all means, let them accompany their merchandise,"

coolly observed an author. "It will be a noble funeral pile!"

The truth was, that the human race had now reached a stage of progress so far beyond what the wisest and wittiest men of former ages had ever dreamed of that it would have been a manifest absurdity to allow the earth to be any longer encumbered with their poor achievements in the literary line. Accordingly, a thorough and searching investigation had swept the booksellers' shops, hawkers' stands, public, and private libraries, and even the little book-shelf by the country fireside, and had brought the world's entire mass of printed paper, bound or in sheets, to swell the already mountain bulk of our illustrious bonfire. Thick, heavy folios, containing the labors of lexicographers, commentators and encyclopedists, were flung in, and falling among the embers with a leaden thump, smouldered away to ashes like rotten wood. The small, richly gilt French tomes of the last age, with the hundred volumes of Voltaire among them, went off in a brilliant shower of sparkles and little jets of flame; while the current literature of the same nation burned red and blue, and threw an infernal light over the visages of the spectators, converting them all to the aspect of party-colored fiends. A collection of German stories emitted a scent of brimstone. The English standard authors made excellent fuel, generally exhibiting the properties of sound oak logs. Milton's works, in particular, sent up a powerful blaze, gradually reddening into a coal, which promised to endure longer than almost any other material of the pile. From Shakespeare there gushed a flame of such marvellous splendor that men shaded their eyes as against the sun's meridian glory; nor even when the works of his own elucidators were flung upon him did he cease to flash forth a dazzling radiance from beneath the ponderous heap. It is my belief that he is blazing as fervidly as ever.

"Could a poet but light a lamp at that glorious flame," remarked I, "he might then consume the midnight oil to some good purpose."

"That is the very thing which modern poets have been too apt to do, or at least to attempt," answered a critic. "The chief benefit to be expected from this conflagration of past literature undoubtedly is, that writers will henceforth be compelled to light their lamps at the sun or stars."

"If they can reach so high," said I; "but that task requires a giant, who may afterwards distribute the light among inferior men. It is not every one that can steal the fire from heaven like Prometheus; but, when once he had done the deed, a thousand hearths were kindled by it."

It amazed me much to observe how indefinite was the proportion between the physical mass of any given author and the property of brilliant and long-continued combustion. For instance, there was not a quarto volume of the last century—nor, indeed, of the present—that could compete in that particular with a child's little gilt-covered book, containing Mother Goose's Melodies. The Life and Death of Tom Thumb outlasted the biography of Marlborough. An epic, indeed a dozen of them, was converted to white ashes before the single sheet of an old ballad was half consumed. In more than one case, too, when volumes of applauded verse proved incapable of anything better than a stifling smoke, an unregarded ditty of some nameless bard—perchance in the corner of a newspaper—soared up among the stars with a flame as brilliant as their own. Speaking of the properties of flame, methought Shelley's poetry emitted a purer light than almost any other productions of his day, contrasting beautifully with the fitful and lurid gleams and gushes of black vapor that flashed and eddied from the volumes of Lord Byron. As for Tom Moore, some of his songs diffused an odor like a burning pastil.

I felt particular interest in watching the combustion of American authors, and scrupulously noted by my watch the precise numbers of moments that changed most of them from shabbily-printed books to indistinguishable ashes. It would be invidious, however, if not perilous, to betray these awful secrets; so that I shall content myself with observing that it was not invariably the writer most frequently in the public mouth that made the most splendid appearance in the bonfire. I especially remember that a great deal of excellent inflammability was exhibited in a thin volume of poems by Ellery Channing, although, to speak the truth, there were certain portions that hissed and spluttered in a very disagreeable fashion. A curious phenomenon occurred in reference to several writers, native as well as foreign. Their books, though of highly respectable figure, instead of bursting into a blaze, or even smouldering out their substance in smoke, suddenly melted away in a manner that proved them to be ice.

If it be no lack of modesty to mention my own words, it must here be confessed that I looked for them with fatherly interest, but in vain. Too probably they were changed to vapor by the first action of the heat; at best, I can only hope that, in their quiet way, they contributed a glimmering spark or two to the splendor of the evening.

"Alas! and woe is me!" thus bemoaned himself a heavy-looking gentleman in green spectacles. "The world is utterly ruined, and there is nothing to live for any longer. The business of my life is snatched from me. Not a volume to be had for love or money!"

"This," remarked the sedate observer beside me, "is a bookworm—one of those men who are born to gnaw dead thoughts. His clothes, you see, are covered with the dust of libraries. He has no inward fountain of ideas; and, in good earnest, now that the old stock is abolished, I do not see what is to become of the poor fellow. Have you no word of comfort for him?"

"My dear sir," said I to the desperate bookworm, "is not Nature better than a book? Is not the human heart deeper than any system of philosophy? Is not life replete with more instruction than past observers have found it possible to write down in maxims? Be of good cheer. The great book of Time is still spread wide open before us; and, if we read it aright, it will be to us a volume of eternal truth."

"Oh, my books, my books, my precious printed books!" reiterated the forlorn bookworm. "My only reality was a bound volume; and now they will not leave me even a shadowy pamphlet!"

In fact, the last remnant of the literature of all the ages was now descending upon the blazing heap in the shape of a cloud of pamphlets from the press of the New World. These like-wise were consumed in the twinkling of an eye, leaving the earth, for the first time since the days of Cadmus, free from the plague of letters—an enviable field for the authors of the next generation.

"Well, and does anything remain to be done?" inquired I somewhat anxiously. "Unless we set fire to the earth itself, and then leap boldly cff into infinite space. I know not that we can carry reform to any farther point."

"You are vastly mistaken, my good friend," said the ob-server. "Believe me, the fire will not be allowed to settle down without the addition of fuel that will startle many persons who have lent a willing hand thus far."

Nevertheless there appeared to be a relaxation of effort for a little time, during which, probably, the leaders of the move-ment were considering what should be done next. In the interval, a philosopher threw his theory into the flames,—a sacrifice which, by those who knew how to estimate it, was pronounced the most remarkable that had yet been made. The combustion, however, was by no means brilliant. Some in-defatigable people, scorning to take a moment's ease, now employed themselves in collecting all the withered leaves and fallen boughs of the forest, and thereby recruited the bonfire to a greater height than ever. But this was mere by-play.

"Here comes the fresh fuel that I spoke of," said my com-panion.

To my astonishment, the persons who now advanced into the vacant space around the mountain fire bore surplices and other priestly garments, mitres, crosiers, and a confusion of Popish and Protestant emblems, with which it seemed their purpose to consummate the great act of faith. Crosses from the spires of old cathedrals were cast upon the heap with as little remorse as if the reverence of centuries, passing in long array beneath the lofty towers, had not looked up to them as the holiest of symbols. The font in which infants were con-secrated to God, the sacramental vessels whence piety received the hallowed draught, were given to the same destruction. Perhaps it most nearly touched my heart to see among these devoted relics fragments of the humble communion tables and undecorated pupils which I recognized as having been torn from the meeting-houses of New England. Those simple edifices might have been permitted to retain all of sacred embellishment that their Puritan founders had bestowed, even though the mighty structure of St. Peter's had sent its spoils to the fire of this terrible sacrifice. Yet I felt that these were but the externals of religion, and might most safely be relinquished by spirits that best know their deep significance.

"All is well," said I, cheerfully. "The woodpaths shall be the aisles of our cathedral,—the firmament itself shall be its ceiling. What needs an earthly roof between the Deity and his worshippers? Our faith can well afford to lose all the drapery that even the holiest men have thrown around it, and linquished by spirits that best knew their deep significance.

"True," said my companion; "but will they pause here?"

The doubt implied in his question was well founded. In the general destruction of books already described, a holy volume, that stood apart from the catalogue of human literature, and yet, in one sense, was at its head, had been spared. But the Titan of innovation,—angel or fiend, double in his nature, and capable of deeds befitting both characters,—at first shaking down only the old and rotten shapes of things, had now, as it appeared, laid his terrible hand upon the main pillars which supported the whole edifice of our moral and spiritual state. The inhabitants of the earth had grown too enlightened to define their faith within a form of words, or to limit the spiritual by any analogy to our material existence. Truths which the heavens trembled at were now but a fable of the world's infancy. Therefore, as the final sacrifice of human error, what else remained to be thrown upon the embers of that awful pile except the book which, though a celestial revelation to past ages, was but a voice from a lower sphere as regarded the present race of man? It was done! Upon the blazing heap of falsehood and wornout truth—things that the earth had never needed, or had ceased to need, or had grown childishly weary of—fell the ponderous church Bible, the great old volume that had lain so long on the cushion of the pulpit, and whence the pastor's solemn voice had given holy utterance on so many a Sabbath day. There, likewise, fell the family Bible, which the long-buried patriarch had read to his children,—in prosperity or sorrow, by the fireside and in the summer shade of trees,—and had bequeathed downward as the heirloom of generations. There fell the bosom Bible, the little volume that had been the soul's friend of some sorely-tried child of dust, who thence took courage, whether his trial were for life or death, steadfastly confronting both in the strong assurance of immortality.

All these were flung into the fierce and riotous blaze; and then a mighty wind came roaring across the plain with a desolate howl, as if it were angry lamentation of the earth for the loss of heaven's sunshine; and it shook the gigantic pyramid of flame and scattered the cinders of half-consumed abominations around upon the spectators.

"This is terrible!" said I, feeling that my cheek grew pale, and seeing a like change in the visages about me.

"Be of good courage yet," answered the man with whom I had so often spoken. He continued to gaze steadily at the spectacle with a singular calmness, as if it concerned him merely as an observer. "Be of good courage, nor yet exult too much; for there is far less both of good and evil in the effect of this bonfire than the world might be willing to believe."

"How can that be?" exclaimed I, impatiently. "Has it not consumed everything? Has it not swallowed up or melted down every human or divine appendage of our mortal state that had substance enough to be acted on by fire? Will there be anything left us tomorrow morning better or worse than a heap of embers and ashes?"

"Assuredly there will," said my grave friend. "Come hither to-morrow morning, or whenever the combustible portion of the pile shall be quite burned out, and you will find among the ashes everything really valuable that you have seen cast into the flames. Trust me, the world of to-morrow will again enrich itself with the gold and diamonds which have been cast off by the world of to-day. Not a truth is destroyed nor buried so deep among the ashes but it will be raked up at last."

This was a strange assurance. Yet I felt inclined to credit it, the more especially as I beheld among the wallowing flames a copy of the Holy Scripture, the pages of which, instead of being blackened into tinder, only assumed a more dazzling whiteness as the finger marks of human imperfection were purified away. Certain marginal notes and commentaries, it is true, yielded to the intensity of the fiery test, but without detriment to the smallest syllable that had flamed from the pen of inspiration.

"Yes; there is the proof of what you say," answered I, turning to the observer; "but if only what is evil can feel the action of the fire, then, surely, the conflagration has been of inestimable utility. Yet, if I understand aright, you intimate a doubt whether the world's expectation of benefit would be realized by it."

The persons whom he indicated consisted of that brutal and most earthy figure who had stood forth so furiously in defence of the gallows,—the hangman, in short,—together with the last thief and the last murderer, all three of whom were clustered about the last toper. The latter was liberally passing the brandy bottle, which he had rescued from the general destruction of wines and spirits. This little convivial party seemed at the lowest pitch of despondency, as considering that the purified world must needs be utterly unlike the sphere that they had hitherto known, and therefore but a strange and desolate abode for gentlemen of their kidney.

"The best counsel for all of us is," remarked the hangman, "that, as soon as we have finished the last drop of liquor, I help you, my three friends, to a comfortable end upon the nearest tree, and then hang myself on the same bough. This is no world for us any longer."

"Poh, poh, my good fellows!" said a dark-complexioned personage, who now joined the group,—his complexion was indeed fearfully dark, and his eyes glowed with a redder light than that of the bonfire; "be not so cast down, my dear friends; you shall see good days yet. There's one thing that these wise-acres have forgotten to throw into the fire, and without which all the rest of the conflagration is just nothing at all; yes, though they had burned the earth itself to a cinder."

"And what may that be?" eagerly demanded the last murderer.

"What but the human heart itself?" said the dark-visaged stranger, with a portentous grin. "And, unless they hit upon some method of purifying that foul cavern, forth from it will reissue all the shapes of wrong and misery—the same old shapes or worse ones—which they have taken such a vast deal of trouble to consume to ashes. I have stood by this livelong night and laughed in my sleeve at the whole business. Oh, take my word for it, it will be old world yet!"

This brief conversation supplied me with a theme for lengthened thought. How sad a truth, if true it were, that man's agelong endeavor for perfection had served only to render him the mockery of the evil principle, from the fatal circumstances of an error at the very root of the matter! The heart, the heart,—there was the little yet boundless sphere wherein existed the original wrong of which the crime and misery of this outward world were merely types. Purify that inward sphere, and the many shapes of evil that haunt the outward, and which now seem almost our only realities, will turn to shadowy phantoms and vanish of their own accord; but if we go no deeper than the intellect, and strive, with merely that feeble instrument, to discern and rectify what is wrong, our whole accomplishment will be a dream, so unsubstantial that it matters little whether the bonfire, which I have so faithfully described, were what we choose to call a real event and a flame that would scorch the finger, or only a phosphoric radiance and a parable of my own brain.

MAIN
STREET

A respectable-looking individual makes his bow and addresses the public. In my daily walks along the principal street of my native town, it has often occurred to me, that, if its growth from infancy upward, and the vicissitude of characteristic scenes that have passed along this thoroughfare during the more than two centuries of its existence, could be presented to the eye in a shifting panorama, it would be an exceedingly effective method of illustrating the march of time. Acting on this idea, I have contrived a certain pictorial exhibition, somewhat in the nature of a puppet-show, by means of which I propose to call up the multiform and many-colored Past before the spectator, and show him the ghosts of his forefathers, amid a succession of historic incidents, with no greater trouble than the turning of a crank. Be pleased, therefore, my indulgent patrons, to walk into the show-room, and take your seats before yonder mysterious curtain. The little wheels and springs of my machinery have been well oiled; a multitude of puppets are dressed in character, representing all varieties of fashion, from the Puritan cloak and jerkin to the latest Oak Hall coat; the lamps are trimmed, and shall brighten into noontide sunshine, or fade away in moonlight, or muffle their brilliancy in a November cloud, as the nature of the scene may require;

First published in Peabody, E. P., ed., *Aesthetic Papers,* 1849.

and, in short, the exhibition is just ready to commence. Unless something should go wrong,—as, for instance, the misplacing of a picture, whereby the people and events of one century might be thrust into the middle of another; or the breaking of a wire, which would bring the course of time to a sudden period,—barring, I say, the casualties to which such a complicated piece of mechanism is liable,—I flatter myself, ladies and gentlemen, that the performance will elicit your generous approbation.

Ting-a-ting-ting! goes the bell; the curtain rises; and we behold—not, indeed, the Main Street—but the track of leaf-strewn forest-land over which its dusty pavement is hereafter to extend.

You perceive, at a glance, that this is the ancient and primitive wood,—the ever-youthful and venerably old,—verdant with new twigs, yet hoary, as it were, with the snowfall of innumerable years, that have accumulated upon its intermingled branches. The white man's axe has never smitten a single tree; his footstep has never crumpled a single one of the withered leaves, which all the autumns since the flood have been harvesting beneath. Yet, see! along through the vista of impending boughs, there is already a faintly traced path, running nearly east and west, as if a prophecy or foreboding of the future street had stolen into the heart of the solemn old wood. Onward goes this hardly perceptible track, now ascending over a natural swell of land, now subsiding gently into a hollow; traversed here by a little streamlet, which glitters like a snake through the gleam of sunshine, and quickly hides itself among the underbrush, in its quest for the neighboring cove; and impeded there by the massy corpse of a giant of the forest, which had lived out its incalculable term of life, and been overthrown by mere old age, and lies buried in the new vegetation that is born of its decay. What footsteps can have worn this half-seen path? Hark! Do we not hear them now rustling softly over the leaves? We discern an Indian woman,—a majestic and queenly woman, or else her spectral image does not represent her truly,—for this is the great Squaw Sachem, whose rule, with that of her sons, extends from

Mystic to Agawam. That red chief, who stalks by her side, is Wappacowet, her second husband, the priest and magician, whose incantations shall hereafter affright the pale-faced settlers with grisly phantoms, dancing and shrieking in the woods at midnight. But greater would be the affright of the Indian necromancer, if, mirrored in the pool of water at his feet, he could catch a prophetic glimpse of the noonday marvels which the white man is destined to achieve; if he could see, as in a dream, the stone front of the stately hall, which will cast its shadow over this very spot; if he could be aware that the future edifice will contain a noble Museum, where, among countless curiosities of earth and sea, a few Indian arrow-heads shall be treasured up as memorials of a vanished race!

No such forebodings disturb the Squaw Sachem and Wappacowet. They pass on, beneath the tangled shade, holding high talk on matters of state and religion, and imagine, doubtless, that their own system of affairs will endure forever. Meanwhile, how full of its own proper life is the scene that lies around them! The gray squirrel runs up the trees, and rustles among the upper branches. Was not that the leap of a deer? And there is the whirr of a partridge! Methinks, too, I catch the cruel and stealthy eye of a wolf, as he draws back into yonder impervious density of underbrush. So, there, amid the murmur of boughs, go the Indian queen and the Indian priest; while the gloom of the broad wilderness impends over them, and its sombre mystery invests them as with something preternatural; and only momentary streaks of quivering sunlight, once in a great while, find their way down, and glimmer among the feathers in their dusky hair. Can it be that the thronged street of a city will ever pass into this twilight solitude,—over those soft heaps of the decaying tree-trunks, and through the swampy places, green with water-moss, and penetrate that hopeless entanglement of green trees, which have been uprooted and tossed together by a whirlwind? It has been a wilderness from the creation. Must it not be a wilderness forever?

Here an acidulous-looking gentleman in blue glasses, with

bows of Berlin steel, who has taken a seat at the extremity of the front row, begins, at this early stage of the exhibition, to criticise.

"The whole affair is a manifest catchpenny!" observes he, scarcely under his breath. "The trees look more like weeds in a garden than a primitive forest; the Squaw Sachem and Wappacowet are stiff in their pasteboard joints; and the squirrels, the deer, and the wolf move with all the grace of a child's wooden monkey, sliding up and down a stick."

"I am obliged to you, sir, for the candor of your remarks," replies the showman, with a bow. "Perhaps they are just. Human art has its limits, and we must now and then ask a little aid from the spectator's imagination."

"You will get no such aid from mine," responds the critic. "I make it a point to see things precisely as they are. But come! go ahead! the stage is waiting!"

The showman proceeds.

Casting our eyes again over the scene, we perceive that strangers have found their way into the solitary place. In more than one spot, among the trees, an upheaved axe is glittering in the sunshine. Roger Conant, the first settler in Naumkeag, has built his dwelling, months ago, on the border of the forest-path; and at this moment he comes eastward through the vista of woods, with his gun over his shoulder, bringing home the choice portions of a deer. His stalwart figure, clad in a leathern jerkin and breeches of the same, strides sturdily onward, with such an air of physical force and energy that we might almost expect the very trees to stand aside and give him room to pass. And so, indeed, they must; for, humble as is his name in history, Roger Conant still is of that class of men who do not merely find, but make, their place in the system of human affairs; a man of thoughtful strength, he has planted the germ of a city. There stands his habitation, showing in its rough architecture some features of the Indian wigwam, and some of the log-cabin, and somewhat, too, of the straw-thatched cottage in Old England, where this good yeoman had his birth and breeding. The dwelling is surrounded by a cleared space of a few acres, where Indian corn grows thrivingly among the stumps of the trees; while the dark forest hems it in, and seems to gaze silently and solemnly, as if wondering at the breadth of sunshine which the white man spreads around him. An Indian, half hidden in the dusky shade, is gazing and wondering too.

Within the door of the cottage you discern the wife, with her ruddy English cheek. She is singing, doubtless, a psalm tune, at her household work; or, perhaps, she sighs at the remembrance of the cheerful gossip, and all the merry social life, of her native village beyond the vast and melancholy sea. Yet the next moment she laughs, with sympathetic glee, at the sports, of her little tribe of children; and soon turns round, with the homelook in her face, as her husband's foot is heard approaching the rough-hewn threshold. How sweet must it be for those who have an Eden in their hearts, like Roger Conant and his wife, to find a new world to project it into, as they have, instead of dwelling among old haunts of men, where so many household fires have been kindled and burnt out, that the very glow of happiness has something dreary in it! Not that this pair are alone in their wild Eden, for here comes Goodwife Massey, the young spouse of Jeffrey Massey, from her home hard by, with an infant at her breast. Dame Conant has another of like age; and it shall hereafter be one of the disputed points of history which of these two babies was the first townborn child.

But see! Roger Conant has other neighbors within view. Peter Palfrey, likewise, has built himself a house, and so has Balch, and Norman, and Woodbury. Their dwellings, indeed,—such is the ingenious contrivance of this piece of pictorial mechanism,—seem to have arisen, at various points of the scene, even while we have been looking at it. The forest-track, trodden more and more by the hobnailed shoes of these sturdy and ponderous Englishmen, has now a distinctness which it never could have acquired from the light tread of a hundred times as many Indian moccasins. It will be a street, anon. As we observe it now, it goes onward from one clearing to another, here plunging into a shadowy strip of woods, there open to the sunshine, but everywhere showing a decided line, along which human interests have begun to hold their career. Over yonder swampy spot, two trees have been felled, and laid side by side to make a causeway. In another place, the axe has cleared away a confused intricacy of fallen trees and clustered boughs, which had been tossed together by a hurricane. So now the little children, just beginning to run alone, may trip along the path, and not often stumble over an impediment, unless they stray from it to gather wood-berries beneath the trees. And, besides the feet of grown people and children, there are the cloven hoofs of a small herd of cows, who seek their subsistence from the native grasses, and help to deepen the track of the future thoroughfare. Goats also browse along it, and nibble at the twigs that thrust themselves across the way. Not seldom, in its more secluded portions, where the black shadow of the forest strives to hide the trace of human footsteps, stalks a gaunt wolf, on the watch for a kid or a young calf; or fixes his hungry gaze on the group of children gathering berries, and can hardly forbear to rush upon them. And the Indians, coming from their distant wigwams to view the white man's settlement, marvel at the deep track which he makes, and perhaps are saddened by a flitting presentiment that this heavy tread will find its way over all the land; and that the wild woods, the wild wolf, and the wild Indian will be alike trampled beneath it. Even so shall it be. The pavements of the Main Street must be laid over the red man's grave.

Behold! here is a spectacle which should be ushered in by the peal of trumpets, if Naumkeag had ever yet heard that cheery music, and by the roar of cannon, echoing among the woods. A procession,—for, by its dignity, as marking an epoch in the history of the street, it deserves that name,—a procession advances along the pathway. The good ship Abigail has arrived from England, bringing wares and merchandise, for the comfort of the inhabitants and traffic with the Indians; bringing passengers too, and, more important than all, a governor for the new settlement. Roger Conant and Peter Palfrey, with their companions, have been to the shore to welcome him; and now, with such honor and triumph as their rude way of life permits, are escorting the sea-flushed voyagers to their habitations. At the point where Endicott enters upon the scene, two venerable trees unite their branches high above his head; thus forming a triumphal arch of living verdure, beneath which he pauses, with his wife leaning on his arm, to catch the first impression of their new-found home. The old settlers gaze not less earnestly at him, than he at the hoary woods and the rough surface of the clearings. They like his bearded face, under the shadow of the broad-brimmed and steeple-crowned Puritan hat,—a visage resolute, grave, and thoughtful, yet apt to kindle with that glow of a cheerful spirit by which men of strong character are enabled to go joyfully on their proper tasks. His form, too, as you see it, in a doublet and hose of sad-colored cloth, is of a manly make, fit for toil and hardship, and fit to wield the heavy sword that hangs from his leathern belt. His aspect is a better warrant for the ruler's office than the parchment commission which he bears, however, fortified it may be with the broad seal of the London council. Peter Palfrey nods to Roger Conant. "The worshipful Court of Assistants have done wisely," say they between themselves. "They have chosen for our governor a man out of a thousand." Then they toss up their hats,—they, and all the uncouth figures of their company, most of whom are clad in skins, inasmuch as their old kersey and linsey-woolsey garments have been torn and tattered by many a long month's wear,—they all toss up their hats, and salute their new governor and captain with a hearty English shout of welcome. We seem to hear it with our own ears, so perfectly is the action represented in this life-like, this almost magic, picture!

But have you observed the lady who leans upon the arm of Endicott?—a rose of beauty from an English garden, now to be transplanted to a fresher soil. It may be that, long years —centuries indeed—after this fair flower shall have decayed, other flowers of the same race will appear in the same soil, and gladden other generations with hereditary beauty. Does not the vision haunt us yet? Has not Nature kept the mould unbroken, deeming it a pity that the idea should vanish from mortal sight forever, after only once assuming earthly substance? Do we not recognize, in that fair woman's face, the model of features which still beam, at happy moments, on what was then the woodland pathway, but has long since grown into a busy street?

"This is too ridiculous!—positively insufferable!" mutters the same critic who had before expressed his disapprobation. "Here is a pasteboard figure, such as a child would cut out of a card, with a pair of very dull scissors; and the fellow modestly requests us to see in it the prototype of hereditary beauty!"

"But, sir, you have not the proper point of view," remarks the showman. "You sit altogether too near to get the best effect of my pictorial exhibition. Pray, oblige me by removing to this other bench, and I venture to assure you the proper light and shadow will transform the spectacle into quite another thing."

"Pshaw!" replies the critic; "I want no other light and shade. I have already told you that it is my business to see things just as they are."

"I would suggest to the author of this ingenious exhibition," observes a gentlemanly person, who has shown signs of being much interested,—"I would suggest that Anna Gower, the first wife of Governor Endicott, and who came with him from England, left no posterity; and that, consequently, we cannot be indebted to that honorable lady for any specimens of feminine loveliness now extant among us."

Having nothing to allege against this genealogical objection, the showman points again to the scene.

During this little interruption, you perceive that the Anglo-Saxon energy—as the phrase now goes—has been at work in the spectacle before us. So many chimneys now send up their smoke, that it begins to have the aspect of a village street;

although everything is so inartificial and inceptive, that it seems as if one returning wave of the wild nature might overwhelm it all. But the one edifice which gives the pledge of permanence to this bold enterprise is seen at the central point of the picture. There stands the meeting-house, a small structure, low-roofed, without a spire, and built of rough timber, newly hewn, with the sap still in the logs, and here and there a strip of bark adhering to them. A meaner temple was never consecrated to the worship of the Deity. With the alternative of kneeling beneath the awful vault of the firmament, it is strange that men should creep into this pent-up nook, and expect God's presence there. Such, at least, one would imagine, might be the feeling of these forest-settlers, accustomed, as they had been, to stand under the dim arches of vast cathedrals, and to offer up their hereditary worship in the old ivy-covered churches of rural England, around which lay the bones of many generations of their forefathers. How could they dispense with the carved altar-work?—how, with the pictured windows, where the light of common day was hallowed by being transmitted through the glorified figures of saints?—how, with the lofty roof, imbued, as it must have been, with the prayers that had gone upward for centuries?—how, with the rich peal of the solemn organ, rolling along the aisles, pervading the whole church, and sweeping the soul away on a flood of audible religion? They needed nothing of all this. Their house of worship, like their ceremonial, was naked, simple, and severe. But the zeal of a recovered faith burned like a lamp within their hearts, enriching everything around them with its radiance; making of these new walls, and this narrow compass, its own cathedral; and being, in itself, that spiritual mystery and experience, of which sacred architecture, pictured windows, and the organ's grand solemnity are remote and imperfect symbols. All was well, so long as their lamps were freshly kindled at the heavenly flame. After a while, however, whether in their time or their children's, these lamps began to burn more dimly, or with a less genuine lustre; and then it might be seen how hard, cold, and confined was their system,—how like an iron cage was that which they called Liberty.

Too much of this. Look again at the picture, and observe how the aforesaid Anglo-Saxon energy is now trampling along the street, and raising a positive cloud of dust beneath its sturdy footsteps. For there the carpenters are building a new house, the frame of which was hewn and fitted in England, of English oak, and sent hither on shipboard; and here a black-smith makes huge clang and clatter on his anvil, shaping out tools and weapons; and yonder a wheelwright, who boasts himself a London workman, regularly bred to his handicraft, is fashioning a set of wagon-wheels, the track of which shall soon be visible. The wild forest is shrinking back; the street has lost the aromatic odor of the pine-trees, and of the sweet-fern that grew beneath them. The tender and modest wild-flowers, those gentle children of savage nature that grew pale beneath the ever-brooding shade, have shrunk away and disappeared, like stars that vanish in the breadth of light. Gardens are fenced in, and display pumpkin-beds and rows of cabbages and beans; and, though the governor and the minister both view them with a disapproving eye, plants of broad-leaved tobacco, which the cultivators are enjoined to use privily, or not all. No wolf, for a year past, has been heard to bark, or known to range among the dwellings, except that single one, whose grisly head, with a plash of blood beneath it, is now affixed to the portal of the meeting-house. The partridge has ceased to run across the too-frequented path. Of all the wild life that used to throng here, only the Indians still come into the settlement, bringing the skins of beaver and otter, bear and elk, which they sell to Endicott for the wares of England. And there is little John Massey, the son of Jeffry Massey and first-born of Naumkeag, playing beside his father's threshold, a child of six or seven years old. Which is the better grown infant,—the town or the boy?

The red men have become aware that the street is no longer free to them, save by the sufferance and permission of the settlers. Often, to impress them with an awe of English power, there is a muster and training of the town-forces, and a stately march of the mail-clad band, like this which we now see advancing up the street. There they come, fifty of them or more; all with their iron breastplates and steel caps well burnished, and glimmering bravely against the sun; their ponderous muskets on their shoulders, their bandoliers about their waists, their lighted matches in their hands, and the drum and fife playing cheerily before them. See! do they not step like martial men? Do they not manœuvre like soldiers who have seen stricken fields? And well they may; for this band is composed of precisely such materials as those with which Cromwell is preparing to beat down the strength of a kingdom; and his famous regiment of Ironsides might be recruited from just such men. In everything at this period, New England was the essential spirit and flower of that which was about to become uppermost in the mother-country. Many a bold and wise man lost the fame which would have accrued to him in English history, by crossing the Atlantic with our forefathers. Many a valiant captain, who might have been foremost at Marston Moor or Naseby, exhausted his martial ardor in the command of a log-built fortress, like that which you observe on the gently rising ground at the right of the pathway,—its banner fluttering in the breeze, and the culverins and sakers showing their deadly muzzles over the rampart.

A multitude of people were now thronging to New England: some, because the ancient and ponderous framework of Church and State threatened to crumble down upon their heads; others, because they despaired of such a downfall. Among those who came to Naumkeag were men of history and legend, whose feet leave a track of brightness along any pathway which they have trodden. You shall behold their life-like images—their spectres, if you choose so to call them—passing, encountering with a familiar nod, stopping to converse together, praying, bearing weapons, laboring, or resting from their labors, in the Main Street. Here, now, comes Hugh Peters, an earnest, restless man, walking swiftly, as being impelled by that fiery activity of nature which shall hereafter thrust him into the conflict of dangerous affairs, make him the chaplain and counsellor of Cromwell, and finally bring him to a bloody end. He pauses, by the meeting-house, to exchange a greeting with Roger Williams, whose face indicates, methinks, a gentler spirit, kinder and more expansive, than that of Peters; yet not less active for what he discerns to be the will of God, or the welfare of mankind. And look! here is a guest for Endicott, coming forth out of the forest, through which he has been journeying from Boston, and which, with its rude branches, has caught hold of his attire, and has wet his feet with its swamps and streams. Still there is something in his mild and venerable, though not aged presence—a propriety, an equilibrium, in Governor Winthrop's nature— that causes the disarray of his costume to be unnoticed, and gives us the same impression as if he were clad in such grave and rich attire as we may suppose him to have worn in the Council Chamber of the colony. Is not this characteristic wonderfully perceptible in our spectral representative of his person? But what dignitary is this crossing from the other side to greet the governor? A stately personage, in a dark velvet cloak, with a hoary beard, and a gold chain across his breast; he has the authoritative port of one who has filled the highest civic station in the first of cities. Of all men in the world, we should least expect to meet the Lord Mayor of London—as Sir Richard Saltonstall has been, once and again—in a forest-bordered settlement of the western wilderness.

Farther down the street, we see Emanuel Downing, a grave and worthy citizen, with his son George, a stripling who has a career before him; his shrewd and quick capacity and pliant conscience shall not only exalt him high, but secure him from a downfall. Here is another figure, on whose characteristic make and expressive action I will stake the credit of my pictorial puppet-show. Have you not already detected a quaint, sly humor in that face,—an eccentricity in the manner,—a certain indescribable waywardness,—all the marks, in short, of an original man, unmistakably impressed, yet kept down by a sense of clerical restraint? That is Nathaniel Ward, the minister of Ipswich, but better remembered as the simple cobbler of Agawam. He hammered his sole so faithfully, and stitched his upper-leather so well, that the shoe is hardly yet worn out, though thrown aside for some two centuries past. And next, among the Puritans and Roundheads, we observe the very model of a Cavalier, with the curling lovelock, the fantastically trimmed beard, the embroidery, the ornamented rapier, the gilded dagger, and all other foppishnesses that distinguished the wild gallants who rode headlong to their overthrow in the cause of King Charles. This is Morton of Merry Mount, who has come hither to hold a council with Endicott, but will shortly be his prisoner. Yonder pale, decaying figure of a white-robed woman, who glides slowly along the street, is the Lady Arabella, looking for her own grave in the virgin soil. That other female form, who seems to be talking—we might almost say preaching or expounding—in the centre of a group of profoundly attentive auditors, is Ann Hutchinson. And here comes Vane—

"But, my dear sir," interrupts the same gentleman who before questioned the showman's genealogical accuracy, "allow me to observe that these historical personages could not possibly have met together in the Main Street. They might, and probably did, all visit our old town, at one time or another, but not simultaneously; and you have fallen into anachronisms that I positively shudder to think of!"

"The fellow," adds the scarcely civil critic, "has learned a bead-roll of historic names, whom he lugs into his pictorial puppet-show, as he calls it, helter-skelter, without caring whether they were contemporaries or not,—and sets them all by the ears together. But was there ever such a fund of impudence? To hear his running commentary, you would suppose that these miserable slips of painted pasteboard, with hardly the remotest outlines of the human figure, had all the character and expression of Michael Angelo's pictures. Well! go on, sir!"

"Sir, you break the illusion of the scene," mildly remonstrates the showman.

"Illusion! What illusion?" rejoins the critic, with a contemptuous snort. "On the word of a gentleman, I see nothing illusive in the wretchedly bedaubed sheet of canvas that forms your background, or in these pasteboard slips that hitch and jerk along the front. The only illusion, permit me to say, is in the puppet-showman's tongue,—and that but a wretched one, into the bargain!"

"We public men," replies the showman, meekly, "must lay our account, sometimes, to meet an uncandid severity of criticism. But—merely for your own pleasure, sir—let me entreat you to take another point of view. Sit farther back, by that young lady, in whose face I have watched the reflection of every changing scene; only oblige me by sitting there; and, take my word for it, the slips of pasteboard shall assume spiritual life, and the bedaubed canvas become an airy and changeable reflex of what it purports to represent."

"I know better," retorts the critic, settling himself in his seat, with sullen but self-complacent immovableness. "And, as for my own pleasure, I shall best consult it by remaining precisely where I am."

The showman bows, and waves his hand; and, at the signal, as if time and vicissitude had been awaiting his permission to move onward, the mimic street becomes alive again.

Years have rolled over our scene, and converted the forest-track into a dusty thoroughfare, which being intersected with lanes and cross-paths, may fairly be designated as the Main Street. On the ground-sites of many of the log-built sheds, into which the first settlers crept for shelter, houses of quaint architecture have now risen. These later edifices are built, as you see, in one generally accordant style, though with such subordinate variety as keeps the beholder's curiosity excited, and causes each structure, like its owner's character, to produce its own peculiar impression. Most of them have one huge chimney in the center, with flues so vast that it must have been easy for the witches to fly out of them, as they were wont to do, when bound on an aerial visit to the Black Man in the forest. Around this great chimney the wooden house clusters itself in a whole community of gable-ends, each ascending into its own separate peak; the second story, with its lattice windows, projecting over the first; and the door, which is perhaps arched, provided on the outside with an iron hammer, wherewith the visitor's hand may give a thundering rat-a-tat. The timber framework of these houses, as compared with those of recent date, is like the skeleton of an old giant, beside the frail bones of a modern man of fashion. Many of them, by the vast strength and soundness of their oaken substance, have been preserved through a length of time which would have tried the stability of brick and stone; so that, in all the progressive decay and continual reconstruction of the street, down to our own days, we shall still behold these old edifices occupying their long-accustomed sites. For instance, on the upper corner of that green lane, which shall hereafter be North Street, we see the Curwen House, newly built, with the carpenters still at work on the roof nailing down the last sheaf of shingles. On the lower corner stands another dwelling, —destined, at some period of its existence, to be the abode of an unsuccessful alchemist,—which shall likewise survive to our own generation, and perhaps long outlive it. Thus, through the medium of these patriarchal edifices, we have now established a sort of kindred and hereditary acquaintance with the Main Street.

Great as is the transformation produced by a short term of years, each single day creeps through the Puritan settlement sluggishly enough. It shall pass before your eyes, condensed into the space of a few moments. The gray light of early morning is slowly diffusing itself over the scene; and the bellman, whose office it is to cry the hour at the street-corners, rings the last peal upon his hand-bell, and goes wearily homewards, with the owls, the bats, and other creatures of the night. Lattices are thrust back on their hinges, as if the town were opening its eyes, in the summer morning. Forth stumbles the still drowsy cowherd, with his horn; putting which to his lips, it emits a bellowing bray, impossible to be represented in the picture, but which reaches the pricked-up ears of every cow in the settlement, and tells her that the dewy pasture-hour is come. House after house awakes, and sends the smoke up curling from its chimney, like frosty breath from living nostrils; and as those white wreaths of smoke, though impregnated with earthy admixtures, climb skyward, so, from each dwelling, does the morning worship—its spiritual essence bearing up its human imperfection—find its way to the heavenly Father's throne.

The breakfast-hour being passed, the inhabitants do not, as usual, go to their fields or workshops, but remain within doors; or perhaps walk the street, with a grave sobriety, yet a disengaged and unburdened aspect, that belongs neither to a holiday nor a Sabbath. And, indeed, this passing day is neither, nor is it a common week-day, although partaking of all the three. It is the Thursday Lecture; an institution which New England has long ago relinquished, and almost forgotten, yet which it would have been better to retain, as bearing relations to both the spiritual and ordinary life, and bringing each acquainted with the other. The tokens of its observance, however, which here meet our eyes, are of rather a questionable cast. It is, in one sense, a day of public shame; the day on which transgressors, who have made themselves liable to the minor severities of the Puritan law, receive their reward of ignominy. At this very moment, the constable has bound an idle fellow to the whipping-post, and is giving him his deserts with a cat-o'-nine-tails. Ever since sunrise, Daniel Fairfield has been standing on the steps of the meeting-house, with a halter about his neck, which he is condemned to wear visibly throughout his lifetime; Dorothy Talby is chained to a post at the corner of Prison Lane, with the hot sun blazing on her matronly face, and all for no other offence than lifting her hand against her husband; while, through the bars of that great wooden cage, in the centre of the scene, we discern either a human being or a wild beast, or both in one, whom this public infamy causes to roar, and gnash his teeth, and shake the strong oaken bars, as if he would break forth, and tear in pieces the little children who have been peeping at him. Such are the profitable sights that serve the good people to while away the earlier part of lecture-day. Betimes in the forenoon, a traveller—the first traveller that has come hitherward this morning—rides slowly into the street on his patient steed. He seems a clergyman; and, as he draws near, we recognize the minister of Lynn, who was pre-engaged to lecture here, and has been revolving his discourse as he rode through the hoary wilderness. Behold, now, the whole town thronging into the meeting-house, mostly with such sombre visages that the sunshine becomes little better than a shadow when it falls upon them. There go the Thirteen Men, grim ruler of a grim community. There goes John Massey, the first town-born child, now a youth of twenty, whose eye wanders with peculiar interest towards that buxom damsel who comes up the steps at the same instant. There hobbles Goody Foster, a sour and bitter old beldam, looking as if she went to curse and not to pray, and whom many of her neighbors suspect of taking an occasional airing on a broomstick. There, too, slinking shamefacedly in, you observe that same poor do-nothing and good-for-nothing whom we saw castigated just now at the whipping-post. Last of all, there goes the tithing-man, lugging in a couple of small boys, whom he has caught at play beneath God's blessed sunshine, in a back lane. What native of Naumkeag, whose recollections go back more than thirty years, does not still shudder at that dark ogre of his infancy, who perhaps had long ceased to have an actual existence, but still lived in his childish belief, in a horrible idea, and in the nurse's threat as the Tidy Man!

It will be hardly worth our while to wait two, or it may be three, turnings of the hour-glass, for the conclusion of the lecture. Therefore, by my control over light and darkness, I cause the dusk, and then the starless night, to brood over the street; and summon forth again the bellman, with his lantern casting a gleam about his footsteps, to pace wearily from corner to corner, and shout drowsily the hour to drowsy or dreaming ears. Happy are we, if for nothing else, yet because we did not live in those days. In truth, when the first novelty and stir of spirit had subsided,—when the new settlement, between the forest-border and the sea, had become actually a little town,—

its daily life must have trudged onward with hardly anything
to diversify and enliven it, while also its rigidity could not
fail to cause miserable distortions of the moral nature. Such
a life was sinister to the intellect, and sinister to the heart;
especially when one generation had bequeathed its religious
gloom, and the counterfeit of its religious ardor, to the next;
for these characteristics, as was inevitable, assumed the form
both of hypocrisy and exaggeration, by being inherited from
the example and precept of other human beings, and not from
an original and spiritual source. The sons and grandchildren
of the first settlers were a race of lower and narrower souls
than their progenitors had been. The latter were stern, severe,
intolerant, but not superstitious, not even fanatical; and endowed, if any men of that age were, with a far-seeing worldly
sagacity. But it was impossible for the succeeding race to
grow up, in heaven's freedom, beneath the discipline which
their gloomy energy of character had established; nor, it may
be, have we even yet thrown off all the unfavorable influences,
which, among many good ones, were bequeathed to us by our
Puritan forefathers. Let us thank God for having given us
such ancestors; and let each successive generation thank Him,
not less fervently, for being one step further from them in
the march of ages.

"What is all this?" cries the critic. "A sermon? If so, it is not
in the bill."

"Very true," replies the showman; "and I ask pardon of the
audience."

Look now at the street, and observe a strange people entering it. Their garments are torn and disordered, their faces
haggard, their figures emaciated; for they have made their
way hither through pathless deserts, suffering hunger and hardship, with no other shelter than a hollow tree, the lair of a
wild beast, or an Indian wigwam. Nor, in the most inhospitable and dangerous of such lodging-places, was there half the
peril that awaits them in this thoroughfare of Christian men,
with those secure dwellings and warm hearths on either side
of it, and yonder meeting-house as the central object of the

scene. These wanderers have received from Heaven a gift that, in all epochs of the world, has brought with it the penalties of mortal suffering and persecution, scorn, enmity, and death itself,—a gift that, thus terrible to its possessors, has ever been most hateful to all other men, since its very existence seems to threaten the overthrow of whatever else the toilsome ages have built up,—the gift of a new idea. You can discern it in them, illuminating their faces—their whole persons, indeed, however earthly and cloddish—with a light that inevitably shines through, and makes the startled community aware that these men are not as they themselves are,—not brethren nor neighbors of their thought. Forthwith, it is as if an earthquake rumbled through the town, making its vibrations felt at every hearthstone, and especially causing the spire of the meeting-house to totter. The Quakers have come. We are in peril! See! they trample upon our wise and well-established laws in the person of our chief magistrate; for Governor Endicott is passing, now an aged man, and dignified with long habits of authority,—and not one of the irreverent vagabonds has moved his hat. Did you note the ominous frown of the white-bearded Puritan governor, as he turned himself about, and, in his anger, half uplifted the staff that has become a needful support to his old age? Here comes old Mr. Norris, our venerable minister. Will they doff their hats, and pay reverence to him? No: their hats stick fast to their ungracious heads, as if they grew there; and—impious varlets that they are, and worse than the heathen Indians!—they eye our reverend pastor with a peculiar scorn, distrust, unbelief, and utter denial of his sanctified pretensions, of which he himself immediately becomes conscious; the more bitterly conscious, as he never knew nor dreamed of the like before.

But look yonder! Can we believe our eyes? A Quaker woman, clad in sackcloth, and with ashes on her head, has mounted the steps of the meeting-house. She addresses the people in a wild, shrill voice,—wild and shrill it must be to suit such a figure,—which makes them tremble and turn pale, although they crowd open-mouthed to hear her. She is bold against established authority, she denounces the priest and his steeple-house. Many of her hearers are appalled; some weep; and others listen with a rapt attention, as if a living truth had now, for the first time, forced its way through the crust of habit, reached their hearts, and awakened them to life. This matter must be looked to; else we have brought our faith across the seas with us in vain; and it had been better that the old forest were still standing here, waving its tangled boughs and murmuring to the sky out of its desolate recesses, instead of this goodly street, if such blasphemies be spoken in it.

So thought the old Puritans. What was their mode of action may be partly judged from the spectacles which now pass before your eyes. Joshua Buffum is standing in the pillory. Cassandra Southwick is led to prison. And there a woman,—it is Ann Coleman,—naked from the waist upward, and bound to the tail of a cart, is dragged through the Main Street at the pace of a brisk walk, while the constable follows with a whip of knotted cords. A strong-armed fellow is that constable; and each time that he flourishes his lash in the air, you see a frown wrinkling and twisting his brow, and, at the same instant, a smile upon his lips. He loves his business, faithful officer that he is, and puts his soul into every stroke, zealous to fulfil the injunction of Major Hawthorne's warrant, in the spirit and to the letter. There came down a stroke that has drawn blood! Ten such stripes are to be given in Salem, ten in Boston, and ten in Dedham; and, with those thirty stripes of blood upon her, she is to be driven into the forest. The crimson trail goes wavering along the Main Street; but Heaven grant that, as the rain of so many years has wept upon it, time after time, and washed it all away, so there may have been a dew of mercy to cleanse this cruel blood-stain out of the record of the persecutor's life!

Pass on, thou spectral constable, and betake thee to thine own place of torment. Meanwhile, by the silent operation of the mechanism behind the scenes, a considerable space of time would seem to have lapsed over the street. The older dwellings now begin to look weather-beaten, through the effect of the many eastern storms that have moistened their unpainted shingles and clapboards, for not less than forty years. Such is the age we would assign to the town, judging by the aspect of John Massey, the first town-born child, whom his neighbors now call Goodman Massey, and whom we see yonder, a grave, almost autumnal-looking man, with children of his own about him. To the patriarchs of the settlement, no doubt, the Main Street is still but an affair of yesterday, hardly more antique, even if destined to be more permanent, than a path shovelled through the snow. But to the middle-aged and elderly men who came hither in childhood or early youth, it presents the aspect of a long and well-established work, on which they have expended the strength and ardor of their life. And the younger people, native to the street, whose earliest recollections are of creeping over the paternal threshold, and rolling on the grassy margin of the track, look at it as one of the perdurable things of our mortal state,—as old as the hills of the great pasture, or the headland at the harbor's mouth. Their fathers and grandsires tell them how, within a few years past, the forest stood here with but a lonely track beneath its tangled shade. Vain legend! They cannot make it true and read to their conceptions. With them, moreover, the Main Street is a street indeed, worthy to hold its way with the thronged and stately avenues of cities beyond the sea. The old Puritans tell them of the crowds that hurry along Cheapside and Fleet Street and the Strand, and of the rush of tumultuous life at Temple Bar. They describe London Bridge, itself a street, with a row of houses on each side. They speak of the vast structure of the Tower, and the solemn grandeur of Westminster Abbey. The children listen, and still inquire if the streets of London are longer and broader than the one before their father's door; if the Tower is bigger than the jail in Prison Lane; if the old Abbey will hold a larger congregation than our meeting-house. Nothing impresses them, except their own experience.

It seems all a fable, too, that wolves have ever prowled here; and not less so that the Squaw Sachem, and the Sagamore her son, once ruled over this region, and treated as sovereign potentates with the English settlers, then so few and storm-beaten, now so powerful. There stand some school-boys, you observe, in a little group around a drunken Indian, himself a prince of the Squaw Sachem's lineage. He brought hither some beaver-skins for sale, and has already swallowed the larger portion of their price, in deadly draughts of fire-water. Is there not a touch of pathos in that picture? and does it not go far towards telling the whole story of the vast growth and prosperity of one race, and the fated decay of another?—the children of the stranger making game of the great Squaw Sachem's grandson!

But the whole race of red men have not vanished with that wild princess and her posterity. This march of soldiers along the street betokens the breaking out of King Philip's war; and these young men, the flower of Essex, are on their way to defend the villages on the Connecticut; where, at Bloody Brook, a terrible blow shall be smitten, and hardly one of that gallant band be left alive. And there, at that stately mansion, with its three peaks in front, and its two little peaked towers, one on either side of the door, we see brave Captain Gardner issuing forth, clad in his embroidered buff-coat, and his plumed cap upon his head. His trusty sword, in its steel scabbard, strikes clanking on the doorstep. See how the people throng to their doors and windows, as the cavalier rides past, reining his mettled steed so gallantly, and looking so like the very soul and emblem of martial achievement,—destined, too, to meet a warrior's fate, at the desperate assault on the fortress of the Narragansetts!

"The mettled steel looks like a pig," interrupts the critic, "and Captain Gardner himself like the Devil, though a very tame one, and on a most diminutive scale."

"Sir, sir!" cries the persecuted showman, losing all patience, —for, indeed, he had particularly prided himself on these figures of Captain Gardner and his horse,—"I see that there is no hope of pleasing you. Pray, sir, do me the favor to take back your money, and withdraw!"

"Not I!" answers the unconscionable critic. "I am just beginning to get interested in the matter. Come! turn your crank, and grind out a few more of these fooleries!"

The showman rubs his brow impulsively, whisks the little rod with which he points out the notabilities of the scene, but, finally, with the inevitable acquiescence of all public servants, resumes his composure and goes on.

Pass onward, onward, Time! Build up new houses here, and tear down thy works of yesterday, that have already the rusty moss upon them! Summon forth the minister to the abode of the young maiden, and bid him unite her to the joyful bridegroom! Let the youthful parents carry their first-born to the meeting-house, to receive the baptismal rite! Knock at the door, whence the sable line of the funeral is next to issue! Provide other successive generations of men, to trade, talk, quarrel, or walk in friendly intercourse along the street, as their fathers did before them! Do all thy daily and accustomed business, Father Time, in this thoroughfare, which thy footsteps, for so many years, have now made dusty! But here, at last, thou leadest along a procession which, once witnessed, shall appear no more, and be remembered only as a hideous dream of thine, or a frenzy of thy old brain.

"Turn your crank, I say," bellows the remorseless critic, "and grind it out, whatever it be, without further preface!"

The showman deems it best to comply.

Then, here comes the worshipful Captain Curwen, sheriff of Essex, on horseback, at the head of an armed guard, escorting a company of condemned prisoners from the jail to their place of execution on Gallows Hill. The witches! There is no mistaking them! The witches! As they approach up Prison Lane, and turn into the Main Street, let us watch their faces, as if we made a part of the pale crowd that presses so eagerly about them, yet shrinks back with such shuddering dread, leaving an open passage betwixt a dense throng on either side. Listen to what the people say.

There is old George Jacobs, known hereabouts, these sixty years, as a man whom we thought upright in all his way of life, quiet, blameless, a good husband before his pious wife

was summoned from the evil to come, and a good father to
the children whom she left him. Ah! but when that blessed
woman went to heaven, George Jacobs's heart was empty, his
hearth lonely, his life broken up; his children were married,
and betook themselves to habitations of their own; and Satan,
in his wanderings up and down, beheld this forlorn old man,
to whom life was a sameness and a weariness, and found the
way to tempt him. So the miserable sinner was prevailed with
to mount into the air, and career among the clouds; and he is
proved to have been present at a witch-meeting as far off as
Falmouth, on the very same night that his next neighbors saw
him, with his rheumatic stoop, going in at his own door. There
is John Willard, too; an honest man we thought him, and so
shrewd and active in his business, so practical, so intent on
every-day affairs, so constant at his little place of trade, where
he bartered English goods for Indian corn and all kinds of
country produce! How could such a man find time, or what
could put it into his mind, to leave his proper calling, and
become a wizard? It is a mystery, unless the Black Man
tempted him with great heaps of gold. See that aged couple,—
a sad sight, truly,—John Proctor, and his wife Elizabeth. If
there were two old people in all the county of Essex who
seemed to have led a true Christian life, and to be treading
hopefully the little remnant of their earthly path, it was this
very pair. Yet have we heard it sworn, to the satisfaction of the
worshipful Chief-Justice Sewell, and all the court and jury,
that Proctor and his wife have shown their withered faces at
children's bedsides, mocking, making mouths, and affrighting
the poor little innocents in the night-time. They, or their
spectral appearances, have stuck pins into the Afflicted Ones,
and thrown them into deadly fainting-fits with a touch or but
a look. And, while we supposed the old man to be reading
the Bible to his old wife,—she meanwhile knitting in the
chimney-corner,—the pair of hoary reprobates have whisked
up the chimney, both on one broomstick, and flown away to a
witch-communion, far into the depths of the chill, dark forest.
How foolish! Were it only for fear of rheumatic pains in their
old bones, they had better have stayed at home. But away they

went; and the laughter of their decayed, cackling voices has been heard at midnight, aloft in the air. Now, in the sunny noontide, as they go tottering to the gallows, it is the Devil's turn to laugh.

Behind these two,—who help one another along, and seem to be comforting and encouraging each other, in a manner truly pitiful, if it were not a sin to pity the old witch and wizard,—behind them comes a woman, with a dark proud face that has been beautiful, and a figure that is still majestic. Do you know her? It is Martha Carrier, whom the Devil found in a humble cottage, and looked into her discontented heart, and saw pride there, and tempted her with his promise that she should be Queen of Hell. And now, with that lofty demeanor, she is passing to her kingdom, and, by her unquenchable pride, transforms this escort of shame into a triumphal procession, that shall attend her to the gates of her infernal palace, and seat her upon the fiery throne. Within this hour, she shall assume her royal dignity.

Last of the miserable train comes a man clad in black, of small stature and a dark complexion, with a clerical band about his neck. Many a time, in the years gone by, that face has been uplifted heavenward from the pulpit of the East Meeting-House, when the Rev. Mr. Burroughs seemed to worship God. What!—he? The holy man!—the learned!—the wise! How has the Devil tempted him? His fellow-criminals, for the most part, are obtuse, uncultivated creatures, some of them scarcely half-witted by nature, and others greatly decayed in their intellects through age. They were an easy prey for the destroyer. Not so with this George Burroughs, as we judge by the inward light which glows through his dark countenance, and, we might almost say, glorifies his figure, in spite of the soil and haggardness of long imprisonment,—in spite of the heavy shadow that must fall on him, while death is walking by his side. What bribe could Satan offer, rich enough to tempt and overcome this man? Alas! it may have been in the very strength of his high and searching intellect that the Tempter found the weakness which betrayed him. He yearned for knowledge; he went groping onward into a world of mystery; at first, as the witnesses have sworn, he summoned up the ghosts of his two dead wives, and talked with them of matters beyond the grave; and, when their responses failed to satisfy the intense and sinful craving of his spirit, he called on Satan, and was heard. Yet—to look at him—who, that had not known the proof, could believe him guilty? Who would not say, while we see him offering comfort to the weak and aged partners of his horrible crime,—while we hear his ejaculations of prayer, that seem to bubble up out of the depths of his heart, and fly heavenward, unawares,—while we behold a radiance brightening on his features as from the other world, which is but a few steps off,—who would not say, that, over the dusty track of the Main Street, a Christian saint is now going to a martyr's death? May not the Arch-Fiend have been too subtle for the court and jury, and betrayed them—laughing in his sleeve the while—into the awful error of pouring out sanctified blood as an acceptable sacrifice upon God's altar? Ah! no; for listen to wise Cotton Mather, who, as he sits there on his horse, speaks comfortably to the perplexed multitude, and tells them that all has been religiously and justly done, and that Satan's power shall this day receive its death-blow in New England.

Heaven grant it be so!—the great scholar must be right; so lead the poor creatures to their death! Do you see that group of children and half-grown girls, and, among them, an old, hag-like Indian Woman, Tituba by name? Those are the Afflicted Ones. Behold, at this very instant, a proof of Satan's power and malice! Mercy Parris, the minister's daughter, has been smitten by a flash of Martha Carrier's eye, and falls down in the street, writhing with horrible spasms and foaming at the mouth, like the possessed one spoken of in Scripture. Hurry on the accursed witches to the gallows, ere they do more michief!—ere they fling out their withered arms, and scatter pestilence by handfuls among the crowd!—ere, as their parting legacy, they cast a blight over the land, so that henceforth it may bear no fruit nor blade of grass, and be fit for nothing but a sepulchre for their unhallowed carcasses! So on they go; and old George Jacobs has stumbled, by reason of his infirmity; but Goodman Proctor and his wife lean on one another, and walk at a reasonably steady pace, considering their age. Mr. Burroughs seems to administer counsel to Martha Carrier, whose face and mien, methinks, are milder and humbler than they were. Among the multitude, meanwhile, there is horror, fear, and distrust; and friend looks askance at friend, and the husband at his wife, and the wife at him, and even the mother at her little child; as if, in every creature that God has made, they suspected a witch, or dreaded an accuser. Never, never again, whether in this or any other shape, may Universal Madness riot in the Main Street!

I perceive in your eyes, my indulgent spectators, the criticism with which you are too kind to utter. These scenes, you think, are all too sombre. So, indeed, they are; but the blame must rest on the sombre spirit of our forefathers, who wove their web of life with hardly a single thread of rose-color or gold, and not on me, who have a tropic-love of sunshine, and would gladly gild all the world with it, if I knew where to find so much. That you may believe me, I will exhibit one of the only class of scenes, so far as my investigation has taught me, in which our ancestors were wont to steep their tough old hearts in wine and strong drink, and indulge an outbreak of grisly jollity.

Here it comes, out of the same house whence we saw brave Captain Gardner go forth to the wars. What! A coffin, borne on men's shoulders, and six aged gentlemen as pall-bearers, and a long train of mourners, with black gloves and black hat-bands, and everything black, save a white handkerchief in each mourner's hand, to wipe away his tears withal. Now, my kind patrons, you are angry with me. You were bidden to a bridal-dance, and find yourselves walking in a funeral procession. Even so; but look back through all the social customs of New England, in the first century of her existence, and read all her traits of character; and if you find one occasion, other than a funeral feast, where jollity was sanctioned by universal practice. I will set fire to my puppet-show without

another word. These are the obsequies of old Governor Bradstreet, the patriarch and survivor of the first settlers, who,
having intermarried with the Widow Gardner, is now
resting from his labors, at the great age of ninety-four.
The white-bearded corpse, which was his spirit's earthly
garniture, now lies beneath yonder coffin-lid. Many a cask of
ale and cider is on tap, and many a draught of spiced wine
and aqua-vitæ has been quaffed. Else why should the bearers
stagger, as they tremulously uphold the coffin?—and the aged
pall-bearers, too, as they strive to walk solemnly beside it?—
and wherefore do the mourners tread on one another's heels?
—and why, if we may ask without offence, should the nose
of the Rev. Mr. Noyes, through which he has just been de-
livering the funeral discourse, glow, like a ruddy coal of fire?
Well, well, old friends! Pass on, with your burden of morality,
and lay it in the tomb with jolly hearts. People should be
permitted to enjoy themselves in their own fashion; every man
to his taste; but New England must have been a dismal abode
for the man of pleasure when the only boon-companion was
Death!

Under cover of a mist that has settled over the scene, a few
years flit by, and escape our notice. As the atmosphere becomes
transparent, we perceive a decrepit grandsire, hobbling along
the street. Do you recognize him? We saw him, first, as the
baby in Goodwife Massey's arms, when the primeval trees were
flinging their shadow over Roger Conant's cabin; we have seen
him, as the boy, the youth, the man, bearing his humble part
in all the successive scenes, and forming the index-finger
whereby to note the age of his coeval town. And here he is,
old Goodman Massey, taking his last walk,—often pausing,—
often leaning over his staff,—and calling to mind whose
dwelling stood at such and such a spot, and whose field or
garden occupied the site of those more recent houses. He can
render a reason for all the bends and deviations of the thoroughfare, which, in its flexible and plastic infancy, was
made to swerve aside from a straight line, in order to visit
every settler's door. The Main Street is still youthful; the
coeval man is in his latest age. Soon he will be gone, a patri-

arch of four-score, yet shall retain a sort of infantine life in our local history, as the first town-born child.

Behold here a change, wrought in the twinkling of an eye, like an incident in a tale of magic, even while your observation has been fixed upon the scene. The Main Street has vanished out of sight. In its stead appears a wintry waste of snow, with the sun just peeping over it, cold and bright, and tingeing the white expanse with the faintest and most ethereal rose-color. This is the Great Snow of 1717, famous for the mountain-drifts in which it buried the whole country. It would seem as if the street, the growth of which we have noted so attentively, following it from its first phase, as an Indian track, until it reached the dignity of sidewalks, were all at once obliterated, and resolved into a drearier pathlessness than when the forest covered it. The gigantic swells and billows of the snow have swept over each man's metes and bounds, and annihilated all the visible distinctions of human property. So that now the traces of former times and hitherto accomplished deeds being done away, mankind should be at liberty to enter on new paths, and guide themselves by other laws than heretofore; if, indeed, the race be not extinct, and it be worth our while to go on with the march of life, over the cold and desolate expanse that lies before us. It may be, however, that matters are not so desperate as they appear. That vast icicle, glittering so cheerlessly in the sunshine, must be the spire of the meeting-house, incrusted with frozen sleet. These great heaps, too, which we mistook for drifts, are houses, buried up to their eaves, and with their peaked roofs rounded by the depth of snow upon them. There, now, comes a gush of smoke from what I judge to be the chimney of the Ship Tavern; and another—another—and another—from the chimneys of other dwellings, where fireside comfort, domestic peace, the sports of children, and the quietude of age are living yet, in spite of the frozen crust above them.

But it is time to change the scene. Its dreary monotony shall not test your fortitude like one of our actual New England winters, which leaves so large a blank—so melancholy a death-spot—in lives so brief that they ought to be all summer-time.

Here, at least, I may claim to be ruler of the seasons. One turn of the crank shall melt away the snow from the Main Street, and show the trees in their full foliage, the rose-bushes in bloom, and a border of green grass along the sidewalk. There! But what! How! The scene will not move. A wire is broken. The street continues buried beneath the snow, and the fate of Herculaneum and Pompeii has its parallel in this catastrophe.

Alas! my kind and gentle audience, you know not the extent of your misfortune. The scenes to come were far better than the past. The street itself would have been more worthy of pictorial exhibition; the deeds of its inhabitants not less so. And how would your interest have deepened, as, passing out of the cold shadow of antiquity, in my long and weary course, I should arrive within the limits of man's memory, and, leading you at last into the sunshine of the present, should give a reflex of the very life that is flitting past us! Your own beauty, my fair townswomen, would have beamed upon you out of my scene. Not a gentleman that walks the street but should have beheld his own face and figure, his gait, the peculiar swing of his arm, and the coat that he put on yesterday. Then, too,—and it is what I chiefly regret,—I had expended a vast deal of light and brilliancy on a representation of the street in its whole length, from Buffum's Corner downward, on the night of the grand illumination for General Taylor's triumph. Lastly, I should have given the crank one other turn, and have brought out the future, showing you who shall walk the Main Street to-morrow, and, perchance, whose funeral shall pass through it!

But these, like most other human purposes, lie unaccomplished; and I have only further to say, that any lady or gentleman who may feel dissatisfied with the evening's entertainment shall receive back the admission fee at the door.

"Then give me mine," cries the critic, stretching out his palm. "I said that your exhibition would prove a humbug, and so it has turned out. So hand over my quarter!"

Prefaces

THE
OLD MANSE
THE AUTHOR MAKES THE READER
ACQUAINTED WITH HIS ABODE

Between two gateposts of rough-hewn stone (the gate itself having fallen from its hinges at some unknown epoch) we beheld the gray front of the old parsonage terminating the vista of an avenue of black ash-trees. It was now a twelvemonth since the funeral procession of the venerable clergyman, its last inhabitant, had turned from that gateway towards the village burying-ground. The wheel-track leading to the door, as well as the whole breadth of the avenue, was almost overgrown with grass, affording dainty mouthfuls to two or three vagrant cows and an old white horse who had his own living to pick up along the roadside. The glimmering shadows that lay half asleep between the door of the house and the public highway were a kind of spiritual medium, seen through which the edifice had not quite the aspect of belonging to the material world. Certainly it had little in common with those ordinary abodes which stand so imminent upon the road that every passer-by can thrust his head, as it were, into the domestic circle. From these quiet windows the figures of passing travelers looked too remote and dim to disturb the sense of privacy. In its near retirement and accessible seclusion it was the very spot for the residence of a clergyman,—a man not estranged from human life, yet enveloped in the midst of it with a veil woven of intermingled gloom and brightness.

It was worthy to have been one of the time-honored parsonages of England in which, through many generations, a succession of holy occupants pass from youth to age, and bequeath each an inheritance of sanctity to pervade the house and hover over it as with an atmosphere.

Nor, in truth, had the Old Manse ever been profaned by a lay occupant until that memorable summer afternoon when I entered it as my home. A priest had built it, a priest had succeeded to it; other priestly men from time to time had dwelt in it; and children born in its chambers had grown up to assume the priestly character. It was awful to reflect how many sermons must have been written there. The latest inhabitant alone—he by whose translation to Paradise the dwelling was left vacant—had penned nearly three thousand discourses, besides the better, if not the greater, number that gushed living from his lips. How often, no doubt, had he paced to and fro along the avenue, attuning his meditations to the sighs and gentle murmurs, and deep and solemn peals of the wind among the lofty tops of the trees! In that variety of natural utterances he could find something accordant with every passage of his sermon, were it of tenderness or reverential fear. The boughs over my head seemed shadowy with solemn thoughts as well as with rustling leaves. I took shame to myself for having been so long a writer of idle stories, and ventured to hope that wisdom would descend upon me with the falling leaves of the avenue, and that I should light upon an intellectual treasure in the Old Manse well worth those hoards of long-hidden gold which people seek for in moss-grown houses. Profound treatises of morality; a layman's unprofessional and therefore unprejudiced views of religion; histories (such as Bancroft might have written had he taken up his abode here as he once purposed) bright with picture, gleaming over a depth of philosophic thought,—these were the works that might fitly have flowed from such a retirement. In the humblest event I resolved at least to achieve a novel that should evolve some deep lesson and should possess physical substance enough to stand alone.

In furtherance of my design, and as if to leave me no

pretext for not fulfilling it, there was in the rear of the house
the most delightful little nook of a study that ever afforded its
snug seclusion to a scholar. It was here that Emerson wrote
Nature; for he was then an inhabitant of the Manse, and
used to watch the Assyrian dawn and Paphian sunset and
moonrise from the summit of our eastern hill. When I first
saw the room its walls were blackened with the smoke of
unnumbered years, and made still blacker by the grim prints
of Puritan ministers that hung around. These worthies looked
strangely like bad angels, or at least like men who had wrestled
so continually and so sternly with the devil that somewhat of
his sooty fierceness had been imparted to their own visages.
They had all vanished now, a cheerful coat of paint and
golden-tinted paper-hangings lighted up the small apartment;
while the shadow of a willow-tree that swept against the overhanging eaves attempered the cheery western sunshine. In place
of the grim prints there was the sweet and lovely head of one
of Raphael's Madonnas and two pleasant little pictures of
the Lake of Como. The only other decorations were a purple
vase of flowers, always fresh, and a bronze one containing
graceful ferns. My books (few, and by no means choice, for they
were chiefly such waifs as chance had thrown in my way)
stood in order about the room, seldom to be disturbed.

The study had three windows, set with little, old-fashioned
panes of glass, each with a crack across it. The two on the
western side looked, or rather peeped, between the willow
branches down into the orchard, with glimpses of the river
through the trees. The third, facing northward, commanded
a broader view of the river at a spot where its hitherto obscure
waters gleam forth into the light of history. It was at this window
that the clergyman who then dwelt in the Manse stood watching
the outbreak of a long and deadly struggle between two nations; he saw the irregular army of his parishioners on the
farther side of the river and the glittering line of the British
on the hither bank. He awaited in an agony of suspense the
rattle of the musketry. It came, and there needed but a gentle
wind to sweep the battle smoke around this quiet house.

Perhaps the reader, whom I cannot help considering as my

guest in the Old Manse and entitled to all courtesy in the way of sight-showing,—perhaps he will choose to take a nearer view of the memorable spot. We stand now on the river's brink. It may well be called the Concord, the river of peace and quietness; for it is certainly the most unexcitable and sluggish stream that ever loitered imperceptibly towards its eternity—the sea. Positively, I had lived three weeks beside it before it grew quite clear to my perception which way the current flowed. It never has a vivacious aspect except when a north-western breeze is vexing its surface on a sunshiny day. From the incurable indolence of its nature, the stream is happily incapable of becoming the slave of human ingenuity, as is the fate of so many a wild, free mountain torrent. While all things else are compelled to subserve some useful purpose, it idles its sluggish life away in lazy liberty, without turning a solitary spindle or affording even waterpower enough to grind the corn that grows upon its banks. The torpor of its movement allows it nowhere a bright, pebbly shore, nor so much as a narrow strip of glistening sand, in any part of its course. It slumbers between broad prairies, kissing the long meadow grass, and bathes the overhanging boughs of elder bushes and willows or the roots of elms and ash-trees and clumps of maples. Flags and rushes grow along its plashy shore; the yellow water-lily spreads its broad, flat leaves on the margin; and the fragrant white pond-lily abounds, generally selecting a position just so far from the river's brink that it cannot be grasped save at the hazard of plunging in.

It is a marvel whence this perfect flower derives its loveliness and perfume, springing as it does from the black mud over which the river sleeps, and where lurk the slimy eel and speckled frog and the mud turtle, whom continual washing cannot cleanse. It is the very same black mud out of which the yellow lily sucks its obscene life and noisome odor. Thus we see, too, in the world that some persons assimilate only what is ugly and evil from the same moral circumstances which supply good and beautiful results—the fragrance of celestial flowers—to the daily life of others.

The reader must not, from any testimony of mine, contract a dislike towards our slumberous stream. In the light of a calm and golden sunset it becomes lovely beyond expression; the more lovely for the quietude that so well accords with the hour, when even the wind, after blustering all day long, usually hushes itself to rest. Each tree and rock, and every blade of grass, is distinctly imaged, and, however unsightly in reality, assumes ideal beauty in the reflection. The minutest things of earth and the broad aspect of the firmament are pictured equally without effort and with the same felicity of success. All the sky glows downward at our feet; the rich clouds float through the unruffled bosom of the stream like heavenly thoughts through a peaceful heart. We will not, then, malign our river as gross and impure while it can glorify itself with so adequate a picture of the heaven that broods above it; or, if we remember its tawny hue and the muddiness of its bed, let it be a symbol that the earthliest human soul has an infinite spiritual capacity and may contain the better world within its depths. But, indeed, the same lesson might be drawn out of any mud puddle in the streets of a city; and, being taught us everywhere, it must be true.

Come, we have pursued a somewhat devious track in our walk to the battle-ground. Here we are, at the point where the river was crossed by the old bridge, the possession of which was the immediate object of the contest. On the hither side grow two or three elms, throwing a wide circumference of shade, but which must have been planted at some period within the three-score years and ten that have passed since the battle day. On the farther shore, overhung by a clump of elder-bushes, we discern the stone abutment of the bridge. Looking down into the river, I once discovered some heavy fragments of the timbers, all green with half a century's growth of water-moss; for during that length of time the tramp of horses and human footsteps have ceased along this ancient highway. The stream has here about the breadth of twenty strokes of a swimmer's arm,—a space not too wide when the bullets were whistling across. Old people who dwell hereabouts will point out the very spots on the western bank where our countrymen fell down and died; and on this side of the river an obelisk of granite has grown up from the soil that was fertilized with British blood. The monument, not more than twenty feet in height, is such as it befitted the inhabitants of a village to erect in illustration of a matter of local interest rather than what was suitable to commemorate an epoch of national history. Still, by the fathers of the village this famous deed was done; and their descendants might rightfully claim the privilege of building a memorial.

A humbler token of the fight, yet a more interesting one than the granite obelisk, may be seen close under the stone-wall which separates the battle-ground from the precincts of the parsonage. It is the grave—marked by a small, mossgrown fragment of stone at the head and another at the foot—the grave of two British soldiers who were slain in the skirmish, and have ever since slept peacefully where Zechariah Brown and Thomas Davis buried them. Soon was their warfare ended; a weary night march from Boston, a rattling volley of musketry across the river, and then these many years of rest. In the long procession of slain invaders who passed into eternity from the battle-fields of the revolution, these two nameless soldiers led the way.

Lowell, the poet, as we were once standing over this grave, told me a tradition in reference to one of the inhabitants below. The story has something deeply impressive, though its circumstances cannot altogether be reconciled with probability. A youth in the service of the clergyman happened to be chopping wood, that April morning, at the back door of the Manse, and when the noise of battle rang from side to side of the bridge he hastened across the intervening field to see what might be going forward. It is rather strange, by the way, that this lad should have been so diligently at work when the whole population of town and country were startled out of their customary business by the advance of the British troops. Be that as it might, the tradition says that the lad now left his task and hurried to the battle-field with the axe still in his hand. The British had by this time retreated, the Americans were in pursuit; and the late scene of strife was thus deserted by both parties. Two soldiers lay on the ground—one was a corpse; but, as the young New Englander drew nigh, the other Briton raised himself painfully upon his hands and knees and gave a ghastly stare into his face. The boy,—it must have been a nervous impulse, without purpose, without thought, and betokening a sensitive and impressible nature rather than a hardened one,—the boy uplifted his axe and dealt the wounded soldier a fierce and fatal blow upon the head.

I could wish that the grave might be opened; for I would fain know whether either of the skeleton soldiers has the mark of an axe in his skull. The story comes home to me like truth. Oftentimes, as an intellectual and moral exercise, I have sought to follow that poor youth through his subsequent career, and observe how his soul was tortured by the blood-stain, contracted as it had been before the long custom of war had robbed human life of its sanctity, and while it still seemed murderous to slay a brother-man. This one circumstance has borne more fruit for me than all that history tells us of the fight.

Many strangers come in the summer time to view the battle-ground. For my own part, I have never found my imagination much excited by this or any other scene of historic celebrity; nor would the placid margin of the river have lost any of its charm for me had men never fought and died there. There is a wilder interest in the tract of land—perhaps a hundred yards in breadth—which extends between the battle-field and the northern face of our Old Manse, with its contiguous avenue and orchard. Here, in some unknown age, before the white man came, stood an Indian village, convenient to the river, whence its inhabitants must have drawn so large a part of their subsistence. The site is identified by the spear and arrowheads, the chisels, and other implements of war, labor, and the chase, which the plough turns up from the soil. You see a splinter of stone, half hidden beneath a sod; it looks like nothing worthy of note; but, if you have faith enough to pick it up, behold a relic! Thoreau, who has a strange faculty of finding what the Indians have left behind them, first set me on the search; and I afterwards enriched myself with some very perfect specimens, so rudely wrought that it seemed almost as if chance had fashioned them. Their great charm consists in this rudeness and in the individuality of each article, so different from the productions of civilized machinery, which shapes everything on one pattern. There is exquisite delight, too, in picking up for one's self an arrowhead that was dropped centuries ago and has never been handled since, and which we thus receive directly from the hand of the red hunter, who purposed to shoot it at his game or at an enemy. Such an incident builds up again the Indian village and its encircling forest, and recalls to life the painted chiefs and warriors, the squaws at their household toil, and the children sporting among the wigwams, while the little windrocked pappoose swings from the branch of the tree. It can hardly be told whether it is a joy or a pain, after such a momentary vision, to gaze around in the broad daylight of reality and see stone fences, white houses, potato fields, and men doggedly hoeing in their shirt-sleeves and homespun pantaloons. But this is nonsense. The Old Manse is better than a thousand wigwams.

The Old Manse! We had almost forgotten it, but will return thither through the orchard. This was set out by the last clergyman, in the decline of his life, when the neighbors laughed at the hoary-headed man for planting trees from which he could have no prospect of gathering fruit. Even had that been the case, there was only so much the better motive for planting them, in the pure and unselfish hope of benefiting his successors,—an end so seldom achieved by more ambitious efforts. But the old minister, before reaching his patriarchal age of ninety, ate the apples from his orchard during many years, and added silver and gold to his annual stipend by disposing of the superfluity. It is pleasant to think of him walking among the trees in the quiet afternoons of early autumn and picking up here and there a windfall, while he observes how heavily the branches are weighed down, and computes the number of empty flour barrels that will be filled by their burden. He loved each tree, doubtless, as if it had been his own child. An orchard has a relation to mankind, and readily connects itself with matters of the heart. The trees possess a domestic character; they have lost the wild nature of their forest kindred, and have grown humanized by receiving the care of man as well as by contributing to his wants. There is so much individuality of character, too, among apple-trees that it gives them an additional claim to be the objects of human interest. One is harsh and crabbed in its manifestations; another gives us fruit as mild as charity. One is churlish and illiberal, evidently grudging the few apples that it bears; another exhausts itself in free-hearted benevolence. The variety of grotesque shapes into which apple-trees contort themselves has its effect on those who get acquainted with them: they stretch out their crooked branches, and take such hold of the imagination that we remember them as humorists and odd-fellows. And what is more melancholy than the old apple-trees that linger about the spot where once stood a homestead, but where there is now only a ruined chimney rising out of a grassy and weed-grown cellar? They offer their fruit to every wayfarer,—apples that are bitter sweet with the moral of Time's vicissitude.

I have met with no other such pleasant trouble in the world as that of finding myself, with only the two or three mouths which it was my privilege to feed, the sole inheritor of the old clergyman's wealth of fruits. Throughout the summer there were cherries and currants; and then came autumn, with his immense burden of apples, dropping them continually from his overladen shoulders as he trudged along. In the stillest afternoon, if I listened, the thump of a great apple was audible, falling without a breath of wind, from the mere necessity of perfect ripeness. And, besides, there were pear-trees, that flung down bushels upon bushels of heavy pears; and peach-trees, which, in a good year, tormented me with peaches, neither to be eaten nor kept, nor, without labor and perplexity, to be given away. The idea of an infinite generosity and exhaustless bounty on the part of our Mother Nature was well worth obtaining through such cares as these. That feeling can be enjoyed in perfection only by the natives of summer islands, where the bread-fruit, the cocoa, the palm, and the orange grow spontaneously and hold forth the ever-ready meal; but likewise almost as well by a man long habituated to city life, who plunges into such a solitude as that of the Old Manse, where he plucks the fruit of trees that he did not plant, and which therefore, to my heterodox taste, bear the closest resemblance to those that grew in Eden. It has been an apothegm these five thousand years, that toil sweetens the bread it earns. For my part (speaking from hard experience, acquired while belaboring the rugged furrows of Brook Farm), I relish best the free gifts of Providence.

Not that it can be disputed that the light toil requisite to cultivate a moderately-sized garden imparts such zest to kitchen vegetables as is never found in those of the market gardener. Childless men, if they would know something of the bliss of paternity, should plant a seed,—be it squash, bean, Indian corn, or perhaps a mere flower or worthless weed,—should plant it with their own hands, and nurse it from infancy to maturity altogether by their own care. If there be not too many of them, each individual plant becomes an object of separate interest. My garden, that skirted the avenue of the Manse, was of precisely the right extent. An hour or two of morning labor was all that it required. But I used to visit and revisit it a dozen times a day, and stand in deep contemplation over my vegetable progeny with a love that nobody could share or conceive of who had never taken part in the process of creation. It was one of the most bewitching sights in the world to observe a hill of beans thrusting aside the soil, or a row of early peas just peeping forth sufficiently to trace a line of delicate green. Later in the season the humming-birds were attracted by the blossoms of a peculiar variety of bean; and they were a joy to me, those little spiritual visitants, for deigning to sip airy food out of my nectar cups. Multitudes of bees used to bury themselves in the yellow blossoms of the summer squashes. This, too, was a deep satisfaction, although when they had laden themselves with sweets they flew away to some unknown hive, which would give back nothing in requital of what my garden had contributed. But I was glad thus to fling a benefaction upon the passing breeze with the certainty that somebody must profit by it, and that there would be a little more honey in the world to allay the sourness and bitterness which mankind is always complaining of. Yes, indeed; my life was the sweeter for that honey.

Speaking of summer squashes, I must say a word of their beautiful and varied forms. They presented an endless diversity of urns and vases, shallow or deep, scalloped or plain, moulded in patterns which a sculptor would do well to copy, since Art has never invented anything more graceful. A hundred squashes in the garden were worthy, in my eyes at least, of being rendered indestructible in marble. If ever Providence (but I know it never will) should assign me a superfluity of gold, part of it shall be expended for a service of plate, or most delicate porcelain, to be wrought into the shapes of summer squashes gathered from vines which I will plant with my own hands. As dishes for containing vegetables they would be peculiarly appropriate.

But not merely the squeamish love of the beautiful was gratified by my toil in the kitchen garden. There was a hearty enjoyment, likewise, in observing the growth of the crook-necked winter squashes, from the first little bulb, with the withered blossom adhering to it, until they lay strewn upon the soil, big, round fellows, hiding their heads beneath the leaves, but turning up their great yellow rotundities to the noontide sun. Gazing at them, I felt that by my agency something worth living for had been done. A new substance was born into the world. They were real and tangible existences, which the mind could hold of and rejoice in. A cabbage, too,—especially the early Dutch cabbage, which swells to a monstrous circumference, until its ambitious heart often bursts asunder,—is a matter to be proud of when we can claim a share with the earth and sky in producing it. But, after all, the hugest pleasure is reserved until these vegetable children of ours are smoking on the table, and we, like Saturn, make a meal of them.

What with the river, the battle-field, the orchard and the garden, the reader begins to despair of finding his way back into the Old Manse. But in agreeable weather it is the truest hospitality to keep him out-of-doors. I never grew quite acquainted with my habitation till a long spell of sulky rain had confined me beneath its roof. There could not be a more sombre aspect of external nature than as then seen from the windows of my study. The great willow-tree had caught and retained among its leaves a whole cataract of water, to be shaken down at intervals by the frequent gusts of wind. All day long, and for a week together, the rain was drip-drip-dripping and splash-splash-splashing from the eaves, and bubbling and foaming into the tubs beneath the spouts. The old, unpainted shingles of the house and out-buildings were black with moisture; and the mosses of ancient growth upon the walls looked green and fresh, as if they were the newest things and afterthought of Time. The usually mirrored surface of the river was blurred by an infinity of raindrops; the whole landscape had a completely water-soaked appearance, conveying the impression that the earth was wet through like a sponge; while the summit of a wooded hill, about a mile distant, was enveloped in a dense mist, where the demon of the tempest seemed to have his abiding-place and to be plotting still direr inclemencies.

Nature has no kindness, no hospitality, during a rain. In the fiercest heat of sunny days she retains a secret mercy, and welcomes the wayfarer to shady nooks of the woods whither the sun cannot penetrate; but she provides no shelter against her storms. It makes us shiver to think of those deep, umbrageous recesses, those overshadowing banks, where we found such enjoyment during the sultry afternoons. Not a twig of foliage there but would dash a little shower into our faces. Looking reproachfully towards the impenetrable sky,—

if sky there be above that dismal uniformity of cloud,—we are apt to murmur against the whole system of the universe, since it involves the extinction of so many summer days in so short a life by the hissing and spluttering rain. In such spells of weather—and it is to be supposed weather came—Eve's bower in Paradise must have been but a cheerless and aguish kind of shelter, nowise comparable to the old parsonage, which had resources of its own to beguile the week's imprisonment. The idea of sleeping on a couch of wet roses!

Happy the man who in a rainy day can betake himself to a huge garret, stored, like that of the Manse, with lumber that each generation has left behind it from a period before the revolution. Our garret was an arched hall, dimly illuminated through small and dusty windows; it was but a twilight at the best; and there were nooks, or rather caverns, of deep obscurity, the secrets of which I never learned, being too reverent of their dust and cobwebs. The beams and rafters, roughly hewn and with strips of bark still on them, and the rude masonry of the chimneys, made the garret look wild and uncivilized,—an aspect unlike what was seen elsewhere in the quiet and decorous old house. But on one side there was a little whitewashed apartment which bore the traditionary title of the Saint's Chamber, because holy men in their youth had slept and studied and prayed there. With its elevated retirement, its one window, its small fireplace, and its closet, convenient for an oratory, it was the very spot where a young man might inspire himself with solemn enthusiasm and cherish saintly dreams. The occupants, at various epochs, had left brief records and ejaculations inscribed upon the walls. There, too, hung a tattered and shrivelled roll of canvas, which on inspection proved to be the forcibly wrought picture of a clergyman, in wig, band, and gown, holding a Bible in his hand. As I turned his face towards the light he eyed me with an air of authority such as men of his profession seldom assume in our days. The original had been pastor of the parish more than a century ago, a friend of Whitefield, and almost his equal in fervid eloquence. I bowed before the effigy of the

dignified divine, and felt as if I had now met face to face with
the ghost by whom, as there was reason to apprehend, the
Manse was haunted.

Houses of any antiquity in New England are so invariably
possessed with spirits that the matter seems hardly worth
alluding to. Our ghost used to heave deep sighs in a particular corner of the parlor, and sometimes rustled paper, as if he
were turning over a sermon in the long upper entry,—where
nevertheless he was invisible in spite of the bright moonshine
that fell through the eastern window. Not improbably he
wished me to edit and publish a selection from a chest full of
manuscript discourses that stood in the garret. Once, while
Hillard and other friends sat talking with us in the twilight,
there came a rustling noise as of a minister's silk gown, sweeping through the very midst of the company so closely as almost
to brush against the chairs. Still there was nothing visible.
A yet stranger business was that of a ghostly servant-maid,
who used to be heard in the kitchen at deepest midnight
grinding coffee, cooking, ironing,—performing, in short, all
kinds of domestic labor,—although no traces of anything accomplished could be detected the next morning. Some neglected duty of her servitude—some ill-starched ministerial
band—disturbed the poor damsel in her grave and kept her
at work without any wages.

But to return from this digression. A part of my predecessor's library was stored in the garret,—no unfit receptacle indeed for such dreary trash as comprised the greater number
of volumes. The old books would have been worth nothing at
an auction. In this venerable garret, however, they possessed
an interest, quite apart from their literary value, as heirlooms,
many of which had been transmitted down through a series
of consecrated hands from the days of the mighty Puritan
divines. Autographs of famous names were to be seen in faded
ink on some of their fly-leaves; and there were marginal observations or interpolated pages closely covered with manuscript in illegible shorthand, perhaps concealing matter of
profound truth and wisdom. The world will never be the

better for it. A few of the books were Latin folios, written by Catholic authors; others demolished Papistry, as with a sledge-hammer, in plain English. A dissertation on the book of Job—which only Job himself could have had patience to read—filled at least a score of small, thickset quartos, at the rate of two or three volumes to a chapter. Then there was a vast folio body of divinity—too corpulent a body, it might be feared, to comprehend the spiritual element of religion. Volumes of this form dated back two hundred years or more, and were generally bound in black leather, exhibiting precisely such an appearance as we should attribute to books of enchantment. Others equally antique were of a size proper to be carried in the large waistcoat pockets of old times,—diminutive, but as black as their bulkier brethren, and abundantly interfused with Greek and Latin quotations. These little old volumes impressed me as if they had been intended for very large ones, but had been unfortunately blighted at an early stage of their growth.

The rain pattered upon the roof and the sky gloomed through the dusty garret windows, while I burrowed among these venerable books in search of any living thought which should burn like a coal of fire, or glow like an inextinguish-able gem, beneath the dead trumpery that had long hidden it. But I found no such treasure; all was dead alike; and I could not but muse deeply and wonderingly upon the humil-iating fact that the works of man's intellect decay like those of his hands. Thought grows mouldy. What was good and nourishing food for the spirits of one generation affords no sustenance for the next. Books of religion, however, cannot be considered a fair test of the enduring and vivacious proper-ties of human thought, because such books so seldom really touch upon their ostensible subject, and have, therefore, so little business to be written at all. So long as an unlettered soul can attain to saving grace, there would seem to be no deadly error in holding theological libraries to be accumula-tions of, for the most part, stupendous impertinence.

Many of the books had accrued in the latter years of the

last clergyman's lifetime. These threatened to be of even less interest than the elder works, a century hence, to any curious inquirer who should then rummage them as I was doing now. Volumes of the *Liberal Preacher* and *Christian Examiner*, occasional sermons, controversial pamphlets, tracts, and other productions of a like fugitive nature took the place of the thick and heavy volumes of past time. In a physical point of view there was much the same difference as between a feather and a lump of lead; but, intellectually regarded, the specific gravity of old and new was about upon a par. Both also were alike frigid. The elder books, nevertheless, seemed to have been earnestly written, and might be conceived to have possessed warmth at some former period; although, with the lapse of time, the heated masses had cooled down even to the freezing-point. The frigidity of the modern productions, on the other hand, was characteristic and inherent, and evidently had little to do with the writer's qualities of mind and heart. In fine, of this whole dusty heap of literature I tossed aside all the sacred part, and felt myself none the less a Christian for eschewing it. There appeared no hope of either mounting to the better world on a Gothic staircase of ancient folios or of flying thither on the wings of a modern tract.

Nothing, strange to say, retained any sap except what had been written for the passing day and year without the remotest pretension or idea of permanence. There were a few old newspapers, and still older almanacs, which reproduced to my mental eye the epochs when they had issued from the press with a distinctness that was altogether unaccountable. It was as if I had found bits of magic looking-glass among the books, with the images of a vanished century in them. I turned my eyes towards the tattered picture above mentioned, and asked of the austere divine wherefore it was that he and his brethren, after the most painful rummaging and groping into their minds, had been able to produce nothing half so real as these newspaper scribblers and almanac makers had thrown off in the effervescence of a moment. The portrait responded not; so I sought an answer for myself. It is the age itself that writes newspapers and almanacs, which, therefore, have a distinct purpose and meaning at the time, and a kind of intelligible truth for all times; whereas most other works—being written by men who, in the very act, set themselves apart from their age—are likely to possess little significance when new, and none at all when old. Genius, indeed, melts many ages into one, and thus effects something permanent, yet still with a similarity of office to that of the more ephemeral writer. A work of genius is but the newspaper of a century, or perchance of a hundred centuries.

Lightly as I have spoken of these old books, there yet lingers with me a superstitious reverence for literature of all kinds. A bound volume has a charm in my eyes similar to what scraps of manuscript possess for the good Mussulman. He imagines that those wind-wafted records are perhaps hallowed by some sacred verse; and I, that every new book or antique one may contain the 'open sesame,'—the spell to disclose treasures hidden in some unsuspected cave of Truth. Thus it was not without sadness that I turned away from the library of the Old Manse.

Blessed was the sunshine when it came again at the close of another stormy day, beaming from the edge of the western horizon; while the massive firmament of clouds threw down all the gloom it could, but served only to kindle the golden light into a more brilliant glow by the strongly contrasted shadows. Heaven smiled at the earth, so long unseen, from beneath its heavy eyelid. Tomorrow for the hill-tops and the wood-paths.

Or it might be that Ellery Channing came up the avenue to join me in a fishing excursion on the river. Strange and happy times were those when we cast aside all irksome forms and straitlaced habitudes, and delivered ourselves up to the free air, to live like the Indians or any less conventional race during one bright semicircle of the sun. Rowing our boat against the current, between wide meadows, we turned aside into the Assabeth. A more lovely stream than this, for a mile above its junction with the Concord, has never flowed on earth,—nowhere, indeed, except to lave the interior regions of a poet's imagination. It is sheltered from the breeze by woods and a hillside; so that elsewhere there might be a hurricane, and here scarcely a ripple across the shaded water. The current lingers along so gently that the mere force of the boatman's will seems sufficient to propel his craft against it. It comes flowing softly through the midmost privacy and deepest heart of a wood which whispers it to be quiet; while the stream whispers back again from its sedgy borders, as if river and wood were hushing one another to sleep. Yes, the river sleeps along its course and dreams of the sky and of the clustering foliage, amid which fall showers of broken sunlight, imparting specks of vivid cheerfulness, in contrast with the quiet depth of the prevailing tint. Of all this scene, the slumbering river has a dream picture in its bosom. Which, after all, was the most real—the picture, or the original?—the objects palpable to our grosser senses, or their apotheosis in the stream beneath? Surely the disembodied images stand in closer relation to the soul. But both the original and the reflection had here an ideal charm; and, had it been a thought more wild, I could have fancied that this river had strayed forth out of the rich scenery of my companion's inner world; only the vegetation along its banks should then have had an Oriental character.

Gentle and unobtrusive as the river is, yet the tranquil woods seem hardly satisfied to allow its passage. The trees are rooted on the very verge of the water, and dip their pendent branches into it. At one spot there is a lofty bank, on the slope of which grow some hemlocks, declining across the stream with outstretched arms, as if resolute to take the plunge. In other places the banks are almost on a level with the water; so that the quiet congregation of trees set their feet in the flood, and are fringed with foliage down to the surface. Cardinal flowers kindle their spiral flames and illuminate the dark nooks among the shrubbery. The pond-lily grows abundantly along the margin—that delicious flower, which, as Thoreau tells me, opens its virgin bosom to the first sunlight and perfects its being through the magic of that genial kiss. He has beheld beds of them unfolding in due succession as the sunrise stole gradually from flower to flower—a sight not to be hoped for unless when a poet adjusts his inward eye to a proper focus with the outward organ. Grape-vines here and there twine themselves around shrub and tree and hang their clusters over the water within reach of the boatman's hand. Oftentimes they unite two trees of alien race in an inextricable twine, marrying the hemlock and the maple against their will, and enriching them with a purple offspring of which neither is the parent. One of these ambitious parasites has climbed into the upper branches of a tall, white pine, and is still ascending from bough to bough, unsatisfied till it shall crown the tree's airy summit with a wreath of its broad foliage and a cluster of its grapes.

The winding course of the stream continually shut out the scene behind us, and revealed as calm and lovely a one before. We glided from depth to depth, and breathed new seclusion at every turn. The shy kingfisher flew from the withered branch close at hand to another at a distance, uttering a shrill cry of anger or alarm. Ducks that had been floating there since the preceding eve were startled at our approach, and skimmed along the glassy river, breaking its dark surface with a bright streak. The pickerel leaped from among the lily-pads. The turtle, sunning itself upon a rock or at the root of a tree, slid suddenly into the water with a plunge. The painted Indian who paddled his canoe along the Assabeth three hundred years ago could hardly have seen a wilder gentleness displayed upon its banks and reflected in its bosom than we did. Nor could the same Indian have prepared his noontide meal with more simplicity. We drew up our skiff at some point where the over-arching shade formed a natural bower, and there kindled a fire with the pine cones and decayed branches that lay strewn plentifully around. Soon the smoke ascended among the trees, impregnated with a savory incense, not heavy, dull, and surfeiting, like the steam of cookery within doors, but sprightly and piquant. The smell of our feast was akin to the woodland odors with which it mingled: there was no sacrilege committed by our intrusion there: the sacred solitude was hospitable, and granted us free leave to cook and eat in the recess that was at once our kitchen and banqueting hall. It is strange what humble offices may be performed in a beautiful scene without destroying its poetry. Our fire, red gleaming among the trees, and we beside it, busied with culinary rites and spreading out our meal on a moss-grown log, all seemed in unison with the river gliding by and the foliage rustling over us. And, what was strangest; neither did our mirth seem to disturb the propriety of the solemn woods; although the hobgoblins of the old wilderness and the will-of-the-wisps that glimmered in the marshy places might have come trooping to share our table-talk, and have added their shrill laughter to our merriment. It was the very spot in which to utter the extremest nonsense or the profoundest wisdom, or that ethereal product of the mind which partakes of both, and may become one or the other, in correspondence with the faith and insight of the auditor.

So amid sunshine and shadow, rustling leaves and sighing waters, up gushed our talk like the babble of a fountain. The evanescent spray was Ellery's; and his, too, the lumps of golden thought that lay glimmering in the fountain's bed and brightened both our faces by the reflection. Could he have drawn out that virgin gold and stamped it with the mint mark that alone gives currency, the world might have had the profit, and he the fame. My mind was the richer merely by the knowledge that it was there. But the chief profit of those wild days to him and me, lay, not in any definite idea, not in any angular or rounded truth, which we dug out of the shapeless mass of problematical stuff, but in the freedom which we thereby won from all custom and conventionalism and fettering influences of man on man. We were so free today that it was impossible to be slaves again to-morrow. When we crossed the threshold of the house or trod the thronged pavements of a city, still the leaves of the trees that overhang the Assabeth were whispering to us, 'Be free! be free!' Therefore along that shady riverbank there are spots, marked with a heap of ashes and half-consumed brands, only less sacred in my remembrance than the hearth of a household fire.

And yet how sweet, as we floated homeward adown the golden river at sunset,—how sweet was it to return within the system of human society, not as to a dungeon and a chain, but as to a stately edifice, whence we could go forth at will into statelier simplicity! How gently, too, did the sign of the Old Manse, best seen from the river, overshadowed with its willow and all environed about with the foliage of its orchard and avenue,—how gently did its gray, homely aspect rebuke the speculative extravagances of the day! It had grown sacred in connection with the artificial life against which we inveighed; it had been a home for many years in spite of all; it was my home too; and, with these thoughts, it seemed to me that all the artifice and conventionalism of life was but an impalpable thinness upon its surface, and that the depth below was none the worse for it. Once, as we turned our boat to the bank, there was a cloud, in the shape of an immensely gigantic figure of a hound, couched above the house, as if keeping guard over it. Gazing at this symbol, I prayed that the upper influences might long protect the institutions that had grown out of the heart of mankind.

If ever my readers should decide to give up civilized life, cities, houses, and whatever moral or material enormities in addition to these the perverted ingenuity of our race has contrived, let it be in the early autumn. Then Nature will love him better than at any other season, and will take him to her bosom with a more motherly tenderness. I could scarcely endure the roof of the old house above me in those first autumnal days. How early in the summer, too, the prophecy of autumn comes! Earlier in some years than in others; sometimes even in the first weeks of July. There is no other feeling like what is caused by this faint, doubtful, yet real perception—if it be not rather a foreboding—of the year's decay, so blessedly sweet and sad in the same breath.

Did I say that there was no feeling like it? Ah, but there is a half-acknowledged melancholy like to this when we stand in the perfected vigor of our life and feel that Time has now given us all his flowers, and that the next work of his never idle fingers must be to steal them one by one away.

I have forgotten whether the song of the cricket be not as early a token of autumn's approach as any other,—that song which may be called an audible stillness; for though very loud and heard afar, yet the mind does not take note of it as a sound, so completely is its individual existence merged among the accompanying characteristics of the season. Alas for the pleasant summer time! In August the grass is still verdant on the hills and in the valleys; the foliage of the trees is as dense as ever, and as green; the flowers gleam forth in richer abundance along the margin of the river, and by the stone walls, and deep among the woods; the days, too, are as fervid now as they were a month ago; and yet in every breath of wind and in every beam of sunshine we hear the whispered farewell and behold the parting smile of a dear friend. There is a coolness amid all the heat, a mildness in the blazing noon. Not a breeze can stir but it thrills us with the breath of autumn. A pensive glory is seen in the far golden gleams, among the shadows of the trees. The flowers—even the brightest of them, and they are the most gorgeous of the year—have this gentle sadness wedded to their pomp, and typify the character of the delicious time each within itself. The brilliant cardinal flower has never seemed gay to me.

Still later in the season Nature's tenderness waxes stronger. It is impossible not to be fond of our mother now; for she is so fond of us! At other periods she does not make this impression on me, or only at rare intervals, but in those genial days of autumn, when she has perfected her harvests and accomplished every needful thing that was given her to do, then she overflows with a blessed superfluity of love. She has leisure to caress her children now. It is good to be alive at such times. Thank Heaven for breath—yes, for mere breath—when it is made up of a heavenly breeze like this! It comes with a real kiss upon our cheeks; it would linger fondly around us if it might; but, since it must be gone, it embraces us with its whole kindly heart and passes onward to embrace likewise the next thing that it meets. A blessing is flung abroad and scattered far and wide over the earth, to be gathered up by all who choose. I recline upon the still unwithered grass and whisper to myself, 'O perfect day! O beautiful world! O beneficent God!' And it is the promise of a blessed eternity; for our Creator would never have made such lovely days and have given us the deep hearts to enjoy them, above and beyond all thought, unless we were meant to be immortal. This sunshine is the golden pledge thereof. It beams through the gates of paradise and shows us glimpses far inward.

By and by, in a little time, the outward world puts on a drear austerity. On some October morning there is a heavy hoarfrost on the grass and along the tops of the fences; and at sunrise the leaves fall from the trees of our avenue without a breath of wind, quietly descending by their own weight. All summer long they have murmured like the noise of waters; they have roared loudly while the branches were wrestling with the thunder gust; they have made music both glad and solemn; they have attuned my thoughts by their quiet sound as I paced to and fro beneath the arch of intermingling boughs. Now they can only rustle under my feet. Henceforth the gray parsonage begins to assume a larger importance, and draws to its fireside,—for the abomination of the airtight stove is reserved till wintry weather,—draws closer and closer to its fireside the vagrant impulses that had gone wandering about through the summer.

When summer was dead and buried the Old Manse became as lonely as a hermitage. Not that ever—in my time at least— it had been thronged with company; but, at no rare intervals, we welcomed some friend out of the dusty glare and tumult of the world, and rejoiced to share with him the transparent obscurity that was floating over us. In one respect our precincts were like the Enchanted Ground through which the pilgrim travelled on his way to the Celestial City! The guests, each and all, felt a slumberous influence upon them; they fell asleep in chairs, or took a more deliberate siesta on the sofa, or were seen stretched among the shadows of the orchard, looking up dreamily through the boughs. They could not have paid a more acceptable compliment to my abode, nor to my own qualities as a host. I held it as a proof that they left their cares behind them as they passed between the stone gate-posts at the entrance of our avenue, and that the so powerful opiate was the abundance of peace and quiet within and all around us. Others could give them pleasure and amusement or instruction—these could be picked up anywhere; but it was for me to give them rest—rest in a life of trouble. What better could be done for those weary and world-worn spirits?—for him whose career of perpetual action was impeded and harassed by the rarest of his powers and the richest of his acquirements?—for another who had thrown his ardent heart from earliest youth into the strife of politics, and now, perchance, began to suspect that one lifetime is too brief for the accomplishment of any lofty aim?—for her on whose feminine nature had been imposed the heavy gift of intellectual power, such as a strong man might have staggered under, and with it the necessity to act upon the world?—in a word, not to multiply instances, what better could be done for anybody who came within our magic circle than to throw the spell of a tranquil spirit over him? And when it had wrought its full effect, then we dismissed him, with but misty reminiscences, as if he had been dreaming of us.

Were I to adopt a pet idea, as so many people do, and fondle it in my embraces to the exclusion of all others, it would be, that the great want which mankind labors under at this present period is sleep. The world should recline its vast head on the first convenient pillow and take an age-long nap. It has gone distracted through a morbid activity, and, while preternaturally wide-awake, is nevertheless tormented by visions that seem real to it now, but would assume their true aspect and character were all things once set right by an interval of sound repose. This is the only method of getting rid of old delusions and avoiding new ones; of regenerating our race, so

that it might in due time awake as an infant out of dewy
slumber; of restoring to us the simple perception of what is
right, and the single-hearted desire to achieve it, both of
which have long been lost in consequence of this weary activity
of brain and torpor or passion of the heart that now afflict the
universe. Stimulants, the only mode of treatment hitherto
attempted, cannot quell the disease; they do but heighten the
delirium.

Let not the above paragraph ever be quoted against the
author; for, though tinctured with its modicum of truth, it is
the result and expression of what he knew, while he was
writing, to be but a distorted survey of the state and prospects
of mankind. There were circumstances around me which made
it difficult to view the world precisely as it exists; for, severe
and sober as was the Old Manse, it was necessary to go but a
little way beyond its threshold before meeting with stranger
moral shapes of men than might have been encountered elsewhere in a circuit of a thousand miles.

These hobgoblins of flesh and blood were attracted thither
by the widespreading influence of a great original thinker, who
had his earthly abode at the opposite extremity of our village.
His mind acted upon other minds of a certain constitution
with wonderful magnetism, and drew many men upon long
pilgrimages to speak with him face to face. Young visionaries
—to whom just so much of insight had been imparted as to
make life all a labyrinth around them—came to seek the clew
that should guide them out of their self-involved bewilderment. Gray-headed theorists—whose systems, at first air, had
finally imprisoned them in an iron frame-work—travelled
painfully to his door, not to ask deliverance, but to invite the
free spirit into their own thraldom. People that had lighted
on a new thought, or a thought that they fancied new, came
to Emerson, as the finder of a glittering gem hastens to a
lapidary, to ascertain its quality and value. Uncertain,
troubled, earnest wanderers through the midnight of the moral
world beheld his intellectual fire as a beacon burning on a
hill-top, and, climbing the difficult ascent, looked forth into

the surrounding obscurity more hopefully than hitherto. The light revealed objects unseen before,—mountains, gleaming lakes, glimpses of a creation among the chaos; but also, as was unavoidable, it attracted bats and owls and the whole host of night birds, which flapped their dusky wings against the gazer's eyes, and sometimes were mistaken for fowls of angelic feather. Such delusions always hover nigh whenever a beacon fire of truth is kindled.

For myself, there had been epochs of my life when I, too, might have asked of this prophet the master word that should solve me the riddle of the universe; but now, being happy, I felt as if there were no question to be put, and therefore admired Emerson as a poet of deep beauty and austere tenderness, but sought nothing from him as a philosopher. It was good, nevertheless, to meet him in the wood-paths, or sometimes in our avenue, with that pure intellectual gleam diffused about his presence like the garment of a shining one; and he so quiet, so simple, so without pretension, encountering each man alive as if expecting to receive more than he could impart. And, in truth, the heart of many an ordinary man had, perchance, inscriptions which he could not read. But it was impossible to dwell in his vicinity without inhaling more or less the mountain atmosphere of his lofty thought, which, in the brains of some people, wrought a singular giddiness,—new truth being as heady as new wine. Never was a poor little country village infested with such a variety of queer, strangely-dressed, oddly-behaved mortals, most of whom took upon themselves to be important agents of the world's destiny, yet were simply bores of a very intense water. Such, I imagine, is the invariable character of persons who crowd so closely about an original thinker as to draw in his unuttered breath and thus become imbued with a false originality. This triteness of novelty is enough to make any man of common sense blaspheme at all ideas of less than a century's standing, and pray that the world may be petrified and rendered immovable in precisely the worst moral and physical state that it ever yet arrived at, rather than be benefited by such schemes of such philosophers.

And now I begin to feel—and perhaps should have sooner felt—that we have talked enough of the Old Manse. Mine honored reader, it may be, will vilify the poor author as an egotist for babbling through so many pages about a mossgrown country parsonage, and his life within its walls and on the river and in the woods, and the influences that wrought upon him from all these sources. My conscience, however, does not reproach me with betraying anything too sacredly individual to be revealed by a human spirit to its brother or sister spirit. How narrow—how shallow and scanty too—is the stream of thought that has been flowing from my pen, compared with the broad tide of dim emotions, ideas, and associations which swell around me from that portion of my existence! How little have I told and of that little, how almost nothing is even tinctured with any quality that makes it exclusively my own! Has the reader gone wandering, hand in hand with me, through the inner passages of my being? and have we groped together into all its chambers and examined their treasures or their rubbish? Not so. We have been standing on the greensward, but just within the cavern's mouth, where the common sunshine is free to penetrate, and where every footstep is therefore free to come. I have appealed to no sentiment or sensibilities save such as are diffused among us all. So far as I am a man of really individual attributes I veil my face; nor am I, nor have I ever been, one of those supremely hospitable people who serve up their own hearts, delicately fried, with brain sauce, as a tidbit for their beloved public.

Glancing back over what I have written, it seems but the scattered reminiscences of a single summer. In fairyland there is no measurement of time; and, in a spot so sheltered from the turmoil of life's ocean, three years hastened away with a noiseless flight, as the breezy sunshine chases the cloud shadows across the depths of a still valley. Now came hints, growing more and more distinct, that the owner of the old house was pining for his native air. Carpenters next appeared, making a tremendous racket among the out-buildings, strewing the green grass with pine shavings and chips of chestnut joists, and vexing the whole antiquity of the place with their discordant renovations. Soon, moreover; they divested our abode of the veil of woodbine which had crept over a large portion of its southern face. All the aged mosses were cleared unsparingly away; and there were horrible whispers about brushing up the external walls with a coat of paint—a purpose as little to my taste as might be that of rouging the venerable cheeks of one's grandmother. But the hand that renovates is always more sacrilegious than that which destroys. In fine, we gathered up our household goods, drank a farewell cup of tea in our pleasant little breakfast-room,—delicately fragrant tea, an unpurchasable luxury, one of the many angel gifts that had fallen like dew upon us,—and passed forth between the tall stone gateposts as uncertain as the wandering Arabs where our tent might next be pitched. Providence took me by the hand, and—an oddity of dispensation which, I trust, there is no irreverence in smiling at—has led me, as the newspapers announce while I am writing from the Old Manse into a custom house. As a story-teller, I have often contrived strange vicissitudes for my imaginary personage, but none like this.

The treasure of intellectual good which I hoped to find in our secluded dwelling had never come to light. No profound treatise of ethics, no philosophic history, no novel even, that could stand unsupported on its edges. All that I had to show, as a man of letters, were these few tales and essays, which had blossomed out like flowers in the calm summer of my heart and mind. Save editing (an easy task) the journal of my friend of many years, the African Cruiser, I had done nothing else. With these idle weeds and withering blossoms I have intermixed some that were produced long ago—old, faded things, reminding me of flowers pressed between the leaves of a book,—and now offer the bouquet, such as it is, to any whom it may please. These fitful sketches, with so little of external life about them, yet claiming no profundity of purpose,—so reserved, even while they sometimes seem so frank,—often but half in earnest, and never, even when most so, expressing satisfactorily the thoughts which they profess to image,—such trifles, I truly feel, afford no solid basis for a literary reputation. Nevertheless, the public—if my limited number of readers, whom I venture to regard rather as a circle of friends, may be termed a public—will receive them the more kindly, as the last offering, the last collection, of this nature which it is my purpose ever to put forth. Unless I could do better, I have done enough in this kind. For myself the book will always retain one charm—as reminding me of the river, with its delightful solitudes, and of the avenue, the garden, and the orchard, and especially the dear Old Manse, with the little study on its western side, and the sunshine glimmering through the willow branches while I wrote.

Let the reader, if he will do me so much honor, imagine himself my guest, and that, having seen whatever may be worthy of notice within and about the Old Manse, he has finally been ushered into my study. There, after seating him in an antique elbow chair, an heirloom of the house, I take forth a roll of manuscript and entreat his attention to the following tales—an act of personal inhospitality, however, which I never was guilty of, nor ever will be, even to my worst enemy.

PREFACE
TO THE 1851 EDITION
OF *TWICE-TOLD TALES*

The Author of "TWICE-TOLD TALES" has a claim
to one distinction, which, as none of his literary brethren will
care about disputing it with him, he need not be afraid to
mention. He was, for a good many years, the obscurest man
of letters in America.

These stories were published in magazines and annuals, extending over a period of ten or twelve years, and comprising
the whole of the writer's young manhood, without making (so
far as he has ever been aware) the slightest impression on the
public. One or two among them, the "Rill from the Town
Pump," in perhaps a greater degree than any other, had a
pretty wide newspaper circulation; as for the rest, he had no
grounds for supposing that, on their first appearance, they
met with the good or evil fortune to be read by anybody.
Throughout the time above specified, he had no incitement to
literary effort in a reasonable prospect of reputation or profit,
nothing but the pleasure itself of composition—an enjoyment
not at all amiss in its way, and perhaps essential to the merit
of the work in hand, but which, in the long run, will hardly
keep the chill out of a writer's heart, or the numbness out of
his fingers. To this total lack of sympathy, at the age when
his mind would naturally have been most effervescent, the
public owe it (and it is certainly an effort not to be regretted

on either part) that the Author can show nothing for the thought and industry of that portion of his life, save the forty sketches, or thereabouts, included in these volumes.

Much more, indeed, he wrote; and some very small part of it might yet be rummaged out (but it would not be worth the trouble) among the dingy pages of fifteen-or-twenty-year-old periodicals, or within the shabby morocco covers of faded souvenirs. The remainder of the works alluded to had a very brief existence, but, on the score of brilliancy, enjoyed a fate vastly superior to that of their brotherhood, which succeeded in getting through the press. In a word, the Author burned them without mercy or remorse, and, moreover, without any subsequent regret, and had more than one occasion to marvel that such very dull stuff, as he knew his condemned manuscripts to be, should yet have possessed inflammability enough to set the chimney on fire!

After a long while the first collected volume of the "Tales" was published. By this time, if the Author had ever been greatly tormented by literary ambition (which he does not remember or believe to have been the case), it must have perished, beyond resuscitation, in the dearth of nutriment. This was fortunate; for the success of the volume was not such as would have gratified a craving desire for notoriety. A moderate edition was "got rid of" (to use the publisher's very significant phrase) within a reasonable time, but apparently without rendering the writer or his productions much more generally known than before. The great bulk of the reading public probably ignored the book altogether. A few persons read it, and liked it better than it deserved. At an interval of three or four years, the second volume was published, and encountered much the same sort of kindly, but calm, and very limited reception. The circulation of the two volumes was chiefly confined to New England; nor was it until long after this period, if it even yet be the case, that the Author could regard himself as addressing the American public, or, indeed, any public at all. He was merely writing to his known or unknown friends.

As he glances over these long-forgotten pages, and considers his way of life while composing them, the Author can very clearly discern why all this was so. After so many sober years, he would have reason to be ashamed if he could not criticise his own work as fairly as another man's; and, though it is little his business, and perhaps still less his interest, he can hardly resist a temptation to achieve something of the sort. If writers were allowed to do so, and would perform the task with perfect sincerity and unreserve, their opinions of their own productions would often be more valuable and instructive than the works themselves.

At all events, there can be no harm in the Author's remarking that he rather wonders how the "TWICE-TOLD TALES" should have gained what vogue they did than that it was so little and so gradual. They have the pale tint of flowers that blossomed in too retired a shade,—the coolness of meditative habit, which diffuses itself through the feeling and observation of every sketch. Instead of passion there is sentiment; and, even in what purport to be pictures of actual life, we have allegory, not always so warmly dressed in its habiliments of flesh and blood as to be taken into the reader's mind without a shiver. Whether from lack of power, or an unconquerable reserve, the Author's touches have often an effect of tameness; the merriest man can hardly contrive to laugh at his broadest humor; the tenderest woman, one would suppose, will hardly shed warm tears at his deepest pathos. The book, if you would see anything in it, requires to be read in the clear, brown, twilight atmosphere in which it was written; if opened in the sunshine, it is apt to look exceedingly like a volume of blank pages.

With the foregoing characteristics, proper to the production of a person in retirement (which happened to be the Author's category at the time), the book is devoid of others that we should quite as naturally look for. The sketches are not, it is hardly necessary to say, profound; but it is rather more remarkable that they so seldom, if ever, show any design on the writer's part to make them so. They have none of the abstruseness of idea, or obscurity of expression, which mark the written communications of a solitary mind with itself. They never need translation. It is, in fact, the style of a man of society. Every sentence, so far as it embodies thought or sensibility, may be understood and felt by anybody who will give himself the trouble to read it, and will take up the book in a proper mood.

This statement of apparently opposite peculiarities leads us to a perception of what the sketches truly are. They are not the talk of a secluded man with his own mind and heart (had it been so, they could hardly have failed to be more deeply and permanently valuable), but his attempts, and very imperfectly successful ones, to open an intercourse with the world.

The Author would regret to be understood as speaking sourly or querulously of the slight mark made by his earlier literary efforts on the Public at large. It is so far the contrary, that he has been moved to write this Preface chiefly as affording him an opportunity to express how much enjoyment he has owed to these volumes, both before and since their publication. They are the memorials of very tranquil and not unhappy years. They failed, it is true,—nor could it have been otherwise,—in winning an extensive popularity. Occasionally, however, when he deemed them entirely forgotten, a paragraph or an article, from a native or foreign critic, would gratify his instincts of authorship with unexpected praise,—too generous praise, indeed, and too little alloyed with censure, which, therefore, he learned the better to inflict upon himself. And, by the by, it is a very suspicious symptom of a deficiency of the popular element in a book when it calls forth no harsh criticism. This has been particularly the fortune of the "TWICE-TOLD TALES." They made no enemies, and were so little known and talked about that those who read, and chanced to like them, were apt to conceive the sort of kindness for the book which a person naturally feels for a discovery of his own.

This kindly feeling (in some cases, at least) extended to

the Author, who, on the internal evidence of his sketches, came to be regarded as a mild, shy, gentle, melancholic, exceedingly sensitive, and not very forcible man, hiding his blushes under an assumed name, the quaintness of which was supposed, somehow or other, to symbolize his personal and literary traits. He is by no means certain that some of his subsequent productions have not been influenced and modified by a natural desire to fill up so amiable an outline, and to act in consonance with the character assigned to him; nor, even now, could he forfeit it without a few tears of tender sensibility. To conclude, however: these volumes have opened the way to most agreeable associations, and to the formation of imperishable friendships; and there are many golden threads interwoven with his present happiness, which he can follow up more or less directly, until he finds their commencement here; so that his pleasant pathway among realities seems to proceed out of the Dreamland of his youth, and to be bordered with just enough of its shadowy foliage to shelter him from the heat of the day. He is therefore satisfied with what the "TWICE-TOLD TALES" have done for him, and feels it to be far better than fame.

PREFACE
TO *THE SNOW IMAGE AND*
OTHER TWICE-TOLD TALES
TO HORATIO BRIDGE, ESQ., U. S. N.

Ｍy Dear Bridge:

Some of the more crabbed of my critics, I understand, have pronounced your friend egotistical, indiscreet, and even impertinent, on account of the Prefaces and Introductions with which, on several occasions, he has seen fit to pave the reader's way into the interior edifice of a book. In the justice of this censure I do not exactly concur, for the reasons, on the one hand, that the public generally has negatived the idea of undue freedom on the author's part, by evincing, it seems to me, rather more interest in these aforesaid Introductions than in the stories which followed,—and that, on the other hand, with whatever appearance of confidential intimacy, I have been especially careful to make no disclosures respecting myself which the most indifferent observer might not have been acquainted with, and which I was not perfectly willing that my worst enemy should know. I might further justify myself, on the plea that, ever since my youth, I have been addressing a very limited circle of friendly readers, without much danger of being overheard by the public at large; and that the habits thus acquired might pardonably continue, although strangers may have begun to mingle with my audience.

But the charge, I am bold to say, is not a reasonable one, in

589

any view which we can fairly take of it. There is no harm, but, on the contrary, good, in arraying some of the ordinary facts of life in a slightly idealized and artistic guise. I have taken facts which relate to myself, because they chance to be nearest at hand, and likewise are my own property. And, as for egotism, a person, who has been burrowing, to his utmost ability, into the depths of our common nature, for the purposes of psychological romance,—and who pursues his researches in that dusky region, as he needs must, as well by the tact of sympathy as by the light of observation,—will smile at incurring such an imputation in virtue of a little preliminary talk about his external habits, his abode, his casual associates, and other matters entirely upon the surface. These things hide the man, instead of displaying him. You must make quite another kind of inquest, and look through the whole range of his fictitious characters, good and evil, in order to detect any of his essential traits.

Be all this as it may, there can be no question as to the propriety of my inscribing this volume of earlier and later sketches to you, and pausing here, a few moments, to speak of them, as friend speaks to friend; still being cautious, however, that the public and the critics shall overhear nothing which we care about concealing. On you, if on no other person, I am entitled to rely, to sustain the position of my Dedicatee. If anybody is responsible for my being at this day an author, it is yourself. I know not whence your faith came; but, while we were lads together at a country college,—gathering blue-berries, in study-hours, under those tall academic pines; or watching the great logs, as they tumbled along the current of the Androscoggin; or shooting pigeons and gray squirrels in the woods; or bat-fowling in the summer twilight; or catching trouts in that shadowy little stream which, I suppose, is still wandering riverward through the forest,— though you and I will never cast a line in it again,—two idle lads, in short (as we need not fear to acknowledge now), doing a hundred things that the Faculty never heard of, or else it had been the worse for us,—still it was your prognostic of your friend's destiny, that he was to be a writer of fiction.

And a fiction-monger, in due season, he became. But, was there ever such a weary delay in obtaining the slightest recognition from the public, as in my case? I sat down by the wayside of life, like a man under enchantment, and a shrubbery sprung up around me, and the bushes grew to be saplings, and the saplings became trees, until no exit appeared possible, through the entangling depths of my obscurity. And there, perhaps, I should be sitting at this moment, with the moss on the imprisoning tree-trunks, and the yellow leaves of more than a score of autumns piled above me, if it had not been for you. For it was through your interposition,—and that, moreover, unknown to himself,—that your early friend was brought before the public, somewhat more prominently than theretofore, in the first volume of "Twice-Told Tales." Not a publisher in America, I presume, would have thought well enough of my forgotten or never noticed stories, to risk the expense of print and paper; nor do I say this with any purpose of casting odium on the respectable fraternity of book-sellers, for their blindness to my wonderful merit. To confess the truth, I doubted of the public recognition quite as much as they could do. So much the more generous was your confidence; and knowing, as I do, that it was founded on old friendship rather than cold criticism, I value it only the more for that.

So, now, when I turn back upon my path, lighted by a transitory gleam of public favor, to pick up a few articles which were left out of my former collections, I take pleasure in making them the memorial of our very long and unbroken connection. Some of these sketches were among the earliest that I wrote, and, after lying for years in manuscript, they at last skulked into the Annuals or Magazines, and have hidden themselves there ever since. Others were the productions of a later period; others, again, were written recently. The comparison of these various trifles—the indices of intellectual condition at far separated epochs—affects me with a singular complexity of regrets. I am disposed to quarrel with the earlier sketches, both because a mature judgment discerns so many faults, and still more because they come so nearly up to the standard of the best that I can achieve now. The ripened autumnal fruit tastes but little better than the early windfalls. It would, indeed, be mortifying to believe that the summertime of life has passed away, without any greater progress and improvement than is indicated here. But,—at least, so I would fain hope,—these things are scarcely to be depended upon as measures of the intellectual and moral man. In youth, men are apt to write more wisely than they really know or feel; and the remainder of life may be not idly spent in realizing and convincing themselves of the wisdom which they uttered long ago. The truth that was only in the fancy then may have since become a substance in the mind and heart.

I have nothing further, I think, to say; unless it be that the public need not dread my again trespassing on its kindness, with any more of these musty and mouse-nibbled leaves of old periodicals, transformed, by the magic arts of my friendly publishers, into a new book. These are the last. Or, if a few still remain, they are either such as no paternal partiality could induce the author to think worth preserving, or else they have got into some very dark and dusty hiding-place, quite out of my own remembrance and whence no researches can avail to unearth them. So there let them rest.

Very sincerely yours,

N.H.

Lenox, November 1st, 1851

Journalism

PASSAGES FROM
CHIEFLY ABOUT
WAR MATTERS

BY A PEACEABLE MAN.

[This article appeared in the "Atlantic Monthly" for July, 1862, and is now first reprinted among Hawthorne's collected writings. The editor of the magazine objected to sundry paragraphs in the manuscript, and these were canceled with the consent of the author, who himself supplied all the foot-notes that accompanied the article when it was published. It has seemed best to retain them in the present reproduction. One of the suppressed passages, in which President Lincoln is described, has since been printed, and is therefore restored to its proper place in the following pages.—G. P. L.]

There is no remoteness of life and thought, no hermetically sealed seclusion, except, possibly, that of the grave, into which the disturbing influences of this war do not penetrate. Of course, the general heart-quake of the country long ago knocked at my cottage-door, and compelled me, reluctantly, to suspend the contemplation of certain fantasies, to which, according to my harmless custom, I was endeavoring to give a sufficiently life-like aspect to admit of their figuring in a romance. As I make no pretensions to state-craft or soldier-ship, and could promote the common weal neither by valor nor counsel, it seemed, at first, a pity that I should be debarred from such unsubstantial business as I had contrived for my-self, since nothing more genuine was to be substituted for it. But I magnanimously considered that there is a kind of trea-son in insulating one's self from the universal fear and sorrow, and thinking one's idle thoughts in the dread time of civil war; and could a man be so cold and hard-hearted, he would better deserve to be sent to Fort Warren than many who have found their way thither on the score of violent, but mis-directed sympathies. I remembered the touching rebuke administered by King Charles to that rural squire the echo of whose hunting-horn came to the poor monarch's ear on the morning before a battle, where the sovereignty and constitution of England were to be set at a stake. So I gave myself up to reading newspapers and listening to the click of the telegraph, like other people; until, after a great many months of such pastime, it grew so abominably irksome that I determined to look a little more closely at matters with my own eyes.

Accordingly we set out—a friend and myself—towards Washington, while it was still the long, dreary January of our Northern year, though March in name; nor were we unwilling to clip a little margin off the five months' winter, during which there is nothing genial in New England save the fireside. It was a clear, frosty morning, when we started. The sun shone brightly on snow-covered hills in the neighbor-hood of Boston, and burnished the surface of frozen ponds; and the wintry weather kept along with us while we trundled through Worcester and Springfield, and all those old, familiar towns, and through the village-cities of Connecticut. In New York the streets were afloat with liquid mud and slosh. Over New Jersey there was still a thin covering of snow, with the face of Nature visible through the rents in her white shroud, though with little or no symptom of reviving life. But when we reached Philadelphia, the air was mild and balmy; there was but a patch or two of dingy winter here and there, and the bare, brown fields about the city were ready to be green. We had met the Spring half-way, in her slow progress from the South; and if we kept onward at the same pace, and could get through the Rebel lines, we should soon come to fresh grass, fruit-blossoms, green peas, strawberries, and all such delights of early summer.

On our way, we heard many rumors of the war, but saw few signs of it. The people were staid and decorous, according to their ordinary fashion; and business seemed about as brisk as usual,—though, I suppose, it was considerably diverted from its customary channels into warlike ones. In the cities, especially in New York, there was a rather prominent display of military goods at the shop windows,—such as swords with gilded scabbards and trappings, epaulets, carbines, revolvers, and sometimes a great iron cannon at the edge of the pavement, as if Mars had dropped one of his pocket-pistols there, while hurrying to the field. As railway-companions, we had now and then a volunteer in his French-gray great-coat, returning from furlough, or a new-made officer travelling to join his regiment, in his new-made uniform, which was perhaps all of the military character that he had about him,—but proud of his eagle-buttons, and likely enough to do them honor before the gilt should be wholly dimmed. The country, in short, so far as bustle and movement went, was more quiet than in ordinary times, because so large a proportion of its restless elements had been drawn towards the seat of the conflict. But the air was full of a vague disturbance. To me, at least, it seemed so, emerging from such a solitude as has been hinted at, and the more impressible by rumors and indefinable presentiments, since I had not lived, like other men, in an atmosphere of continual talk about the war. A battle was momentarily expected on the Potomac; for, though our army was still on the hither side of the river, all of us were looking towards the mysterious and terrible Manassas, with the idea that somewhere in its neighborhood lay a ghastly battlefield, yet to be fought, but foredoomed of old to be bloodier than the one where we had reaped such shame. Of all haunted places, methinks such a destined field should be thickest thronged with ugly phantoms, ominous of mischief through ages beforehand.

Beyond Philadelphia there was a much greater abundance of military people. Between Baltimore and Washington a guard seemed to hold every station along the railroad; and frequently, on the hill-sides, we saw a collection of weather-beaten tents, the peaks of which, blackened with smoke, indicated that they had been made comfortable by stove-heat throughout the winter. At several commanding positions we saw fortifications, with the muzzles of cannon protruding from the ramparts, the slopes of which were made of the yellow earth of that region, and still unsodded; whereas, till these troublous times, there have been no forts but what were grass-grown with the lapse of at least a lifetime of peace. Our stopping-places were thronged with soldiers, some of whom came through the cars asking for newspapers that contained accounts of the battle between the Merrimack and Monitor, which had been fought the day before. A railway-train met us, conveying a regiment out of Washington to some unknown point; and reaching the capital, we filed out of the station between lines of soldiers, with shouldered muskets, putting us in mind of similar spectacles at the gates of European cities. It was not without sorrow that we saw the free circulation of the nation's life-blood (at the very heart, moreover) clogged with such strictures as these, which have caused chronic diseases in almost all countries save our own. Will the time ever come again, in America, when we may live half a score of years without once seeing the likeness of a soldier, except it be in the festal march of a company on its summer tour? Not in this generation, I fear, nor in the next, nor till the Millennium; and even that blessed epoch, as the prophecies seem to intimate, will advance to the sound of the trumpet.

One terrible idea occurs in reference to this matter. Even supposing the war should end to-morrow, and the army melt into the mass of the population within the year, what an incalculable preponderance will there be of military titles and pretensions for at least half a century to come! Every country-neighborhood will have its general or two, its three or four colonels, half a dozen majors, and captains without end,—besides non-commissioned officers and privates, more than the recruiting offices ever knew of,—all with their campaign-stories, which will become the staple of fireside-talk forever-more. Military merit, or rather, since that is not so readily estimated, military notoriety, will be the measure of all claims to civil distinction. One bullet-headed general will succeed another in the Presidential chair; and veterans will hold the offices at home and abroad, and sit in Congress and the state legislatures, and fill all the avenues of public life. And yet I do not speak of this deprecatingly, since, very likely, it may sub-stitute something more real and genuine, instead of the many shams on which men have heretofore founded their claims to public regard; but it behooves civilians to consider their wretched prospects in the future, and assume the military but-ton before it is too late.

We were not in time to see Washington as a camp. On the very day of our arrival sixty thousand men had crossed the Potomac on their march towards Manassas; and almost with their first step into the Virginia mud, the phantasmagory of a countless host and impregnable ramparts, before which they had so long remained quiescent, dissolved quite away. It was as if General McClellan had thrust his sword into a gigantic enemy, and, beholding him suddenly collapse, had discovered to himself and the world that he had merely punctured an enormously swollen bladder. There are instances of a similar character in old romances, where great armies are long kept at bay by the arts of necromancers, who build airy towers and battlements, and muster warriors of terrible aspect, and thus feign a defence of seeming impregnability, until some bolder champion of the besiegers dashes forward to try an encounter with the foremost foeman, and finds him melt away in the death-grapple. With such heroic adventures let the march upon Manassas be hereafter reckoned. The whole business, though connected with the destinies of a nation, takes inevitably a tinge of the ludicrous. The vast preparation of men and warlike material,—the majestic patience and docility with which the people waited through those weary and dreary months,—the martial skill, courage, and caution, with which our movement was ultimately made,—and, at last, the tremendous shock with which we were brought suddenly up against nothing at all! The Southerners show little sense of humor nowadays, but I think they must have meant to provoke a laugh at our expense, when they planted those Quaker guns. At all events, no other Rebel artillery has played upon us with such overwhelming effect.

The troops being gone, we had the better leisure and opportunity to look into other matters. It is natural enough to suppose that the centre and heart of Washington is the Capitol; and certainly, in its outward aspect, the world has not many statelier or more beautiful edifices, nor any, I should suppose, more skilfully adapted to legislative purposes, and to all accompanying needs. But, etc., etc.[1]

• • •

Of course, there was one other personage, in the class of statesmen, whom I should have been truly mortified to leave Washington without seeing; since (temporarily, at least, and by force of circumstances) he was the man of men. But a private grief had built up a barrier about him, impeding the customary free intercourse of Americans with their chief magistrate; so that I might have come away without a glimpse of his very remarkable physiognomy, save for a semi-official

---

1 We omit several paragraphs here, in which the author speaks of some prominent Members of Congress with a freedom that seems to have been not unkindly meant, but might be liable to misconstruction. As he admits that he never listened to an important debate, we can hardly recognize his qualifications to estimate these gentlemen, in their legislative and oratorical capacities.

opportunity of which I was glad to take advantage. The fact is, we were invited to annex ourselves, as supernumeraries, to a deputation that was about to wait upon the President, from a Massachusetts whip-factory, with a present of a splendid whip.

Our immediate party consisted only of four or five (including Major Ben Perley Poore, with his notebook and pencil), but we were joined by several other persons, who seemed to have been lounging about the precincts of the White House, under the spacious porch, or within the hall, and who swarmed in with us to take the chances of a presentation. Nine o'clock had been appointed as the time for receiving the deputation, and we were punctual to the moment; but not so the President, who sent us word that he was eating his breakfast, and would come as soon as he could. His appetite, we were glad to think, must have been a pretty fair one; for we waited about half an hour in one of the antechambers, and then were ushered into a reception-room, in one corner of which sat the Secretaries of War and of the Treasury, expecting, like ourselves, the termination of the Presidential breakfast. During this interval there were several new additions to our group, one or two of whom were in a working-garb, so that we formed a very miscellaneous collection of people, mostly unknown to each other, and without any common sponsor, but all with an equal right to look our head-servant in the face.

By and by there was a little stir on the staircase and in the passage-way, and in lounged a tall, loose-jointed figure, of an exaggerated Yankee port and demeanor, whom (as being about the homeliest man I ever saw, yet by no means repulsive or disagreeable) it was impossible not to recognize as Uncle Abe.

Unquestionably, Western man though he be, and Kentuckian by birth, President Lincoln is the essential representative of all Yankees, and the veritable specimen, physically, of what the world seems determined to regard as our characteristic qualities. It is the strangest and yet the fittest thing in the jumble of human vicissitudes, that he, out of so many

millions, unlooked for, unselected by any intelligible process
that could be based upon his genuine qualities, unknown to
those who chose him, and unsuspected of what endowments
may adapt him for his tremendous responsibility, should have
found the way open for him to fling his lank personality into
the chair of state,—where, I presume, it was his first impulse
to throw his legs on the council-table, and tell the Cabinet
Ministers a story. There is no describing his lengthy awk-
wardness, nor the uncouthness of his movement; and yet it
seemed as if I had been in the habit of seeing him daily, and
had shaken hands with him a thousand times in some village
street; so true was he to the aspect of the pattern American,
though with a certain extravagance which, possibly, I exaggerated still further by the delighted eagerness with which I
took it in. If put to guess his calling and livelihood, I should
have taken him for a country schoolmaster as soon as anything else. He was dressed in a rusty black frock-coat and
pantaloons, unbrushed, and worn so faithfully that the suit
had adapted itself to the curves and angularities of his figure,
and had grown to be an outer skin of the man. He had shabby
slippers on his feet. His hair was black, still unmixed with
gray, stiff, somewhat bushy, and had apparently been acquainted with neither brush nor comb that morning, after
the disarrangement of the pillow; and as to a night-cap,
Uncle Abe probably knows nothing of such effeminacies. His
complexion is dark and sallow, betokening, I fear, an in-
salubrious atmosphere around the White House; he has thick
black eyebrows and an impending brow; his nose is large, and
the lines about his mouth are very strongly defined.

The whole physiognomy is as coarse a one as you would
meet anywhere in the length and breadth of the States; but,
withal, it is redeemed, illuminated, softened, and brightened
by a kindly though serious look out of his eyes, and an expression of homely sagacity, that seems weighted with rich
results of village experience. A great deal of native sense; no
bookish cultivation, no refinement; honest at heart, and
thoroughly so, and yet, in some sort, sly,—at least, endowed

with a sort of tact and wisdom that are akin to craft, and would impel him, I think, to take an antagonist in flank, rather than to make a bull-run at him right in front. But, on the whole, I like this sallow, queer, sagacious visage, with the homely human sympathies that warmed it; and, for my small share in the matter, would as lief have Uncle Abe for a ruler as any man whom it would have been practicable to put in his place.

Immediately on his entrance the President accosted our member of Congress, who had us in charge, and, with a comical twist of his face, made some jocular remark about the length of his breakfast. He then greeted us all round, not waiting for an introduction, but shaking and squeezing everybody's hand with the utmost cordiality, whether the individual's name was announced to him or not. His manner towards us was wholly without pretence, but yet had a kind of natural dignity, quite sufficient to keep the forwardest of us from clapping him on the shoulder and asking him for a story. A mutual acquaintance being established, our leader took the whip out of its case, and began to read the address of presentation. The whip was an exceedingly long one, its handle wrought in ivory (by some artist in the Massachusetts State Prison, I believe), and ornamented with a medallion of the President, and other equally beautiful devices; and along its whole length there was a succession of golden bands and ferrules. The address was shorter than the whip, but equally well made, consisting chiefly of an explanatory description of these artistic designs, and closing with a hint that the gift was a suggestive and emblematic one, and that the President would recognize the use to which such an instrument should be put.

This suggestion gave Uncle Abe rather a delicate task in his reply, because, slight as the matter seemed, it apparently called for some declaration, or intimation, or faint foreshadowing of policy in reference to the conduct of the war, and the final treatment of the Rebels. But the President's Yankee aptness and not-to-be-caughtness stood him in good stead, and he jerked or wiggled himself out of the dilemma with an uncouth dexterity that was entirely in character; although, without his gesticulation of eye and mouth,—and especially the flourish of the whip, with which he imagined himself touching up a pair of fat horses,—I doubt whether his words would be worth recording, even if I could remember them. The gist of the reply was, that he accepted the whip as an emblem of peace, not punishment; and, this great affair over, we retired out of the presence in high good-humor, only regretting that we could not have seen the President sit down and fold up his legs (which is said to be a most extraordinary spectacle), or have heard him tell one of those delectable stories for which he is so celebrated. A good many of them are afloat upon the common talk of Washington, and are certainly the aptest, pithiest, and funniest little things imaginable; though, to be sure, they smack of the frontier freedom, and would not always bear repetition in a drawing-room, or on the immaculate page of the Atlantic.[1]

Good Heavens! what liberties have I been taking with one of the potentates of the earth, and the man on whose conduct more important consequences depend than on that of any other historical personage of the century! But with whom is an American citizen entitled to take a liberty, if not with his own chief magistrate? However, lest the above allusions to President Lincoln's little peculiarities (already well known to the country and to the world) should be misinterpreted, I deem it proper to say a word or two in regard to him, of

[1] The above passage relating to President Lincoln was one of those omitted from the article as originally published, and the following note was appended to explain the omission, which had been indicated by a line of points:—

We are compelled to omit two or three pages, in which the author describes the interview, and gives his idea of the personal appearance and deportment of the President. The sketch appears to have been written in a benign spirit, and perhaps conveys a not inaccurate impression of its august subject; but it lacks *reverence,* and it pains us to see a gentleman of ripe age, and who has spent years under the corrective influence of foreign institutions, falling into the characteristic and most ominous fault of Young America.

unfeigned respect and measurable confidence. He is evidently a man of keen faculties, and, what is still more to the purpose, of powerful character. As to his integrity, the people have that intuition of it which is never deceived. Before he actually entered upon his great office, and for a considerable time afterwards, there is no reason to suppose that he adequately estimated the gigantic task about to be imposed on him, or, at least, had any distinct idea how it was to be managed; and I presume there may have been more than one veteran politician who proposed to himself to take the power out of President Lincoln's hands into his own, leaving our honest friend only the public responsibility for the good or ill success of the career. The extremely imperfect development of his statesmanly qualities, at that period, may have justified such designs. But the President is teachable by events, and has now spent a year in a very arduous course of education; he has a flexible mind, capable of much expansion, and convertible towards far loftier studies and activities than those of his early life; and if he came to Washington a backwoods humorist, he has already transformed himself into as good a statesman (to speak moderately) as his prime-minister.

• • •

Appendix

Introduction
To the First Edition

NATHANIEL HAWTHORNE:
SELECTED TALES AND
SKETCHES
THE ACHIEVEMENT OF THE TALES

"Flowers that blossomed in too retired a shade," Hawthorne once called his tales. Allegories, later realists called them, thus, according to the taste of the time, damning them. Even Henry James, who sympathized with Hawthorne while he patronized him and who found much to admire in certain of the tales, put forward their merits apologetically, confessing that it would be easy to claim too much for such "small things." But it is not easy to claim too much for them, provided one makes the right sort of claim, and there is no very clear relationship in art between merit and bulk. It is long past time for us to assert without qualification that Nathaniel Hawthorne's short tales represent a literary achievement of the first order.

For the inadequate, the timid, the apologetic statements of the value of the tales—the novels have been more adequately assessed—we have chiefly to blame two accidents of history. First, Hawthorne wrote late in the romantic movement; his reputation did not become firmly established until the roman-

tic fashion was giving way to the realistic, so that the generation of Henry James could not take him quite seriously, as
we never can those who follow fashions from which we are
endeavoring to free ourselves. Second, most of those who have
had Hawthorne's reputation in their keeping for the past fifty
years have been historians rather than critics of literature,
content to accept the judgments of the later nineteenth century
or, when they have attempted criticism at all, drawing their
assumptions about literature from the scientific movement
and the mode of literary realism.

Naturally then there has been until the last few years very
little serious study of the art of Hawthorne's tales. Naturally
also the tales have been misread, read in terms of the simplest
abstract ideas in them; and, since the tales are works of art,
not illustrated sermons or propaganda pieces, even these
abstract ideas have been very often misconstrued. To those
readers whose acquaintance with the tales is limited to several
of the simplest read in grade or high school, it may come as a
surprise to learn that most of the distinctions of critical importance for an understanding and assessment of Hawthorne's
tales still remain to be made. For even in these days when
the close critical analysis which for thirty years has been given
to poetry is being applied to fiction, our lingering realistic
assumptions often prevent, or make difficult, a just evaluation
of Hawthorne. We have tended to like only those of his tales
which to some slight degree approximate the realistic story;
we have the impression, irrational but persistent, that Hawthorne was an early minor contributor to the tradition
climaxed by such writers as Arnold Bennett and Theodore
Dreiser, a writer who now and then by accident produced a
story almost realistic.

But Hawthorne wrote the symbolic story. Of the two chief
sources of modern prose fiction, the poetic epic and the verse
romance on the one hand and the documents of history—
journals, letters, biographies and autobiographies—on the
other, Hawthorne was in that unbroken tradition which has
its closest connections with the mythic and poetic source. The

two traditions have differed, of course, only in degree, not in kind: *Pilgrim's Progress* has a realistic surface and *Robinson Crusoe* has its simple symbolic overtones. Fiction that has no symbolic significance at all is perhaps more accurately classified as fabricated history than as literature; and fiction that does not maintain any "illusion of reality" would seem to be nearer to philosophy or to propaganda than to art. As it may be said of *Rasselas* that despite its very interesting philosophic content it remains a minor novel, so it may be said of *A Journal of the Plague Year* that though it cleverly simulates history it is not important as fiction. Modern taste at least—and I believe that an analysis of the chief classics of fiction could show that our preference is something more than a passing fashion —modern taste prefers fiction that maintains a difficult tension between the abstract universal of pure allegory and the concrete particular of pure realism.

Except perhaps in some of his very early tales of New England history, Hawthorne was more strongly attracted by the abstract universal than by the concrete particular. Yet his less successful tales are weak not, as has so often been said, because they are "too allegorical" but because in them Hawthorne's craftsmanship or creative energy or sensibility failed. His taste faltered and his usual humanity seems lacking in "Mrs. Bullfrog"; he failed to develop the idea of "The Lily's Quest" into an effective story, though the tale that resulted from the rudimentary development has wonderful Hawthornesque possibilities; and he seemed not to realize that the theme of "Feathertop" is so worn and so slight as to make the freshness that the story actually has an evidence of pure virtuosity. The most common weakness in Hawthorne's fiction is suggested by the difficulty one has in classifying many of his short pieces: Are they really stories, or are they just sketches? But we must not draw the wrong conclusion from this difficulty: if, as a great many readers feel, "Young Goodman Brown" is Hawthorne's greatest story, it is noteworthy that it is also one of the most intricately symbolic or allegorical of them all. On the whole it is the more "realistic" and less symbolic historical tales and sketches that are the least interesting today, while the tales that, like "Roger Malvin's Burial" and "Young Goodman Brown," are dense with New England history but move from the historical into the universal through symbolism seem to us today to be Hawthorne's greatest. Symbolism, whether carefully elaborated into allegory or scattered and fragmentary, came naturally to Hawthorne. As his notebooks show and some of the weaker among his tales suggest, he had conscientiously to "work up" his facts, his backgrounds, the specifications which give life to fiction, while he found his themes ready in his mind, often long before he had decided how they could be embodied. His work, then, is nearer to allegory than to realism. It is somewhat off center in the direction of the abstract.

But the center is a vaguely defined area. If some of Hawthorne's tales are so lacking in substantiality, in specification, in the kind of sharp actuality that we usually call realism that we must distinguish them rather sharply from some, though by no means all, of the works of modern symbolism, from, say, Katherine Anne Porter's "Flowering Judas" and Ernest Hemingway's "Big Two-Hearted River," then we should not forget that the best of the tales are symbolic in much the same way as *Moby Dick*. The fact that Hawthorne once thought of entitling a group of his tales "Allegories of the Heart" should not mislead us: words shift in value, and our word *symbolism* was not available to Hawthorne. Though he wrote in the tradition of Spenser and Bunyan, he made of allegory a very different thing from what either of them had made of it. He usually called his symbols *emblems* or *types,* but they are not different in kind from the symbols of Kafka or even of Hemingway. Hawthorne was an allegorical symbolist, Hemingway is a realistic symbolist; but Hawthorne's tales and romances are no more mere moral ideas than Hemingway's are mere transcriptions of the external world. The difference between the stories of these two men, though it is as great perhaps as one may find within the realm of fiction that is significant art, is one of emphasis, determined by fashion as

well as by temperament, not one of essence. Criticism may
one day decide that Hawthorne and Hemingway are equally
near the center.

Certain images recur throughout Hawthorne's work. Those
that recur most frequently are symbols of guilt, of self-contemplation, of isolation, of secrecy, of emotional rigidity or coldness, of death. Though only a close and sensitive reading of
each story, a reading which gives due emphasis to every part
in relation to every other part, can take us to the meaning
(finally impossible to state except in terms of the story itself)
and to the value of a story, a study of Hawthorne's recurrent
images can take us closer to the core of his unique achievement
as an artist than we are likely to get in any other way. We
begin, for instance, to understand the significance in the stories
of what the Puritans called natural depravity and what Hawthorne called guilt when we note that Hawthorne usually
symbolized it by a secret which cannot be shared and which
thereby isolates its possessor, as Reuben Bourne was isolated
even from those he loved, or by a stain, a mark, an imperfection, like the mark of the hand on Georgiana's cheek. Such
images extend in one direction into theology, in the other into
psychology, Hawthorne's and our own; and only a careful
study of them can reveal the far-reaching symbolic density of
the stories.

Or again, one of Hawthorne's most persistent themes is the
opposition between *head* and *heart,* and we conclude after
reading the works that he means by the terms roughly what
psychiatrists mean when they talk about the conscious and the
unconscious minds; but we come nearer to understanding
Hawthorne as artist when we return to the symbols in which
he embodied these concepts: for *head,* the scientific reasoning
of an Aylmer or a Rappaccini, the cold and passionless curiosity of an Ethan Brand, the manipulative power knowledge of
a Dr. Heidegger; for *heart,* the cavern to which the man of
adamant retreated ("the human heart to be allegorized as a

cavern," so goes one of Hawthorne's notes for stories), the
fiery furnace of the lime burner, the central chamber of the
decaying old house of seven gables, the graves, the tombs, the
closed dark places, even the glade in the dark forest in "Roger
Malvin's Burial." And we get a further sense of Hawthorne's
richness and complexity when we realize that these symbols
of the human heart also operate as symbols of the other chief
themes without ceasing to be symbols of the heart. The man
of adamant's cave is a closed, a secret place, a place of solitude,
of isolation, so that the story works another variation on Hawthorne's great theme of withdrawal and return that runs
through most of the works. The narrator in "Alice Doane's
Appeal" knew death in ice, while Ethan Brand perished in
fire; they shared not only an experience of death but an ap-
palling isolation. The catacombs of Rome in the romance of
the marble faun and the dark forest where young Goodman
Brown lost his innocence have overlapping symbolic functions:
in both, spectres walk and shameful secrets are known. Though
the heart of Reuben Bourne is a place of guilt and dread, we
note that Rappaccini spreads death around him because in his
search for knowledge and power he has lived by reason alone.
What is feared is also needed, the place of shame is also the
well of life, so that only when head and heart work together
is there a possibility of health and goodness. "Egotism" is thus
one of the few stories Hawthorne ever wrote with an unforced
happy ending, for the bosom serpent departed when the voices
of love and reason (or heart and head) in the person of wife
and friend spoke to tormented Elliston. And though the
serpent's departure left Elliston cured of his awful disease,
the place to which the serpent returned was the place from
which he had come, the fountain: so that here as elsewhere
we find that interpenetration of themes and density of symbolic functions characteristic of Hawthorne: for fountains
and pools, like mirrors, are normally in Hawthorne symbols
of self-contemplation and self-knowledge, and so, by extension,
of that inward, secret, elusive but real person known only to
each as he looks within. Both the cause and the cure of El-

liston's disease, we are justified in concluding, lay in the heart, though the heart was helpless so long as it was alone.

These and other recurrent symbols in Hawthorne are of interest to the psychological critic, and their psychological values contribute to the richness of texture of the tales, but we must never lose sight of the fact that Hawthorne was a more than usually conscious and controlled artist, more so I think than Poe, who boasted of the calculation with which he composed, and certainly more than Melville. With a few exceptions his stories reveal no more than we may assume they were meant to reveal, and reveal perfectly what they were meant to reveal. (Which is not to say that their "meaning" is synonymous with the "morals" with which they frequently end.) There are of course exceptions, where the artist failed and the man spoke. "Alice Doane's Appeal," in which parts of a very early tale were salvaged for publication by the addition of an apologetic framing essay, is such a work. The story almost certainly means more to the modern reader than Hawthorne consciously intended it should. In the framing essay Hawthorne tells us how he once took a walk up Gallows Hill in Salem in the company of two young women and how he tried to give them a sense of the tragic history of the spot by reading to them a tale of murder and witchcraft that he had written years before. The tale itself Hawthorne partly quotes and partly summarizes for us, apologizing meanwhile for the ineptness of an immature work. The fragments which he relates tell how Leonard Doane, who is inordinately attached to his sister, kills Walter Brome, the man who had made love to her, only to discover, to his horror, that the man he has slain strikingly resembles himself, and is indeed his very "counterpart." After experiencing a hallucination in which the dead enemy suddenly takes on the likeness of Doane's dead father, Leonard tries to bury his victim in an icy pond, and, later, visits a wizard whose chuckles and comments suggest that he has foreknown, and perhaps through the power of his magic has caused, the murder. Finally, Doane and his sister watch the dead of Salem dance on their graves and go through the actions habitual to them in life. The tale's strong hints of an incestuous relation between brother and sister are only the beginning of what seems clearly a group of unintended revelations here. There are, for example, Doane's destruction of his self-image in the person of the cold and sinister villain and the hallucination, or, as Hawthorne calls it, "the vision," in which enemy and father merge and Doane feels himself guilty of both murders (though his father has actually been murdered by Indians). There is the structurally extraneous but striking description of the icy village where eyes and hearts are as frozen as the streets, suggesting to us the inner cold that was the source of Hastings' pain in "The Christmas Banquet" and that Hawthorne was to use so often in later tales. There is the witchcraft theme, with its suggestion that Doane is controlled from beyond his conscious mind in both thought and deed. There is the scene in which *all* the former inhabitants of Salem rise from their graves and are recognized as damned. These are symbols which, because the tale or sketch or whatever one chooses to call it is obviously fragmentary and chaotic, invite psychological rather than structural criticism. The springs of his imagination are here revealed, but Hawthorne was not in this tale in command of his art. His symbols controlled him rather than being controlled by him, and they tell more than he wished, later, when he had perfected his public self, to tell.

Some of these symbols appear again in later tales, but there they are disguised, rationalized, controlled. The coldness of the frozen village is to be seen again not only in Hastings but in Rappaccini and in most of the other villains. The sense of universal depravity objectified in the dance on the graves receives its conceptual statement at the end of "Fancy's Show Box" and is symbolized with power and precision in "Young Goodman Brown." The blending of images of guilt, death, and isolation found in the vision of the murdered enemy-self-father is likewise found in "The Hollow of the Three Hills" and "Roger Malvin's Burial." The Oedipus theme is seen in another form in the search for and loss of the kinsman in the tale of Major Molineux.

But again one returns to the fact that Hawthorne was a conscious, even a coldly conscious, artist, and that the secret of his power lies very largely in the calculated skill with which he manipulated his archetypal material. What makes such an early masterpiece as "The Canterbury Pilgrims" interesting is not the revelation of the young Hawthorne contemplating the subject of marriage, though such a revelation is present, and not the "local color" realism, though its sketch of an aspect of the life of old New England is authentic and valuable, but its symbolic and structural and thematic richness and balance, so that one wonders how so apparently slight a tale can say so much so justly and so unobtrusively. Returning for a second reading, one finds that its very opening sentence introduces that note of ambiguity that is maintained throughout; for the moonlight, which completes the romantic setting for young love, is also made to recall the false moonshine of the popular literary "romance." Again one notes that the Shaker settlement is on a high hill, so that the physical establishment is as lofty as the ideal of other-worldliness that created it; but the incoming pilgrims continue toward it as toward death. The quiet detachment of a style at once humorous and grave, the delicate play of irony, the subtle shifts of tone, these too tell the story behind the story. The conclusion, which affirms neither the naïve optimism of the lovers nor the tired cynicism of the incoming travelers, takes the form not of an appended moral but of an emergent attitude that we can understand and accept only after we have read the story with the closest attention. What the story affirms finally is not an adage or indeed any abstraction at all, though one may, leaving the story behind, generalize from and about it, but the validity of the double vision. Ambiguity is here as elsewhere at the center of Hawthorne's art.

So one must ask whether it was saintliness or spiritual pride that moved Mr. Hooper to wear the black veil, that "ambiguity," as Hawthorne called it, "of sin or sorrow." Was the killing of the son in "Roger Malvin's Burial" really accidental, or accidental only in the sense that accidents happen to people who have a psychological need of them? Was it not rather the culminating act of expiation in a compulsive return to the spot where the guilt originated? Hawthorne does not say and we cannot know, for the story says among other things that the springs of conduct are obscurely compounded of accident, reason, and unreason, and that good and evil, like human motives, are never pure. Was there indeed any need for expiation, had Reuben Bourne done anything for which he need have felt ashamed?

Again, is Beatrice Rappaccini really poisonous, or does dull Giovanni merely imagine that he sees living things die at her touch? In just what sense is this beautiful but corrupt garden of the proud and heartless scientist an "Eden of the present world," as Hawthorne calls it? Unless we are familiar with the outlines of the traditional Christian dogma symbolized in the Eden myth, we are not apt to get far beyond a threshold understanding of this tale. For if we accept Beatrice's apparent poisonousness as real rather than imaginary—and these two possibilities exist in the story without destroying each other—then the girl is both corrupted (by the sin of the father) and good (by God's grace and the operation of her own free will: she voluntarily takes the "antidote" knowing it will mean her death). Lovely and dreadful, beautiful and corrupt, made for eternal life and incapable of lasting happiness, she is, in this reading of the story, a "type" of the central Christian paradox. The themes of the story are clearly related to the classic Christian theological conceptions of the revolt in pride, the original sin, the fall of man, and the present ambiguous state of man and nature. The tale has conventionally been interpreted not in terms of this complex symbolic relationship of girl and garden and father but in terms of the symbolic function of Rappaccini alone as a representative of lust for knowledge and pride of intellect. This may mean either that the story has been given an inadequate reading or that it is so rich that any single reading, even though partially valid, is insufficient to exhaust the tale's possibilities. Like the falling branch in "Roger Malvin's Burial," like the triadic structure that subtly pervades "Egotism," like the moonlight in "The Canterbury

Pilgrims" and the falling petals in "The Maypole of Merry-mount," the details of this story, from the ruinousness of the fountain and the color of the poisonous flower to the precise indications of the character of Giovanni and the shape of the mark on his flesh, all are significant, none may be disregarded, all are symbolic. In a great story nothing is wasted, nothing meaningless. Only an imperfect reading of "Rappaccini's Daughter" or of any of the rest of Hawthorne's best tales finds any waste, any disorder, anything but art of the purest sort.

Hawthorne once projected an essay "on the various kinds of death." Again he planned to write a tale in which "a figure of a gay, laughing, handsome youth, or a young lady, all at once, in a natural, unconcerned way, takes off its face like a mask, and shows the grinning, bare skeleton face beneath." The explicit theme of "David Swan" is that "We can be but partially acquainted even with the events which actually influence our course through life, and our final destiny. There are innumerable other events—if such they may be called—which come close upon us, yet pass away without actual results, or even betraying their near approach, by the reflection of any light or shadow across our minds." And at the end of the frail sketch Hawthorne wondered if it did not "argue a superintending Providence that, while viewless and unexpected events thrust themselves continually athwart our path, there should still be regularity enough in mortal life to render foresight even partially available." Like Dr. Johnson, who occupied a prominent place among his favorite authors, like Pascal and Bunyan and T. S. Eliot, Hawthorne saw the skull beneath the skin and realized the truth of E. A. Robinson's phrase, "how little we have to do with what we are."

Such a sensibility and such attitudes ran counter to the main currents of Hawthorne's age. Hawthorne was born in 1804 and began his mature writing about the time of his graduation from college in 1825, when Scott was the popular novelist and Poe was about to begin his ultra-romantic explorations of the

terrors that were "not of Germany but of the soul." But
Spenser, Bunyan, Swift, and Samuel Johnson meant more to
Hawthorne than his immediate predecessors and his contemporaries: beneath his use of current Gothic fashions there
is an element in Hawthorne's work that was old-fashioned
even when he began to write. This element is revealed in
remarks, in "The Old Manse," on the latest writings of the
liberal theologians and in his spirited and humorous defense
of Bunyan against these same religious modernists in "The
Celestial Railroad." It appears in his naming of his first daughter Una out of *The Fairy Queen,* in his pilgrimage to the
spot where Dr. Johnson had once stood as a penitent, and in
his caricature of the romantic poet in "The Canterbury
Pilgrims." All these things and more should be kept in mind
along with the themes of most of his stories: there can be no
doubt that in most essential respects neither Hawthorne's
sensibility nor his views were like those of his "advanced"
contemporaries. If his tales must be called romantic in their
insistence on the strange, the wild, and the mysterious, in their
lack of concern for the details of the actual, and in their use
of the materials of the dream-world, the world of the haunted
mind, they must be called something else again, perhaps
antiromantic, in their themes and in the sensibility which they
exhibit. Hawthorne's late definition of himself as a writer
not of "novels" but of "romances" is thus partly misleading.
Hawthorne was a conservative who did not share many of the
leading ideas we have come to associate with the romantic
period. To most of what his age believed and to most of what
it assumed without thinking about, he said no.

I shall not praise Hawthorne for having been antiromantic:
the romantic period achieved great and permanently valid insights and produced great writers. Yet one of the reasons why
most young people today are more interested in Hawthorne
than in, say, Emerson, is that while Emerson was the spokesman for his age, Hawthorne was the doubter and the critic,
and we have come to be especially sensitive to the fallacies
of the century which preceded and shaped our own. Haw-

thorne's views and attitudes, in short, seem to us—and here we are outside the realm of literary criticism—such as we can take seriously, as we cannot take seriously Emersonian ideas like the goodness of the natural man or the moral lessons to be found in nature. Hitler and the attempted extermination of a whole race, Freudian psychology and anthropology, these and much more have intervened between transcendental optimism and ourselves, and the voices of the romantic nature mystics grow a little shrill. When Hawthorne denied the innate goodness of the natural man and wrote instead about universal guilt, he countered one of the chief trends of his age. When he denied the inevitable rightness of instinct or impulse, thus contradicting Emerson's first premise, he stood apart from the age fathered by Rousseau. When he took what was for Emerson the greatest virtue, *self*-reliance, and interpreted it as pride, when he devoted story after story to a critique of the atomistic individualism characteristic of his age and offered in its place a concept of "the magnetic chain of humanity," when he scoffed, as in "Earth's Holocaust," at the idea of inevitable progress, he took his stand against the liberals of his day and prepared the way for our own increased sympathy for him and for his work.

But despite all these denials, Hawthorne's outlook is not primarily negative. What his work negates is a particular set of doctrines; it affirms another set. The general nature of those doctrines can only be suggested briefly by three words that have lost their edge, so that they arouse merely stock responses, but there are no others to take their place: Hawthorne's views were those of democratic Christian humanism, and the key word here is Christian. Emerson was a great democrat, as John Dewey has pointed out, and in one sense of the word at least he was a humanist, but he was in no historic sense of the word a Christian. (He was, rather, a romantic naturalist and a modernist.) Hawthorne's sensibility was primarily religious, and his instinct was for the central catholic tradition of Christian humanism. He was skeptical of the dogmas of his Puritan forefathers and he deplored their bigotry, but he preferred them to the religious modernists of his time. He criticized them from within their own frame of reference, for their lack of Christian charity and for their spiritual pride, which in his view effectually shut them out, as it did the man of adamant, the type of the Puritan bigot, from the very salvation to which their lives were supposedly dedicated; but he did not ignore them, as most of the "better minds" of his age were doing, or dismiss their problems as unreal. With the Puritans, and with Thomas Aquinas and Dante, he considered pride the worst of the mortal sins; with them he believed in the incurable imperfection of human nature and the consequent folly of secular utopianism; with them he distinguished between truth and fact and considered that truth is the proper understanding of the ends and purposes of life and is, consequently, always religious in nature; with them he set a high value on the rational understanding but held that character is more essential to salvation than intellect, the possession of true charity and humility more important than mastery of the scientific knowledge which he symbolized in the magical lore of Aylmer and Rappaccini. The central theme of Dickens's *David Copperfield*, "A loving heart is better than wisdom," was likewise Hawthorne's central theme. For all his skepticism, Hawthorne agreed as fully as his ancestors with the intent of Micah when he asked, "What doth the Lord require of thee but to do justice, love mercy, and walk humbly with thy God?" It is a fact worth noting that Hawthorne's most persistent theme is pride in its several manifestations; for this worst of sins from the Christian point of view is considered the worst just because it is wholly incompatible with the fulfillment of either of the two commandments which were given the central place in Christian doctrine by Jesus Himself: "Thou shalt love the Lord thy God with all thy heart, and with all thy soul, and with all thy mind. . . . And thou shalt love thy neighbor as thyself. On these two commandments hang all the law and the prophets" (Matthew, 22: 35-40). Pride is incompatible with both of the commandments because it isolates man both from God and from his fellow man, it denies human imperfection and human brotherhood, it is the reverse of humility. In the face of man's common nature and common fate, Hawthorne felt, pride is an absurd or a tragic perversion, depending on the position from which we view it. Hawthorne's stories embody the doctrines that inform the work of Christian writers of all ages, from Dante to T. S. Eliot. Reflecting on these matters, we get a sense of Hawthorne's catholicity and perhaps a new insight into the meaning of his works.

But there is another way of getting at Hawthorne's general meaning for us, a way that avoids theological terminology and so may have for our most untheological age more immediacy. It is to ask ourselves simply what attitudes and ideas the tales implicitly assert, and to answer with specific tales in mind. We find that they assert many things, but perhaps most insistently these: First, the reality, the positive existence, of evil. While Emerson agreed, for once, with Roman Catholic theologians in defining evil as the mere absence of good, Hawthorne felt it as a positive force. He shared, to this extent, the Manichean tendency of his Puritan forebears; he even went beyond them to assert the existence not only of moral but of natural evil. Ethan Brand sins in the way he searches for sin in others while forgetting to look for it in himself, gaining in the process great knowledge but losing love. The ambitious guest, on the other hand, is the victim of natural evil in a world where the rain, and avalanches, fall on the just and the unjust alike.

The tales assert both the fact and the obligation of interdependence. As the penalty for the greatest evil in Hawthorne's work is alienation, so the reward most to be desired is the reunion that comes when pride is conquered and heart and head work together to find freedom in acceptance of dependence. This is the major theme of *The House of Seven Gables*, in which everything, from seemingly casual or nonfunctional images to plot as symbol, presents and is dominated by a rhythm of withdrawal and return; and it is likewise to be found, with major or minor emphasis, in most of the tales, from the early "Wakefield" to the late "Ethan Brand." Hawthorne's meaning here is like Melville's in the monkey rope scene in *Moby Dick*, in which Ishmael, on deck, found himself literally tied to Queequeg, who stood in danger below on the carcass of the whale. It is not a meaning which is easy to accept, so it is not popular. We find it easier to inquire for whom the bell tolls than to acknowledge that we are members one of another. But it is a significant part of Hawthorne's achievement that long before Hemingway popularized Donne's phrase about sending to know for whom the bell tolls, Hawthorne, in the century bemused by the sentimental dream of the naturally good and perfectly free individual, demonstrated the identity of the spiritual injunction and the psychological law: for he showed us better than any other the consequences of living as though one were an island rather than a part of the main.

The tales also assert what we may call the independence of fact. Emerson admitted on one occasion and demonstrated often that his philosophy could easily dispose of the most disagreeable facts. Hawthorne found facts recalcitrant. Though his sympathies were with Beatrice, he could not dispose of the disagreeable fact of her corruption. He plainly sympathized with the element of idealism in Aylmer, but he could not dispose of the disagreeable fact that man's best efforts are insufficient to enable him to attain and keep perfection. Like Pascal before him, Hawthorne was well acquainted with the process we now call rationalization long before the psychologists discovered it. He tried, more successfully than most of us, to avoid wishful thinking.

Again, Hawthorne's tales assert the opacity of experience. Here, it seems to me, Hawthorne laid hold of a truth implicit in the great tragic poets and emphasized, perhaps overemphasized, by recent Existentialists: that we see as through a glass darkly, that the hymns we sing are to an Unknown God, that we cannot know that the patterns of meaning we see are discovered, not imposed. As ambiguity is at the center of Hawthorne's vision—so that it expresses itself formally in what may well be his most characteristic device, his alternative explanations, drawn from rumor, legend, and conjecture, of any mysterious event—so mystery is all around it. No one knew, no one can know, Hawthorne makes clear, why Wakefield went off by himself, not even Wakefield. No one can know what different course his own life might have taken had some insignificant or unknown event been otherwise: Mr. Higginbotham learned, the sleeping David Swan never knew, how our lives are involved in forces we neither control nor understand. No one knows why the fancies in his own show box have remained only fancies. Experience is opaque.

And finally the tales of Hawthorne assert the permanent validity and independence of moral distinctions. This was so fundamental an assumption with Hawthorne that he did not need to make it the theme of any tale, but it is implied in all of them. He assumed it as many people today, including all dialectical materialists and many others, assume its opposite, as too obvious to merit argument or examination. Like Conrad after him, with whom he has much in common, Hawthorne took account of the forces destructive of certainty while continuing to resist modernist nominalism and scientism. Unlike Conrad, Hawthorne did not proclaim himself a relativist; like him he emphasized the difference between legal and real justice and assumed the validity of the basic Christian moral imperatives. He read Voltaire when young and allied himself with no church; the sympathies he felt with both American Puritanism and Roman Catholicism (he felt none at all with the advanced Protestant liberalism fashionable in his own time and place) were insufficient to make him a Puritan or a Catholic. But he was so little a modernist that he never thought of viewing moral law as, in Pareto's words, a "derivative" of social facts. If Hawthorne anticipated the psychoanalysts, he only antedated the anthropologists who, by making us acquainted with the irrational taboos of primitive societies, have made us believe that there are no moral imperatives more rational. His conservatism in this matter made him, rather, anticipate the contemporary antimodernist revolt.

No artist has succeeded equally well in all his work. Hawthorne wrote a good many weak stories, though no vulgar or trivial ones. The stream of his creative energy was pure but never abundant. He was beset all his life by the sin of sloth, and his struggle against it was never wholly determined or wholly successful, for his will was not strong. (I think his vision of death was so vivid and so constant that his inclination was always to doubt the worth of any effort, including the effort to shape the hints that lay in his mind and in his notebooks into stories.) If his style is at times too relaxed, even lazy, so that he uses the general rather than the specific word, as easier, and fails to achieve the intensity, the willful, nervous vigor of Emerson or the difficult precision and power of Thoreau, so likewise the fault typical of his weaker stories is that they are undeveloped, mere hints and sketches, essentially fragments. Even "Wakefield," which has considerable charm and interest, is more nearly a relaxed meditative essay than a story. To have given the reflections in it the body and form demanded by fiction would have been much more trouble than merely to set them down along with a scanty outline of a story that remains largely unwritten. The craft of fiction demands a moral discipline which Hawthorne could not readily achieve or long maintain. His taste was almost always pure and his mind clear, but his energy was easily exhausted.

Yet he wrote a small group of stories in which a close reading will reveal a structural and textural beauty that is the outward manifestation of inward order and harmony, and a subtlety, depth, and purity of insight into the human situation that has seldom been equaled in any fiction. His best stories are indeed, to use a word now unfashionable in this connection but a natural choice when one is speaking of Hawthorne, beautiful, and they are profound. Only a close reading of each story, such readings as those I have listed in the bibliographical note which follows this introduction, can bring us to a realization of just how beautiful and profound they are. For in Hawthorne's tales, as in any great fiction, form is significant, technique is revelation, images are functional. It is for this reason that one cannot "summarize" a successful Hawthorne tale in a sentence, or even in a large number of sentences. Hawthorne himself could not do so: the explicit "morals" which he sometimes appended to his tales are no more adequate as interpretations of the great tales than any generalizations that we ourselves might think up. The visual image of the burning eyes and the auditory image of the laughter in "Major Molineux," the actions of the dog and of the child in "Ethan Brand," the allusions to both the classic and the Christian worlds in "Rappaccini's Daughter"—these and other "details" like them are what we shall have to notice if we are to find the evidence for the belief that Hawthorne is one of the first great masters of the short story. If we give them our fullest attention we shall perhaps perceive with more justice than Hawthorne himself what his tales are, flowers that blossomed in the valley's shadow but were watered by a spring pure, cold, and sweet, whose source was deep under the mountain.

Kansas City, Mo.,   H. H. W.
March, 1950

Rinehart Editions